DEATH
SENTENCES

IAN RANKIN is the bestselling author
of the Rebus series.

OTTO PENZLER is the proprietor of
The Mysterious Bookshop in New York City
and an Edgar-award winning anthologist.

DEATH SENTENCES

INTRODUCED BY
IAN RANKIN

EDITED BY
OTTO PENZLER

**20 Stories of
Deathly Books, Murderous Booksellers
and Lethal Literature
from the World's Best
Crime Writers**

HEAD
ZEUS

Each story was individually published in the USA between 2011 and 2013 by The Mysterious Bookshop, and as an anthology by Assembly! Press, an imprint of Bookspan, New York, USA by arrangement with The Mysterious Bookshop.

This anthology first published in the UK in 2014 by Head of Zeus Ltd by arrangement with The Mysterious Bookshop. This revised paperback edition published in the UK in 2019 by Head of Zeus Ltd.

Contents

Introduction   vii

An Acceptable Sacrifice
Jeffery Deaver   1

Pronghorns of the Third Reich
C.J. Box   41

The Book of Virtue
Ken Bruen   65

The Book Thing
Laura Lippman   87

The Scroll
Anne Perry   111

It's in the Book
Mickey Spillane & Max Allan Collins   145

The Long Sonata of the Dead
Andrew Taylor   181

The Caxton Lending Library & Book Depository
John Connolly   207

The Book Case
Nelson Demille   263

Remaindered
Peter Lovesey   317

Mystery, Inc.
Joyce Carol Oates   347

The Compendium of Srem
F. Paul Wilson   409

The Sequel
R.L. Stine   453

The Little Men
Megan Abbott   483

Citadel
Stephen Hunter   523

Every Seven Years
Denise Mina   633

The Travelling Companion
Ian Rankin   661

Seven Years
Peter Robinson   699

Reconciliation Day
Christopher Fowler   747

Hoodoo Harry
Joe R. Lonsdale   781

Introduction

I AM OFTEN ASKED FOR ADVICE by aspiring writers. Most of what I say is changeable, depending on my mood, but there is one constant: it's hard to be a good writer without also being a good reader. When I get together with other writers we always seem to spend the majority of the conversation passing on hot tips for new books we've enjoyed, or reminiscing about great books from the past. There will be anecdotes about bookshops and libraries, and we will vividly remember favourite books from childhood. It is through reading that we became writers, because we found it impossible to conceive of any finer vocation in the world than storytelling.

In the village where I grew up, there was no bookshop. The newsagent had a carousel displaying the works of Sven Hassel and Frederick Forsyth, but the small local library fulfilled additional needs. I would haunt that place, and I still recall the thrill of being told I had reached an age where I need no longer be confined to the Children's Section. Books immersed me in different lives and worlds, far from my immediate surroundings. As soon as I could, I began writing them for my own amusement, copying the styles of favourite authors (and, yes, sometimes stealing bits and pieces of their plots, too). When I went on to university, I studied English and American Literature, eventually specialising in Scottish Literature for a never-to-be-completed PhD. A group of like-minded students would meet after classes in a local hostelry, sometimes inviting a lecturer or two along, so that our discussions could continue. It was around then I gritted my teeth and started buying hardback fiction. The prices were steep for a student (and this was in the days when books had to be sold at the cover-price), but I was unwilling to wait six months or a year for a paperback fix of the latest William Golding or Angela Carter. I cherish those well-thumbed editions to this day – they sit on groaning shelves in my house. And when I visit other people's homes, I'll head directly to the bookshelves to get a sense of the inhabitants' inner lives.

When my first few Inspector Rebus novels were published, they failed to make ripples, but eventually my publisher in the USA decided I should tour there. This was in the late 1980s, and I discovered that many American towns featured at least one small independent bookshop specialising in crime fiction. Flash-forward quarter of a century and most of them have gone, alas, but some remain. One of these is The Mysterious Bookshop in New York, and its owner, Otto Penzler, was an early champion of my work. He was – and is – an expert in the field of crime fiction, a collector, and a fan. He pens bibliographies and scholarly essays, edits short story collections, and for many years has commissioned authors to write one-off Christmas tales which are then presented as gifts to the bookshop's loyal customers. It was Otto who came up with the idea of a series of 'bibliomysteries' – basically stories of a certain length in which books play a crucial role. As a fan of the genre, it seemed irresistible and fun to him, and when he started contacting authors, they agreed. Why wouldn't they? Books have often played an integral or peripheral role in tales of mystery and adventure – Otto's offer proved catnip to so many writers who share a passion for the written word in all its forms.

Hence this collection.

And what treats you have in store! What struck me when I first read these stories was their variety. Anne Perry reworks 'The Maltese Falcon', but adds theology and the supernatural with gripping, twisty aplomb. Jeffery Deaver focuses on a pair of assassins in Mexico as they attempt the execution of a book-loving criminal. Andrew Taylor shifts the action to London in a tale of libraries, lost love, and jealousy both professional and personal. Then there's Mickey Spillane, with an unfinished story brought to a satisfying conclusion by contemporary author Max Allan Collins, a story where the search for a gangster's notebook brings Mike Hammer a series of clients including cops, politicians and the mob.

And those, dear reader, are for starters.

The bibliomystery then is by no means a narrow sub-genre but rather one that contains multitudes, and it is fascinating to see how different authors approach the task. There are books real and imagined, with stories set in past, present and future. Some will prickle the scalp, others raise a smile. You'll nod in appreciation of a piece of sleight-of-hand, or find your pulse quickening as a bomb is primed to explode. There are pleasing twists at the ends of some, while others resonate long in the mind, having left something at their conclusion for the reader to consider and chew on. All show their authors to be masters of their craft, their delight at the challenge set by Otto Penzler evident in the writing and plotting.

Now read on.

Ian Rankin, 2014

An Acceptable Sacrifice

Jeffery Deaver

WEDNESDAY

THEY'D MET LAST NIGHT for the first time and now, mid-morning, they were finally starting to let go a bit, to relax, to trust each other. *Almost* to trust each other.

Such is the way it works when you're partnered with a stranger on a mission to kill.

"Is it always this hot?" P.Z. Evans asked, squinting painfully against the fierce glare. The dense lenses of his Ray-Bans were useless.

"No."

"Thank God."

"Usually is *hotter*," Alejo Díaz replied, his English enriched by a luscious accent.

"You're shitting me."

The month was May and the temperature was around 97. They were in Zaragoza Plaza, the picturesque square dominated by a statue of two stern men Evans had learned were generals. A cathedral, too.

And then there was the sun . . . like burning gasoline.

Evans had flown to Hermosillo from outside D.C., where he lived when he wasn't on the road. In the nation's capital— the nation to the north, that is—the temperature had been a pleasant 75.

"Summer can be warm," Díaz admitted.

"Warm?" Evans echoed wryly.

"But then . . . You go to Arizona?"

"I played golf in Scottsdale once."

"Well, Scottsdale is hundreds of miles *north* of here. Think about that. We are in the middle of a desert. It has to be hot. What you expect?"

"I only played six rounds," Evans said.

"What?"

"In Arizona. For me to only play six rounds . . . I thought I'd die. And we started at seven in the morning. You golf?"

"Me? You crazy? Too hot here." Díaz smiled.

Evans was sipping a Coke from a bottle whose neck he'd religiously cleaned with a Handi-wipe before drinking. Supposedly Hermosillo, the capital of Sonora, was the only city in Mexico that treated its water, which meant that the ice the bottles nestled in was probably safe.

Probably.

He wiped the neck and mouth again. Wished he'd brought a miniature of Jack Daniels to use as purifier. Handi-wipe tasted like crap.

Díaz was drinking coffee, to which he'd added three or four sugars. Hot coffee, not iced. Evans couldn't get his head around that. A Starbucks addict at home and a coffee drinker in any number of the third-world places he traveled to (you didn't get dysentery from boiled water), he hadn't touched the stuff in Hermosillo. He didn't care if he never had a hot beverage again. Sweat tickled under his arms and down his temple and in his crotch. He believed his ears were sweating.

The men looked around them, at the students on the way to school, the businessmen meandering to offices or meetings. No shoppers; it was too early for that, but there were some mothers about, pushing carriages. The men not in suits were wearing blue jeans and boots and embroidered shirts. The cowboy culture, Evans had learned, was popular in Sonora. Pickup trucks were everywhere, as numerous as old American cars.

These two men vaguely resembled each other. Thirties, compact, athletic, with round faces—Díaz's pocked but not detracting from his craggy good looks, reflecting some Pima Indian in his ancestry. Dark hair both. Evans's face was smoother and paler, of course, and a little off kilter, eyes not quite plumb. Handsome too, though, in a way that might appeal to risk-taking women.

They were in jeans, running shoes and short-sleeved shirts, untucked, which would have concealed their weapons but they weren't carrying today.

So far there was no reason for anyone to wish them harm.

That would change.

Some tourists walked by. Hermosillo was a way station for people traveling from the U.S. to the west coast of Sonora. Lots of people driving, lots of buses.

Buses . . .

Evans lowered his voice, though there was no one near. "You talked to your contact this morning, Al?"

Evans had tried out shortening the Mexican agent's name when they first met—to see how he'd react, if he'd be pissed, defensive, hostile. But the man had laughed. "You can call me Al," he'd said, the line from a Paul Simon song. So the test became a joke and Evans had decided then that he could like this guy. The humor also added to the infrastructure of trust. A lot of people working undercover think that saying "fuck" and making jokes about women creates trust. No. It's humor.

"*Sí*. And from what he say . . . I think our job, it will not be easy." He took the lid off his coffee and blew to cool it, which Evans thought was hilarious. "His security, very tight. Always his security man, a good one, Jos, is with him. And word is they know something's planned."

"What?" Evans's face curled up tight. "A leak?"

And this, Díaz seemed to find funny, "Oh, is always a leak. Every egg in Mexico has a crack. They won't know about us exactly but he has heard somebody is in town to kill him. Oh, *sí*, he has heard."

The "he" they were speaking of was Alonso María Carillo, better known as Cuchillo—in Spanish: "Knife." There was some debate about where the nickname came from. It probably wasn't because he used that weapon to kill rivals—he'd never been arrested for a violent crime . . . or *any* crime, for that matter. More likely the name was bestowed because he was brilliant. *Cuchillo*, as in sharp as a. He was supposedly the man behind one of the cartels in Sonora, the Mexican state that, in addition to neighboring Sinaloa, was home to the major drug gangs. But, though it was small, the Hermosillo Cartel was one of the most deadly, responsible for a thousand or more deaths . . . and the production of many tons of drugs—not only cocaine but insidious meth, which was the hot new profit center in the narcotics trade.

And yet Cuchillo was wily enough to avoid prosecution. The cartel was run by other men—who were, the *Federales* were sure, figureheads. To the world, Cuchillo was an innovative businessman and philanthropist. Educated at UCLA, a degree in business and one in English literature. He'd made his fortune, it appeared, through legitimate companies that were known for being good to workers and were environmentally and financially responsible.

So due process wasn't an option to bring him to justice. Hence the joint operation of Alejo Díaz and P.Z. Evans—an operation that didn't exist, by the way, if you happened to bring up the topic to anyone in Washington, D.C., or Mexico City.

"So," Evans said, "he suspects someone is after him. That means we'll need a diversion, you know. Misdirection. Keep him focused on that, so he doesn't figure out what we're really up to."

"Yes, yes, that is right. At least one diversion. Maybe two. But we have another problem: We can't get him into the open."

"Why not?"

"My contact say he's staying in the compound for the next week. Maybe more. Until he think it's safe."

"Shit," Evans muttered.

Their mission was enwrapped with a tight deadline. Intelligence had been received that Cuchillo was planning an attack on a tourist bus. The vehicle would be stopped, the doors wired shut and then the bus set on fire. The attack would occur on Friday, two days from now, the anniversary of the day the Mexican president had announced his most recent war on the cartels. But there the report ended—as had, presumably, the life of the informant. It was therefore impossible to tell which bus would be targeted; there were hundreds of them daily driving many different routes and run by dozens of companies, most of whom didn't want to scare off passengers by suspending service or cooperating with law enforcement. (In his groundwork for the mission, Evans had researched the bus operators and noted one thing their ads all had in common: they began with variations on *Mexico Is Safe!!*)

Even without knowing the specific bus, however, Díaz and Evans had found a way to stop the attack. The biggest cartels in Sinaloa and Sonora were pulling back from violence. It was very bad publicity—not to mention dangerous to one's health—to kill tourists, even accidentally. An *intentional* attack on innocents, especially Americans, could make the drug barons' lives pure hell. No rivals or anyone within his organization would challenge Cuchillo directly but the agents had learned that if he, say, met with an accident his lieutenants would not follow through with the attack.

However, if Cuchillo would be hiding in his compound until after the bus burned down to a scorched shell, then Díaz's contact was right; their job would not be easy. Drone surveillance had revealed that the house was on five acres, surrounded by a tall wall crowned with electric wire, the yard filled with sensors and scanned by cameras. Sniping wouldn't work because all the buildings—the large house, the separate library and detached garage—had thick bulletproof windows. And the walkways between those structures were out of sight of any vantage points where a shooter could set up.

As they sat bathed in the searing sun, Evans wondered if

your mind slowed down the hotter it got. Oatmeal came to mind, steaming sludge.

He wiped his forehead, sipped Coke and asked for more details about Cuchillo's professional and personal life. Díaz had quite a bit of information; the man had been under investigation for the past year. Nodding, Evans took it all in. He'd been a good tactician in the Special Forces; he was a good tactician in his present job. He drained the Coke. His third of the day.

Nine fucking forty-five in the morning.

"Tell me about his weaknesses."

"Cuchillo? He has no weaknesses."

"Whatta you mean? Everybody has weaknesses. Drugs, women, men? Liquor? Gambling?"

Weakness was a very effective tool of the trade in Evans's business, as useful as bullets and C4. Usually, in fact, more so.

Díaz added yet one more sugar to his cup, though there was only a small amount of coffee remaining. He stirred elaborately. Figure eight. He sipped and then looked up. "There is maybe one thing."

"What?"

"Books," the Mexican agent said. "Books might be his weakness."

❧

The weather in Washington, D.C. was pleasant this May evening so he picked a Starbucks with an outdoor patio . . . because, why not?

This was in a yuppie area of the district, if yuppies still existed. Peter Billings's father had been a yuppie. Shit, that was a long time ago.

Billings was drinking regular coffee, black, and no extra shots or foamed milk or fancy additives, which he secretly believed that people asked for sometimes simply because they liked the sound of ordering them.

He'd also bought a scone, which was loaded with calories, but he didn't care. Besides, he'd only eat half of it. At home in Bethesda, his wife would feed him a Lean Cuisine tonight.

Billings liked Starbucks because you could count on being invisible. Business people typing resumes they didn't want their bosses to see, husbands and wives typing emails to their lovers.

And government operatives meeting about issues that were, shall we say, sensitive.

Starbucks was also good because the steam machine made a shitload of noise and covered up the conversation if you were inside and the traffic covered up the conversation if you were outside. At least here on the streets of the District.

He ate some scone and launched the crumbs off his dark blue suit and light blue tie.

A moment later a man sat down across from him. He had a Starbuck's coffee, too, but it'd been doctored up big time—almond or hazelnut, whipped cream, sprinkles. The man was weasely, Billings reflected. When you're in your forties and somebody looks at you and the word weasel is the first thing that comes to mind, you might want to start thinking about image. Gain some weight.

Have a scone.

Billings now said to Harris, "Evening."

Harris nodded then licked whipped cream from the top of his coffee carton.

Billings found it repulsive, the darting, weasely tongue. "We're at the go/no-go point."

"Right."

"Your man down south."

"Adam."

As good a code as any for Harris's contracting agent in Hermosillo, presently dogging Alonso María Carillo, AKA Cuchillo. Harris, of course, wasn't going to name him. Loud traffic on the streets of D.C. is like cappuccino machines, only loud. It masks, it doesn't obliterate, and both Harris and

Billings knew there were sound engineers who could extract incriminating words from cacophony with the precision of a hummingbird sipping nectar in a hover.

"Communication is good?" A near whisper by Billings.

No response. Of course communication would be good. Harris and his people were the best. No need for a nod, either.

Billings wanted to take a bite of scone but was, for some reason, reluctant to do so in front of a man who'd killed at least a dozen people, or so the unwritten resume went. Billings had killed a number of people *indirectly* but, one on one? Only a squirrel. Accidentally. His voice now dropped lower yet. "Has he been in contact with the PIQ?"

Person in Question.

Cuchillo.

"No. He's doing the prep work. From a distance."

"So he hasn't seen, for instance, weapons or product at the compound?"

"No. They're staying clear. Both Adam and his counterpart from the D.F." Harris continued, "All the surveillance is by drone."

Which Billings had seen. And it wasn't helpful.

They fell silent as a couple at a table nearby stood and gathered their shopping bags.

Billings told himself to be a bit subtler with his questions. Harris was on the cusp of becoming curious. And that would not be good. Billings was not prepared to share what had been troubling him for the past several hours, since the new intelligence assessment came in: that he and his department might have subcontracted out a job to assassinate the wrong man.

There was now some doubt that Cuchillo was in fact head of the Hermosillo Cartel.

The intercepts Billings's people had interpreted as referring to drug shipments by the cartel in fact referred to legitimate products from Cuchillo's manufacturing factories, destined for

U.S. companies. A huge deposit into one of his Cayman accounts was perfectly legal—not a laundering scam, as originally thought—and was from the sale of a ranch he had owned in Texas. And the death of a nearby drug supplier they were sure was a hit ordered by Cuchillo turned out to be a real traffic accident involving a drunk driver. Much of the other data on which they'd based the terminate order remained ambiguous.

Billings had hoped that Adam, on the ground in Sonora, might have seen something to confirm their belief that Cuchillo ran the cartel.

But apparently not.

Harris licked the whipped cream again. Caught a few sprinkles in the process.

Billings looked him over again. Yes, weasely, but this wasn't necessarily an insult. After all, a sneaky weasel and a noble wolf weren't a lot different, at least not when they were sniffing after prey.

Harris asked bluntly, "So, do I tell Adam to go forward?"

Billings took a bite of scone. He had the lives of the passengers of the bus to save . . . and he had his career to think of, too. He considered the question as he brushed crumbs. He'd studied law at the University of Chicago, where the theory of cost-benefit analysis had largely been developed. The theory was this: you balanced the cost of preventing a mishap versus the odds of it occurring and the severity of the consequences if it does.

In the Cuchillo assassination, Billings had considered two options: Scenario One: Adam kills Cuchillo. If he's not the head of the cartel and is innocent, then the bus attack happens, because somebody else is behind it. If he's guilty, then the bus incident *doesn't* happen and there'd be no bus incidents in the future. Scenario Two: Adam stands down. Now, if Cuchillo's innocent, the bus incident happens. If he's guilty, the bus incident happens and there'll be more incidents like it in the future.

In other words, the hard and cold numbers favored going forward, even if Cuchillo was innocent.

But the obvious downside was that Billings could be crucified if that was the case . . . and if he and Harris and Adam were discovered.

An obvious solution occurred to him.

Oh, this was good. He finished the scone. "Yeah, Adam's green-lighted. But there's just one thing."

"What's that?"

"Tell him however he does it, all the evidence has to be obliterated. Completely. Nothing can trace the incident back here. Nothing at all."

And looking very much like a crossbreed, a weasel-wolf, Harris nodded and sucked up the last of the whipped cream. "I have no problem with that whatsoever."

&

Díaz and Evans were back in the apartment in a nice section of Hermosillo, an apartment that was paid for by a company owned by a company owned by a company whose headquarters was a post office box in Northern Virginia. Evans was providing not only the technical expertise but most of the money as well. It was the least he could do, he'd joked, considering that it was America that supplied most of the weapons to the cartels; in Mexico it is virtually impossible to buy or possess weapons legally.

The time was now nearly five p.m. and Evans was reading an encrypted email from the U.S. that he'd just received.

He looked up. "That's it. We're green-lighted."

Díaz smiled. "Good. I want that son of a bitch to go to hell."

And they got back to work, poring over data-mined information about Cuchillo's life: his businesses and associates and employees, household staff, his friends and mistresses, the restaurants and bars where he spent many evenings, what he bought, what he downloaded, what computer programs he used, what he enjoyed listening to, what he ate and drank. The information was voluminous; security forces here and in the U.S. had been compiling it for months.

And, yes, much of this information had to do with books.

Weaknesses . . .

"Listen to this, Al. Last year he bought more than a million dollars' worth of books."

"You mean pesos."

"I mean dollars. Hey, you turn the A.C. down?"

Evans had noticed that the late afternoon heat was flowing into the apartment like a slow, oppressive tide.

"Just little," Díaz said. "Air conditioning, it's not so healthy."

"Cold temperature doesn't give you a cold," Evans said pedantically.

"I know that. I mean, the mold."

"What?"

"Mold in the ducts. Dangerous. *That* is what I meant, unhealthy."

Oh. Evans conceded the point. He actually had been coughing a lot since he'd arrived. He got another Coke, wiped the neck and sipped. He spit Handi-wipe. He coughed. He turned the A.C. down a little more.

"You get used to the heat."

"That's not possible. In Mexico, do you have words for winter, spring and fall?"

"Ha, funny."

They returned to the data-mined info. Not only was the credit card data available but insurance information about many of the books was often included. Some of the books were one of a kind, worth tens of thousands of dollars. They seemed to all be first editions.

"And look," Díaz said, looking over the documents. "He never sells them. He only buys."

It was true, Evans realized. There were no sales documents, no tax declarations of making money by selling capital items described as books. He kept everything he bought.

He'd want them around him all the time. He'd covet them. He'd need them.

Many people in the drug cartels were addicted to their own product; Cuchillo, it seemed, was not. Still, he had an addiction.

But how to exploit it?

Evans considered the list. Ideas were forming, as they always did. "Look at this, Al. Last week he ordered a book inscribed by Dickens, *The Old Curiosity Shop*. The price is sixty thousand. Yeah, dollars."

"For a book?" the Mexican agent asked, looking astonished.

"And it's *used*," Evans pointed out. "It's supposed to be coming in, in a day or two." He thought for some moments. Finally he nodded. "Here's an idea. I think it could work . . . . We'll contact this man—" He found a name on the sheet of data-mined printouts. "Señor Davila. He seems to be Cuchillo's main book dealer. What we'll do is tell him we suspect him of money laundering."

"He probably is."

"And he'd pee his pants, thinking if we announce it, Cuchillo will . . . "Evans drew his index finger across his throat.

"Do you do that in America?"

"What?"

"You know. That thing, your finger, your throat? I only saw that in bad movies. Laurel and Hardy."

Evans asked, "Who?"

Alejo Díaz shrugged and seemed disappointed that he'd never heard of them.

Evans continued, "So Davila will do whatever we want."

"Which will be to call Cuchillo and tell him his Dickens book arrived early. Oh, and the seller wants cash only."

"Good. I like that. So somebody will have to meet him in person—to collect the cash."

"And I'll come to his house to deliver the book. His security man probably won't want that but Cuchillo will insist to take delivery. Because he's—"

"Addicted."

The Mexican agent added, "I'll have to meet him, not you. Your Spanish, it is terrible. Why did they send you here on assignment?"

The reason for sending P.Z. Evans to a conflict zone was not because of his language skills. "I like the soft drinks." He opened another Coke. Did the neck cleaning thing. He cleared his throat and tried not to cough.

Díaz said, "We'll need to get the book, though. That Dickens." Nodding at the list.

Evans said, "I'll make some calls to my people in the States, see if they can track one down."

Díaz asked, "Okay, so it is that I'm inside. What do I do then? If I shoot him, they shoot me."

"Effective," Evans pointed out.

"But not the successful plans you're known for, P.Z."

"True. No, what you're going to do is plant a bomb."

"A bomb?" Díaz said uneasily. "I don't like them so much."

Evans gestured to his computer, referring to the email he'd just received. "Instructions are nothing's supposed to remain. Nothing to trace back to our bosses. Has to be a bomb. And one that produces a big honking fire."

Díaz added, "Always collateral damage."

The American agent shrugged. "Cuchillo doesn't have a wife. He doesn't have any children. Lives pretty much alone. Anybody around him is probably as guilty as he is." Evans tapped a drone picture of the compound. "Anything and anyone inside?" A shrug. "They're just acceptable sacrifices."

∾

He liked his nickname.

Alonso María Carillo was actually honored that people thought enough of him to give him a name that sounded like it was attached to some Mafioso out of a movie. Like Joey "The Knife" Vitelli.

"Cuchillo"—like a blade, like a dagger: How he loved that! And it was ironic because he wasn't a thug, wasn't like Tony Soprano at all. He was solid physically and he was tough, yes, but in Mexico a businessman must be tough. Still, his voice was soft and, well, inquisitive sounding. Almost innocent. His manner unassuming. His temper even.

He was in the office of his home not far from the upscale Hidalgo Plaza area of the city. Though the compound was surrounded by high walls, and sported a number of trees, from this spacious room he had a view of the city's grandest mountain, Cerro de la Compana, if a thousand-foot jut of rock can be described thus.

It was quitting time—he'd been working here since six that morning. No breaks. He put his work aside and went online to download some apps for his new iPhone, which he would synchronize to his iPad. He loved gadgets—both in his personal life and in business he always stayed current with the latest technology. (Since his companies had sales reps throughout Mexico and he needed to stay in constant touch with them he used the Cloud and thought it was the best invention of the last ten years.)

Rising from his desk, declaring it the end of the day, he happened to regard himself in a mirror nearby. Not so bad for an old man.

Cuchillo was about five nine and stocky and resembled Fernandez, Mexico's greatest actor and director, in the businessman's opinion. Though he was in scores of films, Fernandez was at his peak as Mapache in *The Wild Bunch*, one of the few truly honest films about Mexico.

Looking over his face, thick black hair. Keen brown eyes. Cuchillo thought again, No, not so bad . . . The women still appreciated him. Sure, he paid some of them—one way or another—but he also had a connection with them. He could converse with them. He listened. He also made love for hours. Not a lot of 57-year-olds could do that.

"You old devil," he whispered.

Then he gave a wry grin at his own vanity and left the office. He told his maid he'd be staying at home for dinner.

And he walked into his most favorite place on earth, his library. The building was large: sixty feet by forty, and very cool, as well as carefully humidity controlled (which was ironic in Hermosillo, in the heart of the Sonoran desert, where there were two or three rainy days a year). Gauze curtains kept the sun from bleaching the jackets and leather bindings of the books.

The ceilings were thirty feet off the ground and the entire space was open, lined with tall shelves on the ground floor and encircled with levels above, which one could reach by climbing an iron spiral staircase to narrow walkways. In the center were three parallel shelves ten feet high. In the front of the room was a library table, surrounded by comfortable chairs and an overstuffed armchair and a floor lamp with a warm yellow bulb. A small bar featured the best brandy and single-malt scotches. Cuchillo enjoyed Cuban cigars. But never here.

The building was home to 22,000 titles, nearly all of them first editions. Many, the only ones in existence.

On a night like this, after a long day working by himself, Cuchillo would normally have gone out into the relatively cool evening and eaten at Sonora Steak and then gone to Ruby's bar with his friends and—of course—his security. But the rumors of this impending attack were too real to ignore and he'd have to stay within the compound until more was learned about the threat.

Ah, what a country we live in, he reflected. The most philanthropic businessman, and the most hardworking farmer, and the worst drug baron all are treated equally . . . treated to fear.

Someday it will be different.

But at least Cuchillo had no problem staying home tonight, in his beloved library. He called his housekeeper and had her prepare dinner, a simple linguine primavera, made with organic vegetables and herbs out of his own garden. A California cabernet, too, and ice water.

He turned on a small high definition TV, the news. There were several stories about the ceremony in the D.F. on Friday, commemorating the latest war against the cartels. The event would include speeches by the country's president and an American official from the DEA. More drug killings in Chihuahua. He shook his head.

In a half hour the food arrived and he sat down at the table, removed his tie—he dressed for work, even when staying home—and stuffed a napkin into his collar. As he ate, his mind wandered to the Dickens that his book dealer, Señor Davila, would be delivering tomorrow. He was delighted that it had arrived early, but pleased, too, that he was getting it for a lower price than originally agreed. The seller whom Davila had found apparently needed cash and would reduce the price by five thousand if Cuchillo paid in U.S. dollars, which he immediately agreed to do. Davila had said he would reduce his percentage of the finder's fee accordingly, but Cuchillo had insisted that he receive the full amount. Davila had always been good to him.

There was a knock on the door and his security chief, José, entered.

He could tell at once: bad news.

"I heard from a contact in the *Federales*, sir. There is intelligence about this bus attack on Friday? The tourist bus? The reports are linking you to it."

"No!"

"I'm afraid so."

"Dammit," he muttered. Cuchillo had uttered only a few obscenities in his life; this was usually the worst his language got. "*Me*? This is absurd. This is completely wrong! They blame me for everything!"

"I'm sorry, sir."

Cuchillo calmed and considered the problem. "Call the bus lines, call the security people, call whoever you have to. Do what you can to make sure passengers are safe in Sonora. You understand, I want to be certain that no one is hurt here. They will blame me if anything happens."

"I'll do what I can, sir, but—"

His boss said patiently, "I understand you can't control the entire state. But use our resources to do whatever you can."

"Yessir, I will."

The man hurried off.

Cuchillo finally shrugged off the anger, finished dinner and, sipping his wine, walked up and down the aisles enjoying the sight of his many titles.

22,000 . . .

He returned to his den and worked some more on the project that had obsessed him for the past few months: opening another auto parts fabrication plant outside of town. There was a huge U.S. automobile manufacturer here in Hermosillo and Cuchillo had made much of his fortune by supplying parts to the company. It would employ another 400 local workers. Though he benefitted from their foolishness, he couldn't understand the Americans' sending manufacturing *away* from their country. He would never do that. Business—no, all of life—was about loyalty.

At ten p.m., he decided to retire early. He washed and walked into his large bedroom, thinking again of *The Old Curiosity Shop* he would receive tomorrow. This buoyed his spirits. He dressed in pajamas and glanced at his bedside table.

What should he read now, he wondered, to lull him to sleep?

He decided he would continue with *War and Peace*, a title that, he thought wryly, perfectly described a businessman's life in Mexico.

❧

In the living room of the apartment with the complicated ownership, P.Z. Evans was hunched over his improvised workbench, carefully constructing the bomb.

The care wasn't necessary because he risked getting turned into red vapor, not yet, in any event; it was simply that the circuits and wiring were very small and he had big hands. In the old days he would have been soldering the connections. But now impro-vised explosive devices were plug and play. He was pressing the circuits into sheets of especially powerful plastic explosive, which he'd packed into the leather cover after slicing it open with a surgeon's scalpel.

It was eleven p.m. and the agents had not had a moment's respite today. They'd spent the past twelve hours acquiring the key items to the project, like the surgeon's instruments, electronics and a leather-bound edition of the play *The Robbers* by Friedrich Schiller, which their new partner—book dealer Señor Davila—had suggested because Cuchillo liked the German author.

Through a jeweler's loupe over his right eye, Evans examined his handiwork and made some small adjustments.

Outside their door they could hear infectious *norteño* in a nearby square. An accordion was prominent. The windows were open because the evening air teased that it was heading toward the bearable, and the A.C. was off. Evans had convinced himself he had a moldinduced cough.

Alejo Díaz sat nearby, not saying anything and seemingly uneasy. This was not because of the bomb, but because he'd apparently found the task of becoming an expert on book collecting and Charles Dickens daunting, to say the least.

Still, Díaz would occasionally look up from Joseph Connolly's *Collecting Modern First Editions*, his eyes on the bomb. Evans thought about diving to the floor, shouting, "Oh, shit! Five . . . four . . . three . . ." But while the Mexican agent had a sense of humor, that might be over the line.

A half hour later he was gluing the leather into place. "Okay, that's it. Done."

Díaz eyed his handicraft. "Is small."

"Bombs are, yes. That's what makes them so nice."

"It will get the job done?"

A brief laugh. "Oh, yeah."

"Nice," Díaz repeated uneasily.

Evans's phone buzzed with an encrypted text. He read it.

"Bait's here."

A moment later there was a knock on the door and, even though the text he'd just received had included all the proper codes, both men drew their weapons.

But the delivery man was just who he purported to be—a man attached to the Economic Development Council for the U.S. consulate in northern Mexico. Evans had worked with him before. With a nod the man handed Evans a small package and turned and left.

Evans opened it and extracted the copy of Charles Dickens's *The Old Curiosity Shop*. Six hours ago it had been sitting in a famed book dealer's store on Warren Street in New York City. It had been bought with cash by the man who had just delivered it, and its journey to Sonora had been via chartered jet.

Killing bad guys is not only dangerous, it's expensive.

The American wrapped the book back up.

Díaz asked, "So, what are the next steps?"

"Well, you—you just keep on reading." A nod toward the book in his hands. "And when you're through with that, you might want to brush up on the history of English literature in general. You never know what subject might come up."

Díaz rolled his eyes and shifted in his chair, stretching. "And while I'm stuck in school, what are you going to do?"

"I'm going out and getting drunk."

"That is not so fair," Díaz pointed out.

"And it's even less fair when I'm thinking I may get laid, too."

THURSDAY

The latter part of his plans did not happen, though Evans had come close.

But Carmella, the gorgeous young woman he met at a nearby

bar, was a little too eager, which set off warning bells that she probably had designs to land a good-looking and apparently employed American husband.

In any event, tequila had intervened big time and the dance of your-place-or-mine never occurred.

It was now ten in the morning and, natch, hot as searing iron. No A.C., but Evans's cough was gone.

Díaz examined his partner. "You look awful. Hey, you know that many of Charles Dickens' most popular novels were first published serially and that he wrote in a style influenced by gothic popular novels of the Victorian era, but with a whimsical touch?"

"You're fucked if you go in talking like that."

"I going to read one of his books. Is Dickens translated into Spanish?"

"I think so. I don't know."

Evans opened an attach case he'd bought yesterday and had rigged with a false compartment. Into this narrow space he added the Schiller he'd doctored last night and sealed it. Then he added receipts, price guides, scraps of paper—everything that a book dealer would carry with him to a meeting with a collector. The Dickens, too, which was packed in bubble wrap. Evans then tested the communications app on the iPad that Díaz would have with him—it would appear to be in sleep mode, but a hypersensitive microphone would be picking up all the conversation between Cuchillo and Díaz. The system worked fine.

"Okay." Evans then checked his 9mm Beretta. He slipped it into his waistband. "Diversion's ready, device is ready. Let's do it."

They walked down to the parking lot. Evans went to a huge old Mercury—yes, a real Mercury, in sun-faded Mercury brown, with an untraceable registration. Díaz's car was a midnight blue Lincoln registered to Davila Collectable Books, which Señor Davila had quickly, almost tearfully, agreed to let them borrow.

According to the unwritten rules of times like these, the

start of a mission, when either or both might be dead within the hour, they said nothing of luck, hope, or the pleasure of working together. Much less did they shake hands.

"See you later."

"*Sí.*"

They climbed in, fired up the engines and hurried out of the lot.

❧

As he drove to Cuchillo's compound, Alejo Díaz could not help but think of the bus.

The people tomorrow, the tourists, who would be trapped and burned to death by this butcher. He recalled P.Z. Evans's words yesterday and reflected that these people were also—to Cuchillo—acceptable sacrifices.

Díaz was suddenly swept with fury at what people like this were doing to his country. Yes, the place was hot and dusty and the economy staggered and it dwelt forever in the shadow of that behemoth to the north—the country that Mexicans both loved and hated.

But this land is our home, he thought. And home, however flawed, deserves respect.

People like Alonso María Cuchillo treated Mexico with nothing but contempt.

Of course, Díaz would have to keep his revulsion deeply hidden when he met Cuchillo. He was just a shopkeeper's assistant; the drug lord was just another rich businessman with a love of books.

If he screwed that up, then many people—himself included—were going to die.

Then he was at the compound. He was admitted through a gate that swung open slowly and he parked near the modest front door. A swarthy, squat man who clearly was carrying a pistol greeted him pleasantly and asked him to step to a table in the entryway. Another guard gently but thoroughly frisked him.

Then the briefcase was searched.

Díaz regarded the operation with surprising detachment, he decided, considering he might be one minute away from being shot.

The detachment vanished and his heart thudded fiercely when the man frowned and dug into the case.

Jesus . . .

The man gazed at Díaz with wide eyes. Then he grinned. "Is this the new iPad?" He pulled it out and displayed it to the other guard.

His breathing stuttering in and out, Díaz nodded and wondered if his question had burst Evans's eardrum.

"Four-G?"

"If there's a server."

"How many gig?"

"Thirty-two," the Mexican agent managed to say.

"My son has that, too. His is nearly filled. Music videos." He man replaced it and handed the briefcase back. The Schiller novel remained undiscovered.

Struggling to control his breathing, Díaz said, "I don't have many videos. I use it mostly for work."

A few minutes later he was led into the living room. He declined water or any other beverage. Alone, the Mexican agent sat with the briefcase on his lap. He opened it again and smoothly freed the Schiller and slipped it into his waistband, absently thinking about the explosive two inches from his penis. The open lid obscured prying eyes or cameras if there were any. He extracted the Dickens and closed the case.

A moment later a shadow spread on the floor and Díaz looked up to see Cuchillo walking steadily forward on quiet feet.

The Knife. The slaughterer of hundreds, perhaps thousands.

The stocky man strode forward, smiling. He seemed pleasant enough, if a bit distracted.

"Señor Abrossa," he said—the cover name Davila had given when he'd called yesterday. Díaz now presented a business card they'd had printed yesterday. "Good day. Delighted to meet you."

"And I'm pleased to meet such an illustrious client of Señor Davila."

"And how is he? I thought he might come himself."

"He sends his regards. He's getting ready for the auction of eighteenth century Bibles."

"Yes, yes, that's right. One of the few books I *don't* collect. Which is a shame. I understand that the plot is very compelling."

Díaz laughed. "The characters, too."

"Ah, the Dickens."

Taking it reverently, the man unwrapped the bubble plastic and examined the volume and flipped through it. "It is thrilling to know that Dickens himself held this very book."

Cuchillo was lost in the book, a gaze of admiration and respect. Not lust or possessiveness.

And in the silence, Díaz looked around and noted that this house was filled with much art and sculpture. All tasteful and subdued. This was not the house of a gaudy drug lord. He had been inside those. Filled with excess—and usually brimming with beautiful and marginally clad women.

It was then that a sudden and difficult thought came to Díaz. Was it at all possible that they'd made a mistake? Was this subdued, cultured man *not* the vicious dog they'd been led to believe? After all, there'd never been any hard proof that Cuchillo was the drug lord many believed him to be. Just because one was rich and tough didn't mean he was a criminal.

Where exactly had the intelligence assigning guilt come from? How reliable was it?

He realized Cuchillo was looking at him with curiosity. "Now, Señor Abrossa, are you *sure* you're the book dealer I've been led to believe?"

Using all his willpower, Díaz kept a smile on his face and dipped a brow in curiosity.

The man laughed hard. "You've forgotten to ask for the money."

"Ah, sometimes I get so caught up in the books themselves that, you're right, I *do* forget it's a business. I personally would give books away to people who appreciate them."

"I most certainly *won't* tell your employer you said that." He reached into his pocket and extracted a thick envelop. "There is the fifty-five thousand. U.S. "Díaz handed him the receipt on Davila's letterhead and signed " *V. Abrossa.*"

"Thank you . . .?" Cuchillo asked, lifting an eyebrow.

"Victor." Díaz put the money in the attach case and closed it. He looked around. "Your home, it is very lovely. I've always wondered about the houses in this neighborhood."

"Thank you. Would you like to see the place?"

"Please. And your collection, too, if possible."

"Of course."

Cuchillo then lead him on a tour of the house, which was, like the living room, filled with understated elegance. Pictures of youngsters—his nieces and nephews who lived in Mexico City and Chihuahua, he explained. He seemed proud of them.

Díaz couldn't help wondering again: Was this a mistake?

"Now, come to my library. As a booklover, I hope you will be impressed."

They walked through the kitchen, where Cuchillo paused and asked the housekeeper how her ailing mother was doing. He nodded as she answered. He told her to take any time off she needed. His eyes were narrow with genuine sympathy.

A mistake . . .?

They walked out the back door and through the shade of twin brick walls, the ones protecting him from sniper shots, and then into the library.

Even as a non-book lover, Díaz was impressed. *More* than impressed.

The place astonished him. He knew the size from the drone images, but he hadn't imagined it would be filled as completely as it was. Everywhere, books. It seemed the walls were made of them, like rich tiles in all different sizes and colors and textures.

"I don't know what to say, sir."

They walked slowly through the cool room and Cuchillo talked about some of the highlights in the collection. "My superstars," he said. He pointed out some as they walked.

The Hound of the Baskervilles by Conan Doyle, *Seven Pillars of Wisdom* by T.E. Lawrence, *The Great Gatsby* by F. Scott Fitzgerald, *The Tale of Peter Rabbit* by Beatrix Potter, *Brighton Rock* by Graham Greene, *The Maltese Falcon* by Dashiell Hammett, *Night and Day* by Virginia Woolf, *The Hobbit* by J.R.R. Tolkien, *The Sound and the Fury* by William Faulkner, *A Portrait of the Artist as a Young Man* by James Joyce, *A La Recherche Du Temps Perdu* by Marcel Proust, *The Wonderful Wizard of Oz* by Frank Baum, *Harry Potter and the Philosopher's Stone* by J.K. Rowling, *The Bridge* by Hart Crane, *The Catcher in the Rye* by J.D. Salinger, *The Thirty-Nine Steps* by John Buchan, *The Murder on the Links* by Agatha Christie, *Casino Royale* by Ian Fleming.

"And our nation's writers too, of course—that whole wall there. I love all books, but it's important for us in Mexico to be aware of *our* people's voice." He strode forward and displayed a few. "Salvador Novo, Jos Gorostiza, Xavier Villaurrutia, and the incomparable Octavio Paz. Whom you've read, of course."

"Of course," Díaz said, praying that Cuchillo would not ask for the name of one of Paz's books, much less a plot or protagonist.

Díaz noted a book near the man's plush armchair. It was in a display case, James Joyce's *Ulysses*. He happened to have read about the title last night on a rare book website. "Is that the original 1922 edition?"

"Yes, that's right."

"It's worth about $150,000."

Cuchillo smiled. "No. It's worth nothing."

"Nothing?"

His arm swept in a slow circle, indicating the room. "This entire *collection* is worth nothing."

"How do you mean, sir?"

"Something has value only to the extent the owner is

willing to sell. I would never sell a single volume. Most book collectors feel this way, more so than about paintings or cars or sculpture."

The businessman picked up *The Maltese Falcon*. "You are perhaps surprised I have in my collection spy and detective stories?"

The agent recited a fact he'd read. "Of course, popular commercial fiction is usually *more* valuable than literature." He hoped he'd got this straight.

He must have. Cuchillo was nodding. "But I enjoy them for their substance as well as their collectability."

This was interesting. The agent said, "I suppose crime is an art form in a way."

Cuchillo's head cocked and he seemed confused. Díaz's heart beat faster.

The collector said, "I don't mean that. I mean that crime and popular novelists are often better craftspeople than so-called literary writers. The readers know this; they appreciate good storytelling over pretentious artifice. Take that book I just bought, *The Old Curiosity Shop*. When it first came out, serialized in weekly parts, people in New York and Boston would wait on the docks when the latest installment was due to arrive from England. They'd shout to the sailors, 'Tell us, is Little Nell dead?'" He glanced at the display case. "I suspect not so many people did that for *Ulysses*. Don't you agree?"

"I do, sir, yes." Then he frowned. "But wasn't *Curiosity Shop* serialized in monthly parts?"

After a moment Cuchillo smiled. "Ah, right you are. I don't collect periodicals, so I'm always getting that confused."

Was this a test, or a legitimate error?

Díaz could not tell.

He glanced past Cuchillo and pointed to a shelf. "Is that a Mark Twain?"

When the man turned Díaz quickly withdrew the doctored Schiller and slipped it onto a shelf just above *Ulysses*, near the drug baron's armchair.

He lowered his arm just as Cuchillo turned back. "No, not there. But I have several. You've read *Huckleberry Finn*?"

"No. I just know it as a collector's item."

"Some people consider it the greatest American novel. I consider it perhaps the greatest novel of the New World. It has lessons for *us* as well." A shake of the head. "And the Lord knows we need some lessons in this poor country of ours."

They returned to the living room and Díaz dug the iPad from the case. "Let me show you some new titles that Señor Davila has just gotten in." He supposed P.Z. Evans was relieved to hear his voice and learn that he had not been discovered and spirited off to a grave in the graceless Sonora desert.

He called up Safari and went to the website. "Now, we have—"

But his phony sales pitch was interrupted when a huge bang startled them all. A bullet had struck and spattered against the resistant glass of a window nearby.

"My God! What's that?" Díaz called.

"Get out of the room, away from the windows! Now!" José, the security man, gestured them toward the doorways leading out of the living room.

"They're bulletproof," Cuchillo protested.

"But they could try armor piercing when they realize! Move, sir!"

Everyone scattered.

∾

P.Z. Evans didn't get a chance to shoot his gun very often.

Although he and Díaz had earlier commented about Cuchillo meeting with an "accident" in a euphemistic way, in fact staging natural deaths was the preferred way to eliminate people. While the police would often *suspect* that the death of a terrorist or a criminal was not happenstance, a good craftsman could create a credible scenario that was satisfactory to avoid further investigation. A fall down stairs, a car crash, a pool drowning.

But nothing was as much fun as pulling out your long-barreled Italian pistol and blasting away.

He was about fifty yards from the compound, standing on a Dumpster behind a luxury apartment complex. There wasn't a support for the gun, but he was strong—shooters have to have good muscles—and he easily hit the window he was aiming for. He had a decent view through the glass and for his first shot aimed where nobody was standing—just in case this window happened not to be bullet proof. But the slugs smacked harmlessly into the strong glass. He emptied one mag, reloaded and leapt off the Dumpster, sprinting to the car, just as the side gate opened and Cuchillo's security people carefully looked out. Evans fired once into the wall to keep them down and then drove around the block to the other side of the compound.

No Dumpsters here, but he climbed on top of the roof of the car and fired three rounds into the window of Cuchillo's bedroom.

Then he hopped down and climbed into the driver's seat. A moment later he was skidding away.

Windows up, A.C. on full. If there was mold in car's vents he'd just take his chances. He was sweating like he'd spent an hour in the sauna.

❧

Inside the house, after the shooter had vanished and calm—relative calm—was restored, Cuchillo did something that astonished Alejo Díaz.

He ordered his security chief to call the police.

This hardly seemed like the sort of thing that a drug baron would do. You'd think he'd want as little attention—and as little contact with the authorities—as possible.

But when a Hermosillo police captain, along with four uniformed officers, arrived twenty minutes later, Cuchillo was grim and angry. "Once again, I've been targeted! People can't accept that I'm just a businessman. They assume because I'm successful that I'm a criminal and therefore I deserve to be shot. It's unfair! You work hard, you're responsible, you give back to your country and your city . . . and still people believe the worst of you!"

The police conducted a brief investigation, but the shooter was, of course, long gone. And no one had seen anything— everyone inside had fled to the den, bedroom or bathroom, as the security chief had instructed. Díaz's response: "I'm afraid I didn't see much, anything really. I was on the floor, hiding." He shrugged, as if faintly embarrassed by his cowardice.

The officer nodded and jotted his words down. He didn't believe him, but nor did he challenge Díaz to be more thorough; in Mexico one was used to witnesses who "didn't see much, anything really."

The police left and Cuchillo, no longer angry but once more distracted, said goodbye to Díaz.

"I'm not much in the mood to consider Señor Davila's books now," he said, with a nod to the iPad. He would check the website later.

"Of course. And thank you, sir."

"It's nothing."

Díaz left, feeling even more conflicted than ever.

You work hard, you're responsible, you give back to your country and your city . . . and still people believe the worst of you . . .

My God, was he a murderous drug baron or a generous businessman?

And whether Cuchillo was guilty or innocent, Díaz realized he was stabbed by guilt at the thought that he'd just planted a bomb that would take the life of a man at his most vulnerable, doing something he loved and found comfort in: reading a book.

❧

An hour later Cuchillo was sitting in his den, blinds closed over the bulletproof windows. And despite the attack, he was feeling relieved.

Actually, *because* of the attack, he was feeling relieved.

He had thought that the rumors they'd heard for the past few days, the snippets of intelligence, were referring to some kind of brilliant, insidious plan to murder him, a plan that he couldn't anticipate. But it had turned out to be a simple shooting, which had been foiled by the bullet proof glass; the assassin was surely headed out of the area.

Jos knocked and entered. "Sir, I think we have a lead about the attack. I heard from Carmella at Ruby's. She spent much of last evening with an American, a businessman, he claimed. He got drunk and said some things that seemed odd to her. She heard of the shooting and called me."

"Carmella," Cuchillo said, grinning. She was a beautiful if slightly unbalanced young woman who could get by on her looks for the time being, but if she didn't hook a husband soon she'd be in trouble.

Not that Cuchillo was in any hurry for that to happen; he'd slept with her occasionally. She was very, very talented.

"And what about this American?"

"He was asking her about this neighborhood. The houses in it. If there were any hotels nearby, even though earlier he'd said he was staying near the bar."

While there were sights to see in the sprawling city of Hermosillo, Cuchillo's compound was in a nondescript residential area. Nothing here would draw either businessmen or tourists.

"Hotel," Cuchillo mused. "For a vantage point for shooting?"

"That's what I wondered. Now, I've gotten his credit card information from the bar and data-mined it. I'm waiting for more information but we know for a fact it's an assumed identity."

"So he's an operative. But who's he working for? A drug cartel from *north* of the border? A hit man from Texas hired by the Sinaloans? . . . The American government?"

"I hope to know more soon, sir."

"Thank you."

Cuchillo rose and, carrying the Dickens, started for the library.

He stopped. "José?"

"Sir?"

"I want to change our plans with the bus."

"Yes sir?"

"I know I said I wanted safe haven for all bus passengers in Sonora on Friday, that nothing should happen to the passengers here."

"Right, I told the men to wait to attack until it crossed the border into Sinaloa."

"But now, tell the men to hit a bus *here* tomorrow morning."

"In Sonora?"

"That's right. Whoever is behind this *must* know that I won't be intimidated. Any attempts on my life will be met with retribution."

"Yes sir."

Cuchillo looked as his security man carefully. "You don't think I should be doing this, do you?" He encouraged those working for him to make their opinions known, even—especially—differing opinions.

"Frankly, sir, not a tourist bus, no. Not civilians. I think it works to our disadvantage."

"I disagree," Cuchillo said calmly. "We need to take a strong stand."

"Of course, sir, if that's what you want."

"Yes, it is." But a moment later he frowned. "But wait. There's something to what you say."

The security man looked his boss's way.

"When your men attack the bus, get the women and children off before you set it on fire. Only burn the men to death."

"Yes sir."

Cuchillo considered his decision a weakness. But José had a point. The new reality was that, yes, sometimes you *did* need to take public relations into account.

∾

At eight p.m. that evening Cuchillo received a call in his library.

He was pleased at what he learned. One of his lieutenants explained that a shooting team was in place and would assault a large bus as it headed along Highway 26 west toward Bahia de Kino tomorrow morning.

They would stop the vehicle, leave the men on board, then wire shut the door and douse the bus in petrol and shoot anybody who tried to leap from the windows.

The communications man on the shooting team would call the press to make sure they arrived for video and photos before the fire was out.

Cuchillo thanked the man and disconnected, thinking of how much he was looking forward to seeing those news accounts.

He hoped the man who had shot at him would be watching the news, too, and would feel responsible for the pain the victims would experience.

Glancing up from his armchair, he happened to notice that a book was out of order.

It was on the shelf above the case containing the *Ulysses*.

He rose and noted the leather spine. *The Robbers*. How had a Schiller gotten here? He disliked disorder of any kind, particularly in his book collection. One of the maids, perhaps.

Just as he plucked the volume from the shelf, the door burst open.

"Sir!"

"What?" he turned quickly to Jos.

"I think there's a bomb here! That man with the book dealer, Davila; he's fake. He was working with the American!"

His eyes first went to the Dickens but, no, he'd flipped through the entire volume and there'd been no explosives inside. The assassins had simply used that as bait to gain access to Cuchillo's compound.

Then he looked down at what he held in his hand. The Schiller.

"What is it, sir?"

"This book . . . It wasn't here earlier. Abrossa! He planted it when I gave him the tour." Cuchillo realized that, yes, the book was heavier than a comparable book of this size.

"Set it down! Run!"

"No! The books!" He glanced around at the library.

22,000 volumes . . .

"It could blow up at any moment."

Cuchillo started to set it down, then hesitated. "I can't do it! You get back, José!" Then still holding the bomb, he ran outside, the security guard remaining loyally beside him. Once they were to the garden, Cuchillo flung the Schiller as far as he could. The men dropped to the ground behind one of the brick walls.

There was no explosion.

When Cuchillo looked he saw that the book had opened. The contents—electronics and a wad of clay—colored explosives—had tumbled out.

"Jesus, Jesus."

"Please, sir. Inside now!"

They hurried into the house and got the staff away from the side of the house where the box lay in the garden. José called the man they used for making their *own* bombs. He would hurry to the house and disarm or otherwise dispose of the device.

Cuchillo poured a large Scotch. "How did you find this out?"

"I got the data-mined information on the American in the bar, the one who was drinking with Carmella. I found records that he was making calls to the book dealer. And he used his credit card to buy electronic parts at a supplier in town—the sort of circuits that are used in IEDs."

"Yes, yes. I see. They threatened Davila to help them. Or paid the bastard. You know, I suspected that man, Abrossa. I suspected him for a moment. Then I decided, no, he was legitimate."

Because I wanted the Dickens so much.

"I appreciate what you did, José. That was a good job. Would you like a drink, too?"

"No, thank you, sir."

Still calm, Cuchillo wrinkled his brow. "Considering how the American tried to kill us—and nearly destroyed a priceless collection of books—how would you feel if we instructed our people on Highway 26 *not* to get the women and children off before setting fire to the bus?"

José smiled. "I think that's an excellent suggestion, sir. I'll call the team."

∾

Several hours later the bomb had been slipped into a steel disposal container and taken away. Cuchillo, the engineer explained, had unwittingly disarmed it himself. The panicked throw had dislodged the wires from the detonator, rendering it safe.

Cuchillo had enjoyed watching the bomb-disposal robot— the same way he liked being in his parts manufacturing operation and his drug synthesizing facilities. He enjoyed watching technology at work. He had always wanted the *Codex Leicester*—the DaVinci manuscript that contained the inventor's musings on mechanics and science. Bill Gates had paid $30 million for it some years ago. Cuchillo could easily afford that, but the book was not presently for sale. Besides, such a purchase would draw too much attention to him, and a man who has tortured hundreds to death and—in the spirit of mercy—painlessly shot perhaps a thousand, does not want too many eyes turned in his direction.

Cuchillo spent the rest of the night on the phone with associates, trying to find more details of the two assassins and any associates they might have, but there was no other information. He'd learn more tomorrow. It was nearly midnight when finally he sat down to a modest dinner of grilled chicken and beans with tomatillo sauce.

As he ate and sipped a very nice cabernet, he found himself relaxed and curiously content, despite the horror of what might have happened today. Neither he nor any of his people had been injured in the attack. His 22,000 volumes were safe.

And he had some enjoyable projects on the horizon: killing Davila, of course. And he'd find the name of the person masquerading as Abrossa, his assistant, and the shooter who'd fired the shots—a clumsy diversionary tactic, he now realized. Probably the American. Those two would not die as quickly as the book dealer. They had destroyed an original Friedrich Schiller (albeit a third printing with water damage on the spine). Cuchillo would stay true to his name and would use a knife on them himself—in his special interrogation room in the basement below his library.

But best of all: he had the burning bus and its scores of screaming passengers to look forward to.

FRIDAY

At one a.m. Cuchillo washed for bed and climbed between the smooth sheets, not silk but luxurious and expensive cotton.

He would read something calming to lull him to sleep tonight. Not *War and Peace*.

Perhaps some poetry.

He picked up his iPad from the bedside table, flipped open the cover and tapped the icon to bring up his e-reader app. Cuchillo, of course, generally preferred traditional books for the most part. But he was a man of the 21st century and found e-books were often more convenient and easier to read than their paper forebears. His iPad library contained nearly a thousand titles.

As he looked at the tablet, though, he realized he must have hit the wrong app icon—the forward camera had opened and he found he was staring at himself.

Cuchillo didn't close the camera right away, however. He took a moment to regard himself. And laughed and whispered the phrase he'd used to describe himself earlier, "Not so bad, you old devil."

∾

Five hundred yards from Cuchillo's compound, Alejo Díaz and P.Z. Evans were sitting in the front seat of the big Mercury. They were leaning forward, staring at the screen of Evans's impressive laptop computer.

What they were observing was the same image that Cuchillo happened to be basking in—his own wide-angle face—which was being beamed from his iPad's camera to the laptop via a surveillance app that Evans had loaded. They could hear the man's voice too.

You old devil . . .

"He's in bed, alone," Evans said. "Good enough for me." Then he glanced at Díaz. "He's all yours."

"*Sí?*" asked the Mexican agent.

"Yep."

"*Gracias.*"

"*Nada.*"

And without any dramatic flair, Díaz pressed a button on what looked like a garage door opener.

In Cuchillo's bedroom, the iPad's leather case, which Evans had stuffed with the potent incendiary explosive last night, detonated. The explosion was far larger than the American agent had expected. Even the bullet-proof windows blew to splinters and a gaseous cloud of flame shot into the night.

They waited until it was clear the bedroom was engulfed in flame—and all the evidence of the attack was burning to vapors, as they'd been instructed to do by Washington—and then Díaz started the car and drove slowly through the night.

After ten minutes of silence, looking over their shoulders for police or other pursuers, Díaz said, "Have to say, *amigo*, you came up with a good plan."

Evans didn't gloat—or act shy with false modesty, either. It *was* a good plan. Data-mining had revealed a lot about Cuchillo (this was often true in the case of targets like him—wealthy and, accordingly, big spenders). Evans and *Díaz* had noted not only his purchases of collectable books, but his high-tech acquisitions too: an iPad, an e-reader app and a number of e-books, as well as a leather case for the Apple device.

Armed with this information, Evans duplicated the iPad and filled the case with the deadly explosive. *This* was the actual weapon that Díaz smuggled into the compound and swapped with Cuchillo's iPad, whose location they could pinpoint thanks to the finder service Evans had hacked into. With Díaz inside, holding the iPad to show Davila's latest inventory of books, Evans had fired into the windows, scattering everyone and giving his partner a chance to slip into the bedroom and switch the devices. He'd fired into that room's windows, too, just in case Díaz had not been alone there.

The bullets would also serve a second purpose—to let Cuchillo and his security people believe the shooting was the assault they'd heard about and lessen their suspicion that another attack was coming.

Lessen, but not eliminate. The Knife was too sharp for that.

And so they needed a second misdirection. Evans let slip fake information about himself—to Carmella, the beautiful woman who was part of Cuchillo's entourage at Ruby's Bar (phone records revealed he called her once or twice a month). He also fed phony data-mined facts that suggested he and Díaz might have snuck a bomb into the library. He'd hollowed out a copy of Schiller's *The Robbers*—Sorry, Fred—and filled it with real explosives and a circuit, but failed to connect the detonators.

Cuchillo would know his library so well it wouldn't take much to find this out-of-place volume, which Díaz had intentionally planted askew.

After finding this device, they would surely think no more threats existed and not suspect the deadly iPad on Cuchillo's bedside table.

Díaz now called José, the security chief for the late drug baron, and explained—in a loud voice due to the chief's sudden hearing loss—that if any bus attacks occurred he would end up in jail accompanied by the rumor that he had sold his boss out. As unpopular as Cuchillo had been among the competing cartel figures, nothing was more unpopular in a Mexican prison than a snitch.

The man assured them that there would be no attacks. Díaz had to say goodbye three times before the man heard him.

A good plan, if a bit complicated. It would have been much easier, of course, simply to get a real bomb into the library and detonate it when drone surveillance revealed Cuchillo inside.

That idea, however, hadn't even been on the table. They would never have destroyed the library. Aside from the moral issue—and P.Z. Evans *did* have his standards—there was the little matter of how such a conflagration would play in the press if word got out about the identity of the two agents who'd orchestrated it and who their employers were.

You can kill drug barons and their henchmen with impunity; 20,000 destroyed classics were not acceptable sacrifices. That was the sort of mar from which careers do not recover.

In a half hour they were back at the hotel and watching the news, which confirmed that indeed Alonso María Carillo, known as Cuchillo, the suspected head of the Hermosillo Cartel, was dead. No one else had been injured in the attack, which was blamed on a rival cartel, probably from Sinaloa.

The news, Evans was surprised to note, wasn't the lead story, which Cuchillo probably would have taken hard. But, in a way, it was his own fault; he'd contributed to the ubiquity of the drug business in Mexico, which made stories about death in the trade unnewsworthy.

Evans supposed it was something like book collecting: the bigger the print run for first editions, the less the interest, the lower the value.

He shut the set off. They decided to get a little dinner and a lot of tequila—though definitely not at Sonora Steak or Ruby's bar, Cuchillo's favorite hangouts. They'd go somewhere across town. They'd probably be safe; the Hermosillo Cartel had been neutralized. Still, both men had their weapons underneath their untucked shirts. And extra magazines in their left pockets.

As they walked to the big old Mercury, Díaz said, "You should have seen all those books in the library. I never saw so many books in my life."

"Uhn," Evans said, not particularly interested.

"What does that mean, that sound? You don't *like* books?"

"I like books."

The Mexican agent gave a fast laugh. "You no sound like you do. You read at all?"

"Of course I read."

"So, what do you read? Tell me."

Evans climbed into the passenger seat and counted three pickup trucks pass by before he answered. "Okay, you want to know? The sports section. That's all I read."

Díaz started the car. "*Sí*, me too."

Evans said, "Could we get that A.C. going, Al? Does it *ever* cool off in this goddamn town?

Pronghorns of the
Third Reich

C.J. Box

A s he did every morning, Paul Parker's deaf and blind old Labrador, Champ, signaled his need by burrowing his nose into Parker's neck and snuffling. If Parker didn't immediately throw back the covers and get up, Champ would woof until he did. So he got up. The dog used to bound downstairs in a manic rush and skid across the hardwood floor of the landing to the back door, but now he felt his way down slowly, with his belly touching each step, grunting, his big nose serving as a kind of wall bumper. Champ steered himself, Parker thought, via echo navigation. Like a bat. It was sad. Parker followed and yawned and cinched his robe tight and wondered how many more mornings there were left in his dog.

Parker glanced at his reflection in a mirror in the stairwell. Six-foot-two, steel-gray hair, cold blue eyes, and a jaw line that was starting to sag into a dewlap. Parker hated the sight of the dewlap, and unconsciously raised his chin to flatten it. Something else: he looked tired. Worn and tired. He looked like someone's old man. Appearing in court used him up these days. Win or lose, the trials just took his energy out of him and it took longer and longer to recharge. As Champ struggled ahead of him, he wondered if his dog remembered *his* youth.

He passed through the kitchen. On the counter was the bourbon bottle he had forgotten to cap the night before, and the coffee maker he hadn't filled or set. He looked out the window over the sink. Still dark, overcast, spitting snow, a sharp wind quivering the bare branches of the trees. The cloud cover was pulled down like a window blind in front of the distant mountains.

Parker waited for Champ to get his bearings and find the back door. He took a deep breath and reached for the door handle, preparing himself for a blast of icy wind in his face.

Lyle and Juan stood flattened and hunched on either side of the back door of the lawyer's house on the edge of town. They wore balaclavas and coats and gloves. Lyle had his stained gray Stetson clamped on his head over the balaclava, even though Juan had told him he looked ridiculous.

They'd been there for an hour in the dark and cold and wind. They were used to conditions like this, even though Juan kept losing his focus, Lyle thought. In the half-light of dawn, Lyle could see Juan staring off into the backyard toward the mountains, squinting against the pinpricks of snow, as if pining for something, which was probably the warm weather of Chihuahua. Or a warm bed. More than once, Lyle had to lean across the back porch and cuff Juan on the back of his skull and tell him to get his head in the game.

"What game?" Juan said. His accent was heaviest when he was cold, for some reason, and sounded like, "*Wha' gaaaame?*"

Lyle started to reach over and shut Juan up when a light clicked on inside the house. Lyle hissed, "Here he comes. Get ready. *Focus*. Remember what we talked about."

To prove that he heard Lyle, Juan scrunched his eyes together and nodded.

Lyle reached behind him and grasped the Colt .45 1911 ACP with his gloved right hand. He'd already racked in a round so there was no need to work the slide. He cocked it and held it alongside his thigh.

Across the porch, Juan drew a .357 Magnum revolver from the belly pocket of the Carat hoodie he wore.

The back door opened and the large blocky head of a dog poked out looking straight ahead. The dog grunted as it stepped down onto the porch and waddled straight away, although Juan had his pistol trained on the back of its head. It was Juan's job to watch the dog and shoot it dead if necessary.

Lyle reached up and grasped the outside door handle and jerked it back hard.

Paul Parker tumbled outside in a heap, robe flying, blue-white bare legs exposed. He scrambled over on his hands and knees in the snow-covered grass and said, "Jesus Christ!"

"No," Lyle said, aiming the pistol at a spot on Parker's forehead. "Just us."

"What do you want?"

"What's coming to me," Lyle said. "What I deserve and you took away."

A mix of recognition and horror passed over Parker's face. Lyle could see the fear in the lawyer's eyes. It was a good look as far as Lyle was concerned. Parker said, "Lyle? Is that you?"

What could Lyle want, Parker thought. There was little of significant value in the house. Not like Angler's place out in the country, that book collection of Western Americana. But Lyle? He *was* a warped version of Western Americana . . .

"Get up and shut the hell up," Lyle said, motioning with the Colt. "Let's go in the house where it's warm."

Next to Parker, Champ squatted and his urine steamed in the grass.

"He don' even know we're here," Juan said. "Some watch dog. I ought to put it out of its misery." *Meeserie.*

"Please don't," Parker said, standing up. "He's my bird dog and he's been a great dog over the years. He doesn't even know you're here." Lyle noticed Parker had dried grass stuck to his bare knees.

"You don't look like such a hotshot now without your lawyer suit," Lyle said.

"I hope you got some hot coffee, mister," Juan said to Parker.

"I'll make some."

"Is your wife inside?" Lyle asked.

"No."

Lyle grinned beneath his mask, "She left you, huh?"

"Nothing like that," Parker lied. "She's visiting her sister in Sheridan."

"Anybody inside?"

"No."

"Don't be lying to me."

"I'm not. Look, whatever it is . . ."

"Shut up," Lyle said, gesturing with his Colt, "Go inside slowly and try not to do something stupid."

Parker cautiously climbed the step and reached out for the door Lyle held. Lyle followed. The warmth of the house enveloped him, even through his coat and balaclava.

Behind them, Juan said, "What about the dog?"

"Shoot it," Lyle said.

"Jesus God," Parker said, his voice tripping.

A few seconds later there was a heavy boom and simultaneous yelp from the back yard, and Juan came in.

Paul Parker sat in the passenger seat of the pickup and Lyle sat just behind him in the crew cab with the muzzle of his Colt kissing the nape of his neck. Juan drove. They left the highway and took a two-track across the sagebrush foothills eighteen miles from town. They were shadowed by a herd of thirty to forty pronghorn antelope. It was late October, almost November, the grass was brown and snow from the night before pooled in the squat shadows of the sagebrush. The landscape was harsh and bleak and the antelope had been designed perfectly for it: their brown and white coloring melded with the terrain and at times it was as if they were absorbed within it. And if the herd didn't feel comfortable about something—like the intrusion of a 1995 beat-up Ford pickup pulling a rattletrap empty stock trailer behind it—they simply flowed away over the hills like molten lava.

"Here they come again," Juan said to Lyle. It was his truck

and they'd borrowed the stock trailer from an outfitter who got
a new one. "They got so many antelopes out here."

"Focus," Lyle said. He'd long since taken off the mask—no
need for it now—and stuffed it in his coat pocket.

Parker stared straight ahead. They'd let him put on pajamas
and slippers and a heavy lined winter topcoat and that was all.
Lyle had ordered him to bring his keys but leave his wallet and
everything else. He felt humiliated and scared. That Lyle Peebles
and Juan Martinez had taken off their masks meant that they
no longer cared if he could identify them, and that was a very
bad thing. He was sick about Champ.

Lyle was close enough to Parker in the cab that he could smell
the lawyer's fear and his morning breath. Up close, Lyle noticed,
the lawyer had bad skin. He'd never noticed in the courtroom.

"So you know where we're going," Lyle said.

"The Angler Place," Parker said.

"That's right. And do you know what we're going to do
there?"

After a long pause, Parker said, "No, Lyle, I don't."

"I think you do."

"Really, I . . ."

"Shut up," Lyle said to Parker. To Juan, he said, "There's a
gate up ahead. When you stop at it I'll get Paul here to come
and help me open it. You drive through and we'll close it behind
us. If you see him try anything hinky, do the same thing to him
you did to that dog."

"Champ," Parker said woodenly.

"*Ho-kay,*" Lyle said.

Juan Martinez was a mystery to Parker. He'd never seen nor
heard of him before that morning. Martinez was stocky and
solid with thick blue/black hair and he wore a wispy gunfighter's
mustache that made his face look unclean. He had piercing
black eyes that revealed nothing. He was younger than Lyle, and
obviously deferred to him. The two men seemed comfortable

with each other and their easy camaraderie suggested long days and nights in each other's company. Juan seemed to Parker to be a blunt object; simple, hard, without remorse.

Lyle Peebles was dark and of medium height and build and he appeared older than his 57 years, Parker thought. Lyle had a hard narrow pinched face, leathery dark skin that looked permanently sun and wind-burned, the spackled sunken cheeks of a drinker, and a thin white scar that practically halved his face from his upper lip to his scalp. He had eyes that were both sorrowful and imperious at the same time, and teeth stained by nicotine that were long and narrow like horse's teeth. His voice was deep with a hint of country twang and the corners of his mouth pulled up when he spoke but it wasn't a smile. He had a certain kind of coiled menace about him, Parker thought. Lyle was the kind of man one shied away from if he was coming down the side-walk or standing in the aisle of a hardware store because there was a dark instability about him that suggested he might start shouting or lashing out or complaining and not stop until security was called. He was a man who acted and dressed like a cowpoke but he had grievances inside him that burned hot.

Parker had hoped that when the trial was over he'd never see Lyle Peebles again for the rest of his life.

Parker stood aside with his bare hands jammed into the pockets of his coat. He felt the wind bite his bare ankles above his slippers and burn his neck and face with cold. He knew Juan was watching him closely so he tried not to make any suspicious moves or reveal what he was thinking.

He had no weapons except for his hands and fists and the ball of keys he'd been ordered to bring along. He'd never been in a fist-fight in his life, but he could fit the keys between his fingers and start swinging.

He looked around him without moving his head much. The prairie spread out in all directions. They were far enough away from town there were no other vehicles to be seen anywhere, no buildings or power lines.

"Look at that," Lyle said, nodding toward the north and west. Parker turned to see lead-colored clouds rolling straight at them, pushing gauzy walls of snow.

"Hell of a storm coming," Lyle said.

"Maybe we should turn back?" Parker offered.

Lyle snorted with derision.

Parker thought about simply breaking and running, but there was nowhere to run.

It was a standard barbed-wire ranch gate, stiff from disuse. Wire loops from the ancient fence post secured the top and bottom of the gate rail. A heavy chain and padlock mottled with rust stretched between the two. "You got the keys," Lyle said, gesturing with his Colt.

Parker dug the key ring out of his pocket and bent over the old lock. He wasn't sure which key fit it, or whether the rusty hasp would unsnap. While he struggled with the lock, a beach-ball-sized tumbleweed was dislodged from a sagebrush by the wind and it hit him in the back of his thighs, making him jump. Lyle laughed.

Finally, he found the right key and felt the mechanism inside give. Parker jerked hard on the lock and the chain dropped away on both sides.

"Stand aside," Lyle said, and shot him a warning look before he put his pistol in his pocket and leaned against the gate. The way to open these tight old ranch gates was to brace oneself on the gate side, thread one's arms through the strands until the shoulder was against the gate rail and reach out to the solid post and pull. The move left Lyle vulnerable.

Parker thought if he was prepared to do something and fight back, this was the moment. He could attack Lyle before Juan could get out of the pickup. He felt his chest tighten and his toes curl and grip within his slippers.

Lyle struggled with it. "Don't just stand there," red-faced

Lyle said to Parker through gritted teeth, "Help me get this goddamned thing open."

Parker leaned forward on the balls of his feet. He considered hurtling himself like a missile toward Lyle, then slashing at the man's face and eyes with the keys. He could tear Lyle's gun away, shoot Lyle, and then use it on Juan. That's what a man of action would do. That's what someone in a movie or on television would do.

Instead, the lawyer bent over so he was shoulder-to-shoulder with Lyle and his added bulk against the gatepost was enough that Lyle could reach up and pop the wire over the top and open it.

Back inside the pickup, they drove into the maw of the storm. It had enveloped them so quickly it was astonishing. Pellets of snow rained across the hood of the pickup and bounced against the cracked windshield. The heater blew hot air that smelled like radiator fluid inside the cab. Parker's teeth finally stopped chattering but his stomach ached from fear and his hands and feet were cold and stiff.

Juan leaned forward and squinted over the wheel, as if it would help him see better.

"This is the kind of stuff we live with every day," Lyle said to Parker. "Me and Juan are out in this shit day after day. We don't sit in plush offices taking calls and sending bills. This is the way it is out here."

Parker nodded, not sure what to say.

"The road forks," Juan said to Lyle in the backseat, "Which way do we go?"

"Left," Lyle said.

"Are you sure?"

"Goddamit, Juan, how many years did I spend out here on these roads?"

Juan shrugged and eased the pickup to the left. They couldn't see more than fifty feet in any direction. The wind swirled the heavy snow and it buffeted the left side of the pickup truck, rocking the vehicle on its springs when it gusted.

Parker said, "When this is over and you've got whatever it is you want, what then?"

Lyle said, "I'm still weighing that one, counselor. But for now just let me concentrate on getting to the house."

"It would he helpful to know what you've got in mind," Parker said, clearing his throat. Trying to sound conversational. "I mean, since I'm playing a role in this I can be of better service if I know your intentions."

Lyle backhanded the lawyer with his free hand, hitting him hard on the ear. Parker winced.

"Just shut up until we get there," Lyle said. "I heard enough talking from you in that courtroom to last the rest of my pea-pickin' life. So just shut up or I'll put a bullet into the back of your head."

Juan appeared to grimace, but Parker determined it was a bitter kind of smile.

Lyle said to Parker, "You got the keys to that secret room old Angler has, right? The one he never let anybody into? The one with the books?"

"How far?" Juan asked. They were traveling less than five miles an hour. The snow was so thick, Parker thought, it was like being inside a cloud. Tall sagebrush just a few feet from the road on either side looked like gray commas. Beyond the brush, everything was two-tone white and light blue.

"What's in the road?" Juan asked, tapping on the brake to slow them down even further.

Parker looked ahead. Six or seven oblong shadows emerged from the whiteout. They appeared suspended in the air. They looked like small coffins on stilts.

The pickup inched forward. The forms sharpened in detail. Pronghorn antelope—part of the same herd or from another herd. A buck and his does. They stood braced into the storm, oblivious to the truck. Juan drove so close to them Parker could see snow packed into the bristles of their hide and their goat-like faces and black eyes. The buck had long eyelashes and flakes of snow caught in them. His horns were tall and splayed, the hooked-back tips ivory colored.

"Fucking antelope," Lyle said. "Push 'em out of the way or run right over them."

Instead, Juan tapped the horn on the steering wheel. The sound was distant and tinny against the wind, but the pronghorns reacted; haunches bunching, heads ducking, and they shot away from the road as if they'd never been there.

Parker wished he could run like that.

"Few miles," Lyle said. "We'll pass under an archway. I helped build that arch, you know."

"I didn't know that," Juan said.

"Me and Juan," Lyle said to Parker, "We've worked together for the past what, twelve years?"

Juan said, "Twelve, yes. Twelve."

"Some of the shittiest places you could imagine," Lyle said. "All over the states of Wyoming and Montana. A couple in Idaho. One in South Dakota. Most of those places had absentee owners with pricks for ranch foremen. They're the worst, those pricks. They don't actually own the places so for them it's all about power. You give pricks like that a little authority and they treat the workingman like shit. Ain't that right, Juan?"

"*Ees* right."

Parker thought: *It's like we're the only humans on earth.* The world that had been out there just that morning—the world of vistas and mountains and people and cars and offices and meetings—had been reduced for him to just this. Three men in the cab of a pickup driving achingly slow through a whiteout where the entire world had closed in around them. Inside the cab there were smells and weapons and fear. Outside the glass was furious white rage.

There was a kind of forced intimacy that was not welcome,

Parker thought. He'd been reduced to the same level as these two no-account ranch hands who between them didn't have a nickel to rub together. They had guns and the advantage, Parker thought, but they were smart in the way coyotes or other predators were smart in that they knew innately how to survive but didn't have a clue how to rise up beyond that. He knew that from listening to Lyle testify in court in halting sentences filled with poorly chosen words. And when Lyle's broken down ninety-eight-year-old grandfather took the stand it was all over. Parker had flayed the old man with whips made of words until there was no flesh left on his ancient bones.

Lyle likely couldn't be reasoned with-he knew that already. No more than a coyote or a raven could be reasoned with. Coyotes would never become dogs. Likewise, ravens couldn't be songbirds. Lyle Peebles would never be a reasonable man. He was a man whose very existence was based on grievance.

"This is getting bad," Juan said, leaning forward in his seat as if getting six inches closer to the windshield would improve his vision. *Thees*.

Parker gripped the dashboard. The tires had become sluggish beneath the pickup as the snow accumulated. Juan was driving more by feel than by vision, and a few times Parker felt the tires leave the two-track and Juan had to jerk the wheel to find the ruts of the road again.

"We picked a bad day for this," Juan said. *Thees*.

"Keep going," Lyle said. "We been in worse than this before. Remember that time in the Pryor Mountains?"

"Si. That was as bad as this."

"That was *worse*," Lyle said definitively.

There was a metallic clang and Parker heard something scrape shrilly beneath the undercarriage of the truck.

"What the hell was that?" Lyle asked Juan.

"A T-post, I think."

"Least that means we're still on the road," Lyle said.

"*Ay-yi-yi*," Juan whistled.

"We could turn around," Parker said.

"We could," Juan agreed. "At least I could follow our tracks back out. As it is, I can't see where we're going."

"We're fine, Godammit," Lyle said. "I know where we are. Keep going. We'll be seeing that old house any time now."

Parker looked out his passenger window. Snow was sticking to it and covering the glass. Through a fist-sized opening in the snow, he could see absolutely nothing.

He realized Lyle was talking to him. "What did you say?"

"I said I bet you didn't expect you'd be doing this today, did you?"

"No."

"You're the type of guy who thinks once a judge says something it's true, ain't you?"

Parker shrugged.

"You thought after you made a fool of my grandpa you were done with this, didn't you?"

"Look," Parker said, "we all have jobs to do. I did mine. It wasn't personal."

Parker waited for an argument. Instead, he felt a sharp blow to his left ear and he saw spangles where a moment ago there had been only snow. The voice that cried out had been his.

He turned in the seat cupping his ear in his hand.

Lyle grinned back. Parker noticed the small flap of skin on the front sight of the Colt. And his fingers were hot and sticky with his blood.

"You say it ain't personal, lawyer," Lyle said. "But look at me. *Look* at me. What do you see?"

Parker squinted against the pain and shook his head slowly as if he didn't know how to answer.

"What you see, lawyer, is a third-generation loser. That's what you see, and don't try to claim otherwise or I'll beat you bloody. I'll ask you again: what do you see?"

Parker found that his voice was tremulous. He said, "I see a working man, Lyle. A good-hearted working man who gets paid for a hard day's work. I don't see what's so wrong with that."

"Nice try," Lyle said, feinting with the muzzle toward Parker's face like the flick of a tongue from a snake. Parker recoiled, and Lyle grinned again.

"That man fucked over my grandpa and set this all in motion," Lyle said. "He cheated him and walked away and hid behind his money and his lawyers for the rest of his life. Can you imagine what my grandpa's life would have been like if he hadn't been fucked over? Can you imagine what my life would have been like? Not like this, I can tell you. Why should that man get away with a crime like that? Don't you see a crime like that isn't a one-shot deal? That it sets things in motion for generations?"

"I'm just a lawyer," Parker said.

"And I'm just a no-account working man," Lyle said. "And the reason is because of people like you."

"Look," Parker said, taking his hand away from his ear and feeling a long tongue of blood course down his neck into his collar, "maybe we can go back to the judge with new information. But we need new information. It can't just be your grandfather's word and his theories about Nazis and . . ."

"They weren't just theories!" Lyle said, getting agitated. "It was the truth."

"It was so long ago," Parker said.

"That doesn't make it less true!" Lyle shouted.

"There was no proof. Give me some proof and I'll represent you instead of the estate."

Parker shot a glance at the rearview mirror to find Lyle deep in thought for a moment. Lyle said, "That's interesting. I've seen plenty of whores, but not many in a suit."

"Lyle," Juan said sadly, "I think we are lost."

The hearing had lasted less than two days. Paul Parker was the lawyer for the Fritz Angler estate, which was emerging from probate after the old man finally died and left no heirs except a disagreeable out-of-wedlock daughter who lived in Houston. From nowhere, Benny Peebles and his grandson Lyle made a claim for the majority of the Angler estate holdings. Benny claimed he'd been cheated out of ownership of the ranch generations ago and he wanted justice. He testified it had happened this way:

Benny Peebles and Fritz Angler, both in their early twenties, owned a Ryan monoplane together. The business model for Peebles/ Peebles Aviation was to hire out their piloting skills and aircraft to ranchers in Northern Wyoming for the purpose of spotting cattle, delivering goods, and transporting medicine and cargo. They also had contracts with the federal and state government for mail delivery and predator control. Although young and in the midst of the Depression, they were two of the most successful entrepreneurs the town of Cody had seen. Still, the income from the plane barely covered payments and overhead and both partners lived hand-to-mouth.

Peebles testified that in 1936 they were hired by a rancher named Wendell Oaks to help round up his scattered cattle. This was an unusual request, and they learned Oaks had been left high-and-dry by all of his ranch-hands because he hadn't paid them for two months. Oaks had lost his fortune in the crash and the only assets he had left before the bank foreclosed on his 16,000-acre spread were his Hereford cattle. He'd need to sell them all to raise $20,000 to save his place, and in order to sell them he'd need to gather them up. The payments to Peebles/ Peebles would come out of the proceeds, he assured them.

Benny said Fritz was enamored with the Oaks Ranch— the grass, the miles of river, the timber, and the magnificent Victorian ranch house that cost Oaks a fortune to build. He told Benny, "This man is living on my ranch but he just doesn't know it yet."

Benny didn't know what Fritz meant at the time, although his partner, he said, always had "illusions of grandiosity," as Benny put it.

Fritz sent Benny north to Billings to buy fence to build a massive temporary corral for the cattle. While he was gone, Fritz said, he'd fly the ranch and figure out where all the cattle were.

Benny returned to Cody four days later followed by a truck laden with rolls of fence and bundles of steel posts. But Fritz was gone, and so was the Ryan. Wendell Oaks was fit to be tied. Bankers were driving out to his place from Cody to take measurements.

Three days later, while Benny and some locals he'd hired on a day-rate were building the corral, he heard the buzz of an airplane motor. He recognized the sound and looked up to see Fritz Angler landing the Ryan in a hay meadow.

Before Benny could confront his partner, Fritz buttonholed one of the bankers and they drove off together into town. Benny inspected their monoplane and saw where Fritz had removed the co-pilot seat and broken out the interior divides of the cargo area to make more space. The floor of the aircraft was covered in white bristles of hair and animal feces. It smelled dank and unpleasant.

The next thing Benny knew, sheriff's deputies descended on the place and evicted Wendell Oaks. Then they ordered Benny and his laborers off the property by order of the sheriff and the bank and new owner of the ranch, Fritz Angler, who had paid off the outstanding loan balance and now owned the paper for the Oaks Ranch.

The arch appeared out of the snow and Juan drove beneath it. Parker was relieved to discover how close they were to the ranch house, and just as frightened to anticipate what might come next.

Lyle was wound up. "That mean old German son-of-a-bitch never even apologized," he said heatedly from the backseat. "He used the airplane my Grandpa owned half of to swindle our family out of this place, and he never even said sorry. If nothing else, we should have owned half of all this. Instead, it turned my family to a bunch of two-bit losers. It broke my Grandpa and ruined my dad and now it's up to me to get what I can out of it. What choice do I have since you cheated us again in that court?"

"I didn't cheat you," Parker said softly, not wanting to argue with Lyle in his agitated state. "There was no proof . . ."

"Grandpa told you what happened!" Lyle said.

"But that story you told . . ."

"He don't lie. Are you saying he lied?"

"No," Parker said patiently. "But I mean, *come on*. Who is going to believe that Fritz Angler trapped a hundred antelope fawns and flew them around the country and sold them to zoos? That he sold some to Adolf Hitler and flew that plane all the way to Lakehurst, New Jersey and loaded a half-dozen animals on the Hindenburg to be taken to the Berlin Zoo? I mean, come on, Lyle."

"It happened!" Lyle shouted. "If Grandpa said it happened, it fucking happened."

Parker recalled the skeptical but patient demeanor of the judge as old Benny Peebles droned on at the witness stand. There were a few snickers from the small gallery during the tale.

Juan shook his head and said to Parker, "I hear this story before. Many times about the plane and the antelopes."

Parker decided to keep quiet. There was no point in arguing. Lyle spoke with the deranged fervor of a true believer, despite the outlandishness of the tale.

Lyle said, "Look around you. There are thousands of antelope on this ranch, just like there were in 1936. Angler used the plane to herd antelope into a box canyon, where he bound them up. Grandpa showed me where he done it. Angler loaded them into the Ryan and started east, selling them all along the way. He had connections with Hitler because he was German! His family was still over there. They were a bunch of fucking Nazis just like Angler. He knew who to call.

"He sold those fawns for $100 to $200 each because they

were so rare outside Wyoming at the time. He could load up to 40 in the plane for each trip. He made enough cash money to buy airplane fuel all the way to New Jersey and back and still had enough to pay off Wendell Oaks' loan. He did the whole thing in a plane co-owned by my Grandpa but never cut him in on a damned thing!

"Then he started buying other ranches," Lyle said, speaking fast, spittle forming at the corners of his mouth, "then they found that damned oil. Angler was rich enough to spend thousands on lawyers and thugs to keep my Grandpa and my dad away from him all those years. Our last shot was contesting that old Nazi's estate—and *you* shut us out."

Parker sighed and closed his eyes. He'd grown up in Cody. He despised men who blamed their current circumstances on past events as if their lives were preordained. Didn't Lyle know that in the West you simply reinvented yourself? That family legacies meant next to nothing?

"I can't take this ranch with me," Lyle said. "I can't take enough cattle or vehicles or sagebrush to make things right. But I sure as hell can take that damned book collection of his. I've heard it's worth hundreds of thousands. Ain't that right, Parker?"

"I don't know," Parker said. "I'm not a collector."

"But you've seen it, right? You've been in that secret room of his?"

"Once." Parker recalled the big dark room with floor-to-ceiling oak bookshelves that smelled of paper and age. Fritz liked to sit in a red-leather chair under the soft yellow light of a Tiffany lamp and read, careful not to fully open or damage the books in any way. It had taken him sixty years to amass his collection of mostly leather-bound first editions. The collection was comprised primarily of books about the American West and the Third Reich in original German. While Parker browsed the shelves he had noted both volumes of *Mein Kampf* with alarm but had said nothing to the old man.

"And what was in there?" Lyle said. "Did you see some of the books I've heard about? Lewis and Clark's original journals? Catlin's books about Indians? A first edition of Irwin Wister?"

"Owen Wister," Parker corrected. "*The Virginian.* Yes, I saw them."

"Ha!" Lyle said with triumph. "I heard Angler brag that the Indian book was worth a half million."

Parker realized two things at once. They were close enough to the imposing old ranch house they could see its Gothic outline emerge from the white. And Juan had stopped the pickup.

"Books!" Juan said, biting off the word. "*We're here for fucking books? You said we would be getting his treasure.*"

"Juan," Lyle said, "his books are his treasure. That's why we brought the stock trailer."

"I don't want no books!" Juan growled, "I thought it was jewelry or guns. You know, *rare* things. I don't know nothing about old books."

"It'll all work out," Lyle said, patting Juan on the shoulder. "Trust me. People spend a fortune collecting them."

"Then they're fools," Juan said, shaking his head.

"Drive right across the lawn," Lyle instructed Juan. "Pull the trailer up as close as you can get to the front doors so we don't have to walk so far."

"*So we can fill it with shitty old books,*" Juan said, showing his teeth.

"Calm down, amigo," Lyle said to Juan. "Have I ever steered you wrong?"

"About a thousand times, amigo."

Lyle huffed a laugh, and Parker watched Juan carefully. He didn't seem to be playing along.

Lyle said, "Keep an eye on the lawyer while I open the front door." To Parker, he said, "Give me those keys."

Parker handed them over and he watched Lyle fight the blizzard on his way up the porch steps. The wind was ferocious and Lyle kept one hand clamped down on his hat. A gust nearly drove him off the porch. If anything, it was snowing even harder.

"*Books*," Juan said under his breath. "He tricked me."

The massive double front doors to the Angler home filled a gabled stone archway and were eight feet high and studded with iron bolt heads. Angler had a passion for security, and Parker remembered noting the thickness of the open door when he'd visited. They were over two inches thick. He watched Lyle brush snow away from the keyhole and fumble with the key ring with gloved fingers.

"Books are not treasure," Juan said.

Parker sensed an opening. "No, they're not. You'll have to somehow find rich collectors who will overlook the fact that they've been stolen. Lyle doesn't realize each one of those books has an *ex libre* mark."

When Juan looked over, puzzled, Parker said, "It's a stamp of ownership. Fritz didn't collect so he could sell the books. He collected because he loved them. They'll be harder than hell to sell on the open market. Book collectors are a small world."

Juan cursed.

Parker said, "It's just like his crazy story about the antelope and the Hindenburg. He doesn't know what he's talking about."

"He's *crazy*."

"I'm afraid so," Parker said. "And he sucked you into this."

"I didn't kill your dog."

"*What*?"

"I didn't kill it. I shot by his head and he yelped. I couldn't shoot an old dog like that. I like dogs if they don't want to bite me."

"Thank you, Juan." Parker hoped the storm wasn't as violent in town and that Champ would find a place to get out of it.

They both watched Lyle try to get the door open. The side of his coat was already covered with snow.

"A man could die just being outside in a storm like this," Parker said. Then he took a long breath and held it.

"Lyle, he's crazy," Juan said. "He wants to fix his family. He don't know how to move on."

"Well said. There's no reason why you should be in trouble for Lyle's craziness," Parker said.

"Mister, I know what you're doing."

"But that doesn't mean I'm wrong."

Juan said nothing.

"My wife . . ." Parker said. "We're having some problems. I need to talk to her and set things right. I can't imagine never talking to her again. For Christ's Sake, my last words to her were, 'Don't let the door hit you on the way out.'"

Juan snorted.

"Please . . ."

"He wants you to help him," Juan said, chinning toward the windshield. Beyond it, Lyle was gesticulating at them on the porch.

"We can just back away," Parker said. "We can go home."

"You mean just leave him here?"

"Yes," Parker said. "I'll never breathe a word about this to anyone. I swear it."

Juan seemed to be thinking about it. On the porch, Lyle was getting angrier and more frantic. Horizontal snow and wind made his coat sleeves and pant legs flap. A gust whipped his hat off, and Lyle flailed in the air for it but it was gone.

"Go," Juan said.

"But I thought . . ."

"Go now," he said, showing the pistol.

Parker was stunned by the fury of the storm. Snow stung his face and he tried to duck his head beneath his upraised arm to shield it. The wind was so cold it felt hot on his exposed bare skin.

"Help me get this goddamned door open!" Lyle yelled. "I can't get the key to work." He handed Parker the keys.

"I don't know which one it is any more than you do," Parker yelled back.

"Just fucking try it, counselor!" Lyle said, jabbing at him with the Colt.

Parker leaned into the door much as Lyle had. He wanted to

block the wind with his back so he could see the lock and the keys and have room to work. He tried several keys and none of them turned. Only one seemed to fit well. He went back to it. He could barely feel his fingers and feet.

He realized Lyle was shouting again.

"Juan! Juan! What the hell are you doing?"

Parker glanced up. Lyle was on the steps, his back to him, shouting and waving his arms at the pickup and trailer that vanished into the snow. Faint pink tail lights blinked out.

At that moment, Parker pulled up on the iron door handle with his left hand while he turned the key with his right. The ancient lock gave way.

Parker slammed his shoulder into the door and stepped inside the dark house and pushed the door shut behind him and rammed the bolt home.

Lyle cursed at him and screamed for Parker to open the door.

Instead, Parker stepped aside with his back against the cold stone interior wall as Lyle emptied his .45 Colt at the door, making eight dime-sized holes in the wood that streamed thin beams of white light to the slate-rock floor.

He hugged himself and shivered and condensation clouds from his breath haloed his head.

Parker roamed through Angler's library, hugging himself in an attempt to keep warm and to keep his blood flowing. There were no lights and the phone had been shut off months before. Muted light filtered through gaps in the thick curtains. Outside, the blizzard howled and threw itself against the old home but couldn't get in any more than Lyle could get in. Snow covered the single window in the library except for one palm-sized opening, and Parker used it to look around outside for Lyle or Lyle's body but he couldn't see either. It had been twenty minutes since he'd locked Lyle out.

At one point he thought he heard a cry, but when he stopped pacing and listened all he could hear was the wind thundering against the windows.

He started a fire in the fireplace using old books as kindling and had fed it with broken furniture and a few decorative logs he'd found in the great room downstairs. Orange light from the flames danced on the spines of the old books.

He wanted a fire to end all fires that would not only warm him but also act as his shield against the storm and the coming darkness outside.

After midnight Parker ran out of wood and he kept the fire going with Angler's books. Mainly the German language volumes. The storm outside seemed to have eased a bit.

As he reached up on the shelves for more fuel, his fingers avoided touching the copies of *Mein Kampf*. The act of actually touching the books terrified Parker in a way he couldn't explain.

Then he reasoned that if books were to be burned, *Mein Kampf* should be one of them. As he tossed the volumes into the flames, a loose square of paper fluttered out of the pages onto the floor.

Parker bent over to retrieve it to flick it into the fire when he realized it was an old photograph. The image in the firelight made him gasp.

Parker ran down the stairs in the dark to the front door and threw back the bolt. The force of the wind opened both the doors inward and he squinted against the snow and tried to see into the black and white maelstrom.

"Lyle!" he shouted to no effect. "Lyle!"

AUTHOR'S NOTE

The story is fiction but the photograph is not.

In 1936, in one of the odder episodes of the modern American West, Wyoming rancher and noted photographer Charles Belden did indeed catch pronghorn antelope fawns on his ranch and deliver them to zoos across the nation in his Ryan monoplane, including a delivery to the German passenger airship LZ 129 *Hindenburg* in Lakehurst, New Jersey, bound for the Berlin Zoo.

The photograph appears courtesy of the Charles Belden Collection, American Heritage Center, University of Wyoming.

I can find no information on the fate of the pronghorn antelope. They would have arrived shortly after the conclusion of Adolf Hitler's '36 Olympics.

—CJB, 2011

The Book of Virtue

Ken Bruen

M Y OLD MAN:
Tough.

Cruel.

Merciless.

And that was on the weekends when he was happy. If a psycho could do happy.

His cop buddies said,

"Frank, Frank is just intense."

Right.

Other kids go,

"My dad took me to the Yankees."

Mine, he took out my teeth.

With intensity.

The horrors of peace. He bought the farm when I was seventeen. My mom, she took off for Boise, Idaho.

Hell of another sort.

They buried my father in the American flag. No argument, he was a patriot.

I played

"Another one bites the dust."

He'd have hated Queen to be the band.

His inheritance?

A book.

Rich, huh?

My father died horribly. A slow, lingering, eat-your-guts-in-pieces cancer. His buddies admired my constant vigil.

Yeah.

I wanted to ensure he didn't have one of those miraculous recoveries. His last hour, we had an Irish priest who anointed him, said,

"He will soon be with God."

The devil, maybe. With any luck.

He was lucid in his last moments. Looked at me with total fear.

I asked,

"Are you afraid?"

He nodded, his eyes welling up. I leaned close, whispered,

"Good, and, you know, it will get worse."

A flash of anger in those dead brown eyes, and I asked,

"What are you going to do, huh? Who you going to call, you freaking bully?"

The death rattle was loud and chilling. The doctor rushed in, held his hand, said,

"I am so sorry."

I managed to keep my smirk in check. He was buried in a cheap box, to accessorize his cheap soul. A week after, I was given his estate.

The single book.

Mind you, it was a beautiful volume, bound in soft leather, gold leaf trim. Heavy, too.

And well thumbed.

I was puzzled. My old man, his reading extended to the sports page in *The Daily News*.

But a book?

WTF?

On the cover, in faded gold was,

Virtue.

Like he'd know any damn thing about that.

Flicked through it

???

In his spidery handwriting, it was jammed with notes. The first page had this:

"You cannot open a book without learning something."

. . . Confucius.

I put the book down.

"Was he trying to educate himself?"

The schmuck.

My cell shrilled.

Brady, my boss. He muttered,

"Sorry about your old man."

Yeah. Yada, yada.

Did the sympathy jig for all of two minutes. Then,

"Grief in the club last night."

The outrider here being

"The hell where you?"

And, unsaid,

"So your old man bought the farm. You're supposed to ensure the club runs smooth."

The Khe San, in midtown.

Home to:

Wise guys

Cops

Strippers

Low lifes

Skels

Power trippers

Politicians.

All R and R-ing in a place of uneasy truce.

My job: to maintain smooth and easy vibe. I didn't ask if they checked their weapons at the door but did try to keep a rack on the rampant egos. I had an assistant—in truth a Mack 5 would have been the biz—but, lacking that, I had—

Cici.

A weapon of a whole deadly calibre.

Brady was a Nam wanna-be, like Bruce in his heyday, a dubious tradition begun by John Wayne with the loathsome Green Berets. Rattle on enough about a lost war and it gave the impression you were there. Sure to be shooting, Brady played "Born in the USA" like his own personal anthem. That he was from the Ukraine seemed neither here nor deceptive there.

I ran the club, and well.

Was taught by the best, my best friend, Scotty, but more of that later.

Had learned to walk the taut line between chaos and safety that growing up with a bully equips you to do. When your mother takes a walk early, you lose any semblance of trust. My old man, second generation Mick, was as sentimental as only a fledging psychopath can be. His MO was simple:

Beat the living shit out of your child, play the suck-heart songs:

"Danny Boy"

"Galway Bay"

"Molly Malone"

Sink a bottle of Jay.

Weep buckets for your own miserable self.

What they term the "Constellation of Disadvantage."

Booze, mental illness, violence.

But books?

Never.

So what the hell was this beautifully bound edition about? I opened another page at random.

Got

"A book must be an ice axe

To break

The seas

Frozen inside our soul."

I was rattled.

If he could quote that, and, Jesus wept, have applied it to his own self, where the fook did that leave my dark finished portrait of him?'

Resolved to run it by Cici.

She was

Brady's babe, in every sense.

Twenty five years of age with the experience of fifty, and all of them dirty.

And ruthless.

Concealed behind a stunning face, she had that rarity, green eyes, and a mouth designed by a *Playboy* deity.

She was a simple girl at heart, really.

All she wanted really was a shitload of cash.

And, like, before the spring.

Her beauty was of that unique stop-you-dead variety.

Worse, she knew it.

Used it.

Sure, I was banging her. If you live a cliché, then that's the most lame of all. But, see, I could talk to her, I think. And,

Get this:

She read.

Our club catered to the young punks, reared on the movies *Casino* and *Wise Guys*.

They spoke a mangled Joe Peschi, convoluted by snatches of Travis Bickle.

Books? Nope.

They didn't know from kindle to *National Enquirer*. But Cici, she'd have a book running alongside her vegetarian Slurpee. Her latest was titled, *Ethics of the Urban Sister*.

I shit thee not.

So, she seemed to know stuff. Couple that with an old soul glint in her amazing eyes and you had, what?

Sensuality with knowledge.

Late February, New York was colder than my old man's eyes.

An hour before the club opened, we were having the usual hassle:

Chef on the piss

Waitresses on the whinge

And a mega tab from an old guy in one of The Families who no one had the *cojones* to ask,

"Yo, fook head, you want to like, settle your freaking bill?"

Translate

Me.

As in having to ass kiss and somehow get some major green from the dangerous bastard.

Cici was down with the young guns' lingo,

Was explaining to me the essence of

"Too school for cool."

And the extreme irrationality of adding NOT to a statement. Like

"I'm happy."

Dramatic pause,

Then,

"Not."

Fook on a bike.

But the word that annoyed me beyond coherent belief was the universal reply to seemingly any situation.

Like

"Your wife was killed."

". . . Whatever!"

Or, even good news:

"You won the State Lottery."

They go

". . .Whatever."

Drives me ape shit.

My old man was dead five months then. Okay, five months and change.

So, I counted. You betcha. Joy can be measured.

Cici had, in a drunken moment, told me that Brady kept a mountain of coke, and a ton of cash, in his apartment. She was laying down the seed of a plan.

Scotty had been dead three months.

We cherished the hour before Brady showed. Cici had taken my music faves on board. We had a ritual down. She'd ask,

"Caf Corretto?"

Basically the Italian version of a pick me up. Caffeine with Jameson.

The tunes: U2, with "Bad."

The Edge proving he was indeed the owner of the driving guitar.

Lorena McKennet, with "Raglan Road."

Vintage regret. The Irish legacy.

The Clash, with "London Calling."

Because they rock, always.

Gretchen Peters' "Bus to San Cloud."

Pining in beauty.

We were midway along when the door whipped open and Brady blasted in. Heavy-set, muscle and fat in contention. A squashed-in face with eyes that never heard of humor.

His opener:

"Turn off that shit."

Meant we'd have

"Born in the USA."

Ad nauseum.

And add ferocity.

His crudity always managed to reach new depths of offense. Like,

"Bitch, the office. I need servicing."

Cute, huh?

Scotty.

My best and, in truth, only friend.

The ubiquitous *them*, whoever the fook they be, say,

"The difference between one friend and none is infinite."

Scotty was the manager of Khe Shan before me. I was taken on as his assistant. I'd been fiercely pressured by my father to follow his footsteps—heavy, brutal, as they were and join the NYPD.

Yeah, right, like hell.

I went to business college at night. Learned that school teaches you one thing: Greed rocks.

I wanted to rock.

I had a job during the day stocking shelves. And,

Get this:

Carrying customers' bags to their cars. All I ever, Christ ever, needed to know about humiliation, being almost literally invisible.

Until,

A Friday, carrying mega-freight for a guy in his forties, driving a Porsche. Dressed casual, but rich. His casual gear wasn't from Gap, unless he owned the branch, and he had that permanent tan that drives New Yorkers nuts.

Envy? Oh, yeah.

And his shoes, those Italian jobs that mock,

"Sucks being poor."

I managed to finally get his heavy bags in the car. He never looked at me, flipped me a buck. I said,

"You're fooking kidding."

He turned, levelled the bluest eyes outside of Hollywood, laughed, said,

"You're the help, be grateful."

One thing genetics bestows: I've a temper.

My fist bunched instantly and he clocked it, asked,

"How dumb are you, T?"

T?

He pulled out a hundred,

"This stir your mojo?"

I gave him the look, the one that goes,

"Keep fooking with me and see how that pans out."

Two things happened that changed my life.

One, I decked him.

Two, my boss saw me do it, rushed out, picked the dude up, muttered profuse, insincere apologies, pledging,

"His ass is so fired."

The guy rubbed his chin, dismissed my boss with a curt,

"Let me have a word."

Asked,

"What are you going to do now, job wise?"

The hundred was still crumpled in his hand, a trickle of blood leaking from his mouth. I fessed up.

"Don't know."

He assessed me anew, then,

"You like clubs, as in nightclubs?"

"Sure, what's not to like?"

"You want to work in The Khe?"

That's how famous/infamous it was. Didn't even need its full title.

Was he kidding?

"Are you kidding?"

No.

Straight up.

He was El Hombre. The guy who transformed it from a seedy mediocrity to the exclusive joint it was. He turned towards the Porsche, said,

"Be there this evening, six sharp. Wear black pants, a clip-on tie, white shirt, and shoes that fly."

My mind was playing catch up, badly. I asked,

"Clip-on?"

"Yeah, the client wants to pulp you, he goes for the tie, every predictable time."

I couldn't help it. I stared at the vanishing Franklin. He laughed.

"For punching your new boss, you're fined the hundred."

As the Porsche went into its beautiful rev, I shouted,

"What's T?"

"T . . . is for Trash."

Later, I would discover the reason for the
    Unflappable
    Laid back
    Luded

Vibe he had.

A blend of Klonapin and Tequila. Keeps not only the demons at bay but awarded a chill of the emotions as outrider.

I duly showed up at the club and muddled through for the next few weeks. Learned the biz the hard way, by mostly screwing up. Scotty was from South Detroit, not so much street wise as street lethal. Steered me through the delicate art of handling the wise guys, as in, if they didn't pick up their tabs, let it slide until the club owner decided to act. He warned,

"If you're told to ask for payment directly, get yourself a very large gun."

Added,

"If you don't adapt to thinking outside the box, you'll be in one."

Right.

Scotty had earned a shit-load of cash, from, as he put it,

"Creative stealing."

Creative, I could do.

We began to hang out on our Sundays, the only day the club closed. I coerced him into coming to Shea Stadium. I didn't convert him from a Yankees fan, but I did get him to at least appreciate Reyes.

Scotty had taken on my choice of Jameson. Our final Sunday, he'd taken me to a pub he frequented, The Blaggard, West 39th Street, between Fifth and Sixth Avenues. They had Guinness on tap. What more recommendation could you need? Scotty looked more tense the more he knocked back, said,

"Brady is connected to the Russian gangs."

One thing I'd absorbed fast was those mothers made the Italians seem tame. And were regular customers. Always with the incredible dames. They carried a built-in smirk, the one that whispered,

"Fook with me, we'll bury you."

I believed.

He asked me,

"You ever see the Korean movie, *I Saw the Devil* ?"

Nope.

I didn't do Oriental unless it was a hooker. Scotty laughed, said,

"You're a piece of work, but hear this: if I disappear, you can be sure, Brady is behind it."

What?

I went,

"What?"

He explained.

He claims to be American as cover for his gang ties. The cocksucker is from Minsk . . . fooking Minsk, yah believe it?

Scotty was so ultra cool, so in freaking control, I couldn't imagine anyone getting the jump. As if he read my thoughts, he added,

"Brady has a small country's money in his apartment. I know because he showed me. The fook is a showboat, almost daring me to rip him off."

I was saturating this, a silence of foreboding over us. Scotty said,

"If, if, you have to step up, and I'm in the wind, amass a pension, then take Brady out before he buys you the farm."

I was so immersed with my father's book that I put this rap down to the Jay. Changing the subject, I told him about my "inheritance."

He laid a mess of twenties on the counter, to the bar lady's delight. No wonder they liked him—and they did. He knocked back his last shot, said,

"Some men, they think if they can give the impression of goodness despite being a first class son of a bitch, then they have rewritten the book of their life."

Deep, huh?

I wasn't buying, asked,

"That's what you figure my father tried to do?"

He stood, shucked on his shearling coat, a cool three thousand bucks worth, looked at me, with something like warmth, said,

"Oh, yeah, his very own *Book of Virtue*."

We walked down Fifth, a wind blowing across our backs like the dead prayer of despair. We stopped at the intersection and Scotty hailed a cab, turned to me, registering my expression of alarm as he raised his arms, and laughed. Asked,

"What, you think I'm going to give you a hug?"

Paused.

"One thing I learned about the Micks: they don't do affection."

I regret very little of the life I've lived, not even the heavy crap, but oh, Sweet jaysus, why didn't I at least say,

"Thanks for being my buddy and hey, you know, you needn't worry, I've got your back."

I didn't.

Didn't have his back, either.

And that's a true Micked pity.

Monday was one of those stunning New York days. A bright, sunny afternoon, cold but crisp. Reason you never left.

Ever.

Scotty didn't show up for work. Two days later, they fished his beaten body out of the East River.

I had literally read in *The Book of Virtue*, as I now termed the book,

"When the incredible happens, add credible to your account."

Brady was in hyper spirits that evening, dancing around, treating the mob factions to champagne, was almost civil to me.

Like that would last.

It didn't.

He sneered at me,

"Scotty has moved on."

And, as if it was a real award,

"You're the new boss."

Did I start checking on Scotty's death then?

Nope, I was too busy amassing my own fortune.

Months trickled by, I read my father's book, went to bed, frequently with Cici.

Did her sleeping with Brady bother me?

Take a flying guess.

Was near the end of *The Book of Virtue* and read,

"What warehouse of the soul awaits me now?"

I muttered,

"As long as it's hot as hell."

Thought,

Scotty, where were you when I needed you?

Conscious of . . .

"Where was I when he went in the East River?"

And the days moved on until Brady began his dismantling of me.

With an awareness of unpaid tabs circulating in the club.

Brady had literally grabbed my arm, hissed,

"Get the tabs settled."

I tried, adding as much steel as I dared.

"Scotty would have dealt discreetly with this."

He gave me a sneer of such malevolence, like he was crowing, said,

"Pity he didn't learn to swim."

Dancing away, he threw,

"D'Agostino owes me, that's what you need to get your focus with."

Meaning, the old Mafiosi whose running bill was getting seriously out of hand. I asked,

"You really want to mess with him?"

He gave his crooked grin, all malice and spite, said,

"I won't be."

Pause.

"You will."

Then added,

"Before Tuesday."

My father's cop buddies were like a vile extension of him. Save for one, Casey. Yeah, second generation of cop and Mick. Almost a caricature.

Boozy

Hard ass

Harp-ed

If Gene Hackman were Irish, he'd be Casey. But he treated me good.

Very.

After my father passed, he'd said,

"You ever need anything . . ."

So.

So met with him, in an Irish bar off Madison Square Garden. He was dressed in a thick offwhite Aran Island sweater, heavy pea jacket, tweed cap, as if he were auditioning for a part in *Mick Does New York*. A shock of wiry white hair and hands that could cover Manhattan and you had the essence of the Irish NYPD legacy. It wasn't that these guys took life as it came. Hell, no. They grabbed it by the throttle, kicked its ass, and, if that failed, they beat the living shit out it.

Casey had the end booth, shielded from prying eyes, though you'd need some *cojones* to stare at Casey. He welcomed,

"I got you a Jay, lad. Sit yer own self down."

The Jay was at least a double, no ice, heaven forbid. Those Micks weren't hot on blasphemy. He didn't reach over and ruffle my hair but the vibe was there. Even if I reached eighty, I'd always be "the kid" to these dinosaurs.

I knew the drill: get some shots down, then approach the subject in a creep-up-on-it fashion. If you were in a hurry, park it elsewhere. Casey ordered a side of fries and a bunch of pickled eggs. He ordered, I swear, by pounding the table, just once. And, you guessed it, offered/commanded,

"Dig in."

Those old timers, the book in their lives was,

"Book 'em, Danno."

Once we had the ritual drinks in, eggs demolished, he leaned back, asked,

"How you holding up, kiddo?"

I lied, said okay, then asked,

"You know anything about Brady, my boss at Khe Shan?"

He sighed. The guy could have sighed for the entire U. S. Shook his huge head, said,

"Piece of shite, connected to the Russian mob. Animals."

Paused.

Gave me the cool slow appraisal, fine-honed in nigh twenty years of staring down the enemy. *Enemy* covered just about the whole planet save cops and family.

He asked,

"This about the schmuck they pulled out of the East River?"

You might ridicule these throw-back nigh vigilante cops but Holy shit, they were on the ball. You didn't trawl the five boroughs for two decades and be stupid.

I advised, if quietly,

"He was my buddy."

Casey snorted and, when you have a Jameson shooter half way to your lips, it's doubly effective, but he never spilled a drop. Drained it, crashed it down on the table with,

"Never had you down as a bollix, much less a stupid one."

I did the smart thing: shut the hell up. Dense silence over us and . . . few things more lethal than a brooding silent Mick. He finally said,

"Lemme educate you, son. Scotty was well known to the Detroit PD, but a slick fook, so they never nailed him. He headed west, hooked up with Brady, another piece of work who'd adopted an Irish name to make him thug-friendly. They made a lot of cold cash and ploughed it into the club to make it seem legit. The past year, Scotty began to make inroads into his own crew to oust Brady."

Paused.

"You get the picture?"

Yeah.

Then he added,

"Brady will let you run the club for a year, tops, then whack you and bring in some other naïve schmuck."

I excused me own self, headed for the restroom, ordered up a fresh batch of the Jay, and punched the wall, hurt the living crap out of me hand. On my return, I changed tack, asked,

"You ever have my old man down for a reader?"

We clinked shots, downed them, and Casey answered,

"No way. You kidding?"

I told him about *The Book of Virtue* and he let a low whistle, said,

"Me, I never was much for no book learning."

Sounding like he was in a bad Western.

We mulled it over, then he went,

"My mother, Lord rest her and all the bad Caseys, she used to sing a Yeats poem, yeah, *sing* it. All I got is,

"The world is more full of weeping than we can understand."

God is good; he didn't sing it. I hadn't enough Jay to ever endure that. Then he leaned over, put his large hand on my shoulder, said,

"Frank had his faults but, deep down, he was a decent guy."

I felt the bile rise, spat,

"Oh, like, *he meant well*?"

He sat back, stunned by my venom, tried,

"Jaysus, Tommy, c'mon, he loved you."

I said,

"That weeping world . . . *Frank* caused his fair share."

And that was the end of the chat.

He warned me to watch my back, and to call if I needed anything.

I got out of there, had a moment of vague regret that I'd busted his balls, then thought, "He was my Dad's buddy, so the hell with him."

My father's book

Was diverted by a note on the binding. Read,

"Sewn binding, the strongest yet the most expensive. The pages are sewn into the book manually with a sewing machine."

Followed by a note, in my father's hand,

"Check out Moleskin diaries, used by Hemingway and Chatwin."

Now I was seriously perplexed.

Too, the oddest thing, just holding the book, it gave me the strangest sensation of, hell, I'm slow to admit this,

Peace?

WTF?

I went online, put in,

www.realbooks.com

Trawled through a ton of sites until I found one dealing exclusively with the physical qualities of a book, not the contents.

Read long-winded boring passages about the creation of a book, the printing, art of binding, and muttered,

"Bibliophiles."

Come the final Wednesday of the virtue saga.

The last page of my father's book had passages of two poems, Francis Thompson's *The Hound of Heaven* and Cafavvy's *Alexandria*. The gist being, he'd been pursued all his life in dread and terror and, secondly, no matter what he did, he couldn't escape his life, as if you fooked up in one place, so you would always do.

If cops were secretly reading this stuff in their leisure time, no wonder they ate their guns.

Cici had the day off and came to my apartment, the top floor of a brownstone that I lavished my savings on. She had a mouth on her, kidding I ain't. She asked,

"How much are you ripping off from the club?"

A lot.

I said,

"As if I would."

She let that slide.

Gave me the hot look.

It burned.

Followed with a blast of white radiance.

After, I had one of my rarest cigs and, God forgive me, one supplied by Cici.

Virginia Slims.

Not too macho. She pulled on one of my faded denim shirts. I had it longer than I had sense. Looked good, looked in heat. Trailing smoke, she went to mix up a batch of Vodka Spritzers.

Most appetites nigh sated, she picked up my dad's book, asked,

"You read?"

What?

Like I was a dumb bastard?

Hello.

She flicked through it, said,

"Now there's a word."

I followed her to the main room, an XL Yankees T-shirt on, asked,

"What's that?"

She read,

"*Schadenfreude.*"

I asked,

"The hell does that mean?"

She pulled a battered dictionary from my battered book collection, found the entry, intoned,

"A pleasure taken from another's misfortune."

Looked at me,

Added,

"Brady."

Got my vote.

Handed me a glass of the freshly blended batch, it tasted,

Cold

Good and

Like

Hope.

As artificial as that.

And as long lasting.

I said,

"Or my old man."

She sat lotus style on the sofa, looked at me for a long beat. Then,

"We need to deal with Brady."

Sure.

How?

I asked,

"How?"

She took a deep gulp of her drink, her eyes watching me over the rim of the glass. And,

"We need to cash his check."

No dictionary needed for that.

"I wanted to develop a curiosity that was oceanic and insatiable as well as a desire to learn every word in the English language that didn't sound pretentious or ditzy."

Pat Conroy.

My Losing Season.

I was beginning to understand that my old man had used his book in a vain attempt at catching an education. Was that admirable? Weighed it against the terror he'd inflicted on me all his miserable life.

Time was running out on my supposed plea to the Mafioso to ask him to settle his tab. No doubt, if I did, he'd see it as the ultimate diss and, man, this was a guy who beat a busboy to pulp for standing too close while the psycho was getting up from a meal—a meal, of course, that he didn't pay for.

Too, the schmuck, horror, never, like, not *ever*, left a tip.

Enough reason right there to whack his tight ass. I owned an illegal Browning Nine. You run my kind of club, you need to pack more than attitude.

Cici had it down.

Brady rented a fook pad on West 45th Street, between Madison and Fifth Avenues. Friday afternoons, he liked Cici to come by and . . . entertain him. She had a key and gave me a copy.

Oh, and a shit-load of coke. Said,

"Scatter it around the bedroom, make it look like a dope gig gone south."

Cici would have a very high profile lunch with some friends, alibi ensuring. Me, I had none and that itself is its own defense.

The gun was untraceable. I'd literally found it a year ago, shoved down behind a seat in the VIP section.

Friday, coming up to noon, I felt calm. Removing Brady would be a downright freaking joy and, in some odd way, like a lash back at me old man. I dressed casual, not sure of the dress code for murder. Old jeans, a battered windbreaker, Converse sneakers that had always been a size too small. Walk in the blood and the cops, gee, they'd have a footprint.

It went like clockwork.

Brady had laughed when I let myself in. He was nose deep in candy, lolling on a sofa, rasped,

"Jesus, never thought you had the *cojones* to attempt a burglary."

Why wasn't he alarmed?

The coke had fried his brain . . . too out there to be alarmed.

Put one in his gut first, let him whine a bit, chalk up serious payback . . . but all fine things must end so added three to his dumb head.

All she wrote.

I then scattered the coke like fragile snow around his pad.

Found the money in a suitcase.

Yeah, believe it, a suitcase.

Enough cash to launch two new clubs.

Got the hell out of there.

Discreetly.

Next day, the cops arrived.

I kid thee not.

Two detectives, one surly and the other surlier. Bad cop by two.

The latter asked,

Pushing a book at me,

"This yours?"

"My dad's book!"

Before I could protest, the first added,

"If it has your fingerprints?"

They had a warrant and found the suitcase in jig time.

Cici.

The bitch.

I did of course try to implicate her but her alibi was solid. More than.

My lawyer was very young, up to speed with the current kid jargon. Said, "You don't have to worry."

Looked at the cop's book, of evidence, added

"Not."

I sat back in the hard prison metal chair, looked at him, said slowly,

"What . . .

   the . . .

      fook . . .

         ever."

The Book Thing

Laura Lippman

Tess Monaghan wanted to love the funky little children's bookshop that had opened just two years ago among the used bookstores that lined Twenty-Fifth Street in North Baltimore. There was so much to admire about it—the brightly painted miniature rockers and chairs on the converted sun porch, the mynah bird who said "Hi, Hon!" and "Hark, who goes there!" and—best of all—"Nevermore."

She coveted the huge Arnold Lobel poster opposite the front door, the one that showed a bearded man-beast happily ensconced in a tiny cottage that was being overtaken by ramshackle towers of books. She appreciated the fact that ancillary merchandise was truly a sideline here; this shop's business was books, with only a few stuffed animals and Fancy Nancy boas thrown into the mix. Tess was grateful that gift-wrapping was free year-round and that the store did out-of-print book searches. She couldn't wait until her own two-year-old daughter, Carla Scout, was old enough to sit quietly through the Saturday story hour, although Tess was beginning to fear that might not be until Carla Scout was a freshman in college. Most of all, she admired the counterintuitive decision to open a bookstore when so many people seemed to assume that books were doomed.

She just thought it would be nice if the owner of The Children's Bookstore actually *liked* children.

"Be careful," the raven-haired owner growled on this unseasonably chilly October day as Carla Scout did her Frankenstein stagger toward a low shelf of picture books. To be fair, Carla Scout's hands weren't exactly clean, as mother and daughter had just indulged in one of mother's favorite vices, dark chocolate peanut clusters from Eddie's grocery. Tess swooped in with a napkin and smiled apologetically at the owner.

"Sorry," she said. "She loves books to pieces. Literally, sometimes."

"Do you need help?" the owner asked, as if she had never seen Tess before. Tess's credit card begged to differ.

"Oh . . . no, we're looking for a birthday gift, but I have some ideas. My aunt was a children's librarian with the city school system."

Tess did not add that her aunt ran her own bookstore in another part of town and would happily order any book that Tess needed—at cost. But Tess wanted this bookstore, so much closer to her own neighborhood, to thrive. She wanted all local businesses to thrive, but it was a tricky principle to live by, as most principles were. At night, her daughter asleep, the house quiet, she couldn't help it if her mouse clicked its way to online sellers who made everything so easy. Could she?

"You're one of those, I suppose," the woman said.

"One of—?"

The owner pointed to the iPad sticking out of Tess's tote. "Oh . . . no. I mean, sure, I buy some digital books, mainly things I don't care about owning, but I use the reading app on this primarily for big documents. My work involves a lot of paper and it's great to be able to import the documents and carry them with me—"

The owner rolled her eyes. "Sure." She pushed through the flowery chintz curtains that screened her work area from

the store and retreated as if she found Tess too tiresome to
talk to.

Sorry, mouthed the store's only employee, a young woman
with bright red hair, multiple piercings and a tattoo of what
appeared to be Jemima Puddleduck on her upper left arm.

The owner swished back through the curtains, purse under
her arm. "I'm going for coffee, Mona, then to the bank." Tess
waited to see if she boarded a bicycle, possibly one with a
basket for errant nipping dogs. But she walked down Twenty-
Fifth Street, head down against the gusty wind.

"She's having a rough time," said the girl with the duck
tattoo. Mona, the owner had called her. "You can imagine. And
the thing that drives her mad are the people who come in with
digital readers—no offense—just to pick her brain and then
download the electronic versions or buy cheaper ones online."

"I wouldn't think that people wanted children's books in
digital."

"You'd be surprised. There are some interactive Dr. Seuss
books—they're actually quite good. But I'm not sure about the
read-to-yourself functions. I think it's still important for parents
to read to their kids."

Tess blushed guiltily. She did have *Hop on Pop* on her iPad,
along with several games, although Carla Scout so far seemed
to prefer opening—and then deleting—her mother's e-mail.

"Anyway," Mona continued, "it's the sudden shrinkage
that's making her cranky. Because it's the most expensive, most
beautiful books. *Hugo*, things like that. A lot of the Caldecott
books, but never the Newberys, and we keep them in the same
section. Someone's clearly targeting the illustrated books. Yet
not the truly rare ones, which are kept under lock-and-key." She
indicated the case that ran along the front of the counter, filled
with old books in mint condition: *Elouise Goes to Moscow*,
various Maurice Sendak titles, *Emily of Deep Valley*, Eleanor
Estes's *100 Dresses*, a book unknown to Tess, *Epaminondas
and His Auntie*, whose cover illustration was deeply un-PC.

Tess found herself switching personas, from harried mom to a professional private investigator who provided security consultations. She studied her surroundings. "All these little rooms—it's cozy, but a shoplifter's paradise. An alarm, and a bell on the door to alert you to the door's movement, but no cameras. Have you thought about making people check totes and knapsacks?"

"We tried, but Octavia got the numbers confused and when she gets harried—let's just say, it doesn't bring out her best."

"Octavia?"

"The owner."

As if her name conjured her up, she appeared just like that, slamming back through the door, coffee in hand. "I always forget that the bank closes at three every day but Friday. Oh well. It's not like I had that much to deposit."

She glanced at Mona, her face softer, kinder. She was younger than Tess had realized, not even forty. It was her stern manner and dyed black hair that aged her. "I can write you a check today, but if you could wait until Friday . . ."

"Sure, Octavia. And it's almost Halloween. People will be doing holiday shopping before you know it."

Octavia sighed. "More people in the store. More distractions. More opportunity." She glanced at Carla Scout, who was sitting on the floor with a Mo Willems book, "reading" it to herself. Tess thought Octavia would have to be charmed in spite of herself. What could be more adorable than a little girl reading, especially this little girl, who had the good sense to favor her father, with fair skin and thick dark hair that was already down to her shoulders. Plus, she was wearing a miniature leather bomber jacket from the Gap, red jeans and a Clash T-shirt. Tess had heard "She's so adorable" at least forty times today. She waited for the forty-first such pronouncement.

Octavia said: "She got chocolate on the book."

So she had. And they already owned *Don't Let the Pigeon Drive the Bus*, but Tess would just have to eat this damaged copy. "I'll add it to my other purchases when I check out," Tess said, knowing it was folly to try to separate Carla Scout from any object that was keeping her quiet and contented.

"I understand you've been having some problems with theft?"

"Mona!" Owner glared at employee. Tess would have cowered under such a glance, but the younger woman shrugged it off.

"It's not shameful, Octavia. People don't steal from us because we're bad people. Or even because we're bad at what we do. They do it because they're opportunistic."

"A camera would go far in solving your problems," Tess offered.

Octavia sniffed. "I don't do gadgets." She shot another baleful look at Tess's iPad, then added, with slightly less edge: "Besides, I can't afford the outlay just now."

Her honesty softened Tess. "Understood. Have you noticed a pattern?"

"It's not like I can do inventory every week," Octavia began, even as Mona said: "It's Saturdays. I'm almost certain it's Saturdays. It gets busy here, what with the story time and more browsers than usual—often divorced dads, picking up a last-minute gift or just trying desperately to entertain their kids."

"I might be able to help—"

Octavia held up a hand: "I don't have money for that, either."

"I'd do it for free," Tess said, surprising herself.

"Why?" Octavia's voice was edged with suspicion. She wasn't used to kindness, Tess realized, except, perhaps, from Mona, the kind of employee who would sit on a check for a few days.

"Because I think your store is good for North Baltimore and I want my daughter to grow up coming here. To be a true city kid, to ride her bike or take the bus here, pick out books on her own. *Betsy-Tacy*, *Mrs. Piggle-Wiggle*, *The Witch of Blackbird Pond*. Edward Eager and E. Nesbit. All the books I loved."

"Everyone wants to pass their childhood favorites on to

their children," Octavia said. "But if I've learned anything in this business, it's that kids have to make their own discoveries if you want them to be true readers."

"Okay, fine. But if I want her to discover books, there's nothing like browsing in a store or a library. There are moments of serendipity that you can't equal." She turned to her daughter just in time to see—but not stop—Carla Scout reaching for another book with her dirty hands. "We'll take that one, too."

Back on Twenty-Fifth Street, Carla Scout strapped in her stroller, Tess was trying to steer with one hand while she held her phone with another, checking e-mails. Inevitably, she ran up on the heels of a man well-known to her, at least by sight.

She and Crow, Carla Scout's father, called him the Walking Man and often wondered about his life, why he had the time and means to walk miles across North Baltimore every day, in every kind of weather, as if on some kind of mission. He might have been handsome if he smiled and stood up straight, but he never smiled and there was a curve to his body that suggested he couldn't stand up straight. When Tess bumped him, he swung sharply away from her, catching Tess with the knapsack he always wore and it was like being hit with a rock. Tess wondered if he weighed it down to help correct his unfortunate posture.

"Sorry," Tess said, but the walking man didn't even acknowledge their collision. He just kept walking with his distinctive, flatfooted style, his body curving forward like a C. There was no bounce, no spring, in Walking Man's stride, only a grim need to put one foot in front of the other, over and over again. He was, Tess thought, like someone under a curse in a fairy tale or myth, sentenced to walk until a spell was broken.

Before her first Saturday shift at the bookstore, Tess consulted her aunt, figuring that she must also see a lot of "shrinkage" at her store.

"Not really," Kitty said. "Books are hard to shoplift, harder to resell. It happens, of course, but I've never seen a systemic ongoing plan, with certain books targeted the way you're describing. This sounds almost like a vendetta against the owner."

Tess thought about Octavia's brusque ways, Mona's stories about how cranky she could get. Still, it was hard to imagine a disgruntled customer going to these lengths. Most people would satisfy themselves by writing a mean review on Yelp.

"I will tell you this," Kitty said. "Years ago—and it was on Twenty-Fifth Street, when it had even more used bookstores— there was a rash of thefts. The owners couldn't believe how much inventory they were losing, and how random it was. But then it stopped, just like that."

"What happened then? I mean, why did it stop? Did they arrest someone?"

"Not to my knowledge."

"I should probably check with the other sellers on the street, see if they're noticing anything," Tess said. "But I wonder why it's happening *now*."

"Maybe someone's worried that there won't be books much longer, that they're going to be extinct."

It was clearly a joke on Kitty's part, but Tess couldn't help asking: "Are they?"

The pause on the other end of the phone line was so long that Tess began to wonder if her cell had dropped the call. When Kitty spoke again, her voice was low, without its usual mirth.

"I don't dare predict the future. After all, I didn't think newspapers could go away. Still, I believe that there will be a market for physical books; I just don't know how large it will be. All I know is that I'm okay—for now. I own my building, I have a strong core of loyal customers, and I have a good walk-in trade from tourists. In the end, it comes down to what people value. Do they value bookstores? Do they value books? I don't know, Tess. Books have been free in libraries for years and that didn't devalue them. The Book Thing here in Baltimore gives books away to anyone who wants them. Free, no strings. Doesn't hurt me at all. For decades, people have bought used books from everywhere-from flea markets to the Smith College Book Sale. But there's something about pressing a button on your computer and buying something so ephemeral for 99 cents, having it whooshed instantly to you. Remember *Charlie and the Chocolate Factory?*"

"Of course." Tess, like most children, had been drawn to Roald Dahl's dark stories. He was another one on her list of writers she wanted Carla Scout to read.

"Well, what if you could do what Willie Wonka did—as Dahl fantasized—reach into your television and pull out a candy bar? What if everything you wanted was always available to you, all the time, on a 24/7 basis? It damn near is. Life has become so a la carte. We get what we want when we want it. But if you ask me, that means it's that much harder to identify what we really want."

"That's not a problem in Baltimore," Tess said. "All I can get delivered is pizza and Chinese—and not even my favorite pizza or Chinese."

"You're joking to get me off this morbid school of thought."

"Not exactly." She wasn't joking. The state of food delivery in Baltimore was depressing. But she also wasn't used to hearing her ebullient aunt in such a somber mood and she was trying to distract her, as she might play switcheroo with Carla Scout. And it worked. It turned out that dealing with a toddler, day in and day out, was actually good practice for dealing with the world at large.

The Children's Bookstore was hectic on Saturdays as promised, although Tess quickly realized that there was a disproportionate relationship between the bustle in the aisles and the activity at the cash register.

She also noticed the phenomenon that Mona had described, people using the store as a real-life shopping center for their virtual needs. She couldn't decide which was more obnoxious—the people who pulled out their various devices and made purchases while standing in the store, or those who waited until they were on the sidewalk again, who hunched over their phones and eReaders almost furtively as if committing a kind of crime. They were and they weren't, Tess decided. It was legal, but they were ripping off Mona's space and time, using her as a curator of sorts.

At the height of the hubbub, a delivery man arrived with boxes of books, wheeling his hand truck through the narrow aisles, losing the top box at one point. He was exceedingly handsome in a preppy way—and exceedingly clumsy. As he tried to work his way to the back of the store, his boxes fell off one, two, three times. Once, the top box burst open, spilling a few books onto the floor.

"Sorry," he said with a bright smile as he knelt to collect them. Except—did Tess see him sweep several books off a shelf and into a box? Why would he do that? After all, the boxes were being delivered; it's not as if he could take them with him.

"Tate is the clumsiest guy in the world," Mona said with affection after he left. "A sweetheart, but just a mess."

"You mean, he drops stuff all the time?"

"Drops things, mixes up orders, you name it. But Octavia dotes on him. Those dimples . . ."

Tess had not picked up on the dimples, but she had a chance to see how they affected Octavia when the delivery man returned fifteen minutes later, looking sheepish.

"Tate!" Octavia said with genuine delight.

"I feel so stupid. One of those boxes I left—it's for Royal Books up the block."

"No problem," Octavia said. "You know I never get around to unpacking the Saturday deliveries until the store clears out late in the day."

He looked through the stack of boxes he had left, showed Octavia that one was addressed to Royal Books and hoisted it on his shoulder. Tess couldn't help noticing that there wasn't any tape on the box; the top had been folded with the overlapping flaps that people used when boxing their own possessions for a move. She ambled out in the street behind him, saw him put the box on his truck—then drive away, west and then north on Howard Street, completely bypassing Royal Books.

He looks like someone, Tess thought. *Someone I know, yet don't know. Someone famous?* He probably just resembled some actor on television.

Back inside the bookstore, she didn't have the heart to tell Octavia what she suspected. Octavia had practically glowed when she saw Tate. Besides, Tess had no proof. Yet.

"So, did you see anything?" Octavia asked at day's end.

"Maybe. If there was anything taken today, it was from this shelf." Tess pointed to the low one next to where the box had fallen, spilling its contents. Mona crouched on her haunches and poked at the titles. "I can't be sure until I check our computer, but the shelf was full yesterday. I mean—there's no Seuss and we always have Seuss."

"If you saw it, why didn't you say something?" Octavia demanded, as peevish as any paying customer. "Or *do* something, for God's sake."

"I wasn't sure I saw anything and I didn't want to offend . . . a potential customer. I'll be back next Saturday. This is a two-person job." Life is unfair. Tess Monaghan, toting her toddler daughter in a baby carrier, was invisible to most of the world, except for leering men who observed the baby's chest-level position and said things like "Best seat in the house."

But when Crow put on the Ergo and shouldered their baby to *his* chest, the world melted, or at least the female half did. So he stood in the bookstore the next Saturday morning, trying to be polite to the cooing women around him, even as he waited to see if he would observe something similar to what Tess had seen the week before. Once again, Tate arrived when story hour was in full swing, six boxes on his hand truck.

No dropped box, Crow reported via text.

Damn, Tess thought. Maybe he was smart enough to vary the days, despite Mona's conviction that the thefts had been concentrated on Saturdays. Maybe she was deluded, maybe—

Her phone pinged again. *Taking one box with him. Says it was on cart by mistake. I didn't see anything, tho. He's good.*

Tess was on her bike, which she had decided was her best bet for following someone in North Baltimore on a Saturday. A delivery guy, even an off-brand one working the weekends, had to make frequent stops, right? She counted on being able to keep up with him. And she did, as he moved through his route, although she almost ran down Walking Man near the Baltimore Museum of Art. Still, she was flying along, watching him unload boxes at stop after stop until she realized the flaw in her plan: How could she know which box was the box from the Children's Bookstore?

She sighed, resigned to donating yet another Saturday to The Children's Bookstore.

And another and another and another. The next four Saturdays went by without any incidents. Tate showed up, delivered his boxes, made no mistakes, dropped nothing. Yet, throughout the week, customer requests would point out missing volumes— books listed as in-stock in the computer, yet nowhere to be found in the store.

By the fifth Saturday, the Christmas rush appeared to be on and the store was even more chaotic when Tate arrived— and dropped a box in one of the store's remote corners, one that could never be seen from the cash register or the story-time alcove on the converted sun porch. Tess, out on the street on her bike, ready to ride, watched it unfold via Facetime on Crow's phone, which he was holding at hip level. The action suddenly blurred—Mona, taken into Tess's confidence, had rushed forward try and help Tate. Tate brushed her away, but not before Carla Scout's sippee cup somehow fell on the box, the lid bouncing off and releasing a torrent of red juice, enough to leave a visible splotch on the box's side, an image that Crow captured and forwarded in a text. Tess, across the street, watched as he loaded it, noted the placement of the large stain.

It was a long, cold afternoon, with no respite for Tess as she followed the truck. No time to grab so much as a cup of coffee, and she wouldn't have risked drinking anything because that could have forced her to search out a bathroom.

It was coming up on four o'clock, the wintry light beginning to weaken, when Tate headed up one of the most notorious hills in the residential neighborhood of Roland Park, not far from where Tess lived. She would have loved to wait at the bottom, but how could she know where he made the delivery? She gave him a five-minute head start, hoping that Tate, like most Baltimore drivers, simply didn't see cyclists.

His truck was parked outside a rambling Victorian, perhaps one of the old summer houses built when people would travel a mere five to fifteen miles to escape the closed-in heat of downtown Baltimore. Yet this house, on a street full of million-dollar houses, did not appear to be holding its end up. Cedar shingles had dropped off as if the house were molting, the roof was inexpertly patched in places, and the chimney looked like a liability suit waiting to happen. The delivery truck idled in the driveway, Tate still in the driver's seat. Tess crouched by her wheel in a driveway three houses down, pretending to be engaged in a repair. Eventually, a man came out, but not from the house. He had been inside the stable at the head of the driveway. Most such outbuildings in the neighborhood had been converted to new uses or torn down, but this one appeared to have been untouched. A light burned inside, but that was all Tess could glimpse before the doors rolled shut again.

That man looks familiar, she thought, as she had thought about Tate the first time she saw him. *Is he famous or do I know him?*

The man who walked to the end of the driveway, she realized, was Walking Man. No backpack, but it was clearly him, his shoulders rounding even farther forward without their usual counterweight. He shook the driver's hand and Tess realized why she thought she had seen Tate before—he was a handsomer, younger version of Walking Man.

Tate handed Walking Man the box with the red stain. No money changed hands. Nothing changed hands. But even in the dim light, the stain was evident. The man took the box into the old stable and muscled the doors back into place.

Tess was faced with a choice, one she hadn't anticipated. She could follow Tate and confront him, figuring that he had the most to lose. His job was on the line. But she couldn't prove he was guilty of theft until she looked inside the box. If she followed Tate, the books could be gone before she returned and she wouldn't be able to prove anything. She had to see what was inside that box.

She texted Crow, told him what she was going to do and walked up the driveway without waiting for his reply, which she supposed would urge caution, or tell her to call the police. But it was only a box of books from a children's bookstore. How high could the stakes be?

She knocked on the stable door. Minutes passed. She knocked again.

"I saw you," she said to the dusk, to herself, possibly to the man inside. "I know you're in there."

Another minute or so passed, a very long time to stand outside as darkness encroached and the cold deepened. But, eventually, the door was rolled open.

"I don't know you," Walking Man said in the flat affect of a child.

"My name is Tess Monaghan and I sort of know you. You're the—"

She stopped herself just in time. Walking Man didn't know he was Walking Man. She realized, somewhat belatedly, that *he* had not boiled his existence down to one quirk. Whoever he was, he didn't define himself as Walking Man. He had a life, a history. Perhaps a sad and gloomy one, based on these surroundings and his compulsive, constant hiking, but he was not, in his head or mirror, a man who did nothing but walk around North Baltimore.

Or was he?

"I've seen you around. I don't live far from here. We're practically neighbors."

He stared at her oddly, said nothing. His arm was braced against the frame of the door—she could not enter without pushing past him. She sensed he wouldn't like that kind of contact, that he was not used to being touched. She remembered how quickly he had whirled around the day she rolled her stroller up on his heels. But unlike most people, who would turn toward the person who had jostled them, he moved away.

"May I come in?"

He dropped his arm and she took that as an invitation—and also as a sign that he believed himself to have nothing to fear. He wasn't acting like someone who felt guilty, or in the wrong. Then again, he didn't know that she had followed the books here.

The juice-stained box sat on a work table, illuminated by an overhead light strung from the ceiling on a long cable. Tess walked over to the box, careful not to turn her back to Walking Man, wishing she had a name for him other than Walking Man, but he had not offered his name when she gave hers.

"May I?" she said, indicating the box, picking up a box cutter next to it, but only because she didn't want him to be able to pick it up.

"It's mine," he said.

She looked at the label. The address was for this house. Cover, should the ruse be discovered? "William Kemper. Is that you?"

"Yes." His manner was odd, off. Then again, she was the one who had shown up at his home and demanded to inspect a box addressed to him. Perhaps he thought she was just another quirky Baltimorean. Perhaps he had a reductive name for her, too. Nosy Woman.

"Why don't you open it?"

He stepped forward and did. There were at least a dozen books, all picture books, all clearly new. He inspected them carefully.

"These are pretty good," he said.

"Good for what?"

He looked at her as if she were quite daft. "My work."

"What do you do?"

"Create."

"The man who brought you the books . . ."

"My younger brother, Tate. He brings me books. He says he knows a place that gives them away free."

"These look brand-new."

He shrugged, uninterested in the observation.

Tess tried again. "Why does your brother bring you books?"

"He said it was better for him to bring them, than for me to get them myself."

Tess again remembered bumping into Walking Man on Twenty-Fifth Street, the hard thwack of his knapsack, so solid it almost left a bruise.

"But you still sometimes get them for yourself, don't you?"

It took him a while to formulate a reply. A dishonest person would have been thinking up a lie all along. An average person would have been considering the pros and cons of lying. William Kemper was just very deliberate with his words.

"Sometimes. Only when they need me."

"Books need you?"

"Books need to breathe after a while. They wait so long. They wait and they wait, closed in. You can tell that no one has read them in a very long time. Or even opened them."

"So you 'liberate' them? Is that your work?"

Walking Man—William—turned away from her and began sorting through the books his brother had brought. He was through with her, or wanted to be.

"These books weren't being neglected. Or ignored."

"No, but they're the only kind of books that Tate knows

how to get. He thinks it's all about pictures. I don't want to tell them they're not quite right. I make do with what he brings, and supplement when I have to." He sighed, the sigh of an older brother used to a sibling's screw-ups. Tess had to think that Tate had done his share of sighing, too

"William—were you away for a while?"

"Yes," he said, flipping the pages, studying the pictures, his mind not really on her or their conversation.

"Did you go to prison?"

"They said it wasn't." Flip, flip, flip. "At any rate, I got to come home. Eventually."

"When?"

"Two winters ago." It seemed an odd way to phrase it, pseudo-Native American stuff, affected. But for a walking man, the seasons probably mattered more.

"And this is your house?"

"Mine and Tate's. As long as we can pay the taxes. Which is about all we can do. Pay the taxes."

Tess didn't doubt that. Even a ramshackle pile in this neighborhood would have a tax bill of at least $15,000, maybe $20,000 per year. But did he actually live in the house? Her eyes now accustomed to the gloom, she realized the stable had been converted to an apartment of sorts. There was a cot, a makeshift kitchen with a hot plate, a mini fridge, a radio. A bathroom wasn't evident, but William's appearance would indicate that he had a way to keep himself and his clothes clean.

Then she noticed what was missing: *Books.* Except for the ones that had just arrived, there were no books in evidence.

"Where are the books, William?"

"There," he said, after a moment of confusion. Whatever his official condition, he was very literal.

"No, I mean the others. There are others, right?"

"In the house."

"May I see them?"

"It's almost dark."

"So?"

"That means turning on the lights."

"Doesn't the house have lights?"

"We have an account. Tate said we should keep the utilities, because otherwise the neighbors will complain, say it's dangerous. Water, gas and electric. But we don't use them, except for the washer-dryer and for showers. If it gets really cold, I can stay in the house, but even with the heat on, it's still cold. It's so big. The main thing is to keep it nice enough so no one can complain."

He looked exhausted from such a relatively long speech. Tess could tell that her mere presence was stressful to him. But it didn't seem to be the stress of *discovery*. He wasn't fearful. Other people made him anxious in general. Perhaps that was another reason that Walking Man kept walking. No one could catch up to him and start a conversation.

"I'd like to see the books, William."

"Why?"

"Because I—represent some of the people who used to own them."

"They didn't love them."

"Perhaps." There didn't seem to be any point in arguing with William. "I'd like to see them."

From the outside, Tess had not appreciated how large the house was, how deep into the lot it was built. Even by the standards of the neighborhood, it was enormous, taking up almost every inch of level land on the lot. There was more land still, but it was a long, precipitous slope. They were high here, with a commanding view of the city and the nearby highway. William took her through the rear door, which led into an ordinary, somewhat old-fashioned laundry room with appliances that appeared to be at least ten to fifteen years old.

"The neighbors might call the police," William said, his tone fretful. "Just seeing a light."

"Because they think the house is vacant?"

"Because they would do anything to get us out. Any excuse

to call attention to us. Tate says it's important not to let them do that."

He led her through the kitchen, the lights still off. Again, out-of-date, but ordinary and clean, if a bit dusty from disuse. Now they were in a long shadowy hall closed off by French doors, which led to a huge room. William opened these and they entered a multi-windowed room, still dark, but not as dark as the hallway.

"The ballroom. Although we never had any balls that I know of," he said.

A ballroom. This was truly one of the grand old mansions of Roland Park.

"But where are the books, William?" Tess asked.

He blinked, surprised. "Oh, I guess you need more light. I thought the lights from the other houses would be enough." He flipped a switch and the light from overhead chandeliers filled the room. Yet the room was quite empty.

"The books, William. Where are they?"

"All around you."

And it was only then that Tess realized that what appeared to be an unusual, slapdash wallpaper was made from pages— pages and pages and pages of books. Some were only text, but at some point during the massive project—the ceilings had to be at least 20, possibly 30 feet high—the children's books began to appear. Tess stepped closer to inspect what he had done. She didn't have a craft-y bone in her body, but it appeared to be similar to some kind of decoupage—there was definitely a sealant over the pages. But it wasn't UV protected because there were sun streaks on the wall that faced south and caught the most light.

She looked down and realized he had done the same thing with the floor, or started to; part of the original parquet floor was still in evidence.

"Is the whole house like this?"

"Not yet," he said. "It's a big house."

"But William—these books, they're not yours. You've destroyed them."

"How?" he said. "You can still read them. The pages are in order. I'm letting them live. They were dying, inside their covers, on shelves. No one was looking at them. Now they're open forever, always ready to be read."

"But no one can see them here either," she said.

"I can. You can."

"William is my half-brother," Tate Kemper told Tess a few days later, over lunch in the Paper Moon Diner, a North Baltimore spot that was a kind of shrine to old toys. "He's fifteen years older than I am. He was institutionalized for a while. Then our grandfather, our father's father, agreed to pay for his care, set him up with an aide, in a little apartment not far from here. He left us the house in his will and his third wife got everything else. My mom and I never had money, so it's not a big deal to me. But our dad was still rich when William was young, so no one worried about how he would take care of himself when he was an adult."

"If you sold the house, you could easily pay for William's care, at least for a time."

"Yes, even in a bad market, even with the antiquated systems and old appliances, it probably would go for almost a million. But William begged me to keep it, to let him try living alone. He said grandfather was the only person who was ever nice to him and he was right. His mother is dead and our father is a shit, gone from both of our lives, disinherited by his own father. So I let William move into the stable. It was several months before I realized what he was doing."

"But he'd done it before, no?"

Tate nodded. "Yes, he was caught stealing books years ago. Several times. We began to worry he was going to run afoul of some repeat offenders law, so grandfather offered to pay for psychiatric care as part of a plea bargain. Then, when he got out, the aide watched him, kept him out of trouble. But once he had access to grandfather's house . . ." He shook his head, sighing in the same way William had sighed.

"How many books have you stolen for him?"

"Fifty, a hundred. I tried to spread it out to several places, but the other owners are, well, a little sharper than Octavia."

No, they're just not smitten with you, Tess wanted to say.

"Could you make restitution?"

"Over time. But what good would it do? William will just steal more. I'm stuck. Besides . . ." Tate looked defiant, proud. "I think what he's doing is kind of beautiful."

Tess didn't disagree. "The thing is, if something happens to you—if you get caught, or lose your job—you're both screwed. You can't go on like this. And you have to make restitution to Octavia. Do it anonymously, through me, whatever you can afford. Then I'll show you how William can get all the books he needs, for free."

"I don't see—"

"Trust me," Tess said. "And one other thing?"

"Sure."

"Would it kill you to ask Octavia out for coffee or something? Just once?"

"Octavia! If I were going to ask someone there out, it would be—"

"Mona, I know. But you know what, Tate? Not everyone can get the girl with the duck tattoo."

The next Saturday, Tess met William outside his house. He wore his knapsack on his back, she wore hers on the front, where Carla Scout nestled with a sippee cup. She was small for her age, not even twenty-five pounds, but it was still quite the cargo to carry on a hike.

"Are you ready for our walk?"

"I usually walk alone," William said. He was unhappy with this arrangement and had agreed to it only after Tate had all but ordered him to do it.

"After today, you can go back to walking alone. But I want to take you some place today. It's almost three miles."

"That's nothing," William said.

"Your pack might be heavier on the return trip."

"It often is," he said.

I bet, Tess thought. He had probably never given up stealing books despite what Tate thought.

They walked south through the neighborhood, lovely even with the trees bare and the sky overcast. William, to Tess's surprise, preferred the main thoroughfares. Given his aversion to people, she thought he would want to duck down less-trafficked side streets, make use of Stony Run Park's green expanse, which ran parallel to much of their route. But William stuck to the busiest streets. She wondered if drivers glanced out their windows and thought: Oh, the walking man now has a walking woman and a walking baby.

He did not speak and shut down any attempt Tess made at conversation. He walked as if he were alone. His face was set, his gait steady. She could tell it made him anxious, having to follow her path, so she began to narrate the route, turn by turn, which let him walk a few steps ahead. "We'll take Roland Avenue to University Parkway, all the way to Barclay, where we'll go left." His pace was slow by Tess's standards, but William didn't walk to get places. He walked to walk. He walked to fill his days. Tate said his official diagnosis was bi-polar with OCD, which made finding the right mix of medications difficult. His work, as William termed it, seemed to keep him more grounded than anything else, which was why Tate indulged it.

Finally, about an hour later, they stood outside a building of blue-and-pink cinderblocks.

"This is it," Tess said.

"This is what?"

"Go in."

They entered a warehouse stuffed with books. And not just any books—these were all unloved books, as William would have it, books donated to this unique Baltimore institution, the

Book Thing, which accepted any and all books on one condition: They would then be offered free to anyone who wanted them.

"Tens of thousands of books," Tess said. "All free, every weekend."

"Is there a limit?"

"Yes," Tess said. "Only ten at a time. But you probably couldn't carry much more, right?" Actually, the limit, according to the Book Thing's rather whimsical website, was 150,000. But Tess had decided her aunt was right about people according more value to things they could not have so readily. If William thought he could have only ten, every week, it would be more meaningful to him.

He walked through the aisles, his eyes strafing the spines. "How will I save them all?" William said.

"One week at a time," Tess said. "But you have to promise that this will be your only, um, supplier from now on. If you get books from anywhere else, you won't be allowed to come here anymore. Do you understand, William? Can you agree to that?"

"I'll manage," William said. "These books really need me."

It took him forty-five minutes to pick his first book, *Manifold Destiny*, a guide to cooking on one's car engine.

"Really?" Tess said. "That's a book that needs to be liberated?"

William looked at her with pity, as if she were a hopeless philistine.

"He spent five hours there, selecting his books," Tess told Crow that evening, over an early supper. Crow worked Saturday evenings, so they ate early in order to spend more time together.

"Did you feel guilty at all? He's just going to tear them apart and destroy them."

"Is he? Destroying them, I mean. Or is he making something beautiful, as his brother would have it? I go back and forth."

Crow shook his head. "An emotionally disturbed man with scissors, cutting up books inside his home, taking a walk with you and our daughter, whose middle name is Scout. And you didn't make one Boo Radley joke the entire time?"

"Not a one," Tess said. "You do the bath. I'll clean up."

But she didn't clean up, not right away. She went into her own library, a cozy sunroom lined with bookshelves. She had spent much of her pregnancy here, reading away, but even in three months of confinement she barely made a dent in the unread books. She had always thought of it as being rich, having so many books she had yet to read. But in William's view, she was keeping them confined. And no one else, other than Crow, had access to them. Was her library that different from William's?

Of course, she had paid for her books—most of them. Like almost every other bibliophile on the planet, Tess had books, borrowed from friends, that she had never returned, even as some of her favorite titles lingered in friends' homes, never to be seen again.

She picked up her iPad. Only seventy books loaded onto it. *Only.* Mainly things for work, but also the occasional self-help guide that promised to unlock the mysteries of toddlers. Forty of the seventy titles were virtually untouched. She wandered into Carla Scout's room, where there was now a poster of a bearded man living in a pile of books, the Arnold Lobel print from The Children's Bookstore. A payment/gift from a giddy Octavia, who didn't know how Tess had stopped her books from disappearing, and certainly didn't know that her crush had anything to do with it. During Carla Scout's bedtime routine, Tess now stopped in front of the poster, read the verse printed there, then added her own couplet. "It's just as much fun as it looks/To live in a house made of books."

It's what's in the book that matters. Standing in her daughter's room, which also had shelves and shelves filled with books, Tess re-membered a character in a favorite story saying that to someone who objected to using the Bible as a fan on a hot summer day. But she could no longer remember which story it was.

Did that mean the book had ceased to live for her? The title she was trying to recall could be in this very room, along with all of Tess's childhood favorites, waiting for Carla Scout to discover them one day. But what if she rejected them all, insisting on her own myths and legends, as Octavia had prophesied? How many of these books would be out of print in five, ten years? What did it mean to be out of print in a world where books could live inside devices, glowing like captured genies, desperate to get back out in the world and grant people's wishes?

Carla Scout burst into the room, wet hair gleaming, cheeks pink.

"Buh," she said, which was her word for book, unless it was her word for ball or, possibly, balloon. "Buh, p'ease."

She wasn't even in her pajamas yet, just her diaper and hooded towel. Tess would have to use the promise of books to coax her through putting on her footed sleeper and gathering up her playthings. How long would she be able to bribe her daughter with books? Would they be shunted aside like the Velveteen Rabbit as other newer, shinier toys gained favor? Would her daughter even read *The Velveteen Rabbit*? William Kemper suddenly seemed less crazy to Tess than the people who managed to live their lives in houses that had no books at all.

"Three tonight," Tess said. "Pick out three. Only three, Carla Scout. One, two, three. You may have three."

They read five.

Author's note:
The Book Thing is a very real thing and its hours and policies are as described here. The Children's Bookstore on 25th Street is my invention, along with all characters.

The Scroll

Anne Perry

THE EARLY WINTER evening was drawing in. In the antiquarian bookshop well away from the High Street in Cambridge, Monty Danforth sat in his room at the back, working on unpacking and cataloguing the books and papers from the last crate of the Greville Estate. Most of it was exactly what he would have expected: the entire works of Dickens and Thackeray, Walter Scott and Jane Austin, all in leather-bound editions; many of the Russian novelists, similarly bound; *Gibbon's Decline and Fall of the Roman Empire*, Churchill's *History of the English Speaking People*. There were also the usual reference books and encyclopaedias, and some rather more interesting and unusual memoirs and books on travel, especially around the Mediterranean. He did not think much of it would re-sell easily, and it would take rather a lot of space to store it.

The owner of the shop, Roger Williams, was not well and staying at his house further north east, towards the wide, flat fen country. He might decide to auction the whole shipment off in one job lot.

Monty peered into the bottom of the crate to make sure he had everything out of it. There was something rather like an old biscuit drum on one side. He reached in and picked it up.

It was too heavy to be empty. He pried the lid off and looked inside. There was definitely something there, but it was hard to make it out.

He took it over to the light and flicked on the switch. A yellow glow filled the room, leaving the corners even more shadowed. There was what looked like an old scroll inside the tin. He teased it out gently and put it on the table right under the light bulb. He unrolled it an inch or two at a time, and stared. There was writing on it, patchy, faded, in several places illegible. He tried to make out words, but it was very definitely not English, even of the very oldest sort. The letters were more like the little he had seen of Hebrew.

He touched the texture of it experimentally with his finger tips. It was soft, smooth and had not the dry fragile feeling of paper, more like vellum. There were several blanks on it, and other places where the words were half-obscured by smudges, or erased altogether.

According to what he had been told, the Greville family had travelled extensively in the Middle East in the nineteenth century and early twentieth. They could have found this scroll anywhere: Egypt, Mesopotamia, Palestine, Jordan, or what was now Israel.

Just in case it really did have some value, he should photocopy it. That could be useful to get a translation, without sending the original.

He stood up and took it over to the machine. He pressed the switch and it came to life. Very carefully he unrolled the first half of the scroll and laid it on the glass, then closed the lid. He pressed it for one copy. The paper rolled out onto the tray.

He picked it up to check it for clarity. It was blank, apart from a couple of smudges.

That was silly. He tried again, with the same result. He checked the ink, the paper, the settings, and tried a third time. Still nothing.

He took the scroll out and tried it with an old letter from a customer.

Perfect, every detail beautifully clear. It was not the machine. Just as well that, as always, he had his mobile phone with him; the camera in it was really rather good. Digital, of course, and you could check immediately on the result, and print it off on the computer later, if you wished.

He took a photograph of a customer's letter, then looked at it on the screen. It was perfect. Taking two books to hold down the ends and keep the scroll flat, he took the photograph. In the viewfinder it was perfect also, every line and smudge was there. He clicked the exposure once, twice, three times, taking the whole length. Then he looked at it. The first exposure was blank, so was the second, and the third. The vellum was clear, even to the shadows it cast on the table where the edges were torn or curled, but there was no writing on it whatsoever.

Monty blinked and rubbed his eyes. How was it possible? What had he done wrong?

He was still staring at it when he heard the shop's bell ring. It startled him, although he thought the moment after that it was not extraordinary for a lover of rare books or prints to call after hours. Sometimes it was convenient for someone who could not leave their work during the day. Quite often it was the desire to examine in privacy whatever it was that interested them. But they made appointments. Was there someone coming whom he had forgotten?

The bell rang again. He put the scroll back in the tin out of sight, then he went to the door and looked out through the glass. On the step was an old man, stooped, grey-haired, his face lined by time and from the look of him, perhaps also grief. Beside him was a child of perhaps eight years old. Her face was fair-skinned, blemishless, her hair soft and with the lamplight on it, its gold looked almost like a halo. She was staring straight back at Monty through the glass.

He opened the door. "Good evening. May I help you?" he asked.

The child gave him a shy smile and moved closer to the old man, presumably her grandfather.

"Good evening, sir," the old man replied. "My name is Judson Garrett. I am a collector of rare books and manuscripts. I believe you have just come into possession of the books from the Greville estate? Am I in the right place?"

"Yes, indeed," Monty answered. "But we've only just got it. It's not catalogued yet and so we can't put a price on it. The books are in very good condition. In fact, honestly, I'd say a good many of them haven't even been read."

Garrett smiled and his dark eyes were full of sadness. "It is the case with too many books, I fear. Old leather, fine paper are all very well, but it is the words that matter. They are the wealth of the mind and the heart."

Monty stepped back, holding the door open. "Come in, and we can discuss the possibilities."

"Thank you," Garrett accepted, stepping in, closely followed by the child.

Monty closed the door behind them and led the way to Roger Williams' office where matters of business were discussed. He turned the light on, making the bookshelves and the easy chairs leap to a warmth and inviting comfort.

"Please sit down, Mr. Garrett. If you give me your particulars, I'll pass them on to Mr. Williams, the owner, and as soon as we know exactly what we have, we can discuss prices."

The old man did not sit. He remained just inside the door, his face still cast in shadows, the little girl at his side, her hand holding his. There was a weariness in his face as if he had travelled too far and found no rest.

"There is only one item I'm interested in," he said quietly. "The rest does not concern me and you may do with it as you wish."

"Really?" Monty was surprised. He had seen nothing of more than slight worth. "What is the item?"

The old man's eyes seemed to look far away, as if he could see an infinite distance, into another realm, perhaps into a past beyond Monty's imagination. "A scroll," he replied. "Very old.

It may be wrapped in some kind of protection. It is written in Aramaic."

Monty felt a chill run through him as if he had been physically touched by something ice-cold. The child was staring at him. She had clear, sky-blue eyes and she seemed hardly to blink.

Monty's first instinct was to deny having found the scroll, but he knew that the old man was already aware of it. It would be ridiculous to lie, perhaps even dangerous. He drew in a deep breath.

"I don't have the authority to sell the scroll, Mr. Garrett, but I will pass on your interest to Mr. Williams as soon as he comes back. If you leave a contact number or address with me, perhaps an email?"

"I shall return, Mr. Danforth," the old man replied. "Please do not consider selling it to anyone else before you give me an opportunity to bid." His eyes on Monty's were steady and so dark as to be almost black. His expression was unreadable.

The child tugged on his hand and her small fingers seemed to tighten on his even further.

"The scroll is of great value," the old man continued. "I hope you appreciate that?"

"No one else is aware of it yet," Monty assured him. "It isn't actually listed in the papers, and I only discovered it . . . maybe half an hour ago. May I ask how you heard it was there?"

The very faintest of smiles flickered on the old man's face, and vanished again before Monty was sure whether it was amusement or something more like regret. "Many people know it is here," he said very quietly. "They will come and offer you many things for it . . . money, but other things as well. Be very careful what you do with it, Mr. Danforth . . . very careful indeed. There is power in it you would be wise to leave."

Again Monty felt the coldness brush by him again, touching him to the bone.

"What is it?" he said huskily.

The old man drew in his breath as if to answer him. The child

tugged at his hand again, and he sighed and changed his mind.
He looked steadily at Monty, and there was long experience
and a knowledge of evil and of pain in his eyes.

"Be careful, Mr. Danforth. It is a dangerous responsibility
you are about to take upon yourself. Perhaps you have no other
honourable choice. That I understand. But it is a heavy weight.
There is destruction and delusion in what you are about to pick
up. Do nothing without great thought."

Monty found himself gulping, swallowing as if there were
something in his throat. "How do I contact you, Mr. Garrett?"

"You do not need to. I shall come back." He shook the child's
hand off him impatiently and turned towards the door, pushing
it open.

Monty followed him to the street entrance. He opened it
and the old man walked through, the child on his heels. The
street beyond was shadowed, the nearest lamp was apparently
broken. When Monty looked again there was no one there.

Monty locked the door this time, not just the latch but the
deadbolt as well, and went back to his room. He opened the
tin again and took out the scroll. The vellum was soft to his
fingers, almost warm. Was it as ancient as the old man had said?
Aramaic? Perhaps from the time of Christ?

If that were so, then it could be any of a number of things,
real or imagined. How did it come to be in the Greville estate?
In their travels could they have found something like the Dead
Sea Scrolls?

It was far more likely that they had been sold a fake. How
difficult was it to make something of that nature? Or even
to find an old scroll which might have been nothing more
interesting than instructions to build a house, or lists of a cargo
shipped from one port to another? Business writings abounded,
just as domestic pottery far outweighed vases for ornament or
the worship of gods.

He unrolled it on the table and weighed down both ends,
putting it directly under the light. It was not very long, perhaps

a thousand words or a little more. That was a lot for a cargo list, and there were no drawings or diagrams on it, so any kind of a plan seemed unlikely.

He peered at it, looking for patterns, repetitions, anything that would give him a clue as to what it was. It was the Hebrew alphabet, which he was vaguely familiar with, but Garrett had said it was Aramaic.

He really had very little idea of what he was doing, and no chance at all of actually reading it, yet he found it almost impossible to look away. Was this some passionate cry of the soul from the tumultuous times of Christ? An account of power and sacrifice, of agony and resurrection?

Or was it simply somebody's laundry list which had chanced to survive, principally because nobody cared enough to steal it?

Monty's imagination created pictures in his mind, men in long robes, sandals, dusty roads, whispers in the dark, blood and pain.

The light flickered and the shadows in the corners of the room moved, wavering and then righting themselves again. He half-expected someone to materialize out of the air, the darkness to come together, intensify and take form. Who could it be? Mephistopheles—to tempt an all too fragile Faust? With what? Forbidden knowledge?

"Don't be so damn silly!" he said aloud. "It's a power brown out! All you need to do is make sure your computer's backed up!" He had always had a weird imagination, a sensitivity to the presence of evil. He told the most excellent ghost stories to the great entertainment of his friends. He was known for it, even loved. People liked to be given a frisson of fear, just enough to get the adrenalin going.

His best friend, Hank Savage, a pragmatic scientist, teased him about it, although even he conceded that evil was real, just not supernatural. No angels, no devils, just human beings, some with rather too much excitability and a tendency to blame others for their own faults. Who easier to blame than the devil?

Monty picked up the scroll and rolled it tight, the vellum soft under his fingertips. Perhaps it was not all that old after all. It certainly wasn't dried up or likely to crack. He put it back in the tin, and then placed the whole thing in the safe, just as a precaution.

It was time he went home and had some supper, and a nice, prosaic cup of tea, or two, strong and with sugar.

The following morning was Saturday and his presence was not necessary at the bookshop. The rest of the Greville estate could wait until Monday. Monty really needed to see Hank Savage and ask his opinion. It would be perfectly sane and logical. There would be no emotional silliness in it, no heightened imagination.

He found Hank pottering in his studio at the back of his lodgings. It was a large attic room with excellent light where Hank enjoyed his hobby of cleaning up and framing old drawings and prints which he bought, often as job lots at auctions. He made a certain amount of money at it, which he gave away. His purpose was the relaxation he gained, and the triumph now and then of finding something really lovely.

He put down the blade with which he was cutting matt for a drawing and regarding Monty with wry affection.

"You look like hell, Monty. What's happened?" he asked cheerfully. Clearly Monty looked worse than his restless night justified.

"Came across an old scroll," Monty answered, sitting sideways on the edge of a pair of steps piled with papers. Hank was a scientist and his mind was exquisitely ordered. His rooms were correspondingly chaotic.

"How old?" Hank was irritatingly literal. He was tall, rather too thin, with dark hair and mild blue eyes. Monty had brown eyes, and to put it in his own words, not tall enough for his weight.

"I don't know. It's in Aramaic, I think, and I can't read it."

Monty was highly satisfied with the sharp interest in Hank's face. "It's on vellum," he added for good measure. "I found it in a biscuit tube at the bottom of the last crate of books from the Greville estate."

"What is it listed as?" Hank asked, abandoning the framing altogether and giving Monty his entire attention.

"It isn't listed at all. I tried to photocopy it. Nothing came out."

"Maybe your printer's broken? I don't suppose it would be a very good idea to take it anywhere else, if it really is as old as you think. Photograph it, until you get someone in to fix the copier," Hank replied.

"I tried to photograph it. It didn't come out." Monty remembered the strange chill he had felt at the time. "And before you suggest it, there's nothing wrong with my camera. Or with the copier either, actually. They both work fine on anything else."

Hank frowned. "So what's your explanation? Other than gremlins."

"I don't have one. But within half an hour or so of my finding the thing, the oddest old man turned up, with his granddaughter aged about eight, and offered to buy it."

"How much?" Hank asked dubiously. "You didn't sell it, I trust?"

"No, of course I didn't!" Monty said tartly. "I hid it before I even let them in. But you didn't ask the obvious question!"

"Who was he?"

"No! How did he know what it was and that I had it?" Monty said with satisfaction. "I didn't tell anyone and I certainly didn't show anyone."

"Didn't Roger know?" Hank was now both puzzled and very curious.

"Roger wasn't there. He's away sick. Has been for several days."

"Well what did this old man say?"

"His name is Judson Garrett, and he wouldn't leave any address or contact. He just said not to sell it to anyone else, and that it could be very dangerous."

Hank's eyebrows rose. "A threat?"

"Actually it sounded rather more like a warning," Monty admitted, remembering the old man's face and the power of darkness and pain in it.

"Did he say why he wanted it?" Hank was still turning it over in his mind.

"No. But he said others would come after it, but he didn't give any idea who they would be."

"Did you look at this scroll, Monty?"

"Of course I did!" He took a breath. "Do you want to see it?"

"Yes, if you don't mind, I really do." There was no hesitation in Hank's voice, no fear, none of the apprehension that Monty felt. There were times when Hank's total sanity irritated him intensely, but now it was comforting, even a kind of safety from the shadows in his own mind.

At the bookshop Monty opened the safe and took out the biscuit drum. The scroll was exactly as he had placed it. It felt the same to the touch as he pulled it out, dry and slightly warm. He unrolled it on the table for Hank to examine.

Hank looked at it for a long time before finally speaking.

"I think it's Aramaic, alright, and from the few words I can recognize here and there, it seems to be during the Roman occupation of Jerusalem. It could be the time of Christ. I see quite a lot of first person grammar, so it might be someone's own account of what they did, or saw . . . a kind of diary. But I don't know enough to be certain. You need an expert on this, Monty, not only to translate it but to date it and authenticate it. But before you do any of that, you must call Roger and tell him what you have. Have you tried again to get a copy?"

"No. Use your phone if you like," Monty suggested. "See if it's any better. You're pretty good technically."

Hank gave him a quick glance, sensing the difference between 'technically' and 'artistically'. But he did not argue. He took his cell phone out of his pocket, adjusted the settings, looked through the view finder and took three separate photographs. He went back to the first one to look at it, frowned, turned to the second, then the third. He looked up at Monty.

Monty felt the chill creep over his skin.

"Nothing," Hank said quietly. "Blank."

"I'll call Roger," Monty grasped for the only useful thing he could do. He picked up the telephone and dialled Roger Williams' number. He let it ring fifteen times. There was no answer.

He tried again the following day, and again Roger did not pick up. Monty was busy cataloguing the rest of the books from the Greville estate when he became aware of someone standing in the doorway watching him. He was round-faced, broad-browed and smiling benignly, but there was a gravity in his dark eyes, and a very definite knowledge of his own importance in his posture. He was dressed in a clergyman's cassock and he had a purple vestment below his high, white collar.

Monty scrambled to his feet. "I'm sorry, sir," he apologized awkwardly. "I didn't hear you come in. Can I help you?"

The man smiled even more widely. "I'm sure you can, Mr. Danforth."

Monty felt a sudden stab of alarm like a prickle on his skin, a warning of danger. This prince of the church knew his name, just as the old man of the previous evening had done. He had not questioned it at the time, but he did now. It was Roger's name on the door and on the company letterhead. Monty's name appeared nowhere. And why had they not assumed he was Roger? Wouldn't that be the natural thing to do?

"You have me at a disadvantage, Your Grace," he said rather crisply. "I am quite sure I would remember if we had met."

The man smiled again. "I'm sure you would. And yet you greeted me correctly, and with courtesy. There is no need as yet for us to go beyond that. I imagine you also know why I am here. You are not only knowledgeable on books of all types, Mr. Danforth, and an intelligent man, you are also, I believe, unusually sensitive to the power of evil, and also of good."

Monty was flattered, and then frightened. He was an excellent raconteur and could tell ghost stories which held his audience of friends spellbound . . . for an evening's entertainment and fellowship. That was hardly something to spread beyond his own circle, which did not include bishops of any faith, Catholic or Protestant. His friends were largely academics like Hank, or else students and artists of one sort or another.

The bishop continued to smile. "You have in your possession at the moment a very unusual piece of ancient manuscript," he continued. "It is part of an estate, and you will in due course offer it for sale, along with the rest of the books, which are insignificant in comparison. No doubt they are in good condition, but editions of them can be obtained in any decent bookshop. The scroll is unique. But then you know that already." His eyes never moved from Monty's face.

Monty was colder, as if someone had opened a door onto the night. Any idea of denying his knowledge melted away. He had to swallow a couple of times before he could speak, and even then his voice sounded a little high-pitched.

"Something as unusual as the scroll will have to wait for Mr. Williams." It sounded like an excuse, even though it was perfectly true. "I imagine you would like it verified as well. It looks old, but no expert has examined it yet, so I have no idea of price. Actually, we don't even know what it is."

The bishop's smile did not waver, but his eyes were sharp and cold. "It is an ancient and very evil document, Mr. Danforth. If it were to pass into the wrong hands and become known to others the damage it could do would be measureless. I assure you, whatever price an expert might put on it, should you take the path of demanding that price, the Church will meet it. We would hope, as a man of principle and goodwill, you would settle for its value in the market place for scrolls of its date and origin."

Monty's hands were stiff, his arms covered in goosebumps. The bishop's figure seemed to float in the air, to become darker, and then lighter, the edges to blur. This was ridiculous! He blinked and shook his head, then looked again, and everything was normal. An elderly bishop, perfectly solid and human, was standing near the door, still smiling at him, still watching him.

Monty gulped. "The price doesn't lie within my control, Your Grace, but I imagine Mr. Williams will be fair. I have never known him not to be otherwise."

"Do not put it up for auction, Mr. Danforth," the bishop said gravely, the pleasantness disappeared from his expression as completely as a cloud passing across the sun robbed the land beneath of light. "It would be a very dangerous mistake, the extent of which I think might well be beyond your imagination, fertile as that is."

"I shall pass on your message to Mr. Williams," Monty promised, but his voice lacked the firmness he wished.

"Something suggests to me, Mr. Danforth, that I am not the only person to approach you on this subject," the bishop observed. "I urge you, with all the power at my disposal, not to sell this scroll elsewhere, no matter what inducement might be offered you to do so."

Now Monty was annoyed. "You say 'inducement' Your Grace, as if I had been offered bribes. That is not so, and I do not care for your implication. That might be the case with people you usually deal with, but it is not so with this bookshop. Bribery does not work, and neither do threats." The moment the words were out of his mouth fear seized him so tightly he found himself shaking.

"Not threats, Mr. Danforth," the bishop said in barely more than a whisper. "A warning. You are dealing with powers so ancient you cannot conceive their beginning, and in your most hideous nightmare you cannot think of their end. You are not a fool. Do not, in your ignorance and hubris, behave like one." Then without adding any more, or explaining himself, he turned and went out of the door. His feet made no sound whatever on the floorboards beyond, nor did the street door click shut behind him.

Monty did not move; in fact, he could not. His imagination soared over one thing after another and he seemed at once hot and cold. Clearly in the bishop's mind the scroll had an even more immense power than Monty had already seen in his own inability to copy it by any mechanical means. Who had written it and when? Was it ancient, or a more modern hoax? Obviously it held some terrible secret, almost certainly to do with the Church. To do with greed? The Catholic Church at least had treasures beyond imagining. Or was it personal sin, or mass abuse of the type only too well known already, but involving someone of extraordinary importance? Bribery, violence, even murder? Or some challenge to a doctrine people dared not argue or question?

The possibilities raged through his mind and every one of them was frightening.

At last he stood up, a little wobbly at first, his limbs too long cramped, went over to the telephone, and tried to get Roger Williams again. He let it ring twenty times. There was no answer. He hung up, and called instead the young man who looked after opening the shop in Roger's absence and told him that he would not be in the next day.

Monty drove to the village where Williams had his house. The countryside was silent in the morning sun, untroubled by rush hour traffic. He passed through gentle fields, mostly flat land. Much of it was agricultural; here and there sheep grazed, heads down.

He was turning over in his mind exactly how to explain to Roger the sense of evil he had felt from both the old man, and then perhaps even more from the bishop who had seemed at once benign and dangerous. Or was it Monty's own imagination that was at the heart of it, coupled with his technical incompetence in not being able to copy the scroll?

But Hank couldn't copy it either. Hank was absent-minded at times, and he had a dry and odd sense of humour, but he was never incompetent.

He glanced up at a field of crops, and saw beyond it a sight that made his heart lurch. The rich, dark earth was littered with human skulls—thousands of them, as if a great army had been slaughtered and their corpses left in the open to rot as a perpetual reminder of death.

His hands slipped on the steering wheel and the car careered over the road, slewed to one side and finished up on the verge, only a foot from the drainage ditch. Another fourteen inches and he would have broken the axle. He drew in gasps of breath. His whole body was shaking and he was drenched with sweat.

Then he steeled himself to look at the field again. He saw white sheep turnips in the mud and weeds, their skull-like surfaces mounded above the soil.

What on earth had he seen for that awful moment? A vision of Armageddon?

He put the car back into gear and backed out very slowly, then sat, still shaking, until he could compose himself and drive the last mile or so to Roger's house. He pulled in the drive and stopped. Stiffly he climbed out of the car, still a little shaky, and went to the front door. He rang the bell and there was no answer. Normally he might have waited, perhaps gone to the pub for a coffee or a beer, and returned later. But today it was too urgent. He tried the door and found it unlocked.

Inside the hall there was a harsh smell of smoke, as if Roger had burned a pan, or even a whole meal.

"Roger!" he called at the foot of the stairs.

There was no answer, and he went up, beginning to fear that perhaps Roger was more seriously ill than he had supposed.

He knocked on the bedroom door and when there was still no answer, he pushed it open.

He stepped back, gasping, hand over his mouth. Now the silence was hideously plain. What was left of Roger's body lay stiff and black on the remains of the bed, charred mattress, blackened carpet beneath it. The whole room was stained with smuts and soot as if some brief but terrible fire had raged here, consuming all in its path, and then gone out.

Monty fumbled his way back down the stairs to the telephone and called the police.

They came from the nearest small town, taking only twenty minutes to get there. They asked Monty to wait.

It was nearly two hours before a grimfaced sergeant from the county town told him that they believed it had been arson, quick and lethal. They asked him a great many more questions, including some about the bookshop, Roger's personal life, and also to account very precisely for his own whereabouts all the previous day. To his great relief he was able to do so.

Then with their permission he drove back to Cambridge and went to see Roger's solicitor, both to inform him of Roger's death, and to ask for instructions regarding the bookshop, for the time being. He was stunned, grieved and too generally disconcerted even to think about his own future.

"I'm afraid it falls on you, Mr. Danforth," Mr. Ingles told him gravely. "The only family Mr. Williams had is a niece in Australia. I can try to get in touch with her, but I already know from Mr. Williams that the young woman is something of an explorer, and it could be a period of time before we can obtain any instructions from her. In the meantime you are named as Mr. Williams' successor in the running of the business. Did he not inform you of that?" He shook his head. "I'm sorry—by the look on your face, clearly he did not. I do apologize. However there is nothing I can do about it now."

Monty was appalled. The scroll! He couldn't possibly make the decision on the sale of that!

"When can you find this woman?" he said desperately. "How long? Can't the Australian police or somebody get in touch with her? Doesn't she have responsibilities? A telephone? An email address? Something!"

"I dare say we will find her within a few weeks, Mr. Danforth," the solicitor said soothingly. "Until then, I advise that you just run the business as usual."

Monty felt as if one by one the walls were falling down and leaving him exposed to the elements of violence and darkness and there was no protection left.

"You don't understand!" He could hear the hysteria rising in his voice but he could not control it. "I have an ancient scroll in the last shipment, and two people are wanting it. I have no idea what it's worth, or which one to sell it to!"

"Can't you get an expert to value it?" Inglis said, his silver eyebrows raised rather high.

"No, I can't, not if it's worth what the two bidders so far are implying. I don't know what it is . . . it's . . ."

"You're upset, Mr. Danforth," Ingles said soothingly. "Roger's death has distressed you, very naturally. I'm sure when you've had a day or two to think about it, or a good night's sleep at least, you'll know what to do. Roger had a very high opinion of you, you know."

At any other time Monty would have been delighted to hear that; right now it was only making things worse. He could see in Ingles' face that already he was thinking of Monty as incompetent and possibly wondering why on earth Roger had thought well of him.

"The Church wants it," he said aloud.

"Then sell it to them, at whatever price an impartial assessor considers to be fair," Inglis replied, rising to his feet.

How could Monty explain the power the old man had exerted, the extraordinary emotions in his face that Monty could not ignore. Put into words it sounded absurd.

"I'll get an assessment," was all he could think of to say.

Ingles smiled. "Good. I'll wait to hear from you."

Monty did not get home until late, and the following day was taken up with matters of business at the shop. There was a great deal of paperwork to be attended to, access to bank accounts, dry but very necessary details.

In the evening Monty went to his favourite pub to have supper in familiar and happy surroundings. He had called Hank to join him, but Hank had not yet returned home and was not answering his mobile, so Monty was obliged to eat alone.

He had a supper that should have been delicious: freshly cooked cold pork pie with sharp, sweet little tomatoes, then homemade pickle with Caerphilly cheese on oatcakes, and a glass of cider. He barely tasted it.

The setting sun was laying a patina of gold over the river bank and the trees were barely moving in the faint breath of wind beyond the wide glass windows. Monty was looking towards the west when he saw the man walking across the grass towards him, up from the riverside path. He seemed to have the light behind him as if he had a halo, a sort of glow to his very being.

To Monty's surprise the man came in through the door and across the room straight towards him, as if they knew each other. He stopped beside Monty's table.

"May I join you, Mr. Danforth?" he said quietly. "We have much to talk about." Without waiting for the reply, he pulled out the second chair and sat down. "I do not need anything to eat, thank you," he went on, as if Monty had offered him something.

"I have nothing to talk about with you, sir," Monty said a little irritably. "We are not acquainted. I have had a very long day. One of my close friends has just died tragically. I would prefer to finish my dinner alone, if you please." He was aware of sounding rude, but he really did not care.

"Ah, yes," the man said sadly. "The death of poor Mr. Williams. Yet another victim of the powers of darkness."

"He was burned to death," Monty said with sudden anger and a very real and biting pain at the thought. "Fire is hardly a weapon of darkness!"

The man was handsome, his face highbrowed, his eyes wide and blue, filled with intelligence. "I was speaking of the darkness of the mind, Mr. Danforth, not of the flesh. And fire has been one of its weapons since the beginning. We imagine it destroys evil, somehow cleanses. We have burned wise women and healers in the superstitious terror that they were witches. We have burned heretics because they dared to question our beliefs. We have burned books because the knowledge or the opinions in them frightened us and we did not wish them to spread. And pardon me for bringing it back to your mind, but you have seen the results of fire very recently. Did you find it cleansing?"

In spite of himself Monty's mind was filled with the stench of burning and the sight of Roger's charred and blackened body on what was left of the bed. It made him feel sick, as though the food he had just eaten were revolting.

"Who are you and what do you want?" he said harshly.

"I am a scholar," the man replied. "I am someone who could add to the world's knowledge, without judgment as to who should know what, and who should be permitted to conceal truth because they do not agree with it, or have decided that this person or that one could find it difficult or uncomfortable. I would force no one, but allow everyone."

"What do you think is in it?" Monty asked curiously.

"A unique testimony from the time of Christ," the scholar replied. "One that may verify our beliefs—or blow them all apart. It will be a new truth—or a very old one"

Monty already knew what he was going to say, but he asked anyhow.

"And why do you approach me at a time of grief and interrupt my supper?"

"Actually you have finished your supper," the man indicated Monty's empty plate with a smile on his finely sculpted face.

"But I find it hard to believe that you do not already know why I have come. I wish to buy from you the scroll, at whatever price you believe to be fair. I would ask you to give it to the world, if I thought that would prevail upon you, but I know that you have some responsibility to the estate of which it is presently a part. And please do not tell me that it is not within your power. With Mr. Williams' most unfortunate death, it is more than within it, it is your obligation."

Monty felt the sweat break out on his brow in spite of the closing in of the evening, now that the sun had definitely faded.

"You are not the only person seeking to buy it," he answered.

"Of course not," the scholar agreed with amusement. "If I were, I would begin to doubt its authenticity. The Church, at the very least, will bid high for it. But surely money is not your only consideration? That would disappoint me very much, Mr. Danforth. I had thought far more highly of you than that."

"I have not yet been able to get anyone in to verify what it is," Monty prevaricated. "It is impossible to put a price on it."

"When you have verified it, it will still be impossible," the scholar responded. "But you are being disingenuous. I think you have at least an educated guess as to what you have. And I assure you it is what you believe it to be."

"I have no beliefs as to what it is," Monty insisted angrily.

The scholar's face was filled with awe, his eyes almost luminous in the waning light. "It is the lost testament of Judas Iscariot," he said so quietly his voice was barely audible. "We have known of its existence for centuries. It has been hunted by all manner of people, each with his own reasons either to hide it or to make it known."

So it was true. Monty sat on the familiar river bank in the English twilight and thought of Jerusalem two thousand years ago, of betrayal and sacrifice, of blood, pain, ordinary human feet trudging in the dust on a journey into immortality. He thought of faith, and grief, and human love.

"Is it?" he asked.

"I think you know that, Monty," the scholar answered. "It

must be given to the world. Mankind has a right to know what is in it—a different story, or the one we all expect. And in simple morality, does not the accused have a right to testify?"

The thought whirled in Monty's head, and he found no words on his tongue. The enormity of it was too great. Little wonder he could not photocopy it!

The scholar leaned across the table closer to him. "You would be a benefactor to justice, Monty," he said, unable to keep the urgency out of his voice. "An honest man, a true scholar who sought the truth above all emotional or financial interest, a man of unsoiled honesty."

For a moment Monty was overwhelmed by temptation. He drew in his breath, and then he remembered the old man with his granddaughter, and the promise he had made him. Why did he want it? He was the only one who had given no reason. He remembered again the knowledge of time and pain in his eyes.

"I will consider it," he said to the scholar in front of him. "If you leave me an address I will be in touch with you. Now please leave me to have another glass of cider and a piece of cake."

Actually he did not bother with more cider, or the cake. He paid his bill and left. As soon as he was in his car he tried Hank again on his cell phone. This time Hank answered.

"I must see you immediately," Monty said before even asking how Hank was or what he was doing. "Please come to the bookshop. I'll wait for you."

"Are you alright?" Hank said anxiously. "You sound terrible. What's happened?"

"Just come to the bookshop," Monty repeated. "Ring the bell. I'll let you in."

Half an hour later Monty and Hank were sitting at the table in Monty's workroom with the scroll open in front of them.

"Who was this scholar?" Hank said gravely. "He must have given you a name."

"No, he didn't," Monty replied. "Like the old man with his granddaughter, and the bishop, or whatever he was, they all knew about this," he glanced at the scroll. "And my name, and where to find me. But I've told no one, except you. I didn't even have a chance to tell Roger."

Hank looked at the scroll again, lifting up his glasses to peer beneath them and see it more intensely. He was silent for so long that Monty became restless. He was about to interrupt him when Hank sat back at last.

"I've been swatting up a bit on Aramaic," he said, his voice quiet and strained, lines of anxiety deeper in his face than usual, perhaps exaggerated by the artificial light. "I can only make out a few words clearly. I'm not really very good. It's a long way from mathematics, but I've always been interested in the teachings of Christ—just as a good man, perhaps morally the greatest."

"And . . .?" Monty's own voice quivered.

Hank's face lit with a gentle smile. "And I have no special illumination, Monty. I can make out a few words, but they seem ambiguous, capable of far more than one interpretation. There are several proper names and I'm almost sure one of them is 'Judas'. But there is so much I don't know that I couldn't even guess at the meaning. It isn't a matter of missing a subtlety. I could omit a negative and come with a completely opposite interpretation."

"But could he be correct . . . the scholar?" Monty insisted. "Could it be the lost testimony of Judas Iscariot?"

"It could be a testimony of anyone, or just a letter," Hank replied. "Or it could be a fake."

"No it couldn't," Monty said with absolute certainty. "Touch it. Try to photograph it. It's real. Even you can't deny that."

Hank chewed his lip, the lines in his face deepening even more. "If it is what the scholar says, that would explain why the bishop is so anxious to have it, and perhaps destroy it. Or at the very least keep it hidden."

"Why? Surely it would make religion, Christianity in particular, really hot news again."

"If it confirms what they have taught for two thousand years," Hank agreed. "But what if it doesn't?"

"Like what?" Monty asked, then immediately knew the answer. It was as if someone were slowly dimming all the lights everywhere, as far as the eye could see, as far as the imagination could stretch.

Hank said nothing.

"You mean a fake crucifixion?" Monty demanded. "No resurrec-tion?" Then he wished he had not even said the words. "That would be awful. It would rob millions of people of the only hope they have, of all idea of heaven, of a justice to put right the griefs we can't touch here." He swallowed painfully. "Of ever seeing again those we love . . . and those who didn't have a chance here . . ."

"I know," Hank said softly. "That is a belief I would never force on others, even if I hold it myself. I would be inclined to give it to Prince of the Church, and let him burn it."

"Book burning? You, Hank?" Monty said incredulously.

"If I had to choose between truth, or what seems to be truth, and kindness . . . then I think I might choose kindness," Hank said gently. "There are too many 'shorn lambs' I wouldn't hurt."

"Temper the wind to the shorn lamb," Monty said in a whisper. "And could you do it without even knowing what the scroll said?"

"That's the rub," Hank agreed. "We don't know what's in it. It might not be that at all. Do you remember what the Bible says Christ said to Judas? 'Go and do what thou must'?"

Monty stared at him.

Hank looked at the scroll. "If there were no betrayal then there would have been no trial, therefore no crucifixion, and no resurrection. Is it possible that Judas did only what he had to, or there would have been no fulfilment of the great plan?"

Monty was speechless, his mind whirling, his thoughts out of control.

"But that would spoil the simplicity of the damnation that

Christendom has always placed on Judas," Hank went on. "It would all suddenly become terribly real, and fearfully complex, much too much to be shared with the whole world, most of whom like their religion very simple. Good and evil. Black and white. No difficult decisions to be made. We don't like difficult decisions. For two thousand years we have been told what to think, and we've grown used to it. And make no mistakes, Monty, if this goes to anyone except the Prince of the Church, it will be on the Internet the day after, and everyone will know."

"The Churchman is obvious," Monty agreed. "Anyone can see why he wants it, and I can't entirely disagree. And I can see why the scholar wants it, regardless of what it destroys or who it hurts. But who is the old man? Why does he want it, and how did any of them know it exists, and that I have it?"

"What did you say his name was?" Hank asked. "He was the only one who gave you a name, wasn't he?"

"Yes. Judson Garrett."

Hank stood motionless. "Judson Garrett? Say it again, Monty, aloud. Could it possibly be . . .?" He stared at the scroll. "Lock it up, Monty. I don't know if it will do any good, but at least try to keep it safe."

Quite early the next morning Monty received a phone call from the police to tell him that it was now beyond question that Roger Williams had been murdered. They asked him if he would come down to the local station at his earliest convenience, preferably this morning. There were several issues with which he could help them.

"Of course," he replied. "I'll be there in a couple of hours."

He was met by a very pleasant policewoman, no more than in her mid-thirties. She introduced herself as Sergeant Tobias.

"Sorry about this, Mr. Danforth," she apologized straight away. "Coffee?"

"Er . . . yes, please." It seemed discourteous to refuse, and he would welcome something to do with his hands. It might make him appear less nervous. Had she seen how tense he was, how undecided as to what to tell her?

"You said Roger was murdered," he began as soon as they were sitting down in her small office. If that were so, why was a mere sergeant dealing with it, and a young woman? It did not sound as if they regarded it as important.

"Yes," she said gravely. "There is no question that the fire was deliberately set. And Mr. Williams was struck on the head before the fire started. I thought you'd like to know that because it means he almost certainly didn't suffer."

For a moment Monty found it difficult to speak. He had refused even to think of what Roger might have felt.

"Thank you," he said awkwardly. "Why? I mean . . . do you know why anyone would kill him?"

"We were hoping that you could help us with that. We have found no indication of any personal reason at all. And the fact that the house was pretty carefully searched, but many very attractive ornaments left, some of considerable value, not to mention all the cutlery, which incidentally is silver and quite old, suggests it was not robbery. All the electronic things were left too, even a couple of very expensive mobile phones and ipods, very easily portable."

Monty shook his head, as if trying to get rid of the idea. "Nobody could have hated Roger like that. Maybe it was people high on something?"

"Maybe," she agreed. "But it was very methodical and well done. The search was meticulous, and nothing was broken or tossed around."

"Then how do you know?"

She smiled a little bleakly. "Marks in the dust," she answered. "Not just here and there, as he might have pulled books out himself since anyone last dusted. They were on every shelf, all recent. What does your bookshop deal in, Mr. Danforth? What would your most expensive item be?"

Now the cold ate through him and the taste of the coffee was bitter in his mouth. There was only one possible answer to that, unless he were to lie to her. That thought was born in his mind, and died.

"Usually just a rare book, sometimes a manuscript or original folio, quite a lot of first editions, of course. They can fetch thousands, even tens of thousands. Just occasionally we get an old manuscript, possibly illuminated."

She looked at him steadily. "And at the moment?" she prompted.

He took a deep breath and let it out in a sigh. "At the moment we have an old manuscript which came in the bottom of a crate of pretty ordinary books, from an estate sale."

"Old?" she asked. "What do you call 'old'?"

What would she know about books? Probably nothing at all. World War II would be ancient history to her.

"Mr. Danforth?" she prompted.

"Possibly the time of Christ," he answered, feeling a little melodramatic.

Her interest was instant and intense. "Really? In what language? Latin? Hebrew? Aramaic?"

"I think it's Aramaic," he replied. "It seems to be important, because I have had three people asking for it already, and I haven't even had it authenticated yet."

"But you advertised it?" she said with a quick note of criticism in her voice.

"No," he answered. "No, I didn't. I don't know how anybody knew of it. And I don't know whether it is Aramaic or not. I have a friend who knows a little, just words here and there, and that's what he thinks it is. I still need an expert."

"Have you any idea at all what it is about?" she pressed. "What is it written on? Parchment, vellum? How long is it?"

He withdrew a little bit. "Why do you want to know?"

She smiled, and her expression was gentle and full of pride. "My father is Eli Tobias. He is an expert in ancient Aramaic scripts. We think Mr. Williams was killed for a rare book of some sort. That is why they put me onto the case."

He sighed. "You're right. Three different men have come to me and offered anything I want if I will sell it to them. I can't even photocopy the thing. It's as if it were . . . possessed."

"Then you need an expert to look at it," she replied. "Perhaps more than one. Did any of these men suggest what it is, or why they want it so much?"

He repeated to her what each of the men had said and she listened to him without interrupting.

"Keep it safe, Mr. Danforth," she said after he had finished and stared at her over the cold coffee. "We shall send two experts tomorrow, or the day after. I think we have found the reason poor Mr. Williams was burned to death. Please . . . please be very careful."

Monty promised to do so, and went out into the street a little shakily. He drove back to Cambridge and worked in the shop until late afternoon. He finished cataloguing the last books of the Greville estate and decided to go home for supper, and then perhaps telephone Hank and tell him the latest news. It would be comforting to speak to him. His sanity was like a breath of clean air, blowing away the stale nonsense that had collected in his mind.

He was surprised to find when he went outside that it had been raining quite heavily, and he had not noticed. The gutters were full and in places slurping over. Thank goodness it had stopped now or he would have been soaked. The sky was darkening in the east, and the red sky to the west promised a good day tomorrow, if you believe the old tales of forecasting.

He turned the corner and the sunlight struck him in the face. He shut his eyes for a moment, then opened them again. The shock took him like a physical blow. The whole tarmac surface was covered with blood. It lay in pools, shining and scarlet. It ran gurgling in the gutters.

He was paralyzed by the sheer horror of it.

A cyclist came racing around the corner, skidded, slewed across the road and hit him, knocking him over. He was bruised and his skin torn, his chest for a moment unable to move, to draw in breath. With difficulty he gasped in air at last and straightened very slowly to his knees, dizzy and aching.

An old lady was hurrying towards him, her face creased with concern.

"Are you alright?" she asked anxiously. "Stupid boys. They're going much too fast. Didn't even stop. Are you injured?" She offered her hand to help him up, but she looked too frail to take any of his weight.

He stood upright, surprised to find that apart from being thoroughly wet from the gutter, he was actually not damaged. His jacket sleeves and his shirt cuffs were sodden with rainwater, dirty grey, his trousers the same. There was a tiny red smear of blood on his palm where he had scratched it.

"Yes, I think I'm all right, thank you," he replied. "I was standing in the way, I think. Just . . . staring . . ." There was nothing left of the images of blood, just an ordinary asphalt road with puddles of rain gleaming in the last of the sunset. He wouldn't tell Hank about this. As he had always said, most supernatural phenomena were just over-excited imaginations painting very human fears onto perfectly normal situations.

Nevertheless when he saw Hank later on, having washed, changed his clothes and had a very good supper, he found him also unusually concerned.

"Can you work out why we can't photograph this scroll yet?" Monty asked as they sat with late coffee and an indulgence of After Eight mints.

"No," Hank said candidly. He gave a slightly rueful smile. "For once, logic eludes me. I can't think of any reasonable answer. I imagine there's an explanation as to how those three men knew of the scroll at all, when you didn't advertise it. I suppose since they knew you had it, it wasn't a great leap to track down poor Roger. Monty . . ."

"What?"

"We have to settle this issue straight away. I don't think I'm being alarmist, but if they'd kill Roger for it, they aren't going to accept a polite delay from you."

The increasing darkness that had been growing in Monty's mind now suddenly took a very specific shape. Heat raced through him as if he felt flames already.

"I've no idea what price to put on it," he said desperately. "I wish I'd never found the thing. Sergeant Tobias said she'd have her father come and look at it some time this week. What if they won't wait? Or won't pay what he says it's worth? I suppose I should tell the Greville Estate solicitors, shouldn't I?"

"No," Hank replied after a moment's thought. "From what you told me, Roger bought the books as a job lot at auction. They belong to his estate, not the Grevilles. But you're right, I don't think you can wait until a valuation is put on the scroll. That could take quite a while, especially if it really is what the scholar claims it is. That would actually make it almost beyond price."

"Then what the hell can I do?" Monty demanded. "Give it to the British Museum?"

Hank bit his lip. "Do you think the bishop, or Mr. Garrett will allow you to do that? Who do you think killed Roger?"

Monty shut his eyes and ran his fingers through his hair. "I don't know," he admitted. "One of them, I suppose. Hank, what can I do?"

Hank sat for a long time without answering.

Monty waited.

Finally Hank spoke, slowly and very quietly. "I don't believe we can wait, Monty. I don't know what this scroll is, but I do know it has great power. Whatever is in the scroll itself, or in what various men believe of it, that power is real, and it is very dangerous. Roger is dead already. I believe that we need to end the matter long before any experts can run their tests and verify it. For a start, I don't think the bishop, or whoever he is, is going to allow that to happen. His whole purpose in buying the scroll is to destroy it, to make sure that mankind never gets to know what is written in it—expert, scholar or ordinary man in the street, or more importantly to him, perhaps, man-in-the- pew."

"What about Mr. Garrett? What does he think it is, and what does he want it for?" Monty asked.

"I don't know who he is, but I have an absurd guess, for which I doubt my own sanity. The reason he wants it, I believe, is to reverse the verdict of history."

"What can we do?" Monty asked, searching Hank's clear blue eyes.

"Tell the men we know of who want it to meet us at Roger's house, and we will hold an auction there, privately for the three of them."

"I don't know how to contact them," Monty pointed out.

"*Times* personal column," Hank said simply. "Although they may have some way of knowing anyway. Funny they should be so wrong about where the scroll was, though."

"What? Oh . . . you mean . . . in Roger's house? Why did they think that? Why did they kill him? He didn't even know about it?"

"Was the crate with the scroll in it addressed to him?"

Monty had a sudden vivid picture of the address label in his mind's eye.

"Yes. Yes it was . . ."

"Then that may be the answer. At that time they did not realize Roger was sick and not coming in to the bookshop. They assumed he would take it home."

"How did they know about it at all?" Monty pursued.

"That is something I can't answer," Hank admitted. "I don't believe in your ghosts, all of whom have a logical explanation in either fact or hysteria. But I will admit that there are things I can't explain, and I am prepared to allow that they could have to do with a more than ordinary evil . . . albeit a highly powerful human one, with manifestations we don't yet understand."

"Generous of you," Monty said with a touch of sarcasm, the sharper because he was afraid.

Hank ignored him. "Put an advertisement in the personal column of the *Times*: 'Gentleman wishes to auction ancient scroll. Regret photocopies impossible. Auction to be held at 7:00 p.m. at home of now deceased owner of shop. Replies unnecessary.' That should reach those with an interest."

Monty's throat was dry, his tongue practically sticking to the roof of his mouth.

"Then what?" he croaked.

"Then we lock up the scroll here and go to Roger's house to wait," Hank answered, but he too was pale and there was knowledge of fear in his eyes.

At seven in the evening Hank and Monty were in Roger's sitting room, too restless to occupy the armchairs. Hank was by the window looking over the back garden and Monty paced from the center of the room to the front windows and back again. The acrid smell of smoke was still sharp in the air. The electric lights were not working since the fire, and as the room grew darker with the fading sun Hank struck a match and lit the hurricane lamp they had brought.

"They're not going to come," Monty said at quarter past seven. "We didn't give them enough time. Or else they've gone to the shop, and they'll break into the safe and steal it while we're here. We shouldn't have come."

"If they were going to steal it they'd have done so anyway," Hank pointed out. "It was there every night, wasn't it?"

"Then why didn't they?" Monty demanded.

"I don't know. Perhaps they need some legitimacy—or maybe they just aren't good at safe cracking. It's a pretty good safe, isn't it?"

"Yes . . ."

The hurricane lamp burned up, sending its glow into the corners of the room and showing the dark outline of an old man with a child beside him, a fair-haired girl of about eight, whose brilliant, ice-cool eyes gleamed almost luminously.

Monty felt the sweat break out on his skin and run down his

body, cold within seconds. He turned to Hank, and instead saw in the doorway the robed and implacable figure of the bishop, his face filled with a scalding contempt.

The smell of old smoke seemed heavier, catching in the throat.

The bishop moved into the room and his place in the doorway was taken by the scholar, a smile on his handsome face, a fire of intense curiosity blazing in his eyes.

Hank looked at Monty. "Perhaps we had better begin the bidding?" he suggested.

Monty cleared his throat again. "I do not know what the scroll is, or whether it is authentic or not. Each of you has offered to purchase it, as it is. Please make a bid according to what it is worth to you."

"Where is it?" the bishop demanded.

"Hush man, it is of no importance," the scholar cut across him. "Mr. Danforth will provide it, when the time is right. We don't want to risk having it destroyed in another fire, or do we?"

The old man smiled. "How wise of you. I fear destruction is what the bishop's purpose is. He will pay any price to that end."

"May the fires of hell consume you!" the bishop shouted hoarsely.

"The fires of hell burn without consuming," the old man said wearily. "You know so little. The truth is deeper, subtler and far better than your edifice of the imagination . . ."

The bishop lunged forward and picked up the hurricane lamp. He smashed it on the floor at Monty's feet. "Betrayer!" he cried as the flames spread across the spilled oil and licked upwards, hungry and hot.

The scholar, who had been watching Hank, charged him and knocked him over, seizing the small attaché case he had been carrying. He picked it up and made for the window, leaving Hank stunned on the floor.

It was the old man who took off his coat and threw it over Monty, smothering the flames at his feet, catching his trousers already burning his legs.

But the oil had spread wider and the sofa was alight. The billows of black smoke grew more intense, choking, suffocating. The bishop was lost to sight. Hank was still on the floor and Judson Garrett was bending over him, talking to him, pulling him to his feet.

Dimly through the black swirls Monty could see the child hopping up and down, her face brilliant with glee, her eyes shining with age-old evil as she watched the fire grow and swell, now reaching the old man's clothes as he lifted Hank up. He was strong, his hair dark again, his face young. He carried Hank over to the window, smashed it and pushed him through as the fire burned behind him, swallowing him up.

Monty fought his way to the door and out into the hall, gasping for breath, the heat all but engulfing him. He flung the front door open and fell out into the cool, clean night. Behind him the flames were roaring up. There was going to be nothing left of the house. He must find Hank, get him out of the way of exploding debris.

He was as far as the corner of the house when he saw Hank staggering towards him, dizzy but definitely upright.

"Monty! Monty!" he called out. "What happened to Garrett?"

Monty caught Hank by the arm. "I don't know. We've got to get away from here. It's all going up any minute. Those dry timbers are like a bomb. Come on!"

Reluctantly Hank allowed himself to be pulled away until they were both seventy yards along the road and finally saw the plume of flame burst through the roof and soar upwards into the sky.

A cloud of crows flung high in the air like jagged pieces of shadow, thousands of them, tens of thousands, all shouting their hoarse cries into the night.

"Did anybody else get out?" Hank asked, his voice shaking.

"No," Monty answered with certainty.

"He thought the scroll was in my case," Hank said. "The bishop. I've had that case for years."

"What was in it?" Monty asked.

"Nothing," Hank replied. "He would have destroyed the scroll."

"And the scholar would have published it, no matter whose faith it broke," Monty replied. "People need their dreams, right or wrong. You have to give them a new one before you break the old."

"What about Garrett?" Hank asked, pain in his voice as if he dreaded the answer.

"He's all right," Monty said, absolutely sure that it was the truth.

Hank stared at him, then at the burning house. "He's in there!"

"No, he isn't, not now. He's all right, Hank."

"And the child?"

"Gone. I think he's free of her . . . it."

"Do you have any idea what you're talking about?" Hank asked, not with doubt but with hope.

"Oh, yes, yes, I think so. I'm talking about sacrifice and redemption, about faith, about hope being stronger than even the demons who dog you with memory and tales of hatred, and who tempt you to justify yourself, at all costs."

"And the scroll? What are you going to do with it now?"

"I think when we go and look, we'll find it's gone," Monty replied. "We aren't ready for it yet."

Hank smiled and together they turned to walk away towards the darkness ahead, no more than the soft folds of the night, with sunrise beyond.

It's in the Book

Mickey Spillane & Max Allan Collins

Co-author's note: It's unclear when Mickey began this story, which I have developed from an unfinished typescript, but internal evidence suggests the 1980s, so I have made that the time period of the tale. M.A.C.

COPS ALWAYS COME in twos. One will knock on the door, but a pair will come in, a duet on hand in case you get rowdy. One uniform drives the squad car, the other answers the radio. One plain-clothes dick asks the questions, the other takes the notes. Sometimes I think the only time they go solo is to the dentist. Or to bed. Or to kill themselves.

I went out into the outer office where a client had been waiting for ten minutes for me to wrap up a phone call. I nodded to him, but the six-footer was already on his feet, brown shoes, brown suit, brown eyes, brown hair. It was a relief his name wasn't Brown.

I said, "I can see you now, Mr. Hanson."

At her reception desk to one side of my inner-office door, Velda—a raven-haired vision in a white blouse and black skirt—was giving me a faintly amused look that said she had made him, too.

Mr. Hanson nodded back. There was no nervous smile, no anxiety in his manner at all. Generally, anybody needing a private investigator is not at ease. When I walked toward him, he extended a hand for me to shake, but I moved right past, going to the door and pulling it open.

His partner was standing with his back to the wall, like a sentry, hands clasped behind his back. He was a little smaller than Hanson, wearing a different shade of brown, going wild with a tie of yellow and white stripes. Of course, he was younger, maybe thirty, where his partner was pushing forty.

"Why don't you come in and join your buddy," I said, and made an after-you gesture.

This one didn't smile either. He simply gave me a long look and, without nodding or saying a word, stepped inside and stood beside Hanson, like they were sharing the wrong end of a firing squad.

Something was tickling one corner of Velda's pretty mouth as I closed the door and marched the cops into my private office.

I got behind my desk and waved at the client's chairs, inviting them to sit down. But cops don't like invitations and they stayed on their feet.

Rocking back, I said, "You fellas aren't flashing any warrants, meaning this isn't a search party or an arrest. So have a seat."

Reluctantly, they did.

Hanson's partner, who looked like his feelings had been hurt, said, "How'd you make us?"

I don't know how to give enigmatic looks, so I said, "Come off it."

"We could be businessmen."

"Businessmen don't wear guns on their hips, or if they do, they could afford a suit tailored for it. You're too clean-cut to be hoods, but not enough to be feds. You're either NYPD or visiting badges from Jersey."

This time they looked at each other and Hanson shrugged. Why fight it? They were cops with a job to do; this was nothing personal. He casually reached in a side suit coat pocket and flicked a folded hundred-dollar bill onto the desk as if leaving a generous tip.

"Okay," I said. "You have my attention."

"We want to hire you."

The way he hated saying it made it tough for me to keep a straight face. "Who is we?"

"You said it before," Hanson said. "NYPD." *He almost choked, getting that out.*

I pointed at the bill on the desktop. "Why the money?"

"To keep this matter legal. To insure confidentiality. Under your licensing arrangement with the state of New York, you guarantee that by acceptance of payment."

"And if I reject the offer?"

For a moment I thought both of them finally would smile, but they stifled the effort, even if their eyes bore a hint of relief.

Interesting—they wanted me to pass.

So I picked up the hundred, filled out a receipt, and handed it to Hanson. He looked at it carefully, folded it, and tucked it into his wallet.

"What's this all about?" I asked them.

Hanson composed himself and folded his hands in his lap. They were big hands, but flexible. He said, "This was *not* the department's idea."

"I didn't think so."

He took a few moments to look for the words. "I'm sure you know, Hammer, that there are people in government who have more clout than police chiefs or mayors."

I nodded. He didn't have to spell it out. Hell, we both knew what he was getting at.

There was the briefest pause and his eyes went to my phone and then around the room. Before he could ask, I said, "Yes, I'm wired to record client interviews . . .no, I didn't hit the switch. You're fine."

But they glanced at each other just the same.

I said, "If you're that worried, we can take it outside . . .onto the street, where we can talk."

Hanson nodded, already getting up. "Let's do it that way then."

The three of us went into the outer office. I paused to tell Velda I wasn't sure how long this would take. The amusement was gone from her dark eyes now that she saw I was heading out with this pair of obvious coppers.

We used the back door to the semi-private staircase the janitor used for emptying the trash, and went down to the street. There you can talk. Traffic and pedestrians jam up microphones, movement keeps you away from listening ears and, stuck in the midst of all those people, you have the greatest privacy in the world.

We strolled. It was a sunny spring morning but cool.

A block and a half later, Hanson said, "A United States senator is in Manhattan to be part of a United Nations conference."

"One of those dirty jobs somebody's gotta do, I suppose."

"While he's in town, there's an item the senator would like you to recover."

Suddenly this didn't sound so big-time, senator or not.

I frowned. "What's this, a simple robbery?"

"No. There's nothing 'simple' about this situation. But there are aspects of it that make you . . .ideal."

My God, he hated to admit that.

I said, "Your people have already been on it?"

"No."

"Why not?"

"Not your concern, Hammer."

Not my concern?

We stopped at a red light at the street corner and I asked, "Where's the FBI in this, if there's investigating to do? A U.S. senator ought to be able pull those strings."

"This is a local affair. Strictly New York."

But not something the NYPD could handle.

The light changed and we started ambling across the intersection in the thick of other pedestrians. There was something strange about the term Hanson used—'recovery.' If not a robbery, was this mystery item something simply . . .lost? Or maybe I was expected to steal something. I deliberately slowed the pace and started looking in store windows.

Hanson said, "You haven't asked who the senator is."

"You said it was strictly New York. That narrows it to two."

"And you're not curious which one?"

"Nope."

Hanson frowned. "Why not?"

"Because you'll tell me when you're ready, or I'll get to meet him myself."

No exasperation showed in the cop's face, and not even in his tone. Strictly in his words: "What kind of private investigator are you, Hammer? Don't you have any other questions?"

I stopped abruptly, turning my back to a display window, and gave them each a look. Anybody going past would have thought we were just three friends discussing where to grab a bite or a quick drink. Only someone knowledgeable would have seen that the way we stood or moved was designed to keep the bulk of a gun well-concealed under suit coats and that the expressions we wore were strictly for the passerby audience.

I said, "No wonder you guys are pissed off. With all the expertise of the NYPD, the senator decides to call *me* in to find a missing geegaw for you. That's worth a horselaugh."

This time Hanson did choke a little bit. "This . . . *'geegaw'* may be small in size, Hammer, but it's causing rumbles from way up top."

"Obviously all the way up to the senator's office."

Hanson said nothing, but that was an answer in itself.

I asked, "What's higher than that?"

And it hit me.

It was crazy, but I heard myself asking the question: "Not . . .the president?"

Hanson swallowed. Then he shrugged again. "I didn't say that, Hammer. But . . .he's top dog, isn't he?"

I grunted out a laugh. "Not *these* days he isn't."

Maybe if they had been feds, I'd have been accused of treason

or sedition or stupidity. But these two—well, Hanson, at least—
knew the answer already. I gave it to them anyway.

"These days," I said, "political parties and bank-rollers and lobbyists call the shots. No matter how important the pol, he's still a chess piece for money to move around. That includes the big man in the Oval Office."

Hanson's partner chimed in: "That's a cynical point of view, Hammer."

A kid on a skateboard wheeled around the corner. When he'd passed, I said, "What kind of recovery job rates this kind of pressure?"

We started walking again.

Hanson said, "It's there, so who cares. We're all just pawns, right, Hammer? Come on. Let's go."

"Where?"

"To see the senator," he said.

We might have been seated in the sumptuous living room of a Westchester mansion, judging by the burnished wood paneling, the overstuffed furnishings, the Oriental carpet. But this was merely the Presidential Suite of the Hotel St. Moritz on Central Park South.

My host, seated in an armchair fit for a king, was not the president, just a United States senator serving his third consecutive term. And Senator Hugh Boylan, a big pale fleshy man with a Leprechaun twinkle, looked as out of place here as I did. His barely pressed off-white seersucker suit and carelessly knotted blue-and-red striped tie went well with shaggy gray hair that was at least a week past due a haircut. His eyebrows were thick dark sideways exclamation points, a masculine contrast to a plumply sensuous mouth.

He had seen to it that we both had beers to drink. Bottles, not poured glasses, a nice common-man touch. Both brews rested without coasters on the low-slung marble coffee table between us, where I'd also tossed my hat. I was seated on a nearby couch with more well-upholstered curves than a high-ticket call girl.

The senator sat forward, his light blue eyes gently hooded and heavily red-streaked. He gestured with a thick-fingered hand whose softness belied a dirt-poor up-bringing. His days as a longshoreman were far behind him.

"Odd that we've never met, Mr. Hammer, over all these years." His voice was rich and thick, like Guinness pouring in a glass. "Perhaps it's because we don't share the same politics."

"I don't have any politics, Senator."

Those Groucho eyebrows climbed toward a shaggy forelock. "You were famously associated with my conservative colleague, Senator Jasper. There was that rather notorious incident in Russia when you accompanied him as a bodyguard."

"That was just a job, sir."

"Then perhaps you won't have any objection to doing a job for a public servant of . . .a *liberal* persuasion."

"As long as you don't try to persuade me, Senator."

"Fair enough," he said with a chuckle, and settled back in the chair, tenting his fingers. "I would hope as a resident of our great state that you might have observed that I fight for my constituency and try to leave partisan politics out of it. That I've often been at odds with my party for the good of the people."

"Senator, you don't have to sell me. No offense, but I haven't voted in years."

A smile twitched in one corner of his fleshy face. "I am only hoping that you don't view me as an adversary. That you might have some small regard for my efforts."

"You're honest and you're a fighter. That goes a good distance with me."

His pale cheeks flushed red. *Had I struck a nerve without intending?*

"I appreciate that," he said quietly.

Sunshine was filtering through sheer curtains, exposing dust motes—even the St. Moritz had dust. Horns honked below, but faintly, the city out there paying no heed to a venerable public servant and an erstwhile tabloid hero.

"Nicholas Giraldi died last night," he said.

What the hell?

Don Nicholas Giraldi, head of New York's so-called sixth Mafia family, had died in his sleep yesterday afternoon in his private room at St. Luke's Hospital. It had been in the evening papers and all over the media: "Old Nic," that most benign of a very un-benign breed, finally gone.

"I heard," I said.

Boylan's smile was like a priest's, blessing a recalcitrant parishioner. "You knew him. There are rumors that you even did jobs for him occasionally. That he trusted you."

I sipped my Miller Lite and shrugged. "Why deny it? That doesn't make me a wiseguy any more than taking on a job for you makes me a liberal."

He chuckled. "I didn't mean to suggest it did. It does seem . . .forgive me, Mr. Hammer . . . it does seem a trifle strange that a man who once made headlines killing mobsters would form an alliance with one."

"Alliance is too strong a word, Senator. I did a handful of jobs for him, unrelated to his . . .business. Matters he didn't want corrupted by his own associates."

"Could you be more specific?"

"No. Him dying doesn't mean client confidentiality goes out the window. That cop Hanson, in the other room, has the receipt for that C-note that I signed before coming. Spells it out in the small print, if you're interested."

The dark eyebrows flicked up and down. "Actually, that's something of a relief. What I want to ask you dances along the edges of that confidentiality, Mr. Hammer. But I hope you might answer. And that you would trust me to be discreet as well."

"You can ask."

He folded his arms, like a big Irish genie about to grant a wish. "Did you receive something from the old don, shortly before . . .or perhaps *upon* . . . his death?"

"No. What would it have been if I had?"

"A book. A ledger, possibly."

I put the beer bottle back on the coffee table. "No. Is that what you're trying to recover? A ledger?"

He nodded. Now when he spoke it was nearly a whisper: "And here your discretion is key. The don was in power a very long time . . .going back to the late forties. His ways, by modern standards, were old-fashioned, right up to the end. One particular antiquated practice peculiar to Don Giraldi was, apparently, keeping a hand-written record of every transaction, every agreement he ever made. No one knows precisely what was in that book. There were other books kept, accounting records that were largely fictional, intended for the IRS but in this particular volume he was said to record the real events, the actual dealings of his business. When asked about such matters, he would say only, 'It's in the book.'"

I shrugged. "I heard the rumors. That he kept a book under lock and key, or in a safe somewhere, and all his secrets were kept in the thing. But I never believed it."

"Why not?"

I pawed at the air dismissively. "He was too shrewd to write anything down and incriminate himself if it fell into the wrong hands? Naw. It's a myth, Senator. If that's what you want to send me out looking for, my advice is to forget it."

But the big head was shaking side to side. "No, Mr. Hammer, that book is very real. Old Nic told his most innermost associates, when his health began to fail earlier this year, that the book would be given to the person he trusted most."

I frowned, but I also shrugged. "So I'm wrong. Anyway, *I'm* not that person. He didn't send me his damn book. But how is it you know what his 'innermost associates' were told?"

"FBI wiretaps." His smile had a pixieish cast, but his eyes were so hard they might have been glass. "Do you think you could find that ledger, Mr. Hammer?"

I shrugged. "It's a big city. Puts the whole needle-in-a-haystack bit to shame. But what would you do with the thing? Does the FBI think they can make cases out of what's in those pages?"

He swallowed thickly. Suddenly he wasn't looking me in the eye. "There's no question, Mr. Hammer, that names and dates and facts and figures in a ledger would be of interest to law enforcement, both local and federal. There's also no question of its value to the old don's successors."

I was nodding. "Covering their own asses and giving them valuable intel on the other mob families and crooked cops and any number of public figures. The blackmail possibilities alone are . . ."

But I didn't finish. Because the senator's head lowered and his eyes shut briefly, and I knew.

I knew.

"You've always been a straight shooter, Senator. But you didn't come from money. You must have needed help in the early days, getting started. You took money from the don, didn't you?"

"Mr. Hammer . . ."

"Hell. And so did somebody else." I hummed a few nasty off-key bars of "Hail to the Chief."

"Mr. Hammer, your country would be very—"

"Can it. I put in my time in the Pacific. I should let you all swing. I should just sit back and laugh and laugh and let this play out like Watergate was just the cartoon before the main feature."

He looked very soft, this man who had come from such a hard place so long ago. "Is that what you intend to do?"

I sighed. Then I really did laugh, but there wasn't any humor in it. "No. I know what kind of foul waters you have to swim in, Senator. And your public record *is* good. Funny, the president having to send you. Your politics and his couldn't be much more at odds. But you're stuck in the same mire, aren't you? Like dinosaurs in a tar pit."

That made him smile sadly. "Will you walk away and just let us decay, Mr. Hammer?"

"Why shouldn't I?"

"Well, for one thing, somewhere out there, in that big city, or that bigger country beyond, are people that Old Nic trusted. People like you, who aren't tainted by the Mob. And who are now in grave danger."

He was right about that.

"And Mr. Hammer, the way we came looking for you does not compare to the way other interested parties will conduct their search—the other five families, for example. And they may well start with you."

I grunted a laugh. "So I owe you a big thank you, at least, since I would have had no idea I was in anybody's cross-hairs over this. I get that."

"Good. Good." He had his first overdue sip of beer. He licked foam off those rather sensual lips and the Leprechaun twinkle was back. "And what would you say to ten thousand dollars as a fee, Mr. Hammer?"

"Ten thousand dollars of the tax payers' money?" I got up and slapped on my hat. "Sure. Why not? It's a way for me to finally get back some of what I paid in, anyway."

"Bring me the book, Mr. Hammer." His smile was reassuring but the eyes were hard again. "Bring *us* the book."

"See what I can do."

Hoods always come in twos. The bent-nose boys accompany their boss to business meetings, often in restaurants. Sometimes they sit with their boss, other times at an adjacent table. Or one sits nearby while the other stays outside in the car, at the wheel, an eye on the entrance. Or maybe parked in the alley behind a restaurant, which is a smarter move. Mob watchdogs are always teamed up in twos. So are assassins.

This time the guy waiting in the hall outside my office in the Hackard Building was in his twenties, wearing a yellow shirt with a pointy collar and no tie under a light-blue suit that gave no hint of gun bulge. But a piece was under there, all right. He would have been handsome if his nose hadn't been broken into a misshapen thing, stuck on like clay a sculptor hadn't gotten around to shaping. His dark hair was puffy with hair spray and his sideburns were right off the cough-drop box.

Hoods these days.

"Let's go in and join your boss and your buddy," I said.

"What?" His voice was comically high-pitched and his eyes were small and stupid, all but disappearing when he frowned.

I made an educated guess. "You're with Sonny Giraldi's crew. And Sonny and your opposite number are waiting inside. I'm Hammer." I jerked a thumb toward the door. "Like on the glass?"

He was still working that out when I went in and held the door open for him.

John "Sonny" Giraldi, nephew of Don Nicholas Giraldi and assumed heir to the throne, was seated along the side wall like a patient waiting to get in to see the doctor. He was small, slender, olive-complected, with a narrow face, a hook nose, and big dark eyes that had a deceptively sleepy cast. The other bodyguard, bigger than the guy in the hall, was another pointy-collared disco dude with heavy sideburns; he had a protruding forehead and a weak chin, sitting with a chair between himself and his boss.

Sonny's wardrobe, by the way, was likely courtesy of an Italian designer, Armani maybe, a sleekly cut gray number with a black shirt and gray silk tie. No way a gun was under there anywhere. Sonny let his employees handle the artillery.

"I'd prefer, Mr. Hammer," Sonny said, his voice a radio-announcer baritone too big for his small frame, "if you'd let Flavio keep his position in the corridor. This is a . . . uh . . .transitional time. I might attract unwanted company."

"Fine. Let Flavio stand watch. Hell, I know all about unwanted company."

That got a tiny twitch of a smile from Velda, over at her desk, but prior to that she had been sitting as blankly unconcerned as a meter maid making out a ticket. The Giraldi mob's heir apparent would not have suspected that the unseen right hand of this statuesque beauty undoubtedly held a revolver right now.

I shut the door on Flavio and turned to walk toward my inner office door, saying, "Just you, Mr. Giraldi. I take it you're here for a consultation."

He rose on his Italian loafers and gave me a nod, tossing a flat-hand gesture to the seated bodyguard to stay that way. Velda's head swivelled slightly and I flashed her a look that said be ready for anything. She returned that with a barely perceptible nod.

I shut the door and gestured Sonny Giraldi toward the client's chair. I got behind the desk as Sonny removed a silver cigarette case from inside his suit coat. No chance he was going for a gun the way those threads fit. He reached his slender, well-manicured hand out to offer me a smoke from the case and I shook my head.

"I gave those up years ago," I said. "How do you think I managed to live so long?"

He smiled, a smile so delicious he seemed to taste it. "Well, a lot of us were wondering. Mr. Hammer, do you know why I'm here?"

"You want your uncle's ledger."

"Yes. Do you have it?"

"No. Next question."

He crossed his legs as he lighted up a cigarette. He was not particularly manly, though not effeminate, either. "Do you understand why I thought you might have the book?"

"Yeah. On his deathbed, your uncle said he was bequeathing the thing to somebody he trusted."

He nodded slowly, the big dark sleepy eyes in the narrow face fixed on me. "You did a few jobs for the old don, jobs that he didn't feel he could entrust to his own people."

"That's true as far as it goes."

"*Why* did he trust *you*, Mr. Hammer? And why would *you* work for *him*? You're well-known to be an enemy of La Cosa Nostra. Carl Evello. Alberto Bonetti. Two dons, representing two of the six families, and you killed them both. That massacre at the Y and S men's club—*how* many soldiers did you slaughter there, anyway? Thirty?"

"It was never proven I did that. Anyway, who's counting?"

Another tasty smile. There was an ashtray on my desk for the benefit of clients, and he used it, flicking ash with a hand heavy with bejeweled golden rings. The suit might be Armani, but down deep Sonny was still just another tacky goombah.

He was saying, "And yet Don Nicholas, Old Nic himself, not only let you live, he trusted you to do jobs for him. Why?"

"Why did he let me live? Now and then I killed his competitors. Which saved him the trouble. As for why I would do a job for Old Nic . . .let's just say he did me a favor now and then."

"What kind of favor, Mr. Hammer? Or may I call you 'Mike'? After all, you and my uncle were thick as thieves."

"Not that thick, but you can call me Mike . . .Sonny. Let's just say your uncle helped me out of the occasional jam in your world."

The hooded eyes narrowed to slits. "They say he helped you get out of town after the waterfront shoot-out with Sal Bonetti."

I said nothing.

Giraldi exhaled smoke, blowing it off to one side. Thoughtful of him.

"What is the government paying you?" he asked.

"What government? Paying me for what?"

"You were followed to the St. Moritz, Mike. Senator Boylan is staying there. The G wants the book—maybe to try to bring us down, or maybe they got entries in there themself. I don't give two shits either way, Mike. I want that book."

"You've got an army. I'm just one guy. Go find it yourself."

Again he blew smoke to one side. His manner was casual but I could tell he was wound tight.

He said, "I have a feeling you're in a position to know where it is. Call it a hunch. But I don't think that book got sent to anybody in the family business. I was close to my uncle. *He would have given it to me!*"

He slammed a small fist onto my desk and the ashtray jumped. I didn't.

Very softly he repeated, "He would have given it to me."

I rocked back. "What use would somebody outside of the family have for that book?"

"I don't know. I honestly don't know, Mike."

"Does the thing even exist? Do you really believe that your uncle wrote down every important transaction and key business dealing in some ledger?"

He sat forward and the big eyes didn't seem at all sleepy now. "I *saw* him with it. The book exists. He would sit in his study—he wasn't a big man, he was my size, never one of these big fat slobs like so many in our business—a gray little guy always impeccably dressed, bald in his later years, and like . . .like a *monk* goin' over some ancient scroll. After anything big would go down, he'd retire to his study and hunker over that goddamn book."

"What did it look like?"

"It was a ledger, but not a big one, not like an accountant uses. Smaller, more like an appointment book, but not *that* small. Maybe six by four. Beat-up looking brown cover, some kind of leather. But thick—three inches thick, anyway."

"Where did he keep it?"

"Well, it wasn't in his safe in that study, or in a locked drawer, and we've been all over his house, looking." He sat forward and did his best to seem earnest. "Mike, would it mean anything to you if I said the Giraldis are going to stay on the same path as Uncle Nic?"

"You mean prostitution, gambling, loan-sharking, that kind of thing? Am I supposed to be proud of you, Sonny?"

"You know that Uncle Nic never dealt drugs. We're the only one of the six families that stayed out of what he called an 'evil enterprise.' No kiddie or gay porn, neither, no underage hookers."

Did they give a Nobel Prize for conscientious racketeering, I wondered?

He was saying, too quickly, "And we—*I*—am gonna continue contributing to charities, through St. Pat's Old Cathedral in Little Italy. We fund orphanages and drug treatment centers and all kinds of good works, Mike. You know that. We're *alone* in that, of the six families."

"Okay. So you Giraldis are the best of the bad guys. What's that to me?"

He shrugged. "I suspect it's why you were willing to do jobs for my uncle. Not just because he bailed your ass out when crazy Sal Bonetti damn near killed you."

I trotted out my lopsided grin. "Sonny, I don't have the book."

"But you know where to look. There's one-hundred K in it for you, Mike, if you turn that book over to me. Cash."

"That's a lot of green for a ledger whose contents you aren't sure of."

"Find it, Mike. *Find* it."

Sonny got up, stubbed out his cigarette in the ashtray. Smoothed his suit coat. "Do you think I'm the only one who knows you were on the old boy's list of trusted associates? And do you think the other five families aren't going to be looking for that thing?"

Suddenly the government's ten thousand didn't seem like so much loot after all. Even Sonny's hundred K seemed short of generous.

"Of course, you can *handle* yourself, Mike. That's another reason why you're the ideal person to go looking for this particular volume. And any members of the other five families who you might happen to dispose of along the way, well, that's just a bonus for both of us."

He gave me a business card with his private numbers, an after-hours one jotted on the back. Then he went out with a nod of goodbye that I didn't bother to return.

I just sat there thinking. I heard the door close in the outer office, and then Velda was coming in. She skirted the client's chair and leaned her palms on the desk. Her dark eyes were worried.

"What's going on, Mike? First cops, now wiseguys? What next?"

"I missed lunch," I said. "How about an early supper?"

She smirked and shook her head, making the arcs of raven-wing hair swing. "Only you would think of food at a time like this."

"Give Pat a call and have him meet us at the Blue Ribbon in half an hour."

"What makes you think a captain of Homicide is going to drop everything just because you call?"

"He'll drop everything because *you* called, doll. He has a thing for you, remember. And me? I'm the guy who solves half the captain's cases."

The Blue Ribbon Restaurant on West Forty-fourth Street was in its between-lunch-and-supper lull, meaning Velda and I had the restaurant part of the bar damn near to ourselves. We sat at our regular corner table with walls of autographed celebrity photos looking over our shoulders as I put away the knockwurst and Velda had a salad. She worked harder at maintaining her figure than I did.

Pushing her half-eaten rabbit food aside, Velda leaned in and asked, "So . . .you think you can find this ledger? What leads do you have?"

"Just two."

"Such as?"

I gulped from a pilsner of Miller. "Well, one is Father Mandano in Little Italy."

"Makes sense," she said with a nod. "His parish is where Don Giraldi was the primary patron."

I laughed once. "Patron. That's a good way to put it."

"Buying his way into heaven?"

"I don't think these mob guys really believe in God—not the top guys anyway. Buying himself good will is more like it. Like Capone in Chicago opening up soup kitchens in the Depression."

"So you'll talk to the good father."

"I will."

"That's one lead, Mike. You said two."

I looked at her slyly over the rim of my glass. I was almost whispering when I said, "Remember that job we did for Old Nic about twenty years back? That relocation number?"

Velda was nodding, smiling slyly right back at me. Like me, she kept her voice low. "You're right. That's a lead if ever there was one. You want me to come along?"

"I would. She liked you. She'll talk more freely if you're around. But I'll talk to the priest on my own."

"Yeah," she said with a smirk. "Only room for two in a confessional."

Pat came in the revolving door and came straight to us—he knew where we'd be. Enjoying the spring afternoon, he was in a lightweight tan suit, chocolate tie, and no hat—though he and I were two rare New Yorkers who still wore them. He stopped at the bar to grab a beer from George and brought it along with him when he came over, sitting with me on his left and Velda on his right.

"Don't wait for me," he said, noting the meal I was half-way through. "Dig right in."

"I said thirty minutes," I said. "You took forty-five. A man has to eat."

"Yeah, I heard that rumor. You didn't say what this was about, so let *me* tell *you*—old Don Giraldi finally croaking. Everybody and his dog is out looking for that legendary missing ledger of his."

"*Is* it legendary, Pat?"

His expression was friendly but the blue-gray eyes were hard. "Legendary in the sense that it's famous in certain circles. But I think it's very real, considering the stir it's causing among the ziti set."

"The other families?"

"Just one, really—the Pierluigi bunch. They were the family that Old Nic was allied most closely with. Their territories really intertwined, you know. Talking to the OCU guys, they say Old Nic's reputation as the most beneficent of the Mafia capos is bullshit. Specifically, they say he invested in drug trafficking through Pierluigi. That and *other* nasty criminal enterprises that wouldn't have made the old don such a beloved figure around Little Italy."

"Meaning if the don really was keeping a record of his transactions," I said, "that book would be of high interest to the Pierluigi clan."

"Damn straight. But they aren't the only interested parties. There are a couple of underbosses in the Giraldi family who are looking at the old don's passing as an invitation to move up in the world."

"You mean Sonny Giraldi doesn't have the don's chair sewn up."

"He *might* . . .if he had that book. So, Mike," Pat's smile was wide but those eyes of his remained shrewd. "Do you have it?"

"Well, I may be older, but I hope I still have it. What would you say, Vel? Do I still have it?"

"I should say you do," she said.

"Can the comedy," Pat said. "It's well known you had a soft spot for Old Nic, Mike."

"That's horseshit, Pat. I had no illusions about the old boy. He was probably the best man in his world, but what a lousy world, huh?"

Pat sipped beer, then almost whispered: "Word on the street is, that book went to somebody the old don trusted. Are *you* that somebody, Mike?"

"No. Tell me about this guy Hanson."

"Hanson? *What* Hanson?"

"Hanson in the department. He didn't show me his badge but he didn't have to. He had a buddy with him whose name I didn't catch—younger guy."

"That would likely be Captain Bradley."

I grinned at him. "Captain! How about that? A young guy achieving such a rarefied rank. You must be impressed, Pat."

"Screw you, buddy. Hanson is an ass-kisser—sorry, Velda—and a political player from way back. He made inspector at thirty-five. You never ran into him before?"

"No."

"When *did* you run into him?"

I ignored the question. "So this Hanson is strictly a One Police Plaza guy? No wonder I don't know him. But is he honest?"

"Define honest."

"Is he *bent*, Pat? Not just a little, but all the way?"

Pat shook his head. "I don't think so."

"You don't sound very convinced."

"We don't travel in the same orbit, Hanson and me. Mike, I never heard a whisper of corruption in regard to him, but that doesn't make it impossible. I mean, he's a political animal."

I gave him a small, nasty smile. "Could Inspector Hanson be in that ledger?"

Pat had a sip of beer and thought about it. "If he *is* bent, of course he could. But so could any number of bad apples. Why, did he come looking for it?"

I ignored that question, too. "Seems to me there are a lot of people with guns who might like to check this book out of whoever's library it's landed in."

"Brother, you aren't kidding."

I put a hand on his shoulder. "Pat, let me treat you to a platter of this knockwurst. On me."

"What's the occasion for such generosity?"

"I just think it's a pity that average citizens like me don't take the time out, now and again, to properly thank a public servant like you for your stalwart efforts."

"Stalwart, huh? Normally I'd say 'baloney.'"

But instead he had the knockwurst.

St. Patrick's Cathedral on Fifth Avenue, built in the 1870s, was a late arrival compared to old St. Pat's on the corner of Prince and Mott. The original St. Pat's had started saving souls in Little Italy a good seventy years before that midtown upstart.

I sat with Father Mandano in his office in the Prince Street rectory—this was a Wednesday night with no mass at old St. Pat's. Velda sat outside in the reception area, reading an ancient issue of *Catholic Digest*—the desk where her nun equivalent usually sat was empty. This was early evening, after office hours.

The broad-shouldered priest, in casual black and that touch of white, sat with thick-fingered, prayerfully folded hands on the blotter of a massive contradiction of a desk, its austere lines trimmed with ornamental flourishes. The office with its rich wood paneling and arched windows had a conference table to one side and bookcases everywhere, the spacious chamber under-lit by way of a banker's lamp and a few glowing wall-mounted fixtures.

The father was as legendary in Little Italy as that ledger of Don Giraldi's—the old priest deemed tough but fair, his generosity renowned. Still, even in his seventies, he had the well-fed look and hard eyes of a line coach, his white hair cut military short, his square head home to regular features that were distorting with age.

"I have of course heard the tales about this notorious ledger, Michael," he said in a sonorous baritone schooled for the pulpit. "But the late don did not leave it with me."

"You must have had many meetings with Giraldi over the years, Father. Would you have any notion about who he might have entrusted with that book?"

He shook his head once, a solemn and final gesture. "I only met rarely with Mr. Giraldi. For many years, I dealt solely with his wife, Antoinetta, who was a wonderful, devout woman."

"How could she be devout and married to a mob boss?"

"Our Father's house has many mansions."

"Yeah, and compartments, too, I guess. And mob money can build plenty of mansions."

His smile was barely perceptible. "When were you last at mass, Michael? I assume you are of the faith, Irish lad that you are."

"I haven't been a 'lad' for a lot of years, Father, and I haven't been to mass since I got back from overseas."

"The war changed you."

"The war showed me that God either doesn't give a damn or has some sick sense of humor. If you'll forgive my frankness, Father."

The dark eyes didn't look so hard now. "I'm in the forgiveness business, Michael. You hold God responsible for the sins of man?"

"If you mean war, Father, fighting against an evil devil like Hitler isn't considered a sin, is it?"

"No. But I would caution you that holding God responsible for the actions of men is a dangerous philosophy. And I gather, from your words, that you *do* believe in God."

"I do."

There was nothing barely perceptible about his smile now. "Years ago, the headlines were filled with your colorful activities, working against evil men. You were raised in the church, so surely you know of your namesake, St. Michael."

"Yeah, the avenging archangel."

"Well, that's perhaps an over-simplification. Among other things, he leads the army of God against the minions of Satan, the powers of Hell."

"I'm semi-retired from that, Father. Let's just say you don't have time to hear *my* confession, but I bet you heard some beauts from Old Nic."

The smile disappeared and the priest's countenance turned solemn again. "Nicholas Giraldi never came to confession. Not once."

"What?"

"Oh, he will lie in consecrated ground. I gave him bedside Last Rites at St. Luke's. But he never took confession here. And I will confess to *you*, Michael, that I was surprised when, after his wife's death, he continued to fund her charities. If there was any purpose in it, other than his own self-aggrandizement, it might have been to honor her memory."

"The old don bought himself plenty of good will here in Little Italy."

"He did indeed. But I don't believe his good works had anything to do with seeking forgiveness. And, before you ask how I could accept contributions from the likes of Don Giraldi, I will tell you that even a spiritual man, a servant of God, must live in this physical world. If suffering can be alleviated by accepting such contributions, I will accept that penance, whether sincere or cynical. You might consider this in itself a cynical, even selfish practice, Michael. But we were put here in this place, this, this . . ."

"Vale of tears, Father?"

"Vale of tears, son. We were put here in this problem-solving world, this physical purgatory, to exercise our free will. And if I can turn ill-gotten gains into the work of the Lord, I will do so, unashamed."

Why shouldn't he? All he had to do was take confession from some other collar and get his sins washed away for a few Hail Marys. But I didn't say that. Hypocritical or not, Father Mandano had helped a lot of people. He was a practical man and that wasn't a sin in my book.

I got to my feet, my hat in my hands. "Thanks for seeing me at short notice, Father. Listen, if you happen to get a line on that ledger, let me know. It could spark a shooting war out on your streets. And innocent people could die."

"And that troubles you, doesn't it, Michael?"

"Don't kid yourself, Father. This is just a job to me. I have a big payday coming if I pull this off. This is one valuable book."

"In my line of work, Michael," he said, "there is only *one* book of real value."

Wilcox in Suffolk County was a prosperous-looking little beach burg with a single industry: tourism. In a month the population would swell from seven-thousand to who-the-hell-knew, and the business district would be alive and jumping till all hours. Right now, at eight-thirty p.m., it was a ghost town.

Sheila Burrows lived in a two-bedroom brick bungalow on a side street, perched on a small but nicely landscaped yard against a wooded backdrop. The place was probably built in the fifties, nothing fancy, but well-maintained. A free-standing matching brick one-car garage was just behind the house. We pulled in up front. The light was on over the front door. We were expected.

I got out of the car and came around to play gentleman for Velda but she was already climbing out. She had changed into a black pants suit with a gray silk blouse and looked very business-like, or as much as her curves, long legs and all that shoulders-brushing raven hair allowed. She carried a good-size black purse with a shoulder strap. Plenty of room for various female accouterments, including a .22 revolver.

She was looking back the way we came. "I can't shake the feeling we were followed," she said.

"Hard to tell on a damn expressway," I admitted. "But I didn't pick up on anything on that county road."

"Maybe I should stay out here and keep watch."

"No. I can use you inside. I remember you hitting it off with this broad. She was scared of me, as I recall."

Now Velda was looking at the brick house. "Well, for all she knew you were one of Don Giraldi's thugs and she was getting a one-way ride. And maybe something about your manner said that a 'broad' is what you thought she was."

"I wasn't so cultured then."

"Yeah," she said sarcastically, as we started up the walk. "You've come a long way, baby."

Twenty years ago, more or less, Velda and I had moved Sheila Burrows out to these Long Island hinterlands. That hadn't been her name then, and she'd had to leave a Park Avenue penthouse to make the move. The exact circumstances of why Don Giraldi had wanted his mistress to disappear had not been made known to us. But we had suspected.

The woman who met us at the door was barely recognizable as the former Broadway chorus girl we had helped relocate back when LBJ was still president. She had been petite and curvy and platinum blonde. Now she was stout and bulgy and mousy brunette. Her pretty Connie Stevens-ish features, lightly made up, were trapped inside a ball of a face.

"Nice to see you two again," she said as she ushered us inside. She wore a pink top, blue jeans and sandals.

There was no entryway. You were just suddenly in the living room, a formal area with lots of plastic-covered furniture. A spinet piano against the right wall was overseen by a big gilt-framed pastel portrait of our hostess back in all her busty blond glory.

She quickly moved us into a small family room area just off a smallish kitchen with wooden cabinets and up-to-date appliances; a short hallway to the bedrooms was at the rear. She sat us down at a round maple table with captain's chairs and a spring-theme centerpiece of plastic flowers.

She had coffee ready for us. As I stirred milk and sugar into mine, I glanced at the nearby wall where rough-hewn paneling was arrayed with framed pictures. They charted two things: her descent into near obesity, and the birth, adolescence and young manhood of a son. It was all there, from playpen to playground, from high school musical to basketball court, from graduation to what was obviously a recent shot of the handsome young man with an attractive girl outside a building I recognized as part of NYU.

"That's our son," she said, in a breathy second soprano that had been sexy once upon a time.

"We *thought* you were pregnant," Velda said with a tiny smile.

Her light blue eyes jumped. "Really? You knew? Why, I was only a few months gone. Barely showing."

"You just had that glow," Velda said.

Our hostess chuckled. "More like water retention. How *do* you maintain that lovely figure of yours, Miss Sterling? Or are you two *married* by now?"

"Not married," Velda said. "Not quite. Not yet."

"She eats a lot of salad," I said.

That made Sheila Burrows wince, and Velda shot me a look. I'd been rude. Hadn't meant to be, but some things come naturally.

I said, "You probably never figured to see us again."

"That's true," she said. She sipped her coffee. "But I wasn't surprised to hear from you, not exactly."

Velda asked, "Why is that?"

"With Nicholas dying, I figured there would be *some* kind of follow-up. For a long time, there was a lawyer, a nice man named Simmons, who handled the financial arrangements. He would come by every six months and see how I was doing. And ask questions about our son."

I asked, "Any direct contact with Don Giraldi since you moved out here?"

"No. And, at first, I was surprised. I thought after Nick was born . . .our son is Nicholas, too . . .that we might, in some way, resume our relationship. Nicolas Giraldi was a very charming man, Mr. Hammer. Very suave. Very courtly. He was the love of my life."

"You were only with him for, what? Five or six years?"

"Yes, but it was a wonderful time. We traveled together, even went to Europe once, and he practically lived with me during those years. I don't believe he ever had relations with his wife after the early years of their marriage."

"They had three daughters."

"Yes," she said, rather defensively, "but none after our Nick came along."

Funny that she so insistently referred to the son in that fashion—'our Nick'—when the father had avoided any direct contact. And this once beautiful woman, so sexually desirable on and off the stage, had become a homemaker and mother—a suburban housewife. Without a husband.

Velda said, "I can see why you thought Nicholas would come back to you, after your son's birth. If he had *really* wanted you out of his life—for whatever reason—he wouldn't have kept you so close to home."

"Wilcox is a long way from Broadway," she said rather wistfully.

"But it's not the moon," I said. "I had assumed the don felt you'd gotten too close to him—that you'd seen things that could be used against him."

Her eyes jumped again. "Oh, I would never—"

"Not by you, but by others. Police. FBI. Business rivals. But it's clear he wanted his son protected. So that the boy could not be used against him."

She was nodding. "That's right. That's what he told me, before he sent me away. He said our son would be in harm's way, if anyone knew he existed. But that he would *always* look out for young Nick. That someday Nick would have a great future."

Velda said, "You said you had no direct contact with Nicholas. But would I be right in saying that you had . . .*indirect* contact?"

The pretty face in the plump setting beamed. "Oh, yes. Maybe once a year, always in a different way. You see, our Nick is a very talented boy—talented young *man* now. He took part in so many school activities, both the arts and sports. And *so* brilliant; valedictorian of his class! But then his father was a genius, wasn't he?"

I asked, "What do you mean, 'once a year, always in a different way?'"

She was looking past me at the wall of pictures. Fingers that were still slender, graceful, traced memories in the air.

"There Nicholas would be," she said, "looking so proud, in the audience at a concert, or a ball game, or a school play. I think Nick gets his artistic talent from me, if that doesn't sound too stuck up and, best of all, Nicholas came to graduation and heard his son speak."

Velda asked, "Did they ever meet?"

"No." She pointed. "Did you notice that picture? That very first one, high up, at the left?"

A solemn portrait of a kid in army green preceded the first of several baby photos.

"That's a young man who died in Vietnam," she said. "Mr. Simmons, the attorney, provided me with that and other photos, as well as documents. His name was Edwin Burrows and we never met. He was an only child with no immediate family. He won several medals, actually, including a Silver Star, and *that* was the father that Nick grew up proud of."

I asked, "No suspicions?"

"Why should he be suspicious? When he was younger, Nick was very proud of having such an heroic father."

"Only when he was younger?"

"Well . . .you know boys. They grow out of these things."

Not really, but I let it pass.

"Mrs. Burrows," I said, sitting forward, "have you received anything, perhaps in the mail, that might seem to have come from Don Giraldi?"

"No . . ."

"Specifically, a ledger. A book."

Her eyes were guileless. "No," she said. "No. After Mr. Simmons died, and his visits ended, another lawyer came around, just once. I was given a generous amount of money and told I was now on my own. And there's a trust fund for Nick that becomes his on his graduation from NYU."

"Have you talked to your son recently?"

She nodded. "We talk on the phone at least once a week. Why, I spoke to him just yesterday."

"Did he say anything about receiving a ledger from his father?"

"Mr. Hammer, no. As I thought I made clear, as far as Nick

is concerned *his* father is a Vietnam war hero named Edwin Burrows."

"Right," I said. "Now listen carefully."

And I told her about the book.

She might be a suburban hausfrau now, but she had once been the mistress of a mob boss. She followed me easily, occasionally nodding, never interrupting.

"You are on the very short list," I said, "of people who Don Giraldi valued and trusted. You might *still* receive that book. And it's possible some very bad people might come looking for it."

She shook her head, mousy brown curls bouncing. "Doesn't seem possible . . .after all these years. I thought I was safe . . .I thought *Nick* was safe."

"You raise the most pertinent point. I think your son is the logical person the don may have sent that book."

She frowned in concern, but said nothing.

I went on: "I want you to do two things, Mrs. Burrows, and I don't want any argument. I want you to let us stow you away in a safe-house motel we use upstate. Until this is over. You have a car? Velda will drive you in it, and stay with you till I give the word. Just quickly pack a bag."

She swallowed and nodded. "And the other thing?"

"I want you to call your son right now," I said, "and tell him I'm coming to visit him. I'll talk to him briefly myself, so that he'll know my voice. I'll come alone. If more than one person shows up at his door, even if one of them claims to be me, he's not to let them in. If that happens, he's to get out and get away, as fast as he can. Is all of that clear?"

She wore a funny little smile. "You know, Mr. Hammer, I think my impression of you all those years ago was wrong, very wrong."

"Yeah?"

"You really are quite a nice, caring human being."

I glanced at Velda, who didn't bother stifling her grin.

"Yeah," I said. "I get that a lot."

If Wilcox at eight-thirty p.m. was a ghost town, the East Village at eleven-something was a freak show. This was a landscape of crumbling buildings, with as many people living on the streets as walking down them, where in a candy store you could buy a Snickers Bar or an eightball of smack, and when morning came, bodies with bullet holes or smaller but just as deadly ones would be on sidewalks and alleyways like so much trash set out for collection.

Tompkins Square Park was this neighborhood's central gathering place, from oldtimers who had voted for FDR and operated traditional businesses like diners and laundries to students, punkers, artists, and poets seeking life experience and cheap lodging. Every second tenement storefront seemed home to a gallery showcasing work inspired by the tragic but colorful street life around them.

NYU student Nick Burrows lived in a second-floor apartment over a gallery peddling works by an artist whose canvases of graffiti struck me as little different from the free stuff on alley walls.

His buzzer worked, which was saying something in this neighborhood, and he met me on a landing as spongy as the steps coming up had been. He wore a black CBGB T-shirt, jeans and sneakers, a kid of twenty or so with the wiry frame of his father but taller, and the pleasant features of his mother, their prettiness turned masculine by heavy eyebrows.

He offered his hand and we shook under the dim yellowish glow of a single mounted bulb. "I appreciate you helping out my mom, Mr. Hammer. You know, I think I've heard of you."

"A lot of people think they've heard of me," I said, moving past him into the apartment. "They're just not sure anymore."

His was a typical college kid's pad—thrift-shop furnishings, atomic-age stuff that had looked modern in the fifties and seemed quaint now. Plank and cement-block bookcases lined the walls, paperbacks and school books mostly, and the occasional poster

advertising an East Village art show or theatrical production
were taped here and there to the brick walls. The kitchenette
area was off to one side and a doorless doorframe led to a
bedroom with a waterbed. We sat on a thin-cushioned couch
with sparkly turquoise upholstery.

He offered me a smoke and I declined. He got one going,
then leaned back, an arm along the upper cushions, and studied
me like the smart college kid he was. His mother had told him
on the phone that I had something important to talk to him
about. I had spoken to him briefly, as well, but nothing about
the book.

Still, he'd been told there was danger and he seemed unruffled.
There was strength in this kid.

I said, "You know who your real father was, don't you,
Nick?"

He nodded.

I grinned. "I figured a smart kid like you would do some
poking into that Vietnamhero malarkey. Did the don ever get
in touch with you? He came to the occasional school event, I
understand."

He sighed smoke. "Get in touch? No, not in the sense that
he ever introduced himself. But he started seeking me out after
a concert, a basketball game, just to come up and say, 'Good
job tonight,' or 'Nice going out there.' Even shook my hand a
couple of times."

"So you noticed him."

"Yeah, and when I got older, I recognized him. He was in
the papers now and then, you know. I did some digging on my
own, old newspaper files and that kind of thing. Ran across
my mom's picture with him, too, back when she was a real
knockout. She wasn't just a chorus girl, you know, like the press
would have it. She had speaking parts, got mentioned in reviews
sometimes."

"Your mother doesn't know that you know any of this."

"Why worry her?"

"Nick, I'm here because your father kept a ledger, a book said to contain all of his secrets. Word was he planned to give it to the person he trusted most in the world. Are *you* that person?"

He sighed, smiled, allowed himself a private laugh.

Then he asked, "Would you like a beer? You look like a guy who could use a beer."

"Has been a long day."

So he got us cold cans of beer and he leaned back and I did too. And he told me his story.

Two weeks ago, he'd received a phone call from Don Nicholas Giraldi—a breathy voice that had a deathbed ring to it, making a request that young Nick come to a certain hospital room at St. Luke's. No mention of old Nicholas being young Nick's father, not on the phone.

"But when I stood at his bedside," Nick said, "he told me. He said, 'I'm your father.' Very melodramatic. Ever see *Stars Wars?* 'Luke, I am your father'? Like that."

"And what did you say?"

He shrugged. "Just, 'I know. I've known for years.' That seemed to throw the old boy, but he didn't have the wind or the energy to discuss it or ask for details or anything. He just said, 'You're going to come into money when you graduate from the university.'"

"You didn't know there was a trust fund?"

"No. And I still don't know how much is in it. I'll be happy to accept whatever it is, because I think I kind of deserve it, growing up without a father. I'm hoping it'll be enough for me to start a business. Don't let the arty neighborhood fool you, Mr. Hammer. I'm a business major."

"Is that what Old Nic had in mind, you starting up something of your own?"

The young man frowned, shook his head. "I'm not sure. He may have wanted me to step into *his* role in his . . .organization. Or he may have been fine with me going my own way. Who knows? In any event, he said, 'I have something for you. Whatever you do in life, it will be valuable to you.'"

"The book?"

He nodded. "The book, Mr. Hammer. He gave it to me right there in that hospital room. The book of his secrets."

I sat forward. "Containing everything your father knew, a record of every crooked thing he'd done, and all of those he'd conspired with to break God knows how many laws."

"Something like that."

I shook my head. "Even if you go down a straight path, son, that book would be valuable."

He nodded. "It's valuable, all right. But I don't want it, Mr. Hammer. I'm not interested in it or what it represents."

"What are you going to do with the thing?"

"Give it to you." He shrugged. "Do what you will with it. I want only one thing in return."

"Yeah?"

"Ensure that my mother is safe. That she is not in any danger. And do the same for me, if you can. But Mom . . .she did so *much* for me, sacrificed everything, gave her *life* to me . . .I want her *safe*."

"I think I can handle that."

He extended his hand for me to shake, and I did.

He got up and went over to a plank-and-block bookcase under the window onto the neon-winking street. I followed him. He was selecting an ancient-looking sheepskin-covered volume from a stack of books carelessly piled on top when the door splintered open, kicked in viciously, and two men burst in with guns in hand.

First was Flavio, still wearing the light-blue suit and yellow pointy-collar shirt, but I never did get the name of his pal, the big guy with the weak chin and Neanderthal forehead. They come in twos, you know, hoods who work for guys like Sonny Giraldi.

They had big pieces in their fists, matching .357 mags. In this part of town, where gunshots were commonplace, who needed .22 autos with silencers? The big guy fell back to be framed in the doorway like another work of East Village art, and Flavio took two more steps inside, training his .357 on both of us, as young Nick and I were clustered together.

Flavio, in his comically high-pitched voice, said, "Is that the book? Give me that goddamned *book*!"

"Take it," Nick said, frowning, more disgusted than afraid, and stepped forward, holding out the small, thick volume, blocking me as he did.

I used that to whip the .45 out from under my shoulder, and I shoved the kid to the floor and rode him down, firing up.

Flavio may have had a .357, but that's a card a .45 trumps easy, particularly if you get the first shot off, and even more so if you make it a head shot that cuts off any motor action. What few brains the bastard had got splashed in a shower of bone and blood onto his startled pal's puss, and the Neanderthal reacted like he'd been hit with a gory pie, giving me the half second I needed to shatter that protruding forehead with a slug and paint an abstract picture on the brick out in that landing, worthy of any East Village gallery.

Now Nick was scared, taking in the bloody mess on his doorstep. "Jesus, man! What are you going to do?"

"Call a cop. You got a phone?"

"Yeah, yeah, call the cops!" He was pointing. "Phone's over there."

I picked the sheepskin-covered book up off the floor. "No— not the cops. *A* cop."

And I called Pat Chambers.

I didn't call Sonny Giraldi until I got back to the office around three a.m. I had wanted to get that book into my office safe.

The heir to the old don's throne pretended I'd woken him, but I knew damn well he'd been waiting up to hear from his boys. Or maybe some cop in his pocket had already called to say the apartment invasion in the East Village had failed, in which case it was unlikely Sonny would be in the midst of a soothing night's sleep when I used the private number he'd provided me.

Cheerfully I asked, "Did you know that your boy Flavio and his slopehead buddy won a free ride to the county morgue tonight?"

"What?"

"I sent them there. Just like you sent them to the Burrows kid's apartment. They'd been following me, hadn't they? I really *must* be getting old. Velda caught it, but I didn't."

The radio-announcer voice conveyed words in a tumble. "Hammer, I didn't send them. They must be working for one of my rivals or something. I played it absolutely straight with you, I swear to God."

"No, you didn't. You wanted me to lead you to the book, and whoever had it needed to die, because they knew what was in it, and I had to die, too, just to keep things tidy. Right? Who would miss an old broken-down PI like me, anyway?"

"Believe me, Hammer, I—"

"I don't believe you, Sonny. But you can believe me."

Actually, I was about to tell him a whopper, but he'd never know.

I went on: "This book will go in a safe deposit box in some distant bank and will not come out again until my death. If that death is nice and peaceful, I will leave instructions that the book be burned. If I have an unpleasant going away party, then that book will go to the feds. Understood?"

"Understood."

"And the Burrows woman and her son, they're out of this. Any harm befalls either one, that book comes out of mothballs and into federal hands. *Capeesh?*"

"*Capeesh*," he said glumly.

"Then there's the matter of my fee."

"Your *fee!* What the hell—"

"Sonny, I found the book for you. You owe me one-hundred grand."

His voice turned thin and nasty. "I heard a lot of bad things about you, Hammer. But I never heard you were a black-mailing prick."

"Well, you learn something every day, if you're paying attention. I want that hundred K donated to whatever charities that Father Mandano designates. Think of the fine reputation you'll earn, Sonny, continuing your late uncle's good works in Little Italy."

And I hung up on him.

Cops always come in twos, they say, but the next morning, when Hanson entered my private office, he left his nameless crony in the outer one, to read old magazines. Velda wasn't back at her reception desk yet, but she soon would be.

"Have a seat, Inspector," I said, getting behind my desk.

The brown sheepskin volume, its spine ancient and cracked, lay on my blotter at a casual angle, where I'd tossed it in anticipation of his visit.

"*That's* the book," he said, eyes wide.

"That's the book. And it's all yours for ten grand."

"May I?" he asked, reaching for it.

"Be my guest."

He thumbed it open. The pleasure on his face turned to confusion, then to shock.

"My God . . ." he said.

"It's valuable, all right. I'm no expert, though, so you may be overpaying. You may want to hold onto it for a while."

"I'll be damned," he said, leafing through.

"As advertised, it has in it everything the old don knew about dirty schemes and double-dealing. Stuff that applies to crooks and cops and senators and even presidents."

He was shaking his head, eyes still on the book.

"Of course, we *were* wrong about it being a ledger. It's more a how-to-book by another Italian gangster. First-edition English-language translation, though—1640, it says."

"A gangster named Machiavelli," Hanson said dryly.

"And a book," I said, "called *The Prince*."

The Long Sonata
of the Dead

Andrew Taylor

I HADN'T SEEN ADAM in the flesh for over twenty years. I had seen him on television, of course—it was increasingly hard to miss him—but the last time I had met him in person was when we picked up our degrees. Mary had been there too.

"Well," he'd said, punching me gently on the arm. "Thank God it's over. Let's find a drink. We need to celebrate."

"No," I'd said. "I don't want to."

Mary hadn't said anything at all.

I don't deny that it was a shock to see Adam after all this time, and it wasn't a pleasant one. It was the first of the three shocks that happened in swift succession that afternoon.

I was standing at one of the tall windows of the reading room overlooking St. James's Square. It was a Tuesday afternoon in February, just after lunch, and it was raining. I was watching the domes of umbrellas scurrying like wet beetles on the pavements and the steady clockwise flow of traffic round the square. Adam must have walked across the garden in the middle. He came out of the gate in the railings on the north side. He paused for a moment, waiting for a gap in the traffic.

That's when I recognized him. Despite the rain, he didn't

have a hat or umbrella. He was wearing a Burberry raincoat but even that was unbuttoned. He had his head thrown back and his legs a little apart. He was smiling as if the weather was a friend, not an inconvenience.

He had been standing like that the very first time I saw him, which was also in the rain. That had been the first day of our first term at university. I was staring down from my room at the cobbled court below and wishing I was still at home. There was Adam, looking as if he owned the place. Thirty seconds later I discovered that he was my new roommate. He was studying English, too, so we saw each other for a large part of every day for an entire year, apart from the holidays.

The traffic parted before him like the Red Sea. He strolled across the road, swinging his bag. I realized that he was coming here, to the London Library.

Adam looked up at the windows of the reading room. He couldn't have seen me looking down at him—I was too far back from the glass. But I turned and moved away as if I had been caught doing something wrong.

❧

It will help if I explain about the London Library before I go on. It's a building, first of all, an old townhouse that was turned into a private subscription library in 1841. Its members included people like Dickens and Thackeray, Carlyle and George Eliot. Over the years it has been extended down and up, sideways and backwards, until the place has become a maze of literature.

The pillared reading room on the first floor still has the air of a well-appointed gentleman's library, with leather armchairs in front of the fireplace, racks of the latest periodicals and galleries of bookcases far above your head. In all the years I have known it, I have never heard a raised voice there.

There are over a million of books, they say, in over fifty languages, marching along over fifteen miles of shelving. Nowadays they have an electronic universe of information to back them up. But it's the real, printed books that matter. I often think of the sheer weight of all that paper, all that ink, all those words, all those meanings.

The London Library is, in its way, a republic of letters. As long as they pay the subscription and obey the few rules, its members have equal rights and privileges. Perhaps that was the main reason the place was so important to me. In the London Library I was as good as anyone else. Since my marriage had broken up three years ago, I felt more at home in the library than I did in my own flat.

Over the years the collection has grown. As the books have multiplied, so has the space required to house them. Members have free access to the stacks that recede deeper and deeper into the mountain of buildings behind the frontages of St James's Square. Here, in these sternly utilitarian halls of literature, the tall shelves march up and down.

The library is an organic thing that has developed over the decades according to a private logic of its own over many levels and floors. There are hiding places, narrow iron staircases and grubby, rarely-visited alcoves where the paint on the walls hasn't changed since the days of Virginia Woolf. Sometimes I think the library is really a great brain and we, its members who come and go over the years, are no more than its fugitive thoughts and impulses.

You never know quite what you may find in the stacks. There are many forgotten books that perhaps no one has ever looked at since their arrival at the library. Where else would I have found *The Voice of Angels*, for example, or learned about the long sonata of the dead?

Now there was a serpent in my booklined garden of Eden. Its name was Adam.

❧

I went down the paneled stairs to the issue hall on the ground floor. I arrived just as Adam came through the security barrier.

He was putting away the plastic-coated membership card in his wallet. So he was a member, not just a visitor.

He turned right and went into the little side-hall where the lockers are. I was pretty sure that he wouldn't recognize me. He never really noticed people. Anyway, unlike him, I had changed a good deal since he had last seen me. I had put on weight. I had an untidy beard, streaked with grey. I was going bald.

I lingered by the window that looks down into the Lightwell Reading Room. I opened my notebook and pretended to examine one of the pages. The book fell open at the entries I had copied from the computer catalogue when I had first searched for Francis Youlgreave in the name index. Only two of his books were listed there: *The Judgement of Strangers* and *The Tongues of Angels*. They were both reprints from the 1950s.

On the edge of my range of vision I saw Adam crossing the hall to the long counter that divides the staff from the members. He laid down a couple of books for return. The nearest assistant did the little double-take that people do when they encounter the famous and smiled at him. I couldn't see Adam's face but his posture changed—he seemed to grow a little taller, a little wider; he was like a preening peacock.

He turned away and passed behind me into the room where the photocopiers and the catalogues are. The two books remained where they were for the moment. I went over to them and picked up the top one. It was a survey of fin-de-siècle British poetry; it had been written in the 1930s by a man who used to review a good deal for the *Times Literary Supplement*. I had looked at it for my Youlgreave research but there wasn't much there of value and Youlgreave himself was barely mentioned.

The assistant looked up. "I'm sorry, I haven't checked that in yet—would you like to take it out?"

"I'm not sure. But may I look at it? And at this one."

She scanned the labels and handed the books to me. I took them upstairs, back to the reading room, and settled at my table. The other book was a biography of Aubrey Beardsley. Again, I had come across the book myself—Beardsley had provided the illustrations for an 1897 collector's edition of one of Youlgreave's better-known poems, "The Four Last Things." There wasn't much about Beardsley's connection with Youlgreave—merely the usual unsupported claim that they had moved in the same rather louche cultural circle in London, together with an account of Beardsley's struggle to extract payment from Youlgreave's publisher. But the page that mentioned the episode was turned down at the top left corner, an unpleasant habit that some readers have; Adam used to do it with my books and it infuriated me.

I knew then that this must be more than coincidence. That was the second shock of the afternoon. Adam was almost certainly researching Francis Youlgreave. The bastard, I thought, hasn't he got enough already? Hasn't he taken enough from me?

I continued automatically turning the pages. A flash of yellow caught my eye. It was a yellow Post-it note that marked the reference in the sources relating to the Youlgreave commission. That too was typical of Adam—he was always leaving markers in other people's books; I once found a dessicated rasher of streaky bacon in my copy of Sterne's *Sentimental Journey*.

There was something written in pencil on the Post-it note. *You're such a complete shit. You won't get away with it.*

That was the third shock. I recognized the writing, you see, the looping descenders, the slight backward slope, the tendency to turn the dots on the "i"s into tiny but incomplete circles, drawn clockwise, from the left. It had changed significantly over time—for example, the letters were untidier in form and now ran together like a tangle of razor wire on a prison wall.

But there was no doubt about it. A working knowledge of paleography has its advantages. I knew straightaway that the handwriting was Mary's.

❧

Mary was out of my league. She was in the year below mine. I had noticed her around-going to lectures, in the faculty coffee bar and, once, in the saloon bar of the Eagle, sprawled across the lap of a post-graduate student from Harvard who drove a Porsche. As far as I knew she wasn't even aware of my existence.

This changed one night in May when I went to a party at someone's house, taken there by a friend of a friend. We had come on from the pub. Someone was vomiting in the front garden when we arrived. The music was so loud that the windows were rattling in their frames.

We pushed our way through the crowd in the hall and found the kitchen, where the drinks were. That was packed, too. Someone passed me a joint as I came in. Everyone was shouting to make themselves heard over the music. Twenty minutes later, I realized that the joint had been stronger than I'd thought. I had to get away from all the people, the heat and the noise.

The back door was open. I stumbled outside. Cool air touched my skin. There was a little garden full of weeds and rusting metal. A couple was making out on an old mattress. Light and music streamed from the house but both were softened and more bearable. I looked up at the sky, hoping to see stars. There was only the dull yellow glow of a city sky at night.

I sat down on a discarded refrigerator lying on its side against the fence. The dope was still making my thoughts spin but more slowly now, and almost enjoyably. Time passed. The couple on the mattress rustled and groaned in their private world. Then, suddenly, I was not alone.

A change in the light made me look up. Mary was standing in the kitchen doorway. She was wearing a clinging velvet dress the color of red wine. She had a mass of dark hair. Her face was in shadow. The light behind her made a sort of aura around her.

I looked away, not wanting her to think that I was staring at her. I heard her footsteps. I caught a hint of her perfume, mingled with her own smell to make something unique.

"Why do you always look so sad," she said.

Startled, I looked up. "What?"

"Why do you look so sad?"

"I don't know," I said. "I don't feel it."

"Not sad," she said. "That's the wrong word. Like you're thinking tragic, profound thoughts."

"Looks deceive," I said.

"Have you got a cigarette?"

That was an easier question to answer. I found my cigarettes and offered her one. She leant forward when I held up the lighter for her. In the light of the flame I saw the gleam of her eyes, the high cheekbones and the dark, alluring valley between her breasts.

"Move up," she said, as I was lighting my own cigarette. "There's room for two."

There was but only just. I shuffled along the refrigerator. She sat down, her thigh nudging against mine. I felt her warmth through my jeans.

"Christ, it's cold."

"Have my jacket," I suggested.

When we had settled ourselves again we smoked in silence for a moment, listening to the noises from the house and the rather different noises from the mattress.

"Anyway," she said, "you should always look sad."

"Why?"

"Because you look beautiful when you're sad. Sort of soulful."

I couldn't think of anything to say. I wondered if she was stoned. Or if I myself was much, much more stoned than I had thought, and this was some sort of hallucination.

"I've seen you around, haven't I?" she went on. "It's funny we've never actually met. Until now, I mean. What's your name?"

"Tony," I said.

"I'm Mary," she said. Then she kissed me.

∾

You're such a complete shit. You won't get away with it.

The words gave me a sweet, sharp stab of pleasure. The writing was definitely Mary's. The "you" must refer to Adam.

They had been together now for nearly twenty years. They had married a couple of years after university.

Over the years I had looked up Adam in *Who's Who* and Debrett's *People of Today* on several occasions, so I knew the dates. I knew the landmarks of his career, too—the deputy literary editorship at the *New Statesman*, the years at the BBC, the handful of books and the four documentary series, linked to his later books. The documentaries were usually on BBC2, but the last one had graduated to BBC1.

Adam was my age but he looked ten or even fifteen years younger. He was one of those well-known authors who seem far too busy to have much time to write. I'd glanced through his articles in the *Sunday Times* and the *Observer*, and I'd heard him endlessly on radio and seen him on television. Two years earlier, he had chaired the judges of the Man Booker Prize. He was always judging something or another or commenting on something. Even Adam's friendships had a professional or literary flavor—he played tennis with a best-selling novelist, for example, and shared a holiday house in Umbria with the CEO of a major publisher.

I got up to put the books on the trolley for shelving. I was about to return to my seat when I saw Adam himself coming into the reading room by the north door, the one leading to the new staircase that acts as a spine connecting the disparate parts and levels of the library, old and new.

Panic gripped me. He glanced about the room. It all happened so quickly I had no chance to turn away. He was carrying three or four books. For a moment his eyes met mine. There was no sign of recognition in his face, which both relieved and irritated me. He saw an empty seat near the window end of the room and made his way towards it.

The spell that held me broke. I slipped through the glazed doors and onto the landing of the main staircase of the old building. I hurried downstairs, past the portraits of distinguished dead members, a parade of silent witnesses.

Once on the stairs, however, I could think more clearly. I

saw how absurd I was being. Why was I acting as if I had done something wrong, as if Adam were for some reason hunting me down? On the other hand, what on earth was going on between him and Mary? And was he really planning something on Francis Youlgreave? I told myself that I had every reason to be curious.

Besides, Adam was unlikely to leave the reading room for a while.

I continued more slowly down the stairs and into the issue hall. I turned into the passage where the lockers are. These are on the left. On the right is a line of tall cupboards, always open, with hanging spaces for coats and shelves where you can leave your bags.

The Burberry was in the fourth cupboard down, hanging between a tweed overcoat and a torn leather jacket. Adam's bag was on the shelf beneath.

This was the moment when I crossed the line. It didn't seem like that at the time. It seemed quite a natural thing to do in terms of my Youlgreave book. One has to research the possible competition.

I looked over my shoulder. No one was paying me any attention. The bag was one of those canvas-and-leather affairs that look as if they ought to have a bloodstained pheasant or a dead trout inside. I lifted the flap and checked the main compartment and the side pockets. I found nothing but the *Guardian*, the *Spectator* and a couple of crumpled paper handkerchiefs.

Straightening up, I patted the coat. In one pocket was a packet of Polos and a shopping list on the back of an envelope. The list was in Adam's scrawled handwriting: *burgundy, flowers, milk, salad veg*. The other was empty.

I nearly missed the coat's third pocket, which was inside and fastened with a button. It contained something small and rectangular that didn't yield to the touch. I slipped my hand inside and felt the outline of a phone.

It was an iPhone. I had one myself as it happened, though

mine was an older model. The ringer switch was in the off
position. I pressed the control button. The screen lit up.

The phone was locked. But someone had sent a text, and this
was briefly displayed on the screen.

I miss you more and more every moment we're apart. J xxxx

There was no name attached to the text, only a phone
number.

So that explains the Post-it note, I thought. The complete shit
is having an affair.

～

Nothing new there.

So I come back to Mary. She told me later why she kissed me
in the garden at the party: as a demonstration of disdain to her
newly exboyfriend, who was watching us through the kitchen
window. But it developed into something else.

While the party thudded away in the house, we stayed in
the garden and talked and drank and smoked another joint. I
can't remember what we talked about. But I do remember that
for once in my life I seemed to have leapfrogged the paralyzing
shyness that usually characterized my attempts to talk to
attractive girls and landed without any apparent effort into
something approaching friendship.

Later I walked her home, and she kissed me again when
we said goodnight. The next day we met between lectures for
coffee, dispelling my lingering fear that she'd have forgotten me
com-pletely overnight. By the end of the day we had tumbled
into bed together.

I felt as if I'd been turned into someone new and infinitely
preferable, like the frog kissed by a princess. Mary was so
beautiful, so vital. She always knew what she wanted and she
was very direct about getting it. I envied her that. The mystery
was why she wanted me. It was still a mystery.

We lasted nearly a term as a semi-detached couple before
Adam decided he would have her for himself. He and I no

longer shared a room, as we had in our first year. But we still saw a fair amount of each other. I was useful to him—I was the organized one, you see, who knew when the supervisions and lectures were, which library books we needed, how to find the material that could lift your grade from a B to an A.

In a sense, it was Francis Youlgreave who brought Mary and Adam together. I knew something about Youlgreave, even then, because my mother had grown up in Rosington. Youlgreave was a Canon of Rosington Cathedral in the early twentieth century. She had one of his collections of poems, *The Judgement of Strangers*, which had once belonged to my grandparents. I was using this as the basis for my long essay, an extended piece of work we had to do in our final year which counted as a complete module of our degree. I'd made the discovery that there were several advantages to studying obscure literary figures—fewer secondary sources, for a start, and a better than average chance of impressing the examiners with one's initiative.

Mary was waiting for me in my room when Adam turned up one evening. He said he'd wait for me and, while he waited, he investigated the papers on my desk while chatting away to Mary. He found some of the Youlgreave material and Mary told him more.

By the time I returned with an Indian takeaway for two, they were smoking a joint and chatting away like friends on the brink of being something closer. She responded to his charm like a plant to water. He had the priceless knack of seeming to be interested in a person. The takeaway stretched among the three of us. Adam and Mary got very stoned and I sulked.

Next week Mary and I officially broke up. It was one lunchtime in the pub. She did her best to do it tactfully. But all the time she was being kind to me, she was glowing with excitement about Adam like a halloween pumpkin with a candle inside.

As she was going, she said, "Don't take it personally, Tony, will you? I'm always looking for something, you see, and I never quite find it. Maybe one day I'll come round full circle. Or maybe I'll find it. Whatever it is I'm looking for."

∾

I didn't know which disturbed me more: the knowledge that
Adam was having an affair and that his marriage to Mary was
breaking down; or the growing suspicion that he would take
Youlgreave away from me, probably without even knowing
what he was doing.

I knew perfectly well that Francis Youlgreave wasn't "mine"
to lose in the first place. He was just a long-dead clergyman
with eccentric habits, who had written a few minor poems that
sometimes turned up in anthologies. Even I accepted that most
of his poetry wasn't up to much. If half the stories were true, he
had taken too much brandy and opium to do anything very well.

For all that, Youlgreave was an interesting person, always
striving for something out of his reach. He was also interesting
in the wider context of literary history. He was not quite a
Victorian, not quite a modern, but something poised uneasily
between the two.

We were about to reach the hundred-and-fiftieth anniversary
of his birth. Publishers love anniversaries, and I had pitched
the idea of a short biography of Youlgreave with a selection of
his better poems to an editor I'd worked for in the past. To my
surprise she liked the proposal and eventually commissioned it.
The advance was modest. Still, it was a proper book and for a
decent publisher.

I knew there wasn't a great deal of material available
on Youlgreave. It was rather odd, actually, how little had
survived—I suspected that his family had purged his papers
after his death. But when talking to the editor I made a big point
of his friendships with people like Oscar Wilde and Aleister
Crowley, and also his influence on the modernists who came
after him. There were people who claimed to see elements of
Youlgreave's work in T.S. Eliot's *The Wasteland*, which wasn't
as fanciful as it might seem.

Besides, what we did know about him was intriguing. The
second son of a baronet, he had published a volume called

Last Poems while he was still at Oxford. He was ordained and spent the 1890s as a vicar in London. He was made a Canon of Rosington—some people said that his family pulled strings in order to get him away from the temptations of the capital—but had retired early owing to illhealth.

Youlgreave was only in his early forties when he died. I had seen reports of the inquest. He was living at his brother's house. He fell out of a high window. They said it was an accident. But no one really knew what had happened, and they probably never would.

I had one advantage that I made the most of with my editor. Youlgreave had been a member of the London Library for most of his adult life. After his death, his family presented a number of his books to the library.

One of them was his own copy of *The Voice of Angels*. Youlgreave's last collection of poems, published in 1903, was called *The Tongues of Angels*. *Voice* was a privatelyprinted variant of *Tongues* that included an extra poem, "The Children of Heracles." The poem, which has strong elements of cannibalism, was unpleasant even by today's standards; presumably Youlgreave's publisher refused to include it in *Tongues*.

I suspected that the cataloguer hadn't realized how rare this book was. It was not in the British Library or the Bodleian or Cambridge University Library. As far as I knew, the London Library's edition was the only known copy in a collection that was accessible to the public, though there may have been a few in private hands.

The Voice of Angels was valuable not just for its rarity and for the extra poem. This particular copy had penciled marginalia by Youlgreave himself. Some of them are illegible, but not all.

Best of all, on the endpaper at the back, Youlgreave had jotted down a number of disjointed lines and clusters of words-fragments, I believed, of a poem he hadn't lived to write. One phrase leapt out at me when I first saw it: *the long sonata of the dead.*

I recognized the phrase. This was going to be one of the main revelations of my biography. Samuel Beckett had used the identical words in his novel *Molloy*, which he published nearly half a century after Youlgreave's death. It was too unusual to be dismissed as coincidence. To clinch the matter, "The Children of Heracles" included the line: *What words and dead things know.* Beckett had used an almost identical phrase in *Molloy*.

There was only one conclusion: that Beckett had somehow seen *The Voice of Angels*, this very copy that I had found in the London Library, and he had admired it enough to plagiarise at least two of Youlgreave's lines.

Now I had to face the possibility that Adam was going to take that from me too.

⌘

All this passed through my mind as I stood there with Adam's phone in my hand.

I still had one thing in my favor: *The Voice of Angels* was safe on my shelf at home. It wasn't listed in the library's computer catalogue yet, only in the older catalogue, which consists of huge bound volumes with strips of printed titles pasted inside, the margins of the pages crowded with hand-written annotations by long-dead librarians. But, if Adam were serious about Youlgreave, sooner or later he would track it down and put in a request for it. Then I would have to return it to the library.

It was possible he wouldn't notice the discrepancy in the title. It was possible, even, that he wasn't doing anything significant on Youlgreave. That was what I really needed to find out.

I thought of Mary right away. She would know—she was credited as a researcher on the documentaries and in the books. And it would give me an excuse to see her, which was what I wanted to do anyway.

But did I want to see her? The very thought terrified me. Since Adam had walked into the London Library, all the comfortable certainties that shored up my life had crumbled away. Would she even talk to me after all these years? What would happen if I showed her the message on Adam's phone and proved to her that her husband was having an affair?

I had a practical problem to solve first of all. I didn't even know where to find her. Adam hadn't included his private address in his *Who's Who* entry. The library would know it but members' addresses were confidential.

That was when I remembered the crumpled envelope I had found in the Burberry. I took it out again. It was a circular addressed to Adam. There was the address: 23 *Rowan Avenue*.

I glanced over my shoulder. No one was looking at me. I slipped the phone into my trouser pocket.

The library kept a *London A-Z*. Rowan Avenue was out towards Richmond, not far from Kew Gardens.

I gave myself no time to think. I took my coat and left the library. I cut across Pall Mall and the Mall and went into St. James's Park. Hardly anyone was there because of the rain. My hair and my shoulders were soaked by the time I reached Queen Anne's Gate. A moment later I was at the Underground station. I was trembling with cold and, I think, excitement.

Proust was right about his madeleine. Once something unlocks the memories they come pouring out. I was drowning in mine just because I'd seen a man standing in the rain outside the London Library.

Adam had always been a bastard, I thought. People don't change, not really. As time passes, they just become more like themselves.

I didn't have to wait more than a couple of minutes for a Richmond train on the District Line. Kew Gardens was the last stop before Richmond. It was now late afternoon. The carriage was at the end of the train and nearly empty.

I sat down and stared at my reflection in the black glass opposite me. I saw an untidy middle-aged stranger where I half-expected to find a slim, sharp-featured student with shaggy hair.

It was still raining when I left the train and took my bearings. Kew was a nice place, just right for nice people like Adam and

Mary. You couldn't imagine poor people living there. But it wasn't not for the very rich, either, for people who flaunted their money and slapped it in your face. In a perfect world I might have lived there myself.

Rowan Avenue was a gently curving road about five minutes' walk from the station. The houses were terraced or semi-detached-solid Edwardian homes, well-kept and probably unobtrusively spacious. The cars outside were Mercedes, BMWs and the better sort of people carriers designed for shipping around large quantities of nice children.

Number 23 had a little glazed porch with a tiled floor, a green front door and a small stained glass window into the hall beyond. I rang the bell. Adam and Mary had no children—I knew that from *Who's Who*—but there might be a cleaner or a secretary or something. Mary might be out. The longer I waited, the more I hoped she would be.

There were footsteps in the hall. The stained glass rippled as the colors and shapes behind it shifted. My stomach fluttered. I knew it was her.

With a rattle, the door opened a few inches and then stopped. It was on the chain. I felt unexpectedly pleased—London is a dangerous city, growing worse every year; and I was relieved that Mary was taking precautions.

"Hello," she said, giving the word a slight interrogative lift on the second syllable.

"You probably won't remember me." I cleared my throat. "It's been a long time."

I could see only part of her face. She seemed a little smaller than in memory. The hair was carefully styled and much shorter.

She was frowning. "I'm afraid I don't . . ."

"Mary, it's me—Tony." Despair nibbled at me. "Don't you remember?"

"Tony?" Her voice was the same. Slightly breathless and husky. I used to find it unbearably sexy. I still did. "Tony?" she repeated, frowning. "From university?"

"Yes," I said, more loudly than I intended. I touched the beard. "Imagine me without this."

"Tony," she said. I watched recognition creep over her face. "Tony, yes, of course. Come in."

She unhooked the chain and opened the door. She was still Mary, my Mary. She was wearing jeans and a green shirt with a jersey over it. Cashmere, I thought. She was looking at me and I was acutely aware of my own appearance, something I rarely thought about.

For the first time I saw her face properly. "What have you done?" I said. "Are you OK?"

Her upper lip was swollen on the right hand side as if a bee had stung it. Or as if someone had hit her.

"I'm fine. I walked into the bathroom door last night. So stupid."

The hall was large and long, with rugs on stripped boards. Mary took me through to a sitting room dominated by an enormous TV screen. The furniture was modern. There were hardback books lying about—new ones, recently reviewed—and a vase of flowers on the coffee table.

"This is . . . nice," I said, for want of something to say.

She switched on a couple of lamps. "Do you want some tea?"

"No, thanks."

I thought she looked disappointed.

"Do sit down. It's good to see you after all this time."

That's what she said: what she meant was: *Why are you here?*
I sat down on a sofa. There was another sofa at right-angles to mine. She chose that one.

"It's been ages, hasn't it?" she said. "How've you been?"

"Fine. I—"

"What have you been doing?"

"This and that," I said. "I review—I do odds and ends for publishers—reading for them, sub-editing, blurb-writing. I've ghosted some memoirs. That sort of thing. I'm working on the biography of a poet at present."

"Which one?" she asked.

"Francis Youlgreave."

"Really." Her eyes widened as the memory caught up with her. "You always had a thing about him. Funnily enough, Adam's thinking of doing something about him too."

"There's an anniversary coming up," I said.

She nodded. "It's part of a series for him. Another documentary."

"What's it about?"

"Literary culture in the 1890s—*The Naughty Nineties*, I think that's the working title. There's going to be a book, too."

"Of course," I said.

"It's going to be revisionist," she went on. "In the sense that they're arguing the really influential figures aren't the obvious ones like Wilde and Henry James."

"Hence Youlgreave?"

"I suppose. I don't really know. Tony—it's awfully nice to see you, of course, but is there a particular reason for you coming? Like this, I mean, out of the blue."

"This is a bit difficult," I said. I wanted so much to be honest with her. "I saw Adam today—at the London Library. I didn't even know he was a member."

"So he knows you're here?"

"No—I don't think he saw me. But I . . . I happened to see his phone—he'd left it lying around. There was a text."

She sat up sharply, her cheeks coloring with a stain of blood. "A text—what do you mean? You're telling me you've been reading Adam's texts?"

"I didn't mean to, not exactly." I knew I was coloring too. "But, Mary, I think you should see it. That's why I'm here."

I took the iPhone from my pocket and handed it to her. She stared at the screen. I couldn't see her face.

I miss you more and more every moment we're apart. J xxxx.

"He's having an affair, isn't he?" I said. "Did you know?"

She didn't look up. She shrugged.

"Did he hit you, too?"

"If you must know, yes." Mary put down the phone on the arm of the sofa. She stared at me. "We're getting a divorce. We—we can't agree about who gets what. The old story."

"I'm so sorry," I said.

Her expression softened. "I really think you are. Bless you."

"I know what it's like. I was married for a while but it didn't take. Who's 'J'? Do you know?"

"She's called Janine—she used to be his PA. About ten years younger than me." She swallowed. "Nice woman."

"Not that nice."

She stood up suddenly. "I'm going to make some tea. Will you have some now?"

"Is it OK me being here? What if Adam comes back?"

"He's meeting his agent for dinner at Wilton's at nine o'clock. That's what his diary says, anyway. He was going to work in the library until then."

I followed her into the kitchen. She put on the kettle and then stood, arms folded, looking out of the window at the back garden.

"This is going to be so bloody awful," she said. "He's got most of our assets tied up in a couple of companies. One of them is offshore, which makes it even more complicated. And he controls the companies; that's the real problem. I was so naive, you wouldn't believe. I just signed where he told me when he set them up."

I thought of the Post-it note I had found in Adam's library book. *You're such a complete shit. You won't get away with it.* But it looked as if he would get away with it.

"You've talked to a solicitor?"

"Yes. For what it's worth. If I fight Adam for my share, it'll cost a fortune. But I haven't got a fortune. I've hardly got anything. I shouldn't be telling you this—it's not your problem."

"It doesn't matter."

"Anyway, the odds are I'll lose if we go to court."

"What will you do?" I said.

"God knows."

She turned to face me. I couldn't see her face clearly; the window was behind her and the winter afternoon was fading into dusk. Neither of us spoke for a while. The kettle began to hiss quietly at first and then with steadily rising urgency. At last there was a click as it turned itself off.

"I normally have green tea in the afternoon," she said, as if this was a normal conversation on a normal day. "But there's ordinary tea if you prefer, or herbal—"

"Green tea's fine," I said.

She picked up a packet of tea and a spoon. Then she stopped moving and the conversation wasn't normal any more. "I made a mistake, Tony, didn't I?" she said. "I wish . . ."

"What do you wish?" My voice was little more a whisper.

"I wish I could put time back," Mary said. "To when it was just you and me in the garden. Do you remember? At that stupid party? It all seemed so simple then."

∾

On Tuesdays, the London Library stays open until nine p.m. When I got back it was nearly six o'clock. The Burberry was still hanging in the cupboard. I hung my own coat beside it.

I had asked Mary if I should take the phone back and leave it where I had found it. She told me not to bother. Adam often left his phone at home or mislaid it—he wouldn't be surprised if he couldn't find it in his coat. He was careless about his possessions, she said, just as he was careless about people.

The library was much emptier than it had been. I liked the place especially on a winter evening, when the only people there seemed to be a few librarians and a handful of members like me. In the stacks—and most of the place consists of the stacks—each run of shelves has its own set of lights. Members are encouraged to turn off any lights that are not in use. So, on a February evening like this, most of the library consists of pools of light marooned in the surrounding gloom. Sounds are muted. The spines of the books stretch away into an infinity of learning.

Adam wasn't in any of the reading rooms. I guessed that he was either searching for books or working at one of the little tables scattered around the stacks. It didn't matter because I didn't want to find him. I didn't want to see him ever again or hear his voice. I didn't want to think of him.

I sat down and tried to work, which was how I had always intended to spend this evening. But my mind was full of Mary and I couldn't concentrate. I had a pencil in my hand and I wrote the words *the long sonata of the dead* on the inside cover of my notebook. I looked at them for a long time and wondered whether even Francis Youlgreave or Samuel Beckett had known what they meant.

A little after eight-fifteen, I decided I'd had enough. I packed up my work and went downstairs. As I reached the issue hall I nearly bumped into Adam. He had come out of the catalogue room.

We both pulled back at the last moment before a collision became inevitable. We muttered reciprocal apologies. But his words were no more than a polite reflex. He looked through me. I didn't exist for him.

He went over to the enquiries desk. I turned aside and pretended to study a plan of the library on the wall.

"I found a book in the old printed catalogue but I can't see it on the shelves," he said to the librarian. "Can you check if it's out?"

"What is it?" the librarian asked.

"It's by Francis Youlgreave." Adam spelt the surname. "It's called *The Voice of Angels*."

A moment later the librarian said, "I'm afraid it's out. Due back on March the sixth. Would you like to reserve it?"

"Yes, please."

Afterwards Adam went upstairs, glancing at his watch. After a moment I followed him. I was wearing trainers and I made very little noise. He turned into one of the older stacks and walked steadily towards the back. I couldn't see him because the lines of bookcases were in the way. But I heard his footsteps ringing on the iron gratings of the floor. You can look down at the floor below and up at the floor above. I suppose they had to make the floors of iron in order to bear the weight of all the books.

There was a further stack beyond this one, part of the History section. Very few lights were on. I waited near the archway leading into the rear stack. I stood in the shelter of a bookcase containing books on gardening.

The levels on the older stacks are connected internally with steep, narrow iron staircases in a sort of bibliographic snakes and ladders. Some of the staircases still have their original signs—an elegant silhouette of a hand with a pointing finger accompanied by a legend saying something like "Up History" or "Down Society." One of these was nearby, which gave me the reassuring sense that I could slip away if someone else came up behind me.

I listened to Adam's footsteps until they stopped. Then, for several minutes, I heard nothing else except the hum of the strip lighting and a faint crackling sound that might have been rain on a distant skylight or window.

He came out at last. I watched him approaching through the slit between the top of a row of books and the bottom of the shelf above. He had both arms full with a pile of four or five heavy books, a folder of notes and a slim silver laptop. He was wearing a pair of gold-rimmed reading glasses that gave him a scholarly air he didn't deserve.

He passed very close to me. He began to descend the iron stairs. He was in a hurry.

At first, all I did was touch him, rest my hand on his shoulder.

When I touched him, Adam began to turn towards me. But too quickly.

That was the thing: it happened so very quickly. His own momentum still carried him forward. He was encumbered with the weight in his arms. His awareness of the fragility of the books and the laptop perhaps made it harder for him to protect himself.

Then I pushed his shoulder. Not hard, not really—barely more than a gentle nudge, the sort of gesture you might make when you meet an old friend. If you could translate the gesture into words, it would say something like, "Hey—good to see you after all this time."

Except it wasn't good to see him. It wasn't good at all, not for me and not for him.

Adam overbalanced and fell with a terrible scraping crash. The laptop and other objects skipped and clattered down the stairs, making a sound that might have been a form of hard, atonal music.

The long sonata of the dead.

I ran down the stairs. Adam was lying on his front with his books and notes around him. He wasn't moving. He made no sound at all. His head was bleeding. I wondered if the blood would drip through the iron grating and fall to the level beneath. I hoped it wouldn't damage any books.

I listened for sounds elsewhere, for running footsteps, the sound of voices. I heard nothing but the hum and the crackling and, loudest of all, my own rapid breathing.

The laptop had skidded across the floor and come to rest against the base of a bookcase. It looked undamaged. Adam's glasses were beside his head. They were unbroken, too. I remember thinking how easy it is to miss your footing if you forget to take off your reading glasses. Especially if you are going down a flight of stairs.

There was a phone on the floor, just inches from his hand as if he had been carrying that as well.

I picked it up. It was another iPhone. The screen was shattered. Without thinking, I pressed the control button. Nothing happened. The phone was dead. But why was there a phone in the first place?

A dead phone, I thought: *What dead things know.*

I left the library, walked through the rain across the park for the third time and caught a train to Kew.

At this hour, and on a night like this, the train wasn't crowded. Someone had left a copy of the evening's *Metro* on the seat next to mine and I pretended to read it as we trundled wearily westward.

There were four other passengers in the carriage. All of us avoided eye contact. One of them was a thin-faced woman sitting diagonally across the carriage from me. She was younger than I, in her early thirties perhaps, and looked like a character in a Russian novel. She ought to have been travelling by troika rather than London Underground, despite the fact that she was reading something on her Kindle.

When the train stopped at Kew, I hung back, letting the other passengers leave the station first. Three of them took the eastern exit in the direction of Mortlake Road. I left a decent interval and then followed.

It was raining harder than ever. One of the people ahead had turned off. The second one went into a house on the right. That left the thin-face woman, striding down the rainslicked pavement in her long black coat and long black boots, sheltered by an umbrella. She turned into Rowan Avenue.

I didn't want to give her the impression I was stalking her so I waited before following. I took shelter under a tree but there wasn't much point. I was already soaking wet.

A moment later, I turned the corner. Number 23 was on the other side of the road. The lights were on in the hall and behind the blinds of a ground-floor room at the front with a bay window. I had no idea what I would say to Mary. Or even if I would have the courage to ring the bell. But it didn't matter. It would be good to know she was there, in that house. It would be good to know she was alive.

The woman ahead crossed the road. I hesitated. She was approaching the gate of Mary's house. She opened it.

I darted after her and took cover beside a black SUV so absurdly large it would have concealed an elephant. I edged sideways. I could now see her standing in the little porch by the front door. She had closed her umbrella and left it on the tiled floor.

A light was on above her head and she might have been standing on a miniature stage. She glanced over her shoulder. I saw her face, all bones and shadows and glaring white skin.

The door opened. There was Mary. She had changed into a dark blue dress since this afternoon.

"Janine," she said. "Janine."

The women embraced. But it wasn't as friends embrace.

"I'm so sorry," Mary said. "He took my phone, would you believe?"

"So does he know?" Janine said.

"He must have seen the texts. Anyway, come here."

Mary drew the younger woman inside. She was smiling as if she would never stop. The door closed.

I closed my eyes. The rain fell. The raindrops tapped on the dark, shiny roof of the SUV. A car hooted on the Mortlake Road. Traffic grumbled. Tires hissed over wet tarmac. A door opened down the street and, for a moment before it closed again, I heard a piano playing the saddest tune in the world.

My eyes were closed. I listened to the long sonata of the dead.

The Caxton Library &
Book Depository

John Connolly

I

L ET US BEGIN with this:
    To those looking at his life from without, it would have
seemed that Mr. Berger led a dull existence. In fact, Mr. Berger
himself might well have concurred with this view.

He worked for the housing department of a minor English
council, with the job title of "Closed Accounts Registrar." His
task, from year to year, entailed compiling a list of those who
had either relinquished or abandoned the housing provided for
them by the council, and in doing so had left their accounts
in arrears. Whether a week's rent was owed, or a month's, or
even a year's (for evictions were a difficult business and had a
habit of dragging on until relations between council and tenant
came to resemble those between a besieging army and a walled
city), Mr. Berger would record the sum in question in a massive
leather bound ledger known as the Closed Accounts Register.
At year's end, he would then be required to balance the rents
received against the rents that should have been received. If he
had performed his job correctly, the difference between the two
sums would be the total amount contained in the register.

Even Mr. Berger found his job tedious to explain. Rare was

it for a cab driver, or a fellow passenger on a train or bus, to engage in a discussion of Mr. Berger's livelihood for longer than it took for him to describe it. Mr. Berger didn't mind. He had no illusions about himself or his work. He got on perfectly well with his colleagues, and was happy to join them for a pint of ale—but no more than that—at the end of the week. He contributed to retirement gifts, and wedding presents, and funeral wreaths. At one time it had seemed that he himself might become the cause of one such collection, for he entered into a state of cautious flirtation with a young woman in accounts. His advances appeared to be reciprocated, and the couple performed a mutual circling for the space of a year until someone less inhibited than Mr. Berger entered the fray, and the young woman, presumably weary of waiting for Mr. Berger to breach some perceived exclusion zone around her person, went off with his rival instead. It says much about Mr. Berger than he contributed to their wedding collection without a hint of bitterness.

His position as registrar paid neither badly nor particularly well, but enough to keep him clothed and fed, and maintain a roof above his head. Most of the remainder went on books. Mr. Berger led a life of the imagination, fed by stories. His flat was lined with shelves, and those shelves were filled with the books that he loved. There was no particular order to them. Oh, he kept the works of individual authors together, but he did not alphabetize, and neither did he congregate books by subject. He knew where to lay a hand on any title at any time, and that was enough. Order was for dull minds, and Mr. Berger was far less dull than he appeared (to those who are themselves unhappy, the contentment of others can sometimes be mistaken for tedium). Mr. Berger might sometimes have been a little lonely, but he was never bored, and never unhappy, and he counted his days by the books that he read.

I suppose that, in telling this tale, I have made Mr. Berger sound old. He was not. He was thirty-five and, although in no danger of being mistaken for a matinée idol, was not unattractive. Yet perhaps there was in his interiority something that rendered him, if not sexless, then somewhat oblivious to the reality of relations with the opposite sex, an impression strengthened by the collective memory of what had occurred—or not occurred—with the girl from accounts. So it was that Mr. Berger found himself consigned to the dusty ranks of the council's spinsters and bachelors, to the army of the closeted, the odd, and the sad, although he was none of these things. Well, perhaps just a little of the latter: although he never spoke of it, or even fully admitted it to himself, he regretted his failure to express properly his affection for the girl in accounts, and had quietly resigned himself to the possibility that a life shared with another might not be in his stars. Slowly he was becoming a kind of fixed object, and the books he read came to reflect his view of himself. He was not a great lover, and neither was he a tragic hero. Instead he resembled those narrators in fiction who observe the lives of others, existing as dowels upon which plots hang like coats until the time comes for the true actors of the book to assume them. Great and voracious reader that he was, Mr. Berger failed to realize that the life he was observing was his own.

In the autumn of 1968, on Mr. Berger's thirty-sixth birthday, the council announced that it was moving offices. Its various departments had until then been scattered like outposts throughout the city, but it now made more sense to gather them all into one purpose-built environment and sell the outlying buildings. Mr. Berger was saddened by this development. The housing department occupied a set of ramshackle offices in a redbrick edifice that had once been a private school, and there was a pleasing oddness to the manner in which it had been imperfectly adapted to its current role. The council's new headquarters, meanwhile, was a brutalist block designed by one of those acolytes of Le Corbusier whose vision consisted solely of purging the individual and eccentric and replacing it with a uniformity of steel, glass and reinforced concrete. It squatted on the site of what had once been the city's glorious Victorian railway station, itself now replaced by a squat bunker. In time, Mr. Berger knew, the rest of the city's jewels would also be turned to dust, and the ugliness of the built environment would poison the population, for how could it be otherwise?

Mr. Berger was informed that, under the new regimen, there would be no more need for a Closed Accounts Register, and he would be transferred to other duties. A new, more efficient system was to be put in place, although, as with so many other such initiatives, it would later be revealed that it was less efficient, and more costly, than the original. This news coincided with the death of Mr. Berger's elderly mother, his last surviving close relative, and the discovery of a small but significant bequest to her son: her house, some shares, and a sum of money that was not quite a fortune but would, if invested carefully, enable Mr. Berger to live in a degree of restrained comfort for the rest of his life. He had always had a hankering to write, and he now had the perfect opportunity to test his literary mettle.

So it was that Mr. Berger at last had a collection taken up in his name, and a small crowd gathered to bid him farewell and good luck, and he was forgotten almost as soon as he was gone.

2

Mr. Berger's mother had spent her declining years in a cottage on the outskirts of the small town of Glossom. It was one of those passingly pretty English settlements, best suited to those whose time on this earth was drawing slowly to a close, and who wanted to spend it in surroundings that were unlikely to unduly excite them, and thereby hasten the end. Its community was predominantly High Anglican, with a corresponding focus on parish-centered activities: rarely an evening went by without the church hall being occupied by amateur dramatists, or local historians, or quietly concerned Fabians.

It seemed, though, that Mr. Berger's mother had rather kept

herself to herself, and few eyebrows were raised in Glossom when her son chose to do the same. He spent his days outlining his proposed work of fiction, a novel of frustrated love and muted social commentary set among the woolen mills of Lancashire in the nineteenth century. It was, Mr. Berger quickly realized, the kind of book of which the Fabians might have approved, which put something of a dampener on his progress. He dallied with some short stories instead, and when they proved similarly unrewarding he fell back on poetry, the last resort of the literary scoundrel. Finally, if only to keep his hand in, he began writing letters to the newspapers on matters of national and international concern. One, on the subject of badgers, was printed in the *Telegraph*, but it was heavily cut for publication, and Mr. Berger felt that it made him sound somewhat obsessive about badgers when nothing could be further from the truth.

It began to dawn on Mr. Berger that he might not be cut out for the life of a writer, gentleman or otherwise, and perhaps there were those who should simply be content to read. Once he had reached this conclusion, it was as though a great weight had fallen from his shoulders. He packed away the expensive writer's notebooks that he had purchased from Smythson's of Mayfair, and their weight in his pocket was replaced by the latest volume of Anthony Powell's roman fleuve, *A Dance to the Music of Time*.

In the evenings, Mr. Berger was in the habit of taking a walk by the railway line. A disused path, not far from the back gate of his cottage, led through a forest and thus to the raised bank on which the railway ran. Until recently, trains had stopped four times daily at Glossom, but the Beeching cuts had led to the closure of the station. Trains still used the lines, a noisy reminder of what had been lost, but soon even the sound of them would disappear as routes were reorganized. Eventually, the lines through Glossom would become overgrown, and the station would fall into disrepair. There were those in Glossom who had suggested buying it from British Railways and turning it into a museum, although they were unclear as to what exactly might be put in such a museum, the history of Glossom being distinctly lacking in battles, royalty, or great inventors.

None of this concerned Mr. Berger. It was enough that he had a pleasant place in which to walk or, if the weather was conducive, to sit by the lines and read. There was a stile not far from the old station, and he liked to wait there for the passing of the last train south. He would watch the businessmen in their suits flash by, and experience a surge of gratitude that his working life had reached a premature but welcome end.

Now, as winter began to close in, he still took his evening strolls, but the fading of the light and the growing chill in the air meant that he did not pause to take time with his book. Nevertheless, he always carried a volume with him, for it had become his habit to read for an hour at the Spotted Frog over a glass of wine or a pint of mild.

On the evening in question, Mr. Berger had paused as usual to wait for the train. It was, he noticed, running a little late. It had begun to do so more and more of late, which led him to wonder if all of this rationalization was really leading to any kind of improvements at all. He lit his pipe and looked to the west to witness the sun setting behind the woods, the last traces of it like flames upon the denuded branches of the trees.

It was at this point that he noticed a woman passing through the overgrown bushes a little further down the line. He had noticed before a trail of sorts there, for the branches of shrubs had been broken in places, but it was a poor substitute for his own path, and he had no desire to damage his clothing or his skin on briars. The woman was dressed in a dark dress, but what caught Berger's eye was the little red bag that she carried on her arm. It seemed in such stark contrast to the rest of her attire. He tried to see her face, but the angle of her progress concealed it from him.

At that moment he heard a distant whistle, and the stile beneath him started to vibrate. The express, the last train of the evening, was approaching. He could see its lights through the trees as it came. He looked again to his right. The woman had stopped, for she too had heard the train. Mr. Berger expected her to pause and wait for it to pass, but she did not. Instead she hastened her steps. Perhaps she wishes to be across the lines before it comes, thought Mr. Berger, but that was a risky business. It was easy to misjudge distances under such circumstances, and he had heard tales of those who had caught a foot on a sleeper, or stumbled while rushing, and the train had been the end of them.

"Ho!" he called. "Wait!"

Instinctively he stepped down from the stile and walked quickly towards her. The woman turned at the sound of his voice. Even from a distance, Mr. Berger could see that she was beautiful. Her face was pale, but she did not seem distressed. There was about her an eerie, unsettling calm.

"Don't try to cross!" he shouted. "Let the train pass."

The woman emerged from the bushes. She hitched up her skirts, showing a pair of laced ankle boots and a hint of stocking, and proceeded to climb up the embankment. Now Mr. Berger was running, but he continued to call to her, even as the express grew louder behind him before passing him in a flash of noise and light and diesel. His saw the woman cast aside her red bag, draw her head between her shoulders and, with her arms outstretched, throw herself on her knees before the train.

Mr. Berger flinched. The angle of the line meant that he did not witness the moment of impact, and any sounds of distress were lost in the roar of the engine. When he opened his eyes, the woman was gone and the train was continuing on its way.

Mr. Berger ran to the spot at which he had last seen the woman. He steeled himself for the worst, expecting to see the track mired with gore and body parts, but there was nothing. He had no experience of such matters, though, and had no idea whether a train striking a person at such a speed would leave a great mess or none at all. It was possible that the force of it had sent fragments of the woman in all directions, or even that it had carried her broken frame further down the track. After searching the bushes by the point of impact he followed the line for a time, but found no blood, and no sign of a body. He could not even find the woman's discarded red bag. Still, he had seen her, of that he had no doubt. He had not imagined it.

He was now closer to the town than he was to his home. There was no police station in Glossom, but there was one in Moreham, some five miles away. Mr. Berger walked quickly to the public telephone at the old station house, and from there he called the police and told them of what he had witnessed. Then, as instructed, he sat on the bench outside the station and waited for the patrol car to arrive.

3

The police did much the same as Mr. Berger had done, only with greater numbers and at greater expense in man-hours and overtime payments. They searched the bushes and the tracks, and enquiries were made in Glossom in case any female residents had gone missing. The driver of the train was contacted, and the train was kept on the platform at Plymouth for an hour while its engine and carriages were examined for any sign of human remains.

Finally Mr. Berger, who had remained seated on his stile throughout, was interviewed for a second time by the inspector from Moreham. His name was Carswell, and his manner when he confronted Mr. Berger was colder than it had originally been. A light rain had begun to fall shortly after the search for a body had commenced, and Carswell and his men were now damp and weary. Mr. Berger was also wet, and found that he had developed a slight but constant shiver. He suspected that he might be in shock. He had never witnessed the death of another person before. It had affected him deeply.

Now Inspector Carswell stood before him, his hat jammed on his head and his hands thrust deep in the pockets of his coat. His men were packing up, and a pair of dogs that had been brought in to help with the search was being led back to the van in which they had arrived. The townspeople who had gathered to watch were also drifting away, but not without a final curious glance at the figure of Mr. Berger.

"Let's go through it again, shall we?" said Carswell, and Mr. Berger told his story one last time. The details remained the same. He was certain of what he had witnessed.

"I have to tell you," said Carswell, when Mr. Berger had finished speaking, "that the driver of the train saw nothing, and was unaware of any impact. As you can imagine, he was quite shocked to hear that a woman had been reported as throwing herself under his wheels. He aided in the examination of the train himself. It turns out that he has some unfortunate experience of such matters. Before he was promoted to driver, he was a fireman on an engine that struck a man near Coleford Junction. He told us that the driver saw the man on the rails but couldn't brake in time. The engine made a terrible mess of the poor fellow, he said. There was no mistaking what had happened. He seems to think that, if he had somehow hit a woman without knowing, we'd have no trouble finding her remains."

Carswell lit a cigarette. He offered one to Mr. Berger, who declined. He preferred his pipe, even though it had long since gone out.

"Do you live alone, sir?" asked Carswell.

"Yes, I do."

"From what I understand, you moved to Glossom fairly recently."

"That's correct. My mother died, and she left me her cottage."

"And you say that you're a writer?"

"Trying to be a writer. I've started to wonder if I'm really destined to be any good at it, to be honest."

"Solitary business, writing, or so I would imagine."

"It does tend to be, yes."

"You're not married?"

"No."

"Girlfriend?"

"No," said Mr. Berger, then added "Not at the moment."

He didn't want Inspector Carswell to think that there might be anything odd or unsavory about his bachelor existence.

"Ah."

Carswell drew deeply on his cigarette.

"Do you miss her?"

"Miss who?"

"Your mother."

Mr. Berger considered it an odd question to ask, but answered nonetheless.

"Of course," he said. "I would visit her when I could, and we spoke on the telephone once a week."

Carswell nodded, as if this explained a lot.

"Must be strange, coming to a new town, and living in the house in which your mother died. She passed away at home, didn't she?"

Mr. Berger thought that Inspector Carswell seemed to know a lot about his mother. Clearly he had not just been asking about a missing woman during his time in Glossom.

"Yes, she did," he replied. "Forgive me, Inspector, but what has this got to do with the death of this young woman?"

Carswell took the cigarette from his mouth and examined the burning tip, as though some answer might be found in the ash.

"I'm beginning to wonder if you might not have been mistaken in what you saw," he said.

"Mistaken? How can one be mistaken about a suicide?"

"There is no body, sir. There's no blood, no clothing, nothing. We haven't even been able to find the red bag that you mentioned. There's no sign that anything untoward happened on the track at all. So . . ."

Carswell took one last drag on his cigarette, then dropped it on the dirt and ground it out forcefully with the heel of his shoe.

"Let's just say that you were mistaken, and leave it at that, shall we? Perhaps you might like to find some other way to occupy your evenings, now that winter is setting in. Join the bridge club, or take up singing in the choir. You might even find a young lady to walk out with. What I'm saying is, you've had a traumatic time of it, and it would be good for you not to spend so much time alone. That way, you'll avoid making mistakes of this nature again. You do understand me, don't you sir?"

The implication was clear. Being mistaken was not a crime, but wasting police time was. Mr. Berger climbed down from the stile.

"I know what I saw, Inspector," he said, but it was all that he could do to keep the doubt from creeping into his voice, and his mind was troubled as he took the path back to his little cottage.

4

It should come as no surprise to learn that Mr. Berger slept little that night. Over and over he replayed the scene of the woman's demise, and although he had neither witnessed nor heard the impact, still he saw and heard it in the silence of the bedroom. To calm himself, he had taken a large glass of his late mother's brandy upon his arrival home, but he was not used to spirits and the alcohol sat ill with him. He grew delirious in his bed, and so often did the woman's death play out before him that he began to believe that this evening was not the first time he had been present at her passing. A peculiar sense of déjà vu overcame him, one that he was entirely unable to shrug off. Sometimes, when he was ill or feverish, a tune or song would lodge itself in his mind. So entrenched would its hooks become that it would keep him from sleep, and he would be unable to exorcise it until the sickness had passed. Now he was having the same experience with his vision of the woman's death, and its repetitive nature was leading him to believe that he had already been familiar with the scene before he was present at it.

At last, thankfully, weariness overcame him and he was able

to rest, but when he woke the next morning that nagging feeling of familiarity remained. He put on his coat and returned to the scene of the previous evening's excitement. He walked the rough trail, hoping to find something that the police might have missed, a sign that he had not been the victim of an overactive imagination—a scrap of black cloth, the heel of a shoe, or the red bag—but there was nothing.

It was the red bag that bothered him most of all. The red bag was the thing. With his mind unfogged by alcohol—although, in truth, his head still swam slightly in the aftermath—he grew more and more certain that the suicide of the young woman reminded him of a scene in a book: no, not just a scene, but perhaps *the* most famous scene of locomotive-based self-immolation in literature. He gave up on his physical search, and decided to embark on a more literary one.

He had long ago unpacked his books, although he had not yet found shelves for them all, his mother's love of reading not matching his own, and thus leading to her preference for large swathes of bare wall that she had seen fit to adorn only with cheap reproductions of sea views. There was still more room for his volumes than there had been in his own lodgings, due in no small part to the fact that the cottage had more floor space than his flat, and all a true bibliophile needs for his storage purposes is a horizontal plane. He found his copy of *Anna Karenina* sandwiched in a pile on the dining room floor between *War & Peace* and *Master and Man and Other Parables and Tales*, the latter in a nice Everyman's Library edition from 1946 about which he had forgotten, and which almost led him to set aside *Anna Karenina* in favor of a hour or so in its company. Good sense quickly prevailed, although not before he had set *Master and Man* on the dining table for further examination at a more convenient time. There it joined a dozen similarly blessed volumes, all of which had been waiting for days or weeks for their hour to come at last.

He sat in an armchair and opened *Anna Karenina* (Limited Editions Club, Cambridge, 1951, signed by Barnett Freedman, unearthed at a jumble sale in Gloucester and acquired for such a low price that Mr. Berger had later made a donation to charity in order to salve his conscience). He flipped through the pages until he found Chapter XXXI, which began with the words "A bell sounded . . ." From there he read on quickly but carefully, travelling with Anna past Piotr in his livery and top-boots, past the saucy conductor and the woman deformed, past the dirty hunchback *muzhik* until finally he came to this passage:

She was going to throw herself under the first car as its center came opposite where she stood. Her little red travelling-bag caused her to lose the moment; she could not detach it from her arm. She awaited the second. A feeling like that she had experienced once, just before taking a dive in the river, came over her, and she made the sign of the cross. This familiar gesture called back to her soul a whole series of memories of her youth and childhood; and suddenly the darkness which hid every-thing from her was torn asunder. Life, with its elusive joys, glowed for an instant before her. But she did not take her eyes from the car; and when the center, between the two wheels, appeared, she threw away her red bag, drawing her head between her shoulders, and, with outstretched hands, threw herself on her knees under the car. For a second she was horror-struck at what she was doing.

"Where am I? What am I doing? Why?"

She tried to get up, to draw back; but something monstrous, inflexible, struck her head, and threw her on her back.

"Lord, forgive me all!" she murmured, feeling the struggle to be in vain.

A little muzhik *was working on the railroad, mumbling in his beard.*

And the candle by which she had read the book that was filled with fears, with deceptions, with anguish, and with evil, flared up with greater brightness than she had ever known, revealing to her all that before was in darkness, then flickered, grew faint, and went out forever.

Mr. Berger read the passage twice, then leaned back in his chair and closed his eyes. It was all there, right down to the detail of the little red bag, the bag that the woman on the tracks had cast aside before the express had hit her, just as Anna had thrown away her bag before she was struck. The woman's gestures in her final moments had also been similar to Anna's: she too had drawn her head between her shoulders and stretched out her arms, as though the death to come was to take the form of crucifixion rather than iron and wheels. Why, even Mr. Berger's own memory of the incident had been couched in similar phrases.

"My God," said Mr. Berger to the listening books, "perhaps the inspector was right and I have been spending too much time alone with only novels for company. There can be no other excuse for a man believing that he has seen the climactic scene of *Anna Karenina* reenacted on the Exeter to Plymouth railway."

He placed the volume on the arm of the chair and went to the kitchen. He was briefly tempted to reach for the brandy again, but no particular good had come of their previous shared moments, and so he opted for the routine of making a big pot of tea. When all was in place, he took a seat at the kitchen table and drank cup after cup until he had drained the pot dry. For once he did not read, nor did he distract himself with the *Times* crossword, still left untried at this late stage of the morning. He simply stared at the clouds, and listened to birdsong, and wondered if he was not, after all, going gently insane.

Mr. Berger did not read anything else that day. His two examinations of Chapter XXXI of *Anna Karenina* remained his sole contact with the world of literature. He could not recall a day when he had read less. He lived for books. They had consumed every spare moment since the revelation in childhood that he could tackle a novel alone without his mother having to read it to him. He recalled his first halting encounters with the Biggles stories of W.E. Johns, remembering how he had struggled through the longer words by breaking them up into their individual syllables, so that one difficult word became two easier ones. Ever since then, books had been his constant companions. He had, perhaps, sacrificed real friendships to these simulacra, because there were days when he had avoided his chums after school or ignored their knocking on his front door when his parents' house was otherwise empty, taking an alternative route home or staying away from the windows so that he could be sure that no football game or exploration of orchards would get in the way of finishing the story that had gripped him.

In a way, books had also been partly responsible for his fatal tentativeness with the girl from accounts. She seemed to read a little—he had seen her with a Georgette Heyer novel, and the occasional "book in brown" from the two-penny library—but he had the sense that it was not a passion with her. What if she insisted that they spend hours at the theater, or the ballet, or shopping, simply because it meant that they would be "doing things together"? That was, after all, what couples did, wasn't it? But reading was a solitary pursuit. Oh, one could read in the same room as someone else, or beside them in bed at night, but that rather presumed that an agreement had been reached about such matters, and the couple in question consisted of a pair of like-minded souls. It would be a disaster to find oneself embroiled with the sort of person who read two pages of a novel and then began humming, or tapping her fingers to attract attention, or, God help us, started fiddling with the dial on the radio. The next thing one knew, she'd be making "observations" on the text in hand, and once that happened there would be no peace for ever after.

But as he sat alone in the kitchen of his deceased mother's house, it struck Mr. Berger that he had never troubled himself to find out the views of the girl in accounts on the subject of books or, indeed, ballet. Deep inside, he had been reluctant to disturb his ordered lifestyle, a world in which he rarely had to make a more difficult decision than selecting the next book to read. He had lived his life as one removed from the world around him, and now he was paying the price in madness.

5

In the days that followed, Mr. Berger subsisted largely on newspapers and magazines of an improving nature. He had almost convinced himself that what he had seen on the tracks employed by the locomotives of the London and South Western Railway was a psychological anomaly, some form of delayed reaction to the grief he had experienced at his mother's death. He noticed that he was the object of peculiar looks, both poorly concealed and unashamedly open, as he went about his business in the town, but that was to be expected. He did hope that the town's memory of the unproductive police search might fade eventually. He had no desire to be elevated to the role of local eccentric.

But as time wore on, something odd happened. It is usually in the manner of experiences such as Mr. Berger's that, as distance grows from the event in question, so too the memory of it becomes foggier. Mr. Berger should, if the ordinary rules of behavior were being obeyed, have become ever more certain of the psychologically troubling nature of his encounter with the young woman reminiscent of Anna Karenina. But Mr. Berger found himself believing with greater and greater conviction that the opposite was true. He had seen the woman, and she was real, admittedly allowing for a certain latitude in one's definition of reality.

He began reading again, tentatively at first, but soon with his previous immersion. He also returned to walking the path that wound down to the railway line, and sitting on his stile to watch the trains go by. Each evening, with the approach of the train from Exeter to Plymouth, he would set aside his book, and watch the rougher trail to the south. It was darker now, and the trail was harder to see, but Mr. Berger's eyes were still keen, and through habit he grew practiced at picking out the difference in the density of the bushes.

But the trail remained undisturbed until February came, and the woman returned.

6

It was a cold but bracing evening. There was no damp in the air, and Mr. Berger enjoyed the sight of his breath pluming as he took his evening constitutional. There was music in the Spotted Frog that evening: some form of folk revivalism, for which Mr. Berger had a sneaking fondness. He intended to drop in for an hour or two, once he had watched the train go by. His vigil at the stile had become something of a ritual for him, and although he told himself that it was no longer connected to the business of the woman with the red bag, he secretly knew that it was. He was haunted by the image of her.

He took his seat on the stile, and lit his pipe. From somewhere to the east, he heard the sound of the approaching train. He glanced at his watch, and saw that it was just after six. The train was early. This was unheard of. If he had still been in the habit of writing letters to the *Telegraph*, he might well have popped off a missive announcing this turn-up for the books, much in the manner of those twitchers who liked to let the populace know of the appearance of the first cuckoo of spring.

He was already composing the letter in his head when he was distracted by a commotion to his right. Someone was coming down the trail, and in some hurry. Mr. Berger dropped from the stile and began walking in the direction of the sounds. The sky was clear, and the moon was already silvering the undergrowth, but even without the aid of its light Mr. Berger would have been able to pick out the woman rushing to meet the train, and the red bag that hung from her arm.

Mr. Berger dropped his pipe, but managed to retrieve it. It was, after all, a good pipe.

While it would not be untrue to say that he had become obsessed with the woman, he had no real expectation of ever seeing her again. After all, people did not make a habit of throwing themselves under trains. It was the kind of act that tended to be performed once, or not at all. In the case of the former, any possible repeat of the incident was likely to be ruled out by the action of a heavy engine or, in the unlikely event of survival, sufficient recall of the painfulness of the first attempt to render most unwelcome any further repetition of it. Yet here, without a shadow of a doubt, was the same young woman carrying the same red bag and making the same rush towards self-destruction that Mr. Berger had previously witnessed.

It must be a ghost, thought Mr. Berger. There can be no other explanation. This is the spirit of some poor woman who died some time ago—for he saw that her clothing was not of this century—and she is doomed to repeat her final moments over and over until—

Until what? Mr. Berger wasn't certain. He had read his share of M.R. James and W.W. Jacobs, of Oliver Onions and William Hope Hodgson, but had never come across anything quite like this in their stories. He had a vague notion that digging up a forgotten corpse and reburying it in a more appropriate location sometimes helped, while James tended to favor restoring ancient artifacts to their previous resting place, thereby calming the spirits associated with them, but Mr. Berger had no idea where the young woman might be interred, and he had not picked so much as a flower while on his walks, let alone some old whistle or manuscript. All of this would have to be dealt with later, he realized. There was more important business to attend to.

The early arrival of the train had obviously caught the woman, spectral or otherwise, by surprise, and the branches seemed to be conspiring to keep her from her date with mortality. They caught at her dress, and at one point she took a tumble that sent her to her knees. Despite all of these hindrances, it was obvious to Mr. Berger that she was still likely to make it to the tracks in time to receive the full impact of the train.

Mr. Berger ran, and as he did so he screamed and shouted, and waved his arms. He ran faster than he had ever run before, so that he managed to reach the base of the trail some time before the woman did. She drew up short, seemingly surprised to see him. Perhaps she had been so intent on her own demise that she had failed to hear his cries, but she was now faced with the physical reality of Mr. Berger, and he with hers. She was younger than he, and her skin was unusually pale, although that might just have been the moonlight. Her hair was the blackest that Mr. Berger had ever seen. It seemed to consume the light.

The woman tried to dart to her right, and then to her left, to avoid Mr. Berger, but the bushes were too thick. He felt the ground vibrating, and the noise of the approaching train was deafeningly loud. He was aware of its whistle sounding. The driver had probably spotted him by the tracks. Mr. Berger raised his right hand and waved to let the driver know that all was okay. The woman was not going to get past him, and Mr. Berger had no intention of throwing himself under any trains.

The woman clenched her fists in frustration as the train rushed by. Mr. Berger turned his head to watch it go, some of the passengers staring at him curiously from the window, and when he looked back the woman was gone. It was only as the rattle of the train faded that he heard the sound of bushes rustling and knew that she was making her way back up the hill. He tried to follow, but the same branches that had previously hampered her progress now delayed his. His jacket was torn, he lost his pipe, and he even twisted his left ankle slightly on a root, but he did not give up. He reached the road just in time to see the woman slip into a laneway that ran parallel to Glossom's high street. The back gardens of a row of cottages lay on one side, and on the other the rear wall of what had once been the town's brewery but was now derelict and unused, although a faint smell of old hops still hung about it.

Eventually the laneway diverged, with the path to the left eventually connecting with the main street while the path to the right twisted into darkness. Mr. Berger could see no sign of the woman to his left, for the high street was well lit. He chose instead to go right, and was soon among the relics of Glossom's industrial past: old warehouses, some still in use but most abandoned; a wall that announced the presence of a combined cooperage and chandlery, while the decay of the building behind it left no doubt that it had been some time since either barrels or candles had emerged from within; and, finally, a two-storey redbrick building with barred windows and grass growing by its doorstep. Beyond it was a dead end. As he drew nearer, Mr. Berger could have sworn that he heard a door softly closing.

Mr. Berger stood before the building and stared up at it. There were no lights burning, and the windows were so encrusted with dirt and filth both inside and out that there was no possibility of catching a glimpse of its interior. A name was carved into the brickwork above the door. Mr. Berger had to strain his eyes to read it, for the moonlight seemed to have no desire to aid him here. At last he made out the words "Caxton Private Lending Library & Book Depository."

Mr. Berger frowned. He had made enquiries in the town as to whether there was a library and had been told that there was none, the nearest, as with so much else that Glossom lacked, being in Moreham. There was a newsagent that sold books, but they were mainly detective stories and romances, and there was a limit to how many of either Mr. Berger wished to read. It was, of course, entirely likely that the Caxton Private Lending Library & Book Depository was no longer in business, but if that was the case then why was the grass growing around its doorstep trampled flat in places? Someone was still entering and leaving it on a semi-regular basis, including, if Mr. Berger was not mistaken, a woman, or something phantasmagorical that resembled a woman, with an Anna Karenina fixation.

He took out his matchbook and lit a match. There was a yellowed sign behind a small pane of glass to the right of the door. It read: "For all enquiries, please ring bell." Mr. Berger used up three matches looking in vain for a bell of any kind. There was none. Neither was there a slot or box for mail.

Mr. Berger worked his way round the corner of the building to the right, for any progress to the left was barred by the wall. Here was a smaller laneway, but it ended in another brick wall, and there were no windows on that side of the building, nor was there a door. Behind the wall was a patch of waste ground.

Mr. Berger returned to the front door. He banged on it once with his fist, more in hope than expectation of an answer. He was unsurprised when none came. He examined the single keyhole. It did not look rusted, and when he put a finger to it, the digit came back moistened with a hint of lock oil. It was all most peculiar, and not a little sinister.

There was nothing else to be done for now, Mr. Berger thought. The night was growing steadily colder, and he had not yet eaten. Although Glossom was a quiet, safe town, he did not fancy spending a long night outside a darkened lending library in the hope that a spectral woman might emerge so he could ask her what she thought she was doing, throwing herself repeatedly under trains. There were also some nasty scratches on his hands that could do with a spot of antiseptic.

So, with one final look back at the Caxton Library, and more perturbed than ever, Mr. Berger returned home, and the Spotted Frog was deprived of his custom for that night.

7

Mr. Berger returned to the Caxton Library shortly after 10.00 A.M. the next morning, on the basis that this was a reasonably civilized hour at which to appear, and if the Caxton was still in business then it was likely that someone might be about at this time. The Caxton, though, remained as silent and forbidding as it had the previous evening.

With nothing better to do, Mr. Berger began making

enquiries, but to no avail. General expressions of ignorance about the nature of the Caxton Private Lending Library & Book Depository were his sole reward at the newsagent, the local grocery, and even among the early arrivals at the Spotted Frog. Oh, people seemed to be aware that the Caxton existed, but nobody was able to recall a time when it was actually in business as a lending library, nor could anyone say who owned the building, or if any books still remained inside. It was suggested that he might try the town hall in Moreham, where the records for the smaller hamlets in the vicinity were kept.

So Mr. Berger got in his car and drove to Moreham. As he drove, he considered that there seemed to be a remarkable lack of interest in the Caxton Library among the townsfolk of Glossom. It was not merely that those to whom he spoke had forgotten about its existence until Mr. Berger brought it up, at which point some faint atavistic memory of the building was uncovered before promptly being buried again; that, at least, might be understandable if the library had not been in business for many years. What was more curious was that most people seemed to be entirely unaware of its existence, and didn't care very much to investigate further once it was brought to their attention. Glossom was a close-knit community, as Mr. Berger was only too well aware, for comments about hallucinations and train delays still followed him as he asked about the library. There appeared to be only two types of business in the town: everybody's business, and business that was not yet everybody's but soon would be once the local gossips had got to work on it. The older residents of the town could provide chapter and verse on its history back to the 16th century, and every building, old or recent, had its history.

All, that is, except the Caxton Private Lending Library.

The town hall in Moreham proved to be a source of little illumination on the matter. The library building was owned by the Caxton Trust, with an address at a P.O. Box in London. The

Trust paid all bills relating to the property, including rates and electricity, and that was as much as Mr. Berger could find out about it. An enquiry at the library in Moreham was met with blank looks, and although he spent hours searching back issues of the local weekly paper, the *Moreham & Glossom Advertiser*, from the turn of the century onwards, he could find no reference to the Caxton Library anywhere.

It was already dark when he returned to his cottage. He cooked himself an omelette and tried to read, but he was distracted by the fact of the library's apparent simultaneous existence and non-existence. It was there. It occupied a space in Glossom. It was a considerable building. Why, then, had its presence in a small community passed relatively unnoticed and unremarked for so long?

The next day brought no more satisfaction. Calls to booksellers and libraries, including to the grand old London Library, and the Cranston Library in Reigate, the oldest lending library in the country, confirmed only a general ignorance of the Caxton. Finally, Mr. Berger found himself talking to the British representative of the Special Libraries Association, an organization of whose existence he had previously been unaware. She promised to search their records, but admitted that she had never heard of the Caxton and would be surprised if anyone else had either, given that her own knowledge of such matters was encyclopedic, a judgment that, after an hour-long history of libraries in England, Mr. Berger was unwilling to doubt.

Mr. Berger did consider that he might be mistaken about the woman's ultimate destination. There were other buildings in that part of town in which she could have hidden herself to escape his notice, but the Caxton was still the most likely place in which she might have sought refuge. Where else, he thought, would a woman intent upon repeatedly reenacting the final moments of Anna Karenina choose to hide but an old library?

He made his decision before he went to bed that night. He

would become a detective of sorts, and stake out the Caxton Private Lending Library & Book Depository for as long as it took for it to reveal its secrets to him.

8

As Mr. Berger soon discovered, it was no easy business being a detective on a stakeout. It was all very well for those chaps in books who could sit in a car or a restaurant and make observations about the world in a degree of comfort, especially if they were in Los Angeles or somewhere else with a climate noted for warmth and sunlight. It was quite another thing to hang around among dilapidated buildings in a small English town on a cold, damp February day, hoping that nobody one knew happened by or, worse, some passing busybody didn't take it upon himself to phone the police and report a loiterer. Mr. Berger could just imagine Inspector Carswell smoking another cigarette and concluding that he now most definitely had some form of lunatic on his hands.

Thankfully, Mr. Berger found a sheltered space in the old cooperage and chandlery that afforded a view of the end of the laneway through a collapsed section of wall while allowing him to remain relatively concealed. He had brought a blanket, a cushion, a flask of tea, some sandwiches and chocolate, and two books, one of them a John Dickson Carr novel entitled *The Crooked Hinge*, just to enter into the spirit of the thing, and the other *Our Mutual Friend* by Charles Dickens, the only Dickens he had yet to read. *The Crooked Hinge* turned out to be rather good, if a little fantastical. Then again, Mr. Berger considered, a tale of witchcraft and automatons was hardly more outlandish than apparently witnessing the same woman attempt suicide twice, the first time successfully and the second time less so.

The day passed without incident. There was no activity in the laneway, the rustle of the odd rat apart. Mr. Berger finished the

Dickson Carr and started the Dickens, which, being the author's last completed novel, meant that it was mature Dickens, and hence rather difficult by the standards of *Oliver Twist* or *The Pickwick Papers*, and requiring considerably more patience and attention. When the light began to fade, Mr. Berger set aside the book, unwilling to risk drawing attention by using a torch, and waited another hour in the hope that darkness might bring with it some activity at the Caxton Library. No illumination showed in the old building, and Mr. Berger eventually gave up the watch for the night, and took himself to the Spotted Frog for a hot meal and a restorative glass of wine.

His vigil recommenced early the next morning, although he chose to alternate Dickens with Wodehouse. Once again, the day passed with little excitement, the appearance of a small terrier dog apart. The dog began yapping at Mr. Berger, who shooed it ineffectually until its owner gave a shrill whistle from nearby and the dog departed. Still, the day was warmer than the one before, which was a small blessing: Mr. Berger had woken that morning with stiff limbs, and had determined to wear two overcoats if the new day proved as chilly as the last.

Darkness started to descend, and with it doubts on the part of Mr. Berger about the wisdom of his course of action. He couldn't hang around laneways indefinitely. It was unseemly. He leaned into a corner and found himself starting to doze. He dreamed of lights in the Caxton Library, and a train that rolled down the laneway, its complement of passengers consisting entirely of dark-haired ladies carrying small red bags, all of them steeling themselves for self-destruction. Finally he dreamed of footsteps on gravel and grass, but when he woke he could still hear the footsteps. Someone was coming. Tentatively he rose from his resting place and peered at the library. There was a figure on its doorstep carrying what looked like a carpet bag, and he heard the rattle of keys.

Instantly Mr. Berger was on his feet. He climbed through the gap in the wall and emerged into the laneway. An elderly man was standing before the door of the Caxton Library, his key already turning in the lock. He was shorter than average, and wore a long grey overcoat and a trilby hat with a white feather in the band. A remarkable silver handlebar mustache adorned his upper lip. He looked at Mr. Berger with some alarm and hurriedly opened the door.

"Wait!" said Mr. Berger. "I have to talk to you."

The old gent was clearly in no mood to talk. The door was wide open now, and he was already inside when he realized that he had forgotten his carpet bag, which remained on the ground. He reached for it, but Mr. Berger got there at the same time, and an unseemly tug-of-war began with each man holding on to one of the straps.

"Hand it over!" said the old man.

"No," said Mr. Berger. "I want to talk with you."

"You'll have to make an appointment. You'll need to telephone in advance."

"There's no number. You're not listed."

"Then send a letter."

"You don't have a postbox."

"Look, you must come back tomorrow and ring the bell."

"There is no bell!" shouted Mr. Berger, his frustration getting the better of him as his voice jumped an octave. He gave a final hard yank on the bag and won the struggle, leaving only a handle in the grip of the old man.

"Oh, bother!" said the old man. He looked wistfully at his bag, which Mr. Berger was clutching to his chest. "I suppose you'd better come in, then, but you can't stay long. I'm a very busy man."

He stepped back, inviting Mr. Berger to enter. Now that the opportunity had at last presented itself, that worthy gentleman experienced a twinge of concern. The interior of the Caxton Library looked very dark, and who knew what might be waiting inside? He was throwing himself at the mercy of a possible madman, armed only with a hostage carpet bag. But he had come this far in his investigation, and he required an answer of some sort if he was ever to have peace of mind again. Still holding on to the carpet bag as though it were a swaddled infant, he stepped into the library.

9

Lights came on. They were dim, and the illumination they offered had a touch of jaundice to it, but they revealed lines of shelves stretching off into the distance, and that peculiar musty smell distinctive to rooms in which books are aging like fine wines. To his left was an oak counter, and behind it cubbyholes filled with paperwork that appeared not to have been touched in many years, for a fine film of dust lay over it all. Beyond the counter was an open door, and through it Mr. Berger could see a small living area with a television, and the edge of a bed in an adjoining room.

The old gent removed his hat, and his coat and scarf, and hung them on a hook by the door. Beneath them he was wearing a dark suit of considerable vintage, a white shirt, and a very wide gray-and-white striped tie. He looked rather dapper, in a slightly decaying way. He waited patiently for Mr. Berger to begin, which Mr. Berger duly did.

"Look," said Mr. Berger, "I won't have it. I simply won't."

"Won't have what?"

"Women throwing themselves under trains, then coming back and trying to do it again. It's just not on. Am I making myself clear?"

The elderly gentleman frowned. He tugged at one end of his mustache and sighed deeply.

"May I have my bag back, please?" he asked.

Mr. Berger handed it over, and the old man stepped behind the counter and placed the bag in the living room before returning. By this time, though, Mr. Berger, in the manner of bibliophiles everywhere, had begun to examine the contents of the nearest shelf. The shelves were organized alphabetically, and by chance Mr. Berger had started on the letter 'D'. He discovered an incomplete collection of Dickens' work, seemingly limited to the best known of the writer's works. *Our Mutual Friend* was conspicuously absent, but *Oliver Twist* was present, as were *David Copperfield*, *A Tale of Two Cities*, *Pickwick Papers*, and a handful of others. All of the editions looked very old. He took *Oliver Twist* from the shelf and examined its points. It was bound in brown cloth with gilt lettering and bore the publisher's imprint at the foot of the spine. The title page attributed the work to Boz, not Charles Dickens, indicating a very early edition, a fact confirmed by the date of publisher and date of publication: Richard Bentley, London, 1838. Mr. Berger was holding the first edition, first issue, of the novel.

"Please be careful with that," said the old gent, who was hovering nervously nearby, but Mr. Berger had already replaced *Oliver Twist* and was now examining *A Tale of Two Cities*, perhaps his favorite novel by Dickens: Chapman & Hall, 1859, original red cloth. It was another first edition.

But it was the volume marked *Pickwick Papers* that contained the greatest surprise. It was oversized, and contained within it not a published copy but a manuscript. Mr. Berger knew that most of Dickens' manuscripts were held by the Victoria & Albert Museum as part of the Forster Collection, for he had seen them when they were last on display. The rest were held by the British Library, the Wisbech Museum, and the Morgan Library in New York. Fragments of *Pickwick Papers* formed part of the collection of the New York Public Library, but as far as Mr. Berger was aware, there was no complete manuscript of the book anywhere.

Except, it seemed, in the Caxton Private Lending Library & Book Depository of Glossom, England.

"Is it—?" said Mr. Berger. "I mean, can it—?"

The old gentleman gently removed the volume from Mr. Berger's hands and placed it back in its place on the shelf.

"Indeed," said the gentleman.

He was looking at Mr. Berger a little more thoughtfully than before, as though his visitor's obvious appreciation for the books had prompted a reassessment of his probable character.

"It's in rather good company as well," he said.

He gestured expansively at the rows of shelves. They stretched into the gloom, for the yellow lights had not come on in the farther reaches of the library. There were also doors leading off to the left and right. They were set into the main walls, but Mr. Berger had seen no doors when he had first examined the building. They could have been bricked up, but he had seen no evidence of that either.

"Are they all first editions?" he asked.

"First editions, or manuscript copies. First editions are fine for our purposes, though. Manuscripts are merely a bonus."

"I should like to look, if you don't mind," said Mr. Berger. "I won't touch any more of them. I'd just like to see them."

"Later, perhaps," said the gent. "You still haven't told me why you're here."

Mr. Berger swallowed hard. He had not spoken aloud of his encounters since the unfortunate conversation with Inspector Carswell on that first night.

"Well," he said, "I saw a woman commit suicide in front of a train, and then some time later I saw her try to do the same thing again, but I stopped her. I thought she might have come in here. In fact, I'm almost certain that she did."

"That is unusual," said the gent.

"That's what I thought," said Mr. Berger.

"And do you have any idea of this woman's identity?"

"Not exactly," said Mr. Berger.

"Would you care to speculate?"

"It will seem odd."

"No doubt."

"You may think me mad."

"My dear fellow, we hardly know each other. I wouldn't dare to make such a judgment until we were better acquainted."

Which seemed fair enough to Mr. Berger. He had come this far: he might as well finish the journey.

"It did strike me that she might be Anna Karenina." At the last minute, Mr. Berger hedged his bets. "Or a ghost, although she did appear remarkably solid for a spirit."

"She wasn't a ghost," said the gent.

"No, I didn't really believe so. There was the issue of her substantiality. I suppose you'll tell me now that she wasn't Anna Karenina either."

The old gent tugged at his mustache again. His face was betrayed his thoughts as he carried on an internal debate with himself.

Finally, he said "No, in all conscience I could not deny that she is Anna Karenina."

Mr. Berger leaned in closer, and lowered his voice significantly. "Is she a loony? You know . . . someone who thinks that she's Anna Karenina?"

"No. You're the one who thinks that she's Anna Karenina, but she *knows* that she's Anna Karenina."

"What?" said Mr. Berger, somewhat thrown by the reply. "So you mean she *is* Anna Karenina? But Anna Karenina is simply a character in a book by Tolstoy. She isn't real."

"But you just told me that she was."

"No, I told you that the woman I saw *seemed* real."

"And that you thought she might be Anna Karenina."

"Yes, but you see, it's all very well saying that to oneself, or even presenting it as a possibility, but one does so in the hope that a more rational explanation might present itself."

"But there isn't a more rational explanation, is there?"

"There might be," said Mr. Berger. "I just can't think of one at present."

Mr. Berger was starting to feel light-headed.

"Would you like a cup of tea?" said the old gent.

"Yes," said Mr. Berger, "I rather think I would."

10

They sat in the gentleman's living room, drinking tea from china cups and eating some fruitcake that he kept in a tin. A fire had been lit, and a lamp burned in a corner. The walls were decorated with oils and watercolors, all of them very fine and very old. The style of a number of them was familiar to Mr. Berger. He wouldn't have liked to swear upon it, but he was fairly sure that there was at least one Turner, a Constable, and two Romneys, a portrait and a landscape, among their number.

The old gentleman had introduced himself as Mr. Gedeon, and he had been the librarian at the Caxton for more than forty years. His job, he informed Mr. Berger, was "to maintain and, as required, increase the collection; to perform restorative work on the volumes where necessary; and, of course, to look after the characters."

It was this last phrase that made Mr. Berger choke slightly on his tea.

"The characters?" he said.

"The characters," confirmed Mr. Gedeon.

"What characters?"

"The characters from the novels."

"You mean: they're alive?"

Mr. Berger was beginning to wonder not only about his own sanity but that of Mr. Gedeon as well. He felt as though he had wandered into some strange bibliophilic nightmare. He kept hoping that he would wake up at home with a headache to find that he had been inhaling gum from one of his own volumes.

"You saw one of them," said Mr. Gedeon.

"Well, I saw someone," said Mr. Berger. "I mean, I've seen

chaps dressed up as Napoleon at parties, but I didn't go home thinking I'd met Napoleon."

"We don't have Napoleon," said Mr. Gedeon.

"No?"

"No. Only fictional characters here. It gets a little complicated with Shakespeare, I must admit. That's caused us some problems. The rules aren't hard and fast. If they were, this whole business would run a lot more smoothly. But then, literature isn't a matter of rules, is it? Think how dull it would be if it was, eh?"

Mr. Berger peered into his teacup, as though expecting the arrangement of the leaves to reveal the truth of things. When they did not, he put the cup down, clasped his hands, and resigned himself to whatever was to come.

"All right," he said. "Tell me about the characters . . ."

It was, said Mr. Gedeon, all to do with the public. At some point, certain characters became so familiar to readers—and, indeed, to many non-readers—that they reached a state of existence independent of the page.

"Take Oliver Twist, for example," said Mr. Gedeon. "More people know of Oliver Twist than have ever read the work to which he gave his name. The same is true for Romeo and Juliet, and Robinson Crusoe, and Don Quixote. Mention their names to the even averagely educated man or woman on the street and, regardless of whether they've ever encountered a word of the texts in question, they'll be able to tell you that Romeo and Juliet were doomed lovers, that Robinson Crusoe was marooned on an island, and Don Quixote was involved in some business with windmills. Similarly, they'll tell you that Macbeth got above himself, that Ebenezer Scrooge came right in the end, and that D'Artagnan, Athos, Aramis and Porthos were the names of the musketeers.

"Admittedly, there's a limit to the number of those who achieve that kind of familiarity. They end up here as a matter of course. But you'd be surprised by how many people can tell you something of Tristram Shandy, or Tom Jones, or Jay Gatsby.

I'm not sure where the point of crossover is, to be perfectly honest. All I know is that, at some point, a character becomes sufficiently famous to pop into existence and, when they do so, they materialize in or near the Caxton Private Lending Library & Book Depository. They always have, ever since the original Mr. Caxton set up the first depository shortly before his death in 1492. According to the history of the library, he did so when some of Chaucer's pilgrims turned up on his doorstep in 1477."

"Some of them?" said Mr. Berger. "Not all?"

"Nobody remembers all of them," said Mr. Gedeon. "Caxton found the Miller, the Reeve, the Knight, the Second Nun, and the Wife of Bath all arguing in his yard. Once he became convinced that they were not actors or lunatics, he realized that he had to find somewhere to keep them. He didn't want to be accused of sorcery or any other such nonsense, and he had his enemies: where there are books, there will always be haters of books alongside the lovers of them.

"So Caxton found a house in the country for them, and this also served as a library for parts of his own collection. He even established a means of continuing to fund the library after he was gone, one that continues to be used to this day. Basically, we mark up what should be marked down, and mark down what should be marked up, and the difference is deposited with the Trust."

"I'm not sure that I understand," said Mr. Berger.

"It's simple, really. It's all to do with ha'pennys, and portions of cents, or lire, or whatever the currency may be. If, say, a writer was due to be paid the sum of nine pounds, ten shillings, and sixpence ha'penny in royalties, the ha'penny would be shaved off and given to us. Similarly, if a company owes a publisher seventeen pounds, eight shillings and sevenpence ha'penny, they're charged eightpence instead. This goes on all through the industry, even down to individual books sold. Sometimes we're dealing in only fractions of a penny, but when we take them from all round the world and add them together, it's more than enough to fund the Trust, maintain the library, and house the characters here. It's now so embedded in the system of books and publishing that nobody even notices anymore."

Mr. Berger was troubled. He would have had no time for such accounting chicanery when it came to the Closed Accounts Register. It did make sense, though.

"And what is the Trust?"

"Oh, the Trust is just a name that's used for convenience. There hasn't been an actual Trust in years, or not one on which anyone sits. For all intents and purposes, this is the Trust. I am the Trust. When I pass on, the next librarian will be the Trust. There's not much work to it. I rarely even have to sign checks."

While the financial support structure for the library was all very interesting, Mr. Berger was more interested in the question of the characters.

"To get back to these characters, they live here?"

"Oh, absolutely. As I explained, they just show up outside when the time is right. Some are obviously a little confused, but it all becomes clear to them in the days that follow, and they start settling in. And when they arrive, so too does a first edition of the relevant work, wrapped in brown paper and tied with string. We put in on a shelf and keep it nice and safe. It's their life story, and it has to be preserved. Their history is fixed in those pages."

"What happens with series characters?" asked Mr. Berger. "Sherlock Holmes, for example? Er, I'm assuming he's here somewhere."

"Of course," said Mr. Gedeon. "We numbered his rooms as 221B, just to make him feel at home. Dr. Watson lives next door. In their case, I do believe that the library received an entire collection of first editions of the canonical works."

"The Conan Doyle books, you mean?"

"Yes. Nothing after Conan Doyle's death in 1930 actually counts. It's the same for all of the iconic characters here. Once the original creator passes on, then that's the end of their story as far as we, and they, are concerned. Books by other authors who take up the characters don't count. It would all be unmanageable otherwise. Needless to say, they don't show up here until after their creators have died. Until then, they're still open to change."

"I'm finding all of this extremely difficult to take in," said Mr. Berger.

"Dear fellow," said Mr. Gedeon, leaning over and patting Mr. Berger's arm reassuringly, "don't imagine for a moment that you're the first. I felt exactly the same way the first time that I came here."

"How did you come here?"

"I met Hamlet at a number 48B bus stop," said Mr. Gedeon. "He'd been there for some time, poor chap. At least eight buses had passed him by, and he hadn't taken any of them. It's to be expected, I suppose. It's in his nature."

"So what did you do?"

"I got talking to him, although he does tend to soliloquize so one has to be patient. Saying it aloud, I suppose it seems nonsensical in retrospect that I wouldn't simply have called the police and told them that a disturbed person who was under the impression he was Hamlet was marooned at the 48B bus stop. But I've always loved Shakespeare, you see, and I found the man at the bus stop quite fascinating. By the time he'd finished speaking, I was convinced. I brought him back here and restored him to the safe care of the librarian of the day. That was old Headley, my predecessor. I had a cup of tea with him, much as we're doing now, and that was the start of it. When Headley retired, I took his place. Simple as that."

It didn't strike Mr. Berger as very simple at all. It seemed complicated on a quite cosmic scale.

"Could I—?" Mr. Berger began to say, then stopped. It struck him as a most extraordinary thing to ask, and he wasn't sure that he should.

"See them?" said Mr. Gedeon. "By all means! Best bring your coat, though. I find it can get a bit chilly back there."

Mr. Berger did as he was told. He put on his coat and followed Mr. Gedeon past the shelves, his eyes taking in the titles as he went. He wanted to touch the books, to take them down and stroke them, like cats, but he controlled the urge. After all, if Mr. Gedeon was to be believed, he was about to have a far more extraordinary encounter with the world of books.

11

In the end, it proved to be slightly duller than Mr. Berger had expected. Each of the characters had a small but clean suite of rooms, personalized to suit their time periods and dispositions. Mr. Gedeon explained that they didn't organize the living areas by authors or periods of history, so there weren't entire wings devoted to Dickens or Shakespeare.

"It just didn't work when it was tried in the past," said Mr. Gedeon. "Worse, it caused terrible problems, and some awful fights. The characters tend to have a pretty good instinct for these things themselves, and my inclination has always been to let them choose their own space."

They passed Room 221B where Sherlock Holmes appeared to be in an entirely drug-induced state of stupor, while in a nearby suite Tom Jones was doing something unspeakable with Fanny Hill. There was a brooding Heathcliff, and a Fagin with rope burns around his neck, but like animals in a zoo, a lot of the characters were simply napping.

"They do that a lot," said Mr. Gedeon. "I've seen some of them sleep for years, decades even. They don't get hungry as such, although they do like to eat to break the monotony. Force of habit, I suppose. We try to keep them away from wine. That makes them rowdy."

"But do they realize that they're fictional characters?" said Mr. Berger.

"Oh, yes. Some of them take it better than others, but they all learn to accept that their lives have been written by someone else, and their memories are a product of literary invention, even if, as I said earlier, it gets a bit more complicated with historical characters."

"But you said it was only fictional characters who ended up here," Mr. Berger protested.

"That is the case, as a rule, but it's also true that some historical characters become more real to us in their fictional forms. Take Richard III: much of the public perception of him is a product of Shakespeare's play and Tudor propaganda, so in a sense that Richard III is a fictional character. Our Richard III is aware that he's not actually *the* Richard III but *a* Richard III. On the other hand, as far as the public is concerned he is *the* Richard III, and is more real in their minds than any products of later revisionism. But he's the exception rather than the rule: very few historical characters manage to make that transition. All for the best, really, otherwise this place would be packed to the rafters."

Mr. Berger had wanted to raise the issue of space with the librarian, and this seemed like the opportune moment.

"I did notice that the building seems significantly larger on the inside than on the outside," he remarked.

"It's funny, that," said Mr. Gedeon. "Doesn't seem to matter much what the building looks like on the outside: it's as though, when they all move in, they bring their own space with them. I've often wondered why that might be, and I think I've come up with an answer of sorts. It's a natural consequence of the capacity of a bookstore or library to contain entire worlds, whole universes, and all contained between the covers of books. In that sense, every library or bookstore is practically infinite. This library takes that to its logical conclusion."

They passed a pair of overly ornate and decidedly gloomy rooms, in one of which an ashen-faced man sat reading a book, his unusually long fingernails gently testing the pages. He turned to watch them pass, and his lips drew back to reveal a pair of elongated canines.

"The Count," said Mr. Gedeon, in a worried manner. "I'd move along if I were you."

"You mean Stoker's Count?" said Mr. Berger. He couldn't help but gawp. The Count's eyes were rimmed with red, and there was an undeniable magnetism to him. Mr. Berger found his feet dragging him into the room as the Count set aside his book and prepared to welcome him.

Mr. Gedeon's hand grasped his right arm and pulled him back into the corridor.

"I told you to move along," he said. "You don't want to be spending time with the Count. Very unpredictable, the Count. Says he's over all that vampiric nonsense, but I wouldn't trust him farther than I could throw him."

"He can't get out, can he?" asked Mr. Berger, who was already rethinking his passion for evening walks.

"No, he's one of the special cases. We keep those books behind bars, and that seems to do the trick for the characters as well."

"But some of the others wander," said Mr. Berger. "You met Hamlet, and I met Anna Karenina."

"Yes, but that's really most unusual. For the most part, the characters exist in a kind of stasis. I suspect a lot of them just close their eyes and relive their entire literary lives, over and over. Still, we do have quite a competitive bridge tournament going, and the pantomime at Christmas is always good fun."

"How do they get out, the ones who ramble off?"

Mr. Gedeon shrugged. "I don't know. I keep the place well locked up, and it's rare that I'm not here. I just took a few days off to visit my brother in Bootle, but I've probably never spent more than a month in total away from the library in all of my years as librarian. Why would I? I've got books to read, and characters to talk to. I've got worlds to explore, all within these walls."

At last they reached a closed door upon which Mr. Gedeon knocked tentatively.

"*Oui?*" said a female voice.

"*Madame, vous avez un visiteur,*" said Mr. Gedeon.

"*Bien. Faites le entrer, s'il vous plaît.*"

Mr. Gedeon opened the door, and there was the woman whom Mr. Berger had watched throw herself beneath the wheels of a train, and whose life he felt that he had subsequently saved, sort of. She was wearing a simple black dress, perhaps even the very one that had so captivated Kitty in the novel, her curly hair in disarray, and a string of pearls hanging around her firm neck. She seemed startled at first to see him, and he knew that she recalled his face.

Mr. Berger's French was a little rusty, but he managed to dredge up a little from memory.

"*Madame, je m'appelle Monsieur Berger, et je suis enchanté de vous rencontrer.*"

"*Non,*" said Anna, after a short pause, "*tout le plaisir est pour moi, Monsieur Berger. Veuillez vous assoir, s'il vous plaît.*"

He took a seat, and a polite conversation commenced. Mr. Berger explained, in the most delicate terms, that he had been a witness to her earlier encounter with the train, and it had haunted him. Anna appeared most distressed, and apologized profusely for any trouble that she might have caused him, but Mr. Berger waved it away as purely minor, and stressed that he was more concerned for her than for himself. Naturally, he said, when he saw her making a second attempt—if attempt was the right word for an act that had been so successful first time round—he had felt compelled to intervene.

After some initial hesitancy, their conversation grew easier. At some point Mr. Gedeon arrived with more tea, and some more cake, but they barely noticed him. Mr. Berger found much of his French returning, but Anna, having spent so long in the environs of the library, also had a good command of English. They spoke together long into the night, until at last Mr. Berger noticed the hour, and apologized for keeping Anna up so late. She replied that she had enjoyed his company, and she slept little anyway. He kissed her hand, and begged leave to return the next day, and she gave her permission willingly.

Mr. Berger found his way back to the library without too much trouble, apart from an attempt by Fagin to steal his wallet, which the old reprobate put down to habit and nothing more. When he reached Mr. Gedeon's living quarters, he discovered the librarian dozing in an armchair. He woke him gently, and Mr. Gedeon opened the front door to let him out.

"If you wouldn't mind," said Mr. Berger, as he stood on the doorstep, "I should very much like to return tomorrow to speak with you, and Ms. Karenina, if that wouldn't be too much of an imposition."

"It wouldn't be an imposition at all," said Mr. Gedeon. "Just knock on the glass. I'll be here."

With that the door was closed, and Mr. Berger, feeling both more confused and more elated than he had in all his life, returned to his cottage in the darkness, and slept a deep, dreamless sleep.

12

The next morning, once he had washed and breakfasted, Mr. Berger returned to the Caxton Library. He brought with him some fresh pastries that he had bought in the local bakery in order to replenish Mr. Gedeon's supplies, and a book of Russian poetry in translation of which he was unusually fond, but which he now desired to present to Anna. Making sure that he was not being observed, he took the laneway that led to the library and knocked on the glass. He was briefly fearful that Mr. Gedeon might have spirited away the contents of the premises—books, characters, and all—overnight, fearful that the discovery by Mr. Berger of the library's true nature might bring some trouble upon them all, but the old gentleman opened the door to Mr. Berger's knock on the glass and seemed very pleased to see him return.

"Will you take some tea?" asked Mr. Gedeon, and Mr. Berger agreed, even though he had already had tea at breakfast and was anxious to return to Anna. Still, he had questions for Mr. Gedeon, particularly pertaining to Anna.

"Why does she do it?" he asked, as he and Mr. Gedeon shared an apple scone between them.

"Do what?" said Mr. Gedeon. "Oh, you mean throw herself under trains?"

He picked a crumb from his waistcoat and put it on his plate.

"First of all, I should say that she doesn't make a habit of it," said Mr. Gedeon. "In all the years that I've been here, she's done it no more than a dozen times. Admittedly, the incidents have been growing more frequent, and I have spoken to her about them in an effort to find some way to help, but she doesn't seem to know herself why she feels compelled to relive her final moments in the book. We have other characters that return to their fates—just about all of our Thomas Hardy characters appear obsessed by them—but she's the only one who reenacts her end. I can only give you my thoughts on the matter, and I'd say this: she's the titular character, and her life is so tragic, her fate so awful, that it could be that both are imprinted upon the reader, and herself, in a particularly deep and resonant way. It's in the quality of the writing. It's in the book. Books have power. You must understand that now. It's why we keep all of these first editions so carefully. The fate of characters is set forever in those volumes. There's a link between those editions and the characters that arrived here with them."

He shifted in his chair, and pursed his lips.

"I'll share something with you, Mr. Berger, something that I've never shared with anyone before," he said. "Some years ago, we had a leak in the roof. It wasn't a big one, but they don't need to be big, do they? A little water dripping for hours and hours can do a great deal of damage, and it wasn't until I got back from the picture house in Moreham that I saw what had happened. You see, before I left I'd set aside our manuscript copies of *Alice in Wonderland* and *Moby Dick*. "

"*Moby Dick*? " said Mr. Berger. "I wasn't aware that there were any extant manuscripts of *Moby Dick*. "

"It's an unusual one, I'll admit," said Mr. Gedeon. "Somehow it's all tied up with confusion between the American and British first editions. The American edition, by Harper & Brothers, was set from the manuscript, and the British edition, by Bentley's, was in turn set from the American proofs, but there are some six hundred differences in wording between the two editions. But in 1851, while Melville was working on the British edition based on proofs that he himself had paid to be set and plated before an American publisher had signed an agreement, he was also still writing some of the later parts of the book, and in addition he took the opportunity to rewrite sections that had already been set for America. So which is the edition that the library should store: the American, based on the original manuscript, or the British, based not on the manuscript but on a subsequent rewrite? The decision made by the Trust was to acquire the British edition and, just to be on the safe side, the manuscript. When Captain Ahab arrived at the Library, both editions arrived with him."

"And the manuscript of *Alice in Wonderland*? I understood that to be in the collection of the British Museum."

"Some sleight-of-hand there, I believe," said Mr. Gedeon. "You may recall that the Reverend Dodgson gave the original ninety-page manuscript to Alice Liddell, but she was forced to sell it in order to pay death duties following her husband's death in 1928. Sotheby's sold it on her behalf, suggesting a reserve of four thousand pounds. It went, of course, for almost four times that amount, to an American bidder. At that point, the Trust stepped in, and a similar manuscript copy was substituted and sent to the United States."

"So the British Museum now holds a fake?"

"Not a fake, but a later copy, made by Dodgson's hand at the Trust's instigation. In those days, the Trust was always thinking ahead, and I've tried to keep up that tradition. I've always got an eye out for a book or character that may be taking off.

"So the Trust was very keen to have Dodgson's original *Alice*: so many iconic characters, you see, and then there were the illustrations too. It's an extremely powerful manuscript.

"But all of this is beside the point. Both of the manuscripts needed a bit of attention—just a careful clean to remove any dust or other media with a little polyester film. Well, I almost cried when I returned to the library. Some of the water from the ceiling had fallen on the manuscripts: just drops, nothing more, but enough to send some of the ink from *Moby Dick* on to a page of the *Alice* manuscript."

"And what happened?" asked Mr. Berger.

"For one day, in all extant copies of *Alice in Wonderland*, there was a whale at the Mad Hatter's tea party," said Mr. Gedeon solemnly.

"What? I don't remember that."

"Nobody does, nobody but I. I worked all day to clean the relevant section, and gradually removed all traces of Melville's ink. *Alice in Wonderland* went back to the way it was before, but for that day every copy of the book, and all critical commentaries on it, noted the presence of a white whale at the tea party."

"Good grief! So the books can be changed?"

"Only the copies contained in the library's collection, and they in turn affect all others. This is not just a library, Mr. Berger: it's the *ur*-library. It has to do with the rarity of the books in its collection and their links to the characters. That's why we're so careful with them. We have to be. No book is really a fixed object. Every reader reads a book differently, and each book works in a different way on each reader. But the books here are special. They're the books from which all later copies came. I tell you, Mr. Berger, not a day goes by in this place that doesn't bring me one surprise or another, and that's the truth."

But Mr. Berger was no longer listening. He was thinking again of Anna and the awfulness of those final moments as the train approached, of her fear and her pain, and how she seemed doomed to repeat them because of the power of the book to which she had given her name.

But the contents of the books were not fixed. They were open not just to differing interpretations, but to actual change.

Fates could be altered.

13

Mr. Berger did not act instantly. He had never considered himself a duplicitous individual, and he tried to tell himself that his actions in gaining Mr. Gedeon's confidence were as much to do with his enjoyment of that gentleman's company, and his fascination with the Caxton's contents, as with any desire he might have harbored to save Anna Karenina from further fatal encounters with locomotives.

There was more than a grain of truth to this. Mr. Berger did enjoy spending time with Mr. Gedeon, for the librarian was a vast repository of information about the library and the history of his predecessors in the role. Similarly, no bibliophile could fail to be entranced by the library's inventory, and each day among its stacks brought new treasures to light, some of which had been acquired purely for their rarity value rather than because of any particular character link: annotated manuscripts dating back to the birth of the printed word, including poetical works by Donne, Marvell, and Spenser; not one but two copies of the First Folio of Shakespeare's works, one of them belonging to Edward Knight himself, the book-holder of the King's Men and the presumed proofreader of the manuscript sources for the Folio, and containing his handwritten corrections to the errors that had crept into his particular edition, for the Folio was still being proofread during the printing of the book, and there were variances between individual copies; and what Mr. Berger suspected might well be notes, in Dickens's own hand, for the later, uncompleted chapters of *The Mystery of Edwin Drood*.

This latter artifact was discovered by Mr. Berger in an uncatalogued file that also contained an abandoned version of the final chapters of F. Scott Fitzgerald's *The Great Gatsby*, in which Gatsby, not Daisy, is behind the wheel when Myrtle is killed. Mr. Berger had glimpsed Gatsby briefly on his way to visit Anna Karenina. By one of the miracles of the library, Gatsby's quarters appeared to consist of a pool house and a swimming pool, although the pool was made marginally less welcoming by the presence in it of a deflated, bloodstained mattress.

The sight of Gatsby, who was pleasant but haunted, and the discovery of an alternate ending to the book to which Gatsby, like Anna, had given his name, caused Mr. Berger to wonder what might have happened had Fitzgerald published the version held by the Caxton instead of the book that eventually appeared, in which Daisy is driving the car on that fateful night. Would it have altered Gatsby's eventual fate? Probably not, he decided: there would still have been a bloodstained mattress in the swimming pool, but Gatsby's end would have been rendered less tragic, and less noble.

But the fact that he could even think in this way about endings that might have been confirmed in him the belief that Anna's fate might be altered, and so it was that he began to spend more and more time in the section devoted to Tolstoy's works, and familiarized himself with the history of *Anna Karenina*. His researches revealed that even this novel, described as "flawless" by both Dostoevsky and Nabokov, presented problems when it came to its earliest appearance. While it was originally published in installments in the *Russian Messenger* periodical from 1873 onwards, an editorial dispute over the final part of the story meant that it did not appear in its complete form until the first publication of the work as a book in 1878. The library held both the periodical version and the Russian first edition, but Mr. Berger's knowledge of Russian was limited, to put it mildly, and he didn't think that it would be a good idea to go messing around with it in its original language. He decided that the library's first English language edition, published by Thomas Y. Crowell & Co. of New York in 1886, would probably be sufficient for his needs.

The weeks and months went by, but still he did not act. Not only was he afraid to put in place a plan that involved tinkering with one of the greatest works of literature in any language, but Mr. Gedeon was a perpetual presence in the library. He had not yet entrusted Mr. Berger with his own key, and he still kept a careful eye on his visitor. Meanwhile, Mr. Berger noticed that Anna was becoming increasingly agitated, and in the middle of their discussions of books and music, or their occasional games of whist or poker, she would grow suddenly distant and whisper the name of her children or her lover. She was also, he thought, taking an unhealthy interest in certain railway timetables.

Finally, fate presented him with the opportunity he had been seeking. Mr. Gedeon's brother in Bootle was taken seriously ill, and his departure from this earth was said to be imminent. Mr. Gedeon was forced to leave in a hurry if he was to see his brother again before he passed away and, with only the faintest of hesitations, he entrusted the care of the Caxton Private Lending Library & Book Depository to Mr. Berger. He left Mr. Berger with the keys, and the number of Mr. Gedeon's sister-in-law in Bootle in case of emergencies, then rushed off to catch the last evening train north.

Alone for the first time in the library, Mr. Berger opened the suitcase that he had packed upon receiving the summons from Mr. Berger. He removed from it a bottle of brandy, and his favorite fountain pen. He poured himself a large snifter of brandy—larger than was probably advisable, he would later accept—and retrieved the Crowell edition of Anna Karenina from its shelf. He laid it on Mr. Gedeon's desk and turned to the relevant section. He took a sip of brandy, then another, and another. He was, after all, about to alter one of the great works of literature, so a stiff drink seemed like a very good idea.

He looked at the glass. It was now almost empty. He refilled it, took another strengthening swig, and uncapped his pen. He offered a silent prayer of apology to the god of letters, and with three swift dashes of his pen removed a single paragraph.

It was done.

He took another drink. It had been easier than expected. He let the ink dry on the Crowell edition, and restored it to its shelf. He was, by now, more than a little tipsy. Another title caught his eye as he returned to the desk: *Tess of the d'Urbervilles* by Thomas Hardy, in the first edition by Osgood, McIlvaine and Co., London, 1891.

Mr. Berger had always hated the ending of *Tess of the d'Urbervilles*.

Oh well, he thought: in for a penny, in for a pound.

He took the book from the shelf, stuck it under his arm, and was soon happily at work on Chapters LVIII and LIX. He worked all through the night, and by the time he fell asleep the bottle of brandy was empty, and he was surrounded by books.

In truth, Mr. Berger had gotten a little carried away.

14

In the history of the Caxton Private Lending Library & Book Depository, the brief period that followed Mr. Berger's "improvements" to great novels and plays is known as the "Confusion" and has come to be regarded as a lesson in why such experiments should generally be avoided.

The first clue Mr. Gedeon had that something was amiss was when he passed the Liverpool Playhouse on his way to catch the train back to Glossom, his brother having miraculously recovered to such an extent that he was threatening to sue his physicians, and discovered that the theatre was playing *The Comedy of Macbeth*. He did a quick double-take, and immediately sought out the nearest bookshop. There he found a copy of *The Comedy of Macbeth*, along with a critical commentary labeling it "one of the most troubling of Shakespeare's later plays, due to its curious mixture of violence and inappropriate humor bordering on early bedroom farce."

"Good Lord," said Mr. Gedeon aloud. "What has he done? For that matter, what *else* has he done?"

Mr. Gedeon thought hard for a time, trying to recall the novels or plays about which Mr. Berger had expressed serious reservations. He seemed to recall Mr. Berger complaining that the ending of *A Tale of Two Cities* had always made him cry. An examination of a copy of the book in question revealed that it now ended with Sydney Carton being rescued from the guillotine by an airship piloted by the Scarlet Pimpernel, with a footnote advising that this had provided the inspiration for a later series of novels by Baroness Orczy.

"Oh, God," said Mr. Gedeon.

Then there was Hardy.

Tess of the d'Urbervilles now ended with Tess's escape from prison, engineered by Angel Clare and a team of demolitions experts, while *The Mayor of Casterbridge* had Michael Henchard living in a rose-covered cottage near his newly-married stepdaughter and breeding goldfinches. At the conclusion of *Jude the Obscure*, Jude Fawley escaped the clutches of Arabella and survived his final desperate visit to Sue in the freezing weather, whereupon they both ran away and went to live happily ever after in Eastbourne.

"This is terrible," said Mr. Gedeon, although even he had to admit that he preferred Mr. Berger's endings to Thomas Hardy's.

Finally he came to *Anna Karenina*. It took him a little while to find the change, because this one was subtler than the others: a deletion instead of an actual piece of bad rewriting. It was still wrong, but Mr. Gedeon understood Mr. Berger's reason for making the change. Perhaps if Mr. Gedeon had experienced similar feelings about one of the characters in his care, he might have found the courage to intervene in a similar way. He had been a witness to the sufferings of so many of them, the consequences of decisions made by heartless authors, the miserable Hardy not least among them, but his first duty was, and always had been, to the books. This would have to be put right, however valid Mr. Berger might have believed his actions to be.

Mr. Gedeon returned the copy of *Anna Karenina* to its shelf, and made his way to the station.

15

Mr. Berger woke to the most terrible hangover. It took him a while even to recall where he was, never mind what he might have done. His mouth was dry, his head was thumping, and his neck and back were aching from having fallen asleep at Mr. Gedeon's desk. He made himself some tea and toast, most of which he managed to keep down, and stared in horror at the pile of first editions that he had violated the night before. He had a vague sense that they did not represent the entirety of his efforts, for he dimly recalled returning some to the shelves, singing merrily to himself as he went, although he was damned if he could bring to mind the titles of all the books involved. So ill and appalled was he that he could find no reason to stay awake. Instead he curled up on the couch in the hope that, when he opened his eyes again, the world of literature might somehow have self-corrected, and the intensity of his headache might have lessened. Only one alteration did he not immediately regret, and that was his work on *Anna Karenina*. The actions of his pen in that case had truly been a labour of love.

He rose to sluggish consciousness to find Mr. Gedeon standing over him, his face a mixture of anger, disappointment, and not a little pity.

"We need to have words, Mr. Berger," he said. "Under the circumstances, you might like to freshen up before we begin."

Mr. Berger took himself to the bathroom, and bathed his face and upper body with cold water. He brushed his teeth, combed his hair, and tried to make himself as presentable as possible. He felt a little like a condemned man hoping to make a good impression on the hangman. He returned to the living room and smelled strong coffee brewing. Tea, in this case, was unlikely to be sufficient for the task at hand.

He took a seat across from Mr. Gedeon, who was examining the altered first editions, his fury now entirely undiluted by any other emotions.

"This is vandalism!" he said. "Do you realize what you've done? Not only have you corrupted the world of literature, and altered the histories of the characters in our care, but you've damaged the library's collection. How could someone who considers himself a lover of books do such a thing?"

Mr. Berger couldn't meet the librarian's gaze.

"I did it for Anna," he said. "I just couldn't bear to see her suffer in that way."

"And the others?" said Mr. Gedeon. "What of Jude, and Tess, and Sydney Carton? Good grief, what of Macbeth?"

"I felt sorry for them, too," said Mr. Berger. "And if their creators knew that, at some future date, they might take on a physical form in this world, replete with the memories and experiences forced upon them, would they not have given some thought to their ultimate fate? To do otherwise would be tantamount to sadism!"

"But that isn't how literature works," said Mr. Gedeon. "It isn't even how the world works. The books are written. It's not for you or me to start altering them at this stage. These characters have power precisely because of what their creators have put them through. By changing the endings, you've put at risk their place in the literary pantheon and, by extension, their presence in the world. I wouldn't be surprised if we were to go back to the lodgings and find a dozen or more unoccupied rooms, with no trace that their occupants ever existed."

Mr. Berger hadn't thought of that. It made him feel worse than ever.

"I'm sorry," he said. "I'm so very, very sorry. Can anything be done?"

Mr. Gedeon left his desk and opened a large cupboard in the corner of the room. From it he removed his box of restorer's equipment: his adhesives and threads, his tapes and weights and rolls of buckram cloth, his needles and brushes and awls. He placed the box on his desk, added a number of small glass bottles of liquid, then rolled up his sleeves, turned on the lamps, and summoned Mr. Berger to his side.

"Muriatic acid, citric acid, oxalic acid, and Tartureous acid," he said, tapping each bottle in turn.

He carefully mixed a solution of the latter three acids in a bowl, and instructed Mr. Berger to apply it to his inked changes to *Tess of the d'Urbervilles*.

"The solution will remove ink stains, but not printer's ink," said Mr. Gedeon. "Be careful, and take your time. Apply it, leave it for a few minutes, then wipe it off and let it dry. Keep repeating until the ink is gone. Now begin, for we have many hours of work ahead of us."

They worked through the night, and into the next morning. Exhaustion forced them to sleep for a few hours, but they both returned to the task in the early afternoon. By late in the evening, the worst of the damage had been undone. Mr. Berger even remembered the titles of the books that he had returned to the shelves while drunk, although one was forgotten. Mr. Berger had set to work on making *Hamlet* a little shorter, but had got no further than Scenes IV and V, from which he had cut a couple of Hamlet's soliloquies. The consequence was that Scene IV began with Hamlet noting that the hour of twelve had struck, and the appearance of his father's ghost. However by halfway through Scene V, and after a couple of fairly swift exchanges, it was already morning. When Mr. Berger's excisions were discovered many decades later by one of his successors, it was decided to allow them to stand, as she felt that *Hamlet* was quite long enough as it was.

Together they went to the lodgings and checked on the characters. All were present and correct, although Macbeth appeared in better spirits than before, and remained thus ever after.

Only one book remained unrestored: *Anna Karenina*.

"Must we?" said Mr. Berger. "If you say 'yes', then I will accept your decision, but it seems to me that she is different from the rest. None of the others are compelled to do what she does. None of them is so despairing as to seek oblivion over and over. What I did does not fundamentally alter the climax of the novel, but adds only a little ambiguity, and it may be that a little is all that she requires."

Mr. Gedeon considered the book. Yes, he was the librarian, and the custodian of the contents of the Caxton Private Lending Library & Book Depository, but he was also the guardian of its characters. He had a duty to them and to the books. Did one supersede the other? He thought of what Mr. Berger had said: if Tolstoy had known that, by his literary gifts, he would doom his heroine to be defined by her suicide, might he not have found a way to modify his prose even slightly, and thus give her some peace?

And was it not also true that Tolstoy's ending to the novel was flawed in any case? Rather than give us some extended reflection on Anna's death, he chose instead to concentrate on Levin's return to religion, Kozyshev's support for the Serbs, and Vronsky's commitment to the cause of the Slavs. He even gave the final word on Anna's death to Vronsky's rotten mother: "Her death was the death of a bad woman, a woman without religion." Surely Anna deserved a better memorial than that?

Mr. Berger had crossed out three simple lines from the end of Chapter XXXI:

The little muzhik *ceased his mumblings, and fell to his knees by the broken body. He whispered a prayer for her soul, but if her fall had been unwitting then she was past all need of prayer, and she was with God now. If it were otherwise, then prayer could do her no good. But still he prayed.*

He read the preceding paragraph:

And the candle by which she had read the book that was filled with fears, with deceptions, with anguish, and with evil, flared up with greater brightness than she had ever known, revealing to her all that before was in darkness, then flickered, grew faint, and went out forever.

You know, thought Mr. Gedeon, Chapter XXXI could end just as easily there, and there would be peace for Anna.

He closed the book, allowing Mr. Berger's change to stand.

"Let's leave it, shall we?" he said. "Why don't you put it back on its shelf?"

Mr. Berger took the book reverently, and restored it gently, lovingly to its place in the stacks. He thought about visiting Anna one last time, but it did not seem appropriate to ask Mr. Gedeon's permission. He had done all that he could for her, and he hoped only that it was enough. He returned to Mr. Gedeon's living room and placed the key to the Caxton Library on the desk.

"Goodbye," he said. "And thank you."

Mr. Gedeon nodded but did not answer, and Mr. Berger left the library and did not look back.

16

In the weeks that followed Mr. Berger thought often of the Caxton Library, and of Mr. Gedeon, and of Anna most of all, but he did not return to the laneway, and he consciously avoided walking near that part of the town. He read his books, and resumed his evening walks to the railway track. Each evening he waited for the last train to pass, and it always did so without incident. Anna, he believed, was troubled no more.

One evening, as summer drew to its close, there came a knocking on his door. He answered it to find Mr. Gedeon standing on his doorstep, two suitcases by his side, and a taxi waiting for him by the garden gate. Mr. Berger was surprised to see him, and invited him to step inside, but Mr. Gedeon declined.

"I'm leaving," he said. "I'm tired, and I no longer have the energy that I once had. It's time for me to retire, and entrust the care of the Caxton to another. I suspected as much on that first night, when you followed Anna to the library. The library always finds its new librarian, and leads him to its door. I thought that I might have been mistaken when you altered the books, and I resigned myself to waiting until another came, but slowly I came to understand that you were the one after all. Your only fault was to love a character too much, which caused you to do the wrong thing for the right reasons, and it may be that we both learned a lesson from that incident. I know that the Caxton and its characters will be safe in your care until the next librarian comes along. I've left a letter for you containing all that you need to know, and a number at which you can call me should you have any questions, but I think you'll be just fine."

He held out to Mr. Berger a great ring of keys. After only a moment's hesitation, Mr. Berger accepted them, and he saw that Mr. Gedeon could not stop himself from shedding a tear as he entrusted the library and its characters to its new custodian.

"I shall miss them terribly, you know," said Mr. Gedeon.

"You should feel free to visit us anytime," said Mr. Berger.

"Perhaps I will," said Mr. Gedeon, but he never did.

They shook hands for the final time, and Mr. Gedeon departed, and they did not meet or speak again.

17

The Caxton Private Lending Library & Book Depository is no longer in Glossom. At the beginning of this century the town was discovered by developers, and the land beside the library was earmarked for houses, and a modern shopping mall. Questions started to be asked about the peculiar old building at the end of the laneway, and so it was that one evening a vast fleet of anonymous trucks arrived driven by anonymous men, and in the space of a single night the entire contents of the Caxton Private Lending Library & Book Depository—books, characters and all—were spirited away and resettled in a new home in a little village not far from the sea, but far indeed from cities and, indeed, trains. The librarian, now very old and not a little stooped, liked to walk on the beach in the evenings, accompanied by a small terrier dog and, if the weather was good, by a beautiful, pale woman with long, dark hair.

One night, just as summer was fading into autumn, there was a knock on the door of the Caxton Private Lending Library & Book Depository, and the librarian opened it to find a young woman standing on the doorstep. She had in her hand a copy of *Vanity Fair*.

"Excuse me," she said, "I know this may sound a little odd, but I'm absolutely convinced that I just saw a man who looked like Robinson Crusoe collecting seashells on the beach, and I think he returned with them to this—" she looked at the small brass plate to her right—"*library*?"

Mr. Berger opened the door wide to admit her.

"Please come in," he said. "It may sound equally odd, but I think I've been expecting you ..."

The Book Case

Nelson DeMille

OTIS PARKER WAS dead. Killed by a falling bookcase whose shelves were crammed with very heavy reading. Total weight about a thousand pounds which flattened Mr. Parker's slight, 160 pound body. A tragic accident. Or so it seemed.

To back up a bit, I'm Detective John Corey, working out of the First Precinct Detective Squad, which is located – if you ever need me – on Ericsson Place in Lower Manhattan, New York City.

It was a cold, blustery March morning, a Tuesday, and I was sitting in a coffee shop on Hudson Street, a few blocks from my precinct, trying to translate ham and eggs over easy into Spanish for my English-challenged waiter. "Huevos flippo. Hambo and blanco toasto. Okay?"

My cell phone rang at 8:34, and it was my boss, Lieutenant Ed Ruiz who said, "I notice you're not at your desk."

"Are you sure?"

"Where are you?"

I told him and he said, "Good. You're up. We have a body at the Dead End Bookstore on North Moore. Discovered by a clerk reporting for work."

I knew the bookstore, which specialized in crime and mystery novels, and I'd actually been a customer a few times. I love murder mysteries. I can always guess the killer – without peeking at the end. Well…hardly ever. My job should be so easy.

Ruiz continued, "The deceased is the store owner, a Mr. Otis Parker."

"Oh…hey, I know him. Met him a few times."

"Yeah? How?"

"I bought a book."

"Really? Why?"

I ignored that and inquired, "Robbery?"

"No. Who robs a bookstore? You rob places that have money or goods you can sell."

"Right. So? What?"

"Well," replied Lt. Ruiz, "it looks like a ground ball," cop talk for something easy. He explained about the falling bookcase, then added, "Appears to be an accident, but the responding officer, Rourke, says it might need another look before they clean up the mess."

"Okay. Hey, how do you say fried egg on a roll to go in Spanish?"

"You say hasta la vista and get over to the bookstore."

"Right." I hung up and went out into the cold March morning. Lower Manhattan at this hour is jammed with people and vehicles, everyone on their way to work, and all thrilled to be doing that. Me, too.

It was quicker to walk than to get my squad car at the precinct, so I began the four block trek up Hudson, bucking into a strong north wind that roared down the avenue. A flasher on the corner opened his trench coat and got lifted into a holding pattern over the Western Union building. Just kidding.

I turned into North Moore, a quiet cobblestoned street that runs west toward the river. Up ahead on the right I saw two RMPs and a bus, which if you read NYPD detective novels you'll know is two radio cars and an ambulance. One car would be the sector car that responded, and the other the patrol sergeant's car.

As I approached the Dead End Bookstore I saw there was

no crime scene tape, and the police activity hadn't drawn much attention on the street; it hardly ever does in New York unless it's something interesting or culturally significant, like a mob hit. Even then, it's not worth more than a minute of your time. Also, this was not a lively street; mostly older apartment and loft buildings with lots of vacancy signs. Mr. Otis Parker had located his bookstore badly, but named it well.

I clipped my shield on my trench coat and approached a cop whose name tag said Conner. I asked him, "Is the M.E. here?"

"Yeah. Dr. Hines. I think he's waiting for you."

Hines was an okay guy. Looked like an undertaker and didn't try to play detective. I glanced at my cell phone clock. It was now 8:51 A.M. On the off chance that this was something more than an unfortunate example of Newton's law of gravity, I'd need to fill out a DD-5 and begin a homicide file. Otherwise, I was just stopping by.

I looked at the front of the bookstore which took up the whole ground floor of an old five-story brick building, sandwiched between two equally old buildings. The glass door had a Closed sign hanging on it, along with a notice of store hours – open every day except Sundays, 9 A.M. to 6 P.M. Basically, banking hours that insured the minimum number of customers. There were two display windows, one on each side of the door, and in the windows were…well, books. What this street really needed was a bar.

Anyway, in the left window were mostly classic crime novels – Chandler, Dorothy Sayers, Agatha Christie, Conan Doyle, and so forth. The window on the right featured contemporary bestselling authors like Brad Meltzer, James Patterson, David Baldacci, Nelson DeMille, and others who make more money writing about what I do than I make doing what I do.

I asked Officer Conner, "Who's the boss?"

He replied, "Sergeant Tripani." He added, "I'm his driver."

You want to get the lay of the land before you burst on the scene so I also asked, "Who else is in there?"

He replied, "The two paramedics, and the responding

officers, Rourke and Simmons, and an employee named Scott who discovered the body when he came to work."

"And Otis Parker," I reminded him.

"Yeah. He's still there."

"Did you see the body?"

"Yeah."

"What do you think?"

Officer Conner replied, "My boss thinks it's an accident."

"And you think?"

"Whatever he thinks."

"Right." I advised him, "If anyone comes by and identifies themselves as a customer or a friend, show them in."

"Will do."

I entered the bookstore which looked like it did the last time I was here – no customers, no staff, cobwebs on the cash register and, unfortunately no coffee bar. Lots of books.

The store had a two-story high ceiling, and there was a wrought-iron spiral staircase toward the rear that lead up to an open loft area where I could see Sergeant Tripani, whom I knew, standing near the railing. He saw me and said, "Up here."

I walked to the staircase that had a sign saying Private and began the corkscrew climb. On the way, I tried to recall the two or three times I'd interacted with Mr. Otis Parker here in his store. He was a bearded guy in his early 60's, but could have looked younger if he'd bought a bottle of Grecian Formula. He dressed well, and I remember thinking – the way cops do – that he must have had another source of income. Maybe this store was a front for something. Or maybe I read too many crime novels.

I also recalled that Mr. Parker was a bit churlish – though I'd heard him once talking enthusiastically to a customer about collectors' editions which he sold in the back of the store. I'd sized him up as a man who liked his books more than he liked the people who bought them. In short, a typical bookstore owner.

I reached the top of the stairs and stepped up into the open loft which was a large, wood paneled office. In the office was Officer Rourke, the two paramedics, Dr. Hines – wearing the same black suit he'd worn for twenty years – and Sergeant Tripani who greeted me, "Good morning, detective."

"Good morning, sergeant."

There's always a pecking order, and Sergeant Tripani, the patrol supervisor, was the head pecker until Detective Corey from the squad showed up. Of course Mr. Parker's death was not a suspected homicide – at least not by Sergeant Tripani – but here I was to check it out, and Sergeant Tripani was happy to turn it over to me. In fact, he said, "It's all yours, John."

"Ruiz just asked me to stop by." I pointed out, "I still have my coat on."

He didn't reply.

I snagged a pair of latex gloves from a paramedic, then I surveyed the scene of the crime or the accident: It was a nice office, and there was an oriental rug on the floor, strewn with lots of leather bound books around a big mahogany writing desk. The legs of the desk had collapsed under the weight of the falling bookcase behind it, as had the legs and arms of the desk chair and side chair. The tipsy bookcase in question had been uprighted and leaned back against the wall revealing Mr. Otis Parker whose sprawled, splayed, and flattened body lay half on the collapsed desk and half on the floor. The desk items – telephone, Rolodex, pencil holder and so forth – had miraculously remained on the desk as had the blotter which was soaking up some fresh blood on and around the deceased's head and face. Fortunately, Mr. Parker's brains remained where they belonged. I don't like to see brains.

Also on the desk was a framed black and white photo. The glass was cracked but I could see a dark haired woman, maybe in her late thirties. If this was his wife, it would be an old photo. But if it wasn't old, then Mr. Parker had a young wife. Or, maybe it was his daughter. In any case, the lady was not bad looking.

Otis Parker, I noted, was wearing good shoes, and good slacks, and a nice white shirt. His snappy sports jacket hung on a coat tree nearby. I couldn't tell if he was wearing a tie because he was face down. So, obviously, he'd been sitting at his desk when the bookcase behind him had somehow tipped away from the wall and silently fallen on him, his desk and his chair. He may have seen or felt a few books landing around him, but basically he never knew what hit him. Indeed, it looked like an accident. Except, why did a thousand-pound bookcase fall forward? Well, shit happens. Ironic, too, that Otis Parker was killed by the books he loved. Okay, the bookcase killed him. But that's not what the New York Post would say. They'd say, Killed by the books he loved.

I greeted Officer Rourke and inquired as to the whereabouts of his partner, Simmons.

Rourke replied, "He's in the stockroom downstairs with Scott Bixby, the clerk who found the body." He added, "Bixby is writing a statement."

"Good." Everyone seemed to be accounted for so I greeted Dr. Hines and we shook hands. I asked him, "Do you think he's dead?"

Dr. Hines replied to my silly question, "The responding officers" – he motioned to Officer Rourke – "pulled the bookcase off the victim with the assistance of the clerk and they found no signs of life at that time." He further briefed me, "The EMTs" – he indicated the two paramedics – "arrived three minutes later and also found no signs of life." He informed me, "I have pronounced him dead."

"Assuming Mr. Parker did not object, that makes it official."

Dr. Hines doesn't appreciate the dark humor that is a necessary part of tragic situations, and he made a dismissive sound.

I asked him, "Cause of death?"

"I don't know." He elaborated, "Crushed."

"Instantaneous?"

"Probably. No sign of struggle." He speculated, "A bigger man might have survived the impact."

I looked at Otis Parker and nodded. If he'd eaten right and lifted weights...

Dr. Hines continued, "I suspect his neck or vertebrae were broken, or he died of a massive cranial trauma. Or maybe cardiac trauma." He added, "I'll do the autopsy this afternoon and let you know."

"Okay." When someone dies alone, with no witnesses, even if it's an obvious accident, the taxpayers pay for an autopsy. Why? Because the M.E. has to list a cause of death before he signs the certificate, and "crushed" is not a medical term. Also, you do the autopsy because things are not always what they seem to be. That's why I'm here.

I asked him, "Time of death?"

"Recent."

I glanced back at the body and said, "His watch stopped at seven-thirty-two. That's your time of death."

He looked surprised, then walked to the body and peered at the watch on Mr. Parker's wrist. He informed me, "The watch is still running."

"Must be shockproof."

Dr. Hines looked at his own watch and announced, "I have another call." He said to me, "If you discover anything that doesn't look like an accident, let me know before I begin the autopsy."

"I always do, doc." I added, "Hold off on the meat wagon until you hear from me."

"I always do, detective." He added, "But let's not take too long. I want the body in the cooler."

"Right." The drill is this: the ambulance can't take a dead body away, so we needed the morgue van, affectionately known as the meat wagon. But, if I, Detective John Corey, suspected foul play, then we actually needed the Crime Scene Unit who would take charge of the stiff and the premises.

But maybe we didn't need the CSU people at all. I needed to make a determination here and I needed to do it in a relatively short amount of time. I mean, if you cry wolf and there is no wolf, you look like an idiot. Or worse, you look like a guy who has no regard for the budget. But if you say "accident," and it turns out later that it was something else, then you got some explaining to do. I could hear Ruiz now. "Do you know what the word detective means? It means detecting things, detective." And so on.

Dr. Hines had left during my mental exercises and so had the two paramedics. Remaining now in the loft office with me was Sergeant Tripani and the responding officer, Rourke. And Mr. Parker, who, if he could talk might say, "How the hell do I know what happened? I'm just sitting here minding my own business and the next thing I know I'm pressed meat."

I already knew what Sergeant Tripani thought, but in case he'd changed his mind, I asked him, "What do you think, Lou?"

He shrugged, looked at the body and said, "I think it is what it looks like." He explained more fully, "An accident waiting to happen."

I nodded, but it wasn't a real positive nod. I looked at the bookcase that had been leaned at a steep angle against the paneled wall to ensure that it didn't repeat its strange forward motion away from the wall. "Objects in motion," I said, quoting Sir Isaac Newton, "tend to stay in motion. Objects at rest tend to stay at rest."

Sergeant Tripani had no comment on that and asked me, "Do you need me here while you're deciding what this is?"

"No. But I need to speak to Officers Rourke and Simmons and the clerk who found the body."

"Okay."

I asked him, "Do we know next of kin? Any notifications made?"

He replied, "Wife. The clerk called her after he found the body and after he called us. He left a message on her cell phone and home phone saying there's been an accident. Then when Rourke and Simmons arrived, Rourke did the same thing, and he asked Mrs. Parker to call his cell and/or to come immediately to the store."

"Where does she live?"

"The clerk said East Twenty-third."

I asked, "Did you send a car around to her home?"

"We did. No reply to the buzzer and no doorman."

"Does she have a place of business?"

"She works at home, according to the clerk."

"Doing what?"

"I didn't ask."

I wondered why Mrs. Parker had not answered her home phone or even her cell phone and why she hadn't returned those obviously urgent calls or answered her door. Sleeping? Long shower? Doesn't pick up her messages? I'm not married, though I do date, and my experience with ladies and phone messages is mixed. I will say no more on that subject.

Sergeant Tripani started toward the spiral staircase, then turned and said to me, "If you find anything that doesn't look like an accident –"

"Then you buy me breakfast."

"You're on."

"Can your driver get me a ham and egg on a roll?"

"Sure. You want a Lipitor with that?"

"Coffee black. Get a receipt."

Lou Tripani made his way down the spiral staircase and I asked Officer Rourke, "What do you think?"

He replied, "With all due respect for other opinions, I'm just not buying that this bookcase tipped over by itself." He added, "Or that it tipped over at the exact time when this guy was at his desk – when the store was empty with no witnesses to see it and no one around who could've helped him."

I informed him, "Shit happens." I did concede, "Could be more than bad luck."

"Yeah."

"Did you interview the clerk?"

"Sure." He informed me, "He seemed not quite right."

"Meaning?"

"Something off there. Like he seemed more nervous than shocked."

I don't like to be prejudiced before I do an interview, but the clerk's reaction, close to the time he discovered the body, was important and interesting. By now Scott had calmed down and I might see another emotion. I said to Rourke, "Stick around. Put the Open sign on the door and if by some miracle there's a customer, let them in and give me a holler."

"Right."

"And if and when Mrs. Parker shows up, let me handle the notification."

He nodded.

"And let me know when my breakfast arrives."

Officer Rourke went down the staircase. Not every uniformed cop wants to be a detective, but most of them have good instincts and experience, and a lot of cases have been solved or advanced because of the cop who first came on the scene. Rourke seemed smart and he had a suspicious nature. I wouldn't want to be Mrs. Rourke.

I looked at the bookcase again. It looked like an antique, like most of the expensive junk in this office. It was one of those... let's say, ponderous Victorian pieces that decorators hate, but men like.

I looked back at the deceased and mentally pictured the bookcase falling on top of him while he worked at his desk. The force of the object would be increased by its falling speed, like that apple that hit Sir Isaac on the head. But if this was murder, it was a risky way to do it. I mean, there was no guarantee that the bookcase would kill him. Score one against homicide.

But if it was murder, how was it done? It would take two people – or maybe one strong guy – to topple this bookcase. And obviously, it would be someone he knew who was in his office at this hour. And the person or persons would say to him,

"You just sit there Otis while we stand behind you and admire your books." Then, "Okay, one, two, three – timber!"

Maybe. But without the one, two, three.

I noticed that the ten-foot high bookcase was taller than it was wide, and the depth of the bookcase at the bottom was the same at the top, making it inherently unstable. Score another point against the bookcase being a murder weapon; it was, as Tripani said, an accident waiting to happen.

I looked at the splatter pattern of the books, the way you look at blood splatter, and I noticed that most of the books were laying near the front of the desk, with only a few toward the rear, indicating to me that the shelves had held more books toward the top, adding to the instability. Mr. Parker, who seemed smart to me, was not too smart about the danger of top-heavy objects.

I looked at the wall behind the bookcase and at the solid back of the piece to see if there were any screws or bolts that had pulled loose from the wood paneling. But there was nothing securing this massive piece of furniture to the wall – though I did see some old holes in the bookcase, indicating that previous owners had screwed this monster to something solid.

Most accidents, I'm convinced, are God's way of getting rid of stupid people. Or if you believe in Darwinism, you wonder why there are any stupid people left in the world. Well, I guess they can reproduce before they remove themselves from the gene pool.

I also noticed that the oak floor had a slope to it, not uncommon in these creaky old buildings. The floor pitched a bit toward the desk and toward the edge of the loft. I've been in a thousand buildings like this, built in the last century, and the wooden rafters that hold up the floors are uneven, bowed, or warped, giving the floors some interesting tilts.

But what was it that caused this stationary object to suddenly topple away from the wall? Objects at rest, and all that. Well, if not human hands, then a few other things could have done it, the most obvious being the building settling. This can happen even after a hundred years. That's how these places collapse now and then. Also, you get some heavy truck rumbling on the street, and that can cause a vibration that would topple an unstable object. Same with construction equipment and guys working underground. Vibrations are also caused by heating and air conditioning units starting up. Even badly vented plumbing or steam pipes could cause a bang in the pipes which could possibly topple something that was on the verge of toppling. That's exactly what happened in my old East Side tenement building to my mother's prized Waterford crystal vase that her rich aunt gave her. Actually, I broke it. But that's another story.

I was about to rule this a dumbicide, but then something caught my eye. I noticed on the oak floor that there was a faint outline where the bookcase had sat for some years, caused obviously by the fact that no one had washed or waxed the floor under the bookcase since it had been there. And I also noticed that there were outlines of two small objects that had sat on the floor and protruded from the front of the bookcase. You don't have to be a detective to determine that these two outlines were made by furniture chocks or wedges – wood or rubber – that tipped the tall, heavy piece back against the wall for safety. So, Mr. Parker was not so stupid – though I would have also shot some big bolts into the wall.

Point was, the bookcase was probably not on the verge of toppling forward by itself if those wedges were there. And they were there. But where were they now? Not on the floor. I looked around the room, but I couldn't find them.

I went to the rail and saw Officer Rourke sitting behind the counter reading a borrowed book. I called down to him, "Hey, did you see any furniture wedges on the floor when you got up here?"

"Any…? What?"

I explained and he replied, "No. Simmons and I ran up the stairs with the clerk and we lifted the bookcase and leaned it back against the wall where you see it. I didn't notice any furniture wedges on the floor." He let me know, "Other than feeling for a pulse and heartbeat, we didn't touch anything." He added, "EMS arrived about three minutes later."

"Okay." So, this has become the Case of the Missing Furniture Wedges. Let's assume that no one who responded to the 911 call stole two furniture wedges. Let's assume instead that the killer took them. Right. This was no accident. Otis Parker was murdered.

I said to Rourke, "Mum's the word on furniture wedges."

I turned away from the rail and stared at Otis Parker and the bookcase. Someone was in this room with him, someone he probably knew, and that person – or persons – had previously removed the two wedges from under the bookcase. Right. Two people. One to tip the heavy bookcase back a bit and the other to slide the wedges out and pocket them. Now the bookcase is unstable, and maybe made more so if someone transferred some of the books from the lower shelves to the higher ones. Maybe this was done yesterday, or a few days ago. And unfortunately for Otis Parker he hadn't noticed this slight lean of his bookcase away from the wall or that the wedges were missing.

So, early this morning, Otis Parker arrives and sits at his desk. Someone accompanied him, or met him here, probably by appointment. That person – or persons – goes to his bookcase to admire his leather bound collection, or maybe get a book. And while they're at it, he, she, or they cause – in a manner not yet known – the bookcase to topple away from the wall, and the expected trajectory of the falling bookcase intersects with the seated victim. Splat! No contest.

I looked around the room. Now that I suspected murder, everything looked different. And everything and anything could be a clue. Stuff in the waste basket, the victim's date book, his cell phone, the contents of his pockets and the contents of his stomach, and on and on. Hundreds of things that needed to be looked at, bagged, tagged, and parceled out to the forensic labs, the evidence storage room, and so forth, while Otis Parker himself was sliced and diced by Dr. Hines. What a difference a few minutes can make.

I surveyed the office, noting its masculine, old clubby feel. There was a large leather couch to the right of the bookcase, a few book-themed prints on the walls, and a rolling bar near the spiral staircase. I pictured Mr. Parker in here, entertaining an author, or even a lady friend, after hours.

On the far side of the room was a long table stacked with books and I realized that all the books were the same. Beneath the table were five open boxes that had obviously held the books. I walked to the table and saw that the book title was *Death Knocks Once*, and the author was Jay K. Lawrence, an author whom I'd read once or twice. I also noticed a box of Sharpies on the table, and I deduced that Jay K. Lawrence was going to be here today or in the very near future to sign his new book for the store. Or, he'd already done so.

I snapped on my latex gloves and opened one of the books, but there was no autograph on the title page. Too bad. I would have liked to buy a signed copy. But maybe Jay Lawrence would be arriving shortly, and in anticipation of this I opened to the back flap where there was a bio and photo of Jay K. Lawrence. Most male crime writers look like they used their mug shot for the book jacket, but Mr. Lawrence was a bit of a pretty boy with well-coiffed hair, maybe a touch of makeup, and a little air brushing. Jay Lawrence's main character, I recalled, was a tough Los Angeles homicide detective named Rick Strong and I wondered where in Mr. Lawrence's pretty head this tough guy lived.

I read the short bio under the photo and learned that Jay Lawrence lived in L.A. There was no mention of a wife and family, so he probably lived with his mommy and ten cats, and he loved to cook.

The next thing I had to do was call Lieutenant Ruiz. But if I did that, this place would get real crowded. I needed to talk to Scott the clerk and to Mrs. Parker before this was announced as a homicide investigation, because when you say "homicide" the whole game changes and people get weird or they get a lawyer. So, for the record, I didn't see anything suspicious, and this is still an accident investigation.

I heard the door open below, and I looked down to see if it was Mrs. Parker, or maybe Jay Lawrence. But it was Officer Conner with my egg sandwich which made me just as happy. I asked Conner to leave the bag on the counter.

My tummy was growling, but I needed to get as much done here as I could before Ruiz called me to ask what the story was. I called down to Rourke, "There may be an author coming in to sign books. Jay Lawrence. Just say there's been an accident. I want to talk to him."

He nodded and I turned back to the office.

I'm not supposed to touch or move too many things, but I did eyeball everything while my mind was in overdrive.

There was a door to the left of the bookcase, and I opened it and walked into a small room filled with file cabinets. To the right was an open bathroom door and I stepped inside. The lights were on, and the toilet seat was down, indicating that a lady had used it last, or that Otis Parker had a bowel movement. I also noticed that the sink was wet, and there was a damp paper towel in the trash can, and that paper towel would have lots of someone's DNA on it. It's amazing how much evidence is left behind in a bathroom. I'd have the CSU people start here.

I also noticed a toilet plunger standing on the floor in the corner. In the back of my mind I'd been looking for something...I didn't know what it was, but I was sure I'd know it when I saw it. And this could be it.

Somebody – a Greek guy – once said, "Give me a lever long enough, and a place to stand, and I can move the world." Or a bookcase.

Still wearing my latex gloves, I picked up the plunger, and examined the wooden handle. One side of the rounded tip was slightly discolored and there was a small dent or crease about halfway up the handle, on the opposite side of the discoloration.

I carried the plunger into the office and stood on the left side of the bookcase. I now noticed two things – a small dimple in the wood paneling and a small crease in the back edge of the bookcase, both about chest high. These marks were barely noticeable in the hard, dark wood, but they would match perfectly with the marks on the lighter and softer wood of the plunger handle. So, it was obvious to me, as it would be obvious to the CSU team, the D.A., and hopefully a jury, that the killer, after excusing him or herself to use the bathroom, returned quietly to the office and quickly slipped the plunger handle between the bookcase and the wood paneled wall. Then that person pulled on the handle, using it as a lever to tilt the unbalanced bookcase an inch or so forward until gravity took over. For every action, said Sir Isaac Newton, there is an equal and opposite reaction.

I returned Part B of the murder weapon to the bathroom.

Now I knew two things: Otis Parker was murdered, and I also knew how he was murdered.

The only thing left to discover was who murdered him. And why. If you get the why, you usually get the who. As I've discovered in this business, when motive and opportunity coalesce, you get a crime. And when the crime is made to look like an accident, you look for someone close to the victim.

I needed a lot more time in this office, but the office wasn't going anywhere and someone close to the victim – Scott the clerk – was cooling his heels in the stockroom and he needed to be interviewed.

I removed my gloves and went down the stairs. I asked Rourke, "Where's the stockroom?"

He indicated a closed door in the rear of the long bookstore. My ham and egg on a roll was calling my name, but it's not professional to interview a witness with your mouth full, so I just grabbed the coffee and went through the door into the stockroom.

It was a fluorescent-lit space lined with metal shelving that held hundreds of books. The deep shelves looked stable enough, but after seeing what happened to poor Mr. Parker, the place made me nervous.

There was a long table in the center of the room, also stacked with books and paperwork, and at the table sat a uniformed officer – Simmons – and a young gent who must be Scott. I thought I may have seen him once or twice in the store.

There was a metal security door that lead out to the back, and I opened the door and looked out into a paved yard surrounded by a brick wall about ten feet high. There were no gates leading to the adjoining backyards, but the walls could be scaled if you had something to stand on – or if you had a cop hot on your tail. Been there, done that – on both sides of the law. There was also a fire escape leading up to the top floor.

I closed the door and turned to Scott. I identified myself, pointing to my shield – the way the lady cop did in Fargo. Funny scene.

Officer Simmons, who'd been babysitting the witness as per procedure, asked, "Do you need me?"

"No. But stick around."

He nodded, got up and left.

I smiled at Scott who did not return my smile. He still looked nervous and unhappy, maybe concerned about his future at the Dead End Bookstore.

My coffee was tepid, but I spotted a microwave sitting on a small table wedged between two bookcases, and I put my paper cup in the microwave. Twenty seconds? Maybe thirty.

There was a bulletin board above the table with a work schedule, and I saw that Scott was scheduled to come in at 8:30 A.M. today, and someone named Jennifer had a few afternoon hours scheduled this week. Not much of a staff, which meant not many people to interview. There was also a post-it note saying, "J. Lawrence – 10 A.M. Tuesday." Today.

I retrieved my coffee from the microwave and sat across from Scott. He was a soft-looking guy in his mid-twenties, short black hair, black T-shirt and pants, and a diamond stud in his left earlobe which I think means he's a Republican. Maybe I got that wrong. Anyway, I did remember him now – more for his almost surly attitude than his helpfulness.

I flipped through the dozen or so pages of Scott's handwritten statement and saw he hadn't yet finished with his account of who, what, where, and when. In this business, short statements are made by people with nothing to hide; long statements are a little suspicious and this was a long statement.

As I perused his tight, neat handwriting, I said to him, "This seems to be a very helpful account of what happened here."

"Thank you."

I asked him, "Do you think the police arrived promptly?"

He nodded.

"Good. And the EMS?"

"Yeah..."

"Good." And are you now thinking I'm here to evaluate the response to your 911 call? I'm not. I dropped his written statement on the table and asked him, "How you doin'?"

He seemed unsure about how he was doing, but then replied, "Not too good."

"Must have been a shock."

"Yeah."

"How long have you worked here?"

"Three years this June."

"Right after college?"

"Yeah."

"Good job?"

"It's okay." He volunteered, "Pays the bills while I'm writing my novel."

"Good luck." Every store clerk and waiter in this town wants you to know they're really a writer, an actor, a musician or an artist. Just in case you thought they were a clerk or a waiter. I asked Scott, "What time did you get here this morning?"

He replied, "As I told the other policeman, I got here about seven-thirty."

"Right. Why so early?"

"Early?"

"You're scheduled for eight-thirty."

"Yeah...Mr. Parker asked me to get here early."

"Why?"

"To stock shelves."

"The shelves look stocked. When's the last time you sold a book?"

"I had some paperwork to do."

"Yeah? Okay, take me through it, Scott. You got here, opened the door – front door?"

"Yeah." He reminded me, "It's all in my statement."

"Good. And what time was that?"

"I opened the door a little before seven-thirty."

"And it was locked?"

"Yeah."

"Did you know that Mr. Parker was here?"

"No. Well, not at first. I noticed the lights were on in his office up in the loft, so I called up to him."

"I assume he didn't answer."

"No...he...so, I thought maybe he was in here – in the stockroom – so I came in here to get to work."

"And when you saw he wasn't here, what did you think?"

"I...thought maybe he was in his bathroom upstairs."

"Or maybe he ducked out for a ham and egg on a roll."

"Uh...he...if he went out, he'd turn off the lights." Scott informed me, "He's strict about saving energy. Was."

"Right." Now he wasn't using any energy. I said, "Please continue."

"Well...as I said in my statement, after about twenty minutes I carried some books to the counter up front, and I called up to him again. He didn't answer, but then I noticed something...I couldn't see the top of his bookshelf."

In fact, I'd noticed that bookshelf myself on my two or three visits here. You could see the top two or three shelves from the front of the store. But not this morning.

Scott continued, "I didn't know what to make of that at first...and I kept staring up at the office...then I went half way up the stairs and called out again, then I went all the way up and..."

Rourke said Scott looked nervous, but now Scott looked appropriately distraught as he relived that moment of horror when he found his boss flattened by a half ton of mahogany and books.

I didn't say anything as he spoke, but I nodded sympathetically.

Scott continued, "I shouted his name, but... there was no answer and no movement..."

"How'd you know he was under there?"

"I could see...I wasn't all the way up the stairs, so I could see under the bookcase..."

"Right. I thought you said you went all the way up the stairs."

"I...I guess I didn't. But then I did. I tried to move the bookcase, but I couldn't. So I called 911 on my cell phone."

"Good thinking." I glanced at his statement and said, "Then you called Mrs. Parker."

"Yeah."

"How well do you know her?" He thought about that, then replied, "I've known her about three years. Since they started dating."

"So they're newlyweds."

"Yeah." He volunteered, "Married last June."

"Previous marriage for him?"

"Yeah. Before my time."

"How about her?"

"I think so."

Recalling the photo on the deceased's desk, I asked Scott, "How old is she?"

"I...guess about forty."

Booksellers always get the young chicks.

I asked Scott, "Was she a nice lady?"

"I...guess. I didn't see her much. She hardly ever comes to the store."

By now Scott was wondering about my line of questioning,

so I volunteered, "I like to get a feeling for the victim's next of kin before I break the news to them."

He seemed to buy that and nodded.

I asked Scott directly, "Did the Parkers have a happy marriage?"

He shrugged, then replied, "I don't know. I guess." He then asked me, "Why do you ask?"

"I just told you, Scott."

Recalling that Scott told Tripani that Mrs. Parker worked at home, I asked him, "What does she do for a living?"

"She's a decorator. Interior designer. Works at home."

"Do you have any idea where she is this morning?"

"No. Maybe on a job."

"Could she be out of town?"

"Could be." He informed me, "She's from L.A. She has clients there."

"Yeah?" L.A. Who else do I know from L.A.? Ah! Jay Lawrence. Small world. I asked him, "Did she decorate this place?"

He hesitated, then replied, "No. I mean, not the store."

"His office?"

"I don't know. Yeah. I guess."

"That's three different answers to the same question. Did she decorate his office? Yes or no?"

"Yes."

"How long ago was that?"

"Uh...I think about two years ago."

"When they were dating?"

"Yeah."

"So she put the bookcase up there?"

He didn't reply immediately, then said, "I guess."

Scott was a crappy witness. Typical of his generation, if I may be judgmental here. A little fuzzy in his thinking, his brain probably half baked on controlled substances, educated far beyond his ambitions, marking time while he wrote the Great

American Novel. But he did get to work early. So, he had some ambition.

As for Mrs. Parker, I was concerned that she'd take it very badly if she was the person who bought that bookcase and failed to secure it to the wall. I mean, that would be hard to live with. Especially if she took those furniture wedges for another job...well, too early to speculate on that.

I asked Scott, "Was her business successful?"

"I don't know."

"Is this bookstore successful?"

"I don't know. I'm just a clerk."

"Answer the question."

"I...I think he makes ends meet." He let me know, "I get paid."

"Does the rent get paid?"

"He owns the building."

"Yeah? Who's on the top three floors?"

"Nothing. Nobody. Loft space. Unrented."

"Why unrented?"

"Needs heat, a new fire escape, and the freight elevator doesn't work."

And there's no money to do the work. I was wondering what Mr. Parker was thinking when he bought this building, but then Scott, reading my mind, volunteered, "He inherited the building."

I nodded. And he should have sold it to a developer. But he wanted to own a bookstore. Otis Parker, bibliophile, was living his dream, which was actually a nightmare. And Mrs. Parker's decorating career could be a hobby job – or she did okay and had to support her husband's book habit.

Motive is tricky, and you can't ascribe a motive and then try to make it fit the crime. I mean, even if Otis Parker was worth more dead than alive – this building, or at least the property, was worth a couple mil, even in this neighborhood – that didn't mean that his young wife wanted him dead. She might just want him to sell the building and stop sinking time and money into this black hole – this Dead End Bookstore – and go get a real job. Or at least turn the place into a bar.

Maybe I was getting ahead of myself. For all I knew the Parkers were deeply in love and his death – caused by her bookcase – would cause the grief-stricken widow to enter a nunnery.

Meanwhile, I made a mental note to check for a mortgage on the building, plus Mr. Parker's life insurance policies, and if there was a prenup agreement. Money is motive. In fact, statistically, it is the main motive in most crimes.

I returned to the subject at hand and said, "So, after you called 911, you called her."

He nodded.

"From upstairs or downstairs?"

"Downstairs. I ran down to unlock the door."

"And you used your cell phone."

"Yeah."

"Her home number is in your cell phone?"

"Yeah…I have their home number to call if there's a problem here."

"Right. And you have her cell phone number in your cell phone in case…what?"

"In case I can't get Mr. Parker on his cell phone."

"Right." And when I look at everyone's phone records, I might see some interesting calls made and received.

The thing is, if a murder actually does appear to be an accident, there's not much digging beyond the cause and manner of death. But when a cop thinks it looks fishy, then the digging gets deeper, and sometimes something gets dug up that doesn't jibe with peoples' statements.

It had taken me less than fifteen minutes to determine that I was most probably investigating a homicide, so I was already into the digging stage while everyone else – except maybe Officer Rourke – thought we were talking about a bizarre and tragic accident.

Scott – baked brains aside – was getting the drift of some of my questions. In fact, he was looking a bit nervous again, so I asked him bluntly, "Do you think this was something more than an accident?"

He replied quickly and firmly, "No. But that other officer did."

I suggested, "He reads too many detective novels. Do you?"

"No. I don't read this stuff."

He seemed to have a low opinion of detective novels and that annoyed me. On that subject, I asked him, "Is Jay Lawrence scheduled to come in today?"

He nodded. "Yeah. To sign his new book. He's on a book tour. He's supposed to come in sometime around ten A.M."

I looked at my watch and said, "He's late."

"Yeah. Authors are usually late."

"Where's he staying in New York?"

"I don't know."

"Do you have his cell number?"

"Yeah...someplace."

"Have you met him?"

"Yeah. A few times."

"How well does he – did he – know Mr. Parker?"

"I guess they knew each other well. They see each other at publishing events."

"And Mrs. Parker?"

"Yeah...I guess he knew her, too."

"From L.A.?"

"Yeah...I think so."

Out of curiosity, or maybe for some other reason, I asked Scott, "Is Jay Lawrence a big bestseller?"

Scott replied with some professional authority, "He was. Not anymore." He added, "We can hardly give his books away."

"Yeah? But you bought five boxes of them for him to sign."

Scott sort of sneered and replied, "That's a courtesy. Like, a favor. Because they know each other and because he was coming to the store."

"Right." It could be awkward if there were only two books here for Jay Lawrence to sign.

Well, you learn something new every day on this job. Jay Lawrence, who I thought was a bestselling author, was not. Goes to show you. Maybe I make more money doing what I do than he makes writing about what I do.

I had more questions to ask Scott, but there was a knock on the door and Officer Simmons opened it and said, "There's a guy here – a writer named Jay Lawrence, to see the deceased." He added, "Rourke notified him that there had been an accident in the store, but not a fatality."

I looked at my watch. It was 10:26, for the record, and I said to Simmons, "Keep Scott company." I said to Scott, "Keep writing. You may have the beginning of a bestseller."

I went out into the bookstore where Mr. Jay K. Lawrence was sitting in a wingback chair, wearing a black cashmere topcoat, his legs crossed, looking impatient. He should be looking concerned – cops, accident and all that – and maybe he was, but he hid it with feigned impatience. On the other hand, authors are all ego, and if they're detained or inconvenienced by say, an earthquake or a terrorist attack, they take it personally and get annoyed.

I identified myself to Mr. Lawrence and again pointed to my shield. I have to get that stupid movie scene out of my head or people will think I'm an idiot. Actually, it's not a bad thing for a suspect to think that. Not that Jay Lawrence was a suspect. But he had some potential.

Before he could stand – if he intended to – I sat in the chair beside him.

He looked like his photo – coiffed and airbrushed – and I could see that under his open topcoat he wore a green suede sports jacket, a yellow silk shirt and a gold-colored tie. His tan trousers were pressed and creased and his brown loafers had tassels. I don't like tassels.

Anyway, I got to the point and informed him, "I'm sorry to have to say this, but Otis Parker is dead."

He seemed overly shocked – as though the police presence here gave him no clue that something bad had happened.

He composed himself, then asked me, "How did it happen?"

"How did what happen?"

"How did he die?"

"An accident. A bookcase fell on him."

Mr. Lawrence glanced up at the loft, then said softly, "Oh, my God."

"Right. The bookcase in his office. Not the stockroom."

Mr. Lawrence didn't reply, so I continued, "Scott found the body."

He nodded, then asked me, "Who's Scott?"

"The clerk." I said to him, "We left a message on Mrs. Parker's cell phone and home phone, but we haven't heard from her." I asked, "Would you know where she is?"

"No...I don't."

"Were you close to the Parkers?"

"Yes..."

"Then it might be good if you stayed here until she arrives."

"Oh...yes. That might be a good idea." He added, "I can't believe this..."

I had to keep in mind that this guy wrote about what I do, so I needed to be careful with my questions. I mean, I wouldn't want him to get the idea that I suspected foul play. On that subject, there was no crime scene tape outside, and no CSU team present, so he had no reason to believe that he'd walked into a homicide investigation. If he had nothing to do with that, it was a moot point. If he did have something to do with it, he was breathing easier than he'd been on his way here for his scheduled book signing. Also, I'd left my trench coat on, giving him, and anyone else, the impression that I wasn't staying long.

To make him feel a little better, I said to him, "I read two of your books."

He seemed to brighten a bit and asked, "Which ones?"

"The one about the writer who plotted to murder his literary agent."

He informed me, "That was a labor of love."

"Yeah? I guess that's what all writers dream about."

"Most. Some want to murder their editors."

I smiled, then continued, "And I read *Dead Marriage* about the young woman who kills her older husband. Great book."

He stayed silent a second, then said, "I didn't write a book with that theme."

"No? Oh...sorry. Sometimes I get the books confused."

He didn't reply, and in what may have been a Freudian slip, he asked me, "Does Mia know?"

"Who?"

"Mrs. Parker."

"Oh, right. Mia. No. We never say that in a phone message." I added, "We'll wait another fifteen minutes or so, then we have to get the body to the morgue." I suggested, "Why don't you call her?"

He hesitated, then said, "That's not a call I want to make."

"Right. I'll call. Do you have her number?"

"Not with me."

"Not in your cell phone?"

"Uh...I'm not sure." He asked, "Don't you have her number?"

"Not with me." I suggested, "Take a look in your directory. I really want to get her here. That's better than her having to go to the morgue."

"All right..." He retrieved his cell phone, scrolled through his directory and said, "Here's their home phone...Otis' cell phone...and yes, here's Mia's cell phone."

"Good." I put my hand out and he reluctantly gave me his cell phone. If I was brazen, I'd have checked his call log, but I could do that later, if necessary. I speed-dialed Mia Parker's cell phone and she answered, "Jay, where are you?"

Sitting next to a detective at the Dead End Bookstore. She had a nice voice. I said to her, "This is Detective Corey, Mrs. Parker."

"Who...?"

"Detective Corey. NYPD. I'm using Mr. Lawrence's cell phone."

Silence.

I continued, "I'm at the Dead End Bookstore, ma'am. I'm afraid there's been an accident."

"Accident?"

"Did you get the messages that were left on your cell phone?"

"No…what message?"

"About the accident."

"Where's Jay?"

Who's on first? I replied, "He's here with me."

"Why do you have his cell phone? Let me speak to him."

She didn't seem that interested in the accident, or who had the accident, so I handed the phone to Jay.

He said to her, "It's me."

Me, Mia. Mama mia, Mia. Otis is rigor mortis.

He informed her, again, "There's been an accident at the bookstore. Otis is…" He looked at me and I shook my head. He said, "Badly hurt."

She said something, then he asked her, "Where are you? Can you get here quickly?" He listened, nodded to me, then said to her, "I'll be here."

He hung up and said to me, "She's in her apartment. She'll be here in about ten or fifteen minutes."

Thinking out loud, I said, "I wonder why we couldn't reach her earlier?"

He explained, "She said she was writing a proposal. She has an office in the apartment, and she blots out the world when she's working on a project."

"Yeah? Do you do that?"

"I do."

"I need a room like that." Actually, I drink Scotch whiskey to blot out the world and any room will do. I said to him, "She took your call."

"She just finished."

"I see." Again, thinking out loud, I said, "Most accident victims who are badly hurt wind up in the hospital. Not the bookstore."

He didn't reply.

"And yet, Mrs. Parker saw nothing odd about coming to the bookstore."

We made eye contact, and he said to me, "I think she knows it's more than an accident, detective. I think, like most people who get a call like that, she's very distraught and partly in denial." He asked me, "You follow?"

"I do. Thank you."

Two things here. First, I didn't like Jay Lawrence and he didn't like me. Loathing at first sight. And to think he glamorized the police in his novels. Rick Strong, LAPD. This was really a disappointment. But maybe he did like cops. It was *me* he didn't like. I have that effect on pompous asses.

Which brought me to my second point. He was a smooth customer and he had a quick reply to my somewhat leading questions. I've seen lots of guys like this – and they're mostly guys – egotistical, self-absorbed, usually charming, and great liars, i.e., sociopaths. Not to mention narcissistic. Also, as a fiction writer, he bullshitted for a living.

But maybe I was judging Mr. Jay K. Lawrence too quickly and too harshly. And it didn't matter what I thought of him. I'd never see him again – unless I locked him up for murder.

For sure, I wouldn't read any more of his books. Well, maybe I'd take them out of the library to screw him out of the royalty.

I said to Jay Lawrence, "I noticed a pile of your books in Mr. Parker's office." I asked him, "Would you like to sign them while you're waiting?"

He didn't reply, perhaps actually considering this. I mean, a signed book is a sold book. And he needed the sales. Right? I assured him, "You don't have to go upstairs. Unless you want to. I can have Scott bring the books down here."

He replied, a bit coolly, "I don't think it would be appropriate for me to sign books at this time, detective."

"Maybe you're right. But…I hate to ask, but could you personalize one for me?" And leave your DNA and fingerprints on the book?

"Maybe later."

"Okay." I remained seated beside him and asked, "Where are you staying?"

"The Carlyle."

"Nice hotel."

"My publisher pays for it."

"When did you get to New York?"

"Last night."

"How long are you staying?"

"I leave tonight for Atlanta."

"Do you think you can make it back for the funeral?"

He thought about that, then said, "I'll have to check with my publicist." He explained, "These tours are scheduled months in advance. I know it sounds callous, but…"

"I understand. A busy life is scheduled – a sudden death is not." I offered, "You can use that line in your next book."

He ignored my offer and said, "If you'll excuse me, I have some phone calls to make." He explained, "I need to let my publicist know I can't make my other bookstore appointments today, or my media interviews."

"Right." I stood and said, "When Mrs. Parker arrives, I'll let you break the news to her."

He didn't reply.

Well, Mr. Lawrence was sitting in the bookstore with Officer Rourke keeping him company, Scott was in the stockroom with Officer Simmons, writing his bestseller, and Otis Parker was alone in his office, reaching room temperature by now. Time for breakfast.

I retrieved the brown paper bag from the counter and went outside. It was still cold and windy and there weren't many people on North Moore Street. I noticed now that in the store window was a copy of *Death Knocks Once* by Jay K. Lawrence, and a small sign under the book announced, Autographed. Well, not yet.

I got in the passenger seat of Rourke's patrol car, unwrapped my ham and egg sandwich and took a bite. Room temperature.

I called Lieutenant Ruiz before he could call me. He answered, and I said, "I'm still at the Dead End Bookstore."

"What's the story?"

"Well…" I'm about to lie to you. No. Not a good idea. Ruiz, like me, is more interested in results and arrests than silly technicalities, so I said to him, "I have some reason to believe this was a homicide."

"Yeah?"

"But I don't want to announce that at this time."

No reply.

I took another bite and said, "I think the bookcase was tipped over by a person or persons unknown."

"Are you eating?"

"No. I'm chewing on my tie."

He ignored that and asked, "You need assistance?"

"No. I need about thirty or forty minutes."

"Where's the body?"

"Where it was found."

"Suspects?"

"Looks like an inside job."

"I heard from Sergeant Tripani. He says it looks like an accident."

"No. It looks like he owes me breakfast."

Rule number one between cops who are making shit up is Get Your Stories Straight, and Lieutenant Ruiz said to me, "So you're saying you believe it was an accident."

I replied, "At this time, I believe it was an accident."

"Call me in half an hour."

I hung up and got out of the car. I went back into the store and saw that Mr. Lawrence was on his cell phone at the back of the store, out of earshot of Rourke. I didn't know who he was calling, but I'd know when I subpoenaed his phone records.

I stood near the door and looked into the street as a taxi pulled up and discharged a lady who, based on the photo I saw, looked like Mrs. Parker.

She glanced at the police car and strode quickly toward the door. The expression on her face showed some concern, but not exactly sick with worry over her husband's accident. I mean, I've seen it all by now, and Mrs. Parker looked to me like someone who needed to get through some slightly unpleasant business.

She opened the door, glanced at me, then at Officer Rourke, then spotted Jay Lawrence in the rear of the store as he spotted her. They hurried toward one another and met at the Bargain Book table.

It was an awkward moment as they vacillated between embracing, grasping each other's hands, or high-fiving.

He took both her hands in his, and I heard him say, "Mia, I am so sorry...Otis is..."

Dead. Come on, Jay. I've got thirty minutes before I have to announce a suspected homicide.

She got the drift and they embraced. He looked over her shoulder at me and caught me looking at my watch while I took another bite of my sandwich. I really felt like a turd.

I mean, what if neither of them had anything to do with Otis Parker's murder? I knew it had to be an inside job, but it could have been Scott or Otis' ex-wife, or Jennifer the part-time clerk, or other persons not yet known who had off-hour access to the store and to Otis Parker. Right?

On the subject of motive, there are, generally speaking, six major motives for murder. Ready? They are: profit, revenge, jealousy, concealment of a crime, avoidance of humiliation or disgrace, and homicidal mania. There are variations, of course, and combinations, but if you focus on those, and try to match them to a suspect – even to an unlikely suspect – then you can conduct an intelligent investigation.

Sometimes, of course, you don't need to go that route. Sometimes you have lots of forensic evidence – like someone's fingerprints on the murder weapon. But that's not my job. I'm a detective and I deal with the human condition first, then the clues I can see with my own eyes, and the statements people make, or don't make. If I'm smart and lucky, I can wrap it up before the CSU people and the Medical Examiner are done.

While I was thinking about all this, I was observing Mr. Lawrence and Mrs. Parker. They were sitting side by side in the reading chairs now, he with his hand on her shoulder, she dabbing her eyes with his handkerchief.

For the record, she was easy to look at. A little younger than Scott thought – maybe late thirties, long raven black hair, Morticia makeup, and I'm sure a good figure under her black lambskin coat, which was open now revealing a dark gray knit dress that looked expensive. She also wore long, black boots, a cashmere scarf, and gloves which she'd taken off. A well-dressed lady, complete with a gold watch, wedding band, and a nice rock.

I tried to picture her plodding away at her paperwork in her apartment in this outfit. Well, maybe she had an appointment later.

I had let a respectable amount of time elapse, so I ditched my sandwich on the counter, then I walked over to the grieving widow and her friend. I introduced myself to her without pointing to my shield.

She looked up at me but did not respond.

I said, "I'm very sorry about your husband."

She nodded.

I spoke to her, in a soft and gentle voice, "Sometimes the bereaved wants to see the body. Sometimes it helps bring closure. Sometimes it's too painful." And sometimes the bereaved totally loses it and confesses on the spot. I assured her, "It's your choice."

She didn't think too long before replying, "I don't want to… see him."

"I understand." I said to her, "I'd like you like to stay here until the body is removed." I explained, "You may have to sign paperwork."

She replied in a weak voice, "I want to go home."

"All right. I'll call for a police car to take you home." Later.

Jay Lawrence, without consulting the bereaved widow, said, "I will accompany her."

I really wanted to question Mia Parker, but I couldn't keep her here. I also wanted to question Jay Lawrence, but he was latched onto the grieving widow, and you want to question suspects separately, so that you can pick up inconsistencies in their stories. Also, the courts have ruled that a cop is allowed to lie to a suspect in order to draw out some information. Like, "Okay, Mr. Lawrence, you say A, but Mrs. Parker and Scott told me B. Who's lying, Mr. Lawrence?" Actually, it would be me who was lying. But you can't play one against the other if both suspects are sitting together. I did, however, have some info from Scott, though not a lot.

Also, of course, this was not a homicide investigation and therefore there were no suspects, and therefore I couldn't pull these two off separately for questioning.

I mean, I knew beyond a doubt that Otis Parker had been murdered, and I was fairly sure there were two people involved, and it was an inside job, and it was premeditated. And the two people sitting in front of me filled the bill as potential suspects. But I had to tread lightly and treat them as a bereaved widow and a very upset friend, who was also a crime writer with some savvy. Basically, I was at a dead end at the Dead End Bookstore, and the clock was ticking.

So maybe I should just say it. "Sorry to inform you, but I believe Otis Parker was murdered, and I'd like you both to come to the precinct with me to see if you can help the police with this investigation."

I was about to do that, but I had some time to kill before I had to call Ruiz, so I pulled up a chair, put on my sympathetic face and asked Mrs. Parker, "Can I get you some water? Coffee?"

"No, thank you."

I offered, "I can see if there's something stronger in Mr. Parker's office."

She shook her head.

I said, conversationally, "I understand you decorated his office. It's very nice."

Our eyes met, and she hesitated, then said to me, "I *told* him...I told him to have it fastened to the wall...and he said he'd done that."

"You mean the bookcase?"

She nodded.

"Well, unfortunately he didn't."

"Oh..." She sobbed, "Oh, if only he'd listened to me."

Right. If men listened to their wives, they'd live longer and better lives. But, married men, I think, have a death wish. That's why they die before their wives. They want to. Okay, I'm getting off the subject.

I said to her, "Please don't blame yourself." Let me do that.

She put her hands over her face, sobbed again, and said, "I should have checked when I was in his office...but I always believed what Otis said to me."

Making you the first wife in the history of the world to do that. Sorry, I digress again.

Actually, I could imagine that she did like her husband. Maybe he was a father figure. Despite her Morticia look, she seemed pleasant and she had a sweet voice. Maybe I was on the wrong track. But...my instincts said otherwise.

Under the category of asking questions that you already know the answer to, I asked her, "Do you and Mr. Lawrence know each other from L.A.?"

It was Mr. Lawrence who replied, "Yes, we do. But I don't see what difference that makes."

Of course you do, Jay. This is the stuff you write about. Anyway, I winged a response and said, "I need to say in my accident report what your relationship is to the widow."

He didn't say, "Bullshit!" but his face did. Good. Sweat, you pompous ass.

Mia Parker, who seemed clueless from Los Angeles, said to me, "Jay and I have been friends for years. We saw each other socially with our former spouses."

I nodded, then said to her, "Scott tells me you were married last June."

At the mention of her June wedding, her eyes welled with tears, she nodded and covered her face again.

I let a few seconds pass, then I said, "I've spoken to Scott and I think I have enough details for my accident report, but if not I'll speak to him again, and bother you as little as possible."

She nodded and blew here nose into her friend's handkerchief.

Her friend understood that I had a statement from the clerk and that I was, perhaps, a tiny bit suspicious.

There wasn't much more I could do or say to these two at this time, but I had at least hinted to Jay Lawrence that he probably wasn't getting on that flight to Atlanta. I could see he was a bit concerned. I mean, if he'd plotted this – like one of his novels – he had fully expected it to be ruled an accident, and he'd hoped that the body would be gone when he got here half an hour late, and the sign on the door would say Closed. Or, if the cops were still here, they'd say, "Sorry, there's been an accident. The store is closed."

Right. But Mr. Jay K. Lawrence did not imagine a Detective John Corey, called on the scene because a patrolman was suspicious. The ironic thing was that Jay Lawrence's cop character, Rick Strong, was smarter than his creator. But neither Jay Lawrence nor Rick Strong were as smart as John Corey. I was, however, out of bright ideas.

I stood and said to Mrs. Parker, "To let you know, the city requires an autopsy in cases...like this. So, it may be two days before the body is released." I added, "You should make plans accordingly." I also added, "In the unlikely event that the Medical Examiner feels that he needs to...well, do further tests, then someone will notify you."

Mr. Lawrence stood and asked, "What do you mean by that?"

I looked him in the eye and replied, "You understand what I mean."

He didn't reply, but clearly he was getting a bit jumpy.

I was now going to call Ruiz and advise him that I was officially making this a homicide investigation. I had two suspects, but no evidence to hold them. In fact, not enough evidence to even advise them that they were persons of interest – though I'd ask them to meet me later at the station house, to help in the investigation.

But just when you think you've played your last card, you remember the card up your sleeve. The Joker.

I said, "The Medical Examiner should be arriving shortly. Please remain here until then." I assured them, "I'll call for a police car to take you home after the M.E. arrives."

Mr. Lawrence reminded me, "You said we could leave now. And we can find our own transportation."

"I changed my mind. Remain on the premises until the M.E. arrives."

"Why?" asked Mr. Lawrence.

I replied a bit curtly, "Because, Mr. Lawrence, the Medical Examiner may want a positive identification. Or he may need some information as to date of birth, place of residence, and so forth." I said to him, "Actually, *you* may leave. Mrs. Parker cannot."

He didn't reply, but sat again and took her hand. A real gentleman. Or maybe he didn't want her alone with me.

I went to Officer Rourke who was still sitting behind the counter, apparently engrossed in his book, but undoubtedly listening to every word. I made eye contact with him and said, "Let me know when the M.E. arrives and send him up." Wink.

He nodded, and I could see his brain in high gear wondering what the brilliant detective was up to.

I climbed the spiral staircase into Otis Parker's office and looked at his body. Right. He could have survived. Then he could have told me what happened.

But I already knew what happened. I needed Otis Parker to tell me who did it.

Cops, as I said, are allowed to lie. Half the confessions you get are a result of lying to a suspect.

I let a few more seconds pass, then I shouted, "Get an ambulance!" I ran to the rail and shouted to Rourke, "He's alive! He's moving! Get an ambulance!"

Rourke, thank God, didn't shout back, "He's dead as a doornail!" Instead, he got on his hand radio and pretended – I hope – to call for an ambulance.

I glanced at Mia Parker and Jay Lawrence. They didn't seem overjoyed at this news. I shouted to them, "We'll have an ambulance here in three or four minutes!" Great news. Right? Try to contain your feelings of hope and joy. I resisted shouting, "It's a miracle!" I did say, "Mrs. Parker can ride in the ambulance."

They looked...well, stunned. And that wasn't play acting. Also, I didn't see Mrs. Parker running up the stairs to smother her awakening husband with kisses. If she did come upstairs, it might be to smack him in the head with a book. Well...that's just me being cynical and suspicious again.

I disappeared from the rail and let a minute pass, then I walked slowly and deliberately down the spiral staircase and headed toward two worried-looking people. The expression on my face told them they were in deep doo-doo. Actually, if this didn't work, I *was* in deep, deep doo-doo.

I stopped in front of them and said, "He's speaking."

No response.

I looked them both in the eye and said, "He spoke to me."

Very smart people would have shouted in unison, "Bullshit!" But they were so unstrung – actually shaking – that all they could do was stare at me. Also, I'm a good liar. Ask the last guy I tricked into a confession.

I let a few seconds pass, then said, "I saw that someone had removed the furniture wedges from under the bookcase. I also saw that someone had used the toilet plunger to lever the bookcase away from the wall." I paused for dramatic effect, then said, "And now I know who that was." Actually, I didn't. But they did.

I would have bet money that it would be Mia Parker who

cracked – but it was Jay Lawrence. He said, "Then you know I had nothing to do with it. I was in my hotel all morning and I can prove it."

When someone says that, you assume they're telling the truth, i.e. they've established their alibi for the time of death. Or they think they have. Meanwhile, Mia Parker was staring at her friend, who continued, "I had room service at six-thirty, then I had it cleared at seven-thirty."

"All that proves is that you had breakfast." And I didn't.

I looked at Mia Parker and said to her, "Mrs. Parker, based on the statement your husband just made, I am charging you with attempted murder."

I was about to go into my Right-to-Remain-Silent spiel, but she fainted. Just like that. Crumbled to the floor. Ideally, a suspect should be awake when you read them Miranda, so I turned my attention to Jay Lawrence.

He was just standing there, looking not too well himself. Hello? Jay? Your friend just fainted.

I would have come to Mrs. Parker's assistance, but Rourke was already coming toward us.

I looked at Jay Lawrence and I said, "I have reason to believe that you were an accomplice. That it was you who assisted Mrs. Parker in removing the two furniture wedges from under the bookcase. Probably last night after you arrived from L.A." I informed him, "So your alibi for this morning, even if it proves to be true, does not exclude you as an accessory to attempted murder." He didn't faint, but he did go pale.

Rourke had run out to his squad car and returned with a first aid kit. He was now reviving Mrs. Parker with an ammonium nitrate capsule. This was good because now I only had to give the Miranda warning once. A small point, I know, but...anyway, I asked Jay Lawrence, "Do you have anything to say?"

He did. He said, "You're out of your mind." He added, "I had nothing to do with this."

"That's for a jury to decide."

Rourke had gotten Mrs. Parker into the wingback chair and

she looked awake enough, so I began, "You both have the right to remain silent –"

Jay Lawrence chose not to remain silent and interrupted, "I can prove conclusively that I came directly to the hotel from the airport and that I was in the Carlyle all evening, and until ten this morning."

That wasn't what I wanted to hear, but I needed to hear more, so I asked, "How can you prove that?"

He hesitated, then said, "I was with a woman. All night."

Apparently he did better than I did last night. I watched *Bonanza*.

He continued, "I will give you her name and cell phone number and you can speak to her, and she will confirm that."

Okay...so we have the nearly airtight in-bed-with-a-lady alibi. But sometimes this is not so airtight. Still, this was a problem.

I was about to ask him for the lady's name and number, but Mrs. Parker, fully awake now, shouted, "You were *where*?" She stood and shouted again, "You said you had interviews to do. You bastard!"

I've been here, and so has Rourke apparently, because we both stepped between Mrs. Parker and Mr. Lawrence to head off a physical assault.

Mrs. Parker was releasing a string of obscenities and expletives which Jay Lawrence took well, knowing he deserved them. And knowing, too, that his lover's wrath was a lot better than being charged with accessory to attempted murder – which was actually a successful attempt. But that was my secret.

Mia Parker was still screaming and I had the thought that I should have left her on the floor. But my main concern was that I'd gotten this wrong. About Jay Lawrence, I mean. But not about Mia Parker, who confirmed my charge of attempted murder by shouting, "I did this for *you*, you cheating bastard! So we could be together! You *knew* what I was going to –"

Jay Lawrence jumped right in there and shouted back, "I did *not* know what you –"

"You did!"

"Did not!"

And so forth. Rourke was nodding, letting me know he was a witness to this while at the same time he kept repositioning himself so that the wronged lady could not get at her two-timing lover. I kind of hoped that she got around Rourke and dug her nails into Jay's pretty face. I certainly wasn't going to get between them. Hell hath no fury and all that.

Well, I was sure that the Dead End Bookstore hadn't seen so much excitement since the upstairs toilet backed up.

Meanwhile, neither of the now ex-lovers seemed to notice that over five minutes had passed and there was no ambulance pulling up to rush Otis Parker to the hospital.

By now, I should have had Rourke slap the cuffs on Mia Parker, but, well…I was enjoying this. She was really pissed and she shouted to her fellow Angelino, "We could have bought that house in Malibu…we could have been together again…"

Where's Malibu? California? Why did she want to go back there? No one wants to leave New York. This annoyed me.

She broke down again, sobbing and wailing, then collapsed in the chair. She was babbling now. "I hate it here…I hate this store…I hate him…I hate the cold…I want to go home…"

Well, sorry, lady, but you're going to be a guest of the State of New York for awhile.

As much as I wanted to cuff Jay Lawrence, I wasn't certain what his role, if any, was in this murder. Well, he *knew* about it, according to Mia Parker. But did he actually *conspire* in the murder? And assuming she had help, who helped her? Not Jay who was in the sack with his alibi witness.

I motioned for him to follow me and he did so without protest. I led him to the rear of the store, away from his pissed off girlfriend, and I said to him, "You get one chance to assist in this investigation. After that, you get charged with conspiracy to commit murder, and/or as an accessory. Understand?"

He didn't respond verbally, and I didn't even get a nod. Instead, he just stood there, with a blank expression on his face.

I glanced at my watch to indicate the clock was ticking. Then, I said, "Okay, you're under arrest as an accessory –"

"Wait! I...okay, I knew she wanted him...out of the way... and she asked me...like, how would you do this in a novel... but I didn't think she was serious. So, I just made a joke of it."

I informed him, "I think Otis Parker will live, and he can tell us what happened up there and who was in the room at that time."

"Good. Then you'll know that I'm telling the truth."

And he probably was. Mia Parker committed the actual murder herself. But, with all due respect to her apparent intelligence, she didn't think of that bookcase and that plunger and those furniture wedges by herself. That was Jay Lawrence. And that's what she'd say, and he would deny it. She said, he said. Not good in court.

I said to him, "She seemed to think she was going to be with you in..." Where was that place? "Malibu."

He replied, "She's...let's say, mistaken. Actually, delusional. I made no such promise." He made sure I understood, "It was just an affair. A long distance affair."

He was desperately trying to save his ass, and not doing a bad job of it. He was clever, but I am John Corey. Arrogant? No. Just a fact.

I said to him in a tone suggesting he was my cooperating witness, "That bookcase has been sitting there for over two years. Do you think she put it there – right behind his desk – knowing what she was going to do with it?"

He hesitated, then replied, "I don't know. How would I know that?"

He was smart, and he didn't want to admit to any pre-knowledge of premeditated murder – not even as speculation. But he *was* willing to throw his girlfriend under the bus if it kept him out of jail. He was walking the old tightrope without a balancing bar.

By now, Jay Lawrence was thinking about exercising his right to remain silent and his right to an attorney. So I had to be careful I didn't push him too far. On the other hand, time was ticking by and I needed to go in for the kill. I said, "Look, Jay – can I call you Jay? Look, *someone* removed those wedges from under the bookcase, and it wasn't little Mia all by herself. Hell, I don't think I could do that without help. Are you telling me there was someone *else* involved?"

He seemed to think about that, then said, "I haven't been to New York in several months. And I can account for every minute of my time since my plane landed at five-thirty-six last night." He informed me, "I have a taxi receipt, a check-in time at the Carlyle, dinner in the hotel…with my lady friend, the hotel bar –"

"All right, I get it." I didn't want to hear about the adult movie he'd rented from his room. Basically, Jay Lawrence had covered his ass and he had the receipts to prove it. And he'd done this because he knew, in advance, what was going to happen early this morning. But maybe he didn't know about an accomplice.

I asked him for the name and phone number of his lady friend which he gave me. It was, in fact, his publicist in New York; the lady who booked his publicity tour and who could also provide an alibi for his free evening. *Bang publicist*: 7 P.M.-10 A.M. Dinner and breakfast in hotel.

Jay Lawrence was, as Mia Parker said, a two-timing bastard. And also a conniving coward who let his lover do the dirty work while he was establishing an alibi for the crime. He totally bullshited her. And if it had gone right, he was onboard for the payoff, which I guess was his share of all the worldly possessions of the deceased Otis Parker – including his wife. The wife, I'm sure, thought it was all about love and being together. In Malibu. Wherever that was. And none of this would have happened, I'm sure, if Jay Lawrence had sold more books.

Meanwhile, there was still the question of the furniture wedges. Who helped her with that? Jay didn't seem to know, or he wasn't saying. But Mia knew.

I said to him, "Stay right here."

I walked to where Mia Parker was sitting in the wingback

chair, looking a bit more composed, and without any preamble I asked her, "Who helped you remove the furniture wedges?"

She replied, "Jay."

I was fairly certain that was not true and not possible.

"When?"

"Last...early this morning."

"Are you telling me the truth?"

"Why would I lie?"

Well, because Jay was screwing a babe all night, and you are very pissed off.

Mrs. Parker needed less sympathy and understanding and more shock treatment, so I said to Rourke, "Cuff her." But softie that I am, I instructed front cuffs instead of back – so she could dab her eyes and blow her nose.

Rourke told her to stand, gave her a quick but thorough pat down, then cuffed her wrists in the front.

I said to Rourke, "Call for a car." I added, "I'll be riding with her to the precinct."

Mia Parker, now cuffed, under arrest, and about to be taken to the station house for booking, was undergoing a transformation. Early this morning, she was a married lady with a boyfriend and an inconvenient husband. Now she had no boyfriend and no husband. And no future. I've seen this too many times, and if I said it didn't get to me, I'd be lying.

The person who I felt most sorry for, of course, was Otis Parker. He ran a crappy bookstore and he didn't give service with a smile, but he didn't deserve to die.

I asked Mrs. Parker, "If he dies, is all this yours?"

She looked around, then replied, "I hate this store."

"Right. Answer the question."

She nodded, then informed me, "We had a prenup...I didn't get much in a divorce...but..."

"You got a lot under his will." I asked, "Life insurance?"

She nodded again, then, continued, "I also got the building and the...business." She laughed and said, "The stupid business...he owes the publishers a fortune. The business is worth nothing."

"Don't forget the fixtures and the good will."

She laughed again. "Good will? His customers *hate* him. *I* hate him."

"Right."

She continued, "This store was draining us dry...he was going to mortgage the building...I had to do something..."

"Of course." I've heard every justification possible for spousal murder, and most of them are amazingly trivial. Like, "My wife thought cooking and fucking were two cities in China." Or, "My husband watched sports all weekend, drank beer and farted." Sometimes I think being a cop is less dangerous than being married.

Anyway, Mrs. Parker forgot to mention that she'd planned this long before the marriage, or that she had a boyfriend. But I never nitpick a confession.

I inquired, "Do you have a buyer for the building?"

She nodded.

I guessed, "Two million?"

"Two and a half."

Not bad. Good motive.

She also let me know, "His stupid collector books are worth about fifty thousand." She added, "He buys them, but can't seem to sell them."

"Has he tried the internet?"

"That's where he *buys* them." She confided to me, "He's an idiot."

"Put that in your statement," I suggested.

She seemed to notice that she was cuffed, and I guess it hit her all at once that the morning had not gone well, and she knew why. She let me know, "All men are idiots. And liars."

"What's your point?"

She also let me know, "Those books in his office are worth about ten thousand."

"Really?" Poetic justice?

As I said, I'm not married, but I have considered it, so to learn something about that I asked her, "Why'd you marry him?"

She didn't think the question was out of line, or too personal, and she replied, "I was divorced...lonely..."

"Broke?"

She nodded and said, "I met him at a party in LA...he said he was well off...he painted a rosy picture of life in New York..." She thought a moment, then said, "Men are deceitful."

"Right. And when did you think about whacking him?"

She totally ignored my question and went off into space awhile. Then she looked at Jay in the back of the store and asked me, "Why isn't *he* under arrest?"

I don't normally answer questions like that, but I replied, "He has an alibi." I reminded her, "The lady he spent the night with." I shared with her, "His publicist, Samantha –"

"That whore!"

The plot thickens. But that might be irrelevant. More to the point, Mrs. Parker was getting worked up again and I said to her, "If you can convince me – with facts – that he conspired with you in this attempt on your husband's life, then I'll arrest him."

She replied, "We planned this together for over two years. And I can prove it." She added, "It was *his* idea." She let me know, "He's nearly broke."

"Right." I confessed, "I didn't like his last book." I already knew the answer to my next question, but I asked for the record, "Why'd you wait so long?"

"Because," she replied with some impatience, "it took Otis two years to marry me."

"Right." Guys just can't commit. Meanwhile, that bookcase is just waiting patiently to fall over. This was the most premeditation I'd ever seen. Cold, calculating and creepy. I mean, when Otis Parker said, "I do," his blushing bride was saying, "You're done."

The good news is that property values have gone up in the last two or three years. I don't know about collectible books, though.

I tried to reconstruct the crime, to make sure I was getting it right. D-Day for Otis Parker was the day after Jay Lawrence came to town to promote his new book. Today. Jay was supposed to help Mia last night to set up the bookcase for a tumble, then maybe a drink and a little boom-boom at the Carlyle, and some pillow talk about being together, and psyching each other up for the actual murder. And this morning, Jay would be here to comfort the widow.

But Jay, at some point, as the big day approached, got cold feet. All his Rick Strong books ended with the bad guy in jail, and Jay didn't want that ending for himself. So he made a date with his publicist and ditched Mia, leaving Mia to do it all by herself. She had the balls. He had the shakes.

One of the things that bothered me was that Otis Parker was in his office early on the morning that he was going to be whacked. That wasn't coincidence. Not if this was all planned in advance.

I went back to my original thought that Otis Parker had an appointment. And who was that appointment with? And why didn't Scott know about it?

Maybe he did.

I said to Rourke, "I'll be in the stockroom. Keep an eye on these two. Let me know when the car gets here."

That made Mia think of something and she asked me, "Where's the ambulance?"

"I don't know. Stuck in traffic."

She stared at me and shouted, "You bastard! You lied to me!"

"You lied to me first."

"You...you..."

I was glad she was cuffed. Rourke put his hands on her shoulders and pushed her into the chair.

Meanwhile, Jay heard some of this, or figured it out and he walked quickly toward me and asked, "Why isn't the ambulance here?"

I confessed, "Otis Parker doesn't need an ambulance."

Jay looked as stunned as when I had pronounced Otis alive.

People don't like to be tricked, and Mia let loose again. Sweet voice aside, she swore like a New Yorker. Good girl.

Jay Lawrence recovered from his shock and informed me, "You...that was not...that's not admissible..."

"Hey, he looked like he was trying to stand. I'm not a doctor."

"You...you said he spoke to you..."

"Right. Then he died. Look, Jay, here's a tip for your next book. I am allowed to lie. You are allowed to remain silent."

"I'm calling my attorney."

"That's your right. Meanwhile, you're under arrest for conspiracy to commit murder." I gave Rourke my cuffs and said, "Cuff him."

I walked to the back of the store and into the stockroom.

Officer Simmons was talking on his cell phone and Scott was still at the table, reading a book – *How to Get Published for Dummies.*

I sat opposite Scott and asked him, "Why was Mr. Parker here so early?"

He put down his book and said, "I don't know. I guess to do paperwork."

"Did he tell you he was coming in early?"

"No...I didn't know he was going to be here."

"But he asked you to come in early."

"Yeah..."

"But never mentioned that he would be coming in early."

"Uh...maybe he did."

"That's not what you said to me, or what you wrote in your statement."

Officer Simmons was off the phone, and he took up a position behind Scott. This was getting interesting.

Scott, meanwhile, was unraveling fast, and he swallowed, then said in a weak voice, "I...guess I forgot."

"Even after you saw the lights in his office?"

"Yeah...I mean...I remembered that he said he might be in."

"Who put those five boxes of books in his office?"

"I did."

"When?"

"Last night."

"Why last night?"

"So…Jay Lawrence could sign them…Mr. Parker likes the authors to sign in his office."

"Jay Lawrence wasn't coming in until ten A.M."

"Yeah…but…I don't know. I do what I'm told."

"What time did Mr. Parker think that Jay Lawrence would be in?"

"Ten –"

"No. Otis Parker thought that Jay Lawrence was coming in very early. About seven-thirty or eight in the morning. That's why he asked you to bring the books up last night, and that's why he was here this morning."

Scott didn't reply and I asked him, "Who wrote that note on the bulletin board that said 10 A.M.?"

"Me. That's when he was supposed to come in."

My turn to lie. I said, "Mrs. Parker just told me that her husband said he had to get to the store early to meet Jay Lawrence."

"Uh…I didn't know that."

"Mr. Parker never told you that when you carried the books upstairs last night?"

"Uh…I don't –"

"Cut the bullshit, Scott." I informed him, "Two people are going down for murder. The third person involved is the government witness." I asked him, "Which one do you want to be?"

He started to hyperventilate or something, and I said to Simmons, "Get him some water."

Simmons grabbed a bottled water off the counter and put it on the table in front of Scott. I said to him, "Drink."

He screwed the cap off with a trembling hand and drank, then took a deep breath.

I took a shot and said to him, "Mrs. Parker told me you met her here last night, after Mr. Parker left for the day."

He took another deep breath and replied, "I...she asked me to stay and meet her here."

"And she asked you to help her with some furniture in her husband's office"

He nodded.

"And you did that."

He nodded again.

"Did you know *why* you were doing that?"

"No."

"Try again. I need a truthful witness for the prosecution."

He drank more water, then said, "I told her...it wasn't safe to –"

"One more time."

"I...didn't know...she said don't ask questions..."

"What did she offer you?"

He closed his eyes, then replied, "Ten thousand. But I said no."

"Yeah? Did you want more?"

He didn't reply.

I thought a moment and asked, "Did you both have a drink in his office?"

He nodded.

"On the couch?"

"Yeah..."

What a deal. He gets ten thousand bucks, drinks the boss' liquor, and fucks the boss' wife on the boss' couch. And all he has to do in return is push the bookcase back a bit while Mia Parker slides the wedges out. How could you say no to that? Well, Jay Lawrence said no, but he was older and wiser, and he already fucked Mia Parker. Also, he got scared.

I made eye contact with Simmons, who was shaking his head in disbelief.

As I said, I've seen it all, but it's new and shocking every time.

Scott was staring blankly into space, maybe thinking about Mia Parker on the couch. Maybe thinking it seemed like a good idea at the time.

Well, aside from money, you have what I call dick crimes. Dicks get you in trouble.

I had another thought and asked Scott, "Did she say she'd get Jay Lawrence to help you get your book published?"

He seemed surprised that I knew this. I didn't, but it all fit.

Scott was fidgeting with the empty bottle now, then he said, "I didn't know what she was going to do...I *swear* I didn't."

"Right. So, this morning you let her in at about seven-thirty."

He nodded.

"Mr. Parker was already here."

He nodded again.

"He told you his wife was coming by to say hello to Jay Lawrence, her friend from L.A."

"Yeah..."

"She went up to his office and they waited for Jay Lawrence."

He nodded.

"And you went...where?"

"Out back."

"Could you hear the crash?"

He closed his eyes again and said, "No..."

"What time did you come back to the stockroom?"

"About...seven forty-five..."

"Then you carried some books to the counter, just like you said in your statement, and you called up to him."

He nodded.

"And there was no answer, so you knew she was already gone. And where did you think he was? In the bathroom? Or under the bookcase?"

No reply.

"Did you actually go up the stairs?"

"Yeah...I didn't know...I swear I didn't know what she –"

"Right. She needed the furniture wedges for another job. And she paid you ten thousand bucks and had sex with you for your help. And she gave you a script for this morning."

He didn't reply.

I looked at my watch. 11:29. Almost lunch time. I stood and

said to Scott, "I'm placing you under arrest as an accomplice to murder."

I nodded to Officer Simmons, who already had his cuffs out, and he said to Scott, "Stand up." Scott stood unsteadily and Simmons cuffed his hands behind his back.

I said to Simmons, "Read him his rights."

I walked toward the door, then turned and looked at Scott. I almost felt sorry for him. Young guy, bad job, lousy boss, maybe short on cash, and wishing he was back in college, or wishing he could be the guy autographing his books. Meanwhile, other peoples' unhappiness and money problems – Mia's and Jay's – were about to intersect with his life. Of course, he could have just said "no" to Mia and called the police. Instead, he made a bad choice, and one person was dead, two were going to jail for a long time, and Scott, if he was lucky and cooperative, would be out before his thirtieth birthday, a little older and wiser. I wanted to give him an enduring piece of advice, some wisdom that would guide him in the future. I thought of several things, then finally said to him, "Never have sex with a woman who has more problems than you do."

I walked back into the store as my cell phone rang. It was Lieutenant Ruiz who said to me, "I'm waiting for your call, John."

"Sorry, boss."

"What's happening?"

"Three arrests. Wife for premeditated murder, her boyfriend for conspiracy to commit, the clerk who found the body as an accomplice."

"No shit?"

"Would I lie?"

"Confessions or suspicion?"

"Confessions."

"Good work."

"Thank you."

"You coming to work today?"

"After lunch."

We hung up, and I looked at Mia Parker and Jay Lawrence, both sitting now side by side in the wingback chairs, cuffed and quiet. They were together, finally, but they didn't seem to have much to say to each other. I had the thought that the marriage wouldn't have worked anyway.

I also thought about telling Jay that his girlfriend banged the clerk to get the kid to do what Jay wouldn't do. But that would make him feel bad – and he felt bad enough – though it might shut her up about Jay banging his publicist. I resisted the temptation to stir the shit a little, and I let it go. They'd find all this out in the pre-trial anyway.

Later, while we were waiting for the three squad cars to take the perps away, I asked Jay Lawrence to sign a book for me. He graciously agreed, and I took his book out of the display window.

He was able to hold a Sharpie with his cuffed hands, and I held the book open for him. "To John," I requested, "The greatest detective since Sherlock Holmes."

He scrawled something, and I said, "Thanks. No hard feelings."

I put thirty bucks in the cash register.

When all the perps were in the cars, I opened the book and read the inscription:

To John, Fuck You, Jay.

Well...maybe it will be worth something someday.

Remaindered

Peter Lovesey

AGATHA CHRISTIE DID IT. The evidence was plain to see, but no one *did* see for more than a day. Robert Ripple's corpse was cold on the bookshop floor. It must have been there right through Monday, the day Precious Finds was always closed. Poor guy, he was discovered early Tuesday in the section he called his office, in a position no bookseller would choose for his last transaction, face down, feet down and butt up, jack-knifed over a carton of books. The side of the carton had burst and some of the books had slipped out and fanned across the carpet, every one a Christie.

Late Sunday Robert had taken delivery of the Christie novels. They came from a house on Park Avenue, one of the best streets in Poketown, Pennsylvania, and they had a curious history. They were brought over from England before World War II by an immigrant whose first job had been as a London publisher's rep. He'd kept the books as a souvenir of those tough times trying to interest bookshop owners in whodunits when the only novels most British people wanted to read were by Jeffrey Farnol and Ethel M. Dell. After his arrival in America, he'd switched to selling Model T Fords instead and made a sizeable fortune. The Christies had been forgotten about, stored in the attic of the fine old weatherboard house he'd bought after making his first million. And now his playboy grandson planned to demolish the building and replace it with a space-age dwelling of glass and concrete. He'd cleared the attic and wanted to dispose of the books. Robert had taken one look and offered five hundred dollars for the lot. The grandson had pocketed the check and gone away pleased with the deal.

Hardly believing his luck, Robert must have waited until the shop closed and then stooped to lift the carton onto his desk and check the contents more carefully.

Mistake.

Hardcover books are heavy. He had spent years humping books around, but he was sixty-eight, with a heart condition, and this was one box too many.

Against all the odds, Robert had stayed in business for twenty-six years, dealing in used books of all kinds. But Precious Finds had become more than a bookshop. It was a haven of civilized life in Poketown, a center for all manner of small town activities—readers' groups, a writers' circle, coffee mornings and musical evenings. Some of the locals came and went without even glancing at the bookshelves. A few bought books or donated them out of loyalty, but it was difficult to understand how Robert had kept going so long. It was said he did most of his business at the beginning through postal sales and later on the Internet.

Robert's sudden death created problems all round. Tanya Tripp, the bookshop assistant, who had been in the job only a few months, had the nasty shock of discovering the body, and found herself burdened with dealing with the emergency, first calling a doctor, then an undertaker and then attempting to contact Robert's family. Without success. Not a Ripple remained. He had never married. It became obvious that his loyal customers would have to arrange the funeral. Someone had to take charge, and this was Tanya. Fortunately she was a capable young woman, as sturdy in character as she was in figure. She didn't complain about the extra workload, even to herself.

Although all agreed that the effort of lifting the Agatha Christies had been the cause of death, an autopsy was inescapable. The medical examiner found severe bruising to the head and this was attributed to the fall. A coronary had killed Robert.

Simple.

The complications came after. Tanya was unable to find a will. She searched the office where Robert had died, as well as his apartment upstairs, where she had never ventured before. Being the first to enter a dead man's rooms would have spooked the average person. Tanya was above average in confidence and determination. She wasn't spooked. She found Robert's passport, birth certificate and tax returns, but nothing resembling a will. She checked with his bank and they didn't have it.

Meanwhile one of the richest customers offered to pay for the funeral and the regulars clubbed together to arrange a wake at Precious Finds. The feeling was that Robert would have wished for a spirited send-off.

The back room had long been the venue for meetings. The books in there were not considered valuable. Every second-hand bookshop has to cope with items that are never likely to sell: thrillers that no longer thrill, sci-fi that has been overtaken by real science and romance too coy for modern tastes. The obvious solution is to refuse such books, but sometimes they come in a job lot with things of more potential such as nineteenth century magazines containing engravings that can be cut out, mounted and sold as prints. Robert's remedy had been to keep the dross in the back room. The heaviest volumes were at floor level, outdated encyclopedias, dictionaries and art books. Higher up were the condensed novels and book club editions of long-forgotten authors. Above them, privately published fiction and poetry. On the top, fat paperbacks turning brown and curling at the edges, whole sets of Michener, Hailey, and Clavell.

The saving grace of the back room was that the shelves in the center were mounted on wheels and could be rolled aside to create a useful space for meetings. A stack of chairs stood in one corner. Robert made no charge, pleased to have people coming right through the shop and possibly pausing to look at the desirable items shelved in the front rooms. So on Tuesdays the bookshop hosted the Poketown history society, Wednesdays the art club, Thursdays, the chess players. Something each afternoon and every night except Sundays and Mondays.

And now the back room was to be used for the wake.

The music appreciation group knew of an Irish fiddler who brought along four friends, and they set about restoring everyone's spirits after the funeral. The place was crowded out. The event spilled over into the other parts of the shop.

It was a bitter-sweet occasion. The music was lively and there was plenty of cheap wine, but there was still anxiety about what would happen after. For the time being the shop had stayed open under Tanya's management. There was no confidence that this could continue.

"It has to be sold," Tanya said in a break between jigs. "There's no heir."

"Who's going to buy a bookstore in these difficult times?" George Digby-Smith asked. He was one of the Friends of England, who met here on occasional Friday nights, allegedly to talk about cricket and cream teas and other English indulgences. Actually, George was more than just a friend of England. He'd been born there sixty years ago. "Someone will want to throw out all the books and turn the building into apartments."

"Over my dead body," Myrtle Rafferty, another of the Friends of England, piped up.

"We don't need another fatality, thank you," George said.

"We can't sit back and do nothing. We all depend on this place."

"Get real, people," one of the Wednesday morning coffee group said. "None of us could take the business on, even if we had the funds."

"Tanya knows about books," George said at once. "She'll be out of a job if the store closes. What do you say, Tanya?"

The young woman looked startled. It was only a few months since she had walked in one morning and asked if Robert would take her on as his assistant. In truth, he'd badly needed some help and she'd earned every cent he paid. Softly spoken, almost certainly under thirty, she had been a quiet presence in the shop, putting more order into the displays, but leaving Robert to deal with the customers.

"I couldn't possibly buy it."

"I'm not suggesting you do. But you could manage it. In fact, you'd do a far better job than old Robert ever did."

"That's unkind," Myrtle said.

George turned redder than usual. "Yes, it was."

"We are all in debt to Robert," Myrtle said.

"Rest his soul," George agreed, raising his glass. "To Robert, a bookman to the end, gone, but not forgotten. In the best sense of the word, remaindered."

"What's that meant to mean?"

"Passed on, but still out there somewhere."

"More like boxed and posted," the man from the coffee club murmured. "Or pulped."

Myrtle hadn't heard. She was thinking positively. "Tanya didn't altogether turn down George's suggestion. She'd want to continue, given the opportunity."

Tanya was silent.

"When someone dies without leaving a will, what happens?" George asked.

Ivor Ciplinsky, who knew a bit about law, and led the history society, said, "An administrator will have to be appointed and they'll make extensive efforts to trace a relative, however distant."

"I already tried," Tanya said. "There isn't anyone."

"Cousins, second cousins, second cousins once removed."

"Nobody."

Myrtle asked Ivor, "And if no relative is found?"

"Then the property escheats to the state's coffers."

"It *what*?"

"Escheats. A legal term, meaning it reverts to the state by default."

"What a ghastly-sounding word," George said.

"Ghastly to think about," Myrtle said. "Our beloved bookshop grabbed by the bureaucrats."

"It goes back to feudal law," Ivor said.

"It should have stayed there," Myrtle said. "Escheating. Cheating comes into it, for sure. Cheating decent people out of their innocent pleasures. We can't allow that. Precious Finds is the focus of our community."

"If you're about to suggest we club together and buy it, don't," Ivor said. "Paying for a wake is one thing. You won't get a bunch of customers, however friendly, taking on a business as precarious as this. You can count me out straight away."

"So speaks the history society," Myrtle said with a sniff. "Caving in before the battle even begins. Well, the Friends of England are made of sterner stuff. The English stood firm at Agincourt, a famous battle six hundred years ago, in case you haven't covered it on Tuesday evenings, Ivor. Remember who faced off the Spanish Armada."

"Not to mention Wellington at Waterloo and Nelson at Trafalgar," George added.

"Michael Caine," Edward said. He was the third member of the Friends of England.

There were some puzzled frowns. Then George said, "*Zulu*— the movie. You're thinking of the battle of 'Rorke's Drift.'"

"The Battle of Britain," Myrtle finished on a high, triumphant note.

"Who *are* these people?" the coffee club man asked.

It was a good question. Myrtle, George and Edward had been meeting in the back room on occasional Friday nights for longer than anyone could recall. They must have approached Robert at some point and asked if they could have their meetings there. An Anglophile himself, at least as far as books were concerned, Robert wouldn't have turned them away. But nobody else had ever joined the three in their little club. This was because they didn't announce their meetings in advance. If you weren't told which Fridays they met, you couldn't be there, even if you adored England, drank warm beer and ate nothing but roast beef and Yorkshire pudding.

George was the only one of the three with a genuine English connection. You wouldn't have known it from his appearance. He'd come over as a youth in the late sixties, a hippie with flowers in his hair and weed in his backpack, living proof of that song about San Francisco. In middle age he'd given up the flowers, but not the weed. However, he still had the long hair, now silver and worn in a ponytail, and his faded T-shirts and torn jeans remained faintly psychedelic.

Edward, by contrast, dressed the part of the English gent, in blue blazer, white shirt and cravat and nicely ironed trousers. He had a David Niven pencil mustache and dark-tinted crinkly hair with a parting. Only when he spoke would you have guessed he'd been born and raised in the Bronx.

Myrtle, too, was New York born and bred. She colored her hair and it was currently orange and a mass of loose curls. She had a face and figure she was proud of. Back in the nineties, her good looks had reeled in her second husband, Butch Rafferty, a one-time gangster, who had treated her to diamond necklaces and dinners at the best New York restaurants. Tragically, Butch had been gunned down in 2003 by Gritty Bologna, a rival hood he had made the mistake of linking up with. The widowed Myrtle had quit gangland and moved out here to Pennsylvania. She wasn't destitute. She still lived in some style in a large colonial house at the better end of town. No one could fathom her affiliation to the old country except there was not much doubt that she slept (separately) with George and Edward. She had travelled to England a number of times with each of them. Either they were not jealous of each other or she controlled the relationship with amazing skill.

Little was known of what went on at the Friends of England meetings in the bookshop. Comfortable and cozy as the back room was, it was not furnished for middle-aged sex. Tanya, understandably curious, had questioned Robert closely about how the Friends passed their evenings. He'd said he assumed they spent their time looking at travel brochures and planning their next trip. The meetings did seem to be followed quite soon after by visits to England, always involving Myrtle, usually in combination with one or other of her fellow Friends.

The three were now in a huddle at the far end of the back room, where they always gathered for their meetings and where—appropriately—three out-of-date sets of the *Encyclopedia Britannica* took up the entire bottom shelf.

"If the shop is... what was that word?" Edward said when the music once more calmed down enough for conversation.

"Escheated."

"If that happens, they'll want a quick sale and we're in deep shit."

"But there's a precious window of opportunity before it gets to that stage," George said. "They have to make completely sure no one has a claim on the estate and that can't be done overnight. We need to get organized. Myrtle was talking about a trip to the Cotswolds before the end of the month. Sorry, my friends, but I think we must cancel."

"Shucks," Myrtle said. "I was counting the days to that trip. You figure we should stay here and do something?"

"We can't do nothing."

"Do what?" Edward said, and it was clear from his disenchanted tone that it had been his turn to partner Myrtle to England.

George glanced right and left and then lowered his voice. "I have an idea, a rather bold idea, but this is not the time or the place."

"Shall we call a meeting?" Myrtle said, eager to hear more. "How about this Friday? We don't need Robert's permission anymore."

"In courtesy, we ought to mention it to Tanya," George said.

"Tell her your idea?"

"Heavens, no. Just say we need a meeting, so she can book us in."

On Friday they had the back room to themselves. Tanya was in the office at the front end of the shop and there were no browsers. The footfall in Precious Finds had decreased markedly after Robert's death had been written up in the *Poketown Observer*.

Even Edward, still sore that his trip to the Cotswolds with Myrtle had been cancelled, had to agree that George's plan was smart.

"It's not just smart, it's genius," Myrtle said. "We can save the shop and carry on as before." She leaned back in her chair and caressed the spines of the *Encyclopedia Britannica*. "The Friends of England can go on indefinitely."

"For as long as the funds hold up, at any rate," George said. "We've been sensible up to now. Let's keep it like that."

George had to be respected. His wise, restraining advice had allowed the three of them to enjoy a comfortable retirement that might yet continue. If the truth were told, the Friends of England Society was a mutual benefit club. George and Edward had once been members of Butch Rafferty's gang and they were still living off the spoils of a security van heist.

"My dear old Butch would love this plan," Myrtle said with a faraway look. "I can hear him saying, 'Simple ain't always obvious.'"

"If Butch hadn't messed up, we wouldn't be here," Edward said, still moody. "We'd be back in New York City, living in style."

"Don't kid yourself," Myrtle said. "You'd have gambled away your share inside six months. New York, maybe—but by now you'd be sleeping rough in Central Park. I know you better than you know yourself, Edward."

"There are worse places than Central Park," he said. "I've had it up to here with Poketown, Pennsylvania. We should have got outta here years ago."

"Oh, come on."

"It's only because we live in Pennsylvania that my plan will work," George said.

Edward's lip curled. "It had better work."

"And I'm thinking we should bring Tanya in at an early stage," George said.

"No way," Edward said. "What is it with Tanya? You got something going with her?"

"How ridiculous. You're the one who can't keep his eyes off her."

Myrtle said, "Leave it, George. Act your age, both of you. I'm with Edward here. Keep it to ourselves."

Edward almost purred. "Something else Butch once said: 'The more snouts in the trough, the less you get.'"

"As you wish," George said. "We won't say anything to Tanya. She'll get a beautiful surprise."

"So how do we divide the work?" Myrtle said.

"Unless you think otherwise, I volunteer to do the paperwork," George said. "I'm comfortable with the English language."

"Keep it short and simple. Nothing fancy."

"Is that agreed, then?"

Edward agreed with a shrug.

"But we should all join in," Myrtle said. "Another thing Butch said, 'Everyone must get their hands dirty.'"

"Suits me—but what else is there to do?" Edward said.

"I need one of Robert's credit cards," George said.

Edward shook his head. "The hell you do. We're not going down that route. That's a sure way to get found out."

George took a sharp, impatient breath. "We won't be using it to buy stuff."

"So what do we want it for?" Edward said, and immediately knew the answer. "The signature on the back."

"Right," Myrtle said. "Can you take care of that?"

"Tricky," Edward said.

"Not at all. Robert must have used plastic. Everyone does."

"How do we get hold of one?"

"How do *you* get hold of one," Myrtle said. "That's how you get your hands dirty. My guess is they're still lying around the office somewhere."

"Tanya's always in there."

Myrtle rolled her eyes. "God help us, Edward, if you can't find a way to do this simple thing you don't deserve to be one of us."

George, becoming the diplomat, said, "Come on, old friend, it's no hardship chatting up Tanya. You can't keep your eyes off her ample backside."

Myrtle said at once. "Cut that out, George." She turned to Edward. "Get her out of the office on some pretext and have a nose around."

"It's not as if you're robbing the Bank of England," George said.

"Okay, I'll see what I can do," Edward said without much grace, and then turned to Myrtle. "And how will you get your hands dirty?"

"Me? I'm going to choose the perfect place to plant the thing."

Almost overnight, Tanya had been transformed from bookshop assistant to manager of Robert's estate as well as his shop. It wasn't her choice, but there was no one else to step into the breach. At least she continued to be employed. She decided she would carry on until someone in authority instructed her to stop. She would allow the shop to remain open and operate on a cash only basis, buying no new stock and keeping accurate accounts. She couldn't touch the bank account, but there was money left in the till and there were occasional sales.

Meanwhile she did her best to get some order out of the chaos that had been Robert's office. He had given up on the filing system years ago. She spent days sorting through papers, getting up to date with correspondence and informing clients what had happened. Someone at some point would have to make an inventory of the stock. What a task *that* would be. Nothing was on computer, not even the accounts. He had still been using tear-out receipt books with carbon sheets.

She glanced across the room at the carton of Agatha Christies that had been the death of poor Robert. After his body had been taken away she had repaired the carton with sticky tape, replaced the loose books and slid the heavy load alongside the filing cabinet. She really ought to shelve them in the mystery section in the next room. But then she wasn't certain how to price them. Robert had paid five hundred for them, so they weren't cheap editions. The copy of the invoice was in one of the boxes. The titles weren't listed there. It simply read: *Agatha Christie novels as agreed.*

She went over and picked up *The Mysterious Affair at Styles*, the author's first novel, obviously in good condition and still in its dust jacket. A first edition would be worth a lot, but she told herself this must be a second printing or a facsimile. It was easy to be fooled into thinking you'd found a gem. According to the spine the publisher was the Bodley Head, so this copy had been published in England. Yet when she looked inside at the publication details and the 1921 date, she couldn't see any evidence that the book was anything except a genuine first edition. It had the smell of an old book, yet it was as clean as if it had not been handled much.

Was it possible?

She was still learning the business, but her heart beat a little faster. Robert himself had once told her that early Agatha Christies in jackets were notoriously rare because booksellers in the past were in the habit of stripping the books of their paper coverings at the point of sale to display the cloth bindings.

Among the reference works lining the office back wall were some that listed auction prices. She took one down, thumbed through to the right page, and saw that a 1921 Bodley Head first edition *without* its original dust jacket had sold last year for just over ten thousand dollars. No one seemed to have auctioned a copy in its jacket in the past fifty years.

She handled the book with more respect and looked again at the page with the date. This had to be a genuine first edition.

"Oh my God!" she said aloud.

No wonder Robert had snapped up the collection. This volume alone was worth many times the price he had paid for them all. He was sharp enough to spot a bargain, which was why the Christie collection had so excited him. It was easy to imagine his emotional state here in the office that Sunday evening. His unhealthy heart must have been under intolerable strain.

The find of a lifetime had triggered the end of a lifetime.

And now Tanya wondered about her own heart. She had a rock band playing in her chest.

If a copy without its jacket fetched ten grand, how much was this little beauty worth? Surely enough to cover her every need for months, if not years, to come.

So tempting.

Robert had never trusted the computer. He'd used it as a glorified typewriter and little else. His contact details for his main customers were kept in a card index that Tanya now flicked through, looking for wealthy people interested in what Robert had called 'British Golden Age mysteries'. She picked out five names. On each card were noted the deals he had done and the prices paid for early editions of Agatha Christie, Dorothy L. Sayers and Anthony Berkeley. They weren't five figure sums, but the books almost certainly hadn't been such fine copies as these.

It wouldn't hurt to phone some of these customers and ask if they would be interested in making an offer for a 1921 Bodley Head first edition of *The Mysterious Affair at Styles*—with a dust jacket.

"I'd need to see it," the first voice said, plainly trying to sound laid back. Then gave himself away by adding, "You haven't even told me who you are. Where are you calling from? I don't mind getting on a plane."

Tanya was cautious. "In fairness, I need to speak to some other potential buyers."

"How much do you have in mind?" he said. "I can arrange a transfer into any account you care to name and no questions asked. Tell me the price you want."

Collecting can be addictive.

"It's not decided yet," she said. "This is just an enquiry to find out who is interested. As I said, I have other calls to make."

"Are you planning to auction it, or what?"

"I'm not going through an auctioneer. It would be a private sale, but at some point I may ask for your best offer."

"You say it has the original jacket? Is it complete? Sometimes they come with a panel detached or missing."

"Believe me, it's complete."

There was a pause at the end of the line. Then: "I'd be willing to offer a six figure sum. If I can examine it for staining and so on and you tell me the provenance, I could run to more than that."

A six figure sum? Did he really mean that?

"Thank you," Tanya succeeded in saying in a small, shocked voice. "I must make some more calls now."

"Screw it, a hundred and twenty grand."

She swallowed hard. "I'm not yet accepting offers, but I may come back to you."

"One forty." He was terrified to put the phone down.

"I'll bear that in mind," Tanya said, and closed the call.

She tried a second collector of Golden Age mysteries and this one wasn't interested in staining or provenance. He couldn't contain his excitement. "Lady, name your price," he said. "I'd kill for that book." Without any prompting, he offered a hundred and fifty thousand, "In used banknotes, if you want."

She didn't bother to call the others. She needed to collect her thoughts. Robert's sudden death had come as such a shock that no one else had given a thought to the value of the Agatha Christies. She was the only person in Poketown with the faintest idea and she could scarcely believe what she'd been offered. Could the existence of a dust jacket—a sheet of paper printed on one side—really mean a mark-up of more than a hundred grand?

She lifted more books out, first editions all. *The Murder on the Links*, *The Secret of Chimneys* and *The Murder of Roger Ackroyd*. The beauty of this was that there was no written evidence of how many were in the carton. The invoice had lumped them all together. *Agatha Christie novels as agreed*. She could take a dozen home and no one would be any the wiser. But she would be richer. Unbelievably richer.

Her time as stand-in manager would soon end. There was already talk of an administrator being appointed.

The phone on the desk buzzed. She jerked in surprise. Guiltily, as if someone was in the room with her, she turned the books face down and covered them with her arm.

"Miss Tripp?"

"Speaking."

"Al Johnson here, from the bank, about the late Mr. Ripple's estate."

She repeated automatically, "Mr. Ripple's estate."

"You were planning a further search for his will when we last spoke. I guess you'd have called me if you'd been successful."

"I guess."

"Are you okay, Miss Tripp? You sound a little distracted."

"There's a lot going on," she said. "Sorry. You asked about the will. It didn't turn up. I looked everywhere I could think of."

"How long has it been now—five weeks? I think we're fast approaching the point of assuming he died intestate."

"I'm afraid so."

"Neglecting to provide for one's death is not as unusual as you might suppose, even among the elderly. The law is quite straightforward here in Pennsylvania. We get an administrator appointed and he or she will calculate the total assets and make a search for relatives who may inherit."

She made a huge effort not to think about the Agatha Christies. "I tried to contact the family before the funeral, but there doesn't seem to be anyone left. He was unmarried, as you know, and had no brothers or sisters. I couldn't even trace any cousins."

"If that's really so, then the Commonwealth of Pennsylvania will collect. Robert's main asset was the bookshop and his apartment upstairs, of course. Do you have other plans yet?"

"Plans?" Sure, she had plans, but this wasn't the moment to speak about them.

"To move on, get another job."

"Not really. How long have I got?"

"In the shop? About a week, I'd say. It's up to me to ask for the administrator to take over and there's usually no delay over that. Everything is then put on hold."

"We have to close?"

"Between you and me, you should have closed already, but I turned a blind eye, knowing what a blow this will be for our community."

After the call, Tanya reached for a Precious Finds tote-bag and filled it with Agatha Christie firsts. She couldn't help the community, but she'd be crazy if she didn't help herself.

Edward, the David Niven lookalike from the Friends of England, was waiting outside the office door, immaculate as always, a carnation in his lapel, when Tanya unlocked next morning. He held a coffee cup in each hand.

"Howya doin?" The charm suffered when he opened his mouth.

"Pretty good," she said, and meant it. "But it's looking bad for the shop. I think we'll be in administration by the end of the week." She was trying to sound concerned.

"Soon as that? Too bad." Strangely, Edward didn't sound over-worried either. "I picked up a coffee for you, Tanya. Skinny latte without syrup, in a tall cup, right?" He handed it over.

"How did you know?"

"I was behind you in Starbucks the other morning."

"And you remembered? What a kind man you are. Why don't you come in?" She could offer no less.

He looked around for a chair but there wasn't a spare one, so he stood his coffee on the filing cabinet Tanya had been trying to get back into some kind of order. He appeared to stand it there. In fact the cup tipped over, the lid shot off and his black Americano streamed down the side of the metal cabinet.

Tanya screamed, "Ferchrissake!" She grabbed some Kleenex from the box on her desk and moved fast.

"No sweat," Edward said after rapidly checking his clothes. "Missed me."

She was on her knees, dragging the remaining Agatha Christies away from the still dripping coffee, her voice shrill in panic. "It's all over the books."

He stepped around the cabinet for a closer look. "Aw, shit." He pulled the pristine white handkerchief from his top pocket and sacrificed it to mop the surface of the filing cabinet. Then, seeing Tanya's frantic efforts to dry the books in the box, he stooped and began dabbing at them.

"Don't—you'll make it worse," she said.

"Are they special?"

"Special?" She felt like strangling him, the idiot. Words poured from her before she realized how much she was giving away. "They're first edition Agatha Christies, worth a fucking fortune. Help me lift them out. The coffee has ruined most of them."

He started picking out soggy books and carrying them to her desk. "Agatha Christies, huh? And you say they're valuable?"

"They were until you—" She stopped in mid-sentence, realizing she'd said too much. She tried to roll back some of what she had revealed. "Okay, it was an accident, I know, but Robert paid five hundred dollars for these."

He whistled. "Five hundred bucks for used books? I thought people gave them away."

"Not these. Most of them are more than seventy years old and with hardly a stain on them… until now."

"You can still read them when they're dry."

Tanya sighed. The blundering fool didn't get it. He had no conception of the damage he'd done—but maybe this was a good thing. After the initial shock she was trying to calm down.

They had finished emptying the carton. She told herself this could have been a far worse disaster. Fortunately the real plums of the collection were safe in her apartment. The ones she'd left were there for show, in case anyone asked about Robert's last book deal.

Edward gave another rub to the filing cabinet, as if *that* was the problem. "You tidied this place good."

"Sorting it out," she said, still shaking. "Robert wasn't the best organized person in the world."

"And you never found the will?"

"The will?" She forced herself to think about it. "Let's face it. There isn't one—which is why we don't have any future."

"Where did he keep his personal stuff?"

"All over. Birth certificate upstairs. Tax forms and credit card statements down here in the desk drawers. His bank documents were at the back of the filing cabinet."

"Driving license?"

"In the car outside on the street. I even looked there for the will."

"Credit cards?"

"A bunch of them were in a card case in his back pocket. They came back from the morgue last week. I shredded them after making a note of the numbers."

"Good thinking," Edward said, but his facial muscles went into spasm.

"So it's the end of an era here in Poketown," Tanya said and she was beginning to get a grip on herself. "What will happen to your Friends of England group? Will you be able to go somewhere else?"

Edward shook his head. "Wouldn't be the same."

"The end of the line for you, then?"

"Seems so." But he still didn't appear depressed at the prospect. He glanced at the line of sad, damp books. "I wanna find some way of saying sorry. How about lunch?"

"It's not necessary."

"After what I just did, it's the least I can do. Someone I knew used to say, 'You shoot yourself in the foot, you gotta learn to hop.'"

She managed a smile. "Okay. What time?"

They lunched at Jimmy's, the best restaurant on Main Street. By then Tanya had recovered most of her poise. After all, she had enough undamaged Agatha Christies at home to make her rich. And this tête-à-tête with Edward was as good a chance as she would get to discover the main thing she had come to Poketown to find out.

She waited until she had finished her angel-hair pasta with Thai spiced prawns—by which time Edward had gone through three glasses of Chablis.

"Now that Precious Finds is coming to an end, do you mind if I ask something?"

"Sure. Go ahead."

"What exactly went on at the meetings?"

"Meetings?" he said as if he didn't understand the word. She hoped he hadn't drunk too much to make sense.

"Of the Friends. I asked Robert once, but I don't think he knew. He was pretty vague about it, in that way he had of telling you nothing."

Edward gave a guarded answer. "We don't do much except talk."

"In that case, you could talk in some other place. It's not a total disaster if the shop closes, as it will."

He seemed to be avoiding eye contact. "It's not so simple. We can't just shift camp."

"I don't understand why not."

"You don't need to."

She should have waited for him to sink a fourth glass of the wine. "But you can tell me how you three got together."

"We know each other from way back, when we all lived in New York City."

"And Myrtle was married to that man who was murdered?"

He nodded. "Butch Rafferty."

"Mr. Rafferty had a hard reputation as a gang leader, didn't he? I can understand a woman being attracted to that kind of guy." She noted his eyes widen and his chest fill out. "Did you know him?"

"Did I know Butch!" Out to impress, he jutted his jaw a fraction higher.

"Closely, then?"

Edward put down his glass, made a link with his pinkies and pulled them until they turned red. "We were like that."

"Wow! They must have been dangerous times for any friend of Butch Rafferty. Is that why you moved away?"

"We didn't run," he said.

"When you say 'we', do you mean yourself, Myrtle and George? You knew each other in New York?"

"Sure. It suited us to come here."

"I heard there was a big robbery of a security van that in some way caused the falling-out between Butch and Gritty Bologna."

His mouth tightened. "You seem to know a lot about it."

She felt herself color a little. "It was in the papers at the time. I looked it up later after I heard who Myrtle's husband had been. I was curious."

"Curiosity killed the cat," Edward said and ended that line of conversation. It wasn't one of Butch's sayings.

"Well, thanks for the meal. I really enjoyed it," Tanya said a few minutes later.

"Let's do it again tomorrow," Edward said, and it was music to her ears.

"Why not? And I'll pay." She could afford to, now she was dealing in first edition Agatha Christies. She'd get him talking again after a few drinks, no problem.

Her mention of the robbery hadn't put him off entirely, she was pleased to discover. And now Edward played the assertive male. "This afternoon I'm gonna check the filing cabinet."

"There's no need. It was locked," she said.

"Some of my coffee could have seeped inside. I'll take a look."

*

"What in the name of sanity is Edward up to?" George asked Myrtle later that week. "I saw them leaving Jimmy's at lunch today. It's become a regular date."

"He's keeping her sweet, I figure," Myrtle said. "We encouraged him, if you remember."

"That was when we needed the credit card with Robert's signature. He found an old receipt book full of Robert's signatures in the filing cabinet, but that was three days ago. He handed it to me and it's all I want. His work is done. He has no reason to be lunching with Tanya every day."

"Silly old fool," Myrtle said. "He stands no chance with her. Smart clothes can only do so much for a guy. God help him when he takes them off."

"Is that one of Butch's sayings?"

"No. I said it."

"I'm worried, Myrtle." George showed the stress he was under by pulling the end of his silver ponytail across his throat. "We don't want him telling her anything."

"About this?"

"No—about the heist of the van."

"She isn't interested in that. She has too much on her mind, and soon she'll have a whole lot more. How's the project going?"

"My part is complete," George said, reaching into his pocket. "It's over to you now."

"Fine," Myrtle said. "I'll plant the little beauty tomorrow lunchtime, while Edward is working his charm on her in Jimmy's."

"I was thinking," Tanya said, at the next lunch date.

"Yeah?" Edward had already finished the bottle of Chablis and was on Bourbon. His glazed eyes looked ready for a cataract operation.

"About Robert," she went on, "and how you three linked up with him. Was he ever in New York?"

"Sure," he said, with a flap of the hand, "but way back, when we were all much younger."

"In Butch Rafferty's gang?"

"I wouldn't say Robert was in the gang," he said, starting to slur the words, "but we all knew him. He was a bartender then, some place in the Bowery where we used to meet."

"Someone you trusted?"

"Right on. Like one of the family."

"Butch's family?"

"Yeah. Butch liked the guy and so did the rest of us. Robert knew how to keep his mouth shut. Jobs were discussed. It didn't matter."

"A bartender in New York? That's a far cry from owning a bookshop."

"He had a dream to get out of town and open a bookstore and that's what he did when he had the money."

"Just from his work in the bar?" she said, disbelieving.

"Butch helped him. Butch was like that. And it wasn't wasted. Butch knew if he ever needed a bolt-hole he could lay up for a while here in Poketown, Pennsylvania." He shook his head slowly. "Too bad he was shot before he had the chance."

Tanya knew all this, but there was more she didn't know. "So after Butch was killed, some of you left town and came here?"

He nodded. "Myrtle's idea. She knew where Robert had set up shop."

"Was she an active member of the gang?"

"She didn't go on jobs, but she has a good brain and she's cool. She helped Butch with the planning." He blinked and looked sober for a second. "You're not an undercover cop, by any chance?"

She laughed. "No way. I'm starstruck by how you guys operate."

Reassured, he reached for the Bourbon and topped up his glass. "Sexy, huh?"

"It's a turn-on. I'll say that."

"You're a turn-on without saying a word."

"Flatterer." She was still on her first glass of wine, picking her questions judiciously. The process required care, even with a half-cut would-be seducer like this one. The query about the undercover cop was a warning. Edward couldn't have been more wrong, but it would be a mistake to underestimate him. "What is it with the Friends of England? Is that the only way you can meet in private?"

"We could meet anywhere. It's a free country."

"Be mysterious, then," she said, smiling.

He grinned back. "You bet I will. There's gotta be mystery in a relationship."

"Who said anything about…" She didn't get any further. His hand was on her thigh.

She'd got him just as she wanted.

He needed support as he tottered back to Precious Finds and Tanya supplied it, allowing him to put his arm around her shoulder.

"Why don't we close the shop for the afternoon?" he said.

"What a good idea," she said. "I was thinking the same thing." She'd already closed for lunch and didn't have to reopen. She let them inside, fastened the bolts and left the closed notice hanging on the door.

Inside, she said, "After all that wine, some coffee might be a good plan."

"I can think of a better one," Edward said, reaching for her breasts.

She swayed out of range. "Coffee first. I only have instant, but I'm not sending you to Starbucks again. Tell you what. I'll make it here and we'll carry it through to the back room, so we can both have a chair."

"And if I spill it, I can't do so much damage," he said with a grin.

She carried both mugs through the shop after the coffee was made, insisting he went ahead. She didn't want him behind her.

Edward managed to lift two chairs from the stack in the back room and sank into one of them. "Never thought I'd get to be alone with you."

And so drunk you can't do anything about it, Tanya thought, but she said, "Yes, it's great to relax. And in the company of a famous New York mobster."

He looked stupidly flattered.

"I'd love to hear about the last big job you did—the security van," she said. "I thought they were so well protected no robber would even think about a hold-up."

"Takes brains," he said.

"Was it your idea, then?"

"The part that worked, yeah." He ogled her. "You wanna hear about it? I'll tell you. In a job like this you go for the weak spot. You know what that is?"

"The tires?"

"The people. You surprise the guard in his own home, before he reports for work. You tell him his mother has been kidnapped and he has to cooperate. You tape dummy explosives to his chest and tell him you can detonate them by remote whenever you want."

"Brilliant," Tanya said. "Was that you, doing all that?"

"Most of it. From there on, he's so scared he'll do anything. He drives you to where the vans are kept. You're wearing a uniform just like his. He drives the security van to the depot where the bank stores the money. He does the talking and you help load the van."

"How much? Squillions?" She was wide-eyed, playing the innocent.

"They don't deal in peanuts," Edward said. "And when you're outta there and on the street, your buddies follow in the transit van."

"George?"

"He was one of the bunch, yeah. Some were Butch's people and some worked for Gritty Bologna. Gritty had a line into the security outfit, which was how we got the uniform and the guard's address. You drive to the warehouse where you transfer the loot and that's it."

"What about the guard?"

"Tied up and locked in his van. No violence."

"How much did you get?"

"Just under a million pounds."

"Pounds?"

Edward looked sheepish. "Yeah. We screwed up. We thought this van was delivering to the major banks like all the others. Too bad we picked the one supplying British money to currency exchanges at all the major airports in New York."

"You had a vanload of useless money."

"Uh huh. Crisp, new banknotes for tourists to take on their vacations."

"What a letdown."

"Tell me about it. Gritty went bananas. He blamed Butch. There was a shootout and Butch was the loser. Some of us figured Gritty wouldn't stop at one killing, so we left town."

"You and George and Myrtle?" She'd been incredibly patient waiting for the pay-off.

"Myrtle remembered Robert here in Poketown, and this is where we came."

"With the pounds?"

"With the pounds. I figured we might think of a way to use them. It took a while, but with Robert's help we worked it."

"All those trips to England? That's neat."

"Twenty, thirty grand at a time. Some notes we exchange and bring dollars back. Some we spent over there. It's small scale. Has to be, with new, numbered bank-notes."

"And this is why you call it the Friends of England? I love it!" She clapped her hands. "Edward, you're a genius. Is there any left, or is it all spent?"

"More than half is left."

"Who's got it?"

"It's right here in the safe. That's why we can't let the place close."

He was losing her now.

"I haven't found the safe," she said as casually as if she was talking about the one copy of Jane Austen the shop didn't stock. "I don't know what you're talking about."

He just smiled.

"When you say 'right here' do you mean the back room?"

He wagged his finger like a parent with a fractious infant. "Secret."

Infuriating. To her best knowledge there wasn't a safe on the premises. Robert had always left the takings in the till. There wasn't enough to justify using a safe. She gathered herself and gave Edward a smoldering look. "If that's how you want to play this, I won't be showing you my secret either."

"Whassat?" he asked, gripping the chair-arms.

"Wouldn't you like to know, naughty boy."

She watched the struggle taking place in front of her, rampant desire taking over from reality. "You gotta do better than that," he said.

"Okay. To show you my secret we have to go upstairs, to the bedroom."

"Hell," he said, shifting in the chair as if he was suddenly uncomfortable. "Is that an offer?"

She hesitated, then gave a nod.

He groomed his moustache with finger and thumb and took a deep, tremulous breath. "The safe is right where you are. You could touch it with your knee."

She looked down. "Get away."

"The Encyclopedia Brit... Brit..." He couldn't complete the word.

"Britannica?"

"Middle five volumes. False front."

She stooped and studied the spines of the large books that took up the whole of the bottom shelf. With their faded lettering and scuffed cloth bindings they looked no different from the others.

"1911 edition," Edward said. "Green. Press that showy gold

bit on volume twelve and see what happens."

She pressed her thumb against the royal coat of arms and felt it respond. Just as Edward had said, the five spines were only a façade attached to a small, hinged door that sprang open and revealed the gray metal front of a safe with a circular combination lock.

Eureka.

"That's amazing."

"If I could see straight, I'd open it for you," he said, "but there's only stacks of notes in there."

"You have to know the combination."

"Zero-four-two-three-one-nine-six-four, but I didn't tell you that, okay?"

"Smart. How do you remember?"

"It's Myrtle's birthday. April twenty-three, sixty-four. Shut it now and we'll go upstairs."

In his inebriated state, he couldn't have stopped her if she'd walked out and left him there. But, hell, she wanted the satisfaction of showing him her secret, as she'd put it.

"Will you make it?"

He chuckled. "You bet I will, baby." And he did, even though he took the last few stairs on all fours. "So which one is the bedroom?" he asked between deep breaths.

"That's another adventure, loverboy. Next floor."

"Stuff that. There must be a sofa right here."

Tanya shook her head and pointed her finger at the ceiling.

After some hesitation Edward seemed to accept that this had to be on Tanya's terms. "Which way, then?"

"The spiral staircase at the end of the corridor."

Gamely, he stepped towards it and hauled himself to the top. "Makes you kind of dizzy."

"That's not the fault of the staircase." She pushed open a door. "In here, buster."

Robert's bedroom matched the size of the back room downstairs. It overlooked the yard at the rear of the property so it was built over the same foundations. The king-size bed was constructed of oak, with headboard and footboard graciously curved and upholstered in a French empire style. All the furniture matched and there was plenty of it, dressing table, ward-robes, chests of drawers and easy chairs, but no sense of crowding. More books lined the facing wall and there was a fifty-inch plasma TV as well as a sound system with chest-high speakers. There was an open door to an *en suite* shower room. A second door connected to a fire escape.

"This'll do," Edward said, stepping towards Tanya.

She moved aside. "Not so fast."

"C'mon, I showed you *my* secret." He patted the bed.

"Fair enough. Here's mine." She crossed to the dressing-table, swung the mirror right over and revealed a manila envelope fastened to the back. "It's ridiculous. I checked the mirror a week ago, and nothing was there. This morning I found this. Robert's will."

"Yeah?" he said, his thoughts elsewhere.

"You'd better listen up, because it names you." She slipped the document from the envelope and started to read. "'This is the last will and testament of Robert Ripple, of Precious Finds Bookshop, Main Street, Poketown, Pennsylvania, being of sound mind and revoking all other wills and codicils. I wish to appoint as co-executors my good friends George Digby-Smith and Edward Myers.' That's you. Unfortunately as an executor you're not allowed to profit from the estate."

"No problem," Edward said. "Now why don't you put that down so we can give this bed a workout?"

"Listen to this part: 'I leave my house and shop in trust to become the sole property of my devoted assistant manager, Tanya Tripp, on condition that she continues to trade as a bookseller on the premises for ten years from the date of my decease.' Nice try."

"Don't ya like it?" Edward said, frowning.

"It stinks. This wasn't drafted by Robert. It's a fake. I know why you wanted his credit cards the other day and why in the end you walked off with that old receipt book. So you could fake his signature. Well, it's a passable signature, I'll give you that, but you forgot something. A will needs to be witnessed. There are no witnesses here."

"No witnesses, huh?" He raised his right hand in a semi-official pose and intoned in a more-or-less coherent manner, "The state of Pennsylvania doesn't require witnesses to a will. You're in the clear, sweetheart. It's all yours, the house and the shop. Just be grateful someone thought of you."

"Thought of *me*? You were only thinking of yourselves, keeping up the old arrangement, taking your stolen pounds from the safe and spending them in England. I'm supposed to give up ten years of my life to keep this smelly old heap of wood and plaster going just to make life dandy for you guys. Well, forget it. I don't buy it." She held the will high and ripped it apart.

The force of the action somehow penetrated the alcohol in Edward's brain. Suddenly he seemed to realize that there was much more at stake than getting this young woman into bed. "I've got your number. You figure you can do better for yourself with those Agatha Christies you have in the office. Worth a fucking fortune, you said. Few spots of coffee didn't harm them much. You're aiming to take them with you when the shop closes down and cash in big time."

Tanya felt the blood drain from her face. She'd been hoping her agitated words the other day had passed unnoticed. This was dangerous, desperately dangerous. It wasn't quite true because the best books weren't stained. They were safe in her apartment. Even so, this stupid, drink-crazed man could put a stop to everything.

She still had ammunition and her reaction was to use it. "You don't know who I am. I can bring down you and your thieving friends. I'm Gritty Bologna's daughter, Teresa. That money in the safe isn't yours to spend. We spent years tracking you to this place. I took the job with Robert to find out where the banknotes are and now I know."

"You're Teresa Bologna?" he said in amazement. "You were

in school at the time of the heist."

"I'm family, and family doesn't give up."

He moved fast for a drunk. Fear and rage mingled in his face. He came at her like a bull.

He was blocking her route to the door and the *en suite* would be a trap. Her only option was to use the fire escape. She turned and hit the panic bar and the door swung open. She grabbed the rail and swung left just as Edward charged through.

No one's movements are reliable after heavy drinking. Edward pitched forward, failed to stop, hit the rail hard with his hips and couldn't stop his torso from tipping him over. He may have screamed. Tanya (or Teresa) didn't remember. But the sickening thud of the body hitting the concrete forty feet below would stay in her memory forever.

The autopsy revealed substantial alcohol in Edward's blood. No one could say what he had been doing above the bookshop in the dead owner's bedroom. Those who might have thrown some light had all left Poketown overnight and were not heard of again. So an open verdict was returned at the inquest.

In the absence of a will from Robert Ripple, Precious Finds was duly put under the control of an administrator and escheated to the state of Pennsylvania. It ceased trading as a bookshop and was converted into apartments.

About a year later, a married couple set up home on a remote Scottish island. He was thought to be an ex-hippy, she an American. They called themselves Mr. and Mrs. English and they helped the home tourist industry by forever taking holidays in different towns.

Copies of several rare Agatha Christie first editions in dust jackets enlivened the book market in the years that followed, changing hands for huge sums. Their provenance was described as uncertain, but they were certainly genuine.

Mystery, Inc.

Joyce Carol Oates

I AM VERY excited! For at last, after several false starts, I have chosen the perfect setting for my bibliomystery.

It is Mystery, Inc., a beautiful old bookstore in Seabrook, New Hampshire, a town of less than two thousand year-round residents overlooking the Atlantic Ocean between New Castle and Portsmouth.

For those of you who have never visited this legendary bookstore, one of the gems of New England, it is located in the historic High Street district of Seabrook, above the harbor, in a block of elegantly renovated brownstones originally built in 1888. Here are the offices of an architect, an attorney-at-law, a dental surgeon; here are shops and boutiques—leather goods, handcrafted silver jewelry, the Tartan Shop, Ralph Lauren, Esquire Bootery. At 19 High Street a weathered old sign in black and gilt creaks in the wind above the sidewalk:

MYSTERY, INC. BOOKSELLERS
New & Antiquarian Books,
Maps, Globes, Art
Since 1912

The front door, a dark-lacquered red, is not flush with the

sidewalk but several steps above it; there is a broad stone stoop, and a black wrought iron railing. So that, as you stand on the sidewalk gazing at the display window, you must gaze *upward*.

Mystery, Inc. consists of four floors with bay windows on each floor that are dramatically illuminated when the store is open in the evening. On the first floor, books are displayed in the bay window with an (evident) eye for the attractiveness of their bindings: leatherbound editions of such 19th-century classics as Wilkie Collins's *The Moonstone* and *The Woman in White*, Charles Dickens's *Bleak House* and *The Mystery of Edwin Drood*, A. Conan Doyle's *The Adventures of Sherlock Holmes*, as well as classic 20th-century mystery-crime fiction by Raymond Chandler, Dashiell Hammett, Cornell Woolrich, Ross Macdonald, and Patricia Highsmith and a scattering of popular American, British, and Scandinavian contemporaries. There is even a title of which I have never heard—*The Case of the Unknown Woman: The Story of One of the Most Intriguing Murder Mysteries of the 19th Century*, in what appears to be a decades-old binding.

As I step inside Mystery, Inc. I feel a pang of envy. But in the next instant this is supplanted by admiration—for envy is for small-minded persons.

The interior of Mystery, Inc. is even more beautiful than I had imagined. Walls are paneled in mahogany with built-in bookshelves floor to ceiling; the higher shelves are accessible by ladders on brass rollers, and the ladders are made of polished wood. The ceiling is comprised of squares of elegantly hammered tin; the floor is parquet, covered in small carpets. As I am a book collector myself—and a bookseller—I note how attractively books are displayed without seeming to overwhelm the customer; I see how cleverly books are positioned upright to intrigue the eye; the customer is made to feel welcome as in an old-fashioned library with leather chairs and sofas scattered casually about. Here and there against the walls are glass-fronted cabinets containing rare and first-edition books, no doubt under lock and key. I do feel a stab of envy, for of the mystery bookstores I own, in what I think of as my modest mystery-bookstore empire in New England, not one is of the class of Mystery, Inc., or anywhere near.

In addition, it is Mystery, Inc.'s online sales that present the gravest competition to a bookseller like myself, who so depends upon such sales ...

Shrewdly I have timed my arrival at Mystery, Inc. for a half-hour before closing time, which is 7 P.M. on Thursdays, and hardly likely to be crowded. (I think there are only a few other customers—at least on the first floor, within my view.) In this wintry season dusk has begun as early as 5:30 PM. The air is wetly cold, so that the lenses of my glasses are covered with a fine film of steam; I am vigorously polishing them when a young woman salesclerk with tawny gold, shoulder-length hair approaches me to ask if I am looking for anything in particular, and I tell her that I am just browsing, thank you—"Though I would like to meet the proprietor of this beautiful store, if he's on the premises."

The courteous young woman tells me that her employer, Mr. Neuhaus, is in the store, but upstairs in his office; if I am interested in some of the special collections or antiquarian holdings, she can call him ...

"Thank you! I am interested indeed but just for now, I think I will look around."

What a peculiar custom it is, the *openness of a store*. Mystery, Inc. might contain hundreds of thousands of dollars of precious merchandise; yet the door is unlocked, and anyone can step inside from the street into the virtually deserted store, carrying a leather attaché case in hand, and smiling pleasantly.

It helps of course that I am obviously a gentleman. And one might guess, a book-collector and book-lover.

As the trusting young woman returns to her computer at the check-out counter, I am free to wander about the premises. Of course, I will avoid the other customers. I am impressed to see that the floors are connected by spiral staircases, and not ordinary utilitarian stairs; there is a small elevator at the rear which doesn't tempt me as I suffer from mild claustrophobia. (Being locked in a dusty closet as a child by a sadistic older brother surely is the root of this phobia, which I have managed to disguise from most people who know me, including my bookstore employees who revere me, I believe, for being a frank, forthright, commonsensical sort of man free of any sort of neurotic compulsion!) The first floor of Mystery, Inc. is American books; the second floor is British and foreign-language books, and Sherlock Holmesiana (an entire rear wall); the third floor is first editions, rare editions, and leatherbound sets; the fourth floor is maps, globes, and antiquarian art-works associated with mayhem, murder, and death.

It is here on the fourth floor, I'm sure, that Aaron Neuhaus has his office. I can imagine that his windows overlook a view of the Atlantic, at a short distance, and that the office is beautifully paneled and furnished.

I am feeling nostalgic for my old habit of *book theft*—when I'd been a penniless student decades ago, with a yearning for books. The thrill of thievery—and the particular reward, a *book*! In fact for years my most prized possessions were books stolen from Manhattan bookstores along Fourth Avenue that had no great monetary value—only just the satisfaction of being stolen. Ah, those days before security cameras!

Of course, there are security cameras on each floor of Mystery, Inc. If my plan is successfully executed, I will remove the tape and destroy it; if not, it will not matter that my likeness will be preserved on the tape for a few weeks, then destroyed. In fact I am *lightly disguised*— these whiskers are not mine, and the black-plastic-framed tinted glasses I am wearing are very different than my usual eyeglasses.

Just before closing time at Mystery, Inc. there are only a few customers, whom I intend to outstay. One or two on the first floor; a solitary individual on the second floor perusing shelves of Agatha Christie; a middle-aged couple on the third floor looking for a birthday present for a relative; an older man on the fourth floor perusing the art on the walls— reproductions of fifteenth-century German woodcuts titled "Death and the Maiden," "The Dance of Death," and "The Triumph of Death"—macabre lithographs of Picasso, Munch, Schiele, Francis Bacon—, reproductions of Goya's "Saturn Devouring His Children," "Witches' Sabbath," and "The Dog." (Too bad it would be imprudent of me to strike up a conversation with this gentleman, whose taste in macabre art-work is very similar to my own, judging by his absorption in Goya's Black Paintings!) I am indeed admiring— it is remarkable that Aaron Neuhaus can sell such expensive works of art in this out-of-the-way place in Seabrook, New Hampshire, in the off-season.

By the time I descend to the first floor, most of these customers have departed; the final customer is making a purchase at the check-out counter. To bide my time, I take a seat in one of the worn old leather chairs that seems almost to be fitted to my buttocks; so comfortable a chair, I could swear it was my own, and not the property of Aaron Neuhaus. Close by is a glass-fronted cabinet containing first editions of novels by Raymond Chandler— quite a treasure trove! There is a virtual *itch* to my fingers in proximity to such books.

I am trying not to feel embittered. I am trying simply to feel *competitive*—this is the American way!

But it's painfully true—not one of my half-dozen mystery bookstores is so well-stocked as Mystery, Inc., or so welcoming to visitors; at least two of the more recently acquired stores are outfitted with ugly utilitarian fluorescent lights which give me a headache, and fill me with despair. Virtually none of my customers are so affluent-appearing as the customers here in Mystery, Inc., and their taste in mystery fiction is limited primarily to predictable, formulaic bestsellers—you would not see shelves devoted to Ellery Queen in a store of mine, or an entire glass-fronted case of Raymond Chandler's first editions, or a wall of Holmesiana. My better stores carry only a few first editions and antiquarian books—certainly, no art-works! Nor do I seem able to hire attractive, courteous, intelligent employees like this young woman— perhaps because I can't afford to pay them much more than the minimum wage, and so they have no compunction about quitting abruptly.

In my comfortable chair it is gratifying to overhear the friendly conversation between this customer and the young woman clerk, whose name is Laura—for, if I acquire Mystery, Inc., I will certainly want to keep attractive young Laura on the staff as my employee; if necessary, I will pay her just slightly more than her current salary, to insure that she doesn't quit.

When Laura is free, I ask her if I might examine a first-edition copy of Raymond Chandler's *Farewell My Lovely*. Carefully she unlocks the cabinet, and removes the book for me—its publication date is 1940, its dust jacket in good, if not perfect, condition, and the price is $1,200. My heart gives a little leap—I already have one copy of this Chandler novel, for which, years ago, I paid much less; at the present time, in one of my better stores, or online, I could possibly resell it for $1,500...

"This is very attractive! Thank you! But I have a few questions, I wonder if I might speak with ..."

"I will get Mr. Neuhaus. He will want to meet *you*."

Invariably, at independently owned bookstores, proprietors are apt to want to meet customers like *me*.

Rapidly I am calculating—how much would Aaron Neuhaus's widow ask for this property? Indeed, how much is this property worth, in Seabrook? New Hampshire has suffered from the current, long-term recession through New England, but Seabrook is an affluent coastal community whose population more than quadruples in the summer, and so the bookstore may be worth as much as $800,000 ... Having done some research, I happen to know that Aaron Neuhaus owns the property outright, without a mortgage. He has been married, and childless, for more than three decades; presumably, his widow will inherit his estate. As I've learned from past experiences, widows are notoriously vulnerable to quick sales of property; exhausted by the legal and financial responsibilities that follow a husband's death, they are eager to be free of encumbrances, especially if they know little about finances and business. Unless she has children and friends to advise her, a particularly distraught widow is capable of making some very unwise decisions.

Dreamily, I have been holding the Raymond Chandler first edition in my hands without quite seeing it. The thought has come to me—*I must have Mystery, Inc. It will be the jewel of my empire.*

"Hello?"—here is Aaron Neuhaus, standing before me.

Quickly I rise to my feet and thrust out my hand to be shaken—"Hello! I'm very happy to meet you. My name is—" As I proffer Neuhaus my invented name I feel a wave of heat lifting into my face. Almost, I fear that Neuhaus has been observing me at a little distance, reading my most secret thoughts while I'd been unaware of him.

He knows me. But—he cannot know me.

As Aaron Neuhaus greets me warmly it seems clear that the proprietor of Mystery, Inc. is not at all suspicious of this stranger who has introduced himself as "Charles Brockden." Why would he be? There are no recent photographs of me, and no suspicious reputation has accrued to my invented name; indeed, no suspicious reputation has accrued about my actual name as the owner of a number of small mystery bookstores in New England.

Of course, I have studied photographs of Aaron Neuhaus. I am surprised that Neuhaus is so youthful, and his face so unlined, at sixty-three.

Like any enthusiastic bookseller, Neuhaus is happy to answer my questions about the Chandler first edition and his extensive Chandler holdings; from this, our conversation naturally spreads to other, related holdings in his bookstore— first editions of classic mystery-crime novels by Hammett, Woolrich, James M. Cain, John D. MacDonald, and Ross Macdonald, among others. Not boastfully but matter-of-factly Neuhaus tells me that he owns one of the two or three most complete collections of published work by the pseudonymous

"Ellery Queen"—including novels published under other pseudonyms and magazines in which Ellery Queen stories first appeared. With a pretense of naïveté I ask how much such a collection would be worth—and Aaron Neuhaus frowns and answers evasively that the worth of a collection depends upon the market and he is hesitant to state a fixed sum.

This is a reasonable answer. The fact is, any collectors' items are worth what a collector will pay for them. The market may be inflated, or the market may be deflated. All prices of all things—at least, useless beautiful things like rare books—are inherently absurd, rooted in the human imagination and in the all-too-human predilection to desperately want what others value highly, and to scorn what others fail to value. Unlike most booksellers in our financially distressed era, Aaron Neuhaus has had so profitable a business he doesn't need to sell in a deflated market but can hold onto his valuable collections—indefinitely, it may be!

These, too, the wife will inherit. So I am thinking.

The questions I put to Aaron Neuhaus are not duplicitous but sincere—if somewhat naïve-sounding—for I am very interested in the treasures of Aaron Neuhaus's bookstore, and I am always eager to extend my bibliographical knowledge.

Soon, Neuhaus is putting into my hands such titles as *A Bibliography of Crime & Mystery Fiction 1749-1990; Malice Domestic: Selected Works of William Roughead, 1889–1949; My Life in Crime: A Memoir of a London Antiquarian Bookseller (1957); The Mammoth Encyclopedia of Modern Crime Fiction;* and an anthology edited by Aaron Neuhaus, *One Hundred and One Best American Noir Stories of the 20th Century.* All of these are known to me, though I have not read one of them in its entirety; Neuhaus's *One Hundred and One Best American Noir Stories* is one of the backlist bestsellers in most of my stores. To flatter Neuhaus I tell him that I want to buy his anthology, along with the Chandler first edition—" And maybe something else, besides. For I have to confess, I seem to have fallen in love with your store."

At these words a faint flush rises into Neuhaus's face. The irony is, they are quite sincere words even as they are coolly intended to manipulate the bookseller.

Neuhaus glances at his watch—not because he's hoping that it's nearing 7 P.M., and time to close his store, but rather because he hopes he has more time to spend with this very promising customer.

Soon, as booksellers invariably do, Aaron Neuhaus will ask his highly promising customer if he can stay a while, past closing-time; we might adjourn to his office, to speak more comfortably, and possibly have a drink.

Each time, it has worked this way. Though there have been variants, and my first attempt at each store wasn't always successful, necessitating a second visit, this has been the pattern.

Bait, bait taken.

Prey taken.

Neuhaus will send his attractive sales clerk home. The last glimpse Laura will have of her (beloved?) employer will be a pleasant one, and her recollection of the last customer of the day—(the last customer of Neuhaus's life)—will be vivid perhaps, but misleading. *A man with ginger-colored whiskers, black plastic-framed glasses, maybe forty years old—or fifty ... Not tall, but not short ... Very friendly.*

Not that anyone will suspect *me*. Even the brass initials on my attaché case—*CB*—have been selected to mislead.

Sometime this evening Aaron Neuhaus will be found dead in his bookstore, very likely his office, of natural causes, presumably of a heart attack—if there is an autopsy. (He will be late to arrive home: his distraught wife will call. She will drive to Mystery, Inc. to see what has happened to him and/or she will call 911 to report an emergency long after the "emergency" has expired.) There could be no reason to think that an ordinary-seeming customer who'd arrived and departed hours earlier could have had anything to do with such a death.

Though I am a wholly rational person, I count myself one of those who believe that some individuals are so personally vile, so disagreeable, and make the world so much less pleasant a place, it is almost our duty to eradicate them. (However, I have not acted upon this impulse, yet—my eradications are solely in the service of business, as I am a practical-minded person.)

Unfortunately for me, however, Aaron Neuhaus is a very congenial person, exactly the sort of person I would enjoy as a friend— if I could afford the luxury of friends. He is soft-spoken yet ardent; he knows everything about mystery-detective fiction, but isn't overbearing; he listens closely, and never interrupts; he laughs often. He is of moderate height, about five feet nine or ten, just slightly taller than I am, and not quite so heavy as I am. His clothes are of excellent quality but slightly shabby, and mismatched: a dark brown Harris tweed sport coat, a red cashmere vest over a pale beige shirt, russet-brown corduroy trousers. On his feet, loafers. On his left hand, a plain gold wedding band. He has a sweetly disarming smile that offsets, to a degree, something chilly and Nordic in his gray-green gaze, which most people (I think) would not notice. His hair is a steely gray, thinning at the crown and curly at the sides, and his face is agreeably youthful. He is rather straight-backed, a little stiff, like one who has injured his back and moves cautiously to avoid pain. (Probably no one would notice this except one like myself who is by nature sharp-eyed, and has had bouts of back pain himself.)

Of course, before embarking up the coast to Seabrook, New Hampshire, in my (ordinary- seeming, unostentatious) vehicle, attaché case on the seat beside me, and plan for the elimination of a major rival memorized in every detail, I did some minimal research into my subject who has the reputation, in bookselling and antiquarian circles, of being a person who is both friendly and social and yet values his privacy highly; it is held to be somewhat perverse that many of Neuhaus's male friends have never met his wife, who has been a public school teacher in Glastonbury, N.H. for many years. (Dinner invitations to Neuhaus and his wife, from residents in Seabrook, are invariably declined "with regret.") Neuhaus's wife is said to be his high school sweetheart whom he first met in 1965 and married in 1977, in Clarksburg, N.C. So many years—faithful to one woman! It may be laudable in many men, or it may bespeak a failure of imagination and courage, but in Aaron Neuhaus it strikes me as exasperating, like Neuhaus's success with his bookstore, as if the man has set out to make the rest of us appear callow.

What I particularly resent is the fact that Aaron Neuhaus was born to a well-to-do North Carolina family, in 1951; having inherited large property holdings in Clarksburg County, N.C., as well as money held for him in trust until the age of twenty-one, he has been able to finance his bookstore(s) without the fear of bankruptcy that haunts the rest of us.

Nor was Neuhaus obliged to attend a large, sprawling, land-grant university as I did, in dreary, flat Ohio, but went instead to the prestigious, white-column'd University of Virginia, where he majored in such dilettantish subjects as classics and philosophy. After graduation Neuhaus remained at Virginia, earning a master's degree in English with a thesis titled *The Aesthetics of Deception: Ratiocination, Madness, and the Genius of Edgar Allan Poe*, which was eventually published by the University of Virginia Press. The young Neuhaus might have gone on to become a university professor, or a writer, but chose instead to apprentice himself to an uncle who was a (renowned, much-respected) antiquarian bookseller in Washington, D.C. Eventually, in 1980, having learned a good deal from his uncle, Neuhaus purchased a bookstore on Bleecker Street, New York City, which he managed to revitalize; in 1982, with the sale of this bookstore, he purchased a shop in Seabrook, N.H., which he renovated and refashioned as a chic, upscale, yet "historic" bookstore in the affluent seaside community. All that I have learned about Neuhaus as a businessman is that he is both "pragmatic" and "visionary"—an annoying contradiction. What I resent is that Neuhaus seems to have weathered financial crises that have sent other booksellers into despair and bankruptcy, whether as a result of shrewd business dealings or—more likely—the unfair advantage an independently well-to-do bookseller has over booksellers like myself with a thin profit margin and a fear of the future. *Though I do not hate Aaron Neuhaus, I do not approve of such an unfair advantage—it is contrary to Nature.* By now, Neuhaus might have been out of business, forced to scramble to earn a living in the aftermath of, for instance, those hurricanes of recent years that have devastated the Atlantic coastline and ruined many small businesses.

But if Mystery, Inc. suffers storm damage, or its proprietor loses money, it does not matter—there is the *unfair advantage* of the well-to-do over the rest of us.

I want to accuse Aaron Neuhaus: "How do you think you would do if our 'playing field' were level—if you couldn't bankroll your bookstore in hard times, as most of us can't? Do you think you would be selling Picasso lithographs upstairs, or first editions of Raymond Chandler; do you think you would have such beautiful floor-to-ceiling shelves, leather chairs and sofas? Do you think you would be such a naïve, gracious host, opening your store to a ginger-whiskered predator?"

It is difficult to feel indignation over Aaron Neuhaus, however, for the man is so damned *congenial*. Other rival booksellers haven't been nearly so pleasant, or, if pleasant, not nearly so well-informed and intelligent about their trade, which has made my task less of a challenge in the past.

The thought comes to me—Maybe we could be friends? Partners? If …

It is just 7 P.M. In the near distance a church bell tolls—unless it is the dull crashing surf of the Atlantic a quarter-mile away.

Aaron Neuhaus excuses himself, and goes to speak with his young woman clerk. Without seeming to be listening I hear him tell her that she can go home now, he will close up the store himself tonight.

Exactly as I have planned. But then, such *bait* has been dangled before.

Like any predator I am feeling excited—there is a pleasurable surge of adrenaline at the prospect of what will come next, very likely within the hour.

Timing is of the essence! All predators/hunters know this.

But I feel, too, a stab of regret. Seeing how the young blond woman smiles at Aaron Neuhaus, it is clear that she reveres her employer—perhaps loves him? Laura is in her mid-twenties, possibly a college student working part-time. Though it seems clear that there is no (sexual, romantic) intimacy between them, she might admire Neuhaus as an older man, a fatherly presence in her life; it will be terribly upsetting to her if something happens to him ... When I acquire Mystery, Inc., I will certainly want to spend time in this store. It is not far-fetched to imagine that I might take Aaron Neuhaus's place in the young woman's life.

As the new owner of Mystery, Inc., I will not be wearing these gingery-bristling whiskers. Nor these cumbersome black plastic-framed glasses. I will look younger, and more attractive. I have been told that I resemble the great film actor James Mason ... Perhaps I will wear Harris tweeds, and red cashmere sweater vests. Perhaps I will go on a strenuous diet, jogging along the ocean each morning, and will lose fifteen pounds. I will commiserate with Laura—*I did not know your late employer but 'Aaron Neuhaus' was the most highly regarded of booksellers—and gentlemen. I am so very sorry for your loss, Laura!*

Certainly I will want to rent living quarters in Seabrook, or even purchase property in this beautiful spot. At the present time, I move from place to place—like a hermit crab that occupies the empty shells of other sea creatures with no fixed home of its own. After acquiring an old, quasi-legendary mystery bookstore in Providence, Rhode Island, a few years ago, I lived in Providence for a while overseeing the store, until I could entrust a manager to oversee it; after acquiring a similar store in Westport, Connecticut, I lived there for a time; most recently I've been living in Boston, trying to revive a formerly prestigious mystery bookstore on Beacon Street. One would think that Beacon Street would be an excellent location for a quality mystery bookstore, and so it is—in theory; in reality, there is too much competition from other bookstores in the area. And of course there is too much competition from online sales, as from the damned, unspeakable Amazon.

I would like to ask Aaron Neuhaus how he deals with book theft, the plague of my urban-area stores, but I know the answer would be dismaying—Neuhaus's affluent customers hardly need to steal.

When Aaron Neuhaus returns, having sent the young woman home, he graciously asks if I would like to see his office upstairs. And would I like a cup of cappuccino?

"As you see, we don't have a café here. People have suggested that a café would help book sales but I've resisted—I'm afraid I am just too old-fashioned. But for special customers, we do have coffee and cappuccino—and it's very good, I can guarantee."

Of course, I am delighted. My pleasurable surprise at my host's invitation is not feigned.

In life, there are predators, and prey. A predator may require *bait*, and prey may mistake *bait* for sustenance.

In my leather attaché case is an arsenal of subtle weaponry. It is a truism that the most skillful murder is one that isn't detected as *murder* but simply *natural death*.

To this end, I have cultivated toxins as the least cumbersome and showy of murder weapons, as they are, properly used, the most reliable. I am too fastidious for bloodshed, or for any sort of violence; it has always been my feeling that violence is *vulgar*. I abhor loud noises, and witnessing the death throes of an innocent person would be traumatic for me. Ideally, I am nowhere near my prey when he (or she) is stricken by death, but miles away, and hours or even days later. There is never any apparent connection between the subject of my campaign and me—of course, I am far too shrewd to leave "clues" behind.

In quasipublic places like bookstores, fingerprints are general and could never be identified or traced; but if necessary, I take time to wipe my prints with a cloth soaked in alcohol. I am certainly not obsessive or compulsive, but I am *thorough*. Since I began my (secret, surreptitious) campaign of eliminating rival booksellers in the New England area nine years ago, I have utilized poisoned hypodermic needles; poisoned candles; poisoned (Cuban) cigars; poisoned sherry, liqueur, and whiskey; poisoned macaroons; and poisoned chocolates— all with varying degrees of success.

That is, in each case my campaign was successful. But several campaigns required more than one attempt and exacted a strain on nerves already strained by economic anxieties. In one unfortunate instance, after I'd managed to dispose of the bookseller, the man's heirs refused to sell the property though I'd made them excellent offers ... It is a sickening thing to think that one has expended so much energy in a futile project and that a wholly innocent party has died in vain; nor did I have the heart to return to that damned bookstore in Montclair, New Jersey, and take on the arrogant heirs as they deserved.

The method I have selected to dispatch the proprietor of Mystery, Inc. is one that has worked well for me in the past: chocolate truffles injected with a rare poison extracted from a Central American flowering plant bearing small red fruits like cranberries. The juice of these berries is so highly toxic, you dare not touch the outside of the berries; if the juice gets onto your skin it will burn savagely, and if it gets into your eyes—the very iris is horribly burnt away, and total blindness follows. In preparing the chocolates, which I carefully injected with a hypodermic needle, I wore not one but two pairs of surgical gloves; the operation was executed in a deep sink in a basement that could then be flooded with disinfectant and hot water. About three-quarters of the luxury chocolates have been injected with poison and the others remain untouched in their original Lindt box, in case the bearer of the luxury chocolates is obliged to sample some portion of his gift.

This particular toxin, though very potent, is said to have virtually no taste, and it has no color discernible to the naked eye. As soon as it enters the blood stream and is taken to the brain, it begins a virulent and irrevocable assault upon the central nervous system: within minutes the subject will begin to experience tremors and mild paralysis; consciousness will fade to a comatose state; by degrees, over a period of several hours, the body's organs cease to function; at first slowly, then rapidly, the lungs collapse and the heart ceases to beat; finally, the brain is struck blank and is annihilated. If there is an observer it will appear to him—or her—as though the afflicted one has had a heart attack or stroke; the skin is slightly clammy, not fevered; and there is no expression of pain or even discomfort, for the toxin is a paralytic, and thus merciful. There are no wrenching stomach pains, hideous vomiting as in the case of cyanide or poisons that affect the gastric-intestinal organs; stomach contents, if autopsied, will yield no information. The predator can observe his prey ingesting the toxin and can escape well in time to avoid witnessing even mild discomfort; it is advised that the predator take away with him his poisoned gift, so that there will be no detection. (Though this particular poison is all but undetectable by coroners and pathologists. Only a chemist who knew exactly what he was testing for could discover and identify this rare poison.) The aromatic lavender poisoned candles I'd left with my single female victim, a gratingly flirtatious bookseller in New Hope, Pennsylvania, had to work their dark magic in my absence and may have sickened, or even killed, more victims than were required ... No extra poisoned cigars should be left behind, of course; and poisoned alcoholic drinks should be borne prudently away. Though it isn't likely that the poison would be discovered, there is no point in being careless.

My gracious host Aaron Neuhaus takes me to the fourth floor of Mystery, Inc. in a small elevator at the rear of the store that moves with the antique slowness of a European elevator; by breathing deeply, and trying not to think of the terrible darkness of that long-ago closet in which my cruel brother locked me, I am able to withstand a mild onslaught of claustrophobia. Only a thin film of perspiration on my forehead might betray my physical distress, if Aaron Neuhaus were to take particular notice; but, in his affably entertaining way, he is telling me about the history of Mystery, Inc.—"Quite a fascinating history, in fact. Someday, I must write a memoir along the lines of the classic *My Life in Crime*."

On the fourth floor Aaron Neuhaus asks me if I can guess where his office door is—and I am baffled at first, staring from one wall to another, for there is no obvious sign of a door. Only by calculating where an extra room must be, in architectural terms, can I guess correctly: between reproductions of Goya's Black Paintings, unobtrusively set in the wall, is a panel that exactly mimics the room's white walls that Aaron Neuhaus pushes inward with a boyish smile.

"Welcome to my *sanctum sanctorum*! There is another, purely utilitarian office downstairs, where the staff works. Very few visitors are invited *here*."

I feel a frisson of something like dread, and the deliciousness of dread, passing so close to Goya's icons of Hell.

But Aaron Neuhaus's office is warmly lighted and beautifully furnished, like the drawing room of an English country gentleman; there is even a small fire blazing in a fireplace. Hardwood floor, partly covered in an old, well-worn yet still elegant Chinese carpet. One wall is solid books, but very special, well-preserved antiquarian books; other walls are covered in framed art-works including an oil painting by Albert Pinkham Ryder that must have been a study for the artist's famous "The Race Track" ("Death on a Pale Horse")—that dark-hued, ominous and yet beautiful oil painting by the most eccentric of nineteenth-century artists. A single high window overlooks, at a little distance, the rough waters of the Atlantic that appear in moonlight like shaken foil—the very view of the ocean I'd imagined Aaron Neuhaus might have.

Neuhaus's desk is made of dark, durable mahogany, with

many drawers and pigeonholes; his chair is an old-fashioned swivel chair, with a well-worn crimson cushion. The desk top is comfortably cluttered with papers, letters, galleys, books; on it are a Tiffany lamp of exquisite colored glass and a life-sized carved ebony raven—no doubt a replica of Poe's Raven. (On the wall above the desk is a daguerreotype of Edgar Allan Poe looking pale-skinned and dissolute, with melancholy eyes and drooping mustache; the caption is *Edgar Allan Poe Creator of C. Auguste Dupin 1841*.)

Unsurprisingly, Neuhaus uses fountain pens, not ballpoint; he has an array of colored pencils, and an old-fashioned eraser. There is even a brass letter-opener in the shape of a dagger. On such a desk, Neuhaus's state-of-the-art console computer appears out of place as a sleek, synthetic monument in an historic graveyard.

"Please sit, Charles! I will start the cappuccino machine and hope the damned thing will work. It is very Italian—*temperamental*."

I take a seat in a comfortable, well-worn leather chair facing Neuhaus's desk and with a view of the fireplace. I have brought my attaché case with the brass initials *CB*, to rest on my knees. Neuhaus fusses with his cappuccino machine, which is on a table behind his desk; he prefers cappuccino made with Bolivian coffee and skim milk, he says. "I have to confess to a mild addiction. There's a Starbucks in town but their cappuccino is nothing like mine."

Am I nervous? Pleasurably nervous? At the moment, I would prefer a glass of sherry to cappuccino!

My smile feels strained, though I am sure Aaron Neuhaus finds it affable, innocent. It is one of my stratagems to ply a subject with questions, to deflect any possible suspicion away from me, and Neuhaus enjoys answering my questions which are intelligent and well-informed, yet not overly intelligent and well-informed. The bookseller has not the slightest suspicion that he is dealing with an ambitious rival.

He is ruefully telling me that everyone who knew him,

including an antiquarian bookseller uncle in Washington, D.C., thought it was a very naïve notion to try to sell works of art in a bookstore in New Hampshire—"But I thought I would give myself three or four years, as an experiment. And it has turned out surprisingly well, especially my online sales."

Online sales. These are the sales that particularly cut into my own. Politely, I ask Neuhaus how much of his business is now online?

Neuhaus seems surprised by my question. Is it too personal? Too—*professional?* I am hoping he will attribute such a question to the naïveté of Charles Brockden.

His reply is curious—"In useless, beautiful art-works, as in books, values wax and wane according to some unknown and unpredictable algorithm."

This is a striking if evasive remark. It is somehow familiar to me, and yet—I can't recall why. I must be smiling inanely at Aaron Neuhaus, not knowing how to reply. *Useless, beautiful ... Algorithm ...*

Waiting for the cappuccino to brew, Neuhaus adds another log to the fire and prods it with a poker. What a bizarre gargoyle, the handle of the poker! In tarnished brass, a peevish grinning imp. Neuhaus shows it to me with a smile—"I picked this up at an estate sale in Blue Hill, Maine, a few summers ago. Curious, isn't it?"

"Indeed, yes."

I am wondering why Aaron Neuhaus has shown this demonic little face to *me*.

Such envy I've been feeling in this cozy yet so beautifully furnished *sanctum santorum*! It is painful to recall my own business offices, such as they are, utilitarian and drab, with nothing sacred about them. Outdated computers, ubiquitous fluorescent lights, charmless furniture inherited from bygone tenants. Often in a bookstore of mine the business office is also a storage room crammed with filing cabinets, packing crates, even brooms and mops, plastic buckets and step-ladders, and a lavatory in a corner. Everywhere, stacks of books rising from the floor like stalagmites. How ashamed I would be if Aaron Neuhaus were to see one of those!

I am thinking—*I will change nothing in this beautiful place. The very fountain pens on his desk will be mine. I will simply move in.*

Seeing that he has a very admiring and very curious visitor, Aaron Neuhaus is happy to chat about his possessions. The bookseller's pride in the privileged circumstances of his life is almost without ego—as one might take pleasure in any natural setting, like the ocean outside his window. Beside the large, stark daguerreotype of Poe are smaller photographs by the surrealist photographer Man Ray, of nude female figures in odd, awkward poses. Some of them are nude torsos lacking heads—very pale, marmoreal as sculpted forms. The viewer wonders uneasily: are these human beings, or mannequins? Are they human female *corpses*? Neuhaus tells me that the Man Ray photographs are taken from the photographer's *Tresor interdite* series of the 1930s—"Most of the work is inaccessible, in private collections, and never lent to museums." Beside the elegantly sinister Man Ray photographs, and very different from them, are crudely sensational crime photographs by the American photographer Weegee, taken in the 1930s and 1940s: stark portraits of men and women in the crises of their lives, beaten, bleeding, arrested and handcuffed, shot down in the street to lie sprawled, like one welldressed mobster, face down in their own blood.

"Weegee is the crudest of artists, but he is an artist. What is notable in such 'journalistic' art is the absence of the photographer from his work. You can't comprehend what, if anything, the photographer is thinking about these doomed people ..."

Man Ray, yes. Weegee, no. I detest crudeness, in art as in life; but of course I don't indicate this to Aaron Neuhaus, whom I don't want to offend. The man is so boyishly enthusiastic, showing off his treasures to a potential customer.

Prominent in one of Neuhaus's glassfronted cabinets is a complete set of the many volumes of the famous British criminologist William Roughead—"Each volume signed by Roughead"; also bound copies of the American detective pulps *Dime Detective, Black Mask,* and a copy of *The Black Lizard Big Book of Pulps.* These were magazines in which such greats as Dashiell Hammett and Raymond Chandler published stories, Neuhaus tells me, as if I didn't know.

In fact, I am more interested in Neuhaus's collection of great works of the "Golden Era of Mystery"—signed first editions by John Dickson Carr, Agatha Christie, and S.S. Van Dine, among others. (Some of these must be worth more than five thousand dollars apiece, I would think.) Neuhaus confesses that he would be very reluctant to sell his 1888 first edition of *A Study in Scarlet* in its original paper covers (priced at $100,000), or a signed first edition of *The Return of Sherlock Holmes* (priced at $35,000); more reluctantly, his first edition of *The Hound of the Baskervilles,* inscribed and signed, with handsome illustrations of Holmes and Watson (priced at $65,000). He shows me one of his "priceless" possessions—a bound copy of the February 1827 issue of *Blackwood's Magazine* containing Thomas de Quincy's infamous essay, "On Murder Considered as One of the Fine Arts." Yet more impressively, he has the complete four volumes of the first edition (1794) of *Mysteries of Udolpho* (priced at $10,000). But the jewel of his collection, which he will never sell, he says, unless he is absolutely desperate for money, is the 1853 first edition, in original cloth with "sepia cabinet photograph of author" of Charles Dickens's *Bleak House* (priced at $75,000), signed by Dickens in his strong, assured hand, in ink that has scarcely faded!

"But this is something that would particularly interest you, 'Charles Brockden'"— Neuhaus chuckles, carefully taking from a shelf a very old book, encased in plastic, with a loose, faded binding and badly yellowed pages—Charles Brockden Brown's *Wieland; or The Transformation: An American Tale,* 1798.

This is extraordinary! One would expect to see such a rare book under lock and key in the special collections of a great university library, like Harvard.

For a moment I can't think how to reply. Neuhaus seems almost to be teasing me. It was a careless choice of a name, I suppose— "Charles Brockden." If I'd thought about it, of course I would have realized that a bookseller would be reminded of Charles Brockden Brown.

To disguise my confusion, I ask Aaron Neuhaus how much he is asking for this rare book, and Neuhaus says, "'Asking'—? I am not 'asking' any sum at all. It is not for sale."

Again, I'm not sure how to reply. Is Neuhaus laughing at me? Has he seen through my fictitious name, as through my disguise? I don't think that this is so, for his demeanor is good-natured; but the way in which he smiles at me, as if we are sharing a joke, makes me uneasy.

It's a relief when Neuhaus returns the book to its shelf, and locks up the glassfronted cabinets. At last, the cappuccino is ready!

All this while, the fire has been making me warm—over-warm.

The ginger-colored whiskers that cover my jaws have begun to itch.

The heavy black plastic glasses, so much more cumbersome than my preferred wire rim glasses, are leaving red marks on the bridge of my nose. Ah, I am looking forward to tearing both whiskers and glasses from my face with a cry of relief and victory in an hour—or ninety minutes—when I am departing Seabrook in my vehicle, south along the ocean road ...

"Charles! Take care, it's very hot."

Not in a small cappuccino cup but in a hearty coffee mug, Aaron Neuhaus serves me the pungent brewed coffee, with its delightful frothed milk. The liquid is rich, very dark, scalding-hot as he has warned. I am wondering if I should take out of my attaché case the box of Lindt chocolates to share with my host, or whether it is just slightly too soon—I don't want to arouse his suspicion. If—when— Aaron Neuhaus eats one of these potent chocolates I will want to depart soon after, and our ebullient hour together will come to an abrupt conclusion. It is foolish of me perhaps, but I am almost thinking—well, it is not very realistic, but indeed, I am thinking—*Why could we not be partners? If I introduce myself as a serious book collector, one with unerring taste (if not unlimited resources, as he seems to have)—would not Aaron Neuhaus be impressed with me? Does he not, already, like me—and trust me?*

At the same time, my brain is pragmatically pursuing the more probable course of events: if I wait until Aaron Neuhaus lapses into a coma, I could take away with me a select few of his treasures, instead of having to wait until I can purchase Mystery, Inc. Though I am not a *common thief*, it has been exciting to see such rare items on display; almost, in a sense, dangled before me, by my clueless prey. Several of the less-rare items would be all that I could dare, for it would be a needless risk to take away, for instance, the Dickens first edition valued at $79,000—just the sort of greedy error that could entrap me.

"Are you often in these parts, Charles? I don't think that I have seen you in my store before."

"No, not often. In the summer, sometimes …" My voice trails off uncertainly. Is it likely that a bookstore proprietor would see, and take note, of every customer who comes into his store? Or am I interpreting Aaron Neuhaus too literally?

"My former wife and I sometimes drove to Boothbay, Maine. I believe we passed through this beautiful town, but did not stop." My voice is somewhat halting, but certainly sincere. Blindly I continue, "I am not married now—unfortunately. My wife had been my high school sweetheart but she did not share my predilection for precious old books, I'm afraid."

Is any of this true? I am hoping only that such words have the ring of plausibility.

"I've long been a lover of mysteries—in books and in life. It's wonderful to discover a fellow enthusiast, and in such a beautiful store …"

"It is! Always a wonderful discovery. I, too, am a lover of mysteries, of course—in life as in books."

Aaron Neuhaus laughs expansively. He has been blowing on his mug of cappuccino, for it is still steaming. I am intrigued by the subtle distinction of his remark, but would require some time to ponder it—if indeed it is a significant remark, and not just casual banter.

Thoughtfully, Neuhaus continues: "It is out of the profound mystery of life that 'mystery books' arise. And, in turn, 'mystery books' allow us to see the mystery of life more clearly, from perspectives not our own."

On a shelf behind the affable bookseller's desk are photographs that I have been trying to see more clearly. One, in an antique oval frame, is of an extraordinarily beautiful, young, black-haired woman—could this be Mrs. Neuhaus? I think it must be, for in another photograph she and a youthful Aaron Neuhaus are together, in wedding finery—a most attractive couple.

There is something profoundly demoralizing about this sight—such a beautiful woman, married to this man not so very different from myself! Of course—(I am rapidly calculating, cantilevering to a new, objective perspective)—the young bride is no longer young, and would be, like her husband, in her early sixties. No doubt Mrs. Neuhaus is still quite beautiful. It is not impossible to think that, in the devastated aftermath of losing her husband, the widow might not be adverse, in time, to remarriage with an individual who shares so much of her late husband's interests, and has taken over Mystery, Inc. ... Other photographs, surely family photos, are less interesting, though suggesting that Neuhaus is a "family man" to some degree. (If we had more time, I would ask about these personal photos; but I suppose I will find out eventually who Neuhaus's relatives are.)

Also on the shelf behind Neuhaus's desk is what appears to be a homemade art-work— a bonsai-sized tree (fashioned from a coat hanger?)—upon which small items have been hung: a man's signet ring, a man's wristwatch, a brass belt buckle, a pocket watch with a gold chain. If I didn't know that Neuhaus had no children, I would presume that this amateurish "art" has found a place amid the man's treasures which its artistry doesn't seem to merit.

At last, the cappuccino is not so scalding. It is still hot, but very delicious. Now I am wishing badly that I'd prepared a box of macaroons, more appropriate here than chocolate truffles.

As if I have only just now recalled it, I remove the Lindt box from my attaché case. An unopened box, I suggest to Aaron Neuhaus— freshly purchased and not a chocolate missing.

(It is true, I am reluctant to hurry our fascinating conversation, but—there is a duty here that must be done.)

In a display of playful horror Neuhaus half-hides his eyes— "Chocolate truffles—my favorite chocolates—and my favorite truffles! Thank you, Charles, but—I should not. My dear wife will expect me to be reasonably hungry for dinner." The bookseller's voice wavers, as if he is hoping to be encouraged.

"Just one chocolate won't make any difference, Aaron. And your dear wife will never know, if you don't tell her."

Neuhaus is very amusing as he takes one of the chocolate truffles—(from the first, poisoned row)—with an expression both boyishly greedy and guilty. He sniffs it with delight and seems about to bite into it—then lays it on his desk top as if temporarily, in a show of virtue. He winks at me as at a fellow conspirator—"You are quite right, my dear wife needn't know. There is much in marriage that might be kept from a spouse, for her own good. Though possibly, I should bring my wife one of these also—if you could spare another, Charles?"

"Why of course—but—take more than one ... Please help yourself—of course."

This is disconcerting. But there is no way for me to avoid offering Neuhaus the box again, this time somewhat awkwardly, turning it so that he is led to choose a chocolate truffle out of a row of non-poisoned truffles. And I will eat one with much appetite, so that Neuhaus is tempted to eat his.

How warm I am! And these damned whiskers itching!

As if he has only just thought of it, Aaron Neuhaus excuses himself to call his wife—on an old-fashioned black dial phone, talisman of another era. He lowers his voice out of courtesy, not because he doesn't want his visitor to overhear. "Darling? Just to alert you, I will be a little late tonight. A most fascinating customer has dropped by—whom I don't want to short-change." *Most fascinating.* I am flattered by this, though saddened.

So tenderly does Neuhaus speak to his wife, I feel an almost overwhelming wave of pity for him, and for her; yet, more powerfully, a wave of envy, and anger. *Why does this man deserve that beautiful woman and her love, while I have no one—no love—at all?*

It is unjust, and it is unfair. It is intolerable.

Neuhaus tells his wife he will be home, he believes, by at least 8:30 PM. Again it is flattering to me, that Neuhaus thinks so well of me; he doesn't plan to send me away for another hour. Another wife might be annoyed by such a call, but the beautiful (and mysterious) Mrs. Neuhaus does not object. "Yes! Soon. I love you too, darling." Neuhaus unabashedly murmurs these intimate words, like one who isn't afraid to acknowledge emotion.

The chocolate truffle, like the cappuccino, is indeed delicious. My mouth waters even as I eat it. I am hoping that Neuhaus will devour his, as he clearly wants to; but he has left both truffles untouched for the moment, while he sips the cappuccino. There is something touchingly childlike in this procrastination— putting off a treat, if but for a moment. I will not allow myself to think of the awful possibility that Neuhaus will eat the unpoisoned truffle and bring the poisoned truffle home to his wife.

To avoid this, I may offer Neuhaus the entire box to take home to his wife. In that way, both the owner of Mystery, Inc. and the individual who would inherit it upon his death will depart this earth. Purchasing the store from another, less personally involved heir might be, in fact, an easier stratagem.

I have asked Aaron Neuhaus who his customers are in this out-of-the-way place, and he tells me that he has a number of "surprisingly faithful, stubbornly loyal" customers who come to his store from as far away as Boston, even New York City, in good weather at least. There are local regulars, and there are the summertime customers—"Mystery, Inc. is one of the most popular shops in town, second only to Starbucks." Still, most of his sales in the past twenty-five years have been mail-order and online; the online orders are more or less continuous, emails that come in through the night from his "considerable overseas clientele."

This is a cruel blow! I'm sure that I have *no overseas clientele* at all.

Yet it isn't possible to take offense, for Aaron Neuhaus is not boasting so much as speaking matter-of-factly. Ruefully I am thinking—*The man can't help being superior. It is ironic, he must be punished for something that is not his fault.*

Like my brother, I suppose. Who had to be punished for something that wasn't his fault: a mean-spirited soul, envious and malicious regarding *me*. Though I will regret Aaron Neuhaus's fate, I will never regret my brother's fate.

Still, Aaron Neuhaus has put off eating his chocolate truffle with admirable restraint! By this time I have had a second, and Neuhaus is preparing two more cups of cappuccino. The caffeine is having a bracing effect upon my blood. Like an admiring interviewer I am asking my host where his interest in mystery derives, and Neuhaus replies that he fell under the spell of mystery as a young child, if not an infant—"I think it had to do with my astonishment at peering out of my crib and seeing faces peering at me. Who were they? My mother whom I did not yet know was my mother—my father whom I did not yet know was my father? These individuals must have seemed like giants to me—mythic figures— as in the *Odyssey*." He pauses, with a look of nostalgia. "Our lives are odysseys, obviously— continuous, ever-unexpected adventures. Except we are not journeying home, like Odysseus, but journeying away from home inexorably, like the Hubble universe."

What is this?—"Hubble universe"? I'm not sure that I fully understand what Aaron Neuhaus is saying, but there is no doubt that my companion is speaking from the heart.

As a boy he fell under the spell of mystery fiction—boys'

adventure, Sherlock Holmes, Ellery Queen, Mark Twain's *Pudd'head Wilson*— and by the age of thirteen he'd begun reading true crime writers (like the esteemed Roughead) of the kind most readers don't discover until adulthood. Though he has a deep and enduring love for American hard-boiled fiction, his long-abiding love is for Wilkie Collins and Charles Dickens—"Writers not afraid of the role coincidence plays in our lives, and not afraid of over-the-top melodrama."

This is true. Coincidence plays far more of a role in our lives than we (who believe in free will) wish to concede. And lurid, over-the-top melodrama, perhaps a rarity in most lives, but inescapable at one time or another.

Next, I ask Aaron Neuhaus how he came to purchase his bookstore, and he tells me with a nostalgic smile that indeed it was an accident— a "marvelous coincidence"—that one day when he was driving along the coast to visit relatives in Maine, he happened to stop in Seabrook—"And there was this gem of a bookstore, right on High Street, in a row of beautiful old brownstones. The store wasn't quite as it is now, slightly rundown, and neglected, yet with an intriguing sign out front— *Mystery, Inc.: M. Rackham Books*. Within minutes I saw the potential of the store and the location, and I fell in love with something indefinable in the very air of Seabrook, New Hampshire."

At this time, in 1982, Aaron Neuhaus owned a small bookstore that specialized in mystery, detective, and crime fiction in the West Village, on Bleecker Street; though he worked in the store as many as one hundred hours a week, with two assistants, he was chafing under the burden of circumscribed space, high rent and high taxes, relentless book-theft, and a clientele that included homeless derelicts and junkies who wandered into the store looking for public lavatories or for a place to sleep. His wife yearned to move out of New York City and into the country—she had an education degree and was qualified to teach school, but did not want to teach in the New York City public school system, nor did Neuhaus want her to. And so

Neuhaus made a decision almost immediately to acquire the Seabrook bookstore—"If it were humanly possible."

It was an utterly impulsive decision, Neuhaus said. He had not even consulted with his dear wife. Yet, it was unmistakable— "Like falling in love at first sight."

The row of brownstones on High Street was impressive, but *Mystery, Inc: M. Rackham Books* was not so impressive. In the first-floor bay window were displayed the predictable bestsellers one would see in any bookstore window of the time, but here amid a scattering of dead flies; inside, most of the books were trade paperbacks with lurid covers and little literary distinction. The beautiful floor-to- ceiling mahogany bookshelves—carpentry which would cost a fortune in 1982— were in place, the hammered-tin ceiling, hardwood floors. But so far as the young bookseller could see the store offered no first editions, rare or unusual books, or art-works; the second floor was used for storage, and the upper two floors were rented out. Still, the store was ideally situated on Seabrook's main street overlooking the harbor, and it seemed likely that the residents of Seabrook were generally affluent, well-educated, and discerning.

Not so exciting, perhaps, as a store on Bleecker Street in the West Village—yet, it may be that excitement is an overrated experience if you are a serious bookseller.

"After I'd been in the store for a few minutes, however, I could feel—something ... An atmosphere of tension like the air preceding a storm. The place was virtually deserted on a balmy spring day. There were loud voices at the rear. There came then—in a hurry—the proprietor to speak eagerly with me, like a man who is dying of loneliness. When I introduced myself as a fellow bookseller, from New York City, Milton Rackham all but seized my hand. He was a large, soft-bodied, melancholic older gentleman whose adult son worked with him, or for him. At first Rackham talked enthusiastically of books—his favorites, which included, not surprisingly, the great works of Wilkie Collins, Dickens, and Conan Doyle. Then he began to speak with more emotion of how he'd been a young professor of classics at Harvard who, with his young wife who'd shared his love for books and bookstores, decided to quit the 'sterile, self-absorbed' academic world to fulfill a life's dream of buying a bookstore in a small town and making it into a 'very special place.' Unfortunately his beloved wife had died after only a few years, and his unmarried son worked with him now in the store; in recent years, the son had become "inward, troubled, unpredictable, strange—*a brooding personality*."

It was surprising to Neuhaus, and somewhat embarrassing, that the older bookseller should speak so openly to a stranger of these personal and painful matters. And the poor man spoke disjointedly, unhappily, lowering his voice so that his heavyset, pony-tailed son (whom Neuhaus glimpsed shelving books at the rear of the store with a particular sort of vehemence, as if he were throwing livestock into vats of steaming scalding water) might not hear. In a hoarse whisper Rackham indicated to Neuhaus that the store would soon be for sale—"To the proper buyer."

"Now, I was truly shocked. But also … excited. For I'd already fallen in love with the beautiful old brownstone, and here was its proprietor, declaring that it was for sale."

Neuhaus smiles with a look of bittersweet nostalgia. It is enviable that a man can glance back over his life, and present the crucial episodes in his life, not with pain or regret but with—nostalgia!

Next, the young visitor invited Milton Rackham to speak in private with him, in his office—"Not here: Rackham's office was on the first floor, a cubbyhole of a room containing one large, solid piece of furniture, this very mahogany desk, amid a chaos of books, galleys, boxes, unpaid bills and invoices, dust balls, and desperation"—, about the bookstore, what it might cost with or without a mortgage; when it would be placed on the market, and how soon the new owner could take possession. Rackham brandished a bottle of whiskey, and poured drinks for them in "clouded" glasses; he searched for, and eventually found, a cellophane package of stale sourballs, which he offered to his guest. It was painful to see how Rackham's hands shook. And alarming to see how the older man's mood swerved from embittered to elated, from anxious to exhilarated, as he spoke excitedly to his young visitor, often interrupting himself with laughter, like one who has not spoken with anyone in a long time. He confided in Neuhaus that he didn't trust his son—"'Not with our finances, not with book orders, not with maintaining the store, and not with my life.' He'd once been very close to the boy, as he called him, but their relationship had altered significantly since his son's fortieth birthday, for no clear reason. Unfortunately, he had no other recourse than to keep his son on at the store as he couldn't afford to pay an employee a competitive wage, and the boy, who'd dropped out of Williams College midway through his freshman year, for 'mental' reasons, would have no other employment—' It is a tragic trap, fatherhood! And my wife and I had been so happy in our innocence, long ago.'" Neuhaus shudders, recalling.

"As Rackham spoke in his lowered voice I had a sudden fantasy of the son rushing into the office swinging a hand ax at us ... I felt absolutely chilled—terrified ... I swear, I could see that ax ... It was as if the bookstore were haunted by something that had not yet happened."

Haunted by something that had not yet happened. Despite the heat from the fireplace, I am feeling chilled too. I glance over my shoulder to see that the door, or rather the moving panel, is shut. No one will rush in upon us here in Aaron Neuhaus's *sanctum sanctorum*, wielding an ax ...

Nervously, I have been sipping my cappuccino, which has cooled somewhat. I am finding it just slightly hard to swallow— my mouth is oddly dry, perhaps because of nerves. The taste of the cappuccino is extraordinary: rich, dark, delicious. It is the frothy milk that makes the coffee so special, Neuhaus remarks that it isn't ordinary milk but goat's milk, for a sharper flavor.

Neuhaus continues—"It was from Milton Rackham that I

acquired the complete set of William Roughead which, for some eccentric reason, he'd been keeping in a cabinet at the back of the store under lock and key. I asked him why this wonderful set of books was hidden away, why it wasn't prominently displayed and for sale, and Rackham said coldly, with an air of reproach, 'Not all things in a bookseller's life are for sale, sir.' Suddenly, with no warning, the old gentleman seemed to be hostile to me. I was shocked by his tone."

Neuhaus pauses, as if he is still shocked, to a degree.

"Eventually, Rackham would reveal to me that he was hoarding other valuable first editions— some of these I have shown you, the 'Golden Age' items, which I acquired as part of the store's stock. And the first-edition Mysteries of Udolpho— which in his desperation to sell he practically gave away to me. And a collection of antique maps and globes, in an uncatalogued jumble on the second floor—a collection he'd inherited, he said, from the previous bookseller. Why on earth would anyone hoard these valuable items—I couldn't resist asking—and Rackham told me, again in a hostile voice, 'We gentlemen don't wear our hearts on our sleeves, do we? Do *you*?'"

It is uncanny, when Neuhaus mimics his predecessor's voice, I seem—almost—to be hearing the voice of another.

"Such a strange man! And yet, in a way— a way I have never quite articulated to anyone, before now—Milton Rackham has come to seem to me a kind of *paternal figure* in my life. He'd looked upon me as a kind of son, or rescuer— seeing that his own son had turned against him."

Neuhaus is looking pensive, as if remembering something unpleasant. And I am feeling anxious, wishing that my companion would devour the damned chocolate truffle as he clearly wishes to do.

"Charles, it's a poor storyteller who leaps ahead of his story—but—I have to tell you, before going on, that my vision of Rackham's 'brooding' son murdering him with an ax turned out to be prophetic—that is, true. It would happen exactly three weeks to the day after I'd first stepped into the bookstore—at a time when Rackham and I were negotiating the sale of the property, mostly by phone. I was nowhere near Seabrook, and received an astounding call ..." Neuhaus passes his hand over his eyes, shaking his head.

This is a surprising revelation! For some reason, I am quite taken aback. That a bookseller was murdered in this building, even if not in this very room, and by his own son— this is a bit of a shock.

"And so—in some way—Mystery, Inc. is haunted?"—my question is uncertain.

Neuhaus laughs, somewhat scornfully— "Haunted—now? Of course not. Mystery, Inc. is a very successful, even legendary bookstore of its kind in New England. *You* would not know that, Charles, since you are not in the trade."

These words aren't so harsh as they might seem, for Neuhaus is smiling at me as one might smile at a foolish or uninformed individual for whom one feels some affection, and is quick to forgive. And I am eager to agree— I am not in *the trade*.

"The story is even more awful, for the murderer—the deranged 'boy'—managed to kill himself also, in the cellar of the store—a very dark, dank, dungeon-like space even today, which I try to avoid as much as possible. (Talk of 'haunted'! That is the likely place, not the bookstore itself.) The hand ax was too dull for the task, it seems, so the 'boy' cut his throat with a box cutter—one of those razor-sharp objects no bookstore is without." Casually Neuhaus reaches out to pick up a box cutter, that has been hidden from my view by a stack of bound galleys on his desk; as if, for one not in the "trade," a box cutter would need to be identified. (Though I am quite familiar with box cutters it is somewhat disconcerting to see one in this elegantly furnished office— lying on Aaron Neuhaus's desk!) "Following this double tragedy, the property fell into the possession of a mortgage company, for it had been heavily mortgaged. I was able to complete the sale within a few weeks, for a quite reasonable price since no one else seemed to want it." Neuhaus chuckles grimly.

"As I'd said, I have leapt ahead of my story, a bit. There is more to tell about poor Milton Rackham that is of interest. I asked him how he'd happened to learn of the bookstore here in Seabrook and he told me of how 'purely by chance' he'd discovered the store in the fall of 1957—he'd been driving along the coast on his way to Maine and stopped in Seabrook, on High Street, and happened to see the bookstore— Slater's Mystery Books & Stationers it was called—'It was such a vision!—the bay windows gleaming in the sun, and the entire block of brownstones so attractive.' A good part of Slater's merchandise was stationery, quite high-quality stationery, and other supplies of that sort, but there was an excellent collection of books as well, hardcover and paperback; not just the usual popular books but somewhat esoteric titles as well, by Robert W. Chambers, Bram Stoker, M.R. James, Edgar Wallace, Oscar Wilde (*Salome*), H.P. Lovecraft. Slater seemed to have been a particular admirer of Erle Stanley Gardner, Rex Stout, Josephine Tey, and Dorothy L. Sayers, writers whom Milton Rackham admired also. The floor-to-ceiling mahogany bookshelves were in place—cabinetry that would cost a fortune at the time, as Rackham remarked again. And there were odd, interesting things stocked in the store like antique maps, globes—'A kind of treasure trove, as in an older relative's attic in which you might spend long rainy afternoons under a spell.' Rackham told me that he wandered through the store with 'mounting excitement'—feeling that it was already known to him, in a way; through a window, he looked out toward the Atlantic Ocean, and felt the 'thrill of its great beauty.' Indeed, Milton Rackham would tell me that it had been 'love at first sight'—as soon as he'd glimpsed the bookstore.

"As it turned out, Amos Slater had been contemplating selling the store, which had been a family inheritance; though, as he said, he continued to 'love books and bookselling,' it was no longer with the passion of youth, and so he hoped to soon retire. Young Milton Rackham was stunned by this good fortune. Three weeks later, with his wife's enthusiastic support, he made an offer to Amos Slater for the property, and the offer was accepted almost immediately."

Neuhaus speaks wonderingly, like a man who is recounting a somewhat fantastical tale he hopes his listeners will believe, for it is important for them to believe it.

"'My wife had a faint premonition'—this is Milton Rackham speaking—'that something might be wrong, but I paid no attention. I was heedless then, in love with my sweet young wife, and excited by the prospect of walking away from pious Harvard—(where it didn't look promising that I would get tenure)—and taking up a purer life, as I thought it, in the booksellers' trade. And so, Mildred and I arranged for a thirty-year mortgage, and made our initial payment through the Realtor, and on our first visit to the store as the new owners— when Amos Slater presented us with the keys to the building— it happened that my wife innocently asked Amos Slater how he'd come to own the store, and Amos told her a most disturbing tale, like one eager to get something off his chest …

"'Slater's Books'—this is Amos Slater speaking, as reported by Milton Rackham to me—'had been established by his grandfather Barnabas in 1912. Slater's grandfather was a 'lover of books, rather than humankind'— though one of his literary friends was Ambrose Bierce who'd allegedly encouraged Barnabas's writing of fiction. Slater told Rackham a bizarre tale that at the age of eleven he'd had a 'powerful vision'— dropping by his grandfather's bookstore one day after school, he'd found the store empty— 'No customers, no sales clerks, and no Grandfather, or so I thought. But then, looking for Grandfather, I went into the cellar—I turned on a light and— there was Grandfather hanging from a beam, his body strangely straight, and very still; and his face turned mercifully from me, though there was no doubt who it was. For a long moment I stood paralyzed— I could not believe what I was seeing. I could not even scream, I was so frightened … My grandfather Barnabas and I had not been close. Grandfather had hardly seemed to take notice of me except sneeringly—'Is it a little boy, or a little girl? *What is it?*' Grandfather Slater was a strange man, as people said— short-tempered yet also rather cold and detached—passionate about some things, but indifferent about most things—determined to make his book and stationery store a success but contemptuous with most customers, and very cynical about human nature. It appeared that he had dragged a step-ladder beneath the beam in the cellar, tied a hemp noose around his neck, climbed up the ladder and kicked the ladder away beneath him—he must have died a horrible, strangulated death, gasping for breath and kicking and writhing for many minutes ... Seeing the hanged body of my grandfather was one of the terrible shocks of my life. I don't know quite what happened ... I fainted, I think—then forced myself to crawl to the steps, and made my way upstairs—ran for help ... I remember screaming on High Street ... People hurried to help me, I brought them back into the store and down into the cellar, but there was no one there—no rope hanging from the beam, and no overturned step-ladder. Again, it was one of the shocks of my life—I was only eleven, and could not comprehend what was happening ... Eventually, Grandfather was discovered a few doors away at the Bell, Book & Candle Pub, calmly drinking port and eating a late lunch of pigs' knuckles and sauerkraut. He'd spent most of the day doing inventory, he said, on the second floor of the store, and hadn't heard any commotion.'"

"Poor Amos Slater never entirely recovered from the trauma of seeing his grandfather's hanged body in the cellar of the bookstore, or rather the vision of the hanged body—so everyone who knew him believed. ..."

"As Milton Rackham reported to me, he'd learned from Amos Slater that the grandfather Barnabas had been a 'devious' person who defrauded business partners, seduced and betrayed naïve, virginal Seabrook women, and, it was charged more than once, 'pilfered' their savings; he'd amassed a collection of first editions and rare books, including a copy of Charles Brockden Brown's *Wieland*—such treasures he claimed to have bought at estate auctions and sales, but some observers believed he had taken advantage of distraught widows and grief-stricken heirs, or possibly he'd stolen outright. Barnabas had married a well-to-do local woman several years his senior to whom he was cruel and coercive, who'd died at the age of fifty-two of 'suspicious' causes. Nothing was *proven*—so Amos Slater had been told. 'Growing up, I had to see how my father was intimidated by my grandfather Barnabas, who mocked him as 'less than a man' for not standing up to him. 'Where is the son and heir whom I deserve? Who are these weaklings who surround me?'—the old man would rage. Grandfather Barnabas was one to play practical jokes on friends and enemies alike; he had a particularly nasty trick of giving people sweet treats laced with laxatives … Once, our minister at the Episcopal church here in Seabrook was stricken with terrible diarrhea during Sunday services, as a consequence of plum tarts Barnabas had given him and his family; another time, my mother, who was Grandfather's daughter-in-law, became deathly sick after drinking apple cider laced with insecticide my grandfather had put in the cider—or so it was suspected. (Eventually, Grandfather admitted to putting 'just a few drops' of DDT into the cider his daughter-in-law would be drinking; he hadn't known it was DDT, he claimed, but had thought it was a liquid laxative. 'In any case, I didn't mean it to be *fatal*.' And he spread his fingers, and laughed— it was blood-chilling to hear him.) Yet, Barnabas Slater had an 'obsessive love' of books—mystery-detective books, crime books—and had actually tried to write fiction himself, in the mode of Edgar Allan Poe, it was said.

"Amos Slater told Rackham that he'd wanted to flee Seabrook and the ghastly legacy of Barnabas Slater but—somehow—he'd had no choice about taking over his grandfather's bookstore— 'When Grandfather died, I was designated his heir in his will. My father was ill by that time, and would not long survive. I felt resigned, and accepted my inheritance, though I knew at the time such an inheritance was like a tombstone—if the tombstone toppled over, and you were not able to climb out of the grave in which you'd been prematurely buried, like one of those victims in Poe ... Another cruel thing my grandfather boasted of doing—(who knows if the wicked old man was telling the truth, or merely hoping to upset his listeners)—was experimentation with exotic toxins: extracting venom from poisonous frogs that was a colorless, tasteless, odorless, milky liquid that could be added to liquids like hot chocolate and hot coffee without being detected ... The frogs are known as Poison Dart Frogs, found in the United States in the Florida Everglades, it is said ... "'The Poison Dart Frog's venom is so rare, no coroner or pathologist could identify it even if there were any suspicion of foul play— which there wasn't likely to be. A victim's symptoms did not arouse suspicion. Within minutes (as Grandfather boasted) the venom begins to attack the central nervous system— the afflicted one shivers, and shudders, and can't seem to swallow, for his mouth is very dry; soon, hallucinations begin; and paralysis and coma; within eight to ten hours, the body's organs begin to break down, slowly at first and then rapidly, by which time the victim is unconscious and unaware of what is happening to him. Liver, kidneys, lungs, heart, brain—all collapse from within. If observed, the victim seems to be suffering some sort of attack—heart attack, stroke—'fainting'— there are no gastric-intestinal symptoms, no horrible attacks of vomiting. If the stomach is pumped, there is nothing—no 'food poisoning.' The victim simply fades away ... it is a merciful death, as deaths go.'" Aaron Neuhaus pauses as if the words he is recounting, with seeming precision, from memories of long ago, are almost too much for him to absorb.

"Then, Milton Rackham continued—'The irony is, as Slater told it, after a long and surprisingly successful life as a small town bookseller of quality books, Barnabas Slater did hang himself, it was surmised out of boredom and self-disgust at the age of seventy-two—in the cellar of Slater's Books exactly as his grandson Amos had envisioned. Scattered below his hanging body were carefully typed, heavily edited manuscript pages of what appeared to be several mystery-detective novels— no one ever made the effort of collating the pages and reading them. It was a family decision to inter the unpublished manuscripts with Grandfather.'"

"Isn't this tale amazing? Have you ever heard anything so bizarre, Charles? I mean— in actual life? In utter solemnity poor Milton Rackham recounted it to me, as he'd heard it from Amos Slater. I could sympathize that Rackham was a nervous wreck—he was concerned that his son might do violence against him, and he had to contend with being the proprietor of a store in which a previous proprietor had hanged himself! He went on to say, as Slater had told him, that it had been the consensus in Seabrook that no one knew if Barnabas had actually poisoned anyone fatally— he'd played his little pranks with laxatives and insecticide—but the 'Poison Dart Frog venom' was less evident. Though people did die of somewhat mysterious 'natural causes,' in the Slater family, from time to time. Several persons who knew Barnabas well said that the old man had often said that there are some human beings so vile, they don't deserve to live; but he'd also said, with a puckish wink, that he 'eradicated' people for no particular reason, at times. 'Good, not-so-good, evil'— the classic murderer does not discriminate. Barnabas particularly admired the de Quincy essay 'On Murder Considered One of the Fine Arts' that makes the point that no reason is required for murder, in fact to have a reason is to be rather vulgar—so Barnabas believed also. Excuse me, Charles? Is something wrong?"

"Why, I—I am—utterly confused ..."

"Have you lost your way? My predecessor was Milton Rackham, from whom I bought this property; his predecessor was Amos Slater, from whom he, Rackham, bought the property; and *his predecessor* was a gentleman named Barnabas Slater who seems to have hanged himself in the cellar here—for which reason, as I'd mentioned a few minutes ago, I try to avoid the damned place, as much as possible. (I send my employees down, instead! They don't mind.) I think you were reacting to

Barnabas Slater's philosophy, that no reason is required for murder, especially for murder as an 'art form.'"

"But—why would anyone kill for no reason?"

"Why would anyone kill *for a reason*?" Neuhaus smiles, eloquently. "It seems to me, Slater's grandfather Barnabas may have extracted the essence of 'mystery' from life, as he was said to have extracted venom from the venomous frog. The act of killing is complete in itself, and requires no reason—like any work of art. Yet, if one is looking for a reason, one is likely to kill to protect oneself—one's territory. Our ancestors were fearful and distrustful of enemies, strangers—they were 'xenophobic'—'paranoid.' If a stranger comes into your territory, and behaves with sinister intent, or even behaves without sinister intent, you are probably better off dispatching him than trying to comprehend him, and possibly making a fatal mistake. In the distant past, before God was love, such mistakes could lead to the extinction of an entire species—so it is that *Homo sapiens*, the preemptive species, prefers to err by over-caution, not under-caution."

I am utterly confounded by these words, spoken by my affable companion in a matter-of-fact voice. And that smile!—it is so boyish, and magnanimous. Almost, I can't speak, but stutter feebly.

"That is a—a—surprising thing to say, for you ... Aaron. That is a somewhat cynical thing to say, I think ..."

Aaron Neuhaus smiles as if, another time, I am a very foolish person whom he must humor. "Not at all 'cynical,' Charles—why would you think so? If you are an aficionado of mystery-detective-crime fiction, you know that someone, in fact many people, and many of them 'innocent,' must die for the sake of the art—for *mystery's sake*. That is the bedrock of our business: Mystery, Inc. Some of us are booksellers, and some of us are consumers, or are consumed. But all of us have our place in the noble trade."

There is a ringing in my ears. My mouth is so very dry, it is virtually impossible to swallow. My teeth are chattering for I am very cold. Except for its frothy remains, my second cup of cappuccino is empty—I have set it on Neuhaus's desk, but so shakily that it nearly falls over.

Neuhaus regards me closely with concerned eyes. On his desk, the carved ebony raven is regarding me as well. Eyes very sharp! I am shivering—despite the heat from the fire. I am very cold—except the whiskers on my jaws feel very hot. I am thinking that I must protect myself—the box of Lindt's chocolate truffles is my weapon, but I am not sure how to employ it. Several of the chocolate truffles are gone, but the box is otherwise full; many remain yet to be eaten.

I know that I have been dismissed. I must leave—it is time.

I am on my feet. But I am feeling weak, unreal. The bookseller escorts me out of his office, graciously murmuring, "You are leaving, Charles? Yes, it is getting late. You might come by at another time, and we can see about these purchases of yours. And bring a check—please. Take care on the stairs!—a spiral staircase can be treacherous." My companion has been very kind even in dismissing me, and has put the attaché case into my hands.

How eager I am to leave this hellish, airless place! I am gripping the railing of the spiral staircase, but having difficulty descending. Like a dark rose a vertigo is opening in my brain. My mouth is very dry and also very cold and numb—my tongue feels as if it is swollen, and without sensation. My breath comes ever more quickly, yet without bringing oxygen to my brain. In the semi-darkness my legs seem to buckle and I fall—I am falling, helpless as a rag doll—down the remainder of the metal stairs, wincing with pain.

Above me, two flights up, a man is calling with what sounds like genuine concern— "Charles? Are you all right? Do you need help?"

"No! No thank you—*I do not* ..."

My voice is hoarse, my words are hardly audible.

Outside, I am temporarily revived by cold, fresh wind from the ocean. There is the smell and taste of the ocean. Thank God! I will be all right now, I think. I am safe now, I will escape ... I've left the Lindt chocolates behind, so perhaps—(the predator's thoughts come frantically now)—the poison will have its effect, whether I am able to benefit from it or not.

In the freezing air of my vehicle, with numbed fingers I am jamming a misshapen key into the slot of the ignition that appears to be too small for it. How can this be? I don't understand.

Yet, eventually, as in a dream of dogged persistence, the key goes into the slot, and the engine comes reluctantly to life.

Alongside the moonstruck Atlantic I am driving on a two-lane highway. If I am driving, I must be all right. My hands grip the steering wheel that seems to be moving— wonderfully—of its own volition. A strange, fierce, icy-cold paralysis is blooming in my brain, in my spinal cord, in all the nerves of my body, that is so fascinating to me, my eyes begin to close, to savor it.

Am I asleep? Am I sleeping while driving? Have I never left the place in which I dwell and have I dreamt my visit to Mystery, Inc. in Seabrook, New Hampshire? I have plotted my assault upon the legendary Aaron Neuhaus of Mystery, Inc. Books—I have injected the chocolate truffles with the care of a malevolent surgeon—how is it possible that I might fail? *I cannot fail.*

But now I realize—to my horror—I have no idea in which direction I am driving. I should be headed south, I think—the Atlantic should be on my left. But cold moon-glittering waters lap dangerously high on both sides of the highway. Churning waves have begun to rush across the road, into which I have no choice but to drive.

YPSILANTI, MICHIGAN APRIL 11, 2006

Take my hand, she said.

He did. Lifted his small hand to Mommy's hand. This was maybe five minutes before the abduction.

Did he see their car? she asked him. Did he remember where they'd parked?

It was a kind of game she'd played with him. He was responsible for remembering where they'd parked the car at the mall which was to teach the child to look closely, and to remember.

The car was Daddy's Nissan. A silvery gray-green that didn't stand out amid other parked vehicles.

He was an alert child most of the time, except when tired or distracted as he was now.

Remember? Which store we parked in front of? Was it Home Depot or Kresge Paints?

Mommy narrowed the stores to two, for Robbie's benefit. The mall was too much for his five-year-old brain.

He was staring ahead, straining to see. He took his responsibility for the car seriously.

Mommy began to worry: she'd made too much of the silly game and now her son was becoming anxious.

For he was fretting, Is the car lost, Mommy? How will we get home if the car is lost, Mommy?

Mommy said, with a little laugh, Don't be impatient, sweetie! I promise, the car is not *lost*.

She would remember: the lot that was often a sea of glittering vehicles was now only about one-third filled. For it was nearing dusk of a weekday. She would remember that the arc lights high overhead on tall poles hadn't yet come on.

The harsh bright arc lights of Libertyville Mall. Not yet on.

It was in a row of vehicles facing the entrance to Kresge Paints that she'd parked the Nissan. Five or six cars back. The paint store advertised itself with a festive rainbow painted across the stucco facade of the building.

The Libertyville Mall was a welcoming sort of place. As you approached the entrances, a percolating sort of pop-music emerged out of the very air.

Didn't trust her spatial memory in these massive parking lots and so Dinah never walked away from her car without fixing a landmark in her memory. A visual cue rather than trying to remember the signs: letters and numerals were too easy to forget.

Unless she jotted down the location of the parked car on a scrap of paper, which she had not done.

Searching for the car Robbie was becoming increasingly fretful. Tugging at Mommy's hand in nervous little twitches. And his little face twitched, like a rabbit's.

She assured him: I'm sure the car is just over there. Next row. Behind that big SUV. Perpendicular to the paint store.

Robbie was straining to see. Robbie seemed convinced, the car was *lost*.

And how would they get home, if Daddy's car was *lost*?

Mommy asked Robbie if he knew what *perpendicular* meant but he scarcely listened. Ordinarily new and exotic words were fascinating to Robbie but now he was distracted.

Mommy what if… Lost?

Damn she regretted the silly parking-lot game! Maybe it was a good idea sometimes but not now, evidently. Too much excitement in the mall and Robbie hadn't had a nap and now he was fretting and on the verge of tears and she felt a wave of protective love for him, a powerful wish to shield him, to clutch him close and assure him that he was safe, and she was safe, and the car was only a few yards away, and not *lost*. And they were not *lost*.

Except: when she came upon the row of vehicles in which she was sure she'd parked the Nissan, it wasn't there.

Which meant: she'd parked in the next row. That was all.

It's right here, Robbie. Next row.

You must hide from your child your own foolish uncertainties.

You must hide from your child your own sudden sharp-as-a-razor self-loathing.

Dinah was thinking more positively—(a good mother is one who insists upon thinking "more positively")—what a good thing it is, that a child's fears can be so quickly dispelled. Robbie's anxiety would begin to fade as soon as they sighted the car and would have been totally forgotten by the time they arrived home and Daddy came home for supper.

And Daddy would ask Robbie what they'd done that day and Robbie would tell him about the mall—the items they'd bought, the stores they'd gone into, the plump white pink-nosed Easter bunnies in an enclosure in the atrium at the center of the mall and how he'd petted them through the bars for it was allowed for visitors to pet the bunnies as long as they did not feed them, or frighten them.

PET ME PLEASE DON'T PINCH ME.

And Robbie would climb onto Daddy's lap and ask, as he'd asked Mommy, Could they have an Easter bunny? And Daddy would say as Mommy had said, Not this year but maybe next year at Easter.

And to Mommy in an undertone, Jugged hare, maybe. With red wine.

Pulling Robbie through a maze of parked vehicles and certain now that she saw the Nissan, parked exactly where she'd left it, Dinah was prepared to say in relief and triumph: See, honey? Just where we left it.

CHURCH OF ABIDING HOPE DETROIT, MICHIGAN
APRIL 12, 2006

Shall we not say, we are created in God's image?

Gently the Preacher moved among the flock of starving souls. His blessing fell upon them like precious seed. His eyes bore deep into theirs, in knowledge of their aloneness and their great hunger which only one of the Preacher's spirit could satisfy.

Moses Maimonides tells us that Time is so precious, God gives it to us in atoms. In the smallest units, that we may bear them without harm to ourselves.

For we dare not gaze into the sun. For the sun will blind us.

It is the Preacher who gazes into the sun, and risks harm for the sake of the faithful.

We are a dignified people. We are not a crass cowering cowardly people but a great people, of these United States of North America. We are a people created in God's image and we abide in the great mystery of all Being.

Shall we not say that we cannot know the limit of our grace? That we cannot plumb the depths of our own single, singular souls, let alone the depths of God?

Knowing only that we are brothers and sisters in Being— beneath our separate skins.

The Preacher spoke in a voice of consolation. The Preacher spoke in a voice of tenderness, forgiveness. The Preacher spoke in a voice that did not judge harshly. The Preacher spoke in a voice acquainted with sin.

The Preacher did not stand at the head of the flock and preach to uplifted faces but moved between the rows of seats in the central and side aisles of the little church with the ease and grace of a true shepherd. Often the Preacher reached out to touch a shoulder, a head, an outstretched hand—*Bless you my brother in Christ! Bless you my sister in Christ! God loves you.*

The Preacher was a visitor at the Church of Abiding Hope. He had several times given guest sermons here in the small asphalt-sided church at the intersection of Labrosse and Fifth Street in the inner-city of Detroit in the shadow of the John Lodge Freeway.

The congregation of the Church of Abiding Hope—some seventy-five or eighty individuals of whom most were over fifty and only a scattering were what you'd call *young*—gazed upon the Preacher in a transport of incomprehension. It was *white-man's* speech elevated and wondrous as a hymn of a kind they rarely heard directed toward them and yet in the Preacher's particular voice intimate as a caress.

Understanding, their own minister Reverend Thomas Tindall could provide them.

The Preacher was a tall man of an age no one might have guessed—for his stark sculpted face was unlined, his eyes quick and alert and stone-colored in their deep-set sockets, his beard thick and dark and joyous to behold. His mouth that might have been prim and downturning was a mouth of smiles, a mouth of beckoning.

The Preacher's words were elevated but his eyes sparked. *My brothers in Christ. My sisters in Christ. God bless us all!*

The Preacher wore black: for the occasion was somber. A black light-woolen coat, black trousers with a sharp crease, black shoes.

The Preacher wore a crimson velvet vest: for the occasion was joyous. And at his neck a checked crimson-and-black silk scarf.

The surprise was, the Preacher was not dark-skinned like the faithful of the Church of Abiding Hope or Reverend Tindall who was the Preacher's host. The Preacher's skin was pale and bleached-looking and if you came close, you saw that it was comprised of thin layers, or scales, of transparent skin-tissue, like a palimpsest. The Preacher was the sole *white face* in the church and bore his responsibility with dignity and a sense of his mission.

The Preacher's rusted-iron hair that was threaded with silver like shafts of lightning fell to his shoulders in flaring wings. Parted in the center of his head that was noble and sculpted like a head of antiquity.

The congregation stared hungrily perceiving the Preacher as an emissary from the *white world* who was yet one of their own.

The Preacher spoke warmly of the great leader W. E. B. DuBois who exhorted us to see the beauty in blackness—*In all of our skins, and beneath our skins. The beauty of Christ.*

The Preacher spoke warmly of Reverend Martin Luther King, Jr. who exhorted us to never give up our dream—*Of full integration, and full citizenship, and the beauty of Christ realized in us as Americans.*

Then in an altered voice the Preacher spoke of his "forging" years in Detroit for he'd been born in this city that was beloved of God even as it was severely tested by God.

Forged in the rubble of the old lost neighborhood south of Cass and Woodward. In the rubble of destroyed dreams. Now there were small forests of trees pushing through broken houses. Gigantic weeds and thorns pushing through cracked pavement. The very house of his childhood. His father had worked in the Fisher Body plant long since closed. His grandfather had worked at the Central railroad station long since closed. These mighty buildings, fallen to ruins. The grandeur of Woodward Avenue, fallen to ruins. The tall buildings of Bellevue Avenue, fallen to ruins as in an ancient cataclysm. Yet the spirit of God has not forsaken Detroit. His spirit prevails here and will rise again. A strange and wondrous landscape of colors, flowers, vegetation, birds. Feral creatures breed here. Pollution has given to brick walls a beautiful sepia tint. Shattered glass on roadways shines with the grandeur of God. You might think that God has forsaken Detroit but you would be mistaken for God forsakes no human habitation, as God forsakes no man. The great Christian leader John Calvin said, Nature is a shining garment in which God is concealed but also revealed.

The Preacher was of this soil, for he had been born on the first day of the troubles of July 1967 when Detroit, long smoldering, had erupted into flames.

The Preacher had been born to his mother in a house on Cass Avenue. The Preacher had been born into a time of "racial" troubles and yet—the knowledge is in us nonetheless, *we are blessed.*

For the flaming city on the river had been an emblem of the black man's deep revulsion for his place in these United States, which had been then a place of ignominy and ignorance—deception and duplicity. God had sent flames to reveal this injustice. God was the burning city as the God of the Old Testament had been the burning bush. No one could shut his eyes against such a revelation.

Decades had passed since then. Much had changed since then.

In a bold voice the Preacher spoke. In the voice of one who knows.

And now in the new century it was prophesized, the races would rise together. There would be a dark-skinned President in this new century—the Preacher had had a vision, and the Preacher *knew*.

To all this the congregation listened mesmerized. Scarcely did the congregation draw breath. Of what they could comprehend they could not believe a syllable of such a fantastic vision and yet, in their souls they did believe.

All that the Preacher extolled to them, they did believe.

The Preacher was concluding his sermon. The Preacher was visibly shaken by his own words. On the Preacher's palimpsest-skin there shone sparkling tears.

My sisters and brothers in Christ, we are borne upon a vast journey in uncharted seas. I am not one who provides you with easy answers to your doubts but I am one who tells you, you are beautiful souls and from beauty there issues beauty everlasting.

From my heart to yours, my dear sisters and brothers in Christ, I say to you *Amen*.

Through the church came joyously spoken *Amens*.

The sermon had ended. The Preacher stood to the side, at the pulpit. As the choir began to sing—"I Love to Tell the Story"—"When I Survey the Wondrous Cross"—"There Is a Balm in Gilead"—the Preacher sang with the choir in his deep resonant voice.

Now it did seem that there were younger members of the congregation. At least one-third of the choir was comprised of shining young faces.

At the conclusion of the service Reverend Tindall clasped the Preacher's hand. Tears brimmed in Reverend Tindall's glaucoma-dimmed eyes. His face was of the hue of cracked leather. His scalp was shiny-dark, with a fringe of fleecy white hair. He was a vain old man and yet insecure and well intentioned. You could see that he was very proud of his friendship with the eloquent white preacher.

Thank you, Brother Chester! That was what this congregation was thirsting to hear.

The Preacher was invited to stay for supper with the Reverend and his family. But the Preacher explained he could not stay that night. He was *in transit* for he was badly needed elsewhere.

There is always terrible *need*. Sometimes I think we dare not lay our heads down to sleep, or we will lose all that we've gained.

The Preacher was given to such pronouncements, grave and matter-of-fact. It was not always clear what the Preacher's meaning was, yet you did not doubt that the Preacher knew.

You will come back to us? Brother?

Of course I will come back to you, Brother. In my heart I will not depart.

The collection of $362 was divided between them—Reverend Tindall and the Preacher who was known to the Reverend as Chester Cash.

In the alley beside the asphalt-sided church the Preacher's van was parked.

The van was dark as an undersea creature. Even its windows were dark-tinted. On the roof of the van was a wooden cross painted a luminous white and secured with ropes and on this was written in crimson block letters

THE CHURCH OF ABIDING HOPE USA

The van was a 2000 Chrysler minivan and its chassis dented and scarified but it appeared to have been recently painted. It had been recently painted in some haste for there were smears of iridescent dark-purple paint on several of the windows like fingerprints.

From the threshold of the Church of Abiding Hope, you could see the van parked in the alley. But you could not see into the van for the windows were tinted.

It must have been that the Preacher had no family remaining in Detroit for he had not sought them out and did not seem to wish to speak of them now. When Reverend Tindall asked after the Preacher's mother, the Preacher glanced downward and replied in a murmur—Weeping may remain for a night, but rejoicing comes in the morning.

Reverend Tindall asked after the Preacher's ten-year-old son who'd accompanied the Preacher to the Church of Abiding Hope the previous spring.

The Preacher frowned as if trying to recall this son. As if just perceptibly startled by the question.

Nostradamus has chosen another pathway, it seems. He has gone to live with his mother and her people in the Upper Peninsula.

A fine boy, Reverend Tindall said. You had said, your son would follow you into your ministry?

He was but a child then. He has not put aside childish ways. And he dwells now among Philistines—it is his choice.

The Preacher spoke sadly yet not without a shiver, a twitching of whiskered jaws, as if the memory of a young son's betrayal were fresh to him, and painful.

Reverend Tindall seemed about to ask another question about the lost son but then thought better of it. For the Preacher was breathing quickly and stroking his whiskered jaws unsmiling.

By His light, the Preacher said in a lowered and quavering voice, I walked through darkness.

Brother, Amen!—Reverend Tindall clamped the Preacher on his shoulder.

Because the Preacher was a frugal man, and chose to spend his money solely on necessities, he lived in the minivan much of the time when he was *in transit*. In the van he kept clothes, books and documents, a miniature kerosene stove, canned food. It was a part of the Preacher's ministry to visit small churches across the country and to deliver guest sermons where he was welcomed. Abiding Hope is a family, the Preacher said. We are brothers and sisters in Christ. We are one, inside our skins. Everywhere, we recognize one another.

As he stood on the threshold of the little asphalt-sided church on Labrosse Street, Detroit, speaking with Reverend Tindall in the early evening of April 12, 2006, the Preacher glanced at the van parked in the alley a few yards away. His deep-socketed eyes encircled the van. Clearly there was something about the van, its very stillness, its iridescent-purple chassis and the surprise of the luminous white cross secured to its roof, that riveted his attention.

Brother, are you sure you can't stay the night? Or at least have supper with us?—Reverend Tindall seemed disappointed. His glaucoma-dimmed eyes blinked and blurred.

The Preacher thanked him kindly. The Preacher had now the keys to his van in his hand. With a wide smile the Preacher explained that he was bound for the West Coast, for Carmel, where a new ministry in the Church of Abiding Hope awaited him.

I-80 EAST MICHIGAN, OHIO APRIL 13–14, 2006

Take my hand, he said.

But the child would not.

I say to you, son—*take my hand.*

When the quivering child did not lift his hand, did not obey, Daddy Love seized the hand, and squeezed the little fingers with such force, the smallest finger audibly cracked.

Inside the gag, the child screamed.

On I-80 east a continuous stream of vehicles.

On I-80 east Daddy Love drove at just slightly below the speed limit taking care that the white-painted wooden cross on the roof of his vehicle wouldn't be shaken by wind and blown off. He was a patient driver who took little note that vehicles were constantly passing him. In the wake of enormous trailer-trucks, the Chrysler minivan swayed slightly.

Like souls passing, Daddy Love thought. The stream of vehicles.

He was among them and yet elevated. It was Daddy Love's particular destiny that amid the mass of humankind only a very few like him were possessed of the power to *see*.

Eastern religions believed in the "third eye"—in the forehead, just above the bridge of the nose. Through meditation, through zealous religious practices, the "third eye" opened and vision flooded the brain.

Daddy Love was one of these. From boyhood he'd been gifted with such visions. Like the power of X-rays to see through flesh. Daddy Love *saw*.

It was a particular insight of the brain. An activated and excited area of the brain just behind the eyes. The frontal lobe, it was called. Neurons *fired* in mysterious surges like heat lightning soundless in a black summer sky.

But such scientific terms, mere *words*, meant little to Daddy Love who understood how *words* were purely invented and how if you were a master of *words*, you were a master of men.

Ordinary individuals could not understand. Ordinary individuals comprised somewhere beyond 99 percent of *Homo sapiens*.

You had to suppose that the Buddha achieved enlightenment,

and so Nirvana—(or maybe that was the Hindu heaven not the Buddha heaven)—at about the age of Daddy Love when he'd been, in that long-ago lifetime, a gangling boy named Chester Czechi who'd first *seen*.

He'd known he was a special case. He'd known that he would be forever a pilgrim in his life, embarked upon a (secret, thrilling) pilgrimage, utterly unguessed-at by others.

Even his family. Especially his family.

(Daddy Love smiled, recalling. He had not seen his fucking "family"—fucking "relatives"—who'd betrayed him to the Wayne County, Michigan, juvenile authorities, aged twelve, in twenty-six years.)

Now on the interstate highway what the ordinary eye saw wasn't the Chrysler minivan but the luminous white cross secured to the van's roof.

The cross was approximately four feet in height. The horizontal plank was approximately three feet.

The cross did shudder in the wind. But Daddy Love, who was a natural-born carpenter, a visionary with a talent for *using his hands,* had secured it tight, with both wires and rope.

The cross was a curiosity: some observers might smile. (In recognition of the sacred cross, or in condescension that a cross might be so awkwardly affixed to the roof of a minivan.) Some might try to read the crimson letters hand-printed on the cross.

Most would lose interest and look away after a few seconds.

State troopers looking for a *beige, battered* van on the interstate would take little interest in this iridescent-purple minivan in the service of the Church of Abiding Hope.

Also, the van's license plates were New Jersey. The child had been taken from the Libertyville Mall in Ypsilanti, Michigan.

Daddy Love loved to be *invisible*. In the eyes of ordinary mortals and fools, the superior man can make himself so.

Spray-painting the van iridescent purple and securing the white cross to the van's roof was a means of rendering the van *invisible*.

Daddy Love had cultivated such strategies in the past. To move through life *invisible at will* you had to create distractions that drew the attention of ordinary individuals.

The ordinary individual, Daddy Love had discovered, was not so very different from a child in his perceptions and expectations.

Hunting his prey, for instance, Daddy Love rendered himself close to *invisible*. He wore the clothing of an ordinary man, exactly what an ordinary man might wear to the mall on a weekday afternoon, to buy a few items at Sears, Home Depot.

A nylon jacket, unzipped. T-shirt, jeans or work-trousers. Not-new and not-expensive running shoes.

On his head, a baseball cap. But not a team cap. No discernible color, maybe gray, or beige.

The whiskers were conspicuous, that was a fact. But the whiskers were of a pale powdery-gray color they had not been at the Libertyville Mall and the tinted glasses hiding the eyes rendered the eyes invisible and unidentifiable.

(He'd heard, on the van radio turned low, the bulletin-news. Child-abduction-news out of Ypsilanti, Michigan. "Breaking news" it was breathlessly called. Had to laugh to hear a witness report how, in the mall, a few minutes before the child was taken, the witness hadn't seen anyone watching the mother and child—*no one suspicious.*)

Witnesses never get it right. Witnesses see only what their eyes see, not what is *invisible*.

Once. Daddy Love had wrapped white gauze and tape around his (left, bare) leg to the knee and hobbled most convincingly on a crutch. An old ruse of Ted Bundy's and immediately recognizable to an enlightened eye but the foolish trusting eye of a young mother who'd brought her eight-year-old to a playground—in Carbondale, Illinois—hadn't recognized it. *Excuse me ma'am could you help me—I'm having trouble getting this trunk open—damn crutch gets in the way...*

Hunting his prey at the Libertyville Mall, Ypsilanti. Here was the Midwest. He'd never have risked Ann Arbor which was where the university was, and not really the Midwest for everyone there was from somewhere else or was bound for somewhere else. But Ypsilanti was the very heart of the Midwest: a *nothing-place*.

He'd hunted his prey at the mall for several days in succession. He'd had a premonition, one of his *boys* was being prepared for him, soon.

Both inside the mall, and outside, he'd hunted. And inside again. Mixing easily with other Daddy-shoppers for he was in no hurry.

Kindly Daddy Love held open doors for young-mother shoppers with children. They were grateful murmuring *Thank you! Nice of you.*

Scarcely a glance at Daddy Love, as they passed through the entrance. Some of them pushing strollers and others gripping children's hands.

They moved on. Not a backward glance.

Of every one hundred children perhaps one interested Daddy Love in the depths of his soul. Of every two hundred children perhaps one excited him.

Of every thousand children perhaps one *very much excited him.*

Daddy Love trusted to the higher power that streamed through him, to allow him to *see.*

He would be immediately alerted: a child destined to be *one of his.*

A child who required, for the salvation of his soul, not the merely adequate birth-parent, but a parent like Daddy Love.

The hunt was thrilling. The hunt was ceaseless. The hunt was one in which Daddy Love participated, *invisible.*

In public places: malls, city squares, amusement parks, camping sites and hiking trails, beaches. Rarely near schools, for such territories were dangerous.

And rarely playgrounds of course. (With a few exceptions over the course of twenty-five years.)

The best time for the hunt was late afternoon shading into

dusk. Before lights came on. Before the eye quite adjusted to the fading light.

People were tired then. Young mothers, their shoulders sagging.

Daddy Love was quietly thrilled by the hunt. Daddy Love was not ever impatient or agitated but passed among ordinary individuals as if he were one of them.

Except Daddy Love was not one of *them*. He'd never been!

Daddy Love ceaselessly, ingeniously inventive. Daddy Love had invented the Preacher, for instance.

The Preacher's dark garb, with the surprise of the Preacher's crimson vest and neck-scarf. The Preacher's grave and gracious manner, the blessing of the Preacher's fingers, and the Preacher's joyful smile.

Daddy Love was younger than the Preacher, for sure. Daddy Love was not so self-regarding and so pious. Daddy Love liked to joke, and the Preacher had never been known to joke.

Daddy Love considered the Preacher in the way that you might consider an uncle who's good-hearted and sincere and just not *cool*.

If women touched the Preacher's hand, or drew their fingers along his arm, or leaned to him, to smile, to murmur in his ear inviting him to have dinner with them, the Preacher did not quite know how to respond except with a stiff smile. But Daddy Love knew.

The Preacher was intriguing to Daddy Love, but only for a limited period of time. The Preacher did make money, upon occasion. You could not lock eyes with the Preacher's gravely kindly gaze and not feel the urge to open your wallet to him for in giving money to the Preacher you are giving money to Jesus Christ Himself—so it seemed. Yet with relief Daddy Love tore off the Preacher's clothes, folded them and put them away in his trunk, in the rear of the van. With relief Daddy Love shook and shimmied in his body, loose-limbed as a goose, a younger guy, a guy with a sly smile, a guy who grooved to rock music, rap music, a guy you'd like to have a drink with.

Daddy Love was a man whom other men liked. And certainly, a man whom women liked.

Children, too. Boys younger than twelve.

Daddy Love was that restless American type. Except he'd settled (more or less) in the East, or the Midwest, he'd have looked like a rancher in Wyoming. Or a (slightly older) hitch-hiker making his way to the West Coast.

Daddy Love couldn't say was he happiest in motion, in his van, which he'd painted and repainted several times since its purchase, traveling east or traveling west on I-80, or was he happiest once he'd come to rest for a while, a few months at least, maybe a year, once he'd established a home-site. Wherever Daddy Love was, there was his kingdom.

Such strategies of evasion, flight, and escape! No ordinary individual could hope to understand.

Son you are coming home!

Soon you will be home, and safe.

Son d'you hear me? I think you do son.

Daddy Love loves YOU.

Through the countryside of Ohio, Pennsylvania, and across the Delaware River into New Jersey, these many hours, hours bleeding into hours, Daddy Love never ceased to address the child behind him, in the rear of the van.

Daddy Love is bringing you to your true home for Daddy Love is your true Daddy who loves YOU.

Inside the ingenious Wooden Maiden the child made not a whimper.

Inside the gag, not a muffled cry.

Daddy Love was a stern daddy and yet loving. He'd taped a split to the little broken finger. Child-bones heal quickly but must not heal crookedly.

The child would learn quickly: each act of disobedience, however small, would be immediately punished. *No exceptions!*

Zero tolerance!

And when the child obeyed, and was a true son to Daddy Love, immediately he would be rewarded with food, water, the comfort of Daddy Love's strong arms and the gentle intonations of Daddy Love's voice. *This is my son in whom I am well pleased.*

Quickly then the child would learn. They all did.

He'd read of "conditioning"—the great American psychologist B. F. Skinner and before him the nineteenth-century Russian Ivan Pavlov. But his natural instinct was to reward, and to punish, in such a way as to instill love, fear, respect for and utter allegiance to Daddy Love in the child-subject.

The child was to be played like a musical instrument. Sometimes gently, and sometimes not-so-gently. For Daddy Love was always in control.

When he'd first sighted the child in the mall he had estimated that the child was about four years old. For Daddy Love, this was a quite young child.

By the age of eleven or twelve, the child was less desirable. The child was a pubescent. Daddy Love had little patience with pubescents and still less with adolescents.

The younger the child, the more desirable. Though Daddy Love did not want a *baby*—hardly! In any case, a baby was too much effort. A baby required a female as a caretaker.

An older child had obvious disadvantages: he would remember much of his old family, that would have to be cast off.

This child in the mall, happily chattering as he petted plump white nose-twitching Easter bunnies in an enclosure, was unusually alert, bright, and talkative. Daddy Love had been quite *ravished*!

But, how ordinary the mother.

Not coarse and vulgar like some. The woman's face wasn't luridly made up and her hair was a decent drab-brown brushed back behind her ears and her ears weren't studded with a half-dozen glittering piercings. She wore jeans but not "skinny" jeans. She wore a belted sweater that looked hand-knitted. (The belt was twisted in back, which gave her a disheveled look of which she was blissfully unaware.) Her body was slender, stringy. She had no hips and virtually no breasts. (How had she nursed her baby? Her milk would be watery, curdled. This was not a *mother*.) She wore sneakers. On the third finger of her left hand she wore a plain silver wedding band advertising *Yes! Believe it or not, somebody married me.* She was perhaps thirty years old and not getting any younger: when her face wasn't smiling, "lit up" by the most banal Mommy-love-and-pride, it was a frankly tired face. The husband would soon be unfaithful, if he hadn't been already. Who'd want to climb into bed, sink his dick in *that.* For the woman was clearly ordinary, and hardly fit for the radiant child.

The child's skin was "white"—yet the child's hair was very dark, kinky-curly. Daddy Love felt a thrill of discovery: was this a *mixed-race child?*

Daddy Love had never appropriated a *mixed-race child.* And Daddy Love was no racist.

He'd trailed them in the mall. He'd been patient, and not-visible.

In JCPenney, in Macy's, in Sears, and in the atrium at the center of the mall. The Easter-bunny enclosure that drew children like moths to flame.

Daddy Love's shrewd practiced eye glanced quickly about— in such places, where small children are gathered, laughing, talking shrilly, with (usually) just a single parent nearby, and that parent (usually) the mother, you will often find, indeed Daddy Love invariably found, solitary men of (usually) middle age, standing at a little distance, not too near, not too *visibly near,* observing.

Daddy Love wasn't one of these. Daddy Love was no *registered sex offender.*

Trailing the mother and child outside the mall Daddy Love had known that his mission was just, and necessary, and could not be delayed, when he'd seen the mother pause and fumble in her sweater pocket for—a pack of cigarettes! And quickly light up a cigarette, as the child stood innocently by; several quick deep inhalations, as if the toxic smoke were pure oxygen, and the woman desperate for oxygen; then, with a gesture of disdain, casting the cigarette from her, onto a grassless area abutting the walkway, where other careless and selfish smokers had cast their butts.

A smoker trying to quit. Failing to quit.

A smoker who was ashamed of her weakness. And maybe it was a weakness the child's father did not know about.

It was God-ordained, Daddy Love must take this child as his own.

Daddy Love hurried to his van. He would trail the mother and the child in the lot. He would not let them out of his sight. He had but a few seconds to make his move—he knew how precisely such a move had to be timed, from previous experiences. The narrow window of opportunity, as it was called, had to be coordinated with a clear field and no witnesses.

How many times Daddy Love had circled a target, borne in upon a target, but had to withdraw when a random witness appeared on the scene...

Taking the little boy from the mother was more difficult than Daddy Love had calculated. He'd struck her on the head with a claw hammer—hard; enough to crack her skull, he'd thought. She'd fallen to the pavement like a dead weight and yet, in the next instant, like a comatose boxer struggling to his feet, somehow the woman managed to heave herself up from the ground and stagger after him...

By this time he had the boy in the van. How small and light the child was, yet how frantically he struggled, like a terrified little animal! He'd shaken, punched, and struck the boy with his fist on the side of the boy's head, to calm him.

It was astonishing to Daddy Love, the mother running desperately after the van—that look in her face, and her face streaming blood.

He'd swerved the van around, to run her down. Bitch, daring to defy Daddy Love!

The Compendium of Srem

F. Paul Wilson

I

TOMÁS DE TORQUEMADA opened his eyes in the dark. Was that…?

Yes. Someone knocking on his door.

"Who is it?"

"Brother Adelard, good Prior. I must speak to you." Even if he had not said his name, Tomás would have recognized the French accent. He glanced up at his open window. Stars filled the sky with no hint of dawn.

"It is late. Can it not wait until morning?"

"I fear not."

"Come then."

With great effort, Tomás struggled to bring his eighty-year-old body to a sitting position as Brother Adelard entered the tiny room. He carried a candle and a cloth-wrapped bundle. He set both next to the Vulgate Bible on the rickety desk in the corner.

"May I be seated, Prior?"

Tomás gestured to the room's single straight-back chair. Adelard dropped into it, then bounded up again.

"No. I cannot sit."

"What prompts you to disturb my slumber?"

Adelard was half his age and full of righteous energy—one of the inquisitors the pope had assigned to Tomás four years ago.

He seemed unable to contain that energy now. The candlelight reflected in his bright blue eyes as he paced Tomás's room.

"I know you are not feeling well, Prior, but I thought it best to bring this to you in the dark hours."

"Bring what?"

He fairly leaped to the table where he pulled the cloth from the rectangular bundle, revealing a book. Even from across the room, even with his failing eyesight, Tomás knew this was like no book he had ever seen.

"This," he said, lifting the candle and bringing both closer. He held the book before Tomás, displaying the cover. "Have you ever seen anything like it?"

Tomás shook his head. No, he hadn't.

The covers and spine seemed to be made of stamped metal. He squinted at the strange marks embossed on the cover. They made no sense at first, then seemed to swim into focus. Words… in Spanish… at least one was in Spanish.

Compendio ran across the upper half in large, ornate letters; and below that, half size: *Srem.*

"What do you see?" Adelard said. The candle flame wavered as his hand began to shake.

"The title, I should think."

"The words, Prior. Please tell me the words you see."

"My eyes are bad but I am not blind: *Compendio* and *Srem.*" The candle flame wavered more violently.

"When I look at it, Prior, I too see Srem, but to my eyes the first word is not *Compendio* but *Compendium.*"

Tomás bent closer. No, his eyes had not fooled him.

"It is as plain as day: *Compendio.* It ends in i-o."

"You were raised speaking Spanish, were you not, Prior?"

"As a boy of Valladolid, I should say so."

"As you know, I was raised in Lyon and spent most of my life speaking French before the pope assigned me to assist you."

To rein me in, you mean, Tomás thought, but said nothing.

The current Pope, Alexander VI, thought him too… what word had he had used? *Fervent.* Yes, that was it. How could one be too fervent in safeguarding the Faith? And hadn't he previously narrowed procedures, limiting torture only to those accused by at least two citizens of good standing? Before that, any wild accusation could send someone to the rack.

"Yes-yes. What of it?"

"When…" He swallowed. "When *you* look at the cover, you see *Compendio*, a Spanish word. When I look at the cover I see a French word: *Compendium*."

Tomás pushed the book away and struggled to his feet.

"Have you gone mad?"

Adelard staggered back, trembling. "I feared I was, I was sure I was, but you see it too."

"I see what is stamped in the metal, nothing more!"

"But this afternoon, when Amaury was sweeping my room, he spied the cover and asked where I had learned to read Berber. I asked him what he meant. He grinned and pointed to the cover, saying 'Berber! Berber!'"

Tomás felt himself going cold.

"Berber?"

"Yes. He was born in Almeria where they speak Berber, and to his eyes the two words on the cover were written in Berber script. He can read only a little of the writing, but he saw enough of it growing up. I opened the book for him and he kept nodding and grinning, saying 'Berber' over and over."

Tomás knew Amaury, as did everyone else in the monastery—a simpleminded Morisco who performed menial tasks for the monks, like sweeping and serving at table. He was incapable of duplicity.

"After that, I gave Brother Ramiro a quick look at the cover, and he saw *Compendio*, just as you do." Adelard looked as if he were in physical pain. "It appears to me, good Prior, that whoever looks at this book sees the words in their native tongue. But how can that be? How can that *be*?"

Tomás's knees felt weak. He pulled the chair to his side and lowered himself onto it.

"What sort of deviltry have you brought into our house?"

"I had no idea it was any sort of deviltry when I bought it. I spied it in the marketplace. A Moor had laid it out on a blanket with other trinkets and carvings. I thought it so unusual I bought it for Brother Ramiro—you know how he loves books. I thought he could add it to our library. Not till Amaury made his comment did I realize that it was more than simply a book with an odd cover. It..." He shook his head. "I don't know what it is, Prior, but it has certainly been touched by deviltry. That is why I've brought it to you."

To me, Tomás thought. Well, it would have to be me, wouldn't it.

Yet in all his fifteen years as Grand Inquisitor he had never had to deal with sorcery or witchcraft. Truth be told, he could give no credence to that sort of nonsense. Peon superstitions.

Until now.

"That is not all, Prior. Look at the pattern around the words. What do you see?"

Tomás leaned closer. "I see crosshatching."

"So do I. Now, close your eyes for a count of three."

He did so, then reopened them. The pattern had changed to semicircles, each row facing the opposite way of the row above and below it.

His heart gave a painful squeeze in his chest.

"What do you see?"

"A... a wavy pattern."

"I kept my eyes open and I still see the cross hatching."

Tomás said nothing as he tried to comprehend what was happening here. Finally ...

"There is surely deviltry on the covers. What lies between?"

Adelard's expression was bleak. "Heresy, Prior... the most profound heresy I have ever seen or heard."

"That is an extreme judgment, Brother Adelard. It also means you have read it."

"Not all. Not nearly all. I spent the rest of the afternoon and all night reading it until just before I came to your door. And even so, I have only begun. It is evil, Prior. Unspeakably evil."

He did not recall Adelard being prone to exaggeration, but this last had to be an overstatement.

"Show me."

Adelard placed the tome on the table and opened it. Tomás noticed that the metal cover was attached to the spine by odd interlacing hinges of a kind he had never seen before. The pages looked equally odd. Moving his chair closer, he reached out and ran his fingers over the paper—if it was paper at all—and it felt thinner than the skin of an onion, yet completely opaque. He would have expected such delicate material to be marred by wrinkles and tears, but each page was perfect.

As was the writing that graced those pages—perfect Spanish. It had the appearance of an ornate handwritten script, yet each letter was perfect, and identical to every other of its kind. Every "a" looked like every other "a," every "m" like every other "m." Tomás had seen one of the Holy Bibles printed by that German, Gutenberg, where each letter had been exactly like all its brothers. The Gutenberg book had been printed in two columns per page, however, whereas the script in this compendium flowed from margin to margin.

"Show me heresy," Tomás said.

"Let me show you deviltry first, Prior," said the monk as he began to turn the pages at blinding speed.

"You go too fast. How will you know when to stop?"

"I will know, Prior. I will know."

Tomás saw numerous illustrations fly by, many in color.

"Here!" Adelard said, stopping and jabbing his finger at a page. "Here is deviltry most infernal!"

Tomás felt his saliva dry as he faced a page with an illustration that moved... a globe spinning in a rectangular black void. Lines crisscrossed the globe, connecting glowing dots on its surface.

"Heavenly Lord! It..." He licked his lips. "It moves."

He reached out, but hesitated. It looked as if his hand might pass into the void depicted on the page.

"Go ahead, Prior. I have touched it."

He ran his fingers over the spinning globe. It felt as flat and smooth as the rest of the page—no motion against his fingertips, and yet the globe continued to turn beneath them.

"What sorcery is this?"

"I was praying you could tell me. Do you think that sphere is supposed to represent the world?"

"I do not know. Perhaps. The Queen has just sent that Genoan, Colón, on his third voyage to the New World. He has proven that the world is round... a sphere."

Adelard shrugged. "He has proven only what sailors have been saying for decades."

Ah, yes. Brother Adelard fancied himself a philosopher.

Tomás stared at the spinning globe. Although some members of the Church hierarchy argued against it, most now accepted that the world God had created for Mankind was indeed round; but if this apparition was supposed to be that world, then the perspective was from that of the Lord Himself.

Why now? Why, with his health slipping away like sand— he doubted he would survive the year—did a tome that could only be described as sorcerous find its way to his quarters? In his younger days he would have relished hunting down the perpetrators of this deviltry. But now... now he barely had the strength to drag himself through the day.

He sighed. "Light my candle and leave this abomination to me. I would read it."

"I know you must, dear Prior, but prepare yourself. The heresies are so profound they will... they will steal your sleep."

"I doubt that Brother Adelard." In his years as Grand Inquisitor he had heard every conceivable heresy. "I doubt that very much."

But no matter what its contents, this tome had already stolen his sleep.

After Adelard departed, he looked around at his spare quarters. Four familiar whitewashed walls, bare except for the crucifix over his bed. A white ceiling and a sepia tiled floor. A cot, a desk, a chair, a small chest of drawers, and a Holy Bible comprised the furnishings. As prior, as Grand Inquisitor, as the queen's confessor, no one would have raised an eyebrow had he requisitioned more comfortable quarters. But earthly trappings led to distractions, and he would not be swayed from his Holy Course.

Before opening the *Compendium*, he took his bible, kissed its cover, and laid it in his lap...

2

Tomás read through the night. His candle burned out just as dawn began to light the sky, so he read on, foregoing breakfast. Finally he forced himself to close both the abominable book and his eyes.

As he slumped in his chair he heard the sounds of hammers and saws and axes and the calls of the workmen wafting through his window. Every day was the same—except Sunday, of course. Main construction on the monastery—*Monasterio de Santo Tomás*—had been officially completed four years ago, but always there seemed more to do: a patio here, a garden there. It seemed it would never be finished.

The monastery had become the centerpiece of Ávila. And that it should not be. It had grown too big, too ornate. He thought of the elegant studded pillars ringing the second-floor gallery overlooking the enormous courtyard, beautiful works of art in themselves, but inappropriate for a mendicant order that required a vow of poverty.

It housed three cloisters—one for novitiates, one for silence, and one for the royal family. Since the king and queen had funded the monastery, and used it as their summer residence, he supposed such excess was unavoidable. The queen was why he had moved here from Seville—he had been her confessor for many years.

He opened his eyes and stared at the cover of the *Compendium of Srem.* He wasn't sure if Srem was the name of a town or the fictional civilization it described or the person who had compiled it. But the title mattered not. The content... the content was soul rattling in its heresy, and utterly demonic in the subtle seductiveness of its tone.

The book never denounced the Church, never blasphemed God the Father, Jesus the Son, or the Holy Ghost. Oh, no. That would have been too obvious. That would have set up a barrier between the reader and the unholiness within. Tomás would have found shrill, wild-eyed blasphemy easier to deal with than the alternative presented here: God and His Church were not presented as enemies—in fact, they were never presented at all! *Not one mention.* Impossible as it was, the author pretended to be completely unaware of their existence.

That was bad enough. But the tone... the tone...

The *Compendium* presented itself as a collection of brief essays describing every facet of an imaginary civilization. Where that civilization might exist—or when—was never addressed. Perhaps it purported to describe the legendary Island of Atlas mentioned by Plato in his *Timaeus*, supposedly sunk beneath the waves millennia ago. But no one took those stories seriously. It portrayed a civilization that harnessed the lightning and commanded the weather, defying God's very Creation by fashioning new creatures from the humors of others.

But the tone... it presented these hellish wonders in a perfectly matter-of-fact manner, as if everyone was familiar with them, as if these were mere quotidian truths that the author was simply cataloguing for the record. Usually when imaginary wonders were described—the Greek legends of their gods and goddesses, came to mind—the teller of the tall tale related them in breathless prose and a marveling tone. Not so the *Compendium.* The descriptions were flat and straightforward, almost casual. And the way they interconnected and referred back and forth to each other indicated that a great deal of thought had been invested in these fictions.

Which was what made it all so seductive.

Many times during the night and through the morning Tomás had to force himself to lean back and press the Holy Bible against his fevered brow so as to counteract the spell the *Compendium* was attempting to weave around him.

By the time he closed the covers, he had dipped barely a fingertip into the foul well of its waters, but he had read enough to know that this so-called *Compendium of Srem* was in truth the *Compendium of Satan*, a library of falsehoods fashioned by the Father of Lies himself.

And the most profound lies concerned gods, although he didn't know if "god" was the proper word for the entities described. No, "described" was not the word. The author referred to two vaporous entities at war in the aether. The people of this fictional civilization did not worship these entities. Rather they contended with them, some currying favor with one so as to help defeat the other, and vice versa. They had not bothered to name their gods, and had no images of them. Their gods simply... *were*.

But reading the *Compendium* was not necessary to appreciate its hellish origin. Simply leafing through the pages was all it took. For the book had no end! It numbered one hundred sheets— Tomás had counted them—but when he'd leafed to the last page, he'd found there was no last page. Every time he turned what appeared to be the last page, another lay waiting. And yet the sheet count never varied from one hundred, because a page at the front was disappearing every time a new one appeared at the rear. Yet whenever he closed and reopened the book, it began again with the title page.

Sorcery... sorcery was the only explanation.

3

Brother Adelard and Brother Ramiro arrived together.

Tomás had rewrapped the *Compendium* in Adelard's blanket

and carried it to the tribunal room. He had been shocked at the thick tome's almost negligible weight. Once there, he summoned them and waited in his seat at the center of the long refectory table. The room was similar to the tribunal room at the monastery in Segovia where he had spent most of his term as Grand Inquisitor: the long table, the high-backed leather-upholstered chairs—the highest back reserved for him—facing the door; stained-glass windows to either side, and a near life-size crucifix on the wall above the fireplace behind him. The crucifix was positioned so as to force the accused to look upon the face of their crucified Lord as they stood before the inquisitors and responded to the accusations made against then. They were not allowed to know the names of their accusers, merely the charges against them.

"Good Prior," Adelard said as he entered. "I see in your eyes that you have read it."

Tomás nodded. "Not all of it, of course, but enough to know what we must do." He shifted his gaze to Ramiro. "And you, Brother... have you read it?"

Ramiro was about Adelard's age, but there the resemblance ceased. Ramiro was portly where Adelard was lean, brown-eyed instead of blue, swarthy instead of fair. Those dark eyes were wide now and fixed on the *Compendium*, which Tomás had unwrapped.

"No, Prior. I have seen only the cover, and that is enough."

"You have no desire to peruse its contents?"

He gave his head a violent shake. "Brother Adelard has told me—"

Tomás gave Adelard a sharp look. "Told? Who else have you told?"

"No one, Prior. Since Ramiro had already seen the book, I thought—"

"See that it stops here. Tell no one what you have read. Tell no one that this abomination exists. Knowledge of the book does not spread beyond this room. Understood?"

"Yes, Prior," they said in unison.

He turned to Ramiro. "You have no desire for first-hand knowledge of these heresies?"

Another violent shake of the head. "From what little I have heard from Brother Adelard, they must be contained. Heresies spread with every new set of eyes that behold them. I do not want to add mine."

Tomás was impressed. "You are wise beyond your years, Ramiro." He motioned him closer. "But it is your knowledge of book craft that we need today."

Ramiro was in charge of the monastery's library. He had overseen its construction in the monk's cloister—was still attending to refinements, in fact—and was in charge of acquiring texts to line the shelves.

Ramiro approached the *Compendium* as if it were a coiled viper. He touched it as if it might sear his flesh. Adelard came up behind him to watch over his shoulder.

"I do not know what kind of metal this is," Ramiro said. "It looks like polished steel, but the highlights in the surface are most unusual."

Tomás had wondered at the pearly highlights himself.

"It is not steel," Adelard said.

Tomás raised his eyebrows. "Oh? And you are a metallurgist as well as a philosopher?"

"I seek to learn as much about God's Creation as I can, Prior. But I think it is obvious that the covers are not steel. If they were, the book would weigh much more than it does."

Ramiro gripped the *Compendium* and hefted it. "As light as air."

"Note the hinges that connect the covers to the spine," Tomás said. "Have you ever seen anything like that?" As Ramiro raised it for a closer look, Tomás added, "I ask because we must determine where this was fashioned."

Adelard was nodding his understanding. "Yes, of course. To help us hunt down the heretic who made it."

Ramiro was shaking his head. "I have never seen anything like this. I cannot fathom how it was put together."

"Through sorcery," Tomás said.

Ramiro looked at him, eyes bright. "Yes, that is the only explanation."

He hid his disappointment. If Ramiro had recognized the workmanship, they would have brought them that much closer to naming the heretic.

"This Moor who sold it to you," Tomás said, turning to Adelard. "He was in the marketplace?"

"Yes, Prior."

"Could this be his work?"

"I doubt it. He was poor and ragged with crippled fingers. I cannot see how that would be possible."

"But he may know who did make it."

"Yes, he certainly may." Adelard slapped his palm on the table. "If only we had jurisdiction over Moors!"

Ferdinand and Isabella's edict limited the inquisition's reach to anyone who professed to be Christian, but its focus had always been the *conversos*—the Jews to whom the Alhambra Decree had given the ultimatum of either converting to Christianity or leaving the country.

"We have jurisdiction over the purity of the Faith," Tomás said, pointing to the *Compendium*. "That includes heresy from any source, and this is heresy most foul. Have him brought here."

4

The Moor stood before them, quaking in fear.

Because of the sorcerous nature of the *Compendium* and his determination to keep its very existence secret, Tomás had decided to forego a full tribunal inquiry and limit the proceedings to himself and the two others who already knew of it.

After Adelard identified the Moor, soldiers assigned to the Inquisition had rounded him up and delivered him to the tribunal room.

Tomás studied this poor excuse for a human being. The name he had given upon his arrival was mostly Berber gibberish. Tomás had heard "Abdel" in the mix and decided to call him that. Abdel wore a dirty cloth cap and a ratty beard, both signs of continued adherence to the ways of Mohammed. His left eye was milky white, in stark contrast to the mass of dark wrinkles that made up his face. He had few teeth and his hands were twisted and gnarled. Tomás agreed with Adelard: This man did not craft the *Compendium*.

"Abdel, have you accepted Jesus Christ as your savior?" Adelard said.

The old man bowed. "Yes, sir. Years ago."

"So, you are a Morisco then?"

"Yes, sir."

"And yet you still wear your beard in the style required by the religion you claimed to have given up."

Tomás knew what Adelard was doing: striking fear into the Morisco's heart.

The old Moor's good eye flashed. "I wear it in the style of Jesus as I have seen him portrayed in church."

Tomás rubbed his mouth to hide a smile. Adelard had been outflanked.

"We are not here to question your manner of dress, Abdel," Tomás said, wishing to turn the inquest to the matter that most concerned him. "No accusations have been made."

He saw sudden relief in the Moor's eyes. "Then may I ask why—?"

Tomás lifted the *Compendium* so that the Moor could see the cover. "We *are* here to question why you are selling heresy."

His shock looked genuine. "I did not know! It is just a book I found!"

"Found?" Adelard said. "Found where?"

"In a trunk," he said, head down, voice barely audible.

"And where is this trunk?"

The Moor's voice sank even lower. "I do not know."

Adelard's voice rose. "Do you mean to tell us you have

forgotten?" "Perhaps some time on the rack will improve your memory!"

Tomás raised a hand. He thought he knew the problem.

"You stole it, didn't you, Abdel?"

The Moor's head snapped up, then looked down again without replying.

"Understand, Abdel," Tomás went on, "that we have no jurisdiction against civil crimes. We are concerned by the immorality of your action, yes, and trust that you will confess your sin to your priest, but we can take no action against you for the theft itself." He paused to let this sink in, then added, "Who did you steal it from?"

When the Moor still did not reply, Tomás kept his voice low despite his growing anger. "We cannot punish you for stealing, but we can use every means at our disposal to wring a confession from you as to the source of your heresy." He released his fury and began pounding on the table. "And I will personally see to it that you suffer the tortures of the damned if you do not—"

"Asher ben Samuel!" the Moor cried. "I stole it from Asher ben Samuel!"

Silence in the tribunal room. Ramiro, who had sat silent during the interrogation, finally spoke.

"Asher ben Samuel... at last!"

Samuel was a prominent Jewish importer who converted to Christianity rather than leave the country after the Alhambra Decree, but no one on the inquisition tribunal believed his conversion had been true. They had dispatched townsfolk to spy on him and catch him engaging in Judaist practices. They watched for lack of smoke from his chimney on Saturdays, which would indicate observance of the Jewish Sabbath. They would offer him leavened bread during Passover—if he refused, his true faith would be revealed. But he always ate it without hesitation.

Still, the tribunal had not been convinced.

But now... now they had him.

Or did they?

After Abdel was removed, to be freed again to the streets, Tomás said, "What accusation can be leveled against Asher ben Samuel?"

"Heresy, of course!" Ramiro said.

"Who will accuse him?"

Adelard said, "We will."

"On the word of a disreputable Morisco street merchant who will have to admit to thievery to make the accusation?"

They fell silent at that.

"I have an idea," Ramiro said. "In which are we more interested: exposing a crypto Jew, or learning the origin of this hellish tome?"

Tomás knew the answer immediately. "I think we can all agree that the *Compendium* presents a far greater threat to the Faith than a single *converso*."

"It surely does," Ramiro said. "Although in my heart I believe that Asher ben Samuel is guilty of many heresies, we have not caught him at a single one. But in the course of our attempts to catch him over the years, we have kept too close a watch on him to allow him the opportunity of fashioning this book without our knowing."

Tomás reluctantly agreed. "You are saying that if the book did not originate with him, he must have bought it from someone else."

"Exactly, good Prior. Each owner and subsequent owner is a stepping stone across a stream. Each one brings us closer to shore: the heretic who fashioned it. And so I propose that Brother Adelard and I confront Asher ben Samuel in his home with the book and learn where he obtained it."

"That is most irregular," Tomás said.

"I realize that, Prior," Ramiro said. "But if we wish to limit knowledge of the book's existence, we cannot keep bringing suspect after suspect to the monastery. Who knows how many we will have to interrogate before we find the fashioner? Eventually the other members of the tribunal will begin to ask questions we wish not to answer. And by our own rules of procedure, each accused is allowed thirty days of grace to confess and repent. If the trail is long, the fashioner will have months and months of warning during which he can flee."

All excellent points. He was proud of Brother Ramiro.

"But how will you induce him to speak in his home? The instruments of truth lie two floors below us."

Ramiro shrugged. "I will tell him the truth: that we are more interested in finding the heretic behind the *Compendium* than in punishing those through whose hands it happened to pass. Asher ben Samuel is a wealthy man. He has more to lose than his life. He knows that if brought before the tribunal he will be found guilty, and then not only will he face the cleansing flame at the stake, but all his property will be seized and his wife and daughters cast into the streets." Ramiro smiled. "He will tell us. And then we will move on to the next stepping stone."

Tomás nodded slowly. The plan had merit.

"Do it, then. Begin today." He tapped the *Compendium*'s strange metal cover. "I want this heretic found. The sooner we have him, the sooner his soul can be cleansed by an *auto da fé*.

5

From within the sheltering cowl of his black robe, Adelard regarded the twilit streets of Ávila. He was glad to be out in the air. He left the monastery so seldom these days. Spring had taken control, as evidenced by the bustling townspeople. When summer arrived, the heat would slow all movement until well into the dark hours.

Brother Ramiro carried the carefully wrapped *Compendium* between his chest and his folded arms as they crossed the town square. Adelard glanced at the trio of scorched stakes where heretics were unburdened of their sins by the cleansing flame. He had witnessed many an *auto da fé* here since his arrival from France.

"Note how passersby avert their eyes and give us a wide berth," Ramiro said.

Adelard had indeed noticed that. "I don't know why. They can't know that I am a member of the tribunal."

"They don't. They see the black robes and know us as Dominicans, members of the order that runs the Inquisition, and that is enough. This saddens me."

"Why?"

"You are an inquisitor, I am a simple mendicant. You would not know."

"I was not always an inquisitor, Ramiro."

"But you did not know Ávila before the Inquisition arrived. We were greeted with smiles and welcomed everywhere. Now no one looks me in the eye. What do you think their averted gazes mean? That they have heresies to hide?"

"Perhaps."

"Then you are wrong. It means that the robes of our order have become associated with the public burnings of heretics to the exclusion of all else."

Adelard had never heard his friend talk like this.

"What are you saying, Ramiro?"

"I am saying that we are not an order that stays behind its walls. We have always gone out among the people, helping the sick, feeding the poor, easing pain and sorrow. But the order's involvement in guarding the Faith seems to have erased all memory of our centuries of good works."

"Be careful what you say, Ramiro. You are flirting with heresy."

"Are you going to accuse me?"

"No. You are my friend. I know that you speak from a good, faithful heart, but others might not appreciate that. So please watch your tongue."

Adelard was surprised at Ramiro's familiarity with the people of Ávila. He had imagined him spending all his time in the library or tilling the monastery's fields. He changed the subject.

"I've known you for a number of years now, Ramiro, but I don't know where you are from."

"Toro. A province north of here."

"Do you still have family there?"

"No. My family was wiped out in the Battle of Toro. I was just a boy and barely managed to survive."

Adelard had heard of that—one of the battles in the war for the crown of Castile.

"How did you come to the order?"

"After the horrors I'd seen, I wanted a life of peace and contemplation and good works. And that is what I had until the Inquisition changed everything."

Adelard had come to the Dominicans for very different reasons. The order provided him a place to pursue the philosophy of nature and to write papers explaining God's Creation and how what he had learned bolstered the doctrines of the Church. Sometimes he had to stretch the truth to avoid censure, but in general his papers were well received and seen as a cogent defense of doctrine. As a result, when the pope decided that the Spanish Inquisition needed outside influence, he assigned Adelard to be one of the new inquisitors.

But concerns about doctrine faded as the *Compendium* took command of his thoughts, much as it had since he'd opened it yesterday and begun reading. The ability of its text to appear written in the reader's native tongue certainly seemed sorcerous, and yet... and yet it seemed so congruent with the civilization described within.

Since his youth, Adelard had been fascinated with the philosophy of nature. When his father would bring home small game from the hunt, he would insist on gutting them, but doing so in his own way—methodically, systematically, so that he might understand the inner workings of the creatures. And even now he had reserved a room in the monastery where he could mix various elements and record their interactions.

He wondered if there might be a natural explanation for the marvels described within the *Compendium* and for the wonder of the tome itself—something that would not violate Church orthodoxy.

He would have to ponder this alone. He could not discuss it with Ramiro, who had not read it, and he might be risking his position, perhaps even his life, if he broached the subject with the Grand Inquisitor.

They reached the large plot of land on the edge of town where Asher ben Samuel lived, and started down the long path that led to his house.

"Does it seem right that a Jew should have such fortune?" Adelard said as they passed through a grove of olive trees.

"He is a *converso*—no longer a Jew."

Even though they professed to be Christian, *conversos* were mistrusted and even held in contempt. Especially someone with the financial influence of Samuel. Was his "conversion" simply economic pragmatism, or had he truly rejected his old beliefs? Adelard suspected—nay, was convinced—of the latter. The problem was proving it.

"You are so naïve, Ramiro. Once a Jew, always a Jew."

"I have Jewish blood. And so, no doubt, do you."

"You lie!"

"There's hardly an educated person in Castile who does not carry Jewish blood."

"I was raised in France."

"Probably the same there. Even our own prior—were you aware that a grandfather in the Torquemada line was a Jew?"

Tomás de Torquemada, the Hammer of Heretics, the Queen's confessor... had Jewish blood? How was this possible?

"That can't be true!"

"It is. He makes no secret of it. He has said that the purpose of the Holy Inquisition is not to stamp out Jewish blood, but to stamp out Jewish practices."

"All right, then, if the Prior says it is true, I accept it as true. But even so, his Jewish blood and yours are different from Asher ben Samuel's."

"How?"

"The prior and you were raised in the Faith. *Conversos* like him were not."

At the end of the path they found the high-walled home of Asher ben Samuel.

Ramiro said, "It reminds me of a fortress."

They stopped before the wrought iron gate and pulled the bell cord. An elderly footman exited the house and limped across the gap between.

"Yes?" he said, his eyes full of fear.

"We have come to see your master," Ramiro said.

"On a matter of faith," Adelard added.

The old man turned away. "I must go ask—"

"Open immediately!" Ramiro said. "Members of the Tribunal of the Holy Office of the Inquisition do not wait outside like beggars!"

With trembling hands, the old man unlocked the gate and pulled it open. He led them through a heavy oak door into a large, tiled gallery that opened onto a courtyard. And there sat Asher ben Samuel, reading under a broad chandelier.

A squat man of perhaps fifty years, he rose and came forward as they entered. "Friars! To what do I owe this honor?"

Adelard wondered why he didn't seem surprised or upset. Had he seen them coming?

"We will speak to you in private," he said.

"Of course. Diego, go to your quarters. But first—can I have him bring you some wine?"

Adelard would have loved some good wine, but he would accept no hospitality from this Jew.

"This is not a social call," he said.

Still apparently unperturbed, Samuel waved Diego off and then faced them. "How may I be of service?"

Ramiro pointed to the large illuminated manuscript that lay open on the table behind Samuel. "You can first tell us what you are reading."

Samuel smiled. "The Gospel of Matthew. It is my favorite."

Liar, Adelard thought. He *had* seen them coming.

Ramiro unwrapped the *Compendium* and placed it on the table. "We thought this would have been more to your liking."

Finally Samuel's composure cracked, but only a little.

"How—?"

"How it came to us is not the question. How did it come to you?"

He backed a step and sat heavily in a chair. "I collect books. This was offered to me. Since it was of such unusual construction and written in Hebrew, I snatched it up."

"Written in He—?" Ramiro began, then frowned. "Oh, of course."

"When I began to read it I realized it was a very dangerous book to have in one's possession."

"Why did you not bring it to the tribunal?" Adelard said.

Samuel gave them a withering look. "Really, good friars. For years you have been trying to find a reason to drag me before you. I should provide you with such a reason myself?"

"You know as well as we that many *conversos* pay only lip service to the Church's teachings and hold to their Jewish ways once their doors are closed. One cannot shed one's lifelong faith like an old coat."

"Ah, but you forget that I am a Castilian as well. If my queen and her king want to rule a Christian land, then I become Christian. It is not as if I am forsaking the Jewish God for a pagan idol. As I am sure you know, Jesus was born a Jew. The Old Testament of the Jews leads to the New Testament of Jesus. We worship the same God."

He possessed a persuasive tongue, this Jew; Adelard would give him that.

Ramiro said, "So, instead of bringing this book to the tribunal, you packed it in a trunk. For what purpose?"

"You seem to know so much…"

"Answer the question!"

"I intended to throw it in the river. I did not want such a

dangerous text in my library, nor in anyone else's." He spread his hands. "But when I reached the river, I could not find it. It was gone, as if by magic."

Not magic, Adelard thought. A thieving Morisco.

"Who sold it to you?"

Samuel said nothing for a moment, then took a deep breath. "I hesitate to condemn another man to the rack. Do you understand that?"

"We understand," Adelard said. "We wish to find the author of this heresy as soon as possible. If you assist us in locating him, I have the authority to overlook the time the book was in your possession."

Asher ben Samuel tapped his fingers on the arm of his chair as he pondered this. He knew the enormous cost to him and his family to withhold the name.

Finally he looked up and said, "You will make the same offer to the man I name?"

"We offer you absolution and you dare to bargain with us?"

"I merely asked a question."

Adelard hated conceding to the Jew, but they had to stay focused on their ultimate goal.

"As long as he is not the fashioner. If the book merely passed through his hands, he will not be punished. But the fashioner... the fashioner has committed heresy most foul and will pay a severe penalty."

Samuel smiled. "No possibility of the man in question being your fashioner. He is a simple carpenter. I doubt he can read a dozen words, let alone concoct such a fiction as you have in this book."

"He stole it then?" Ramiro said.

Samuel shrugged. "He told me the book had been freely given to him, but who is to know? He has done work for me, building shelves for my library. He knows of my love of learning and so he came to me to sell it."

Adelard raised his voice. "The name! We want his name, not your empty excuses!"

"The only name I have for him is Pedro the carpenter."

Ramiro was nodding. "I know him. He built shelves for the monastery's library as well. He does excellent work." He looked at Adelard. "But I agree: It is inconceivable that he wrote the *Compendium*."

"Perhaps. But he will be able to tell us how it came to him. And then we will be—as you like to say, Brother Ramiro—one stepping stone closer to the source."

6

Eventually, after asking questions at a number of intersections, they came to a meager shack down near the east bank of the Rio Adaja. The river ran sluggishly here, and stank from the waste thrown in the waters upstream. Faint light flickered through the gaps in the hut's weathered boards. Certainly no more than a single candle burned within.

Adelard stopped in the darkness and stared at the hovel. Ramiro drew close to his side.

"Does it seem fair to you, Ramiro, that a skilled craftsman should live in such poverty while a man who simply buys and sells lives in luxury?"

"We are not to expect fairness in this world, brother, only in the next."

"True, true, but still it rankles."

"Pedro is a simple man. I fear the two of us appearing at his door will terrify him. He might flee and hide. But he knows me. Let me go in and speak to him alone, assure him that he has nothing to fear if he tells us the truth."

"Very well, but be quick about it."

Adelard was exhausted. He had not slept last night. How could he, knowing his aging, ailing prior was up alone reading that hellish tome? All he wanted now was to complete this step in the investigation and return to his cot.

He watched Brother Ramiro approach the door with the

Compendium under his arm, hesitate, then enter without knocking.

Immediately a cry rose from within, a hoarse voice shouting, "No! No, I'm sorry! I did not know!"

And then a scream of pain.

Adelard rushed forward, almost colliding with Ramiro as he stumbled from within.

"What happened?"

Ramiro was shaking. "When he saw me, he grabbed a knife. I feared he was going to attack me, but he thrust it into his own heart!"

Adelard pushed past him and looked inside. A thin man with graying hair lay on the floor with a knife handle jutting from his chest. His unseeing eyes gazed heavenward.

"Do you see?" Ramiro cried. "See what you and your Inquisition have done! This is what I said before: The very sight of this robe terrifies people! Pedro did not see me, he saw torture and burning flesh!"

7

"Do we have no other path to follow?" Tomás said to the two monks standing before him.

He had napped this evening while they were out, but then had waited up for their return. The news they brought was not at all what he had hoped for.

Adelard shook his head. "I fear not, Prior. The carpenter's death cuts off all further avenues of inquiry."

"How did this come to pass?"

Brother Ramiro spread his hands. "As soon as I stepped inside, he began to cry out in fear. Before I had a chance to say a single word, he snatched a knife up from his table and thrust it into his heart."

"He must have thought Brother Ramiro was there to drag him before the tribunal," Adelard said. "He knew he had transgressed and feared the stake."

Tomás shook his head. After all these years of the Holy Inquisition, the common folk remained ignorant of the process. They saw someone taken in for questioning and later saw that same person tied to a stake and screaming as the flames consumed them. They assumed the *auto da fé* was the outcome of every arrest, but nothing could be further from the truth. They forgot that the vast majority of those detained were eventually freed after confessing their guilt and doing penance. The instruments of truth were used only on those who refused to confess. Those consumed at the stake were usually *relapsos*— sinners who returned to their heretical ways after having been released by the tribunal.

"So unnecessary," Ramiro said, shaking his head. "And so frustrating. He lived alone, so we will never know where he obtained the book."

Tomás pounded his fist on the *Compendium*. "We must find this heretic!"

"How?" Adelard said. "Tell us how and we shall do it."

Tomás had no answer for him.

He sighed. "I see only one course now." He gestured to the fireplace behind him. "Consign it to the flames."

The fire had burned low by now. He watched as Adelard and Ramiro added wood and fanned it to a roaring blaze. When the heat had risen to an uncomfortable level, Tomás handed the *Compendium* to Adelard who opened it at the middle and dropped it upon the flames.

Tomás waited for the cover to scorch and then melt, for the pages to smoke and blacken and curl. But the *Compendium* ignored the flames. It lay there unperturbed as the fire burned down to faintly glowing embers around it.

"This cannot be," Tomás muttered.

Ramiro grabbed the tongs and pulled the book from the ashes. As it lay unmarred on the hearth, he held his open palm over it.

"It doesn't seem..." He touched it, then looked up in wonder. "It is not even warm!"

Tomás felt his gut crawl. A heretical text that would not burn... this went beyond his worst nightmare.

"Brother Ramiro..." His voice sounded hoarse. "Bring the headsman's ax."

As Ramiro hurried off, Adelard stepped closer to Tomás.

"I am glad that Ramiro is gone," he said in a low voice. "He has not read the *Compendium* and you and I have. His absence offers us an opportunity to discuss its contents."

"What is there to discuss about heresy?"

"What if..." Adelard seemed hesitant.

"Go on."

"What if this *Compendium* speaks the truth?"

Tomás could not believe his ears. "Have you gone mad?"

"This is just supposition, Prior. We have this strange, strange book before us. I ask you: Is it heresy to theorize about its origins? If you say it is, I shall speak no further."

Tomás considered this. Heresy involved presenting falsehoods about the Faith or the Church as truth. Merely theorizing rather than proselytizing ...

"Go ahead. I shall warn you when you begin to venture into heresy."

"Thank you, Prior." He stepped away and began pacing the tribunal chamber. "I have been thinking. *The Book of Genesis* tells about the Flood: How the evil of Mankind prompted God to bring the Deluge to cleanse the world and start afresh. What if the *Compendium* tells of an evil, godless civilization that existed before the Deluge? What if the *Compendium* is all that is left of that civilization?"

Adelard... ever the philosopher. However...

"The Holy Bible makes no mention of such a civilization."

"Neither does it give specifics about the 'evils of mankind' that triggered God's wrath. The *Compendium*'s civilization could have been the very reason for the Deluge."

Tomás found himself nodding. Adelard's theory would explain why neither the Church nor Jesus were ever mentioned in the book, for neither would have existed when it was supposedly written. His idea was certainly unorthodox, but did not contradict Church doctrine in any way Tomás could see.

"An interesting theory, Brother Adelard."

Adelard stopped his pacing. "If it is true, Prior"—he waved his hands—"no, I mean if we *suppose* it is true, then this tome is an archeological artifact, an important piece of pre-Deluge history—perhaps the last existing piece of the pre-Deluge world. Do we then have a right to destroy it?"

Tomás did not like where this was leading.

"Right? It is not a matter of our *right* to destroy it, we have a sacred *duty* to destroy it."

"But perhaps it should be preserved as a piece of history."

"You tread dangerous ground here, Brother Adelard. Let us suppose that the *Compendium* does predate the Deluge and that the heretical civilization described therein did exist in those ancient days. If the book is preserved and its contents become widely known, then people will begin to ask why it was never mentioned in the *Book of Genesis*. And if *Genesis* makes no mention of that, then it is logical to ask what else *Genesis* fails to mention. And right then and there you have planted a seed of doubt. And from the tiniest seed of doubt can grow vast heresies."

Adelard backed away, nodding. "Yes, I see. I see. Indeed, we must destroy it."

He didn't have to explain to Adelard that questions had no place where faith was concerned. All the answers were there, waiting, no questions necessary. Questions, however, though a necessary part of philosophy and the pursuit of knowledge, were toxic to faith. If one feels the need to question the Faith, then one has already fallen from grace and entered the realm of doubt.

Tomás was well aware that every thinking man contended with doubts about some aspect of the Faith from time to time. He had experienced one or two himself during his middle years, but he overcame them long before he was appointed Grand Inquisitor. As long as a man confined his doubts to his inner struggle, they did not fall under the authority of the Holy Inquisition. But should that man communicate those qualms to others for the purpose of infecting them with his uncertainty, *then* the tribunal stepped in.

"You have an inquiring mind, Brother Adelard. Be careful that it does not lead you astray. And see to it that our discussion here goes no further than this room."

"For certain, Prior."

Ramiro returned then, puffing from the exertion of hurrying his portly frame to the basement two floors below and back up again with the burden of the heavy, long-handled ax.

Not all recalcitrant heretics were allowed the cleansing flame of the *auto da fé*. Some were simply beheaded like common criminals. The ax was stored below and its wide cutting edge kept finely honed.

"Shall I, Prior?" he said, approaching the *Compendium* where it lay open on the hearth.

Tomás nodded. "Split it in two, Ramiro. Then reduce it to tiny scraps that we may scatter to the wind."

Ramiro lifted the ax high above his head. With a snarl and a cry, he swung it down with all his strength and struck the *Compendium* a blow such as would have severed any head from its body, no matter how sturdy the neck that supported it. Yet, to Tomás's wonder and dismay, the blade bounced off the exposed pages without so much as creasing them.

"This cannot be!" Ramiro cried.

He swung again and again, raining blow after blow upon the *Compendium*, but for all the effect he had he might as well have been caressing it with a feather.

Finally, red faced, sweating, panting, Ramiro stopped and faced them.

"Surely this is a thing from hell!"

Tomás would not argue that.

"What do we do?" Ramiro said, still panting. "Asher ben Samuel said he was going to throw it in the river. Perhaps that is the only course that remains to us."

Tomás shook his head. "No. Not a river. Too easy for a fisherman's net to retrieve it from the bottom. The deep ocean would be better. Perhaps we can send one of you on a voyage far out to sea where you can drop it over the side."

Ever the philosopher, Adelard said, "First we must make certain it will sink. But even if it does sink, it will still be intact. It will still exist. And even confined to a briny abyss, there will always remain the possibility that it will resurface. We must find a way to *destroy* it."

"How?" Ramiro said. "It will not burn, it will not be cut."

Adelard said, "Perhaps I can concoct a mixture of elements and humors that will overcome its defenses."

Elements! An idea struck Tomás just then—why hadn't he thought of it before? He pointed to a small table in the corner.

"Adelard, bring the holy water here."

The younger man's eyes lit as he hurried across the room and returned with a flagon of clear liquid. Tomás rose slowly from his chair and approached the book where it lay on the hearth. When Adelard handed him the unstoppered flagon, he blessed it, then poured some of its contents onto the *Compendium*...

... to no effect.

Angered, Tomás began splashing the holy water in the shape of a cross as he intoned, *"In Nomine Patri et Fili et Spiritus Sancti!"*

Then he waited, praying for the holy water to eat away at the pages. But again... nothing.

A pall settled over him. Had they no recourse against this hellish creation?

"Good Prior," Adelard said after a moment, "if I could take the tome and experiment on it, I might be able to discover a vulnerability."

Tomás fought a burst of anger. "You seek to succeed where water blessed in God's name has failed?"

Adelard pointed to the *Compendium*. "That thing was fashioned from the elements of God's earth. I know in my heart that it can be undone by the same."

Could philosophy succeed where faith had failed?

"For the sake of the Faith, let us pray you are right."

8

Tomás did pray—all that night. And in the morning, when he stepped into the hall outside his room, an acrid odor assailed his nostrils. It seemed to issue from Adelard's workroom at the end of the hall. He approached the closed door as quickly as his painful hips would allow and pulled it open without knocking.

Inside he found Adelard holding a pair of steel tongs. The gripping end of the tongs suspended a glass flask of fuming red-orange liquid over the *Compendium*. The *Compendium* itself rested on the tile floor.

Adelard smiled at him. "You are just in time, Prior."

Tomás covered his mouth and nose and pointed to the flask. "What is that?"

"*Aqua regia*. I just now mixed it. The solution will dissolve gold, silver, platinum, almost any metal you care to name."

"Yet the simple glass of its container appears impervious."

"Glass is not metal. But the *Compendium* is."

Tomás felt his hackles rise. "This smacks of alchemy, Brother Adelard."

"Not in the least, Prior. Aqua regia was first compounded over one hundred years ago. It is simply the combination of certain of God's elements in a given ratio. No spells or incantations are required. Anyone with the recipe can do it. I will show you later, if you wish."

"That will not be necessary. What I want to know is, will it work?"

"If gold cannot stand against aqua regia, how can the *Compendium*?"

Tomás remembered having similar confidence about holy water last night.

"Please stand back, Prior. I am going to try a small amount first."

Tomás held his ground. "Start your trial."

He watched as Adelard tilted the flask and allowed a single drop of the smoking liquid to fall onto the cover. It stopped fuming on contact. It neither bubbled nor corroded nor marred the patterned surface in any way. Frowning, Adelard slowly poured a little more over a wider area with similar result. A container of spring water would have had the same effect.

Adelard used his sandaled foot to flip the cover open, revealing a random page onto which he emptied the flask. The corrosive had no more effect there than on the cover.

Adelard's shoulders slumped, and Tomás imagined his own did as well.

"I see no recourse but a deep-sea burial," Tomás said.

Adelard lifted his head. "Not yet, good Prior. I am not yet ready to surrender. Give me three days before I must admit defeat."

Tomás considered this. Yes, they could spare three days.

"Very well. Three days, Brother Adelard, but no more. And may God speed."

9

Tomás spent those three days in prayer, often with Brother Ramiro at his side. Tribunal matters were postponed, meetings were canceled for the time being. Two *relapsos* awaited their *auto da fé* but Tomás delayed the sentence until this more pressing matter was resolved.

They did not know what Brother Adelard was up to, but Tomás was aware of the monk making many trips to and from his workroom carrying mysterious bundles of materials. Questions were raised by other members of the order, inquiring as to the cries of anger and anguish, the cacophony of hammering and sawing and smashing glass issuing from behind the closed door.

Tomás was able to put them off with the simple truth: Brother Adelard was engaged in the Lord's work.

Toward the end of the third day with no results, Tomás called Ramiro to the tribunal room. He squinted at the stains and sawdust on the monk's black robe. Ramiro must have noticed the scrutiny.

"I have been making some changes in the library, Prior—doing the work myself since I no longer have a carpenter to call on."

Tomás wasn't sure if he detected a barb in that last remark. Never mind...

"While Brother Adelard's efforts have been heroic, every time I pass him in the hallway he reports no progress. I have given up hope of success by philosophical means. I see the ocean bottom as the only remaining option."

Ramiro nodded. "Yes, Prior. I am afraid I agree. I will be happy to make the voyage."

Tomás smiled. "How well you anticipate my thoughts. I was just about to tell you that I was assigning you the task. I do not think Brother Adelard has slept at all these past three days and he will be in no condition to make the journey."

"It is the least I can do after all his efforts."

Just then they heard a voice calling in the hallway.

"Prior Tomás! Prior Tomás! I have done it!"

Praying that Adelard was not mistaken, Tomás allowed Ramiro to help him down the hall to the workroom.

"I have been trying one combination of elements after another," Adelard said, leading the way. His eyes looked wild and his robe was pocked with countless holes burned by splashes of the corrosive compounds he had been handling. "Finally I found the one that works—quite possibly the only combination in all Creation that works!"

He reached the door and held it open for them. The workroom was full of fumes, which billowed out and ran along both the floor and ceiling of the hallway.

Ramiro waved his free arm ahead of them, parting the

fumes as they reached the threshold. Tomás squinted through haze to see an odd structure sitting in the middle of the floor. It appeared to be a wooden cabinet but a deep glass bowl took up most of its upper surface. Through the smoke rising from the bowl Tomás spied what appeared to be a rectangular block of metal, immersed in a bubbling, fuming orange solution.

"What is happening here?" Tomás said.

"The *Compendium*! It is dissolving!"

Tomás prayed he wasn't dreaming. The letters and designs had been eaten off the cover, and the whole book appeared to be melting.

"But how—?"

"Through trial and error, Prior! I kept adding different compounds and solutions to the aqua regia until... until *this*! Isn't it wonderful?"

Yes. It was indeed wonderful.

"Praise God. He has worked a miracle." Tomás looked at Ramiro. "Don't you agree?"

Ramiro's expression was troubled, then it cleared and he offered a weak smile. "Yes, Prior. A miracle."

Tomás wondered what was distressing him. Jealous of Adelard's success? Or disappointed that he would not be going on the ocean voyage?

They watched for nearly an hour, with Adelard periodically adding fresh solution, until the *Compendium* was reduced to a mass of semi-molten metal. Adelard used tongs to remove it from the solution and lay it on the floor.

"As you can see," he said, his voice full of pride, "the *Compendium* of Srem is no more. The solution has fused it into a solid mass. It is not even recognizable as a book."

"I'll dispose of the remains," Ramiro said.

Adelard stepped forward. "Not necessary, Brother Ramiro. I—"

"You've done quite enough, Brother Adelard," Tomás said. "Go rest. You have earned it."

"But Prior—"

Tomás lifted his hand, halting discussion.

He did not understand Adelard's uneasy expression.

10

Tomás awoke to soft knocking on his door. It reminded him of that night not too long ago when Adelard had shown up with that accursed tome.

"Yes?"

"It is Brother Ramiro, Prior. I must speak to you on an urgent matter."

"Come, then."

He remained supine in his bed as Ramiro entered with a candle. "Good Prior, I must show you something."

"What is it?"

"It would be better to see with your own eyes."

Tomás looked up at him. "Tell me."

Ramiro took a deep breath and let out a sigh. "I wish to show you the *Compendium*."

"It was not destroyed?" Tomás closed his eyes and groaned. "How is this possible? I thought you buried what was left of it."

"I regret to inform you that what you saw dissolving was not the *Compendium*, Prior. That was a sheaf of tin sheets."

"But—"

"In addition to gold and silver and platinum, aqua regia dissolves tin."

The meaning was suddenly all too clear.

"You are accusing Brother Adelard of deceiving us!"

"Yes, Prior. Much as it pains me to say it, I fear it is so."

"This is a terribly serious charge."

Ramiro bowed his head. "That was why I wanted to show you."

"Show me what?"

"Where he has hidden the *Compendium*."

Tomás realized he would have to see for himself.

"Light my candle and wait for me in the hall."

Ramiro pressed the flame of his candle against the cold wick of the one on the desk and left. Tomás struggled from his cot and slipped on his black robe. He grabbed his cane and joined Ramiro in the hallway, then followed him to Adelard's workroom.

"I found it here," Ramiro said, opening the door.

He stepped to the acid-scarred cabinet in the center of the floor. The glass bowl in the top still contained residue from the dissolution they had witnessed yesterday. He knelt and removed a panel from the side of the cabinet. Then he removed a board from the base of the inner compartment.

"A false floor," Ramiro said.

From within the hidden compartment he removed a blanket-wrapped parcel. He placed it atop the cabinet and unfolded the wrapping, revealing...

The *Compendium*.

For a moment Tomás did not know what to think. Was this a trick? Was Ramiro so jealous of his fellow monk that he would—?

Just then Adelard rushed in, gasping. "Oh, no! Prior, I can explain!"

No denial on the young monk's part, only the offer of an excuse. Tomás felt crushed by this betrayal.

"Oh, Adelard, Adelard," he said, his voice barely audible. "Preserving heresy."

"It is not heresy if it is true!"

"It goes against Church doctrine, and it will raise dangerous questions. We have discussed this."

"But Prior, it won't burn, it won't be cut, it laughs at the most corrosive compounds we have. It is ancient and it is a wonder—truly a wonder. The Colossus of Rhodes, the Hanging Gardens of Babylon, the Lighthouse at Alexandria—six of the Seven Wonders of the Ancient World are gone. Only the Pyramids at Giza remain. Yet we hold the Eighth Wonder here in our hands.

We have no right to keep it from the world!"

Tomás had heard enough—more than enough. Adelard was condemning himself with every word.

"Brother Adelard, you will confine yourself to your quarters until members of the Inquisition Guard bring you before the tribunal."

His eyes widened further. "The tribunal? But I am a member!"

"I am well aware of that. No more discussion. You will await judgment in your quarters."

As the crestfallen Adelard shuffled away toward his room, Tomás had no worries that he might run off. Adelard knew there was no escape from the Holy Inquisition.

What concerned Tomás was bringing a member of the tribunal before the tribunal itself to be judged. It was unprecedented. He would have to give this much thought. In the meantime...

"Brother Ramiro, wrap up that infernal tome and make certain that no one else sees it. Prepare to take it to sea on the earliest possible voyage."

"Yes, Prior."

He watched him fold the blanket around it, then carry it off toward his quarters. Tomás made his way to his own room and was just about to remove his cowled robe when he heard a knock on the door.

Was he never to have another full night's rest?

Ramiro's hushed voice came through the door. "I am so sorry, Prior, but I must speak with you again."

Tomás opened the door and found the portly friar standing on the threshold with a stricken expression. He held the wrapped *Compendium* against his chest. The blanket looked damp.

"It floats," he said.

"What do you mean?"

"I dropped it into a tub of water in the kitchen. It will not sink."

Tomás was not surprised. Why should it sink? That would make it too easy to dispose of.

"We will place it in trunk weighted with lead and wrapped with iron chains and—"

"Trunks rot in salt water, as do chains. Sooner or later it will surface again."

Tomás could not argue with that.

"What do we do, Brother Ramiro?"

"I have an idea…"

11

Tomás stood to the side while the two *relapsos* dug a deep hole at the rear of the Royal Cloister.

King Ferdinand and Queen Isabella would be arriving in a week or two to spend the summer, and the cloister would be empty until then. The queen had wanted a patio on the north side that would be shaded in the afternoon. Since the royal treasury was funding the monastery, her every whim was a command. The area had been cleared and leveled, and was now half paved with interlocking granite blocks. The remainder was bare earth. That was where the *relapsos* labored. Lanterns placed around the hole illuminated their efforts.

"Here, Prior," said Ramiro from behind him. "I brought you a chair."

He set the leather upholstered chair on the pavers and Tomás gladly made use of it. He had been holding the wrapped *Compendium* against his chest. Standing for so long had started an ache in his low back.

"This is a brilliant plan, Ramiro," he whispered.

"I live to serve the Faith. I would like to think that the Lord inspired me."

His plan was simple and yet perfect: Bury the *Compendium* in a section of the grounds that was scheduled to be paved over with heavy blocks. The *Monasterio de Santo Tomás* would stand for centuries, perhaps a thousand years or more. The *Compendium* would never be found. And if it ever were, perhaps the monks of that future time would know then how to destroy it.

But that day might never come. There would be no record anywhere of the existence of the *Compendium of Srem*, let alone where it was hidden. The two *relapsos* had no idea why they were digging the hole, and would not know what went into it. And even if they learned, what matter? Each had been sentenced to an *auto da fé*. Tomás would see to it that they had their time at the stakes early tomorrow.

Only Tomás and Ramiro would know its final resting place. The secret would die with them.

Together they watched the progress of the hole. The *relapsos* took turns in the pit: one would climb down the ladder with a shovel and fill a bucket with earth; the one topside would pull the bucket up on a rope, empty it, and send it back down. This went on until the top of the ten-foot ladder sank to a point where it was level with the surface.

"That is deep enough, I think," Tomás said.

Ramiro ordered the *relapso* down below to come up and pull the ladder from the pit. He tied their hands behind their backs. After blindfolding them, he made them kneel, facing away.

He held out his hands to Tomás. "May I, Prior?"

Tomás handed him the *Compendium* and watched as he unwrapped it. The flickering lantern light revealed the strange cover. The background pattern was crosshatching now. He closed his eyes for a few heartbeats, and when he reopened them it had changed to asymmetrical swirls.

"This is the last time anyone will ever see this book from hell," Ramiro said. He handed Tomás two cords. "I believe you deserve the honor of tying the covering around it."

Tomás tied one cord vertically and one horizontally, forming a cross, then handed it to Ramiro.

"Do you not wish to consign it to the pit?"

Tomás shook his head. His legs were tired and his back pained him. "You do it, Brother Ramiro."

"As you—?" His head shot up. "I believe I just saw a falling star."

"Where?" Tomás searched the cloudless heavens.

"It is gone. A streaking flash that lasted less than the blink of an eye. Do you think that has meaning, seeing one fall at this moment? Is it the Lord blessing our work?"

"Some say they are damned souls being cast into hell, others say they are signs of good luck. And still others say that falling stars are just that: stars that have slipped free from the dome of heaven and are falling to earth."

Ramiro was nodding. "Perhaps it is just as well not to read too much into these things." He held up the tied bundle. "I would carry it myself to the bottom but I fear my girth will not allow it."

He lifted one of the lamps as he approached the pit and held it high over the opening. Tomás watched the *Compendium* drop into the depths. Then Ramiro began shoveling dirt atop it. After half a dozen shovelfuls, he untied the *relapsos* and had them finish the job.

When they were done and the earth had been tamped flat over the hole, he bound them again, but this time he gagged them before leading them back to their cells.

Tomás remained seated, gazing at the bare earth. He would keep close watch on this patio until it was completed. Once the pavers were in place, the *Compendium* would be hidden from Mankind... forever.

12

The *relapsos* finally stopped screaming within their pillars of flame.

Ramiro lurched away from the town square and stumbled back toward the monastery. He had always avoided the square during an *auto da fé* but today he felt obliged to brave the dawn's chill and bear witness. Those two had repeatedly preached against the Church's practice of selling indulgences. In his heart Ramiro agreed with them, but would never be foolish enough to profess that aloud.

He had imagined the horror of seeing someone burned alive, but the reality proved worse than he had ever dreamed. Those *relapsos*, however, were gone for good. They would preach heresy no more, but more important, the location of the hole they had dug last night had been consumed with them.

As he walked along, the people who passed him averted their gaze—as usual.

He hated the Inquisition and what it had done to the Spains. He found it logical that the Church should want to safeguard the doctrines that empowered it, but at what cost? Thousands upon thousands had been tortured, hundreds upon hundreds had died in agony, tens of thousands had been banished from the land. A whole society had been upended.

But preserving the Faith was only part of it. The war for the crown of Castile, in which his family had been slaughtered, plus the war in Grenada—the whole *Reconquista*, in fact—had bankrupted the monarchy. Banishing the Jews and Moors did more than make the Spains a Christian realm. It left the abandoned properties to be looted by the Church and the royal treasury—an equal share between them. The same with heretics: the Church and the treasury divided their property and money down the middle.

Wealth and power—the two Holy Grails of church and state.

When he reached the monastery he ventured around the Royal Cloister to monitor the progress on the patio. The masons were hard at work, fitting the paving blocks snugly together, chipping away at the edges to assure a tighter fit. By tonight, or mid-tomorrow at the latest, the patio would be fully paved.

Satisfied, Ramiro moved on, entering the cloister that housed his quarters. His fellow monks spent spring mornings tilling the monastery's fields for planting. Soon he would join them, but first...

He descended to the basement that housed the heretics and

what Torquemada liked to call the "instruments of truth"—the rack, the wheel, the thumbscrews, the boots. Adelard had been locked in one of the basement's windowless cells. No guards were needed because the doors were thick and the locks sturdy.

He approached the only locked cell and looked through the small iron-barred opening.

"Brother Adelard?" he whispered.

Adelard's face appeared. "Ramiro! Have you news? Have they decided what?"

"I am sorry. I have heard nothing. I feel terrible for betraying you."

"I know. But you had no choice. I might have done the same. I don't… I don't know what came over me. Almost as if that book had put a spell on me. Against all reason, I had to have it, I had to save it."

Ramiro nodded. He knew the feeling well.

He reached through a slit in his robe into a pouch strapped to his ample abdomen. From it he withdrew a small wineskin.

"Here," he said, pushing it between the bars. "For strength. For courage."

Adelard pulled off the stopper and drank greedily.

"They don't feed me and give me very little water."

How does it feel? Ramiro thought. How many have you treated the same to make them weak and more easily persuaded by your tortures?

When Adelard finished the wine he pushed the empty skin back through the opening.

"Thank you. I had no hope of any kindness here."

"I will save you some bread from the midday meal and return with it."

Adelard sobbed. "Bless you, Ramiro. Bless you!"

"I must go. I have no business here and do not wish to be caught."

"Yes. Go. I anxiously await your return."

"Good-bye, brother."

As Ramiro climbed the steps to the ground floor, he knew he would have no reason to return. The poison in the wine would kill Adelard within the hour.

He sighed with relief when he reached the library on the second floor. As usual, he had the library to himself at his time of day.

At the rear of the room he lifted one of the larger tiles and gazed at the *Compendium* of Srem where it rested in the space he had hollowed out for it. He ran his fingers over the cover.

The crimes I have committed for you...

The *Compendium* had been under his family's care seemingly forever, handed down from father to first-born son for more generations than he could count. But no generation had taken credit for fashioning it. The book simply *was*.

Ramiro had not been his family's first son, but after the Battle of Toro he was the only son left. He had guarded the *Compendium* then, from the Inquisition and from others who had been searching for it down the ages. But as the Inquisition progressed, strengthening its hold on the populace and penetrating deeper and deeper into the lives of all within reach, he realized that possessing such a magical tome endangered his life. His anxiety grew to the point where he knew he had to change his ways: either flee to a different land, or hide in the belly of the beast.

He chose the latter and joined the Dominicans. He brought the *Compendium* with him, thinking the last place anyone would look for a heretical book would be in a monastery inhabited by the very order running the Inquisition. His family had never followed any religion, merely pretending to be Christians to fit in. After joining, Ramiro had found it easy to pretend, and came to enjoy the serene life of a monk.

But still his anxiety grew. He kept the *Compendium* hidden in a false bottom of his tiny bureau of drawers, but if someone found it, he would end up on the rack. He decided that he wanted to be done with guarding the *Compendium*. That had been his family's tradition, but he could no longer honor the commitment. He had to rid himself of the book, hide it for some future generation to find. But he could not allow himself to know where it was hidden, for he did not think he could resist digging it up and paging through it one more time. And one more time after that. And again after that...

So he had wrapped it and tied it and given it to Pedro the carpenter. He trusted the simple man to follow his instructions: Do not disturb the wrapping and bury it somewhere safe of his own choosing; he was to tell no one the location, not even Ramiro. Pedro had agreed and hurried off into the night.

Days later, Ramiro had almost swooned with shock when Adelard had invited him into his room to see the wondrous new book he had bought in the marketplace.

Pedro had betrayed him.

Right then and there Ramiro had known he wanted it back. The *Compendium* had to be his again.

He pretended to be ignorant of the book and followed along with Adelard until the trail led them to Pedro. When he'd entered the carpenter's hovel alone, he drew a knife from the sleeve of his robe and stabbed him in the heart. He had felt no remorse then and felt none now. He had trusted Pedro with a task and the man had betrayed him in a way most foul, a way that could have cost him his own life.

Ramiro knew from his family tradition across the generations that the *Compendium* had survived flood and blade and fire. That was why he had attacked it so enthusiastically with the headsman's axe: He had known the book would be impervious.

And then Adelard's pathetic attempt to fool them into thinking he had found a solvent to destroy the *Compendium*. Torquemada's eyes were poor, but Ramiro knew the book too well and had recognized the decoy for what it was. After that it was a simple matter of finding where Adelard had hidden the original.

Regaining possession had been the easiest. After making sure Torquemada had tied up the *Compendium* himself, Ramiro pretended to see a falling star. While the old man was searching the sky, Ramiro reached through the slit in his robe into the same pouch where he had hidden Adelard's wine this morning. He removed Adelard's tin fake, wrapped identically as the original. The true *Compendium* took its place in the pouch and Adelard's fake went into the earth.

Ramiro shook his head. He had lied for the *Compendium*, killed for it, betrayed and killed a friend for it, then stolen it back from the Grand Inquisitor himself.

Perhaps you are from hell, he thought, touching the raised lettering. Look what you've made me do.

But no, the *Compendium* was not from hell. Adelard had been right: It came from the past, from before the Deluge. Indeed, it *was* the Eighth Wonder of the Ancient World. But it must remain hidden from the modern world. Not for Torquemada's reason of a threat to the Faith—Ramiro cared not for any faith—but because the world did not need it yet.

He replaced the tile and headed for the fields.

Pedro and Adelard and the two *relapsos* were dead. One look at Torquemada and anyone could tell that the Grand Inquisitor would soon be joining them. The Morisco from the marketplace was practically illiterate and had no idea what treasure he had held. Only Asher ben Samuel remained, and as a *converso* targeted by the tribunal, he would never talk about it.

The *Compendium* seemed safe... at least for the moment.

Ramiro's family tradition said the *Compendium* was a thing of destiny, with an important role to play in the future. Ramiro had rededicated himself to preserving it for that future. It would be safer hidden under the library floor than in the chest of drawers in his room or buried in a field. Someday it would find its place in the future and fulfill its destiny.

One day he would leave the order and find a wife. He would have a son and start a new tradition of protecting the *Compendium*.

But until then it would belong to him and him alone. No one else could touch it or read of the marvels described and pictured within. Only him.

Ramiro liked it that way.

The Sequel

R.L. Stine

WITNESS ONE ZACHARY Gold, 33. Youthful, tanned, long and lean, tensed over his laptop in the back corner of the coffee shop, one hand motionless over the keyboard.

Casual in a white Polo shirt to emphasize his tan, khaki cargo shorts, white Converse All-Stars. He grips the empty cardboard latte cup, starts to raise it, then sets it down. Should he order a third, maybe a grande this time?

Zachary Gold, an author in search of a plot, begs the gods of caffeine to bring him inspiration. He is an author in the hold of that boring cliché, the Sophomore Slump. And his days of no progress on the second novel have taught him only that clichés are always true.

Not a superstitious man, not a fanciful man. Practical. A realist.

But today he will welcome any magic that will start him writing. An angel, a muse, a shaman, a voice from beyond the grave, enchanted beads, an amulet, a scrawled message on a crinkled-up paper napkin.

Today... perhaps today that magic will arrive.

No, Zachary Gold does not live in *The Twilight Zone*. He lives in a brownstone in the West 70's of Manhattan, a building he bought with the abundant royalties from his first novel.

He tells interviewers that he never reads reviews. But he did read the piece in the *New York Times* that declared him the "once-and-future king of the new American popular literature."

Does the once-and-future king have a future?

Zachary succumbs to a third latte, skim milk with a shot of espresso, and resumes his throne in front of the glaringly blank screen.

The first book wrote itself, he recalls. *I practically wrote it as fast as I could type it. And then I barely had to revise.*

A sigh escapes his throat. The hot cup trembles in his hand. If the first book hadn't crowned him king, he wouldn't be under so much pressure for the second one.

A lot of kings have been beheaded.

And then he scolds himself: Don't be so grim. A lot of authors have had this problem before you.

Zachary has a sense of humor. His wife Kristen says it kept him alive several times when she felt like battering him over the head with a hot frying pan. Kristen is a redhead and—another cliché—has the stormy temperament that is supposed to come with the fiery hair.

Two teenage girls at a table against the wall catch Zachary's attention. They have their green canvas backpacks on the floor and their phones in front of them on the table.

"Mrs. Abrams says we don't have to read *War and Peace*. We can read the Spark Notes instead."

"Mrs. Abrams is awesome."

At the table behind them, a woman with white scraggly hair, round red face, a long blue overcoat buttoned to her throat, two shopping bags at her feet, slumps in her chair as if in defeat, jabbering to herself. Or is she on the phone?

Zachary tells himself he needs the noise, the chatter and movement, the distraction of new faces, to help him concentrate. He wrote most of the first novel in this very coffee shop. He can't stay at home. Not with the baby crying. And the nanny on the phone, speaking torrents of heated Spanish to her boyfriend.

He tried an app that a friend told him about. It offered

background coffee shop noise to play through your home stereo. Like those sound machines that play ocean waves to help you sleep. The app had an endless loop with the clatter of dishes and low chatter of voices. But the sounds weren't stimulating enough to force Zachary to beam his attention to the keyboard. He had to get out.

And now he sits gazing from table to table. Studying the faces of those chatting and those caught in the glow of laptop screens. And he thinks how carefree everyone looks. *Because they don't have to write a book*. Most people leave school and never have to turn in another paper. And they are so happy about it.

Why did he choose to be a writer? Was it because he couldn't think of anything else? Was it because his parents begged him to start a real career, to find something he could "fall back on?"

Was it because the Howard Striver character came to him as if in a dream?

Howard Striver, please don't haunt me.

I like you, Howard. No. I love you. I'll always be grateful, old buddy. But I need to leave you behind.

Zachary sips the latte, already on its way to lukewarm. A flash of an idea. *What if an author's character won't leave him alone? Pursues him in real life?*

It's been done. But it's the start of something.

Zachary leans forward. Shuts his eyes to allow his thoughts to flow. Prepares to type. A shock of pain as a hand squeezes his shoulder.

He turns and gazes up at a big, broad man, fifties, maybe sixty, salt-and-pepper stubble of a beard on a jowly, hazel-eyed face. Sandy hair in disarray. The whole face is blurred, Zachary thinks. Like the man is somehow out of focus.

A homeless man looking for a handout? No. He's too well dressed. Pale blue sport shirt open at the neck, dark suit pants well pressed, polished brown wingtips.

The hand loosens on Zachary's shoulder. "We need to talk," the man says through his teeth. The lips don't move.

The harsh tone makes Zachary lean away. "Do I know you?"

"I'm Cardoza," the man says.

"S-sorry." Zachary has always had a stammer when he's surprised.

"Cardoza," the man repeats. The hazel eyes lock on Zachary. "Cardoza. You know me."

"No. Sorry." Zachary turns away and returns his hands to the keyboard. "Please. I'm working. I don't have time—"

The man named Cardoza lunges forward. He reaches for the lid of the laptop and slams it down hard on Zachary's hands.

Zachary hears a *crack*. Then he feels the pain rage over his hands and shoot up both arms.

His scream cuts through the coffee house chatter. People turn to stare.

"You broke my fingers! I think you broke my fingers."

Cardoza hovers over Zachary.

Zachary frees his hands from the laptop. He tries to rub the pain off his fingers. "What do you want? Tell me—what do you want?"

2

"What do I want? Just what's coming to me."

Cardoza pulls out the chair opposite Zachary and, with a groan, lowers his big body into it. His smile is unpleasant. Not a smile but a cold warning. He spreads his hands over the table, as if claiming it. Large hands, dark hair on the knuckles, a round, sparkly pinky ring on his right hand.

Zachary rubs his aching hands, tests his fingers. They seem to be working properly. If this man intended to frighten him, he has succeeded. Zachary glances around for a store manager, a security guy, maybe. Of course, there is none.

Why can't he get the man's face in focus? It seems to deflect the light.

He slides the latte cup aside. "I really am working here. I don't know you and I really think—"

Cardoza raises a big hand to silence Zachary. His smile fades. "I don't really care what you think."

Zachary glances around again, this time for an escape route. The narrow aisles are clogged with people. Two women have blocked the aisle with enormous baby strollers.

Two of his fingers have started to swell. Zachary rubs them tenderly. "You've attacked me for no reason. I have to ask you to leave me alone now."

The smile again. "Ask all you like."

Zachary doesn't know how to respond to this. Is Cardoza crazy? If he is crazy and wants to fight, Zachary is at a disadvantage. He's never been in a fight in his life, not even on the playground as a kid in Port Washington.

He eyes the man without speaking. He knows he's never seen him before. A tense silence between them. Zachary's laptop case is between his feet on the floor. Can he slide the computer into the case and get ready to make his escape?

Cardoza breaks the silence. He leans over the small, square coffee-stained table. "Having a productive day, Mr. Gold?" He doesn't wait for an answer. He spins the laptop around, opens it, and gazes at the screen. "Blank? A blank screen? Again?"

Zachary grabs the computer and spins it back around. "What do you mean again? What are you talking about?"

The hazel eyes lock on Zachary, now with cold menace. "Isn't that why you stole your book from me?"

"Hah!" Zachary can't help a scornful laugh from escaping. "Is that why you're here, Cardoza? You're crazy. You're messed up. You need to leave now." Zachary jumps to his feet as if to chase the man away.

Cardoza doesn't move. He clasps his hands together on the tabletop. "Word for word, Mr. Gold. Line by line. You stole my book. But I'm not a vindictive man. I just want a little payback."

Zachary's mind spins. Once again, his eyes search the small room for someone who could rescue him. "Cardoza, you need help," he murmurs. "You're deluded."

This man is insane, Zachary thinks. *But is he dangerous?*

And then: *Do other authors have to put up with this kind of harassment?*

And then: *Does he really think I'm going to give him money?*

"Please—leave me alone," Zachary says softly. "I'm asking you nicely."

"I can't, Mr. Gold. "I can't leave you alone. I don't know how you uncovered my manuscript. But you know I'm the one who created the Howard Striver character. He is based on my older brother, after all."

Zachary is still standing, hands on the back of his chair. "I'm begging you—" he starts.

Cardoza shakes his head. "I'm not going anywhere." He motions for Zachary to return to his seat. "I think you and I are going to develop a very close friendship." That cold smile again. "Unless you want the world to know you are a thief and a fraud."

Zachary sees the women push out the front door with their strollers. This is his chance. He ignores his suddenly racing heartbeats, grabs the laptop in one hand, leaves the case on the floor, spins to the front and runs.

"Look out!" A young long-haired young man carrying a muffin and a tall coffee cup leaps back as Zachary bolts past him.

Zachary is out the door. Nearly collides with the two strollers. The women have stopped to adjust the babies in the seats. They glare at him as he stumbles and skids to a stop, turns, and runs up Amsterdam Avenue.

A mild, hazy day of early spring. The air feels cool on his blazing hot face. He dodges two men with handcarts, making a flower delivery to the store next-door. Runs past a man setting up his shawarma cart on the corner, a brief whiff of grilled meat as he passes.

Zachary has to stop at the corner as a large Budweiser truck rumbles through the red light, horn wailing like a siren.

Which way? Which way?

He glimpses a dark blur behind him. Is Cardoza following him?

Zachary shields his eyes with one hand and squints into the sunlight. Yes. The big man is chasing him. Head down like a bull stampeding a toreador. A glint of silver, a flash of light in his hand.

Is he carrying a gun?

3

Maybe it's a phone.

Zachary darts behind the beer truck, crosses the street.

I can outrun him, but it would be better to hide. Especially if that's a gun in his hand.

The branch library stands in the middle of the block. The front window appears dark. Is it open? With the budget cuts, it's closed a lot of days. Zachary trots to the door, tugs the handle. Yes. Open. He swings the door just wide enough to slip inside.

Shouts outside. Is it Cardoza? The sound cuts off as the glass door closes behind him.

The librarian, a young woman, black bangs cropped across her forehead, red-framed glasses glinting in the light over the front desk, perched on a tall wooden stool, almost lost inside a loose camisole dress, very lilac, clashing with the red eyeglasses. She sees Zachary enter, breathing hard, almost wheezing, probably sweat visible on his forehead and cheeks.

He struggles to look calm and collected, as if he intended to visit the library. Flashes her a smile, but she continues to stare warily. He's holding the caseless laptop in one hand. Awkward. *I didn't steal it. Honest.*

She's a librarian. She should recognize him. He was on the *Times* list for forty-two weeks in a row last year.

Tucking the laptop under one armpit, Zachary makes his way to the reading room behind the front desk. It's a big room, deep and wide, lots of dark wood, worn armchairs along one wall, interrupted by a nonworking fireplace. Eight or nine rows of long tables across the middle of the room.

Nearly empty in this late-morning hour. Two bearded Asian men in armchairs reading Chinese newspapers. A middle-aged woman with frizzy, blond-streaked hair, leaning over a table in the front row, seemingly enthralled by an old copy of *People* magazine.

Zachary hurries to the back. Listening hard for the front door to open, for a big man with a gun (or maybe a phone) to burst in, alert to every sound. He drops into the last chair in the back row and hunches low, waiting for his breathing to return to normal, waiting for his eyes to adjust to the pale light from the old cone-shaped fixtures high in the rafters.

A good hiding place. Cardoza must not have seen him slip into the library. He would be here by now.

Do I have to be afraid to leave my apartment?

He opens the laptop. Wipes sweat off his forehead with the sleeve of his Polo shirt. His phone rings. His ringtone is an old-fashioned classic phone ring. It's supposed to be ironic but now everyone has it.

Startled, he tugs the phone from his shorts pocket. The Asian men don't look out from behind their newspapers. The woman in the front ignores it, too.

He takes the call. "Eleanor?" His agent.

"Zachary, how are you?"

"Well... I'm having an interesting morning." He turns his head and talks in a loud whisper. Obviously, phone conversations in the reading room are not encouraged.

"Well, you know my main job. I'm the nudge. How is the sequel coming, Mr. Z?"

He can't hold back an exasperated groan. "I told you, Eleanor. I'm not writing a sequel. Do I have to tattoo it on my chest before you'll believe me?"

"Zachary, should I call back later? Sounds like you're having a bad day."

"A bad day? I'm hiding in the library from a guy who chased me down the street because he says I stole my book from him."

"We all have our problems, Z. Know what my problem is? Getting you to write the sequel."

"Eleanor, please—"

"Why do you think you're having so much trouble getting started on the new book? Because you know your readers want another Howard Striver book. Zachary, why are you fighting it?"

"Been there, done that. Ever hear that phrase?" He sighed. "I don't want to be known as the guy who writes the Howard Striver books. I want to be known as an author. Period."

"Stubborn, stubborn. Let's look at it one other way, okay?"

"If we have to."

"Z, let's talk money. You like money, don't you? I know you and Kristen just got back from the Ocean Club on Paradise Island. That's not-too-shabby a resort. You enjoyed it, right?"

"Well, yes. But we had the baby and—"

"Zachary, do the Striver book, and I can get you a million dollars for any book you want to do next. Seriously. Do the sequel. The next book is an instant check for a million dollars. Can you picture that?"

"Of course. Don't talk to me like I'm an infant."

The *People* magazine woman turns her head and squints at him. He turns his back and hunches lower behind the laptop screen.

"How am I supposed to talk to you when you're acting like a stubborn baby? Hey, think of your baby. Think of all the strained peas a million dollars will buy." She laughs. "Organic artisanal local strained peas, right?"

He didn't reply.

"One last thing, Z, then I'll go. Think of all the new mind powers you can give Howard. Think of all the brain powers you haven't touched upon yet. There have to be a hundred story possibilities."

"Well…"

"Think of the story possibilities. And then picture that million-dollar check. Okay?"

Zachary hears his reply as if it's coming from some other body: "Okay, Eleanor. I'll think about it."

4

Zachary thinks about his first novel. *The Cerebellum Syndrome* is a science thriller. Part Michael Crichton, part *Bourne Identity*, with a hint of the sci-fi novels Zachary devoured as a teenager.

Howard Striver is a brilliant brain surgeon and neurological explorer. Fascinated by the fact that seventy-five percent of the human brain is dormant, he sets about finding a way to stimulate the unused parts of the cerebellum.

Unable to find volunteers, Dr. Striver experiments on his own brain—and succeeds in giving himself extraordinary mind powers. His expanded memory, his newly found kinetic abilities, his ability to retain encyclopedic amounts of knowledge make him a powerful superhero of the mind.

Three different governments, including our own, send agents to kidnap Striver. They are desperate to analyze his brain and learn how to use his newly discovered mind powers for military purposes. He escapes again and again, a thrilling chase scenario.

But even while he flees his pursuers, Howard Striver continues his experiments. He knows he is going too far, expanding his abilities too rapidly to analyze what he has accomplished.

To thwart his pursuers, he escapes into his own mind. He begins living entirely in the unexplored spaces of his brain. He transforms reality into an internal reality of his own making.

That's the basis of the first book. Is it ripe for a sequel?

At home, thinking hard, Zachary paces back and forth in his

study, holding Emily, the baby, in his arms. Emily's expression is serious, attentive, as if she can read the turmoil in his mind. She makes a gurgling sound. Zachary imagines she is trying to comfort him.

He raises her head to his face and gives it a long sniff. Nothing smells as good as baby skin. He runs a finger gently under her chin, a soft tickle.

"Emily, you are so precious to me," he tells her. "Should I give up writing something new? Write the sequel? For you?" Her pink mouth crinkles up. She starts to cry, thrashing her arms out stiffly.

He hands her back to the nanny.

I have to get out of here. I have to start writing. I have to think.

He picks up his laptop and carries it outside, down the front steps of the brownstone. He decides to return to the reading room of the little library on Amsterdam. Quiet and nearly empty. He can sit in the back and start to outline a plot.

But before he can go half a block, he sees the heavyset man leaning on the blue mailbox on the corner. Cardoza. He steps up beside Zachary, matches his quick strides. "You have to acknowledge me, Mr. Gold," he says. He keeps his eyes straight ahead. His big hands swing gently at his sides as he dodges a boy on a silver scooter to keep up with Zachary.

"You can't just walk away. You stole my book."

Zachary tries to sound casual. But his voice is shrill, suddenly breathless. "You have mental problems, Cardoza. Please don't make me call the police."

"That would be a very bad plan," Cardoza replies, still facing forward, keeping pace with Zachary step for step. "You don't want to be exposed. You have only one reputation to keep."

"As I explained, I've never seen you before. My work... It's my own."

Zachary stops as the Don't Walk sign locks on red. A yellow cab swerves to the curb to let off a passenger. Zachary steps back and finally turns to face his accuser.

But Cardoza has vanished.

Zachary gazes behind him, then up and down the side street. No sign of the man. Zachary realizes he is sweating. Not because he feels any guilt. He knows he didn't steal anyone's work.

It's the casual menace on Cardoza's face. The certainty of an insane person.

He knows where I live. He was waiting for me.

The reading room is more crowded than the day before. People occupy the tables and the armchairs. One man has spread his papers over a table, taking up at least six places.

Zachary glances behind him. Despite its size, the room suddenly seems more vulnerable. If Cardoza rumbles in, there's no place to hide. Nowhere to run.

Laptop tucked under his arm, Zachary walks along the aisle to the back. He recognizes the same two bearded Asian men, Chinese newspapers spread out in front of them. A broad stairway leads down. The steps are painted bright yellow, red, and blue. A hand-painted monkey on a poster points down. A dialogue balloon above his head: THIS WAY, KIDS.

Zachary finds himself in the children's room. Shelves on three walls jammed with books. Picture books are scattered on a low, round table surrounded by tiny wooden chairs. Tall cardboard cutouts of book characters stand watch. A bright blue Dr. Seuss creature. Tinkerbell dressed as a Disney princess. A *Star Wars* droid.

Behind them, Zachary spots a long, dark wood table. Grownup height. Chairs on both sides. He positions himself behind the cardboard characters. Sets his laptop down. There is no one here, not even a librarian. The kids are all in school.

Quiet. The air a little warm, a little stuffy and dry. But the perfect place to work, hidden from the world.

He takes a moment to catch his breath. Glances at the framed book cover posters on the wall. All fairy tales. *Rapunzel... Snow White and Rose Red... Hansel and Gretel...*

Dark, nasty stories, he thinks.

He opens the laptop and brings up his *Word* program. He likes to start a book by making random notes. Plot ideas. Characters to populate the story. Story twists. Stream-of consciousness thoughts. The research will come later.

To write the first book, he had to learn almost as much about the brain and its functions as Striver. He types the name: Howard Striver. He types: Book Two?

Am I really going to write a sequel?

He left Dr. Striver living entirely inside his own brain. Striver had expanded his consciousness enough that his inner world was big enough and interesting enough to inhabit without any outside stimulation.

But a sequel could not take place inside Striver's mind. Too constricting for even the cleverest, most brilliant writer.

How do I bring Striver back? How do I pull him from living inside his own mind, into the world where he can interact with people once again?

And once he is back, what will his mission be?

Zachary knows he has already done all he can do in the government-agents-out-to-capture-Striver's-Brain department. To pursue that plot would be writing the exact same book again.

What new brain powers can I give him?

Time travel?

Can the secret to time travel be locked away somewhere in the human brain, waiting to be discovered?

"Too outlandish," Zachary murmurs. "Too science-fictiony. Bor-ring."

He types: Do I really want to write a sequel? Am I fighting it because I know it won't compare to the first book?

He hears voices upstairs. A woman laughs. Chairs scrape the floor. The light shifts from the narrow, high windows up at street level. A gray shadow slants over the table.

Zachary checks the time on his phone. It is two hours later. He has been sitting here for two hours with nothing to show for it. Nothing on the screen. No idea in his head.

Maybe I'll become like Jack Nicholson in The Shining. *Go crazy. Type the same phrase over and over. Even that is better than a blank screen.*

Suddenly weary, he shuts his eyes and rubs them.

He opens them to find a beautiful young woman seated across from him. Round blue eyes, almost too blue to be real. Full red lips, wavy black hair flowing down past the shoulders of her pale blue top.

She reaches across the table and touches the back of his hand. "Can I help you?"

5

They're making better-looking librarians these days, he thinks.

"I'm sorry if I don't belong here," he says. "I just needed a quiet place to write."

She smiles. "I'm not a librarian." The voice is velvety, just above a whisper.

He gazes back at her. She is radiant. The high cheekbones of a model. He even notices her creamy skin, like baby skin. She isn't wearing any makeup.

She doesn't blink. "Sometimes I help writers," she says.

"Help? What do you mean?"

The cheeks darken to pink. The red lips part. "I... do things for them."

She's teasing me. Coming on to me?

She taps the back of his hand again. "I recognized you, Zachary. I loved your book."

"Thank you. I—"

"I can't wait for the sequel." She tosses her hair back with a shake of her head.

Zachary shrugs. "I'm not sure there's going to be a sequel."

She makes a pouty face.

He's tempted to laugh. The expression is so childlike. "Look,

I've been sitting here for two hours thinking about a sequel, and... well, I haven't exactly been inspired."

"I can help you," she says. "Seriously. I like helping writers."

"You want to write it for me?" he jokes.

She doesn't smile. "Maybe." She tugs his hand and starts to stand up. "Come on. Let's go talk about it."

He closes the laptop. "Where are we going?"

"To talk about your book." She has a clear, childlike laugh from deep in her throat. "You look so tense. Come on. Follow me. I can help you."

Outside, the afternoon sun is high in the sky. Two cherry trees across the street have opened their pink-white blossoms. The air smells sweet like springtime.

She is more petite than he imagined. She can't be more than five-five. Her slim-legged jeans emphasize her boyish figure. He wishes he was better at guessing a woman's age, but he hasn't a clue. She could be eighteen or thirty.

He likes the way she takes long strides, almost strutting, her hair swinging behind her.

She leads him to the Beer Keg Tap on the corner. A broken neon sign over the front promises steaks and chops. But the place hasn't served food in thirty years.

Sunlight disappears as he steps into the long, dark bar, and the aroma of spring is replaced by beer fumes. Two men in blue work overalls are perched at the bar, bottles of Bud in front of them, arguing, their hands slashing the air as they both talk at once. A small TV on the wall above them shows a soccer game with the sound off.

The bartender is a pouchy, middle-aged woman with a red bandana tied around henna-colored hair, red cheeks, a long white apron over a yellow *I ♥ Beer* t-shirt. She leans with her back against the bar, eyes raised to the soccer game.

Zachary and his new friend slide into a red vinyl booth at the back. He sets the laptop on the seat beside him. He gazes at the vintage Miller Hi-Life sign on the wall above her head.

"Maybe I'll just have coffee," he tells her. "It's a little early..."

"You're a lot of fun," she says. It takes him a few seconds to realize she's being sarcastic. "Guess what I had for breakfast. Vodka and scrambled eggs. Breakfast of the czars."

"You're serious?"

The bartender appears before she can answer. "What are you drinking?"

She asks for a vodka tonic. Zachary, a little stung by her sarcasm, orders a Heineken. He suddenly remembers: "I haven't had lunch."

She smiles. "Then this is lunch."

At the front, the two men walk out, still arguing.

She pretends to shiver, shaking her slender shoulders. "This is exciting, Zachary. We're the only ones here."

She's a groupie? An author groupie?

"Tell me about your new book."

"I told you. There's no book. There isn't a shred of an idea yet. I'm not blocked or anything. At least, I don't think so. I am just so ambivalent about writing a sequel. I think I'm setting up roadblocks for myself."

The bartender sets the drinks on the table. "Need any nuts or anything?"

"That's okay," he says. She walks back to the bar, the floorboards creaking under her shoes.

They clink bottle against glass.

Then what do they talk about?

Here's where the time warp occurs. Zachary can't remember. Yes, he remembers another beer. No. Another after that.

He never was much of a drinker.

He remembers her red-lipped smile and the way those eyes penetrated his brain, like lasers, like he was the only one on the planet and she was determined not to lose him.

But what did they talk about?

And how did they end up in this pink and frilly studio apartment on the East Side? Such a girly apartment with pink throw rugs, and cornball paintings on the wall of children with huge eyes, and shelves of little unicorn figurines, and a pile of stuffed animals, mostly teddy bears and leopards.

Zachary doesn't remember a cab ride here, or a walk through the park. He feels okay, not drunk, not queasy the way he usually does after three or four beers.

He's sitting on the edge of her pink-and-white bedspread. She leans across the bed and starts to pull his Polo shirt over his head.

When did she get undressed?

She's wearing only blue thong underwear. Her skin so creamy. Small perfect breasts tilt toward him as she works the shirt off.

And now she's kissing his chest. Those full red lips moving down his skin, setting off electric charges. She's kissing him. Licking him. Lowering her face as her lips slide down his body.

Is this really happening?

Oh, my God—it is!

6

Afterwards, Zachary pulls on his clothes. Glances at his phone. He's late. Kristen is at a conference out of town. He has to get home to relieve the nanny. He feels light-headed. The girlish room tilts and spins. He feels as if he's inside a pink-and-white frosted cake.

I've never been unfaithful before.

She watches him from bed, quilted bedspread pulled up to her chin. Her black hair is spread over the pillow. Is that an *amused* expression on her face?

I held that face between my hands as we made love.

"Zachary, my dear, I'm your muse now. No. I'm more than a muse. I'll write that book for you. You can trust me."

The words rattle in his brain like dice clicking together. He can't line them up to make sense of them. Can he be so wasted from three beers? Maybe it was four.

Why is she talking about his nonexistent book? She can't possibly think she can ghostwrite a sequel for him.

"Of course, there will be a price, Zachary," she is saying. "Everything has a price, right?"

He nods in agreement. "Okay," he says. "You write it."

Later, he realizes he wasn't as delirious as he acted. He just didn't want to admit to the reality of what he had just done.

And he didn't want to face the truth of what he was giving her permission to do.

"Yes. Okay, okay. Write the book for me. I don't want to write it. You write it."

"You understand it isn't for free?"

"Yes. You write it."

He tells himself there will be time to let her down easy when her manuscript is unacceptable. Meanwhile, the project will keep her close to him. Yes, he wants to see her again.

I've never been unfaithful before.

He sits on the edge of the bed to tie his sneakers. The room suddenly feels steamy, swampy. His skin prickles.

He stands up to leave. He feels unsteady, but not as unsteady as he'd like. If only he could blame his bad decisions on his dizziness. The little unicorns gaze up at him.

She's so beautiful. She didn't hypnotize him but she could have. He knows he's fallen under some kind of spell, just being near a creature so perfect.

She doesn't lift her head from the pillow. Just lies there watching him, her hair fanned out beneath her head. "Give me a kiss," she says, pleading, teasing.

He bends down to kiss her. She wraps her hands around his neck and holds him down for a long, thrilling kiss. "I'll see you at the library," she says when she finally lets him go.

He starts to feel more like himself as soon as he is out of her apartment. The late afternoon air feels cool on his hot face. Long blue shadows slant across the sidewalk as the sun slowly lowers itself behind the tall apartment buildings across the street.

Where is he? Zachary doesn't recognize the neighborhood. He walks a few blocks, past a Gristedes supermarket, past a Duane-Reade, past a shoe repair store, until he finds a street sign. Surprised to find himself on 2nd Avenue. 2nd and 83rd Street?

How did I get way over here?

He steps off the curb to hail a cab. Several pass with Off-Duty lights on their roofs. It's change-over time. Most daytime drivers are heading to their garage. It might be hard to find a cab.

Zachary suddenly becomes aware of a figure standing in the deep shadow of a building at the next corner. He doesn't have to focus to know it's Cardoza.

A shudder of fear snaps Zachary from any remaining cloudiness of his mind. All is clear now. The sight of this frightening pursuer makes Zachary alert, every muscle tensed for action.

He is stalking me. He is determined to frighten me.

He sees Cardoza begin to lumber toward him. The big man's fists pump at his sides, as if he's warming for a fight.

Zachary turns, considers running. He doesn't need to. A taxi pulls to the curb. Zachary darts to it, pulls open the door, and dives inside.

He breathlessly tells the driver his address. The taxi begins to bump down Second Avenue. Zachary turns and peers out the back window. Cardoza stands with his meaty hands on his waist, still as a statue, watching... watching Zachary escape.

Zachary slumps in the seat, struggling to catch his breath, to slow his hummingbird heartbeats. Someone has left a water bottle on the floor of the taxi. It bumps Zachary's foot. He makes no attempt to set it aside.

Stalking me.

How did he attract these two new people in his life? One accuses him of stealing his book. The other wants to write the next book *for* him.

Zachary turns and stares out the back window again. He has

to make sure he has left Cardoza behind. When he is satisfied that he has escaped, Zachary turns back, settles into the seat—and utters a gasp.

He slaps the seat with his palm. He twists his body and looks behind him on the seat.

No. No.

His laptop.

No. It isn't here.

He left it in her apartment.

7

"Hello?"

"Mr. Z, how's it coming along?"

"And how are *you*, Eleanor? How was your day?"

"I'm hoping you will improve my day, Zachary. I need a yes from you."

"Eleanor, do you ever take a break to be a human? Do you ever stop working?" Zachary balances the baby in one arm, the phone in his other hand. Emily is just the right nestling size. He loves her lightness, the way her round bald head feels on his shoulder.

"Stop working? I don't think that would be fair to my clients."

Zachary laughs. "Just saying. The way you always cut right to business. Sometimes I wonder if you have a life."

"*You* are my life, Z. Enough about me. Now let's talk about the Howard Striver sequel. I need a yes from you today. I wasn't kidding about that million dollars."

"Yes," Zachary says.

"Yes? Did you just say yes?"

"Yes, I'll do the sequel."

Silence at the other end. She's speechless for once. He can *see* the surprise on her face.

"Well, good," she says finally. "I'll let them know. We can have a lunch and discuss delivery date, etcetera."

Emily starts to cry, soft gulps at first, then full-out blasts. He sits down and shifts her to his knee. "Got to run, Eleanor. Baby's crying. I think she's hungry."

"I know the book will be a winner, Mr. Z. And maybe a sequel will help get the movie out of development hell. You never know."

Did she ever congratulate him or compliment him on the baby? He can't remember her ever acknowledging this new addition to his life.

She really isn't *human.*

He clicks off the phone and tosses it onto the couch. He carries Emily to the changing table. Maybe that's why she's crying.

I wish Kristen would get home.

He feels a flash of guilt.

And then more than guilt. He's just promised a new book, and he doesn't even have his laptop. And in a moment of sheer insanity, he told a woman, a total stranger, she could write the book for him.

How crazy was that?

If he could undo the day…

Maybe he still can.

When the nanny arrives the next morning, he hails a taxi and returns to 83rd and 2nd. It shouldn't be difficult to find her building. He passes the shoe repair store, the supermarket, the drugstore. He stops at the corner, shielding his eyes from the low morning sun.

Was it the redbrick building across the street? It doesn't look familiar. He turns and gazes at a tall white apartment building on the east side of 2nd Avenue. Cars are parked in a short, circular driveway that leads to the entrance.

He doesn't remember a driveway in front of her building. But the other buildings don't look familiar, either.

He can't ask for her, he realizes. He doesn't know her name. *I never even asked her name.*

He doesn't know her name and he doesn't know where she lives. And, of course, he was too dazed and besotted to get her phone number.

Classic stupidity. But then the word *library* flashes into his head.

"Whoa. Yes," he murmurs. "The library."

She will return to the library and bring his laptop. Why did he go into such panic mode? Well, can you blame him? Writers don't like to lose their laptops (or leave them with total strangers).

Zachary feels a stab of fear as a large man in a pale blue business suit rapidly crosses 83rd Street. Cardoza? No. Another broad-shouldered, sandy-haired man taking elephant strides.

You're going to have to confront Cardoza. You can't be afraid every time you leave the apartment.

He studies the apartment buildings again. It's useless. He takes a taxi back across town to the library on Amsterdam. The reading room is empty. He nods to the librarian at the front desk, who doesn't look up, and makes his way downstairs to the children's room.

Zachary glances around. No sign of the young woman. The room is empty, as before. A very slender man with tall spiked blond hair over a frog-shaped face, and square, black-framed glasses approaches him. "I'm the children's activity director. Can I help you?"

"Well…" Zachary hesitates. He plans to stay down here and wait for the young woman with his laptop. But it might be awkward sitting by himself in the children's room. "I'm doing research on fairy tales," he says. "Can you direct me to the right shelves?"

He doesn't realize this is only the beginning of a very long week.

8

For five days, he waits at the table in the children's room, a stack of fairy tale books in front of him. He reads every collection, fairy tales from a dozen countries. He becomes an expert on witches and elves and princesses, evil spells, cauldrons of poisoned soups, power-mad queens, orphans lost in the forest, dragons and angels and talking owls. He spends the week in this terrifying otherworld, and the young woman doesn't show up.

Should he forget about her? Chalk the whole thing up to a crazy, weird experience? Buy a new laptop and get back to his life?

He admits to himself that he really wants to see her. He wants to see her beautiful, almost perfect face and hear her whisper-smooth voice. Yes, he has sexual fantasies about her all the time. But he just wants to see the blue eyes, the red lips, the angel-white skin...

When she shows up at his apartment on a Monday afternoon, he freezes at the door, tongue-tied. He can feel his cheeks go hot and knows he's blushing.

"You're here," he utters redundantly.

She laughs. "Can I come in?" He's blocking the door.

She slides into the apartment. She's wearing layers of t-shirts, pale blue and pink, and a short, pleated plaid skirt. Her legs are bare down to her white sneakers.

She brushes her dark hair back with a shake of her head. Then she hands him the laptop. "Did you miss me, honey?" She draws a finger down his cheek.

"Well, yes. I waited for you. At the library. I mean—"

She gazes around the living room, then dives to the baby in the porta-crib on the couch. "Ooh, she's so cute." She rubs Emily's head tenderly. "And she's so bald."

"She had hair when she was born," Zachary says. "But it fell out. Now she's sprouting her real hair." And then a question forces its way to his mind: "How did you know she's a girl?"

She gives the baby head a last rub, then turns to him. "Zachary, I know everything about you." A strange smile, not warm, maybe ironic. "Today we'll find out what you know about *me*."

He blinks. "Excuse me?"

She points to the laptop. "I wrote the sequel for you, dear. I hope you like it."

He crosses the room to her. He has an impulse to toss down the laptop and throw his arms around her tiny waist. Instead, he squints at her. "You wrote the whole book in one week?"

She giggles. "I'm very fast."

"But—"

"And very good. It didn't take long to pick up your style." She pushes him to the couch. "Go ahead. Read it. I can't wait. Read the first chapter. I want to see the look on your face."

He sits down beside the baby and opens the laptop on his lap. She gets down on her knees in front of the porta-crib and makes cooing sounds, petting the baby's head as if she were a puppy.

Zachary opens the file and starts to read. His mind whirs. He's thinking of how he can tell her the work is not right, not acceptable, without making her angry and driving her away.

He wants to kiss her. He wants to hold her. He's aroused to the point of not being able to concentrate on the words. But he reads. Squinting into the glare of the screen, he reads the first chapter.

When he finishes it, he taps the screen with his fingers. "This is good. This is really good."

She smiles. "I thought you'd approve."

"Seriously. It's excellent," Zachary insists. He stares at her as if he's never really seen her. *This young woman is no-kidding-around talented.*

He taps the screen again. "Where is the rest? I need to see more. I'm excited. I think... I think you've really got it."

She climbs to her feet. Then she reaches down and carefully

lifts the baby from the small basket. Emily makes no sound as she lowers her to her shoulder.

"I will show you how to read the rest of the book, Zachary. But, remember, I said you'd have to pay?"

He nods. "That's no problem. We can talk about terms."

She rocks the baby gently on her shoulder. "Don't worry about terms, honey."

"Then… what do you want?"

The blue eyes lock on his. "You just have to tell me my name."

A laugh escapes his throat. "I… what?"

"You don't know my name, do you?"

"Well, I'm embarrassed. But…"

"So go ahead. Guess my name. You want the rest of the book, right? Okay. Guess my name, and the book is yours. That's the deal. Tell me my name. You have three chances."

He closes the computer but leaves it on his lap. "Seriously?"

She doesn't blink. She taps one foot.

Zachary realizes he has to play her game. Okay. No big deal. He guesses. "Uh… Sarah?"

She shakes her head. He sees a flash of merriment in those cold blue eyes. "Two more guesses."

"Jessica?"

"No. Think hard, honey. You're down to your last guess. Make it a good one."

He squints hard at her, studies her as if trying to read her thoughts. *What name does she look like? Well…*

"Ashley?"

She lowers her head, hair falling over her face. "Oh, wow. Sorry, Zachary. That's not my name. And that was your last chance." She walks past him toward the door.

"So, tell me," he cries. "What is it? What is your name?"

She sighs. "Zachary, didn't we meet among the fairy tales?"

"Yes."

"So you should have guessed. You really should have guessed. My name is Rumpelstiltskin."

He gasps. "Huh?"

"My name is Rumpelstiltskin. You didn't guess it. So now the baby is mine."

Zachary shoves the laptop to the couch and struggles to his feet. But before he can stand up, she and the baby are out the door.

9

He tugs open the door and bolts into the hall. He listens for her footsteps on the stairs. But all he can hear are his pounding heartbeats.

She's crazy, and she has my baby.

He takes off, flying down the stairs two at a time. Out onto the stoop. He gazes up and down the sidewalk. No. No. Not here. Breathing so hard, it feels as if his chest might burst.

Don't give yourself a heart attack.

Did she have a car waiting? How did she disappear so quickly?

He pulls himself back up to the living room. He grabs his phone off the couch.

I've got to call the police. She kidnapped my baby.

But what will the police say when he tells them her name is Rumpelstiltskin? He can already hear the derisive laughter when he describes how he's been living in a fairy tale.

"Oh, you lost your baby to Rumpelstiltskin? Why don't you ask Goldilocks to help you find her?" Followed by: "Hawhawhawhawhaw."

Zachary vows to find her on his own. He knows he isn't thinking clearly. He can't really think at all. He only knows he has to run. He has to run across the city, run to the places she might be, run to anywhere he might find her.

He's too frightened, too horrified to stay in one place. If he does, the horror of what he has done will catch up to him and swallow him whole.

He runs to the library. No one has seen her there. He runs to the East Side, back to her block. Which building? Which building? No. No sign of her.

Where to look now? He can't give up.

He's walking up 2nd Avenue almost, to 86th Street, when he sees her seated at a table in a coffee shop window. She has Emily on her shoulder. A plate of scrambled eggs in front of her. And sitting in the opposite chair—Cardoza.

Were they working together?

Of course they were. Cardoza's job was to get him frightened, off-balance, vulnerable, ready for her to step in and do her thing.

Rage overtakes him. He pounds on the window with both fists.

They turn, surprise then alarm on their faces. Before they can jump up, Zachary is through the door, past the group of people at the cash register waiting for a table.

His fists cut the air as he strides up to their table. His head feels ready to explode. He can feel the blood pulsing at his temples. He glares at them, his eyes moving from Cardoza, to the baby, to the woman.

He opens his mouth to speak—and stops. He suddenly feels like a balloon deflating. He can feel the air whoosh from his lungs, feel his whole body sinking... shrinking.

He lowers his fists. His breathing slows. Finally, Zachary finds his voice. "I made you up, didn't I," he says softly.

They both nod, faces blank.

"I made you both up. You're not real," Zachary repeats.

"Yes," she answers in a whisper. "You imagined us."

"You're in my mind. You're a fairy tale. You're not really here." Zachary murmurs.

They watch him expectantly. She holds the baby against her shoulder, her eyes, unblinking, on Zachary.

"I imagined you," he says. "And if I shut my eyes..."

He doesn't wait for them to respond. He shuts his eyes.

And when he opens them, he sees faces—unfamiliar

faces—staring down at him. Faces hovering over him, features tensed, as if they've been waiting for him to do or say something.

He's lying on his back. He raises his head. "Where am I?" he asks.

10

"We put you in this room, Dr. Striver," a chocolate-skinned woman in a pale green uniform replies. Her curly white hair pokes out from her nurse's cap. "We thought you'd be comfortable here."

He nods and settles his head back on the pillow where it had been resting. Cardoza and Rumpelstiltskin linger in his mind.

A woman bumps the nurse out of her way. Her face hovers above his, her eyes disapproving, cheeks wet with tears. "You did it again, Howard," Debra, his wife, says. "I... don't understand. Can you explain it to me? Is living inside your own mind so much better than being with me?"

"No," he replies quickly. He reaches for her but she eludes his arms. The tears glisten on her cheeks. She makes no attempt to rub them away.

"How long have I been out?" he asks.

"Two days," Debra says. "But we had no way of knowing how long you would be away this time." Before he can reply, she continues. "Why do you keep doing this, Howard? Retreating into your own mind. You're trying to escape from me. Just admit it."

"No," he says again. "No. Really." He pulls himself up to a sitting position. He gazes at the doctors and nurses who have retreated to the walls so that Debra can confront him. "The baby," he says to her. "Is the baby okay?"

She narrows her dark eyes at him. "Howard, we don't have a baby. What's *wrong* with you?"

He's trying to get clear. He has to sort things out before he can assure Debra, before he can win her back. "What about my book?" he asks.

She shakes her head. "You keep threatening to write a book about your discoveries. But you'll never have time to write if you keep disappearing into your own mind."

He nods. He's starting to feel stronger. He takes her hand and squeezes it tenderly. "I'm ready to make a new start, Debra. I'll try not to escape again. I promise. Let's make this a new beginning. Part two of our lives. The sequel. Yes, let's start the sequel today."

She eyes him doubtfully, but she doesn't let go of his hand.

"Dr. Striver," the white-haired nurse interrupts. "Those men from the Pentagon have been waiting for two days."

He scratches his head. "What do they want?"

"Remember? They want to talk to you about how the military can make use of your brain powers? Dr. Striver? Dr. Striver?"

Debra drops his hand. She shakes him by the shoulders. "I don't believe it. Howard? Howard? Is he *gone* again? Howard—don't do this. *Howard*?"

The Little Men

Megan Abbott

A T NIGHT, THE sounds from the canyon shifted and changed. The bungalow seemed to lift itself with every echo and the walls were breathing. Panting.

Just after two, she'd wake, her eyes stinging, as if someone had waved a flashlight across them.

And then, she'd hear the noise.

Every night.

The tapping noise, like a small animal trapped behind the wall.

That was what it reminded her of. Like when she was a girl, and that possum got caught in the crawlspace. For weeks, they just heard scratching. They only found it when the walls started to smell.

It's not the little men, she told herself. *It's not.*

And then she'd hear a whimper and startle herself. Because it was her whimper and she was so frightened.

I'm not afraid I'm not I'm not.

It had begun four months ago, the day Penny first set foot in the Canyon Arms. The chocolate and pink bungalows, the high arched windows and French doors, the tiled courtyard, cosseted on all sides by eucalyptus, pepper, and olive trees, miniature date palms—it was like a dream of a place, not a place itself.

This is what it was supposed to be, she thought.

The Hollywood she'd always imagined, the Hollywood of her childhood imagination, assembled from newsreels: Kay Francis in silver lamé and Clark Gable driving down Sunset in his Duesenberg, everyone beautiful and everything possible.

That world, if it ever really existed, was long gone by the time she'd arrived on that Greyhound a half-dozen years ago. It had been swallowed up by the clatter and color of 1953 Hollywood, with its swooping motel roofs and shiny glare of its hamburger stands and drive-ins, and its descending smog, which made her throat burn at night. Sometimes she could barely breathe.

But here in this tucked away courtyard, deep in Beachwood Canyon, it was as if that Old Hollywood still lingered, even bloomed. The smell of apricot hovered, the hush and echoes of the canyons soothed. You couldn't hear a horn honk, a brake squeal. Only the distant *ting-ting* of window chimes, somewhere. One might imagine a peignoired Norma Shearer drifting through the rounded doorway of one of the bungalows, cocktail shaker in hand.

"It's perfect," Penny whispered, her heels tapping on the Mexican tiles. "I'll take it."

"That's fine," said the landlady, Mrs. Stahl, placing Penny's cashier's check in the drooping pocket of her satin housecoat and handing her the keyring, heavy in her palm.

The scent, thick with pollen and dew, was enough to make you dizzy with longing.

And so close to the Hollywood sign, visible from every vantage, which had to mean something.

She had found it almost by accident, tripping out of the Carnival Tavern after three stingers.

"We've all been stood up," the waitress had tut-tutted, snapping the bill holder at her hip. "But we still pay up."

"I wasn't stood up," Penny said. After all, Mr. D. had called, the hostess summoning Penny to one of the hot telephone booths. Penny was still tugging her skirt free from its door hinges when he broke it to her.

He wasn't coming tonight and wouldn't be coming again. He had many reasons why, beginning with his busy work schedule, the demands of the studio, plus negotiations with the union were going badly. By the time he got around to the matter of his wife and six children, she wasn't listening, letting the phone drift from her ear.

Gazing through the booth's glass accordion doors, she looked out at the long row of spinning lanterns strung along the bar's windows. They reminded her of the magic lamp she had when she was small, scattering galloping horses across her bedroom walls.

You could see the Carnival Tavern from miles away because of the lanterns. It was funny seeing them up close, the faded circus clowns silhouetted on each. They looked so much less glamorous, sort of shabby. She wondered how long they'd been here, and if anyone even noticed them anymore.

She was thinking all these things while Mr. D. was still talking, his voice hoarse with logic and finality. A faint aggression.

He concluded by saying surely she agreed that all the craziness had to end.

You were a luscious piece of candy, he said, *but now I gotta spit you out*.

After, she walked down the steep exit ramp from the bar, the lanterns shivering in the canyon breeze.

And she walked and walked and that was how she found the Canyon Arms, tucked off behind hedges so deep you could disappear into them. The smell of the jasmine so strong she wanted to cry.

"You're an actress, of course," Mrs. Stahl said, walking her to Bungalow Number 4.

"Yes," she said. "I mean, no." Shaking her head. She felt like she was drunk. It was the apricot. No, Mrs. Stahl's cigarette. No, it was her lipstick. Tangee, with its sweet orange smell, just like Penny's own mother.

"Well," Mrs. Stahl said. "We're all actresses, I suppose."

"I used to be," Penny finally managed. "But I got practical. I do makeup now. Over at Republic."

Mrs. Stahl's eyebrows, thin as seaweed, lifted. "Maybe you could do me sometime."

It was the beginning of something, she was sure.

No more living with sundry starlets stacked bunk-to-bunk in one of those stucco boxes in West Hollywood. The Sham-Rock. The Sun-Kist Villa. The smell of cold cream and last night's sweat, a brush of talcum powder between the legs.

She hadn't been sure she could afford to live alone, but Mrs. Stahl's rent was low. Surprisingly low. And, if the job at Republic didn't last, she still had her kitty, which was fat these days on account of those six months with Mr. D., a studio man with a sofa in his office that wheezed and puffed. Even if he really meant what he said, that it really was kaput, she still had that last check he'd given her. He must have been planning the brush off, because it was the biggest yet, and made out to cash.

And the Canyon Arms had other advantages. Number 4, like all the bungalows, was already furnished: sun-bleached zebra print sofa and key lime walls, that bright-white kitchen with its cherry-sprigged wallpaper. The first place she'd ever lived that didn't have rust stains in the tub or the smell of moth balls everywhere.

And there were the built-in bookshelves filled with novels in crinkling dustjackets.

She liked books, especially the big ones by Lloyd C. Douglas or Frances Parkinson Keyes, though the books in Number Four were all at least twenty years old with a sleek, high-tone look about them. The kind without any people on the cover.

She vowed to read them all during her time at the Canyon

Arms. Even the few tucked in the back, the ones with brown-paper covers.

In fact, she started with those. Reading them late at night, with a pink gin conjured from grapefruit peel and an old bottle of Gilbey's she found in the cupboard. Those books gave her funny dreams.

"She got one."

Penny turned on her heels, one nearly catching on one of the courtyard tiles. But, looking around, she didn't see anyone. Only an open window, smoke rings emanating like a dragon's mouth.

"She finally got one," the voice came again.

"Who's there?" Penny said, squinting toward the window.

An old man leaned forward from his perch just inside Number Three, the bungalow next door. He wore a velvet smoking jacket faded to a deep rose.

"And a pretty one at that," he said, smiling with graying teeth. "How do you like Number Four?"

"I like it very much," she said. She could hear something rustling behind him in his bungalow. "It's perfect for me."

"I believe it is," he said, nodding slowly. "Of that I am sure."

The rustle came again. Was it a roommate? A pet? It was too dark to tell. When it came once more, it was almost like a voice shushing.

"I'm late," she said, taking a step back, her heel caving slightly.

"Oh," he said, taking a puff. "Next time."

That night, she woke, her mouth dry from gin, at two o'clock. She had been dreaming she was on an exam table and a doctor with an enormous head mirror was leaning so close to her she could smell his gum: violet. The ringlight at its center seemed to spin, as if to hypnotize her.

She saw spots even when she closed her eyes again.

The next morning, the man in Number Three was there again, shadowed just inside the window frame, watching the comings and goings on the courtyard.

Head thick from last night's gin and two morning cigarettes, Penny was feeling what her mother used to call "the hickedty ticks."

So, when she saw the man, she stopped and said briskly, "What did you mean yesterday? 'She finally got one'?"

He smiled, laughing without any noise, his shoulders shaking.

"Mrs. Stahl got one, got you," he said. "As in: Will you walk into my parlor? said the spider to the fly."

When he leaned forward, she could see the stripes of his pajama top through the shiny threads of his velvet sleeve. His skin was rosy and wet looking.

"I'm no chump, if that's your idea. It's good rent. I know good rent."

"I bet you do, my girl. I bet you do. Why don't you come inside for a cup? I'll tell you a thing or two about this place. And about your Number Four."

The bungalow behind him was dark, with something shining beside him. A bottle, or something else.

"We all need something," he added cryptically, winking.

She looked at him. "Look, mister—"

"Flant. Mr. Flant. Come inside, miss. Open the front door. I'm harmless." He waved his pale pink hand, gesturing toward his lap mysteriously.

Behind him, she thought she saw something moving in the darkness over his slouching shoulders. And music playing softly. And old song about setting the world on fire, or not.

Mr. Flant was humming with it, his body soft with age and stillness, but his milky eyes insistent and penetrating.

A breeze lifted and the front door creaked open several inches, and the scent of tobacco and bay rum nearly overwhelmed her.

"I don't know," she said, even as she moved forward.

Later, she would wonder why, but in that moment, she felt it was definitely the right thing to do.

The other man in Number Three was not as old as Mr. Flant but still much older than Penny. Wearing only an undershirt and trousers, he had a moustache and big round shoulders that looked gray with old sweat. When he smiled, which was often, she could tell he was once matinee-idol handsome, with the outsized head of all movie stars.

"Call me Benny," he said, handing her a coffee cup that smelled strongly of rum.

Mr. Flant was explaining that Number Four had been empty for years because of something that happened there a long time ago.

"Sometimes she gets a tenant," Benny reminded Mr. Flant. "The young musician with the sweaters."

"That did not last long," Mr. Flant said.

"What happened?"

"The police came. He tore out a piece of the wall with his bare hands."

Penny's eyebrows lifted.

Benny nodded. "His fingers were hanging like clothespins."

"But I don't understand. What happened in Number Four?"

"Some people let the story get to them," Benny said, shaking his head.

"What story?"

The two men looked at each other.

Mr. Flant rotated his cup in his hand.

"There was a death," he said softly. "A man who lived there, a dear man. Lawrence was his name. Larry. A talented bookseller. He died."

"Oh."

"Boy did he," Benny said. "Gassed himself."

"At the Canyon Arms?" she asked, feeling sweat on her neck despite all the fans blowing everywhere, lifting motes and old skin. That's what dust really is, you know, one of her roommates once told her, blowing it from her fingertips. "Inside my bungalow?"

They both nodded gravely.

"They carried him out through the courtyard," Mr. Flant said, staring vaguely out the window. "That great sheaf of blond hair of his. Oh, my."

"So it's a challenge for some people," Benny said. "Once they know."

Penny remembered the neighbor boy who fell from their tree and died from blood poisoning two days later. No one would eat its pears after that.

"Well," she said, eyes drifting to the smudgy window, "some people are superstitious."

Soon, Penny began stopping by Number Three a few mornings a week, before work. Then, the occasional evening, too. They served rye or applejack.

It helped with her sleep. She didn't remember her dreams, but her eyes still stung lightspots most nights.

Sometimes the spots took odd shapes and she would press her fingers against her lids trying to make them stop.

"You could come to my bungalow," she offered once. But they both shook their heads slowly, and in unison.

Mostly, they spoke of Lawrence. Larry. Who seemed like such a sensitive soul, delicately formed and too fine for this town.

"When did it happen?" Penny asked, feeling dizzy, wishing Benny had put more water in the applejack. "When did he die?"

"Just before the war. A dozen years ago."

"He was only thirty-five."

"That's so sad," Penny said, finding her eyes misting, the liquor starting to tell on her.

"His bookstore is still on Cahuenga Boulevard," Benny told her. "He was so proud when it opened."

"Before that, he sold books for Stanley Rose," Mr. Flant added, sliding a handkerchief from under the cuff of his fraying sleeve. "Larry was very popular. Very attractive. An accent soft as a Carolina pine."

"He'd pronounce 'bed' like 'bay-ed.'" Benny grinned, leaning against the window sill and smiling that Gable smile. "And he said 'bay-ed' a lot."

"I met him even before he got the job with Stanley," Mr. Flant said, voice speeding up. "Long before Benny."

Benny shrugged, topping off everyone's drinks.

"He was selling books out of the trunk of his old Ford," Mr. Flant continued. "That's where I first bought *Ulysses*."

Benny grinned again. "He sold me my first Tijuana Bible. *Dagwood Has a Family Party*."

Mr. Flant nodded, laughed. "*Popeye in The Art of Love*. It staggered me. He had an uncanny sense. He knew just what you wanted."

They explained that Mr. Rose, whose bookstore once graced Hollywood Boulevard and had attracted great talents, used to send young Larry to the studios with a suitcase full of books. His job was to trap and mount the big shots. Show them the goods, sell them books by the yard, art books they could show off in their offices, dirty books they could hide in their big gold safes.

Penny nodded. She was thinking about the special books Mr. D. kept in his office, behind the false encyclopedia fronts. The books had pictures of girls doing things with long, fuzzy fans and peacock feathers, a leather crop.

She wondered if Larry had sold them to him.

"To get to those guys, he had to climb the satin rope," Benny said. "The studio secretaries, the script girls, the publicity office, even makeup girls like you. Hell, the grips. He loved a sexy grip."

"This town can make a whore out of anyone," Penny found herself blurting.

She covered her mouth, ashamed, but both men just laughed.

Mr. Flant looked out the window into the courtyard, the *flip-flipping* of banana leaves against the shutter. "I think he loved the actresses the most, famous or not."

"He said he liked the feel of a woman's skin in 'bay-ed,'"

Benny said, rubbing his left arm, his eyes turning dark, soft. "'Course, he'd slept with his mammy until he was thirteen."

As she walked back to her own bungalow, she always had the strange feeling she might see Larry. That he might emerge behind the rose bushes or around the statue of Venus.

Once she looked down into the fountain basin and thought she could see his face instead of her own.

But she didn't even know what he looked like.

Back in the bungalow, head fuzzy and the canyon so quiet, she thought about him more. The furniture, its fashion at least two decades past, seemed surely the same furniture he'd known. Her hands on the smooth bands of the rattan sofa. Her feet, her toes on the banana silk tassels of the rug. And the old mirror in the bathroom, its tiny black pocks.

In the late hours, lying on the bed, the mattress too soft, with a vague smell of mildew, she found herself waking again and again, each time with a start.

It always began with her eyes stinging, dreaming again of a doctor with the head mirror, or a car careering toward her on the highway, always lights in her face.

One night, she caught the lights moving, her eyes landing on the far wall, the baseboards.

For several moments, she'd see the light spots, fuzzed and floating, as if strung together by the thinnest of threads.

The spots began to look like the darting mice that sometimes snuck inside her childhood home. She never knew mice could be that fast. So fast that if she blinked, she'd miss them, until more came. Was that what it was?

If she squinted hard, they even looked like little men. Could it be mice on their hindfeet?

The next morning, she set traps.

"I'm sorry, he's unavailable," the receptionist said. Even over the phone, Penny knew which one. The beauty marks and giraffe neck.

"But listen," Penny said, "it's not like he thinks. I'm just calling about the check he gave me. The bank stopped payment on it."

So much for Mr. D.'s parting gift for their time together. She was going to use it to make rent, to buy a new girdle, maybe even a television set.

"I've passed along your messages, Miss Smith. That's really all I can do."

"Well, that's not all I can do," Penny said, her voice trembling. "You tell him that."

Keeping busy was the only balm. At work, it was easy, the crush of people, the noise and personality of the crew.

Nights were when the bad thoughts came, and she knew she shouldn't let them.

In the past, she'd had those greasy-skinned roommates to drown out thinking. They all had rashes from cheap studio makeup and the clap from cheap studio men and beautiful figures like Penny's own. And they never stopped talking, twirling their hair in curlers and licking their fingers to turn the magazine pages. But their chatter-chatter-chatter muffled all Penny's thoughts. And the whole atmosphere—the thick muzz of Woolworth's face powder and nylon nighties when they even shared a bed—made everything seem cheap and lively and dumb and easy and light.

Here, in the bungalow, after leaving Mr. Flant and Benny to drift off into their applejack dreams, Penny had only herself. And the books.

Late into the night, waiting for the lightspots to come, she found her eyes wouldn't shut. They started twitching all the time, and maybe it was the night jasmine, or the beachburr.

But she had the books. All those books, these beautiful, brittling books, books that made her feel things, made her long to go places and see things—the River Liffey and Paris, France.

And then there were those in the wrappers, the brown paper soft at the creases, the white baker string slightly fraying.

Her favorite was about a detective recovering stolen jewels from an unlikely hiding spot.

But there was one that frightened her. About a farmer's daughter who fell asleep each night on a bed of hay. And in the night, the hay came alive, poking and stabbing at her.

It was supposed to be funny, but it gave Penny bad dreams.

"Well, she was in love with Larry," Mr. Flant said. "But she was not Larry's kind."

Penny had been telling them how Mrs. Stahl had shown up at her door the night before, in worn satin pajamas and cold cream, to scold her for moving furniture around.

"I don't even know how she saw," Penny said. "I just pushed the bed away from the wall."

She had lied, telling Mrs. Stahl she could hear the oven damper popping at night. She was afraid to tell her about the shadows and lights and other things that made no sense in daytime. Like the mice moving behind the wall on hindfeet, so agile she'd come to think of them as pixies, dwarves. Little men.

"It's not your place to move things," Mrs. Stahl had said, quite loudly, and for a moment Penny thought the woman might cry.

"That's all his furniture, you know," Benny said. "Larry's. Down to the forks and spoons."

Penny felt her teeth rattle slightly in her mouth.

"He gave her books she liked," Benny added. "Stiff British stuff he teased her about. Charmed himself out of the rent for months."

"When he died she wailed around the courtyard for weeks," Mr. Flant recalled. "She wanted to scatter the ashes into the canyon."

"But his people came instead," Benny said. "Came on a train

all the way from Carolina. A man and woman with cardboard suitcases packed with pimento sandwiches. They took the body home."

"They said Hollywood had killed him."

Benny shook his head, smiled that tobacco-toothed smile of his. "They always say that."

"You're awfully pretty for a face-fixer," one of the actors told her, fingers wagging beneath his long makeup bib.

Penny only smiled, and scooted before the pinch came.

It was a Western, so it was mostly men, whiskers, lip bristle, three-day beards filled with dust.

Painting the girl's faces was harder. They all had ideas of how they wanted it. They were hard girls, striving to get to Paramount, to MGM. Or started out there and hit the Republic rung on the long slide down. To Allied, AIP. Then studios no one ever heard of, operating out of some slick guy's house in the Valley.

They had bad teeth and head lice and some had smells on them when they came to the studio, like they hadn't washed properly. The costume assistants always pinched their noses behind their backs.

It was a rough town for pretty girls. The only place it was.

Penny knew she had lost her shine long ago. Many men had rubbed it off, shimmy by shimmy.

But it was just as well, and she'd just as soon be in the warpaint business. When it rubbed off the girls, she could just get out her brushes, her power puffs, and shine them up like new.

As she tapped the powder pots, though, her mind would wander. She began thinking about Larry bounding through the backlots. Would he have come to Republic with his wares? Maybe. Would he have soft-soaped her, hoping her bosses might have a taste for T.S. Eliot or a French deck?

By day, she imagined him as a charmer, a cheery, silver-tongued roué.

But at night, back at the Canyon Arms, it was different.

You see, sometimes she thought she could see him moving, room to room, his face pale, his trousers soiled. Drinking and crying over someone, something, whatever he'd lost that he was sure wasn't ever coming back.

There were sounds now. Sounds to go with the two a.m. lights, or the mice or whatever they were.

Tap-tap-tap.

At first, she thought she was only hearing the banana trees, brushing against the side of the bungalow. Peering out the window, the moon-filled courtyard, she couldn't tell. The air looked very still.

Maybe, she thought, it's the fan palms outside the kitchen window, so much lush foliage everywhere, just the thing she'd loved, but now it seemed to be touching her constantly, closing in.

And she didn't like to go into the kitchen at night. The white tile glowed eerily, reminded her of something. The wide expanse of Mr. D.'s belly, his shirt pushed up, his watch chain hanging. The coaster of milk she left for the cat the morning she ran away from home. For Hollywood.

The mouse traps never caught anything. Every morning, after the rumpled sleep and all the flits and flickers along the wall, she moved them to different places. She looked for signs.

She never saw any.

One night, three a.m., she knelt down on the floor, running her fingers along the baseboards. With her ear to the wall, she thought the tapping might be coming from inside. A *tap-tap-tap*. Or was it a *tick-tick-tick*?

"I've never heard anything here," Mr. Flant told her the following day, "but I take sedatives."

Benny wrinkled his brow. "Once, I saw pink elephants," he offered. "You think that might be it?"

Penny shook her head. "It's making it hard to sleep."

"Dear," Mr. Flant said, "would you like a little helper?"

He held out his palm, pale and moist. In the center, a white pill shone.

That night she slept impossibly deeply. So deeply she could barely move, her neck twisted and locked, her body hunched inside itself.

Upon waking, she threw up in the waste basket.

That evening, after work, she waited in the courtyard for Mrs. Stahl.

Smoking cigarette after cigarette, Penny noticed things she hadn't before. Some of the tiles in the courtyard were cracked, some missing. She hadn't noticed that before. Or the chips and gouges on the sculpted lions on the center fountain, their mouths spouting only a trickle of acid green. The drain at the bottom of the fountain, clogged with crushed cigarette packs, a used contraceptive.

Finally, she saw Mrs. Stahl saunter into view, a large picture hat wilting across her tiny head.

"Mrs. Stahl," she said, "have you ever had an exterminator come?"

The woman stopped, her entire body still for a moment, her left hand finally rising to her face, brushing her hair back under her mustard-colored scarf.

"I run a clean residence," she said, voice low in the empty, sunlit courtyard. That courtyard, oleander and wisteria everywhere, bright and poisonous, like everything in this town.

"I can hear something behind the wainscoting," Penny replied. "Maybe mice, or maybe it's baby possums caught in the wall between the bedroom and kitchen."

Mrs. Stahl looked at her. "Is it after you bake? It might be the dampers popping again."

"I'm not much of a cook. I haven't even turned on the oven yet."

"That's not true," Mrs. Stahl said, lifting her chin triumphantly. "You had it on the other night."

"What?" Then Penny remembered. It had rained sheets and she'd used it to dry her dress. But it had been very late and she didn't see how Mrs. Stahl could know. "Are you peeking in my windows?" she asked, voice tightening.

"I saw the light. The oven door was open. You shouldn't do that," Mrs. Stahl said, shaking her head. "It's very dangerous."

"You're not the first landlord I caught peeping. I guess I need to close my curtains," Penny said coolly. "But it's not the oven damper I'm hearing each and every night. I'm telling you: there's something inside my walls. Something in the kitchen."

Mrs. Stahl's mouth seemed to quiver slightly, which emboldened Penny.

"Do I need to get out the ball peen I found under the sink and tear a hole in the kitchen wall, Mrs. Stahl?"

"Don't you dare!" she said, clutching Penny's wrist, her costume rings digging in. "Don't you dare!"

Penny felt the panic on her, the woman's breaths coming in sputters. She insisted they both sit on the fountain edge.

For a moment, they both just breathed, the apricot-perfumed air thick in Penny's lungs.

"Mrs. Stahl, I'm sorry. It's just—I need to sleep."

Mrs. Stahl took a long breath, then her eyes narrowed again. "It's those chinwags next door, isn't it? They've been filling your ear with bile."

"What? Not about this, I—"

"I had the kitchen cleaned thoroughly after it happened. I had it cleaned, the linoleum stripped out. I put up fresh wallpaper over every square inch after it happened. I covered everything with wallpaper."

"Is that where it happened?" Penny asked. "That poor man who died in Number Four? Larry?"

But Mrs. Stahl couldn't speak, or wouldn't, breathing into her handkerchief, lilac silk, the small square over her mouth suctioning open and closed, open and closed.

"He was very beautiful," she finally whispered. "When they

pulled him out of the oven, his face was the most exquisite red. Like a ripe, ripe cherry."

Knowing how it happened changed things. Penny had always imagined handsome, melancholy Larry walking around the apartment, turning gas jets on. Settling into that club chair in the living room. Or maybe settling in bed and slowly drifting from earth's fine tethers.

She wondered how she could ever use the oven now, or even look at it.

It had to be the same one. That Magic Chef, which looked like the one from childhood, white porcelain and cast iron. Not like those new slabs, buttercup or mint green.

The last tenant, Mr. Flant told her later, smelled gas all the time.

"She said it gave her headaches," he said. "Then one night she came here, her face white as snow. She said she'd just seen St. Agatha in the kitchen, with her bloody breasts."

"I... I don't see anything like that," Penny said.

Back in the bungalow, trying to sleep, she began picturing herself the week before. How she'd left that oven door open, her fine, rain-slicked dress draped over the rack. The truth was, she'd forgotten about it, only returning for it hours later.

Walking to the closet now, she slid the dress from its hanger pressing it to her face. But she couldn't smell anything.

Mr. D. still had not returned her calls. The bank had charged her for the bounced check so she'd have to return the hat she'd bought, and rent was due again in two days.

When all the other crew members were making their way to the commissary for lunch, Penny slipped away and splurged on cab fare to the studio.

As she opened the door to his outer office, the receptionist was already on her feet and walking purposefully toward Penny.

"Miss," she said, nearly blocking Penny, "you're going to have to leave. Mac shouldn't have let you in downstairs."

"Why not? I've been here dozens of—"

"You're not on the appointment list, and that's our system now, Miss."

"Does he have an appointment list now for that squeaking starlet sofa in there?" Penny asked, jerking her arm and pointing at the leather-padded door. A man with a thin moustache and a woman in a feathered hat looked up from their magazines.

The receptionist was already on the phone. "Mac, I need you... Yes, that one."

"If he thinks he can just toss me out like street trade," she said, marching over and thumping on Mr. D.'s door, "he'll be very, very sorry."

Her knuckles made no noise in the soft leather. Nor did her fist.

"Miss," someone said. It was the security guard striding toward her.

"I'm allowed to be here," she insisted, her voice tight and high. "I did my time. I earned the right."

But the guard had his hand on her arm.

Desperate, she looked down at the man and the woman waiting. Maybe she thought they would help. But why would they?

The woman pretended to be absorbed in her *Cinestar* magazine.

But the man smiled at her, hair oil gleaming. And winked.

The next morning she woke bleary but determined. She would forget about Mr. D. She didn't need his money. After all, she had a job, a good one.

It was hot on the lot that afternoon, and none of the makeup crew could keep the dust off the faces. There were so many lines and creases on every face—you never think about it until you're trying to make everything smooth.

"Penny," Gordon, the makeup supervisor said. She had the feeling he'd been watching her for several moments as she pressed the powder into the actor's face, holding it still.

"It's so dusty," she said, "so it's taking a while."

He waited until she finished then, as the actor walked away, he leaned forward.

"Everything all right, Pen?"

He was looking at something—her neck, her chest.

"What do you mean?" she said, setting the powder down.

But he just kept looking at her.

"Working on your carburetor, beautiful?" one of the grips said, as he walked by.

"What? I..."

Peggy turned to the makeup mirror. That was when she saw the long grease smear on her collarbone. And the line of black soot across her hairline too.

"I don't know," Penny said, her voice sounding slow and sleepy. "I don't have a car."

Then, it came to her: the dream she'd had in the early morning hours. That she was in the kitchen, checking on the oven damper. The squeak of the door on its hinges, and Mrs. Stahl outside the window, her eyes glowing like a wolf's.

"It was a dream," she said, now. Or was it? Had she been sleepwalking the night before?

Had she been in the kitchen... *at the oven*... in her sleep?

"Penny," Gordon said, looking at her squintily. "Penny, maybe you should go home."

It was so early, and Penny didn't want to go back to Canyon Arms. She didn't want to go inside Number Four, or walk past the kitchen, its cherry wallpaper lately giving her the feeling of blood spatters.

Also, lately, she kept thinking she saw Mrs. Stahl peering at her between the wooden blinds as she watered the banana trees.

Instead, she took the bus downtown to the big library on South Fifth. She had an idea.

The librarian, a boy with a bowtie, helped her find the obituaries.

She found three about Larry, but none had photos, which was disappointing.

The one in the *Mirror* was the only with any detail, any texture.

It mentioned that the body had been found by the "handsome proprietress, one Mrs. Herman Stahl," who "fell to wailing" so loud it was heard all through the canyons, up the promontories and likely high into the mossed eaves of the Hollywood sign.

"So what happened to Mrs. Stahl's husband?" Penny asked when she saw Mr. Flant and Benny that night.

"He died just a few months before Larry," Benny said. "Bad heart, they say."

Mr. Flant raised one pale eyebrow. "She never spoke of him. Only of Larry."

"He told me once she watched him, Larry did," Benny said. "She watched him through his bedroom blinds. While he made love."

Instantly, Penny knew this was true.

She thought of herself in that same bed each night, the mattress so soft, its posts sometimes seeming to curl inward.

Mrs. Stahl had insisted Penny move it back against the wall. Penny refused, but the next day she came home to find the woman moving it herself, her short arms spanning the mattress, her face pressed into its applique.

Watching, Penny had felt like the Peeping Tom. It was so intimate.

"Sometimes I wonder," Mr. Flant said now. "There were rumors. Black Widow, or Old Maid."

"You can't make someone put his head in the oven," Benny said. "At least not for long. The gas'd get at you, too."

"True," Mr. Flant said.

"Maybe it didn't happen at the oven," Penny blurted. "She found the body. What if she just turned on the gas while he was sleeping?"

"And dragged him in there, for the cops?"

Mr. Flant and Benny looked at each other.

"She's very strong," Penny said.

Back in her bungalow, Penny sat just inside her bedroom window, waiting.

Peering through the blinds, long after midnight, she finally saw her. Mrs. Stahl, walking along the edges of the courtyard.

She was singing softly and her steps were uneven and Penny thought she might be tight, but it was hard to know.

Penny was developing a theory.

Picking up a book, she made herself stay awake until two.

Then, slipping from bed, she tried to follow the flashes of light, the shadows.

Bending down, she put her hand on the baseboards, as if she could touch those funny shapes, like mice on their haunches. Or tiny men, marching.

"Something's there!" she said outloud, her voice surprising her. "It's in the walls."

In the morning, it would all be blurry, but in that moment, clues were coming together in her head, something to do with gas jets and Mrs. Stahl and love gone awry and poison in the walls, and she had figured it out before anything bad had happened.

It made so much sense in the moment, and when the sounds came too, the little *tap-taps* behind the plaster, she nearly cheered.

Mr. Flant poured her glass after glass of amaro. Benny waxed his moustache and showed Penny his soft shoe.

They were trying to make her feel better about losing her job.

"I never came in late except two or three times. I always did my job," Penny said, biting her lip so hard it bled. "I think

I know who's responsible. He kited me for seven hundred and forty dollars and now he's out to ruin me."

Then she told them how, a few days ago, she had written him a letter.

Mr. D.—

I don't write to cause you any trouble. What's mine is mine and I never knew you for an indian giver.

I bought fine dresses to go to Hollywood Park with you, to be on your arm at Villa Capri. I had to buy three stockings a week, your clumsy hands pawing at them. I had to turn down jobs and do two cycles of penicillin because of you. Also because of you, I got the heave-ho from my roommate Pauline who said you fondled her by the dumbwaiter. So that money is the least a gentleman could offer a lady. The least, Mr. D.

Let me ask you: those books you kept behind the false bottom in your desk drawer on the lot—did you buy those from Mr. Stanley Rose, or his handsome assistant Larry?

I wonder if your wife knows the kinds of books you keep in your office, the girls you keep there and make do shameful things?

I know Larry would agree with me about you. He was a sensitive man and I live where he did and sleep in his bed and all of you ruined him, drove him to drink and to a perilous act.

How dare you try to take my money away. And you with a wife with ermine, mink, lynx dripping from her plump, sunk shoulders.

Your wife at 312 North Faring Road, Holmby Hills.

Let's be adults, sophisticates. After all, we might not know what we might do if backed against the wall.

—yr lucky penny

It had made more sense when she wrote it than it did now, reading it to them.

Benny patted her shoulder. "So he called the cops on ya, huh?"

"The studio cops. Which is bad enough," Penny said.

They had escorted her from the makeup department. Everyone had watched, a few of the girls smiling.

"Sorry, Pen," Gordon had said, taking the powder brush from her hand. "What gives in this business is what takes away."

When he'd hired her two months ago, she'd watched as he wrote on her personnel file: MR. D.

"Your man, he took this as a threat, you see," Mr. Flant said, shaking his head as he looked at the letter. "He is a hard man. Those men are. They are hard men and you are soft. Like Larry was soft."

Penny knew it was true. She'd never been hard enough, at least not in the right way. The smart way.

It was very late when she left the two men.

She paused before Number Four and found herself unable to move, cold fingertips pressed between her breasts, pushing her back.

That was when she spotted Mrs. Stahl inside the bungalow, fluttering past the picture window in her evening coat.

"Stop!" Penny called out. "I see you!"

And Mrs. Stahl froze. Then, slowly, she turned to face Penny, her face warped through the glass, as if she were under water.

"Dear," a voice came from behind Penny. A voice just like Mrs. Stahl's. *Could she throw her voice?*

Swiveling around, she saw the landlady standing in the courtyard, a few feet away.

It was as if she were a witch, a shapeshifter from one of the fairytales she'd read as a child.

"Dear," she said again.

"I thought you were inside," Penny said, trying to catch her breath. "But it was just your reflection."

Mrs. Stahl did not say anything for a moment, her hands cupped in front of herself.

Penny saw she was holding a scarlet-covered book in her palms.

"I often sit out here at night," she said, voice loose and tipsy, "reading under the stars. Larry used to do that, you know."

She invited Penny into her bungalow, the smallest one, in back.

"I'd like us to talk," she said.

Penny did not pause. She wanted to see it. Wanted to understand.

Walking inside, she realized at last what the strongest smell in the courtyard was. All around were pots of night-blooming jasmine, climbing and vining up the built-in bookshelves, around the window frame, even trained over the arched doorway into the dining room.

They drank jasmine tea, iced. The room was close and Penny had never seen so many books. None of them looked like they'd ever been opened, their spines cool and immaculate.

"I have more," Mrs. Stahl said, waving toward the mint-walled hallway, some space beyond, the air itself so thick with the breath of the jasmine, Penny couldn't see it. "I love books. Larry taught me how. He knew what ones I'd like."

Penny nodded. "At night, I read the books in the bungalow. I never read so much."

"I wanted to keep them there. It only seemed right. And I didn't believe what the other tenants said, about the paper smelling like gas."

At that, Penny had a grim thought. What if everything smelled like gas and she didn't know it? The strong scent of apricot, of eucalyptus, a perpetual perfume suffusing everything. How would one know?

"Dear, do you enjoy living in Larry's bungalow?"

Penny didn't know what to say, so she only nodded, taking a long sip of the tea. Was it rum? Some kind of liqueur? It was very sweet and tingled on her tongue.

"He was my favorite tenant. Even after…" she paused, her head shaking, "what he did."

"And you found him," Penny said. "That must have been awful."

She held up the red-covered book she'd been reading in the courtyard.

"This was found on... on his person. He must've been planning on giving it to me. He gave me so many things. See how it's red, like a heart?"

"What kind of book is it?" Penny asked, leaning closer.

Mrs. Stahl looked at her, but didn't seem to be listening, clasping the book with one hand while with the other stroked her neck, long and unlined.

"Every book he gave me showed how much he understood me. He gave me many things and never asked for anything. That was when my mother was dying from Bright's, her face puffed up like a carnival balloon. Nasty woman."

"Mrs. Stahl," Penny started, her fingers tingling unbearably, the smell so strong, Mrs. Stahl's plants, her strong perfume—sandalwood?

"He just liked everyone. You'd think it was just you. The care he took. Once, he brought me a brass rouge pot from Paramount studios. He told me it belonged to Paulette Goddard. I still have it."

"Mrs. Stahl," Penny tried again, bolder now, "were you in love with him?"

The woman looked at her, and Penny felt her focus loosen, like in those old detective movies, right before the screen went black.

"He really only wanted the stars," Mrs. Stahl said, running her fingers across her décolletage, the satin of her dressing robe, a dragon painted up the front. "He said their skin felt different. They smelled different. He was strange about smells. Sounds. Light. He was very sensitive."

"But you loved him, didn't you?" Penny's voice more insistent now.

Her eyes narrowed. "Everyone loved him. Everyone. He said yes to everybody. He gave himself to everybody."

"But why did he do it, Mrs. Stahl?"

"He put his head in the oven and died," she said, straightening her back ever so slightly. "He was mad in a way only Southerners and artistic souls are mad. And he was both. You're too young, too simple, to understand."

"Mrs. Stahl, did you do something to Larry?" This is what Penny was trying to say, but the words weren't coming. And Mrs. Stahl kept growing larger and larger, the dragon on her robe, it seemed, somehow, to be speaking to Penny, whispering things to her.

"What's in this tea?"

"What do you mean, dear?"

But the woman's face had gone strange, stretched out. There was a scurrying sound from somewhere, like little paws, animal claws, the sharp feet of sharp-footed men. A gold watch chain swinging and that neighbor hanging from the pear tree.

She woke to the purple creep of dawn. Slumped in the same rattan chair in Mrs. Stahl's living room. Her finger still crooked in the tea cup handle, her arm hanging to one side.

"Mrs. Stahl," she whispered.

But the woman was no longer on the sofa across from her.

Somehow, Penny was on her feet, inching across the room.

The bedroom door was ajar, Mrs. Stahl sprawled on the mattress, the painted dragon on her robe sprawled on top of her.

On the bed beside her was the book she'd been reading in the courtyard. Scarlet red, with a lurid title.

Gaudy Night, it was called

Opening it with great care, Penny saw the inscription:

To Mrs. Stahl, my dirty murderess.
Love, Lawrence.

She took the book, and the tea cup.

She slept for a few hours in her living room, curled on the zebra print sofa.

She had stopped going into the kitchen two days ago, tacking an old bath towel over the doorway so she couldn't even see inside. The gleaming porcelain of the oven.

She was sure she smelled gas radiating from it. Spotted blue light flickering behind the towel.

But still she didn't go inside.

And now she was afraid the smell was coming through the walls.

It was all connected, you see, and Mrs. Stahl was behind all of it. The lightspots, the shadows on the baseboard, the noises in the walls and now the hiss of the gas.

Mr. Flant looked at the inscription, shaking his head.

"My god, is it possible? He wasn't making much sense those final days. Holed up in Number Four. Maybe he was hiding from her. Because he knew."

"It was found on his body," Penny said, voice trembling. "That's what she told me."

"Then this inscription," he said, reaching out for Penny's wrist, "was meant to be our clue. Like pointing a finger from beyond the grave."

Penny nodded. She knew what she had to do.

"I know how it sounds. But someone needs to do something."

The police detective nodded, drinking from his Coca-Cola, his white shirt bright. He had gray hair at the temples and he said his name was Noble, which seemed impossible.

"Well, Miss, let's see what we can do. That was a long time ago. After you called, I had to get the case file from the crypt. I can't say I even remember it." Licking his index finger, he flicked open the file folder, then beginning turning pages. "A gas job, right? We got a lot of them back then. Those months before the war."

"Yes. In the kitchen. My kitchen now."

Looking through the slim folder, he pursed his lips a moment, then came a grim smile. "Ah, I remember. I remember. The little men."

"The little men?" Penny felt her spine tighten.

"One of our patrolmen had been out there the week before on a noise complaint. Your bookseller was screaming in the courtyard. Claimed there were little men coming out of the walls to kill him."

Penny didn't say anything at all. Something deep inside herself seemed to be screaming and it took all her effort just to sit there and listen.

"DTs. Said he'd been trying to kick the sauce," he said, reading the report. "He was a drunk, miss. Sounds like it was a whole courtyard full of 'em."

"No," Penny said, head shaking back and forth. "That's not it. Larry wasn't like that."

"Well," he said, "I'll tell what Larry was like. In his bedside table we found a half-dozen catcher's mitts." He stopped himself, looked at her. "Pardon. Female contraceptive devices. Each one with the name of a different woman. A few big stars. At least they were big then. I can't remember now."

Penny was still thinking about the wall. The little men. And her mice on their hindfeet. Pixies, dancing fairies.

"There you go," the detective said, closing the folder. "Guy's a dipso, one of his high-class affairs turned sour. Suicide. Pretty clear cut."

"No," Penny said.

"No?" Eyebrows raised. "He was in that oven waist deep, Miss. He even had a hunting knife in his hand for good measure."

"A knife?" Penny said, her fingers pressing her forehead. "Of course. Don't you see? He was trying to protect himself. I told you on the phone, detective. It's imperative that you look into Mrs. Stahl."

"The landlady. Your landlady?"

"She was in love with him. And he rejected her, you see."

"A woman scorned, eh?" he said, leaning back. "Once saw a jilted lady over on Cheremoya take a clothes iron to her fellow's face while he slept."

"Look at this," Penny said, pulling Mrs. Stahl's little red book from her purse.

"*Gaudy Night*," he said, pronouncing the first word in a funny way.

"I think it's a dirty book."

He looked at her, squinting. "My wife owns this book."

Penny didn't say anything.

"Have you even read it?" he asked, wearily.

Opening the front to the inscription, she held it in front of him.

"'Dirty murderess.'" He shrugged. "So you're saying this fella knew she was going to kill him and, instead of going to, say, the police, he writes this little inscription, then lets himself get killed?"

Everything sounded so different when he said it aloud, different than the way everything joined in perfect and horrible symmetry in her head.

"I don't know how it happened. Maybe he was going to go to the police and she beat him to it. And I don't know how she did it," Penny said. "But she's dangerous, don't you get it?"

It was clear he did not.

"I'm telling you, I see her out there at night, doing things," Penny said, her breath coming faster and faster. "She's doing something with the natural gas. If you check the gas jets maybe you can figure it out."

She was aware that she was talking very loudly, and her chest felt damp. Lowering her voice, she leaned toward him.

"I think there might be a clue in my oven," she said.

"Do you?" he said, rubbing his chin. "Any little men in there?"

"It's not like that. It's not. I see them, yes." She couldn't look him in the eye or she would lose her nerve. "But I know they're not really little men. It's something she's doing. It always starts at two. Two a.m. She's doing something. She did it to Larry and she's doing it to me."

He was rubbing his face with his hand, and she knew she had lost him.

"I told you on the phone," she said, more desperately now. "I think she drugged me. I brought the cup."

Penny reached into her purse again, this time removing the tea cup, its bottom still brown-ringed.

Detective Noble lifted it, took a sniff, set it down.

"Drugged you with Old Grandad, eh?

"I know there's booze in it. But, detective, there's more than booze going on here." Again, her voice rose high and sharp, and other detectives seemed to be watching now from their desks.

But Noble seemed unfazed. There even seemed to be the flicker of a smile on his clean-shaven face.

"So why does she want to harm you?" he asked. "Is she in love with you, too?"

Penny looked at him, and counted quietly in her head, the dampness on her chest gathering.

She had been dealing with men like this her whole life. Smug men. Men with fine clothes or shabby ones, all with the same slick ideas, the same impatience, big voice, slap-and-tickle, fast with a back-handed slug. Nice turned to nasty on a dime.

"Detective," she said, taking it slowly, "Mrs. Stahl must suspect that I know. About what she did to Larry. I don't know if she drugged him and staged it. The hunting knife shows there was a struggle. What I do know is there's more than what's in your little file."

He nodded, leaning back in his chair once more. With his right arm, he reached for another folder in the metal tray on his desk.

"Miss, can we talk for a minute about *your* file?"

"My file?"

"When you called, I checked your name. S.O.P. Do you want to tell me about the letters you've been sending to a certain address in Holmby Hills?"

"What? I... There was only one."

"And two years ago, the fellow over at MCA? Said you slashed his tires?"

"I was never charged."

Penny would never speak about that, or what that man had tried to do to her in a back booth at Chasen's.

He set the file down. "Miss, what exactly are you here for? You got a gripe with Mrs. Stahl? Hey, I don't like my landlord either. What, don't wanna pay the rent?"

A wave of exhaustion shuddered through Penny. For a moment, she did not know if she could stand.

But there was Larry to think about. And how much she belonged in Number Four. Because she did, and it had marked the beginning of things. A new day for Penny.

"No," Penny said, rising. "That's not it. You'll see. You'll see. I'll show you."

"Miss," he said, calling after her. "Please don't show me anything. Just behave yourself, okay? Like a good girl."

Back at Number Four, Penny laid down on the rattan sofa, trying to breathe, to think.

Pulling Mrs. Stahl's book from her dress pocket, she began reading.

But it wasn't like she thought.

It wasn't dirty, not like the brown-papered ones. It was a detective novel, and it took place in England. A woman recently exonerated for poisoning her lover attends her school reunion. While there, she finds an anonymous poisoned pen note tucked in the sleeve of her gown: "You Dirty Murderess...!"

Penny gasped. But then wondered: Had that inscription just been a wink, Larry to Mrs. Stahl?

He gave her books she liked, Benny had said. *Stiff British stuff that he could tease her about.*

Was that all this was, all the inscription had meant?

No, she assured herself, sliding the book back into her pocket. It's a red herring. To confuse me, to keep me from finding the truth. Larry needs me to find out the truth.

It was shortly after that she heard the click of her mail slot. Looking over, she saw a piece of paper slip through the slit and land on the entry-way floor.

Walking over, she picked it up.

Bungalow Four:
You are past due.
—Mrs. H. Stahl

"I have to move anyway," she told Benny, showing him the note.

"No, kid, why?" he whispered. Mr. Flant was sleeping in the bedroom, the gentle whistle of his snore.

"I can't prove she's doing it," Penny said. "But it smells like a gas chamber in there."

"Listen, don't let her spook you," Benny said. "I bet the pilot light is out. Want me to take a look? I can come by later."

"Can you come now?"

Looking into the darkened bedroom, Benny smiled, patted her forearm. "I don't mind."

Stripped to his undershirt, Benny ducked under the bath towel Penny had hung over the kitchen door.

"I thought you were inviting me over to keep your bed warm," he said as he kneeled down on the linoleum.

The familiar noise started, the *tick-tick-tick*.

"Do you hear it?" Penny said, voice tight. Except the sound was different in the kitchen than the bedroom. It was closer. Not inside the walls but everywhere.

"It's the igniter," Benny said. "Trying to light the gas."

Peering behind the towel, Penny watched him.

"But you smell it, right?" she said.

"Of course I smell it," he said, his voice strangely high. "God, it's awful."

He put his head to the baseboards, the sink, the shuddering refrigerator.

"What's this?" he said, tugging the oven forward, his arms straining.

He was touching the wall behind the oven, but Penny couldn't see.

"What's what?" she asked. "Did you find something?"

"I don't know," he said, his head turned from her. "I... Christ, you can't think with it. I feel like I'm back in Argonne."

He had to lean backward, palms resting on the floor.

"What is it you saw, back there?" Penny asked, pointing behind the oven.

But he kept shaking his head, breathing into the front of his undershirt, pulled up.

After a minute, both of them breathing hard, he reached up and turned the knob on the front of the oven door.

"I smell it," Penny said, stepping back. "Don't you?"

"That pilot light," he said, covering his face, breathing raspily. "It's gotta be out."

His knees sliding on the linoleum, he inched back toward the oven, white and glowing.

"Are you... are you going to open it?"

He looked at her, his face pale and his mouth stretched like a piece of rubber.

"I'm going to," he said. "We need to light it."

But he didn't stir. There was a feeling of something, that door open like a black maw, and neither of them could move.

Penny turned, hearing a knock at the door.

When she turned back around, she gasped.

Benny's head and shoulders were inside the oven, his voice making the most terrible sound, like a cat, its neck caught in a trap.

"Get out," Penny said, no matter how silly it sounded. "Get out!"

Pitching forward, she leaned down and grabbed for him, tugging at his trousers, yanking him back.

Stumbling, they both rose to their feet, Penny nearly huddling against the kitchen wall, its cherry-sprigged paper.

Turning, he took her arms hard, pressing himself against her, pressing Penny against the wall.

She could smell him, and his skin was clammy and goosequilled.

His mouth pressed against her neck roughly and she could feel his teeth, his hands on her hips. Something had changed, and she'd missed it.

"But this is what you want, isn't it, honey?" the whisper came, his mouth over her ear. "It's all you've ever wanted."

"No, no, no," she said, and found herself crying. "And you don't like girls. You don't like girls."

"I like everybody," he said, his palm on her chest, hand heel hard.

And she lifted her head and looked at him, and he was Larry. She knew he was Larry.

Larry.

Until he became Benny again, moustache and grin, but fear in that grin still.

"I'm sorry, Penny," he said, stepping back. "I'm flattered, but I don't go that way."

"What?" She said, looking down, seeing her fingers clamped on his trouser waist. "Oh. Oh."

Back at Number Three, they both drank from tall tumblers, breathing hungrily.

"You shouldn't go back in there," Benny said. "We need to call the gas company in the morning."

Mr. Flant said she could stay on their sofa that night, if they could make room under all the old newspapers.

"You shouldn't have looked in there," he said to Benny, shaking his head. "The oven. It's like whistling in a cemetery."

A towel wrapped around his shoulders, Benny was shivering. He was so white.

"I didn't see anything," he kept saying. "I didn't see a goddamned thing."

She was dreaming.

"You took my book!"

In the dream, she'd risen from Mr. Flant's sofa, slicked with sweat, and opened the door. Although nearly midnight, the courtyard was mysteriously bright, all the plants gaudy and pungent.

Wait. Had someone said something?

"Larry gave it to me!"

Penny's body was moving so slowly, like she was caught in molasses.

The door to Number Four was open, and Mrs. Stahl was emerging from it, something red in her hand.

"You took it while I slept, didn't you? Sneak thief! Thieving whore!"

When Mrs. Stahl began charging at her, her robe billowing like great scarlet wings, Penny thought she was still dreaming.

"Stop," Penny said, but the woman was so close.

It had to be a dream, and in dreams you can do anything, so Penny raised her arms high, clamping down on those scarlet wings as they came toward her.

The book slid from her pocket, and both of them grappled for it, but Penny was faster, grabbing it and pushing back, pressing the volume against the old woman's neck until she stumbled, heels tangling.

It had to be a dream because Mrs. Stahl was so weak, weaker than any murderess could possibly be, her body like that of a yarn doll, limp and flailing.

There was a flurry of elbows, clawing hands, the fat golden beetle ring on Mrs. Stahl's gnarled hand against Penny's face.

Then, with one hard jerk, the old woman fell to the ground with such ease, her head clacking against the courtyard tiles.

The ratatattat of blood from her mouth, her ear.

"Penny!" A voice came from behind her.

It was Mr. Flant standing in his doorway, hand to his mouth.

"Penny, what did you *do*?"

Her expression when she'd faced Mr. Flant must have been meaningful because he had immediately retreated inside his bungalow, the door locking with a click.

But it was time, anyway. Of that she felt sure.

Walking into Number Four, she almost felt herself smiling.

One by one, she removed all the tacks from her makeshift kitchen door, letting the towel drop onto her forearm.

The kitchen was dark, and smelled as it never had. No apricots, no jasmine, and no gas. Instead, the tinny smell of must, wallpaper paste, rusty water.

Moving slowly, purposefully, she walked directly to the oven, the moonlight striking it. White and monstrous, a glowing smear.

Its door shut.

Cold to the touch.

Kneeling down, she crawled behind it, to the spot Benny had been struck by.

What's this? he'd said.

As in a dream, which this had to be, she knew what to do, her palm sliding along the cherry-sprig wallpaper down by the baseboard.

She saw the spot, the wallpaper gaping at its seam, seeming to breathe. Inhale, exhale.

Penny's hand went there, pulling back, the paper glue dried to fine dust under her hand

She was remembering Mrs. Stahl. *I put up fresh wallpaper over every square inch after it happened. I covered everything with wallpaper*

What did she think she would see, breathing hard, her knees creaking and her forehead pushed against the wall?

The paper did not come off cleanly, came off in pieces, strands, like her hair after the dose Mr. D. passed to her, making her sick for weeks.

A patch of wall exposed, she saw the series of gashes, one after the next, as if someone had jabbed a knife into the plaster. A hunting knife. Though there seemed a pattern, a hieroglyphics.

Squinting, the kitchen so dark, she couldn't see.

Reaching up to the oven, she grabbed for a kitchen match.

Leaning close, the match lit, she could see a faint scrawl etched deep.

The little men come out of the walls. I cut off their heads every night. My mind is gone.

Tonight, I end my life.

I hope you find this.

Goodbye.

Penny leaned forward, pressed her palm on the words.

This is what mattered most, nothing else.

"Oh, Larry," she said, her voice catching with grateful tears. "I see them, too."

The sound that followed was the loudest she'd ever heard, the fire sweeping up her face.

The detective stood in the center of the courtyard, next to a banana tree with its top shorn off, a smoldering slab of wood, the front door to the blackened bungalow, on the ground in front of him.

The firemen were dragging their equipment past him. The gurney with the dead girl long gone.

"Pilot light. Damn near took the roof off," one of the patrolman said. "The kitchen looks like the Blitz. But only one scorched, inside. The girl. Or what's left of her. Could've been much worse."

"That's always true," the detective said, a billow of smoke making them both cover their faces.

Another officer approached him.

"Detective Noble, we talked to the pair next door," he said. "They said they warned the girl not to go back inside. But she'd been drinking all day, saying crazy things."

"How's the landlady?"

"Hospital."

Noble nodded. "We're done."

It was close to two. But he didn't want to go home yet. It was a long drive to Eagle Rock anyway.

And the smell, and what he'd seen in that kitchen—he didn't want to go home yet.

At the top of the road, he saw the bar, its bright lights beckoning.

The Carnival Tavern, the one with the roof shaped like a big top.

Life is a carnival, he said to himself, which is what the detective might say, wryly, in the books his wife loved to read.

He couldn't believe it was still there. He remembered it from before the war. When he used to date that usherette at the Hollywood Bowl.

A quick jerk to the wheel and he was pulling into its small lot, those crazy clown lanterns he remembered from all those years ago.

Inside, everything was warm and inviting, even if the waitress had a sour look.

"Last call," she said, leaving him his rye. "We close in ten minutes."

"I just need to make a quick call," he said.

He stepped into one of the telephone booths in the back, pulling the accordion door shut behind him.

"Yes, I have that one," his wife replied, stifling a yawn. "But it's not a dirty book."

Then she laughed a little in a way that made him bristle.

"So what kind of book is it?" he asked.

"Books mean different things to different people," she said.

She was always saying stuff like that, just to show him how smart she was.

"You know what I mean," he said.

She was silent for several seconds. He thought he could hear someone crying, maybe one of the kids.

"It's a mystery," she said, finally. "Not your kind. No one even dies."

"Okay," he said. He wasn't sure what he'd wanted to hear. "I'll be home soon."

"It's a love story, too," she said, almost a whisper, strangely sad. "Not your kind."

After he hung up, he ordered a beer, the night's last tug from the bartender's tap.

Sitting by the picture window, he looked down into the canyon, and up to the Hollywood sign. Everything about the moment felt familiar. He'd worked this precinct for twenty years, minus three to Uncle Sam, so even the surprises were the same.

He thought about the girl, about her at the station. Her nervous legs, that worn dress of hers, the plea in her voice.

Someone should think of her for a minute, shouldn't they?

He looked at his watch. Two a.m. But she won't see her little men tonight.

A busboy with a pencil moustache came over with a long stick. One by one, he turned all the dingy lanterns that hung in the window. The painted clowns faced the canyon now. Closing time.

"Don't miss me too much," he told the sour waitress as he left.

In the parking lot, looking down into the canyon, he noticed he could see the Canyon Arms, the smoke still settling on the bungalow's shell, black as a mussel. Her bedroom window, glass blown out, curtains shuddering in the night breeze.

He was just about to get in his car when he saw them. The little men.

They were dancing across the hood of his car, the canyon beneath him.

Turning, he looked up at the bar, the lanterns in the window, spinning, sending their dancing clowns across the canyon, across the Canyon Arms, everywhere.

He took a breath.

"That happens every night?" he asked the busboy as the young man hustled down the stairs into the parking lot.

Pausing, the busboy followed his gaze, then nodded.

"Every night," he said. "Like a dream."

Citadel

Stephen Hunter

For R. Sidney Bowen,
author of
Dave Dawson with the R.A.F.
and
Red Randall at Pearl Harbor
and so many others, for teaching me
the glory of the story sixty-odd years ago

A book is a physical object in a world of physical objects. It is
a set of dead symbols. And then the right reader comes along
and the words— or, rather, the poetry behind the words, for the
words themselves are mere symbols—spring to life.

—Jorge Luis Borges

FIRST DAY

THE LYSANDER TOOK off in the pitch-dark of 0400 British
Standard War Time, Pilot Officer Murphy using the
prevailing south-southwest wind to gain atmospheric traction,
even though the craft had a reputation for short takeoffs. He
nudged it airborne, felt it surpass its amazingly low stall speed,
held the stick gently back until he reached 150 meters, then
commenced a wide left-hand bank to aim himself and his
passenger toward Occupied France.

Murphy was a pro and had done many missions for his outfit, No. 138 (Special Duties Squadron), inserting and removing agents in coordination with the Resistance. But that didn't mean he was blasé, or without fear. No matter how many times you flew into Nazi territory, it was a first time. There was no predicting what might happen, and he could just as easily end up in a POW camp or against the executioner's wall as back in his quarters at RAF Newmarket.

The high-winged, single-engine plane hummed along just over the 150-meter notch on the altimeter to stay under both British and, twenty minutes on, German radar. It was a moonless night, as preferred, a bit chilly and damp, with ground temperature at about four degrees centigrade. It was early April 1943; the destination, still two hours ahead, was a meadow outside Sur-la-Gane, a village forty-eight kilometers east of Paris. There, God and the Luftwaffe willing, he would deviate from the track of a railroad, find four lights on the ground, and lay the plane down between them, knowing that they signified enough flatness and tree clearance for the airplane. He'd drop his passenger, the peasants of whichever Maquis group was receiving that night (he never knew) would turn the plane around, and in another forty seconds he'd be airborne, now headed west toward tea and jam. That was the ideal, at any rate.

He checked the compass at the apex of the Lysander's primitive instrument panel and double-checked his heading (148° ENE), his fuel (full), and his airspeed (175 mph), and saw through the Perspex windscreen, as expected, nothing. Nothing was good. He knew it was a rare off-night in the war and that no fleets of Lancasters filled the air and radio waves to and from targets deep in Germany, which meant that the Luftwaffe's night fighters, Me110s, wouldn't be up and about. No 110 had ever shot down a Lysander because they operated at such different altitudes and speeds, but there had to be a first time for everything.

Hunched behind him was an agent named Basil St. Florian, a captain in the army by official designation, commissioned in

1932 into the Horse Guards—not that he'd been on horseback in over a decade. Actually Basil, a ruddy-faced, ginger-haired brute who'd once sported a giant moustache, didn't know or care much about horses. Or the fabulous traditions of the Horse Guards, the cavalry, even the army. He'd only ended up there after a youth notorious for spectacular crack-ups, usually involving trysts with American actresses and fights with Argentine polo players. His father arranged the commission, as he had arranged so much else for Basil, who tended to leave debris wherever he went, but once in khaki Basil veered again toward glamorous self-extinction until a dour little chap from Intelligence invited him for a drink at Boodle's. When Basil learned he could do unusual things and get both paid and praised for it, he signed up. That was 1934, and Basil had never looked back.

As it turned out, he had a gift for languages and spoke French, German, and Spanish without a trace of accent. He could pass for any European nationality except Irish, though the latter was more on principle, because he despised the Irish in general terms. They were so loud.

He liked danger and wasn't particularly nonplussed by fear. He never panicked. He took pride in his considerable wit, and his bons mots were famous in his organization. He didn't mind fighting, with fist or knife, but much preferred shooting, because he was a superb pistol and rifle shot. He'd been on safari at fifteen, again at twenty-two, and a third time at twenty-seven; he was quite used to seeing large mammals die by gunshot, so it didn't particularly perturb him. He knew enough about trophy hunting to hope that he'd never end up on another man's wall.

He'd been in the agent trade a long time and had the nightmares to show for it, plus a drawerful of ribbons that someone must organize sooner or later, plus three bullet holes, a raggedy zigzag of scar tissue from a knife (don't ask, please, don't *ever* ask), as well as piebald burn smears on back and hips from a long session with a torturer. He finally talked, and the lies he told the man were among his finest memories. His other favorite memory: watching his torturer's eyes go eightball as Basil strangled him three days later. Jolly fun!

Basil was cold, shivering under an RAF sheepskin over an RAF aircrew jumpsuit over a black wool suit of shabby prewar French manufacture. He sat uncomfortably squashed on a parachute, which he hadn't bothered to put on. The wind beat against him, because on some adventure or another the Lysander's left window had been shot out and nobody had got around to replacing it. He felt vibrations as the unspectacular Bristol Mercury XII engine beat away against the cold air, its energy shuddering through all the spars, struts, and tightened canvas of the aircraft.

"Over Channel now, sir," came the crackle of a voice from the earphones he wore, since there was entirely too much noise for pilot and passenger to communicate without it. "Ten minutes to France."

"Got it, Murphy, thanks."

Inclining toward the intact window to his starboard, Basil could see the black surface of the Channel at high chop, the water seething and shifting under the powerful blast of cold early-spring winds. It somehow caught enough illumination from the stars to gleam a bit, though without romance or beauty. It simply reminded him of unpleasant things and his aversion to large bodies of the stuff, which to him had but three effects: it made you wet, it made you cold, or it made you dead. All three were to be avoided.

In time a dark mass protruded upon the scene, sliding in from beyond to meet the sea.

"I say, Murphy, is that France?"

"It is indeed, sir."

"You know, I didn't have a chance to look at the flight plan. What part of France?"

"Normandy, sir. Jerry's building forts there, to stop an invasion."

"If I recall, there's a peninsula to the west, and the city of Cherbourg at the tip?"

"Yes, sir."

"Tell me, if you veered toward the west, you'd cross the peninsula, correct? With no deviation then, you'd come across coastline?"

"Yes, sir."

"And from that coastline, knowing you were to the western lee of the Cherbourg peninsula, you could easily return home on dead reckoning, that is, without a compass, am I right?"

"Indeed, sir. But I have a compass. So why would—"

Basil leaned forward, holding his Browning .380 automatic pistol. He fired once, the pistol jumping, the flash filling the cockpit with a flare of illumination, the spent casing flying away, the noise terrific.

"Good Christ!" yelped Murphy. "What the bloody hell! Are you mad?"

"Quite the opposite, old man," said Basil. "Now do as I suggested—veer westerly, cross the peninsula, and find me coastline."

Murphy noted that the bullet had hit the compass bang on, shattered its glass, and blown its dial askew and its needle arm into the vapors.

A FEW DAYS EARLIER

"Basil, how's the drinking?" the general asked.

"Excellent, sir," Basil replied. "I'm up to seven, sometimes eight whiskies a night."

"Splendid, Basil," said the general. "I knew you wouldn't let us down."

"See here," said another general. "I know this man has a reputation for wit, as it's called, but we are engaged in serious business, and the levity, perhaps appropriate to the officers' mess, is most assuredly inappropriate here. There should be no laughing here, gentlemen. This is the War Room."

Basil sat in a square, dull space far underground. A few dim bulbs illuminated it but showed little except a map of Europe pinned to the wall. Otherwise it was featureless. The table was large enough for at least a dozen generals, but there were only three of them—well, one was an admiral—and a civilian, all sitting across from Basil. It was rather like orals at Magdalen, had he bothered to attend them.

The room was buried beneath the Treasury in Whitehall, the most secret of secret installations in wartime Britain. Part of a warren of other rooms—some offices for administrative or logistical activities, a communications room, some sleeping or eating quarters—it was the only construction in England that might legitimately be called a lair. It belonged under a volcano, not a large office building. The prime minister would sit in this very place with his staff and make the decisions that would send thousands to their death in order to save tens of thousands. That was the theory, anyway. And that also is why it stank so brazenly of stale cigar.

"My dear sir," said the general with whom Basil had been discussing his drinking habits to the general who disapproved, "when one has been shot at for the benefit of crown and country as many times as Captain St. Florian, one has the right to set the tone of the meeting that will most certainly end up getting him shot at quite a bit more. Unless you survived the first day on the Somme, you cannot compete with him in that regard."

The other general muttered something grumpily, but Basil hardly noticed. It really did not matter, and since he believed himself doomed no matter what, he now no longer listened to those who did not matter.

The general who championed him turned to him, his opposition defeated. His name was Sir Colin Gubbins and he was head of the outfit to which Basil belonged, called by the rather dreary title Special Operations Executive. Its mandate was to Set Europe Ablaze, as the prime minister had said when he invented it and appointed General Gubbins as its leader. It was the sort of organization that would have welcomed Jack the Ripper to its ranks, possibly even promoted, certainly decorated him. It existed primarily to destroy—people, places, things, anything that could be destroyed. Whether all this was just mischief for the otherwise unemployable or long-term strategic wisdom was as yet undetermined. It was up for considerable debate among the other intelligence agencies, one of which was represented by the army general and the other by the naval admiral.

As for the civilian, he looked like a question on a quiz: Which one does not belong? He was a good thirty years younger than the two generals and the admiral, and hadn't, as they did, one of those heavy-jowled authoritarian faces. He was rather handsome in a weak sort of way, like the fellow who always plays Freddy in any production of *Pygmalion*, and he didn't radiate, as did the men of power. Yet here he was, a lad among the Neanderthals, and the others seemed in small ways to defer to him. Basil wondered who the devil he could be. But he realized he would find out sooner or later.

"You've all seen Captain St. Florian's record, highly classified as it is. He's one of our most capable men. If this thing can be done, he's the one who can do it. I'm sure before we proceed, the captain would entertain any questions of a general nature."

"I seem to remember your name from the cricket fields, St. Florian," said the admiral. "Were you not a batsman of some renown in the late twenties?"

"I have warm recollections of good innings at both Eton and Magdalen," said Basil.

"Indeed," said the admiral. "I've always said that sportsmen make the best agents. The playing field accustoms them to arduous action, quick, clever thinking, and decisiveness."

"I hope, however," said the general, "you've left your sense of sporting fair play far behind. Jerry will use it against you, any chance he gets."

"I killed a Chinese gangster with a cricket bat, sir. Would that speak to the issue?"

"Eloquently," said the general.

"What did your people do, Captain?" asked the admiral.

"He manufactured something," said Basil. "It had to do with automobiles, as I recall."

"A bit hazy, are we?"

"It's all rather vague. I believe that I worked for him for a few months after coming down. My performance was rather disappointing. We parted on bad terms. He died before I righted myself."

"To what do you ascribe your failure to succeed in business and please your poor father?"

"I am too twitchy to sit behind a desk, sir. My bum, pardon the French, gets all buzzy if I am in one spot too long. Then I drink to kill the buzz and end up in the cheap papers."

"I seem to recall," the admiral said. "Something about an actress—'31, '32, was that it?"

"Lovely young lady," Basil said, "A pity I treated her so abominably. I always plucked the melons out of her fruit salad and she could not abide that."

"Hong Kong, Malaysia, Germany before and during Hitler, battle in Spain—shot at a bit there, eh, watching our Communists fight the generalissimo's Germans, eh?" asked the army chap. "Czecho, France again, Dieppe, you were there? So was I."

"Odd I didn't see you, sir," said Basil.

"I suppose you were way out front then. Point taken, Captain. All right, professionally, he seems capable. Let's get on with it, Sir Colin."

"Yes," said Sir Colin. "Where to begin, where to begin? It's rather complex, you see, and someone important has demanded that you be apprised of all the nuances before you decide to go."

"Sir, I could save us all a lot of time. I've decided to go. I hereby officially volunteer."

"See, there's a chap with spirit," said the admiral. "I like that."

"It's merely that his bum is twitchy," said the general.

"Not so fast, Basil. I insist that you hear us out," said Sir Colin, "and so does the young man at the end of the table. Is that not right, Professor?"

"It is," said the young fellow.

"All right, sir," said Basil.

"It's a rather complex, even arduous story. Please ignore the twitchy bum and any need you may have for whisky. Give us your best effort."

"I shall endeavor, sir."

"Excellent. Now, hmm, let me see...oh, yes, I think this is how to start. Do you know the path to Jesus?"

THE FIRST DAY (CONT'D.)

Another half hour flew by, lost to the rattle of the plane, the howl of the wind, and the darkness of Occupied France below. At last Murphy said over the intercom, "Sir, the west coast of the Cherbourg Peninsula is just ahead. I can see it now."

"Excellent," said Basil. "Find someplace to put me down."

"Ah..."

"Yes, what is it, Pilot Officer?"

"Sir, I can't just land, you see. The plane is too fragile—there may be wires, potholes, tree stumps, ditches, mud, God knows what. All of which could snarl or even wreck the plane. It's not so much me. I'm not that important. It's actually the plane. Jerry's been trying to get hold of a Lysander for some time now, to use against us. I can't give him one."

"Yes, I can see that. All right then, perhaps drop me in a river from a low altitude?"

"Sir, you'd hit the water at over 100 miles per hour and bounce like a billiard ball off the bumper. Every bone would shatter."

"On top of that, I'd lose my shoes. This is annoying. I suppose then it's the parachute for me?"

"Yes, sir. Have you had training?"

"Scheduled several times, but I always managed to come up with an excuse. I could see no sane reason for abandoning a perfectly fine airplane in flight. That was then, however, and now, alas, is now."

Basil shed himself of the RAF fleece, a heavy leather jacket lined with sheep's wool, and felt the coldness of the wind bite him hard. He shivered. He hated the cold. He struggled with the straps of the parachute upon which he was sitting. He found the going rather rough. It seemed he couldn't quite get the left shoulder strap buckled into what appeared to be the strap nexus, a circular lock-like device that was affixed to the right shoulder strap in the center of his chest. He passed on that and went right to the thigh straps, which seemed to click in admirably, but then noticed he had the two straps in the wrong slots, and he couldn't get the left one undone. He applied extra effort and was able to make the correction.

"I say, how long has this parachute been here? It's all rusty and stiff."

"Well, sir, these planes aren't designed for parachuting. Their brilliance is in the short takeoff and landing drills. Perfect for agent inserts and fetches. So, no, I'm afraid nobody has paid much attention to the parachute."

"Damned thing. I'd have thought you RAF buckos would have done better. Battle of Britain, the few, all that sort of thing."

"I'm sure the 'chutes on Spits and Hurricanes were better maintained, sir. Allow me to make a formal apology to the intelligence services on behalf of the Royal Air Force."

"Well, I suppose it'll have to do," sniffed Basil. Somehow, at last, he managed to get the left strap snapped in approximately where it belonged, but he had no idea if the thing was too tight or too loose or even right side up. Oh, well, one did what one must. Up, up, and play the game, that sort of thing.

"Now, I'm not telling you your job, Murphy, but I think you should go lower so I won't have so far to go."

"Quite the opposite, sir. I must go higher. The 'chute won't open fully at 150 meters. It's a 240-meter minimum, a thousand far safer. At 150 or lower it's like dropping a pumpkin on a sidewalk. Very unpleasant sound, lots of splash, splatter, puddle, and stain. Wouldn't advise a bit of it, sir."

"This is not turning out at all as I had expected."

"I'll buzz up to a thousand. Sir, the trick here is that when you come out of the plane, you must keep hunched up in a ball. If you open up, your arms and legs and torso will catch wind and stall your fall and the tail wing will cut you in half or at least break your spine."

"Egad," said Basil. "How disturbing."

"I'll bank hard left to add gravity to your speed of descent, which puts you in good shape, at least theoretically, to avoid the tail."

"Not sure I care for 'theoretically.'"

"There's no automatic deployment on that device, also. You must, once free of the plane, pull the ripcord to open the 'chute."

"I shall try to remember," said Basil.

"If you forget, it's the pumpkin phenomenon, without doubt."

"All right, Murphy, you've done a fine job briefing me. I shall have a letter inserted in your file. Now, shall we get this nonsense over with?"

"Yes, sir. You'll feel the plane bank, you should have no difficulty with the door, remember to take off earphones and throat mike, and I'll signal go. Just tumble out. Rip cord, and down you go. Don't brace hard in landing—you could break or sprain something. Try to relax. It's a piece of cake."

"Very well done, Murphy."

"Sir, what should I tell them?"

"Tell them what happened. That's all. I'll happily be the villain. Once I potted the compass, it was either do as I say or head home. On top of that, I outrank you. They'll figure it out, and if they don't, then they're too damned stupid to worry about!"

"Yes, sir."

Basil felt the subtle, then stronger pull of gravity as Murphy pulled the stick back and the plane mounted toward heaven. He had to give more throttle, so the sound of the revs and the consequent vibrations through the plane's skeleton increased. Basil unhitched the door, pushed it out a bit, but then the prop wash caught it and slammed it back. He opened it a bit again, squirmed his way to the opening, scrunched to fit through, brought himself to the last point where he could be said to be inside the airplane, and waited.

Below, the blackness roared by, lit here and there by a light. It really made no difference where he jumped. It would be completely random. He might come down in a town square, a haystack, a cemetery, a barn roof, or an SS firing range. God would decide, not Basil.

Murphy raised his hand, and probably screamed "Tally-ho!"

Basil slipped off the earphones and mike and tumbled into the roaring darkness.

A FEW DAYS EARLIER (CONT'D.)

"Certainly," said Basil, "though I doubt I'll be allowed to make the trip. The path to Jesus would include sobriety, a clean mind, obedience to all commandments, a positive outlook, respect for elders, regular worship, and a high level of hygiene. I am happily guilty of none of those."

"The damned insouciance," said the army general. "Is everything an opportunity for irony, Captain?"

"I shall endeavor to control my ironic impulses, sir," said Basil.

"Actually, he's quite amusing," said the young civilian. "A heroic chap as imagined by Noël Coward."

"Coward's a poof, Professor."

"But a titanic wit."

"Gentlemen, gentlemen," said Sir Colin. "Please, let's stay with the objective here, no matter how Captain St. Florian's insouciance annoys or enchants us."

"Then, sir," said Basil, "the irony-free answer is no, I do not know the path to Jesus."

"I don't mean in general terms. I mean specifically *The Path to Jesus*, a pamphlet published in 1767 by a Scottish ecclesiastic named Thomas MacBurney. Actually he listed twelve steps on the way, and I believe you scored high on your account, Basil. You only left out thrift, daily prayer, cold baths, and regular enemas."

"What about wanking, sir? Is that allowed by the Reverend MacBurney?"

"I doubt he'd heard of it. Anyway, it is not the content of the reverend's pamphlet that here concerns us but the manuscript itself. That is the thing, the paper on which he wrote in ink, the actual physical object." He paused, taking a breath. "The piece began as a sermon, delivered to his congregation in that same year. It was quite successful—people talked much about it and requested that he deliver it over and over. He did, and became, one might say, an ecclesiastical celebrity. Then it occurred to him that he could spread the Word more effectively, and make a quid or two on the side—he was a Scot, after all—if he committed it to print and offered it for a shilling a throw. Thus he made a fair copy, which he delivered to a jobbing printer in Glasgow, and took copies around to all the churches and bookstores. Again, it was quite successful. It grew and grew and in the end he became rather prosperous, so much so that—this is my favorite part of the tale—he gave up the pulpit and retired to the country for a life of debauchery and gout, while continuing to turn out religious tracts when not abed with a local tart or two."

"I commend him," said Basil.

"As do we all," said the admiral.

"The fair copy, in his own hand, somehow came to rest in the rare books collection at the Cambridge Library. That is the one he copied himself from his own notes on the sermon, and which he hand-delivered to Carmichael & Sons, printers, of 14 Middlesex Lane, Glasgow, for careful reproduction on September 1, 1767. Mr. Carmichael's signature in receipt, plus instructions to his son, the actual printer, are inscribed in pencil across the title page. As it is the original, it is of course absurdly rare, which makes it absurdly valuable. Its homilies and simple faith have nothing to do with it, only its rarity, which is why the librarian at Cambridge treasures it so raptly. Are you with me, Basil?"

"With you, sir, but not with you. I cannot begin to fathom why this should interest the intelligence service, much less the tiny cog of it known as Basil St. Florian. Do you think exposure to it would improve my moral character? My character definitely needs moral improvement, but I should think any book of the New Testament would do the job as well as the Reverend MacBurney."

"Well, it happens to be the key to locating a traitor, Basil. Have you ever heard of the book code?"

THE SECOND DAY

There was a fallacy prevalent in England that Occupied France was a morose, death-haunted place. It was gray, gray as the German uniforms, and the conquerors goose-stepped about like Mongols, arbitrarily designating French citizens for execution by firing squad as it occurred to them for no reason save whimsy and boredom and Hun depravity. The screams of the tortured pierced the quiet, howling out of the many Gestapo torture cellars. The Horst Wessel song was piped everywhere; swastikas emblazoned on vast red banners fluttered brazenly everywhere. Meanwhile the peasants shuffled about all hangdog, the bourgeoisie were rigid with terror, the civic institutions were in paralysis, and even the streetwalkers had disappeared.

Basil knew this to be untrue. In fact, Occupied France was quite gay. The French barely noted their own conquest before returning to bustling business as usual, or not as usual, for the Germans were a vast new market. Fruit, vegetables, slabs of beef, and other provisions gleamed in every shop window, the wine was ample, even abundant (if overpriced), and the streetwalkers were quite active. Perhaps it would change later in the war, but for now it was rather a swell time. The Resistance, such as it was—and it wasn't much—was confined to marginal groups: students, Communists, bohemians, professors—people who would have been at odds with society in any event; they just got more credit for it now, all in exchange for blowing up a piddling bridge or dynamiting a rail line which would be repaired in a few hours. Happiness was general all over France.

The source of this gaiety was twofold. The first was the French insistence on being French, no matter how many panzers patrolled the streets and crossroads. Protected by their intensely high self-esteem, they thought naught of the Germans, regarding the *feldgrau* as a new class of tourist, to be fleeced, condescended to ("Red wine as an aperitif! *Mon Dieu!*"), and otherwise ignored. And there weren't nearly as many Nazi swastikas fluttering on silk banners as one might imagine.

The second reason was the immense happiness of the occupiers themselves. The Germans loved the cheese, the meals, the whores, the sights, and all the pleasures of France, it is true, but they enjoyed one thing more: that it was Not Russia.

This sense of Not-Russia made each day a joy. The fact that at any moment they could be sent to Is-Russia haunted them and drove them to new heights of sybaritic release. Each pleasure had a melancholy poignancy in that he who experienced it might shortly be slamming 8.8 cm shells into the breach of an antitank gun as fleets of T-34s poured torrentially out of the snow at them, this drama occurring at minus thirty-one degrees centigrade on the outskirts of a town with an unpronounceable name that they had never heard of and that offered no running water, pretty women, or decent alcohol.

So nobody in all of France in any of the German branches worked very hard, except perhaps the extremists of the SS. But most of the SS was somewhere else, happily murdering farmers in the hundreds of thousands, letting their fury, their rage, their misanthropy, their sense of racial superiority play out in real time.

Thus Basil didn't fear random interception as he walked the streets of downtown Bricquebec, a small city forty kilometers east of Cherbourg in the heart of the Cotentin Peninsula. The occupiers of this obscure spot would not be of the highest quality, and had adapted rather too quickly to the torpor of garrison life. They lounged this way and that, lazy as dogs in the spring sun, in the cafés, at their very occasional roadblocks, around city hall, where civil administrators now gave orders to the French bureaucrats, who had not made a single adjustment to their presence, and at an airfield where a flock of Me110 night fighters were housed, to intercept the nightly RAF bomber stream when it meandered toward targets in southern Germany. Though American bombers filled the sky by day, the two-engine 110s were not nimble enough to close with them and left that dangerous task to younger men in faster planes. The 110 pilots were content to maneuver close to the Lancasters, but not too close, to hosepipe their cannon shells all over the sky, then to return to schnapps and buns, claiming extravagant kill scores which nobody took seriously. So all in all, the atmosphere was one of snooze and snore.

Basil had landed without incident about eight kilometers outside of town. He was lucky, as he usually was, in that he didn't crash into a farmer's henhouse and awaken the rooster or the man but landed in one of the fields, among potato stubs just barely emerging from the ground. He had gathered up his 'chute, stripped off his RAF jumpsuit to reveal himself to be a rather shabby French businessman, and stuffed all that kit into some bushes (he could not bury it, because a] he did not feel like it and b] he had no shovel, but c] if he had had a shovel, he still would not have felt like it). He made it to a main road and walked into town, where he immediately treated himself to a breakfast of eggs and potatoes and tomatoes at a railway station café.

He nodded politely at each German he saw and so far had not excited any attention. His only concession to his trade was his Browning pistol, wedged into the small of his back and so flat it would not print under suit and overcoat. He also had his Riga Minox camera taped to his left ankle. His most profound piece of equipment, however, was his confidence. Going undercover is fraught with tension, but Basil had done it so often that its rigors didn't drive him to the edge of despair, eating his energy with teeth of dread. He'd simply shut down his imagination and considered himself the cock of the walk, presenting a smile, a nod, a wink to all.

But he was not without goal. Paris lay a half day's rail ride ahead; the next train left at four, and he had to be on it. But just as he didn't trust the partisans who still awaited his arrival 320 kilometers to the east, he didn't trust the documents the forgery geniuses at SOE had provided him with. Instead he preferred to pick up his own—that is, actual authentic docs, including travel permissions—and he now searched for a man who, in the terrible imagery of document photography, might be considered to look enough like him.

It was a pleasant day and he wandered this way and that, more or less sightseeing. At last he encountered a fellow who would pass for him, a well-dressed burgher in a black homburg and overcoat, dour and official-looking. But the bone structure was similar, given to prominent cheekbones and a nose that looked like a Norman axe. In fact the fellow could have been a long-lost cousin. (Had he cared to, Basil could have traced the St. Florian line back to a castle not 100 kilometers from where he stood now, whence came his Norman forebears in 1044— but of course it meant nothing to him).

Among Basil's skills was pickpocketing, very useful for a

spy or agent. He had mastered its intricacies during his period among Malaysian gunrunners in 1934, when a kindly old rogue with one eye and fast hands named Malong had taken a liking to him and shown him the basics of the trade. Malong could pick the fuzz off a peach, so educated were his fingers, and Basil proved an apt pupil. He'd never graduated to the peach-fuzz class, but the gentleman's wallet and document envelopes should prove easy enough.

He used the classic concealed hand dip and distraction technique, child's play but clearly effective out here in the French hinterlands. Shielding his left hand from view behind a copy of that day's *Le Monde*, he engineered an accidental street-corner bump, apologized, and then said, "I was looking at the air power of *les amis* today." He pointed upward, where a wave of B-17s painted a swath in the blue sky with their fuzzy white contrails as they sped toward Munich or some other Bavarian destination for an afternoon of destruction. "It seems they'll never stop building up their fleet. But when they win, what will they do with all those airplanes?"

The gentleman, unaware that the jostle and rhetoric concealed a deft snatch from inside not merely his overcoat but also his suit coat, followed his interrupter's pointed arm to the aerial array.

"The Americans are so rich, I believe our German visitors are doomed," said the man. "I only hope when it is time for them to leave they don't grow bitter and decide to blow things up."

"That is why it is up to us to ingratiate ourselves with them," said Basil, reading the eyes of an appeaser in his victim, "so that when they do abandon their vacation, they depart with a gentleman's deportment. *Vive la France*."

"Indeed," said the mark, issuing a dry little smile of approval, then turning away to his far more important business.

Basil headed two blocks in the opposite direction, two more in another, then rotated around to the train station. There, in the men's loo, he examined his trove: 175 francs, identity papers for one Jacques Piens, and a German travel authority "for official business only," both of which wore a smeary black-and-white photo of M. Piens, moustachioed and august and clearly annoyed at the indignity of posing for German photography.

He had a coffee. He waited, smiling at all, and a few minutes before four approached the ticket seller's window and, after establishing his bona fides as M. Piens, paid for and was issued a first-class ticket on the four p.m. Cherbourg–Paris run.

He went out on the platform, the only Frenchman among a small group of Luftwaffe enlisted personnel clearly headed to Paris for a weekend pass's worth of fun and frolic. The train arrived, as the Germans had been sensible enough not to interfere with the workings of the French railway system, the continent's best. Spewing smoke, the engine lugged its seven cars to the platform and, with great drama of steam, brakes, and steel, reluctantly halted. Basil knew where first class would be and parted company with the privates and corporals of the German air force, who squeezed into the other carriages.

His car half empty and comfortable, he put himself into a seat. The train sat…and sat…and sat. Finally a German policeman entered the car and examined the papers of all, including Basil, without incident. Yet still the train did not leave.

Hmm, this was troubling.

A lesser man might have fumbled into panic. The mark had noticed his papers missing, called the police, who had called the German police. Quickly enough they had put a hold on the train, fearing that the miscreant would attempt to flee that way, and now it was just a matter of waiting for an SS squad to lock up the last of the Jews before it came for him.

However, Basil had a sound operational principle which now served him well. *Most bad things don't happen.* What happens is that in its banal, boring way, reality bumbles along.

The worst thing one can do is panic. Panic betrays more agents than traitors. Panic is the true enemy.

At last the train began to move.

Ah-ha! Right again.

But at that moment the door flew open and a late-arriving Luftwaffe colonel came in. He looked straight at Basil.

"There he is! There's the spy!" he said.

A FEW DAYS EARLIER (CONT'D)

"A book code," said Basil. "I thought that was for Boy Scouts. Lord Baden-Powell would be so pleased."

"Actually," said Sir Colin, "it's a sturdy and almost impenetrable device, very useful under certain circumstances, if artfully employed. But Professor Turing is our expert on codes. Perhaps, Professor, you'd be able to enlighten Captain St. Florian."

"Indeed," said the young man in the tweeds, revealing himself by name. "Nowadays we think we're all scienced up. We even have machines to do some of the backbreaking mathematics to it, speeding the process. Sometimes it works, sometimes it doesn't. But the book code is ancient, even biblical, and that it has lasted so long is good proof of its applicability in certain instances."

"I understand, Professor. I am not a child."

"Not at all, certainly not given your record. But the basics must be known before we can advance to the sort of sophisticated mischief upon which the war may turn."

"Please proceed, Professor. Pay no attention to Captain St. Florian's abominable manners. We interrupted him at play in a bawdy house for this meeting and he is cranky."

"Yes, then. The book code stems from the presumption that both sender and receiver have access to the same book. It is therefore usually a common volume, shall we say Lamb's *Tales from Shakespeare*. I want to send you a message, say 'Meet me at two p.m. at the square.' I page through the book until I find the word 'meet.' It is on page 17, paragraph 4, line 2, fifth word.

So the first line in my code is 17-4-2-5. Unless you know the book, it is meaningless. But you, knowing the book, having the book, quickly find 17-4-2-5 and encounter the word 'meet.' And on and on. Of course variations can be worked—we can agree ahead of time, say, that for the last designation we will always be value minus two, that is, two integers less. So in that case the word 'meet' would actually be found at 17-4-2-3. Moreover, in picking a book as decoder, one would certainly be prone to pick a common book, one that should excite no excitement, that one might normally have about."

"I grasp it, Professor," said Basil. "But what, then, if I take your inference, is the point of choosing as a key book the Right Reverend MacBurney's *The Path to Jesus*, of which only one copy exists, and it is held under lock and key at Cambridge? And since last I heard, we still control Cambridge. Why don't we just go to Cambridge and look at the damned thing? You don't need an action-this-day chap like me for that. You could use a lance corporal."

"Indeed, you have tumbled to it," said Sir Colin. "Yes, we could obtain the book that way. However, in doing so we would inform both the sender and the receiver that we knew they were up to something, that they were control and agent and had an operation under way, when our goal is to break the code without them knowing. That is why, alas, a simple trip to the library by a lance corporal is not feasible."

"I hope I'm smart enough to stay up with all these wrinkles, gentlemen. I already have a headache."

"Welcome to the world of espionage," said Sir Colin. "We all have headaches. Professor, please continue."

"The volume in the library is indeed controlled by only one man," Turing said. "And he is the senior librarian of the institution. Alas, his loyalties are such that they are not, as one might hope and expect, for his own country. He is instead one of those of high caste taken by fascination for another creed, and it is to that creed he pays his deepest allegiance. He has made himself useful to his masters for many years as a 'talent spotter,' that is, a man who looks at promising undergraduates, picks those with keen policy minds and good connections, forecasts their rise, and woos them to his side as secret agents with all kinds of babble of the sort that appeals to the mushy romantic brain of the typical English high-class idiot. He thus plants the seeds of our destruction, sure to bloom a few decades down the line. He does other minor tasks too, running as a cutout, providing a safe house, disbursing a secret fund, and so forth. He is committed maximally and he will die before he betrays his creed, and some here have suggested a bullet in the brain as apposite, but actually, by the tortured rules of the game, a live spy in place is worth more than a dead spy in the ground. Thus he must not be disturbed, bothered, breathed heavily upon—he must be left entirely alone."

"And as a consequence you cannot under any circumstances access the book. You do not even know what it looks like?" Basil asked.

"We have a description from a volume published in 1932, called *Treasures of the Cambridge Library*."

"I can guess who wrote it," said Basil.

"Your guess would be correct," said Sir Colin. "It tells us little other than that it comprises thirty-four pages of foolscap written in tightly controlled nib by an accomplished freehand scrivener. Its eccentricity is that occasionally apostolic bliss came over the author and he decorated the odd margin with constellations of floating crosses, proclaiming his love of all things Christian. The Reverend MacBurney was clearly given to religious swoons."

"And the librarian is given to impenetrable security," said the admiral. "There will come a time when I will quite happily murder him with your cricket bat, Captain."

"Alas, I couldn't get the bloodstains out and left it in Malay. So let me sum up what I think I know so far. For some reason the Germans have a fellow in the Cambridge library controlling access to a certain 1767 volume. Presumably they have sent an agent to London with a coded message he himself does not know the answer to, possibly for security reasons. Once safely here, he will approach the bad-apple librarian and present him with the code. The bad apple will go to the manuscript, decipher it, and give a response to the Nazi spy. I suppose it's operationally sound. It neatly avoids radio, as you say it cannot be breached without giving notice that the ring itself is under high suspicion, and once armed with the message, the operational spy can proceed with his mission. Is that about it?"

"Almost," said Sir Colin. "In principle, yes, you have the gist of it—manfully done. However, you haven't got the players quite right."

"Are we then at war with someone I don't know about?" said Basil.

"Indeed and unfortunately. Yes. The Soviet Union. This whole thing is Russian, not German."

THE SECOND DAY (CONT'D.)

If panic flashed through Basil's mind, he did not yield to it, although his heart hammered against his chest as if a spike of hard German steel had been pounded into it. He thought of his L-pill, but it was buried in his breast pocket. He thought next of his pistol: Could he get it out in time to bring a few of them down before turning it on himself? Could he at least kill this leering German idiot who...but then he noted that the characterization had been delivered almost merrily.

"You must be a spy," said the colonel, laughing heartily, sitting next to him. "Why else would you shave your moustache but to go on some glamorous underground mission?"

Basil laughed, perhaps too loudly, but in his chest his heart still ran wild. He hid his blast of fear in the heartiness of the fraudulent laugh and came back with an equally jocular, "Oh, that? It seems in winter my wife's skin turns dry and very sensitive, so I always shave it off for a few months to give the beauty a rest from the bristles."

"It makes you look younger."

"Why, thank you."

"Actually, I'm so glad to have discovered you. At first I thought it was not you, but then I thought, Gunther, Gunther, who would kidnap the owner of the town's only hotel and replace him with a double? The English are not so clever."

"The only thing they're any good at," said Basil, "is weaving tweed. English tweed is the finest in the world. "

"I agree, I agree," said the colonel. "Before all this, I traveled there quite frequently. Business, you know."

It developed that the colonel, a Great War aviator, had represented a Berlin-based hair tonic firm whose directors had visions, at least until 1933, of entering the English market. The colonel had made trips to London in hopes of interesting some of the big department stores in carrying a line of lanolin-based hair creams for men, but was horrified to learn that the market was controlled by the British company that manufactured Brylcreem and would use its considerable clout to keep the Germans out.

"Can you imagine," said the colonel, "that in the twenties there was a great battle between Germany and Great Britain for the market advantage of lubricating the hair of the British gentleman? I believe our product was much finer than that English goop, as it had no alcohol and alcohol dries the hair stalk, robbing it of luster, but I have to say that the British packaging carried the day, no matter. We could never find the packaging to catch the imagination of the British gentleman, to say nothing of a slogan. German as a language does not lend itself to slogans. Our attempts at slogans were ludicrous. We are too serious, and our language is like potatoes in gravy. It has no lightness in it at all. The best we could come up with was, 'Our tonic is very good.' Thus we give the world Nietzsche and not Wodehouse. In any event, when Hitler came to power and the air forces were reinvigorated, it was out of the hair oil business and back to the cockpit."

It turned out that the colonel was a born talker. He was on his way to Paris on a three-day leave to meet his wife for a "well-deserved, if I do say so myself" holiday. He had reservations at the Ritz and at several four-star restaurants.

Basil put it together quickly: the man he'd stolen his papers from was some sort of collaborationist big shot and had made it his business to suck up to all the higher German officers, presumably seeing the financial opportunities of being in league with the occupiers. It turned out further that this German fool was soft and supple when it came to sycophancy and he'd mistaken the Frenchman's oleaginous demeanor with actual affection, and he thought it quite keen to have made a real friend among the wellborn French. So Basil committed himself to six hours of chitchat with the idiot, telling himself to keep autobiographical details at a minimum in case the real chap had already spilled some and he should contradict something previously established.

That turned out to be no difficulty at all, for the German colonel revealed himself to have an awesomely enlarged ego, which he expressed through an autobiographical impulse, so he virtually told his life story to Basil over the long drag, gossiping about the greed of Göring and the reluctance of the night fighters to close with the Lancasters, Hitler's insanity in attacking Russia, how much he, the colonel, missed his wife, how he worried about his son, a Stuka pilot, and how sad he was that it had come to pass that civilized Europeans were at each other's throats again, and on and on and on and on, but at least the Jews would be dealt with once and for all, no matter who won in the end. He titillated Basil with inside information on his base and the wing he commanded, Nachtjagdgeschwader-9, and the constant levies for Russia that had stripped it of logistics, communications, and security people, until nothing was left but a skeleton staff of air crew and mechanics, yet still they were under pressure from Luftwaffe command to bring down yet more Tommies to relieve the night bombing of Berlin. Damn the Tommies and their brutal methods of war! The man considered himself fascinating, and his presence seemed to ward off the attention of the other German officers who came and went on the trip to the Great City. It seemed so damned civilized that you almost forgot there was a war on.

It turned out that one of the few buildings in Paris with an actual Nazi banner hanging in front of it was a former insurance company's headquarters at 14 rue Guy de Maupassant in the sixth arrondissement. However, the banner wasn't much, really just an elongated flag that hung limply off a pole on the fifth floor. None of the new occupants of the building paid much attention to it. It was the official headquarters of the Paris district of the Abwehr, German military intelligence, ably run from Berlin by Admiral Canaris and beginning to acquire a reputation for not being all that crazy about Herr Hitler.

They were mostly just cops. And they brought cop attributes to their new headquarters: dyspepsia, too much smoking, cheap suits, fallen arches, and a deep cynicism about everything, but particularly about human nature and even more particularly about notions of honor, justice, and duty. They did believe passionately in one cause, however: staying out of Russia.

"Now let us see if we have anything," said Hauptmann Dieter Macht, chief of Section III-B (counterintelligence), Paris office, at his daily staff meeting at three p.m., as he gently spread butter on a croissant. He loved croissants. There was something so exquisite about the balance of elements—the delicacy of the crust, which gave way to a kind of chewy substrata as you peeled it away, the flakiness, the sweetness of the inner bread, the whole thing a majestic creation that no German baker, ham-thumbed and frosting-crazed, could ever match.

"Hmmm," he said, sifting through the various reports that had come in from across the country. About fifteen men, all ex-detectives like himself, all in droopy plain clothes like himself, all with uncleaned Walthers holstered sloppily on their hips, awaited his verdict. He'd been a Great War aviator, an actual ace in fact, then the star of Hamburg Homicide before this war, and had a reputation for sharpness when it came to seeing patterns in seemingly unrelated events. Most of III-B's arrests came from clever deductions made by Hauptmann Macht.

"Now this is interesting. What do you fellows make of this one? It seems in Sur-la-Gane, about forty kilometers east of here, a certain man known to be connected to inner circles of the Maquis was spotted returning home early in the morning by himself. Yet there has been no Maquis activity in that area since we arrested Pierre Doumaine last fall and sent him off to Dachau."

"Perhaps," said Leutnant Abel, his second-in-command, "he was at a meeting and they are becoming active again. Netting a big fish only tears them down for a bit of time, you know."

"They'd hold such a meeting earlier. The French like their sleep. They almost slept through 1940, after all. What one mission gets a Maquis up at night? Anyone?"

No one.

"British agent insertion. They love to cooperate with the Brits because the Brits give them so much equipment, which can either be sold on the black market or be used against their domestic enemies after the war. So they will always jump lively for the SOE, because the loot is too good to turn down. And such insertions will be late-night or early-morning jobs."

"But," said Leutnant Abel, "I have gone through the reports too, and there are no accounts of aviation activities in that area that night. When the British land men in Lysanders, some farmer always calls the nearby police station to complain about low-flying aviators in the dark of night, frightening the cows. You never want to frighten a peasant's cows; he'll be your enemy for life. Believe me, Hauptmann Macht, had a Lysander landed, we'd know from the complaints."

"Exactly," said Macht. "So perhaps our British visitor didn't arrive for some reason or other and disappointed the Sur-la-Gane Resistance cell, who got no loot that night. But if I'm not mistaken, that same night complaints did come in from peasants near Bricquebec, outside Cherbourg."

"We have a night fighter base there," said Abel. "Airplanes come and go all night—it's meaningless."

"There were no raids that night," said Macht. "The bomber stream went north, to Prussia, not to Bavaria."

"What do you see as significant about that?"

"Suppose for some reason our fellow didn't trust the Sur-la-Gane bunch, or the Resistance either. It's pretty well penetrated, after all. So he directs his pilot to put him somewhere else."

"They can't put Lysanders down just anywhere," said another man. "It has to be set up, planned, torches lit. That's why it's so vulnerable to our investigations. So many people—someone always talks, maybe not to us, but to someone, and it always gets to us."

"The Bricquebec incident described a roar, not a put-put or a dying fart. The roar would be a Lysander climbing to parachute altitude. They normally fly at 500, and any agent who made an exit that low would surely scramble his brains and his bones. So the plane climbs, this fellow bails out, and now he's here."

"Why would he take the chance on a night drop into enemy territory? He could come down in the Gestapo's front yard. Hauptsturmführer Boch would enjoy that very much."

Actually the Abwehr detectives hated Boch more than the French and English combined. He could send them to Russia.

"I throw it back to you, Walter. Stretch that brain of yours beyond the lazy parameters it now sleepily occupies and come up with a theory."

"All right, sir, I'll pretend to be insane, like you. I'll postulate that this phantom Brit agent is very crafty, very old school, clever as they come. He doesn't trust the Maquis, nor should he. He knows we eventually hear everything. Thus he improvises. It's just his bad luck that his airplane awakened some cows near Bricquebec, the peasants complained, and so exactly what he did not want us to know is exactly what we do know. Is that insane enough for you, sir?"

Macht and Abel were continually taking shots at each other, and in fact they didn't like each other very much. Macht was always worried about Is-Russia as opposed to Not-Russia, while the younger Abel had family connections that would keep him far from Stalin's millions of tanks and Mongols and all that horrible snow.

"Very good," said Macht. "That's how I read it. You know when these boys arrive they stir up a lot of trouble. If we don't stop them, maybe we end up on an antitank gun in Russia. Is anyone here interested in that sort of a job change?"

That certainly shut everyone up fast. It frightened Macht even to say such a thing.

"I will make some phone calls," Abel said. "See if there's anything unusual going on."

It didn't take him long. At the Bricquebec prefecture, a policeman read him the day's incident report, from which he learned that a prominent collaborationist businessman had claimed that his papers were stolen from him. He had been arrested selling black-market petrol and couldn't identify himself. He was roughly treated until his identity was proven, and he swore he would complain to Berlin, as he was a supporter of the Reich and demanded more respect from the occupiers.

His name, Abel learned, was Piens.

"Hmmm," said Macht, a logical sort. "If the agent was originally going to Sur-la-Gane, it seems clear that his ultimate destination would be Paris. There's really not much for him to do in Bricquebec or Sur-la-Gane, for that matter. Now, how would he get here?"

"Clearly, the railway is the only way."

"Exactly," said Hauptmann Macht. "What time does the train from Cherbourg get in? We should meet it and see if anyone is traveling under papers belonging to M. Piens. I'm sure he'd want them returned."

A FEW DAYS EARLIER (CONT'D.)

"Have I been misinformed?" asked Basil. "Are we at war with the Russians? I thought they were our friends."

"I wish it were as easy as that," said Sir Colin. "But it never is. Yes, in one sense we are at war with Germany and at peace with Russia. On the other hand, this fellow Stalin is a cunning old brute, stinking of bloody murder to high heaven, and thus he presumes that all are replicas of himself, equally cynical and vicious. So while we are friends with him at a certain level, he still spies on us at another level. And because we know him to be a monster, we still spy on him. It's all different compartments. Sometimes it's damned hard to keep straight, but there's one thing all the people in this room agree on: the moment the rope snaps hard about Herr Hitler's chicken neck, the next war begins, and it is between we of the West and they of the East."

"Rather dispiriting," said Basil. "One would have thought one had accomplished something other than clearing the stage for the next war."

"So it goes, alas and alack, in our sad world. But Basil, I think you will be satisfied to know that the end game of this little adventure we are preparing for you is actually to help the Russians, not to hurt them. It benefits ourselves, of course, no doubt about it. But we need to help them see a certain truth that they are reluctant, based on Stalin's various neuroses and paranoias, to believe."

"You see," said the general, "he would trust us a great deal more if we opened a second front. He doesn't think much of our business in North Africa, where our losses are about one-fiftieth of his. He wants our boys slaughtered on the French beaches in numbers that approach the slaughter of his boys. Then he'll know we're serious about this Allies business. But a second front in Europe is a long way off, perhaps two years. A lot of American men and matériel have to land here before then.

In the meantime we grope and shuffle and misunderstand and misinterpret. That's where you'll fit in, we hope. Your job, as you will learn at the conclusion of this dreadful meeting about two days from now, is to shine light and dismiss groping and shuffling and misinterpretation."

"I hope I can be of help," said Basil. "However, my specialty is blowing things up."

"You have nothing to blow up this time out," said Sir Colin. "You are merely helping us explain something."

"But I must ask, since you're permitting me unlimited questions, how do you know all this?" said Basil. "You say Stalin is so paranoid and unstable he does not trust us and even spies upon us, you know this spy exists and is well placed, and that his identity, I presume, has been sent by this absurd book-code method, yet that is exactly where your knowledge stops. I am baffled beyond any telling of it. You know so much, and then it stops cold. It seems to me that you would be more likely to know all or nothing. My head aches profoundly. This business is damned confounding."

"All right, then, we'll tell you. I think you have a right to know, since you are the one we are proposing to send out. Admiral, as it was your service triumph, I leave it to you."

"Thank you, Sir Colin," said the admiral. "In your very busy year of 1940, you probably did not even notice one of the world's lesser wars. I mean there was our war with the Germans in Europe and all that blitzkrieg business, the Japanese war with the Chinese, Mussolini in Ethiopia, and I am probably leaving several out. 1940 was a very good year for war. However, if you check the back pages of the *Times*, you'll discover that in November of 1939, the Soviet Union invaded Finland. The border between them has been in dispute since 1917. The Russians expected an easy time of it, mustering ten times the number of soldiers as did the Finns, but the Finns taught them some extremely hard lessons about winter warfare, and by early 1940 the piles of frozen dead had gotten immense. The war raged for four long months, killing thousands over a few miles of frozen tundra, and ultimately, because lives mean nothing to Communists, the Russians prevailed, at least to the extent of forcing a peace on favorable terms."

"I believe I heard a bit of it."

"Excellent. What you did not hear, as nobody did, was that in a Red Army bunker taken at high cost by the Finns, a half-burned codebook was found. Now since we in the West abandoned the Finns, they were sponsored and supplied in the war by the Third Reich. If you see any photos from the war, you'll think they came out of Stalingrad, because the Finns bought their helmets from the Germans. Thus one would expect that such a high-value intelligence treasure as a codebook, even half burned, would shortly end up in German hands.

"However, we had a very good man in Finland, and he managed somehow to take possession of it. The Russians thought it was burned. The Germans never knew it existed. Half a code is actually not merely better than nothing, it is *far* better than nothing, and is in fact almost a whole codebook, because a clever boots like young Professor Turing here can tease most messages into comprehension."

"I had nothing to do with it," said the professor. "There were very able men at Bletchley Park before I came aboard."

What, wondered Basil, *would Bletchley Park be?*

"Thus we have been able to read and mostly understand Soviet low- to midlevel codes since 1940. That's how we knew about the librarian at Cambridge and several other sticky lads who, though they speak high Anglican and know where their pinkie goes on the teacup, want to see our Blighty go all red and men like us stood up to the wall and shot for crimes against the working class."

"That would certainly ruin my crease. Anyhow, before we go much further, may I sum up?" said Basil.

"If you can."

"By breaking the Russian crypto, you know that a highly

secure, carefully guarded book code has been given to a forthcoming Russian spy. It contains the name of a highly important British traitor somewhere in government service. When he gets here, he will take the code to the Cambridge librarian, present his bona fides, and the librarian will retrieve the Reverend Thomas MacBurney's *Path to Jesus*—wait. How would the Russians themselves have…Oh, now I see, it all hangs together. It would be easy for the librarian, not like us, to make a photographed copy of the book and have it sent to the Russian service."

"NKVD, it is called."

"I think I knew that. Thus the librarian quickly unbuttons the name and gives it to the new agent, and the agent contacts him at perhaps this mysterious Bletchley Park that the professor wasn't supposed to let slip—"

"That was a mistake, Professor," said Sir Colin. "No milk and cookies for you tonight."

"So somehow I'm supposed to, I don't know what, do something somewhere, a nasty surprise indeed, but it will enable you to identify the spy at Bletchley Park."

"Indeed, you have the gist of it."

"And you will then arrest him."

"No, of course not. In fact, we shall promote him."

THE SECOND DAY / THE THIRD DAY

It was a pity the trip to Paris lasted only six hours with all the local stops, as the colonel had just reached the year 1914 in his life. It was incredibly fascinating. Mutter did not want him to attend flying school, but he was transfixed by the image of those tiny machines in their looping and spinning and diving that he had seen—and described in detail to Basil—in Mühlenberg in 1912, and he was insistent upon becoming an aviator.

This was more torture than Basil could have imagined in the

cellars of the Gestapo, but at last the conductor came through, shouting, "Paris, Montparnasse station, five minutes, end of the line."

"Oh, this has been such a delight," said the colonel. "Monsieur Piens, you are a fascinating conversationalist—"

Basil had said perhaps five words in six hours.

"—and it makes me happy to have a Frenchman as an actual friend, beyond all this messy stuff of politics and invasions and war and all that. If only more Germans and French could meet as we did, as friends, just think how much better off the world would be."

Basil came up with words six and seven: "Yes, indeed."

"But, as they say, all good things must come to an end."

"They must. Do you mind, Colonel, if I excuse myself for a bit? I need to use the loo and prefer the first class here to the *pissoirs* of the station."

"Understandable. In fact, I shall accompany you, *monsieur,* and—oh, perhaps not. I'll check my documents to make sure all is in order."

Thus, besides a blast of blessed silence, Basil earned himself some freedom to operate. During the colonel's recitation—it had come around to the years 1911 and 1912, vacation to Cap d'Antibes—it had occurred to him that the authentic M. Piens, being a clear collaborationist and seeking not to offend the Germans, might well have reported his documents lost and that word might, given the German expertise at counterintelligence, have reached Paris. Thus the Piens documents were suddenly explosive and would land him either in Dachau or before the wall.

He wobbled wretchedly up the length of the car—thank God here in first class the seats were not contained as in the cramped little compartments of second class!—and made his way to the loo. As he went he examined the prospective marks: mostly German officers off for a weekend of debauchery far from their garrison posts, but at least three French businessmen of proper decorum sat among them, stiff, frightened of the Germans and yet obligated by something or other to be there. Only one was anywhere near Basil's age, but he had to deal with things as they were.

He reached the loo, locked himself inside, and quickly removed his M. Piens documents and buried them in the wastebasket among repugnant wads of tissue. A more cautious course would have been to tear them up and dispose of them via the toilet, but he didn't have time for caution. Then he wet his face, ran his fingers through his hair, wiped his face off, and left the loo.

Fourth on the right. Man in suit, rather blasé face, impatient. Otherwise, the car was stirring to activity as the occupants set about readying for whatever security ordeal lay ahead. The war—it was such an inconvenience.

As he worked his way down the aisle, Basil pretended to find the footing awkward against the sway of the train on the tracks, twice almost stumbling. Then he reached the fourth seat on the right, willed his knees to buckle, and, with a squeal of panic, let himself tumble awkwardly, catching himself with his left hand upon the shoulder of the man beneath, yet still tumbling further, awkwardly, the whole thing seemingly an accident as one out-of-control body crashed into the other, in-control body.

"Oh, excuse me," he said, "excuse, excuse, I am so sorry!"

The other man was so annoyed that he didn't notice the deft stab by which Basil penetrated his jacket and plucked his documents free, especially since the pressure on his left shoulder was so aggressive that it precluded notice of the far subtler stratagem of the pick reaching the brain.

Basil righted himself.

"So sorry, so sorry!"

"Bah, you should be more careful," said the mark.

"I will try, sir," said Basil, turning to see the colonel three feet from him in the aisle, having witnessed the whole drama from an advantageous position.

*

Macht requested a squad of *feldpolizei* as backup, set up a choke point at the gate from the platform into the station's vast, domed central space, and waited for the train to rumble into sight. Instead, alas, what rumbled into sight was his nemesis, SS Hauptsturmführer Boch, a toadlike Nazi true believer of preening ambition who went everywhere in his black dress uniform.

"Dammit again, Macht," he exploded, spewing his excited saliva everywhere. "You know by protocol you must inform me of any arrest activities."

"Herr Hauptsturmführer, if you check your orderly's message basket, you will learn that at ten-thirty p.m. I called and left notification of possible arrest. I cannot be responsible for your orderly's efficiency in relaying that information to you."

"Calculated to miss me, because of course I was doing my duty supervising an *aktion* against Jews and not sitting around my office drinking coffee and smoking."

"Again, I cannot be responsible for your schedule, Herr Hauptsturmführer." Of course Macht had an informer in Boch's office, so he knew exactly where the SS man was at all times. He knew that Boch was on one of his Jew-hunting trips; his only miscalculation was that Boch, who was generally unsuccessful at such enterprises, had gotten back earlier than anticipated. And of course Boch was always unsuccessful because Macht always informed the Jews of the coming raid.

"Whatever, it is of no consequence," said Boch. Though both men were technically of the same rank, captains, the SS clearly enjoyed Der Führer's confidence while the Abwehr did not, and so its members presumed authority in any encounter. "Brief me, please, and I will take charge of the situation."

"My men are in place, and disturbing my setup would not be efficient. If an arrest is made, I will certainly give the SS credit for its participation."

"What are we doing here?"

"There was aviation activity near Bricquebec, outside Cherbourg. Single-engine monoplane suddenly veering to parachute altitude. It suggested a British agent visit. Then the documents of a man in Bricquebec, including travel authorization, were stolen. If a British agent were in Bricquebec, his obvious goal would be Paris, and the most direct method would be by rail, so we are intercepting the Cherbourg–Paris night train in hopes of arresting a man bearing the papers of one Auguste M. Piens, restaurateur, hotel owner, and well-known ally of the Reich, here in Paris."

"An English agent!" Boch's eyes lit up. This was treasure. This was a medal. This was a promotion. He saw himself now as Obersturmbannführer Boch. The little fatty all the muscular boys had called Gretel and whose underdrawers they tied in knots, an Obersturmbannführer! That would show them!

"If an apprehension is made, the prisoner is to be turned over to the SS for interrogation. I will go to Berlin if I have to on this one, Macht. If you stand in the way of SS imperatives, you know the consequences."

The consequence: *"Russian tanks at 300! Load shells. Prepare to fire."*

"Sir, I can't see them. The snow is blinding, my fingers are numb from the cold, and the sight is frozen!"

Even though he had witnessed the brazen theft, the colonel said nothing and responded in no way. His mind was evidently so locked in the beautiful year 1912 and the enchantment of his eventual first solo flight that he was incapable of processing new information. The crime he had just seen had nothing whatsoever to do with the wonderful French friend who had been so fascinated by his tale and whose eyes radiated such utter respect, even hero worship; it could not be fitted into any pattern and was thus temporarily disregarded for other pleasures, such as, still ahead, a narration of the colonel's adventures in the Great War, the time he had actually shaken hands with the great Richthofen, and his own flight-ending crash—left arm permanently disabled. Luckily, his tail in tatters, he had made it back to his own lines before going down hard early in '18. It was one of his favorite stories.

He simply nodded politely at the Frenchman, who nodded back as if he hadn't a care in the world.

In time the train pulled into the station, issuing groans and hisses of steam, vibrating heavily as it rolled to a stop.

"Ah, Paris," said the colonel. "Between you and me, M. Piens, I so prefer it to Berlin. And so especially does my wife. She is looking forward to this little weekend jaunt."

They disembarked in orderly fashion, Germans and Frenchmen combined, but discovered on the platform that some kind of security problem lay ahead, at the gate into the station, as soldiers and SS men with machine pistols stood along the platform, smoking but eyeing the passengers carefully. Then the security people screamed out that Germans would go to the left, French to the right, and on the right a few dour-looking men in fedoras and lumpy raincoats examined identification papers and travel authorizations. The Germans merely had to flash leave papers, so that line moved much more quickly.

"Well, M. Piens, I leave you here. Good luck with your sister's health in Paris. I hope she recovers."

"I'm sure she will, Colonel."

"*Adieu.*"

He sped ahead and disappeared through the doors into the vast space. Basil's line inched its way ahead, and though the line was shorter, each arrival at the security point was treated with thorough Germanic ceremony, the papers examined carefully, the comparisons to the photographs made slowly, any bags or luggage searched. It seemed to take forever.

What could he do? At this point it would be impossible to slip away, disappear down the tracks, and get to the city over a fence; the Germans had thrown too many security troops around for that. Nor could he hope to roll under the train; the platform was too close to it, and there was no room to squeeze through.

Basil saw an evil finish: they'd see by the document that his face did not resemble the photograph, ask him a question or two, and learn that he had not even seen the document and had no idea whose papers he carried. The body search would come next, the pistol and the camera would give him away, and it was off to the torture cellar. The L-pill was his only alternative, but could he get to it fast enough?

At the same time, the narrowing of prospects was in some way a relief. No decisions needed to be made. All he had to do was brazen it out with a haughty attitude, beaming confidence, and it would be all right.

Macht watched the line while Abel examined papers and checked faces. Boch meanwhile provided theatrical atmosphere by posing heroically in his black leather trench coat, the SS skull on his black cap catching the light and reflecting impulses of power and control from above his chubby little face.

Eight. Seven. Six. Five.

Finally before them was a well-built chap of light complexion who seemed like some sort of athlete. He could not be a secret agent because he was too charismatic. All eyes would always turn to him, and he seemed accustomed to attention. He could be English, indeed, because he was a sort called "ginger." But the French had a considerable amount of genetic material for the hue as well, so the hair and the piercing eyes communicated less than the Aryan stereotypes seemed to proclaim.

"Good evening, M. Vercois," said Abel in French as he looked at the papers and then at the face, "and what brings you to Paris?"

"A woman, Herr Leutnant. An old story. No surprises."

"May I ask why you are not in a prisoner-of-war camp? You seem military."

"Sir, I am a contractor. My firm, M. Vercois et Fils—I am the son, by the way—has contracted to do much cement work on the coastline. We are building an impregnable wall for the Reich."

"Yes, yes," said Abel in a policeman's tired voice, indicating that he had heard all the French collaborationist sucking-up he needed to for the day. "Now do you mind, please, turning to the left so that I can get a good profile view. I must say, this is a terrible photograph of you."

"I take a bad photograph, sir. I have this trouble frequently, but if you hold the light above the photo, it will resolve itself. The photographer made too much of my nose."

Abel checked.

It still did not quite make sense.

He turned to Macht.

"See if this photo matches, Herr Hauptmann. Maybe it's the light, but—"

At that moment, from the line two places behind M. Vercois, a man suddenly broke and ran crazily down the platform.

"That's him!" screamed Boch. "Stop that man, goddammit, stop that man!"

The drama played out quickly. The man ran and the Germans were disciplined enough not to shoot him, but instead, like football athletes, moved to block him. He tried to break this way, then that, but soon a younger, stronger, faster Untersharführer had him, another reached the melee and tangled him up from behind, and then two more, and the whole scrum went down in a blizzard of arms and legs.

"Someone stole my papers!" the man cried. "My papers are missing, I am innocent. Heil Hitler. I am innocent. Someone stole my papers."

"Got him," screamed Boch. "Got him!" and ran quickly to the melee to take command of the British agent.

"Go on," said Abel to M. Vercois as he and Macht went themselves to the incident.

His face blank, Basil entered the main station as whistles sounded and security troops from everywhere ran to Gate No. 4, from which he had just emerged. No one paid him any attention as he turned sideways to let the heavily armed Germans swarm past him. In the distance German sirens sounded, that strange two-note *caw-CAW* that sounded like a crippled crow, as yet more troops poured to the site.

Basil knew he didn't have much time. Someone smart among the Germans would understand quickly enough what had happened and would order a quick search of the train, where the M. Piens documents would be found in the first-class loo, and they'd know what had transpired. Then they'd throw a cordon around the station, call in more troops, and do a very careful examination of the horde, person by person, looking for a man with the papers of poor M. Vercois, currently undergoing interrogation by SS boot.

He walked swiftly to the front door, though the going was tough. Too late. Already the *feldpolizei* had commanded the cabs to leave and had halted buses. More German troops poured from trucks to seal off the area; more German staff cars arrived. The stairs to the Métro were all blocked by armed men.

He turned as if to walk back, meanwhile hunting for other ways out.

"Monsieur Piens, Monsieur Piens," came a call. He turned and saw the Luftwaffe colonel waving at him.

"Come along, I'll drop you. No need to get hung up in this unfortunate incident."

He ran to and entered the cab, knowing full well that his price of survival would be a trip back to the years 1912 through 1918. It almost wasn't worth it.

A FEW DAYS EARLIER (CONT'D.)

"Promote him!" said Basil. "The games you play. I swear I cannot keep up with them. The man's a traitor. He should be arrested and shot."

But his anguish moved no one on the panel that sat before him in the prime minister's murky staff room.

"Basil, so it should be with men of action, but you posit a world where things are clear and simple," said Sir Colin. "Such a planet does not exist. On this one, the real one, direct action is almost always impossible. Thus one must move on the oblique, making concessions and allowances all the way, never giving up too much for too little, tracking reverberations and rebounds, keeping the upper lip as stiff as if embalmed in concrete. Thus we leave small creatures such as our wretch of a Cambridge librarian alone in hopes of influencing someone vastly more powerful. Professor, perhaps you could put Basil in the picture so he understands what it is we are trying to do, and why it is so bloody important."

"It's called Operation Citadel," said Professor Turing. "The German staff has been working on it for some time now. Even though we would like to think that the mess they engineered on themselves at Stalingrad ended it for them, that is mere wishful dreaming. They are wounded but still immensely powerful."

"Professor, you speak as if you had a seat in the OKW general officers' mess."

"In a sense he does. The professor mentioned the little machines he builds, how they are able to try millions of possibilities and come up with solutions to the German code combinations and produce reasonable decryptions. Thus we have indeed been able to read Jerry's mail. Frankly, I know far more about German plans than about what is happening two doors down in my own agency, what the Americans are doing, or who the Russians have sent to Cambridge. But it's a gift that must be used sagely. If it's used sloppily, it will give up the game and Jerry will change everything. So we just use a bit of it now and then. This is one of those nows or thens. Go on, Professor."

"I defer to a strategic authority."

"General Cavendish?"

Cavendish, the army general, had a face that showed emotions from A all the way to A–. It was a mask of meat shaped in an oval and built bluntly around two ball bearings, empty of light, wisdom, empathy, or kindness, registering only force. He had about a pound of nose in the center of it and a pound of medals on his tunic.

"Operation Citadel," he delivered as rote fact, not interpretation, "is envisioned as the Götterdämmarung of the war in the East, the last titanic breakthrough that will destroy the Russian war-making effort and bring the Soviets to the German table, hats in hand. At the very least, if it's successful, as most think it will be, it'll prolong the war by another year or two. We had hoped to see the fighting stop in 1945; now it may last well into 1947, and many more millions of men may die, and I should point out that a good number of those additional millions will be German. So we are trying to win—yes, indeed— but we are trying to do so swiftly, so that the dying can stop. That is what is at stake, you see."

"And that is why you cannot crush this little Cambridge rat's ass under a lorry. All right, I see that, I suppose, annoyed at it though I remain."

"Citadel, slated for May, probably cannot happen until July or August, given the logistics. It is to take place in southwest Russia, several hundred miles to the west of Stalingrad. At that point, around a city called Kursk, the Russians find themselves with a bulge in their lines—a salient, if you will. Secretly the Germans have begun massing matériel both above and beneath the bulge. When they believe they have overwhelming superiority, they will strike. They will drive north from below and south from above, behind walls of Tigers, flocks of Stukas, and thousands of artillery pieces. The infantry will advance behind the tanks. When the encirclement is complete, they will turn and kill the 300,000 men in the center and destroy the 50,000 tanks. The morale of the Red Army will be shattered, the losses so overwhelming that all the American aid in the world cannot keep up with it, and the Russians will fall back, back, back to the Urals. Leningrad will fall, then Moscow. The war will go on and on and on."

"I'm no genius," said Basil, "but even I can figure it out. You must tell Stalin. Tell him to fortify and resupply that bulge. Then when the Germans attack, they will fail, and it is they who will be on the run, the war will end in 1945, and those millions of lives will have been saved. Plus I can then drink myself to death uninterrupted, as I desire."

"Again, sir," said the admiral, who was turning out to be Basil's most ardent admirer, "he has seen the gist of it straight through."

"There is only one thing, Basil," said Sir Colin. "We have told Stalin. He doesn't believe us."

THE THIRD DAY

"Jasta 3 at Vraignes. Late 1916," said Macht. "Albatros, a barge to fly."

"He was an ace," said Abel. "Drop a hat and he'll tell you about it."

"Old comrade," said Oberst Gunther Scholl, "yes. I was Jasta 7 at Roulers. That was in 1917. God, so long ago."

"Old chaps," said Abel, "now the nostalgia is finished, so perhaps we can get on with our real task, which is staying out of Russia."

"Walter will never go to Russia," said Macht. "Family connections. He'll stay in Paris, and when the Americans come, he'll join up with them. He'll finish the war a lieutenant-colonel in the American army. But he does have a point."

"Didi, that's the first compliment you ever gave me. If only you meant it, but one can't have everything."

"So let's go through this again, Herr Oberst," said Macht to Colonel Scholl. "Walter reminds us that there's a very annoyed SS officer stomping around out there and he would like to send you to the Russian front. He would also like to send all of us to the Russian front, except Walter. So it is now imperative that we catch the fellow you sat next to for six hours, and you must do better at remembering."

The hour was late, or early, depending. Oberst Scholl had imagined himself dancing the night away at Maxim's with Hilda, then retiring to a dawn of love at the Ritz. Instead he was in a dingy room on the rue Guy de Maupassant, being grilled by gumshoes from the slums of Germany in an atmosphere seething with desperation, sour smoke, and cold coffee.

"Hauptmann Macht, believe me, I wish to avoid the Russian front at all costs. Bricquebec is no prize, and command of a night fighter squadron does not suggest, I realize, that I am expected to do big things in the Luftwaffe. But I am happy to fight my war there and surrender when the Americans arrive. I have told you everything."

"This I do not understand," said Leutnant Abel. "You had previously met Monsieur Piens and you thought this fellow was he. Yet the photography shows a face quite different from the one I saw at the Montparnasse station."

"Still, they are close," explained the colonel somewhat testily. "I had met Piens at a reception put together by the Vichy mayor of Bricquebec, between senior German officers and prominent, sympathetic businessmen. This fellow owned two restaurants and a hotel, was a power behind the throne, so to speak, and we had a brief but pleasant conversation. I cannot say I memorized his face, as why would I? When I got to the station, I glanced at the registration of French travelers and saw Piens's name and thus looked for him. I suppose I could say it was my duty to amuse our French sympathizers, but the truth is, I thought I could charm my way into a significant discount at his restaurants or pick up a bottle of wine as a gift. That is why I looked for him. He did seem different, but I ascribed that to the fact that he now had no moustache. I teased him about it and he gave me a story about his wife's dry skin."

The two policemen waited for more, but there wasn't any "more."

"I tell you, he spoke French perfectly, no trace of an accent, and was utterly calm and collected. In fact, that probably was a giveaway I missed. Most French are nervous in German presence, but this fellow was quite wonderful."

"What did you talk about for six hours?"

"I run on about myself, I know. And so, with a captive audience, that is what I did. My wife kicks me when I do so inappropriately, but unfortunately she was not there."

"So he knows all about you but we know nothing about him."

"That is so," said the Oberst. "Unfortunately."

"I hope you speak Russian as well as French," said Abel. "Because I have to write a report, and I'm certainly not going to put the blame on myself."

"All right," said Scholl. "Here is one little present. Small, I know, but perhaps just enough to keep me out of a Stuka cockpit."

"We're all ears."

"As I have told you, many times, he rode in the cab to the Ritz, and when we arrived I left and he stayed in the cab. I don't know where he took it. But I do remember the cabbie's name. They must display their licenses on the dashboard. It was Philippe Armoire. Does that help?"

It did.

That afternoon Macht stood before a squad room filled with about fifty men, a third his own, a third from Feldpolizei Battalion 11, and a third from Boch's SS detachment, all in plain clothes. Along with Abel, the *feldpolizei* sergeant, and Hauptsturmführer Boch, he sat at the front of the room. Behind was a large map of Paris. Even Boch had dressed down for the occasion, though to him "down" was a bespoke pin-striped, double-breasted black suit.

"All right," he said. "Long night ahead, boys, best get used to it now. We think we have a British agent hiding somewhere here," and he pointed at the fifth arrondissement, the Left Bank, the absolute heart of cultural and intellectual Paris. "That is the area where a cabdriver left him early this morning, and I believe Hauptsturmführer Boch's interrogators can speak to the truthfulness of the cabdriver."

Boch nodded, knowing that his interrogation techniques were not widely approved of.

"The Louvre and Notre Dame are right across the river, the Institut de France dominates the skyline on this side, and on the hundreds of streets are small hotels and restaurants, cafés, various retail outlets, apartment buildings, and so forth and so on. It is a catacomb of possibilities, entirely too immense for a dragnet or a mass cordon and search effort.

"Instead, each of you will patrol a block or so. You are on the lookout for a man of medium height, reddish to brownish hair, squarish face. More recognizably, he is a man of what one might call charisma. Not beauty per se, but a kind of inner glow that attracts people to him, allowing him to manipulate them. He speaks French perfectly, possibly German as well. He may be in any wardrobe, from shabby French clerk to priest, even to a woman's dress. If confronted he will offer well-thought-out words, be charming, agreeable, and slippery. His papers don't mean much. He seems to have a sneak thief's skills at picking pockets, so he may have traded off several identities by the time you get to him. The best tip I can give you is, if you see a man and think what a great friend he'd be, he's probably the spy. His charm is his armor and his principle weapon. He is very clever, very dedicated, very intent on his mission. Probably armed and dangerous as well, but please be forewarned. Taken alive, he will be a treasure trove. Dead, he's just another Brit body."

"Sir, are we to check hotels for new registrations?"

"No. Uniformed officers have that task. This fellow, however, is way too clever for that. He'll go to ground in some anonymous way, and we'll never find him by knocking on hotel room doors. Our best chance is when he is out on the street. Tomorrow will be better, as a courier is bringing the real Monsieur Piens's photo up from Bricquebec and our artist will remove the moustache and thin the face, so we should have a fair likeness. At the same time, I and all my detectives will work our phone contacts and listen for any gossip, rumors, and reports of minor incidents that might reveal the fellow's presence. We will have radio cars stationed every few blocks, so you can run to them and reach us if necessary and thus we can get reinforcements to you quickly if that need develops. We can do no more. We are the cat, he is the mouse. He must come out for his cheese."

"If I may speak," said Hauptsturmführer Boch.

Who could stop him?

And thus he delivered a thirty-minute tirade that seemed modeled after Hitler's speech at Nuremberg, full of threats and exotic metaphors and fueled by pulsing anger at the world for its injustices, perhaps mainly in not recognizing the genius of Boch, all of it well punctuated by the regrettable fact that those who gave him evidence of shirking or laziness could easily end up on that cold antitank gun in Russia, facing the Mongol hordes.

It was not well received.

Of course Basil was too foxy to bumble into a hotel. Instead, his first act on being deposited on the Left Bank well after midnight was to retreat to the alleyways of more prosperous blocks and look for padlocked doors to the garages. It was his belief that if a garage was padlocked, it meant the owners of the house had fled for more hospitable climes and he could safely use such a place for his hideout. He did this rather easily, picking the padlock and slipping into a large vault of a room occupied by a Rolls-Royce Phantom on blocks, clear evidence that its wealthy owners were now rusticating safely in Beverly Hills in the United States. His first order of the day was rest: he had, after all, been going full steam for forty-eight hours now, including his parachute arrival in France, his exhausting ordeal by Luftwaffe Oberst on the long train ride, and his miraculous escape from Montparnasse station, also courtesy of the Luftwaffe Oberst, whose name he did not even know.

The limousine was open; he crawled into a back seat that had once sustained the arses of a prominent industrialist, a department store magnate, the owner of a chain of jewelry stores, a famous whore, whatever, and quickly went to sleep.

He awoke at three in the afternoon and had a moment of confusion. Where was he? In a car? Why? Oh, yes, on a mission. What was that mission? Funny, it seemed so important at one time; now he could not remember it. Oh, yes, *The Path to Jesus*.

There seemed no point in going out by day, so he examined the house from the garage, determined that it was deserted, and slipped into it, entering easily enough. It was a ghostly museum of the aristocratic du Clercs, who'd left their furniture under sheets and their larder empty, and by now dust had accumulated everywhere. He amused himself with a little prowl, not bothering to go through drawers, for he was a thief only in the name of duty. He did borrow a book from the library and spent the evening in the cellar, reading it by candlelight. It was Tolstoy's great *War and Peace*, and he got more than three hundred pages into it.

He awakened before dawn. He tried his best to make himself presentable and slipped out, locking the padlock behind himself. The early-morning streets were surprisingly well populated, as workingmen hastened to a first meal and then a day at the job. He melded easily, another anonymous French clerk with a day-old scrub of beard and a somewhat dowdy dark suit under a dark overcoat. He found a café and had a *café au lait* and a large piece of buttered toast, sitting in the rear as the place filled up.

He listened to the gossip and quickly picked up that *les boches* were everywhere today; no one had seen them out in such force before. It seemed that most were plainclothesmen, simply standing around or walking a small patrol beat. They preformed no services other than looking at people, so it was clear that they were on some sort of stakeout duty. Perhaps a prominent Resistance figure—this brought a laugh always, as most regarded the Resistance as a joke—had come in for a meet-up with Sartre at Les Deux Magots, or a British agent was here to assassinate Dietrich von Choltitz, the garrison commander of Paris and a man as objectionable as a summer moth. But everyone knew the British weren't big on killing, as it was the Czechs who'd bumped off Heydrich.

After a few hours Basil went for his reconnaissance. He saw them almost immediately, chalk-faced men wearing either the tight faces of hunters or the slack faces of time-servers. Of the two, he chose the latter, since a loafer was less apt to pay attention and wouldn't notice things and furthermore would go off duty exactly when his shift was over.

The man stood, shifting weight from one foot to the other, blowing into his hands to keep them warm, occasionally rubbing the small of his back, where strain accumulated when he who does not stand or move much suddenly has to stand and move.

It was time to hunt the hunters.

A FEW DAYS AGO (CONT'D.)

"It's the trust issue again," said General Cavendish, in a tone suggesting he was addressing the scullery mice. "In his rat-infested brain, the fellow still believes the war might be a trap, meant to destroy Russia and Communism. He thinks that we may be feeding him information on Operation Citadel, about this attack on the Kursk salient, as a way of manipulating him into overcommitting to defending against that attack. He wastes men, equipment, and treasure building up the Kursk bulge on our say-so, then, come July, Hitler's panzer troops make a feint in that direction but drive en masse into some area of the line that has been weakened because all the troops have been moved down to the Kursk bulge. Hitler breaks through, envelops, takes, and razes Moscow, then pivots, heavy with triumph, to deal with the moribund Kursk salient. Why, he needn't even attack. He can do to those men what was done to Paulus's Sixth Army at Stalingrad, simply shell and starve them into submission. At that point the war in the East is over and Communism is destroyed."

"I see what where you're going with this, gentlemen," said Basil. "We must convince Stalin that we are telling the truth. We must verify the authenticity of Operation Citadel, so that he believes in it and acts accordingly. If he doesn't, Operation Citadel will succeed, those 300,000 men will die, and the war will continue for another year or two. The soldiers now say 'Home alive in '45,' but the bloody reality will be 'Dead in heaven in '47.' Yet more millions will die. We cannot allow that to happen."

"Do you see it yet, Basil?" asked Sir Colin. "It would be so helpful if you saw it for yourself, if you realized what has to be done, that no matter how long the shot, we have to play it. Because yours is the part that depends on faith. Only faith will get you through the ordeal that lies ahead."

"Yes, I do see it," said Basil. "The only way of verifying the Operation Citadel intercepts is to have them discovered and transmitted quite innocent of any other influence by Stalin's most secret and trusted spy. That fellow has to come across them and get them to Moscow. And the route by which he encounters them must be unimpeachable, as it will be vigorously counterchecked by the NKVD. That is why the traitorous librarian at Cambridge cannot be arrested, and that is why no tricky subterfuge of cracking into the Cambridge rare books vault can be employed. The sanctity of the Cambridge copy of *The Path to Jesus* must be protected at all costs."

"Exactly, Basil. Very good."

"You have to get these intercepts to this spy. However— here's the rub—you have no idea who or where he is."

"We know where he is," said the admiral. "The trouble is, it's not a small place. It's a good-sized village, in fact, or an industrial complex."

"This Bletchley, whose name I was not supposed to hear—is that it?"

"Professor, perhaps you could explain it to Captain St. Florian."

"Of course. Captain, as I spilled the beans before, I'll now spill some more. We have Jerry solved to a remarkable degree, via higher mathematical concepts as guidelines for the construction of electronic 'thinking machines,' if you will…"

"Turing engines, they're called," said Sir Colin. "Basil, you are honored by hearing this from the prime mover himself. It's like a chat with God."

"Please continue, your Supreme Beingness," said Basil.

Embarrassed, the professor seemed to lose his place, then came back to it. "…thinking machines that are able to function at high speed, test possibilities, and locate patterns which cut down on the possible combinations. I'll spare you details, but it's quite remarkable. However, one result of this breakthrough is that our location—Bletchley Park, about fifty kilometers out of London, an old Victorian estate in perfectly abominable taste—has grown from a small team operation into a huge bureaucracy. It now employs over eight hundred people, gathered from all over the empire for their specific skills in extremely arcane subject matters.

"As a consequence, we have many streams of communication, many units, many subunits, many sub-subunits, many huts, temporary quarters, recreational facilities, kitchens, bathrooms, a complex social life complete with gossip, romance, scandal, treachery, and remorse, our own slang, our own customs. Of course the inhabitants are all very smart, and when they're not working they get bored and to amuse themselves conspire, plot, criticize, repeat, twist, engineer coups and countercoups, all of which further muddies the water and makes any sort of objective 'truth' impossible to verify. One of the people in this monstrous human beehive, we know for sure from the Finland code, reports to Joseph Stalin. We have no idea who it is—it could be an Oxbridge genius, a lance corporal with Enfield standing guard, a lady mathematician from Australia, a telegraph operator, a translator from the old country, an American liaison, a Polish consultant, and on and on. I suppose it could even be me. All, of course, were vetted beforehand by our intelligence service, but he or she slipped by.

"So now it is important that we find him. It is in fact mandatory that we find him. A big security shakeout is no answer at all. Time-consuming, clumsy, prone to error, gossip, and resentment, as well as colossally interruptive and destructive to our actual task, but worst of all a clear indicator to the NKVD that we know they've placed a bug in our rug. If that is the conclusion they reach, then Stalin will not trust us, will not fortify Kursk, et cetera, et cetera."

"So breaking the book code is the key."

"It is. I will leave it to historians to ponder the irony that in the most successful and sophisticated cryptoanalytic operation in history, a simple book code stands between us and a desperately important goal. We are too busy for irony."

Basil responded, "The problem then refines itself more acutely: it is that you have no practical access to the book upon which the code that contains the name for this chap's new handler is based."

"That is it, in a nutshell," said Professor Turing.

"A sticky wicket, I must say. But where on Earth do I fit in? I don't see that there's any room for a boy of my most peculiar expertise. Am I supposed to—well, I cannot even conjure an end to that sentence. You have me..."

He paused.

"I think he's got it," said the admiral.

"Of course I have," said Basil. "There has to be another book."

THE FOURTH DAY

It had to happen sooner or later, and it happened sooner. The first man caught up in the Abwehr observe-and-apprehend operation was Maurice Chevalier.

The French star was in transit between mistresses on the Left Bank, and who could possibly blame Unterscharführer Ganz for blowing the whistle on him? He was tall and gloriously handsome, he was exquisitely dressed, and he radiated such warmth, grace, confidence, and glamour that to see him was to love him. The sergeant was merely acting on the guidance given the squad by Macht: if you want him to be your best friend, that's probably the spy. The sergeant had no idea who Chevalier was; he thought he was doing his duty.

Naturally, the star was not amused. He threatened to call his good friend Herr General von Choltitz and have them *all* sent to the Russian front, and it's a good thing Macht still had some diplomatic skills left, for he managed to talk the elegant man out of that course of action by supplying endless amounts of unction and flattery. His dignity ruffled, the star left huffily and went on his way, at least secure in the knowledge that in twenty minutes he would be making love to a beautiful woman and these German peasants would still be standing around out in the cold, waiting for something to happen. By eight p.m. he had forgotten entirely about it, and on his account no German boy serving in Paris would find himself on that frozen antitank gun.

As for SS Hauptsturmführer Otto Boch, that was another story. He was a man of action. He was not one for the patience, the persistence, the professionalism of police work. He preferred more direct approaches, such as hanging around the Left Bank hotel where Macht had set up his headquarters and threatening in a loud voice to send them all to Russia if they didn't produce the enemy agent quickly. Thus the Abwehr men took to calling him the Black Pigeon behind his back, for the name took into account his pigeonlike strut, breast puffed, dignity formidable, self-importance manifest, while accomplishing nothing tangible whatsoever except to leave small piles of shit wherever he went.

His SS staff got with the drill, as they were, fanatics or not, at least security professionals, and it seemed that even after a bit they were calling him the Black Pigeon as well. But on the whole, they, the Abwehr fellows, and the 11th Battalion *feldpolizei* people meshed well and produced such results as could be produced. The possibles they netted were not so spectacular as a regal movie star, but the theory behind each apprehension was sound. There were a number of handsome men, some gangsters, some actors, one poet, and a homosexual hairdresser. Macht and Abel raised their eyebrows at the homosexual hairdresser, for it occurred to them that the officer who had whistled him down had perhaps revealed more about himself than he meant to.

Eventually the first shift went off and the second came on. These actually were the sharper fellows, as Macht assumed that the British agent would be more likely to conduct his business during the evening, whatever that business might be. And indeed the results were, if not better, more responsible. In fact one man brought in revealed himself to be not who he claimed he was, and that he was a wanted jewel thief who still plied his trade, Occupation or no. It took a shrewd eye to detect the vitality and fearlessness this fellow wore behind shoddy clothes and darkened teeth and an old man's hobble, but the SS man who made the catch turned out to be highly regarded in his own unit. Macht made a note to get him close to any potential arrest situations, as he wanted his best people near the action. He also threatened to turn the jewel thief over to the French police but instead recruited him as an informant for future use. He was not one for wasting much.

Another arrestee was clearly a Jew, even if his papers said otherwise, even if he had no possible connection to British Intelligence. Macht examined the papers carefully, showed them to a bunco expert on the team, and confirmed that they were fraudulent. He took the fellow aside and said, "Look, friend, if I were you I'd get myself and my family out of Paris as quickly as possible. If I can see through your charade in five seconds, sooner or later the SS will too, and it's off to the East for all of you. These bastards have the upper hand for now, so my best advice to you is, no matter what it costs, get the hell out of Paris. Get out of France. No matter what you think, you cannot wait them out, because the one thing they absolutely will do before they're either chased out of town or put against a wall and shot is get all the Jews. That's what they live for. That's what they'll die for, if it comes to that. Consider this fair warning and probably the only one you'll get."

Maybe the man would believe him, maybe not. There was nothing he could do about it. He got back to the telephone, as, along with his other detectives, he spent most of the time monitoring his various snitches, informants, sympathizers, and sycophants, of course turning up nothing. If the agent was on the Left Bank, he hadn't moved an inch.

And he hadn't. Basil sat on the park bench the entire day, obliquely watching the German across the street. He got so he knew the man well: his gait (bad left hip, Great War wound?); his policeman's patience at standing in one place for an hour, then moving two meters and standing in that place for an hour; his stubbornness at never, ever abandoning his post, except once, at three p.m., for a brief trip to the pissoir, during which he kept his eyes open and examined each passerby through the gap at the pissoir's eye level. He didn't miss a thing—that is, except for the dowdy Frenchman observing him from ninety meters away, over an array of daily newspapers.

Twice, unmarked Citroëns came by and the officer gave a report to two other men, also in civilian clothes, on the previous few hours. They nodded, took careful records, and then hastened off. It was a long day until seven p.m., a twelve-hour shift, when his replacement moseyed up. There was no ceremony of changing the guard, just a cursory nod between them, and then the first policeman began to wander off.

Basil stayed with him, maintaining the same ninety-meter interval, noting that he stopped in a café for a cup of coffee and a sandwich, read the papers, and smoked, unaware that Basil had followed him in, placed himself at the bar, and also had a sandwich and a coffee.

Eventually the German got up, walked another six blocks down Boulevard Saint-Germain, turned down a narrower street called rue de Valor, and disappeared halfway down the first block into a rummy-looking hotel called Le Duval. Basil looked about, found a café, had a second coffee, smoked a Gauloise to blend in, joked with the bartender, was examined by a uniformed German policeman on a random check, showed papers identifying himself as Robert Fortier (picked freshly that morning), was checked off against a list (he was not on it, as perhaps M. Fortier had not yet noted his missing papers), and was then abandoned by the policeman for other possibilities.

At last he left and went back to rue de Valor, slipped down it, and very carefully approached the Hotel Duval. From outside it revealed nothing—a typical Baedeker two-star for commercial travelers, with no pretensions of gentility or class. It would be stark, clean, well run, and banal. Such places housed half the population every night in Europe, except for the past few years, when that half-the-population had slept in bunkers, foxholes, or ruins. Nothing marked this place, which was exactly why whoever was running this show had chosen it. Another pro like himself, he guessed. It takes a professional to catch a professional, the saying goes.

He meekly entered as if confused, noting a few sour-looking individuals sitting in the lobby reading *Deutsche Allgemeine Zeitung* and smoking, and went to the desk, where he asked for directions to a hotel called Les Deux Gentilhommes and got them. It wasn't much, but it enabled him to make a quick check on the place, and he learned what he needed to know.

Behind the desk was a hallway, and down it Basil could see

a larger room, a banquet hall or something, full of drowsy-looking men sitting around listlessly, while a few further back slept on sofas pushed in for just that purpose. It looked police.

That settled it. This was the German headquarters.

He moseyed out and knew he had one more stop before tomorrow.

He had to examine his objective.

A FEW DAYS PREVIOUSLY (CONT'D.)

"Another book? Exactly yes and exactly no," said Sir Colin.

"How could there be a second original? By definition there can be only one original, or so it was taught when I was at university."

"It does seem like a conundrum, does it not?" said Sir Colin. "But indeed, we are dealing with a very rare case of a second original. Well, of sorts."

"Not sure I like the sound of that," said Basil.

"Nor should you. It takes us to a certain awkwardness that, again, an ironist would find heartily amusing."

"You see," said Basil, "I am fond of irony, but only when applied to other chaps."

"Yes, it can sting, can it not?" said General Cavendish. "And I must say, this one stings quite exhaustively. It will cause historians many a chuckle when they write the secret history of the war in the twenty-first century after all the files are finally opened."

"But we get ahead of ourselves," said Sir Colin. "There's more tale to tell. And the sooner we tell it, the sooner the cocktail hour."

"Tell on, then, Sir Colin."

"It all turns on the fulcrum of folly and vanity known as the human heart, especially when basted in ambition, guilt, remorse, and greed. What a marvelous stew, all of it simmering within the head of the Reverend MacBurney. When last we left him, our God-fearing MacBurney had become a millionaire because his pamphlet *The Path to Jesus* had sold endlessly, bringing him a shilling a tot. As I said, he retired to a country estate and spent some years happily wenching and drinking in happy debauchery."

"As who would not?" asked Basil, though he doubted this lot would.

"Of course. But then in the year 1789, twenty-two years later, he was approached by a representative of the bishop of Gladney and asked to make a presentation to the Church. To commemorate his achievement, the thousands of souls he had shepherded safely upon the aforenamed path, the bishop wanted him appointed deacon at St. Blazefield's in Glasgow, the highest church rank a fellow like him could achieve. And Thomas wanted it badly. But the bishop wanted him to donate the original manuscript to the church, for eternal display in its ambulatory. Except Thomas had no idea where the original was and hadn't thought about it in years. So he sat down, practical Scot that he was, and from the pamphlet itself he back-engineered, so to speak, another 'original' manuscript in his own hand, a perfect facsimile, or as perfect as he could make it, even, one must assume, to the little crucifix doodles that so amused the Cambridge librarian. That was shipped to Glasgow, and that is why to this day Thomas MacBurney lounges in heaven, surrounded by seraphim and cherubim who sing his praises and throw petals where he walks."

"It was kind of God to provide us with the second copy," said Basil.

"Proof," said the admiral, "that He is on our side."

"Yes. The provenance of the first manuscript is well established; as I say, it has pencil marks to guide the printer in the print shop owner's hand. That is why it is so prized at Cambridge. The second was displayed for a century in Glasgow, but then the original St. Blazefield's was torn down for a newer, more imposing one in 1857, and the manuscript somehow disappeared. However, it was discovered in 1913 in Paris. Who knows by what mischief it ended up there? But to prevent action by the French police, the owner anonymously donated it to a cultural institution, in whose vaults it to this day resides."

"So I am to go and fetch it. Under the Nazis' noses?"

"Well, not exactly," said Sir Colin. "The manuscript itself must not be removed, as someone might notice and word might reach the Russians. What you must do is photograph certain pages using a Riga Minox. Those are what must be fetched."

"And when I fetch them, they can be relied upon to provide the key for the code and thus give up the name of the Russian spy at Bletchley Park, and thus you will be able to slip into his hands the German plans for Operation Citadel, and thus Stalin will fortify the Kursk salient, and thus the massive German summer offensive will have its back broken, and thus the boys will be home alive in '45 instead of dead in heaven in '47. Our boys, their boys, all boys."

"In theory," said Sir Colin Gubbins.

"Hmm, not sure I like 'in theory,'" said Basil.

"You will be flown in by Lysander, dispatched in the care of Resistance Group Philippe, which will handle logistics. They have not been alerted to the nature of the mission as yet, as the fewer who know, of course, the better. You will explain it to them, they will get you to Paris for recon and supply equipment, manpower, distraction, and other kinds of support, then get you back out for Lysander pickup, if everything goes well."

"And if it does not?"

"That is where your expertise will come in handy. In that case, it will be a maximum hugger-mugger sort of effort. I am sure you will prevail."

"I am not," said Basil. "It sounds awfully dodgy."

"And you know, of course, that you will be given an L-pill so that headful of secrets of yours will never fall in German hands."

"I will be certain to throw it away at the first chance," said Basil.

"There's the spirit, old man," said Sir Colin.

"And where am I headed?"

"Ah, yes. An address on the Quai de Conti, the Left Bank, near the Seine."

"Excellent," said Basil. "Only the Institut de France, the most profound and colossal assemblage of French cultural icons in the world, and the most heavily guarded."

"Known for its excellent library," said Sir Colin.

"It sounds like quite a pickle," said Basil.

"And you haven't even heard the bad part."

THE FOURTH DAY, NEAR MIDNIGHT

In the old days, and perhaps again after the war if von Choltitz didn't blow the place up, the Institut de France was one of the glories of the nation, emblazoned in the night under a rippling tricolor to express the high moral purpose of French culture. But in the war it, too, had to fall into line.

Thus the blazing lights no longer blazed and the cupola ruling over the many stately branches of the singularly complex building overlooking the Seine on the Quai de Conti, right at the toe of the Île de la Cité and directly across from the Louvre, in the sixth arrondissement, no longer ruled. One had to squint, as did Basil, to make it out, though helpfully a searchlight from some far-distant German antiaircraft battery would backlight it and at least accentuate its bulk and shape. The Germans had not painted it *feldgrau*, thank God, and so its white stone seemed to gleam in the night, at least in contrast to other French buildings in the environs. A slight rain fell; the cobblestones glistened; the whole thing had a cinematic look that Basil paid no attention to, as it did him no good at all and he was by no means a romantic.

Instead he saw the architectural tropes of the place, the brilliant façade of colonnades, the precision of the intersecting angles, the dramatically arrayed approaches to the broad steps of the grand entrance under the cupola, from which nexus one proceeded to its many divisions, housed each in a separate wing. The whole expressed the complexity, the difficulty, the arrogance, the insolence, the ego, the whole *je ne sais quoi* of the French: their smug, prosperous country, their easy treachery, their utter lack of conscience, their powerful sense of entitlement.

From his briefing, he knew that his particular goal was the Bibliothèque Mazarine, housed in the great marble edifice but a few hundred meters from the center. He slid that way, while close at hand the Seine lapped against its stone banks, the odd taxi or bicycle taxi hurtled down Quai de Conti, the searchlights crisscrossed the sky. Soon midnight, and curfew. But he had to see.

On its own the Mazarine was an imposing building, though without the columns. Instead it affected the French country palace look, with a cobblestone yard which in an earlier age had allowed for carriages but now was merely a car park. Two giant oak doors, guarding French propriety, kept interlopers out. At this moment it was locked up like a vault; tomorrow the doors would open and he would somehow make his penetration.

But how?

With Resistance help he could have mounted an elaborate ruse, spring himself to the upper floors while the guards tried to deal with the unruliness beneath. But he had chosen not to go that way. In the networks somebody always talked, somebody always whispered, and nothing was really a secret. The Resistance could get him close, but it could also earn him an appetizer of strychnine L-pill.

The other, safer possibility was to develop contacts in the French underworld and hire a professional thief to come in from below or above, via a back entrance, and somehow steal the booklet, then replace it the next day. But that took time, and there was no time.

In the end, he only confirmed what he already knew: there was but one way. It was as fragile as a Fabergé egg, at any time given to yield its counterfeit nature to anyone paying the slightest attention. Particularly with the Germans knowing something was up and at high alert, ready to flood the place with cops and thugs at any second. It would take nerve, a talent for the dramatic, and, most important, the right credentials.

A FEW DAYS PREVIOUSLY (FINI)

"Are you willing?" said Sir Colin. "Knowing all this, are you willing?"

"Sir, you send men to their death every day with less fastidiousness. You consign battalions to their slaughter without blinking an eye. The stricken gray ships turn to coffins and slide beneath the ocean with their hundreds; *c'est la guerre*. The airplanes explode into falling pyres and nobody sheds a tear. Everyone must do his bit, you say. And yet now, for me, on this, you're suddenly squeamish to an odd degree, telling me every danger and improbability and how low the odds of success are. I have to know why. It has a doomed feel to it. If I must die, so be it, but somebody wants nothing on his conscience."

"That is very true."

"Is this a secret you will not divulge?"

"I will divulge, and what's more, now is the time to divulge, before we all die of starvation or alcohol withdrawal symptoms."

"How very interesting."

"A man on this panel has the ear of the prime minister. He holds great power. It is he who insisted on this highly unusual approach, it is he who forces us to overbrief you and send you off with far too much classified information. Let him speak, then."

"General Sir Colin means me," said the professor. "Because of my code-breaking success, I find myself uniquely powerful. Mr. Churchill likes me, and wants me to have my way. That is why I sit on a panel with the barons of war, myself a humble professor, not even at Oxford or Cambridge but at Manchester."

"Professor, is this a moral quest? Do you seek forgiveness beforehand, should I die? It's really not necessary. I owe God a death, and he will take it when he sees fit. Many times over the years he has seen fit not to do so. Perhaps he's bored with me and wants me off the board. Perhaps he tires of my completely overblown legendary wit and sangfroid and realizes I'm just as scared as the next fellow, am a bully to boot, and that it ended on a rather beastly note with my father, a regret I shall always carry. So, Professor, you who have saved millions, if I go, it's on the chap upstairs, not you."

"Well spoken, Captain St. Florian, like the hero I already knew you to be. But that's not quite it. Another horror lies ahead and I must burden you with it, so I will be let alone enough by all those noisy screamers between my ears to do my work if the time comes."

"Please enlighten."

"You see, everyone thinks I'm a genius. Of course I am really a frail man of many weaknesses. I needn't elucidate. But I am terrified of one possibility. You should know it's there before you undertake."

"Go ahead."

"Let us say you prevail. At great cost, by great ordeal, blood, psychic energy, morale, whatever it takes from you. And perhaps other people die as well—a pilot, a Resistance worker, someone caught by a stray bullet, any of the routine whimsies of war."

"Yes."

"Suppose all that is true, you bring it back, you sit before me exhausted, spent, having been burned in the fire, you put it to me, the product of your hard labors, and *I cannot decode the damned thing*."

"Sir, I—"

"*They* think I can, these barons of war. Put the tag 'genius' on a fellow and it solves all problems. However, there are no, and I do mean no, assurances that the pages you bring back will accord closely enough with the original to yield a meaningful answer."

"We've been through this a thousand times, Professor Turing," said the general. "You will be able, we believe, to handle this. We are quite confident in your ability and attribute your reluctance to a high-strung personality and a bit of stage fright, that's all. The variations cannot be that great, and your Turing engine or one of those things you call a bombe ought to be able to run down other possible solutions quickly and we will get what we need."

"I'm so happy the men who know nothing of this sort of work are so confident. But I had to face you, Captain St. Florian, with this truth. It may be for naught. It may be undoable, even by the great Turing. If that is the case, then I humbly request your forgiveness."

"Oh, bosh," said Basil. "If it turns out that the smartest man in England can't do it, it wasn't meant to be done. Don't give it a thought, Professor. I'll simply go off and have an inning, as best I know how, and if I get back, then you have your inning. What happens, then that's what happens. Now, please, gentleman, can we hasten? My arse feels as if Queen Victoria used it for needlepoint!"

ACTION THIS DAY

Of course one normally never went about in anything but bespoke. Just wasn't done. Basil's tailor was Steed-Aspell, of Davies & Son, 15 Jermyn Street, and Steed-Aspell ("Steedy" to his clients) was a student of Frederick Scholte, the Duke of Windsor's genius tailor, which meant he was a master of the English drape. His clothes hung with an almost scary brilliance, perfect. They never just crumpled. As gravity took them, they formed extraordinary shapes, presented new faces to the world, gave the sun a canvas for compositions playing light against dark, with gray working an uneasy region between, rather like the Sudetenland. Basil had at least three jackets for which he had been offered immense sums (Steed-Aspell was taking no new clients, though the war might eventually open up some room on his waiting list, if it hadn't already), and of course

Basil merely smiled drily at the evocations of want, issued a brief but sincere look of commiseration, and moved onward, a lord in tweed, perhaps *the* lord of the tweeds.

Thus the suit he now wore was a severe disappointment. He had bought it in a secondhand shop, and *monsieur* had expressed great confidence that it was of premium quality, and yet its drape was all wrong, because of course the wool was all wrong. One didn't simply use *any* wool, as its provincial tailor believed. Thus it got itself into twists and rumples and couldn't get out, its creases blunted themselves in moments, and it had already popped a button. Its rise bagged, sagged, and gave up. It rather glowed in the sunlight. Buttoned, its two breasts encased him like a girdle; unbuttoned, it looked like he wore several flags of blue pinstripe about himself, ready to unfurl in the wind. He was certain his clubman would not let him enter if he tried.

And he wanted very much to look his best this morning. He was, after all, going to blow up something big with Germans inside.

"I tell you, we should be more severe," argued SS Hauptsturmführer Otto Boch. "These Paris bastards, they take us too lightly. In Poland we enacted laws and enforced them with blood and steel and incidents quickly trickled away to nothing. Every Pole knew that disobedience meant a polka at the end of a rope in the main square."

"Perhaps they were too enervated on lack of food to rebel," said Macht. "You see, you have a different objective. You are interested in public order and the thrill of public obedience. These seem to you necessary goals, which must be enforced for our quest to succeed. My goal is far more limited. I merely want to catch the British agent. To do so, I must isolate him against a calm background, almost a still life, and that way locate him. It's the system that will catch him, not a single guns-blazing raid. If you stir things up, Herr Hauptsturmführer, I guarantee you it will come to nothing. Please trust me on this. I have run manhunts, many times successfully."

Boch had no remonstrance, of course. He was not a professional like Macht and in fact before the war had been a salesman of vacuums, and not a very good one.

"We have observers everywhere," Macht continued. "We have a photograph of M. Piens, delicately altered so that it closely resembles the man that idiot Scholl sat next to, which should help our people enormously. We have good weather. The sun is shining, so our watchers won't hide themselves under shades or awnings to get out of the rain and thus cut down their visibility. The lack of rain also means our roving autos won't be searching through the slosh and squeal of wiper blades, again reducing what they see. We continue to monitor sources we have carefully been nurturing since we arrived. Our system will work. We will get a break today, I guarantee it."

The two sat at a table in the banquet room of the Hotel Duval, amid a batch of snoozing agents who were off shift. The stench of cigarette butts, squashed cigars, and tapped-out pipe tobacco shreds hung heavy in the room, as did the smell of cold coffee and unwashed bodies. But that was what happened on manhunts, as Macht knew and Boch did not. Now nothing could be done except wait for a break, then play that break carefully and…

"Hauptmann Macht?" It was his assistant, Abel.

"Yes?"

"Paris headquarters. Von Choltitz's people. They want a briefing. They've sent a car."

"Oh, Christ," said Macht. But he knew this was what happened. Big politicos got involved, got worried, wanted credit, wanted to escape blame. No one anywhere in the world understood the principle that sometimes it was better not to be energetic and to leave things alone instead of wasting energy in a lot of showy ceremonial nonsense.

"I'll go," said Boch, who would never miss a chance to preen before superiors.

"Sorry, sir. They specified Hauptmann Macht."

"Christ," said Macht again, trying to remember where he'd left his trench coat.

A street up from the Hotel Duval, Basil found the exact thing he was looking for. It was a Citroën Traction Avant, black, and it had a large aerial projecting from it. It was clearly a radio car, one of those that the German man-hunter had placed strategically around the sixth arrondissement so that no watcher was far from being able to notify headquarters and get the troops out.

Helpfully, a café was available across the street, and so he sat at a table and ordered a coffee. He watched as, quite regularly, a new German watcher ambled by, leaned in, and reported that he had seen nothing. Well organized. They arrived every thirty minutes. Each man came once every two hours, so the walk over was a break from standing around. It enabled the commander to get new information to the troops in an orderly fashion, and it changed the vantage point of the watchers. At the same time, at the end of four hours, the car itself fired up and its two occupants made a quick tour of their men on the street corners. The point was to keep communications clear, keep the men engaged so they didn't go logy on duty, yet sacrifice nothing in the way of observation. Whoever was running this had done it before.

He also noted a new element. Somehow they had what appeared to be a photograph. They would look it over, pass it around, consult it frequently in all meetings. It couldn't be of him, so possibly it was a drawing. It meant he had to act today. As the photo or drawing circulated, more and more would learn his features and the chance of his being spotted would become greater by degrees. Today the image was a novelty and would not stick in the mind without constant refreshment, but by tomorrow all who had to know it would know it. The time was now. Action this day.

When he felt he had mastered the schedule and saw a clear break coming up in which nobody would report to the car for at least thirty minutes, he decided it was time to move. It was about three p.m. on a sunny, if chilly, Paris spring afternoon. The ancient city's so-familiar features were everywhere as he meandered across Boulevard Saint-Germain under blue sky. There was a music in the traffic and in the rhythm of the pedestrians, the window shoppers, the pastry munchers, the café sitters, the endless parade of bicyclists, some pulling passengers in carts, some simply solo. The great city went about its business, Occupation or no, action this day or no.

He walked into an alley and reached over to fetch a wine bottle that he had placed there early this morning, while it was dark. It was, however, filled with kerosene drained from a ten-liter tin jug in the garage. Instead of a cork it had a plug of wadded cotton jammed into its throat, and fifteen centimeters of strip hung from the plug. It was a gasoline bomb, constructed exactly to SOE specification. He had never done it before, since he usually worked with Explosive 808, but there was no 808 to be found, so the kerosene, however many years old it was, would have to do. He wrapped the bottle in newspaper, tilted it to soak the wad with the fuel, and then set off jauntily.

This was the delicate part. It all turned on how observant the Germans were at close quarters, whether or not Parisians on the street noticed him, and if so, if they took some kind of action. He guessed they wouldn't; actually, he gambled that they wouldn't. The Parisians are a prudent species.

Fortunately the Citroën was parked in an isolated space, open at both ends. He made no eye contact with its bored occupants, his last glance telling him that one leaned back, stretching, to keep from dozing, while the other was talking on a telephone unit wired into the radio console that occupied the small back seat. He felt that if he looked at them they might feel the pressure of his eyes, as those of predatory nature sometimes do, being weirdly sensitive to signs of aggression.

He approached on the oblique, keeping out of view of the rear

window of the low-slung sedan, all the rage in 1935 but now
ubiquitous in Paris. Its fuel tank was in the rear, which again
made things convenient. In the last moment as he approached,
he ducked down, wedged the bottle under the rear tire, pulled
the paper away, lit his lighter, and lit the end of the strip of
cloth. The whole thing took one second, and he moved away as
if he'd done nothing.

It didn't explode. Instead, with a kind of air-sucking gush, the
bottle erupted and shattered, smearing a billow of orange-black
flame into the atmosphere from beneath the car, and in the next
second the gasoline tank also went, again without explosion as
much as flare of incandescence a hundred meters high, bleaching
the color from the beautiful old town and sending a cascade of
heat radiating outward.

Neither German policeman was injured, except by means
of stolen dignity, but each spilled crazily from his door, driven
by the primal fear of flame encoded in the human race, one
tripping, going to hands and knees and locomoting desperately
from the conflagration on all fours like some sort of beast.
Civilians panicked as well, and screaming became general
as they scrambled away from the bonfire that had been an
automobile several seconds earlier.

Basil never looked back, and walked swiftly down the street
until he reached rue de Valor and headed down it.

Boch was lecturing Abel on the necessity of severity in dealing
with these French cream puffs when a man roared into the
banquet room, screaming, "They've blown up one of our radio
cars. It's an attack! The Resistance is here!"

Instantly men leaped to action. Three ran to a gun rack
in a closet where the MP 40s were stored and grabbed those
powerful weapons up. Abel raced to the telephone and called
Paris command with a report and a request for immediate troop
dispatch. Still others pulled Walthers, Lugers, and P38s from

holsters, grabbed overcoats, and readied themselves to move to the scene and take command.

Hauptsturmführer Boch did nothing. He sat rooted in terror. He was not a coward, but he also, for all his worship of severity and aggressive interrogation methods, was particularly inept at confronting the unexpected, which generally caused his mind to dump its contents in a steaming pile on the floor while he sat in stupefaction, waiting for it to refill.

In this case, when he found himself alone in the room, he reached a refill level, stood up, and ran after his more agile colleagues.

He stepped on the sidewalk, which was full of fleeing Parisians, and fought against the tide, being bumped and jostled in the process by those who had no idea who he was. A particularly hard thump from a hurtling heavyweight all but knocked him flat, and the fellow had to grab him to keep him upright before hurrying along. Thus, making little progress, the Hauptsturmführer pulled out his Luger, trying to remember if there was a shell in the chamber, and started to shout in his bad French, "Make way! German officer, make way!" waving the Luger about as if it were some kind of magic wand that would dissipate the crowd.

It did not, so taken in panic were the French, so he diverted to the street itself and found the going easier. He made it to Boulevard Saint-Germain, turned right, and there beheld the atrocity. Radio Car Five still blazed brightly. German plainclothesmen had set up a cordon around it, menacing the citizens with their MP 40s, but of course no citizens were that interested in a German car, and so the street had largely emptied. Traffic on the busy thoroughfare had stopped, making the approach of the fire truck more laggard—the sound of klaxons arrived from far away, and it was clear that by the time the firemen arrived the car would be largely burned to a charred hulk. Two plainclothesmen, Esterlitz, from his SS unit, and an Abwehr agent, sat on the curb looking completely unglued while Abel tried to talk to them.

Boch ran to them.

"Report," he snapped as he arrived, but nobody paid any attention to him.

"Report!" he screamed.

Abel looked over at him.

"I'm trying to get a description from these two fellows, so we know who we're looking for."

"We should arrest hostages at once and execute them if no information is forthcoming."

"Sir, he has to be in the area still. We have to put people out in all directions with a solid description."

"Esterlitz, what did you see?"

Esterlitz looked at him with empty eyes. The nearness of his escape, the heat of the flames, the suddenness of it all, had disassembled his brain completely. Thus it was the Abwehr agent who answered.

"As I've been telling the lieutenant, it happened so quickly. My last impression in the split second before the bomb exploded was of a man walking north on Saint-Germain in a blue pinstripe that was not well cut at all, a surprise to see in a city so fashion-conscious, and then *whoosh*, a wall of flame behind us."

"The bastards," said Boch. "Attempting murder in broad daylight."

"Sir," said Abel, "with all due respect, this was not an assassination operation. Had he wanted them dead, he would have hurled the Molotov through the open window, soaking them with burning gasoline, burning them to death. Instead he merely ignited the petrol tank, which enabled them to escape. He didn't care about them. That wasn't the point, don't you see?"

Boch looked at him, embarrassed to be contradicted by an underling in front of the troops. It was not the SS way! But he controlled his temper, as it made no sense to vent at an ignorant police rube.

"What are you saying?"

"This was some sort of distraction. He wanted to get us all out here, concentrating on this essentially meaningless event, because it somehow advanced his higher purpose."

"I—I—" stuttered Boch.

"Let me finish the interview, then get the description out to all other cars, ordering them to stay in place. Having our men here, tied up in this jam, watching the car burn to embers, accomplishes nothing."

"Do it! Do it!" screamed Boch, as if he had thought of it himself.

Basil reached the Bibliothèque Mazarine within ten minutes and could still hear fire klaxons sounding in the distance. The disturbance would clog up the sixth arrondissement for hours before it was finally untangled, and it would mess up the German response for those same hours. He knew he had a window of time—not much, but perhaps enough.

He walked through the cobbled yard and approached the doors, where two French policemen stood guard.

"Official business only, *monsieur*. German orders," said one.

He took out his identification papers and said frostily, "I do not care to chat with French policemen in the sunlight. I am here on business."

"Yes, sir."

He entered a vast, sacred space. It was composed of an indefinite number of hexagonal galleries, with vast air shafts between, surrounded by very low railings. From any of the hexagons one could see, interminably, the upper and lower floors. The distribution of the galleries was invariable. Twenty shelves, five long shelves per side, covered all the sides except two; their height, which was the distance from floor to ceiling, scarcely exceeded that of a normal bookcase. The books seemed to absorb and calm all extraneous sounds, so that as his heels clicked on the marble of the floor on the approach to a central desk, a woman behind it hardly seemed to notice him. However, his papers got her attention and her courtesy right away.

"I am here on important business. I need to speak to *le directeur* immediately."

She left. She returned. She bade him follow. They went to an elevator where a decrepit Great War veteran, shoulders stooped, medals tarnished, eyes vacant, opened the gate to a cage-like car. They were hoisted mechanically up two flights, followed another path through corridors of books, and reached a door.

She knocked, then entered. He followed, to discover an old Frenchie in some kind of frock coat and goatee, standing nervously.

"I am Claude De Marque, the director," he said in French. "How may I help you?"

"Do you speak German?"

"Yes, but I am more fluent in my own tongue."

"French, then."

"Please sit down."

Basil took a chair.

"Now—"

"First, understand the courtesy I have paid you. Had I so chosen, I could have come with a contingent of armed troops. We could have shaken down your institution, examined the papers of all your employees, made impolite inquiries as we looked for leverage and threw books every which way. That is the German technique. Perhaps you shield a Jew, as is the wont of your kind of prissy French intellectual. Too bad for those Jews, too bad for those who shield him. Are you getting my meaning?"

"Yes, sir, I—"

"Instead I come on my own. As men of letters, I think it more appropriate that our relationship be based on trust and respect. I am a professor of literature at Leipzig, and I hope to return to that after the war. I cherish the library, this library, any library. Libraries are the font of civilization, do you not agree?"

"I do."

"Therefore, one of my goals is to protect the integrity of the library. You must know that first of all."

"I am pleased."

"Then let us proceed. I represent a very high science office of the Third Reich. This office has an interest in certain kinds of rare books. I have been assigned by its commanding officer to assemble a catalog of such volumes in the great libraries of Europe. I expect you to help me."

"What kinds of books?"

"Ah, this is delicate. I expect discretion on your part."

"Of course."

"This office has an interest in volumes that deal with erotic connections between human beings. Our interest is not limited to those merely between male and female but extends to other combinations as well. The names de Sade and Ovid have been mentioned. There are more, I am sure. There is also artistic representation. The ancients were more forthright in their descriptions of such activities. Perhaps you have photos of paintings, sculptures, friezes?"

"Sir, this is a respectable—"

"It is not a matter of respect. It is a matter of science, which must go where it leads. We are undertaking a study of human sexuality, and it must be done forthrightly, professionally, and quickly. We are interested in harnessing the power of eugenics and seek to find ways to improve the fertility of our finest minds. Clearly the answer lies in sexual behaviors. Thus we must fearlessly master such matters as we chart our way to the future. We must ensure the future."

"But we have no salacious materials."

"And do you believe, knowing of the Germans' attributes of thoroughness, fairness, calm and deliberate examination, that a single assurance alone would suffice?"

"I invite you to—"

"Exactly. This is what I expect. An hour, certainly no more, undisturbed in your rare book vault. I will wear white gloves if you prefer. I must be free to make a precise search and assure my commander that either you do not have such materials, as you claim, or you do, and these are the ones you have. Do you understand?"

"I confess a first edition of Sade's *Justine*, dated 1791, is among our treasures."

"Are the books arranged by year?"

"They are."

"Then that is where I shall begin."

"Please, you can't—"

"Nothing will be disturbed, only examined. When I am finished, have a document prepared for me in which I testify to other German officers that you have cooperated to the maximum degree. I will sign it, and believe me, it will save you much trouble in the future."

"That would be very kind, sir."

At last he and the Reverend MacBurney were alone. *I have come a long way to meet you, you Scots bastard*, he thought. *Let's see what secrets I can tease out of you.*

MacBurney was signified by a manuscript on foolscap, beribboned in a decaying folder upon which *The Path to Jesus* had been scrawled in an ornate hand. It had been easy to find, in a drawer marked *1789*; he had delicately moved it to the tabletop, where, opened, it yielded its treasure, page after page in the round hand of the man of God himself, laden with swoops and curls of faded brown ink. In the fashion of the eighteenth century, he had made each letter a construction of grace and agility, each line a part of the composition, by turning the feather quill to get the fat or the thin, these arranged in an artistic cascade. His punctuation was precise, deft, studied, just this much twist and pressure for a comma, that much for a (more plentiful) semicolon. It was if the penmanship itself communicated the glory of his love for God. All the nouns were capitalized, and the *S*'s and the *F*'s were so close it would take an expert to tell which was which; superscript showed up everywhere, as the man tried to shrink his burden of labor; frequently the word "the" appeared as "ye," as the penultimate letter often stood in for *th* in that era. It seemed the words on the page wore powdered periwigs and silk stockings and buckled, heeled shoes as they danced and pirouetted across the page.

Yet there was a creepy quality to it, too. Splats or droplets marked the creamy luster of the page—some of wine perhaps, some of tea, some of whatever else one might have at the board in the eighteenth century. Some of the lines were crooked, and the page itself felt off-kilter, as though a taint of madness had attended, or perhaps drunkenness, for in his dotage old MacBurney was no teetotaler, it was said.

More psychotic still were the drawings. As the librarian had noticed in his published account of the volume in *Treasures of the Cambridge Library*, the reverend occasionally yielded to artistic impulse. No, they weren't vulvas or naked boys or fornicators in pushed-up petticoats or farmers too in love with their cows. MacBurney's lusts weren't so visible or so nakedly expressed. But the fellow was a doodler after Jesus. He could not compel himself to be still, and so each page wore a garland of crosses scattered across its bottom, a Milky Way of holiness setting off the page number, or in the margins, and at the top silhouetted crucifixions, sketches of angels, clumsy reiterations of God's hand touching Adam's as the great Italian had captured upon that ceiling in Rome. Sometimes the devil himself appeared, horned and ambivalent, just a few angry lines not so much depicting as suggesting Lucifer's cunning and malice. It seemed the reverend was in anguish as he tried desperately to finish this last devotion to the Lord.

Basil got to work quickly. Here of all places was no place to tarry. He untaped the Riga Minox from his left shin, checked that the overhead light seemed adequate. He didn't need flash, as Technical Branch had come up with extremely fast 21.5 mm film, but it was at the same time completely necessary to hold still. The lens had been prefocused for 15 cm, so Basil did not need to play with it or any other knobs, buttons, controls. He took on faith that he had been given the best equipment in the world with which to do the job.

He had seven pages to photograph—2, 5, 6, 9, 10, 13, and 15—for the codebreaker had assured him that those would be the pages on which the index words would have to be located, based on the intercepted code.

In fact, Sade's *Justine* proved very helpful, along with a first edition of Voltaire's *Pensées* and an extra-illustrated edition of *Le Decameron de Jean Boccace*, published in five volumes in Paris in 1757, Ah, the uses of literature! Stacked, they gave him a brace against which he could sustain the long fuselage of the Minox. Beneath it he displayed the page. Click, wind, click again, on to the next one. It took so little time. It was too sodding easy. He thought he might find an SS firing squad just waiting for him, enjoying the little trick they'd played on him.

But when he replaced all the documents in their proper spots, retaped the camera to his leg, and emerged close to an hour later, there was no firing squad, just the nervous Marque, *le directeur*, waiting with the tremulous smile of the recently violated.

"I am finished, *monsieur le directeur*. Please examine, make certain all is appropriate to the condition it was in when I first entered an hour ago. Nothing missing, nothing misfiled, nothing where it should not be. I will not take offense."

The director entered the vault and emerged in a few minutes.

"Perfect," he said.

"I noted the Sade. Nothing else seemed necessary to our study. I am sure copies of it in not so rare an edition are commonly available if one knows where to look."

"I could recommend a bookseller," said *le directeur*. "He specializes in, er, the kind of thing you're looking for."

"Not necessary now, but possible in the future."

"I had my secretary prepare a document, in both German and French."

Basil looked at it, saw that it was exactly as he had ordered, and signed his false name with a flourish.

"You see how easy it is if you cooperate, *monsieur*? I wish I could teach all your countrymen the same."

By the time Macht returned at four, having had to walk the last three blocks because of the traffic snarl, things were more or less functioning correctly at his banquet hall headquarters.

"We now believe him to be in a pinstripe suit. I have put all our watchers back in place in a state of high alert. I have placed cars outside this tangled-up area so that we can, if need be, get to the site of an incident quickly," Abel briefed him.

"Excellent, excellent," he replied. "What's happening with the idiot?"

That meant Boch, of course.

"He wanted to take hostages and shoot one every hour until the man is found. I told him that was probably not a wise move, since this fellow is clearly operating entirely on his own and is thus immune to social pressures such as that. He's now in private communication with SS headquarters in Paris, no doubt telling them what a wonderful job he has been doing. His men are all right, he's just a buffoon. But a dangerous one. He could have us all sent to Russia. Well, not me, ha-ha, but the rest of you."

"I'm sure your honor would compel you to accompany us, Walter."

"Don't bet on it, Didi."

"I agree with you that this is a diversion, that our quarry is completing his mission somewhere very near. I agree also that it is not a murder, a sabotage, a theft, or anything spectacular. In fact, I have no idea what it could be. I would advise that all train stations be double-covered and that the next few hours are our best for catching him."

"I will see to it."

In time Boch appeared. He beckoned to Macht, and the two stepped into the hallway for privacy.

"Herr Hauptmann, I want this considered as fair warning.

This agent must be captured, no matter what. It is on record that you chose to disregard my advice and instead go about your duties at a more sedate pace. SS is not satisfied and has filed a formal protest with Abwehr and others in the government. SS Reichsführer Himmler himself is paying close attention. If this does not come to the appropriate conclusion, all counterintelligence activities in Paris may well come under SS auspices, and you yourself may find your next duty station rather more frosty and rather more hectic than this one. I tell you this to clarify your thinking. It's not a threat, Herr Hauptmann, it's simply a clarification of the situation."

"Thank you for the update, Herr Hauptsturmführer. I will take it under advisement and—"

But at that moment Abel appeared, concern on his usually slack, doughy face. "Hate to interrupt, Herr Hauptmann, but something interesting."

"Yes?"

"One of Unterscharführer Ganz's sources is a French policeman on duty at the Bibliothèque Mazarine, on Quai de Conti, not far from here. An easy walk, in fact."

"Yes, the large complex overlooking the river. The cupola—no, that is the main building, the Institut de France, I believe."

"Yes, sir. At any rate, the report is that at about three p.m., less than twenty minutes after the bomb blast—"

"Flare is more like it, I hear," said Macht.

"Yes, Captain. In any event, a German official strode into the library and demanded to see the director. He demanded access to the rare book vault and was in there alone for an hour. Everybody over there is buzzing because he was such a commanding gentleman, so sure and smooth and charismatic."

"Did he steal anything?"

"No, but he was alone in the vault. In the end, it makes very little sense. It's just that the timing works out correctly, the description is accurate, and the personality seems to match. What British intelligence could—"

"Let's get over there, fast," said Macht.

This was far more than *monsieur le directeur* had ever encountered. He now found himself alone in his office with three German policemen, and none were in a good mood.

"So, if you will, please explain to me the nature of this man's request."

"It's highly confidential, Captain Macht. I had the impression that discretion was one of the aspects of the visit. I feel I betray a trust if I—"

"*Monsieur le directeur,*" said Macht evenly, "I assure you that while I appreciate your intentions, I nevertheless must insist on an answer. There is some evidence that this man may not be who you think he was."

"His credentials were perfect," said the director. "I examined them very carefully. They were entirely authentic. I am not easy to fool."

"I accuse you of nothing," said Macht. "I merely want the story."

And *le directeur* laid it out, rather embarrassed.

"Dirty pictures," said Macht at the conclusion. "You say a German officer came in and demanded to check your vault for dirty pictures, dirty stories, dirty jokes, dirty limericks, and so forth in books of antiquarian value?"

"I told you the reason he gave me."

The two dumpy policemen exchanged glances; the third, clearly from another department, fixed him with beady, furious eyes behind pince-nez glasses and somehow seemed to project both aggression and fury at him without saying a word.

"Why would I make up such a story?" inquired *le directeur*. "It's too absurd."

"I'll tell you what we'll do," said the third officer, a plumper man with pomaded if thinning hair showing much pate between its few strands and a little blot of moustache clearly modeled on either Himmler's or Hitler's. "We'll take ten of your employees to the street. If we are not satisfied with your answers, we'll shoot one of them. Then we'll ask again and see if—"

"Please," the Frenchman implored, "I tell the truth. I am unaccustomed to such treatment. My heart is about to explode. I tell the truth, it is not in me to lie, it is not my character."

"Description, please," said Macht. "Try hard. Try very hard."

"Mid-forties, well-built, though in a terrible-fitting suit. I must say I thought the suit far beneath him, for his carriage and confidence were of a higher order. Reddish-blond hair, blue eyes, rather a beautiful chin—rather a beautiful man, completely at home with himself and—"

"Look, please," said the assistant to the less ominous of the policemen. He handed over a photograph.

"Ahhhh—well, no, this is not him. Still, a close likeness. Same square shape. His eyes are not as strong as my visitor's, and his posture is something rather less. I must say, the suit fits much better."

Macht sat back. Yes, a British agent had been here. What on Earth could it have been for? What in the Mazarine Library was of such interest to the British that they had sent a man on such a dangerous mission, so fragile, so easily discovered? They must have been quite desperate.

"And what name did he give you?" Abel asked.

"He said his name was…Here, look, here's the document he signed. It was exactly the name on his papers, I checked very closely so there would be no mistake. I was trying my hardest to cooperate. I know there is no future in rebellion."

He opened his drawer, with trembling fingers took out a piece of paper, typed and signed.

"I should have shown it to you earlier. I was nonplussed, I apologize, it's not often that I have three policemen in my office."

He yammered on, but they paid no attention, as all bent forward to examine the signature at the bottom of the page.

It said, "Otto Boch, SS Hauptsturmführer, SS-RHSA, 13 rue Madeleine, Paris."

ACTION THIS DAY (CONT'D.)

The train left Montparnasse at exactly five minutes after five p.m. As SS Hauptsturmführer Boch, Gestapo, 13 rue Madeleine, Paris, Basil did not require anything save his identification papers, since Gestapo membership conferred on him an elite status that no rail clerk in the Wehrmacht monitoring the trains would dare challenge. Thus he flew by the ticket process and the security checkpoints and the flash inspection at the first-class carriage steps.

The train eased into motion and picked up speed as it left the marshaling yards resolving themselves toward blur as the darkness increased. He sat alone amid a smattering of German officers returning to duty after a few stolen nights in Paris. Outside, in the twilight, the little toy train depots of France fled by, and inside, the vibration rattled and the grumpy men tried to squeeze in a last bit of relaxation before once again taking up their vexing duties, which largely consisted of waiting until the Allied armies came to blow them up. Some of them thought of glorious death and sacrifice for the fatherland; some remembered the whores in whose embraces they had passed the time; some thought of ways to surrender to the Americans without getting themselves killed, but also of not being reported, for one never knew who was keeping records and who would see them.

But most seemed to realize that Basil was an undercover SS officer, and no one wanted to brook any trouble at all with the SS. Again, a wrong word, a misinterpreted joke, a comment too politically frank, and it was off to that dreaded 8.8 cm antitank gun facing the T-34s and the Russians. All of them preferred their luck with the Americans and the British than with the goddamn Bolsheviks.

So Basil sat alone, ramrod straight, looking neither forward nor back. His stern carriage conveyed seriousness of purpose, relentless attention to detail, and a devotion to duty so hard and true it positively radiated heat. He permitted no mirth to show, no human weakness. Most of all, and hardest for him, he allowed himself to show no irony, for irony was the one attribute that would never be found in the SS or in any Hitlerite true believer. In fact, in one sense the Third Reich and its adventure in mass death was a conspiracy against irony. Perhaps that is why Basil hated it so much and fought it so hard.

Boch said nothing. There was nothing to say. Instead it was Macht who did all the talking. They leaned on the hood of a Citroën radio car in the courtyard of the Bibliothèque Mazarine.

"Whatever it was he wanted, he got it. Now he has to get out of town and fast. He knows that sooner or later we may tumble to his acquisition of Herr Boch's identity papers, and at that point their usefulness comes to an abrupt end and they become absolutely a danger. So he will use them now, as soon as possible, and get as far away as possible."

"But he has purposefully refused any Resistance aid on this trip," said Abel.

"True."

"That would mean that he has no radio contact. That would mean that he has no way to set up a Lysander pickup."

"Excellent point, Walter. Yes, and that narrows his options considerably. One way out would be to head to the Spanish border. However, that's days away, involves much travel and the danger of constant security checks, and he would worry that his Boch identity would have been penetrated."

They spoke of Boch as if he were not there. In a sense, he wasn't. *"Sir, the breech is frozen." "Kick it! They're almost on us!" "I can't, sir. My foot fell off because of frostbite."*

"He could, I suppose, get to Calais and swim to Dover. It's only thirty-two kilometers. It's been done before."

"Even by a woman."

"Still, although he's a gifted professional, I doubt they have anyone quite that gifted. And even if it's spring, the water is four or five degrees centigrade."

"Yes," said Macht. "But he will definitely go by water. He will head to the most accessible seaport. Given his talents for subversion, he will find some sly fisherman who knows our patrol boat patterns and pay the fellow to haul him across. He can make it in a few hours, swim the last hundred yards to a British beach, and be home with his treasure, whatever that is."

"If he escapes, we should shoot the entire staff of the Bibliothèque Mazarine," said Boch suddenly. "This is on them. He stole my papers, yes, he pickpocketed me, but he could have stolen anyone's papers, so to single me out is rather senseless. I will make that point in my report."

"An excellent point," said Macht. "Alas, I will have to add that while he *could* have stolen anyone's papers, he *did* steal yours. And they were immensely valuable to him. He is now sitting happily on the train, thinking of the jam and buns he will enjoy tomorrow morning with his tea and whether it will be a DSC or a DSO that follows his name from now on. I would assume that as an honorable German officer you will take full responsibility. I really don't think we need to go shooting up any library staffs at this point. Why don't we concentrate on catching him, and that will be that."

Boch meant to argue but saw that it was useless. He settled back into his bleakness and said nothing.

"The first thing: which train?" Macht inquired of the air. The air had no answer and so he answered it himself. "Assuming that he left, as *le directeur* said, at exactly three forty-five p.m. by cab, he got to the Montparnasse station by four-fifteen. Using his SS papers, he would not need to stand in line for tickets or checkpoints, so he could leave almost immediately. My question thus has to be, what trains leaving for coastal destinations were available between four-fifteen and four forty-five? He will be on one of those trains. Walter, please call the detectives."

Abel spoke into the microphone by radio to his headquarters and waited. A minute later an answer came. He conveyed it to the two officers.

"A train for Cherbourg left at four-thirty, due to arrive in that city at eleven-thirty p.m. Then another at—"

"That's fine. He'd take the first. He doesn't want to be standing around, not knowing where we are in our investigations and thus assuming the worst. Now, Walter, please call Abwehr headquarters and get our people at Montparnasse to check the gate of that train for late-arriving German officers. I believe they have to sign a travel manifest. At least, I always do. See if Hauptsturmführer—ah, what's the first name, Boch?"

"Otto."

"SS Hauptsturmführer *Otto* Boch, Gestapo, came aboard at the last moment."

"Yes, sir."

Macht looked over at Boch. "Well, Hauptsturmführer, if this pans out, we may save you from your 8.8 in Russia."

"I serve where I help the Führer best. My life is of no consequence," said Boch darkly.

"You may feel somewhat differently when you see the tanks on the horizon," said Macht.

"It hardly matters. We can never catch him. He has too much head start. We can order the train met at Cherbourg, I suppose, and perhaps they will catch him."

"Unlikely. This eel is too slippery."

"Please tell me you have a plan."

"Of course I have a plan," said Macht.

"All right, yes," said Abel, turning from the phone. "Hauptsturmführer Boch did indeed come aboard at the last moment."

*

He sat, he sat, he sat. The train shook, rattled, and clacked. Twilight passed into lightless night. The vibrations played across everything. Men smoked, men drank from flasks, men tried to write letters home or read. It was not an express, so every half hour or so the train would lurch to a stop and one or two officers would leave, one or two would join. The lights flickered, cool air blasted into the compartment, the French conductor yelled the meaningless name of the town, and on and on they went, into the night.

At last the conductor yelled, "Bricquebec, twenty minutes," first in French, then in German.

He stood up, leaving his overcoat, and went to the loo. In it, he looked at his face in the mirror, sallow in the light. He soaked a towel, rubbed his face, meaning to find energy somehow. Action this day. Much of it. A last trick, a last wiggle.

The fleeing agent's enemy is paranoia. Basil had no immunity from it, merely discipline against it. He was also not particularly immune to fear. He felt both of these emotions strongly now, knowing that this nothingness of waiting for the train to get him where it had to was absolutely the worst.

But then he got his war face back on, forcing the armor of his charm and charisma to the surface, willing his eyes to sparkle, his smile to flash, his brow to furl romantically. He was back in character. He was Basil again.

"Excellent," said Macht. "Now, Boch, your turn to contribute. Use that SS power of yours we all so fear and call von Choltitz's adjutant. It is important that I be given temporary command authority over a unit called Nachtjagdgeschwader-9. Luftwaffe, of course. It's a wing headquartered at a small airfield near the town of Bricquebec, less than an hour outside Cherbourg.

Perhaps you remember our chat with its commandant, Oberst Gunther Scholl, a few days ago. Well, you had better hope that Oberst Scholl is on his game, because he is the one who will nab Johnny England for us."

Quite expectedly, Boch didn't understand. Puzzlement flashed in his eyes and fuddled his face. He began to stutter, but Abel cut him off.

"Please, Herr Hauptsturmführer. Time is fleeing."

Boch did what he was told, telling his Uber-Hauptsturmführer that Hauptmann Dieter Macht, of Abwehr III-B, needed to give orders to Oberst Scholl of NJG-9 at Bricquebec. Then the three got into the Citroën and drove the six blocks back to the Hotel Duval, where they went quickly to the phone operator at the board. Though the Abwehr men were sloppy by SS standards, they were efficient by German standards.

The operator handed a phone to Macht, who didn't bother to shed his trench coat and fedora.

"Hullo, hullo," he said, "Hauptmann Macht here, call for Oberst Scholl. Yes, I'll wait."

A few seconds later Scholl came on the phone.

"Scholl here."

"Yes, Oberst Scholl, it's Hauptmann Macht, Paris Abwehr. Have things been explained to you?"

"Hello, Macht. I know only that by emergency directive from Luftwaffe Command I am to obey your orders."

"Do you have planes up tonight?"

"No, the bomber streams are heading north tonight. We have the night off."

"Sorry to make the boys work, Herr Oberst. It seems your seatmate is returning to your area. I need manpower. I need you to meet and cordon off the Cherbourg train at the Bricquebec stop. It's due in at eleven-thirty p.m. Maximum effort. Get your pilots out of bed or out of the bars or brothels, and your mechanics, your ground crews, your fuelers. Leave only a skeleton crew in the tower. I'll tell you why in a bit."

"I must say, Macht, this is unprecedented."

"Oberst, I'm trying to keep you from the Russian front. Please comply enthusiastically so that you can go back to your three mistresses and your wine cellar."

"How did—"

"We have records, Herr Oberst. Anyhow, I would conceal the men in the bushes and inside the depot house until the train has all but arrived. Then, on command, they are to take up positions surrounding the train, making certain that no one leaves. At that point I want you to lead a search party from one end to the other, though of course start in first class. You know who you are looking for. He is now, however, in a dark blue pin-striped suit, double-breasted. He has a dark overcoat. He may look older, more abused, harder, somehow different from when last you saw him. You must be alert, do you understand?"

"Is he armed?"

"We don't know. Assume he is. Listen here, there's a tricky part. When you see him, you must not react immediately. Do you understand? Don't make eye contact, don't move fast or do anything stupid. He has an L-pill. It will probably be in his mouth. If he sees you coming for him, he will bite it. Strychnine—instant. It would mean so much more if we could take him alive. He may have many secrets, do you understand?"

"I do."

"When you take him, order your officers to go first for his mouth. They have to get fingers or a plug or something deep into his throat to keep him from biting or swallowing, then turn him facedown and pound hard on his back. He has to cough out that pill."

"My people will be advised. I will obviously be there to supervise."

"Oberst, this chap is very efficient, very practiced. He's an old dog with miles of travel on him. For years he's lasted in a profession where most perish in a week. Be very careful, be very astute, be very sure. I know you can do this."

"I will catch your spy for you, Macht."

"Excellent. One more thing. I will arrive within two hours in my own Storch, with my assistant, Abel."

"That's right, you fly."

"I do, yes. I have over a thousand hours, and you know how forgiving a Storch is."

"I do."

"So alert your tower people. I'll buzz them so they can light a runway for the thirty seconds it takes me to land, then go back to blackout. And leave a car and driver to take me to the station."

"I will."

"Good hunting."

"Good flying."

He put the phone down, turned to Abel, and said, "Call the airport, get the plane flight-checked and fueled so that we can take off upon arrival."

"Yes, sir."

"One moment," said Boch.

"Yes, Herr Hauptsturmführer?"

"As this is a joint SS-Abwehr operation, I demand to be a part of it. I will go along with you."

"The plane holds only two. It loses its agility when a third is added. It's not a fighter, it's a kite with a tiny motor."

"Then I will go instead of Abel. Macht, do not fight me on this. I will go to SS and higher if I need to. SS must be represented all through this operation."

"You trust my flying?"

"Of course."

"Good, because Abel does not. Now, let's go."

"Not quite yet. I have to change into my uniform."

Refreshed, Basil left the loo. But instead of turning back into the carriage and returning to his seat, he turned the other way, as if it were the natural thing to do, opened the door at the end of the carriage, and stepped out onto the rattling, trembling running board over the coupling between carriages. He waited for the door behind him to seal, tested for speed. Was the train slowing? He felt it was, as maybe the vibrations were further apart, signifying that the wheels churned slightly less aggressively, against an incline, on the downhill, perhaps negotiating a turn. Then, without a thought, he leaped sideways into the darkness.

Will I be lucky? Will the famous St. Florian charm continue? Will I float to a soft landing and roll through the dirt, only my dignity and my hair mussed? Or will this be the night it all runs out and I hit a bridge abutment, a tree trunk, a barbed-wire fence, and kill myself?

He felt himself elongate as he flew through the air, and as his leap carried him out of the gap between the two cars the slipstream hit him hard, sending his arms and legs flying wildly.

He seemed to hang in the darkness for an eternity, feeling the air beat him, hearing the roar of both the wind and the train, seeing nothing.

Then he hit. Stars exploded, suns collapsed, the universe split atomically, releasing a tidal wave of energy. He tasted dust, felt pain and a searing jab in his back, then high-speed abrasion of his whole body, a piercing blow to his left hand, had the illusion of rolling, sliding, falling, hurting all at once, and then he lay quiet.

Am I dead?

He seemed not to be.

The train was gone now. He was alone in the track bed, amid a miasma of dust and blood. At that point the pain clamped him like a vise and he felt himself wounded, though how badly was yet unknown. Could he move? Was he paralyzed? Had he broken any bones?

He sucked in oxygen, hoping for restoration. It came, marginally.

He checked his hip pocket to see if his Browning .380 was

still there, and there indeed it was. He reached next for his shin, hoping and praying that the Minox had survived the descent and landfall.

It wasn't there! The prospect of losing it was so tragically immense that he could not face it and exiled the possibility from his brain as he found the tape, still tight, followed it around, and in one second touched the aluminum skin of the instrument. Somehow the impact of the fall had moved it around his leg but had not sundered, only loosened, the tape. He pried it out, slipped it into his hip pocket. He slipped the Browning into his belt in the small of his back, then counted to three and stood.

His clothes were badly tattered, and his left arm so severely ripped he could not straighten it. His right knee had punched through the cheap pin-striped serge, and it too had been shredded by abrasions. But the real damage was done to his back, where he'd evidently encountered a rock or a branch as he decelerated in the dust, and it hurt immensely. He could almost feel it bruising, and he knew it would pain him for weeks. When he twisted he felt shards of glass in his side and assumed he'd broken or cracked several ribs. All in all, he was a mess.

But he was not dead, and he was more or less ambulatory.

He recalled the idiot Luftwaffe colonel on the ride down.

"Yes, our squadron is about a mile east of the tracks, just out of town. It's amazing how the boys have dressed it up. You should come and visit us soon, *monsieur*. I'll take you on a tour. Why, they've turned a rude military installation in the middle of nothing into a comfortable small German town, with sewers and sidewalks and streets, even a gazebo for summertime concerts. My boys are the best, and our wing does more than its share against the Tommy bombers."

That put the airfield a mile or so ahead, given that the tracks had to run north–south. He walked, sliding between trees and gentle undergrowth, through a rather civilized little forest, actually, and his night vision soon arrived through his headache and the pain in his back, which turned his walk into Frankenstein's lumber, but he was confident he was headed in the right direction. And very shortly he heard the approaching buzz of a small plane and knew absolutely that he was on track.

The Storch glided through the air, its tiny engine buzzing away smoothly like a hummingbird's heart. Spindly from its overengineered landing gear and graceless on the ground, it was a princess in the air. Macht held it at 450 meters, compass heading almost due south. He'd already landed at the big Luftwaffe base at Caen for a refueling, just in case Bricquebec proved outside the Storch's 300-kilometer range. He'd follow the same route back, taking the same fuel precautions. He knew: in the air, take nothing for granted. The western heading would bring him to the home of NJG-9 very soon, as he was flying throttle open, close to 175 km per hour. It was a beautiful little thing, light and reliable; you could feel that it wanted to fly, unlike the planes of the Great War, which had mostly been underpowered and overengineered, so close to the maximum they seemed to want to crash. You had to fight them to keep them in the air, while the Storch would fly all night if it could.

A little cool air rushed in, as the Perspex window was cranked half down. It kept the men cool; it also kept them from chatting, which was fine with Macht. It let him concentrate and enjoy, and he still loved the joy of being airborne.

Below, rural France slipped by, far from absolutely dark but too dark to make out details.

That was fine. Macht, a good flier, trusted his compass and his watch and knew that neither would let him down, and when he checked the time, he saw that he was entering NJG-9's airspace. He picked up his radio phone, clicked it a few times, and said, "Anton, Anton, this is Bertha 9-9, do you read?"

The headset crackled and snapped, and he thought perhaps he was on the wrong frequency, but then he heard, "Bertha 9-9, this is Anton—I have you; I can hear you. You're bearing a little to the southwest. I'd bear a few degrees to the north."

"Excellent, and thanks, Anton."

"When I have you overhead, I'll light a runway."

"Excellent, excellent. Thanks again, Anton."

Macht made the slight correction and was rewarded a minute later with the sudden flash to illumination of a long horizontal V. It took seconds to find the line into the darkness between the arms of the V which signified the landing strip. He eased back on the throttle, hearing the engine rpm's drop, watched his airspeed indicator fall to seventy-five, then sixty-five, eased the stick forward into a gentle incline, came into the cone of lights, and saw grass on either side of a wide tarmac built for the much larger twin-engine Me110 night fighters, throttled down some more, and alit with just the slightest of bumps.

When the plane's weight overcame its decreasing power, it almost came to a halt, but he revved back to taxi speed, saw the curved roofs of hangers ahead, and taxied toward them. A broad staging area before the four arched buildings, where the fighters paused and made a last check before deploying, was before him. He took the plane to it, pivoted it to face outward-bound down the same runway, and hit the kill switch. He could hear the vibrations stop, and the plane went silent.

Basil watched the little plane taxi to the hangers, pause, then helpfully turn itself back to the runway. Perfect. Whoever was flying was counting on a quick trip back and didn't want to waste time on the ground.

He crouched well inside the wire, about 300 meters from the airplane, which put him 350 meters from the four hangars. He knew, because Oberst Scholl had told him, that recent manpower levies had stripped the place of guards and security people, all of whom were now in transit to Russia, where their bodies were needed urgently to feed into the fire. As for the patrol dogs, one had died of food poisoning and the other was so old he could hardly move, again information provided by

Scholl. The security of NJG-9's night fighter base was purely an illusion; all nonessential personnel had been stripped away for something big in Russia.

In each hangar Basil could see the prominent outlines of the big night fighters, each cockpit slid open, resting at the nose-up, tail-down, fifteen-degree angle on the buttress of the two sturdy landing gears that descended from the huge bulge of engine on the broad wings. They were not small airplanes, and these birds wore complex nests of prongs on the nose, radar antennae meant to guide them to the bomber stream 7,600 meters above. The planes were all marked by the stark black Luftwaffe cross insignia, and their metallic snouts gleamed slightly in the lights, until the tower turned them off when the Storch had come to a safe stop.

He watched carefully. Two men. One wore a pilot's leather helmet but not a uniform, just a tent of a trench coat that hadn't seen cleaning or pressing in years. He was the pilot, and he tossed the helmet into the plane, along with an unplugged set of headphones. At the same time he pulled out a battered fedora, which looked like it had been crushed in the pocket of the coat for all the years it hadn't been pressed or cleaned.

No. 2 was more interesting. He was SS, totally, completely, avatar of dark style and darker menace. The uniform—jodhpurs and boots under a smart tunic, tight at the neck, black cap with death's head rampant in silver above the bill at a rakish angle— was more dramatic than the man, who appeared porky and graceless. He was shakier than the pilot, taking a few awkward steps to get his land legs back and drive the dizziness from his mind.

In time a Mercedes staff car emerged from somewhere in the darkness, driven by a Luftwaffer, who leaped out and offered a snappy salute. He did not shake hands with either, signifying his enlisted status as against their commissions, but obsequiously retreated to the car, where he opened the rear door.

The two officers slid in. The driver resumed his place behind the wheel, and the car sped away into the night.

*

"Yes, that's very good, Sergeant," said Macht as the car drove in darkness between the tower and administration complex on the left and the officers' mess on the right. The gate was a few hundred meters ahead. "Now, very quickly, let us out and continue on your way, outside the gate, along the road, and back to the station at Bricquebec, where your commanding officer waits."

"Ah, sir, my instructions are—"

"Do as I say, Sergeant, unless you care to join the other bad boys of the Wehrmacht on an infantry salient on some frozen hill of dog shit in Russia."

"Obviously, sir, I will obey."

"I thought you might."

The car slipped between two buildings, slowed, and Macht eased out, followed by Boch. Then the car rolled away, speeded up, and loudly issued the pretense that it was headed to town with two important passengers.

"Macht," hissed Boch, "what in the devil's name are you up to?"

"Use your head, Herr Hauptsturmführer. Our friend is not going to be caught like a fish in a bucket. He's too clever. He presumes the shortest possible time between his escape from Paris and our ability to figure it out and know what name he travels under. He knows he cannot make it all the way to Cherbourg and steal or hire a boat. No indeed, and since that idiot Scholl has conveniently plied him with information about the layout and operational protocols of NJG-9, as well as, I'm certain, a precise location, he has identified it as his best opportunity for an escape. He means, I suppose, to fly to England in a 110 like the madman Hess, but we have provided him with a much more tempting conveyance—the low, slow, gentle Storch. He cannot turn it down, do you see? It is absolutely his best—his only— chance to bring off his crazed mission, whatever it is. But we will stop him. Is that pistol loaded?"

Boch slapped the Luger under the flap of his holster on his ceremonial belt.

"Of course. One never knows."

"Well, then, we shall get as close as possible and wait for him to make his move. I doubt he's a quarter kilometer from us now. He'll wait until he's certain the car is gone and the lazy Luftwaffe tower personnel are paying no attention, and then he'll dash to the airplane, and off he goes."

"We will be there," said Boch, pulling his Luger.

"Put that thing away, please, Herr Hauptsturmführer. It makes me nervous."

Basil began his crawl. The grass wasn't high enough to cover him, but without lights, no tower observer could possibly pick him out flat against the ground. His plan was to approach on the oblique, locating himself on such a line that the plane was between himself and the watchers in the tower. It wouldn't obscure him, but it would be more data in a crowded binocular view into an already dark zone, and he hoped that the lazy officer up there was not really paying that much attention, instead simply nodding off on a meaningless night of duty far from any war zone and happy that he wasn't out in the godforsaken French night on some kind of insane catch-the-spy mission two kilometers away at the train station.

It hurt, of course. His back throbbed, a bruise on his hip ached, a pain between his eyes would not go away, and the burns on knee and arm from his abrasions seemed to mount in intensity. He pulled himself through the grass like a swimmer, his fear giving him energy that he should not have had, the roughness of his breath drowning out the night noise. He seemed to crawl for a century, but he didn't look up, because, as if he were swimming the English Channel, if he saw how far he had to go, the blow to his morale would be stunning.

Odd filaments of his life came up from nowhere, viewed

from strange angles so that they made only a bit of sense and maybe not even that. He hardly knew his mother, he had hated his father, his brothers were all older than he was and had formed their friendships and allegiances already. Women that he had been intimate with arrived to mind, but they did not bring pride and triumph, only memories of human fallibility and disappointment, theirs and his; and his congenital inability to remain faithful to any of them, love or not, always revealed its ugliness. Really, he had had a useless life until he signed with the crown and went on his adventures—it was a perfect match for his adventurer's temperament, his casual cruelty, his cleverness, his ruthlessness. He had no problem with any of it: the deceit, the swindles, the extortion, the cruel manipulation of the innocent, even the murder. He had killed his first man, a corrupt Malaysian police inspector, in 1935, and he remembered the jump of the big Webley, the smell of cordite, the man's odd deflation as he surrendered to gravity. He thought it would have been so much more; it was, really, nothing, nothing at all, and he supposed that his own death, in a few minutes, a few hours, a few days, a few weeks, or next year or the year after, would mean as little to the man who killed him, probably some Hanoverian conscript with a machine pistol firing blindly into the trees that held him.

So it would go. That is the way of the wickedness called war. It eats us all. In the end, it and it alone is the victor, no matter what the lie called history says. The god of war, Mars the Magnificent and Tragic, always wins.

And then he was there.

He was out of grass. He had come to the hard-packed earth of the runway. He allowed himself to look up. The little plane was less than fifty meters away, tilted skyward on its absurdly high landing-gear struts. He had but to jump to the cockpit, turn it on, let the rpm's mount, then take off the brakes, and it would pull itself forward and up, due north, straight on till morning.

Fifty meters, he thought. *All that's between myself and Blighty.*

He gathered himself for the crouched run to it. He checked: *Pistol still with me, camera in my pocket, all nice and tidy.* He had one last thing to do. He reached into his breast pocket and shoved his fingers down, probing, touching, searching. Then he had it. He pulled the L-pill out, fifty ccs of pure strychnine under a candy shell, and slid it into his mouth, back behind his teeth, far in the crevice between lip and jawbone. One crunch and he got to Neverland instantly.

"There," whispered Boch. "It's him, there, do you see, crouching just off the runway." They knelt in the darkness of the hangar closest to the Storch.

Macht saw him. The Englishman seemed to be gathering himself. *The poor bastard is probably exhausted. He's been on the run in occupied territory over four days, bluffed or brazened his way out of a dozen near misses.* Macht could see a dark double-breasted suit that even from this distance looked disheveled.

"Let him get to the plane," said Macht. "He will be consumed by it, and under that frenzy we approach, keeping the tail and fuselage between ourselves and him."

"Yes, I see."

"You stand off and hold him with the Luger. I will jump him and get this"—he reached into his pocket and retrieved a pipe—"into his mouth, to keep him from swallowing his suicide capsule. Then I will handcuff him and we'll be done."

They watched as the man broke from the edge of the grass, running like an athlete, with surprising power to his strides, bent double as if to evade tacklers, and in a very little time got himself to the door of the Storch's cockpit, pulled it open, and hoisted himself into the seat.

"Now," said Macht, and the two of them emerged from their hiding place and walked swiftly to the airplane.

His Luger out, Boch circled to the left to face the cockpit squarely from the left side while Macht slid along the right side of the tail boom, reached the landing struts, and slipped under them.

"*Halt!*" yelled Boch, and at precisely that moment Macht rose, grabbed the astonished Englishman by the lapels of his suit, and yanked him free of the plane. They crashed together, Macht pivoting cleverly so that his quarry bounced off his hip and went into space. He landed hard, far harder than Macht, who simply rode him down, got a knee on his chest, bent, and stuffed his pipe in the man's throat. The agent coughed and heaved, searching for leverage, but Macht had wrestled many a criminal into captivity and knew exactly how to apply leverage.

"Spit it out!" he cried in English. "Damn you, spit it out!" He rolled the man as he shook him, then slapped him with a hard palm between the shoulder blades, and in a second the pill was ejected like a piece of half-chewed, throat-obstructing meat, riding a propulsive if involuntary spurt of breath, and arched to earth, where Macht quickly put a heavy shoe on it, crushing it.

"Hands up, Englishman, goddamn you," he yelled as Boch neared, pointing the Luger directly into the face of the captive to make the argument more persuasively.

There was no fight left in him, or so it seemed. He put up his hands.

"Search him, Macht," said Boch.

Macht swooped back onto the man, ran his hands around his waist, under his armpits, down his legs.

"Only this," he said, holding aloft a small camera. "This'll tell us some things."

"I think you'll be disappointed, old man," said the Englishman. "I am thinking of spiritual enlightenment, and my photographs merely propose a path."

"Shut up," bellowed Boch.

"Now," said Macht, "we'll—"

"Not so fast," said Boch.

The pistol covered both of them.

It happened so fast. He knew it would happen fast, but not this fast. *Halt!* came the cry, utterly stunning him with its loudness and closeness, and then this demon rose from nowhere, pulled him—the strength was enormous—from the plane, and slammed him to the ground. In seconds the L-pill had been beaten from him. Whoever this chap was, he knew a thing or two.

Now Basil stood next to him. Breathing hard, quite fluttery from exhaustion, and trying not to face the enormity of what had just happened, he tried to make sense, even as one thing, his capture, turned into another—some weird German command drama.

The SS officer had the Luger on both of them.

"Boch, what do you think you are doing?" said the German in the trench coat.

"Taking care of a certain problem," said the SS man. "Do you think I care to have an Abwehr bastard file a report that will end my career and get me shipped to Russia? Did you think I could permit *that*?"

"My friends," said Basil in German, "can't we sit down over a nice bottle of schnapps and talk it out? I'm sure you two can settle your differences amicably."

The SS officer struck him across the jaw with his Luger, driving him to the ground. He felt blood run down his face as the cheek began to puff grotesquely.

"Shut your mouth, you bastard," the officer said. Then he turned back to the police officer in the trench coat.

"You see how perfectly you have set it up for me, Macht? No witnesses, total privacy, your own master plan to capture this spy. Now I kill the two of you. But the story is, he shot you, I shot him. I'm the hero. Moreover, whatever treasure of intelligence that little camera holds, it comes to me. I will weep pious tears at your funeral, which I'm sure will be held under the highest honors, and I will express my profound regrets to your unit as it ships out to Russia."

"You lunatic," said Macht. "You disgrace."

"Sieg Heil," said the SS officer as he fired.

He missed.

This was because his left ventricle was interrupted mid-beat by a .380 bullet fired a split second earlier by Basil's .380 Browning in the Abwehr agent's right hand. Thus Boch jerked and his shot plunged off into the darkness.

The SS officer seemed to melt. His knees hit first—not that it mattered, because he was already quite dead, and he toppled to the left, smashing his nose, teeth, and pince-nez.

"Excellent shot, old man," said Basil. "I didn't even feel you remove my pistol."

"I knew he would be up to something. He was too cooperative. Now, sir, tell me what I should do with you. Should I arrest you and earn the Iron Cross, or should I give you back your pistol and camera and watch you fly away?"

"Even as a philosophic exercise, I doubt I could argue the first proposition with much force," said Basil.

"Give me an argument, then. You saved my life, or rather your pistol did, and you saved the lives of the men in my unit. But I need a justification. I'm German, you know, with that heavy, irony-free, ploddingly logical mind."

"All right, then. I did not come here to kill Germans. I have killed no Germans. Actually the only one who has killed Germans, may I point out, sir, is you. Germans will die, more and more, and Englishmen and Russians and even the odd Frog or two. Possibly an American. That can't be stopped. But I am told that the message on the film, which is completely without military value, by the way, has a possibility of ending the war by as much as two years sooner than expected. I don't know about you, sir, but I am sick to death of war."

"Fair enough. I am, too. Here, take this, and your camera, and get out of here. There's the plane."

"Ah, one question, if I may?"

"Yes?"

"How do you turn it on?"

"You don't fly, do you?"

"Not really, no. At least, not *technically*. I mean I've watched it, I've flown in them, I know from the cinema that one pulls the stick up to climb, down to descend, right and left, with pedals—"

"God, you are something, I must say."

And so the German told him where the ignition was, where the brakes were, what groundspeed he had to achieve to go airborne, and where the compass was for his due north heading.

"Don't go over 150 meters. Don't go over 150 kilometers per hour. Don't try anything fancy. When you get to England, find a nice soft meadow, put her down, and just before you touch down, switch off the magnetos and let the plane land itself."

"I will."

"And remember one thing, Englishman. You were good— you were the best I ever went after. But in the end I caught you."

THE WAR ROOM

"Gentlemen," said Sir Colin Gubbins, "I do hope you'll forgive Captain St. Florian his appearance. He is just back from abroad, and he parked his airplane in a tree."

"Sir, I am assured the tree will survive," said Basil. "I cannot have *that* on my conscience, along with so many other items."

Basil's right arm was encased in plaster of Paris; it had been broken by his fall from the tree. His torso, under his shirt, was encased in strong elastic tape, several miles of it, in fact, to help his four broken ribs mend. The swelling on his face, from the blow delivered by the late SS Hauptsturmführer Boch, had gone down somewhat, but it was still yellowish, corpulent, and quite repulsive, as was the blue-purple wreath that surrounded his bloodshot eye. He needed a cane to walk, and of all his nicks, it was the abraded knee that turned out to hurt the most, other than the headache, constant and throbbing, from the concussion. In the manly British officer way, however, he still managed to wear his uniform, even if his jacket was thrown about his shoulders over his shirt and tie.

"It looks like you had a jolly trip," said the admiral.

"It had its ups and downs, sir," said Basil.

"I think we know why we are here," said General Cavendish, ever irony-free, "and I would like to see us get on with it."

It was the same as it always was: the darkish War Room under the Treasury, the prime minister's lair. That great man's cigar odor filled the air, and too bad if you couldn't abide it. A few posters, a few maps, a few cheery exhortations to duty, and that was it. There were still four men across from Basil, a general, an admiral, Gubbins, and the man of tweed, Professor Turing.

"Professor," said Sir Colin, "as you're just in from the country and new to the information, I think it best for you to acquire the particulars of Captain St. Florian's adventures from his report. But you know his results. He succeeded, though he got quite a thrashing in the process. I understand it was a close-run thing. Now you have had the results of his mission on hand at Bletchley for over a week, and it is time to see whether or not St. Florian's blood, sweat, and tears were worth it."

"Of course," said Turing. He opened his briefcase, took out the seven Minox photos of the pages from *The Path to Jesus*, reached in again, and pulled out around three hundred pages of paper, whose leaves he flipped to show the barons of war. Every page was filled with either numerical computation, handwriting on charts, or lengthy analysis in typescript.

"We have not been lazy," he said. "Gentleman, we have tested everything. Using our decryptions from the Soviet diplomatic code as our index, we have reduced the words and letters to numerical values and run them through every electronic bombe we have. We have given them to our best intuitive code breakers—it seems to be a gift, a certain kind of mind that can solve these problems quickly, without much apparent effort. We have analyzed them up, down, sideways, and backwards. We have tested the message against every classical code known to man. We have compared it over and over, word by word, with the printed words of the Reverend MacBurney. We have measured it to the thousandth of an inch, even tried to project it as a geometric problem. Two PhDs from Oxford even tried to find a pattern in the seemingly random arrangement of the odd crosslike formations doodled across all the pages. Their conclusion was that the *seemingly* random pattern was *actually* random."

He went silent.

"Yes?" said Sir Colin.

"There is no secret code within it," the professor finally said. "As any possible key to a book code, it solves nothing. It unlocks nothing. There is no secret code at all within it."

The moment was ghastly.

Finally Basil spoke.

"Sir, it's not what I went through to obtain those pages that matters. I've had worse drubbings in football matches. But a brave and decent man has put himself at great risk to get them to you. His identity would surprise you, but it seems there are some of them left on the other side. Thus I find it devastating to write the whole thing off and resign him to his fate for nothing. It weighs heavily."

"I understand," said Professor Turing. "But you must understand as well. Book codes work with books, don't they? Because the book is a closed, locked universe—that is the *point*, after all. What makes the book code work, as simple a device as it is, is, after all, that it's a *book*. It's mass-produced on Linotype machines, carefully knitted up in a bindery, festooned with some amusing imagery for a cover, and whether you read it in Manchester or Paris or Berlin or Kathmandu, the same words will be found on the same places on the same page, and thus everything makes sense. This, however, is not a book but a manuscript, in a human hand. Who knows how age, drinking, debauchery, tricks of memory, lack of stamina, advanced syphilis or gonorrhea may have corrupted the author's effort? It will almost certainly get messier and messier as it goes along, and it may in the end not resemble the original at all. Our whole assumption was that it would be a close enough replica to what MacBurney had produced twenty years earlier for us to locate the right letters and unlock the code. Everything about it is facsimile, after all, even to those frequent religious doodles on the pages. If it were a good facsimile, the growth or shrinkage would be consistent and we could alter our calculations by measurable quantities and unlock it. But it was not to be. Look at the pages, please, Captain. You will see that even among themselves, they vary greatly. Sometimes the letters are large, sometimes small. Sometimes a page contains twelve hundred letters, sometimes six hundred, sometimes twenty-three hundred. In certain of them, it seems clear that he was drunk, pen in hand, and the lines are all atumble, and he is just barely in control. His damnable lack of consistency dooms any effort to use this as a key to a code contained in the original. I told you it was a long shot."

Again a long and ghastly silence.

"Well, then, Professor," said Gubbins, "that being the case, I think we've taken you from your work at Bletchley long enough. And we have been absent from our duties as well. Captain St. Florian needs rest and rehabilitation. Basil, I think all present will enthusiastically endorse you for decoration, if it matters, for an astonishing and insanely courageous effort. Perhaps a nice promotion, Basil. Would you like to be a major? Think of the trouble you could cause. But please don't be bitter. To win a war you throw out a million seeds and hope that some of them produce, in the end, fruit. I'll alert the staff to call—"

"Excuse me," said Professor Turing. "What exactly is going on here?"

"Ah, Professor, there seems to be no reason for us to continue."

"I daresay you chaps have got to learn to listen," he said.

Basil was slightly shocked by the sudden tartness in his voice.

"I am not like Captain St. Florian, a witty ironist, and I am not like you three high mandarins with your protocols and all that elaborate and counterfeit bowing and scraping. I am a scientist. I speak in exact truth. What I say is true and nothing else is."

"I'm rather afraid I don't grasp your meaning, sir," said Gubbins stiffly. It was clear that neither he nor the other two mandarins enjoyed being addressed so dismissively by a forty-year-old professor in baggy tweeds and wire-frame glasses.

"I said listen. *Listen!*" repeated the professor, rather rudely, but with such intensity it became instantly clear that he regarded them as intellectual inferiors and was highly frustrated by their rash conclusion.

"Sir," said General Cavendish, rather icily, "if you have more to add, please add it. As General Sir Colin has said, we have other duties—"

"*Secret* code!" interrupted the professor.

All were stupefied.

"Don't you see? It's rather brilliant!" He laughed, amused by the code maker's wit. "Look here," he said. "I shall try to explain. What is the most impenetrable code of all to unlock? You cannot do it with machines that work a thousand times faster than men's brains."

Nobody could possibly answer.

"It is the code that pretends to be a code but isn't at all."

More consternation, impatience, yet fear of being mocked.

"Put another way," said the professor, "the code is the absence of code."

No one was going to deal with that one.

"Whoever dreamed this up, our Cambridge librarian or an NKVD spymaster, he was a smart fellow. Only two people on earth could know the meaning of this communication, though I'm glad to say they've been joined by a third one. Me. It came to me while running. Great for clearing the mind, I must say."

"You have the advantage, Professor," said Sir Colin. "Please, continue."

"A code is a disguise. Suppose something is disguised as itself?"

The silence was thunderous.

"All right, then. Look at the pages. *Look at them!*"

Like chastened schoolboys, the class complied.

"You, St. Florian, you're a man of hard experience in the world. Tell me what you see."

"Ah…" said Basil. He was completely out of irony. "Well, ah, a messy scrawl of typical eighteenth-century handwriting, capitalized nouns, that sort of thing. A splotch of something, perhaps wine, perhaps something more dubious."

"Yes?"

"Well, I suppose, all these little religious symbols."

"Look at them carefully."

Basil alone did not need to unlimber reading spectacles. He saw what they were quickly enough.

"They appear to be crosses," he said.

"Just crosses?"

"Well, each of them is mounted on a little hill. Like Calvary, one supposes."

"Not like Calvary. There were three on Calvary. This is only one. Singular."

"Yes, well, now that I look harder, I see the hill isn't exactly a hill. It's segmented into round, irregular shapes, very precisely drawn in the finest line his nib would permit. I would say it's a pile of stones."

"At last we are getting somewhere."

"I think I've solved your little game, Professor," said General Cavendish. "That pile of stones, that would be some kind of road marker, eh? Yes, and a cross has been inserted into it. Road marker, that is, marking the path, is that what it is? It would be a representation of the title of the pamphlet, *The Path to Jesus.* It is an expression of the central meaning of his argument."

"Not what it *means*. Didn't you hear me? Are you deaf?"

The general was taken aback by the ferocity with which Professor Turing spoke.

"I am not interested in what it means. If it means something, that meaning is different from the thing itself. I am interested in what it *is*. Is, not means."

"I believe," said the admiral, "a roadside marker is called a cairn. So that is exactly what it is, Professor. Is that what you—"

"Please take it the last step. There's only one more. Look at it and tell me what it is."

"Cairn... cross," said Basil. "It can only be called a cairncross. But that means nothing unless..."

"Unless what?" commanded Turing.

"A name," said Sir Colin.

Hello, hello, said Basil to himself. He saw where the path to Jesus led.

"The Soviet spymaster was telling the Cambridge librarian the name of the agent at Bletchley Park so that he could tell the agent's new handler. The device of communication was a 154-year-old doodle. The book-code indicators were false, part of the disguise."

"So there is a man at Bletchley named Cairncross?" asked Sir Colin.

"John Cairncross, yes," said Professor Turing. "Hut 6. Scotsman. Don't know the chap myself, but I've heard his name mentioned—supposed to be first-class."

"John Cairncross," said Sir Colin.

"He's your Red spy. Gentlemen, if you need to feed information to Stalin on Operation Citadel, you have to do it through Comrade Cairncross. When it comes from him, Stalin and the Red generals will believe it. They will fortify the Kursk salient. The Germans will be smashed. The retreat from the East will begin. The end will begin. What was it again? 'Home alive in '45,' not 'Dead in heaven in '47.'"

"Bravo," said Sir Colin.

"Don't *bravo* me, Sir Colin. I just work at sums, like Bob Cratchit. Save your bravos for that human fragment of the Kipling imagination sitting over there."

"I say," said Basil, "instead of a *bravo*, could I have a nice whisky?"

ACKNOWLEDGMENTS

Thanks to Otto Penzler for commissioning this short-form experiment for me and badgering me until I finished. Barrett Tillman was indispensable on German aviation, Lenne Miller on general editing and proofreading, and Gary Goldberg on cyber transmissions. Naturally all failures of taste, plot, and nerve devolve solely to me.

Every Seven Years

Denise Mina

I AM STANDING on a rostrum in my old school library. An audience of thirty or so people is applauding, I am smiling and mouthing "thank you" and I know that they all hate me.

The audience looks like people I used to know seven years ago, but less hopeful and fatter. Actually, they're not fat, they're normal sized, but I'm an actor. We have to stay thin because our bodies are a tool of our trade. A lot of us have eating disorders and that creates an atmosphere of anxiety around food. The applauding audience isn't fat; I'm just London-actress thin, which is almost-too-thin.

I look down. The rostrum is composed of big ply board cubes that fit together. We are standing on five but the corner one is missing; maybe they ran out of cubes, or one is broken. It's like standing on a slide puzzle, where one tile is missing and the picture is jumbled. This seems hugely significant to me while it is happening: we're in a puzzle and a big bit is missing. The whole afternoon feels like a hyper-real dream sequence so far, interspersed with flashes of terror and disbelief. My mum died this morning.

There is no chair on the rostrum, no microphone, no lectern to hide behind. I stand, exposed, on a broken box and justify my career as a minor actress to an audience who doesn't like me.

There are about thirty people in the audience. Not exactly the Albert Hall, but they are appreciative of my time because my mum is ill. She's in the local hospital and that's why I'm back. It has been mentioned several times, in the introductions and during the questioning. So sorry about your mum.

Maybe pity is fueling the applause. Maybe time is moving strangely because I'm in shock. I smile and mouth "thank you" at them for a third time. I want to cry but I'm professional and I swallow the wave of sadness that engulfs me. Never bitter. My mother's words: never bitter, Else. That's not for us. My mum said life is a race against bitterness. She said if you die before bitterness eats you, then you've won. She won.

A fat child is climbing up the side of the rostrum towards me. He can't be more than four or five. He's so round and wobbly he has to swing his legs sideways to walk properly. He comes up to me and—tada!—he shoves a bunch of supermarket flowers at my belly without looking at me. The price is still on them. He must be someone's kid. He's not the kid you would choose to give a visiting celebrity flowers, even a crap celebrity. He turns away and sort of rolls off the side of the platform and runs back to his mum.

He pumps his chunky little arms at his side, leg-swing-run, leg-swing-run, running all the way down the aisle to a big lady sitting at the back. Her face brims with pride. He looks lovely to her. She's just feeding him what she's eating; she doesn't see him as fat. I'm seeing that. I'm probably the only person in the room who is seeing that. Everyone else is seeing a cute wee boy doing a cute wee thing.

It's me. Bitterness comes in many forms. Malevolent gossip, lack of gratitude, even self-damaging diet regimes. Today bitterness is a tsunami coming straight at me. It's a mile-high wall of regret and recrimination. Broken things are carried in the threatening wave: chair legs and dead people and boats. And it is coming for me.

My mum died. This morning. In a hospital nearby. My mum died.

This is going on, this stupid event in a dreary public library on the island where I grew up. At the same time an alternate universe is unfolding, the one where I am a daughter and my mum is no longer alive.

I love cats. On YouTube there's an eight-minute montage of cats crashing into windows and glass doors they thought were open. It went viral; you've probably seen it. Lots of different cats flying gleefully into what they think is empty space, bouncing off glass. It's funny, not because the cats are hurt; they're not hurt. It's funny because of that moment afterward when the cat sits up. They look at the glass, variously astonished or angry or embarrassed. It's funny because it is so recognizably human, that reaction. The WTF reaction.

Hitting the glass is where I am with the fact that my mum has died. I keep forgetting, thinking other things—I need a wee—that woman has got a spot on her neck—I want to sit down—and then BOOM I hit the glass.

But actors are special. We just keep going. If we forget our lines, or the scenery falls, or a colleague has died on stage, we just keep going. So I just keep going.

I'm standing on the rostrum with Karen Little. Karen and I grew up together. She made my life a misery at school and we haven't seen each other for seven years. I can see her eyes narrow when she looks at me. I can see her shoulders rise, her lips tighten. Maybe she hates me even more now. I don't have a system of quantification for hate. I've forgotten what it is to be the recipient of this, so maybe that's why it feels heightened. Life has been kind to me since I left.

My mum died and, frankly, I'm not really giving too much of a shit. I want to tell her that: hey, Karen, d'you know what? The human body renews itself every seven years. Each individual cell and atom is replaced on a seven-year cycle. It's been seven years since we met and I'm different now. You're different now. All that stuff from before? We could just let that go.

But that's not how we do things on the island. Aggression is unspoken here. We're too dependent on one another to have outright fights.

Karen Little, just to fill you in on the background, was in my class. There were thirteen in our year. Eight girls, five boys. Karen was good at everything. Head girl material from the age of twelve, she was bossy, sporty, and academic. She was like all of the Spice Girls in one person. Except Baby Spice. Karen was never soft. Growing up on a farm will do that to you.

She has gray eyes and blond hair, Viking coloring. She looks like a Viking, too. Big, busty, kind of fertile-looking hips. She stands on both feet at the same time, always looks as if she is standing on the prow of a boat.

I'm a sloucher. An academic nothing. A dark-haired incomer. My mother moved here to teach but gave it up before I was born. After the accident, they made it clear they didn't want her. Even the children shunned her.

Karen's a full head taller than me. So it was odd that she had this thing about me. I never understood why she hated me so much. Everyone hated Mum because of the accident, but Karen hated me. It wasn't reciprocated and it was scary.

No one there liked my mother or me but Karen took it to extremes. I saw her looking at me sometimes, as if she'd like to hit me. She didn't do anything. I should emphasis that. But I often saw her staring at me, at parties, across roads, in class. I was scared of her. I think she had a lot going on at home and I became a focus for her ire.

Now, Karen is the librarian in the school library.

My face hits the glass.

There is no one here I can confide in. My. Mum. Died. Three words. I haven't said them to anyone yet. If I don't say it maybe the universe will realize its mistake. It will get sorted out. The governor will call at the last minute and stop her dying of lung cancer. Maybe, if I don't say it.

Or maybe I'm worried that if I say it I will start crying, I'll cry and cry and maybe I will die of it.

No one in the school library knows yet. They will as soon as they leave. Mum is headline news around here. Everyone knows that she isn't well, in the local hospital with lung cancer. Since I got back several people have told me that she will get better because the treatment is better than it was. People tell me happy stories about other people who had cancer but got better and now they run marathons, climb mountains, have second lives. Mention of cancer prompts happy stories, as if people feel jinxed by the word and need to rebalance the narrative. I've learned that you can't make them stop with the positive anecdotes. They need them. No one here can believe that my mother is going to die anymore than I can. My mother is an unfinished song. It's out of character that she will simply die of an illness. My mother has never done a simple thing.

But they know that's why I'm back on the island, in the small town of my birth, standing on a rostrum with Karen Little, listening to interminable clapping.

I mouth "thank you" again and watch the fat kid's mother pull him onto her knee. He looks forward, flush from his run. Behind him the mother shuts her eyes and kisses his hair with a gesture so tender I have to look away.

Karen cornered me in the chemist's. Do come, Else, please. We would be so glad to hear from you, all your exciting experiences! Karen covers her loathing with smiles. They all do. Anywhere else we would have been excluded, picked on. Maybe they would have burnt crosses on our lawn. The hostility would have affected our day-to-day interactions, but the island is small, we are so dependent on each other for survival, that instead, aggression is a background thrum in a superficially pleasant existence.

Tourists fall in love with the white beaches and palm trees. The seeds are washed up here on the Gulf Stream and palm trees grow all over the island. The landscape looks tropical until you step off the coach or out of the hotel or from your rented car. It is bitterly cold here. The vegetation makes it perpetually unexpected. The distillery towns are always dotted with startled tourists from Spain or Japan, all looking for a sweater shop. That's what we're famous for: whisky and sweaters.

Karen is tired of watching me being applauded. It's dying out anyway, so she steps in front of me and blocks my sight lines.

Thank you! Her voice is shrill. Thank you to our local celeb, Miss Else Kennedy!

She has prompted another round of applause. Oh, god. My right knee buckles, as if it knows this will never end and it's decided to go solo and just get the hell out of here.

Karen turns to address me. Her face is too close to mine. She has lipstick on, it is bleeding into a dry patch of skin at the side of her mouth, and I can smell it; she's close. I feel as if she's going to bite my face and it makes me want to cry.

We have a present for you!

She is smiling with her teeth apart looking from me to the audience. Something special is coming, I can see the venom spark in her eye like the flick of a serpent's tail.

Karen's voice continues to trill through my fog of grief and annoyance. Special gift! It will be presented by —— Marie! (I wasn't listening to that bit).

—— Marie is also a bit scary looking. She has an unusually big face, her hair is greasy. She climbs up onto the platform holding a yellow hardback with both hands. She looks as if she's delivering a sacred pizza.

I know this isn't a surreal dream. It's just work-a-day grim and I'm bristling with shock and sorrow. My mum died. I feel the glass bounce me backwards on the decking.

—— Marie takes tiny steps to get to me, the rostrum isn't big enough for three people and I'm making the best of it, a professional smile is nailed to my face.

But then I see what is in her hand.

It's the book. My smile drops.

Karen's voice is loud in my ear.

A lovely book about the famous painter: Roy Lik-Tin-Styne! This is, believe it or not! The very last book Else took out of our library! Isn't that fun? And Anne-Marie is going to present it to her as a memento of this lovely visit!

Karen turns and looks straight at me, giving a loud and hearty laugh. HAHAHA! she says, straight into my face HAHAHA! She is so close her gusty laugh moves my hair.

Anne-Marie drops the big book into one of my hands and shakes the other one. She is smiling vacantly over my shoulder. Then she's gone.

What do you think of that, Else?

I can't speak. I look at it. The flyleaf is ripped but it is the same book. Time-yellowed cover, whitened along the spine from sun exposure. I know then. I will kill Karen Little. And I'll kill her tonight.

Back in the house I sit in my mum's living room with a huge glass of straight vodka in my hand.

I haven't had a drink for seven years and surprise myself by pouring straight Smirnoff into a pint glass. This is what I want. Not a glass of full-bodied red or a relaxing beer. What I want is a sour, bitter drink that will wither my tongue and make me half mad. I want a drink that will make me sick and screw me up.

Before this morning, before the final breath went out of her as I held her hand in the hospital, I thought of Totty as "Mum." Now I find I call her "my mum." In the Scots Gaelic language there is no ownership. It isn't *my* cup of tea. The cup of tea is *with* me. Now that Mum is no longer with me she has become *my* mum. I'm claiming ownership of her.

My mum is all around me in this room, I can smell her. I can see the book she was reading before she went into the hospital, open on the arm of the chair. This house is polluted with books. Her phrase. Polluted. They're everywhere. They're not furniture or mementoes. They're not arranged by spine color on bookcases or anything like that. They're functioning things, on the bathroom floor, in the kitchen by the cooker, on the floor in the hall, as if she had to stop reading that one to pull a coat on and go out. And her tastes were very catholic. Romance, classic, Russian literature, crime fiction. She'd read anything. I've known her to read a book halfway through before realizing that she'd read it before. She didn't read to show off at book groups or for discussion. She never made a show of her erudition. She just liked to be lost.

The book from the school is on the table in front of me. Yellow, accusing. Lichtenstein is on the cover, photographed in black and white. He is standing contraposto in the picture, looking a little fey. The height of the white room behind him implies a studio space.

I can't look at that anymore.

The couch is facing the window. A sloping lawn leads down to an angry sea. America is over there, obscured from view by the curvature of the earth and nothing more. Away is over there.

I sat here often while she was alive, on the couch, planning my exit from this small place. *I will get away.* The day after my sixteenth birthday, I left the island like a rat on fire. Down to London, sleeping on floors, in beds I didn't particularly want to be in, just to be away. I would have sold my soul. But my mum stayed.

She came to visit me in London once I got a place of my own, when I was doing the TV soap and the money was rolling in. Nothing makes you feel rich as much as having been poor. Totty came down to London "for a visit." Always "for a visit." Coming back was not negotiable. She was always going to come back here, to an island that hated her.

I asked her to stay with me in London. I did it several times. Sobbing, drunk, and begging her to stay. She took my hand and said *I love you* and *you know I can't* and *they'll win then.* Finally she said she wouldn't come and visit anymore if I asked her again. And you should stop drinking, Else. You don't have a problem but you drink for the wrong reasons. Get drunk for fun, she said, and only for fun. Never get drunk to give yourself guts. That's what I'm doing now. Sipping the foul vodka as if it were medicine, trying to swallow it before it touches the sides. I need guts tonight.

I look at the book on the table and I'm back at the event in the small, packed library. Why did they even have a podium, I wonder now. Everyone could see me perfectly well. In hindsight it feels like a freak show tent, with me as the freak everyone wants to peer at. Karen planned it all around the giving of the book. She must have known while she watched me speak about my pathetic career, my reality show appearances, the failed comedy series. She must have known when she cornered me in the chemist's.

I look down at the book.

I'm getting drunk and I try to think of an alternative explanation: is this a custom? Do people give people "the last book they took out of their school library"? No.

I should have asked: did someone else suggest this? But I know in my gut that the answer would be no. No one else suggested this. Karen Little suggested giving you this book. No one else would know which was the last book you took out of the school library. And why would they? Why the hell would they? It means nothing to anyone but Karen and me.

I open it. Tech solutions hadn't reached this little corner of Scotland yet. There were no chips or automatic reminders sent by text to the mobiles of borrowers. They still stamped books out of the library. The book has never been taken out since I had it, seven years ago. Of course it hasn't. Its been sitting in Karen's cupboard.

I start to cry and stroke the torn flyleaf. I realize that I'm glad my mum was already dead when Karen gave me this.

I flick through the book, as if casually, but I know, even before the pages fall open, that the handwritten note will still be there. The pages part like the Red Sea. A ripped corner of foolscap paper, narrow, faint lines. Even the small hairs at the ripped edge are flattened perfectly after seven years.

It is facing down, but the ink is showing through. I pick it up and turn it over. There in a careful hand to disguise the writing, it says,

She got herself raped by
Paki Harris. <u>That</u>'s why.

The stock in the school library has always been old. Most of it was second hand, given to the school by well-meaning locals after post mortem clear-outs of family houses. The history books were hangovers from the Empire. Books that referred to "coolies" and other anachronisms. The Lichtenstein book was bang up to date by comparison. It was only fifteen years old and was about a modern painter. I was thrilled when I stumbled across it. I didn't know Lichtenstein's work. I was a pretentious teenager. I imagined myself walking through town with the book in my hand. I imagined myself in New York, in London, discussing Lichtenstein with Londoners. I didn't know until I got there that, one way or another, most Londoners are from small, hateful islands, too.

At the bus stop, on the way home from school, waiting with the book on my knee so anyone passing could see me reading it. *I'd Rather Drown Than Ask Brad For Help.* And then turning the page and finding the note. My whole life story shifting painfully to the side. Who I was. What I was. Looking up. Karen Little standing across the road, doing her death stare. The greatest acting lesson I ever had.

Replace the note in the pages.

Shut the book.

Bite your lip.

Smile past Karen and look for the bus. I thought I might be sick. I thought I might cry. I did neither. I sat, apparently calm, imagined what someone who hadn't just been punched in the heart would look like, and I did that. I looked for the bus.

I scratched my face.

I saw a sheep on the sea front and my eyes followed it calmly for a few minutes. Karen kept her eyes on me the whole time, until the bus came and I got on and smiled at the driver and took my seat. Maybe she thought I didn't get the note. Maybe that's why she's giving it to me again. Karen Little made me an actor anyway. I have to give her that.

When I got to the end of our drive I was struck by terror. Totty might find the book. It might be true and she might tell me so. Why didn't I just throw the note away? It seemed inseparable from the book. I wrapped the book in a plastic bag and tucked it under a thick gorse bush. I left it there all night and picked it up in the morning and took it back to the library. I should have taken the note out but I didn't dare look at it again or touch it.

I wondered about the writing at the time. Did Karen disguise her writing because I knew her? Why stand there, watching me find it at the bus stop? Or did she disguise it in case the police became involved?

I never told Totty about the note. Ever. And I'm glad. And I know I'll be glad about that forever.

I remember that she's gone for the fifteenth time in an hour. My thoughts are flying, racing somewhere and then BANG. Shock. Disbelief.

Totty's gone. The world feels poorer. It feels pointless. The next breath feels pointless.

I sit on the couch and watch the waves break on each other as they struggle inland, then are dragged back out by their heels. Striving pointlessly. Then I make an effort. Studiously, I drink the crazy drink and get crazy drunk.

It's the middle of the night and I wake up on the couch. I'm sweaty and I smell unfamiliar to myself, strange and sour. The sea is howling outside, fierce gray. A self-harming sea. I'm going kill Karen Little. I'm so angry I can hardly breathe in.

The first problem is the car. I get into the car and start the engine and back it into a wall. It sounds as if it was probably a bad crash, from the crumple of metal, but I can't be bothered getting out to look at it. It's windy. The sea spray is as thick as a fog over the windscreen.

It's in *reverse*. That's the problem there. I've solved a problem and feel buoyed.

I change gear. I go for a front-ways one this time and move off. I pass the gorse bush where I hid the Lik-Tin-Stein all those years ago. The engine is groaning and growling, doesn't sound happy, so maybe it's third gear. First gear. That's the one. So I put it in first and it sounds happy now. Am I wearing a coat? Where does Karen even live now? I'll find her. Wherever she lives.

I get all the way up the hill, looking down on the lights of the town and the harbor. Its inky dark up here and the road is disappearing in front of me, swallowed in the blackness. Lights! Of course! My lights are off.

I stop on the top of the hill, over the town. She's down there somewhere. I crank on the hand break and look for the lights. I don't know this car. The switch should be on the wheel but it's not. Not on the dashboard. Why would they hide a thing like that? It's ridiculous, it's not safe. I'm going to write to the company.

A glass-tap and a shout through the sheeting rain—HELLO?

A face. Man-face at the window. Smiling.

I wind the window down. I'm already indignant about the safety flaws in the car and the rain comes in making my leg cold. Now I'm furious.

The hell're you *doing* out here?

Else? He smiles, sweet, as round faced as he ever was. Tam. God, he's handsome.

I heard she died, Else. I was coming to see you.

So there's a dissonant thing going on now: *inside* my head I'm saying "Tam" over and over in different ways, friendly way, surprised, delighted, howthehellareye! ways. But outside my head, I'm making a noise, a squeal like a hurt piglet, very high noise. My face is tight so I can't will it to move and I'm holding the steering wheel tight with both hands. And my face is wet.

Auch, darlin', says Tam.

He opens the door and all the rain's getting on me and he's carrying me to his car and then I'm in the kitchen.

Tam.

Tam's pouring coffee. I hope it's for me because it looks really nice. He's telling me a lot of things that are surprising but also nice. Tam was my first boyfriend and, honestly, I have never stopped loving that man. We were inseparable before I left so abruptly. He knew why. I never wrote to him or called. I never asked him to visit. But Tam isn't bitter. He's winning his race.

Tam's telling me that he's gay and he has a man and he's happy. It makes me feel so pleased, as if a part of me is now gay and has a man and is happy, too.

Now he's telling me very carefully that it wasn't me that turned him gay, you know. Tam? The hell are you on about? He sees that I'm laughing at him. I'm laughing in a loving way because, Tam, you don't need to explain that to me! For godsake! Well, anyway he's laughing, too, now but his laughter is more from relief really.

He explains that he went out with another girl from the other side of the island. Well, she's kind of angry with Tam for being gay. She thinks either she turned him gay by being unattractive or that he tricked her into covering for him. She hasn't settled on one reading of events just yet, but even though it was five years ago, she's still very annoyed about it.

I think about asking how unattractive can she possibly be, but that's a quip and my lips aren't very agile. Nor is my brain. And then the moment for a joke is past. So I just smile and say, Auch, well. People are nuts.

Tam says, Yeah, people are nuts and gives a sad half shrug. Still, he says, not nice to be the cause of hurt, you know?

He means it. However nasty she was to him, he still doesn't

want to be the cause of hurt to her. That's what Tam's like. Like my mum. Better people than me. Good people.

I put my hand on Tam's to say that he's a lovely person, that he always was a lovely person, just like my mum. But he looks at my hand on his and he's a bit alarmed, like he's worried I might be coming on to him and he'll have to explain something else about being gay and how gay isn't just a sometimes type of thing. He's afraid of causing me hurt maybe. So I get out of my seat, sticking my tongue right out and sort of jab it at his face while making a hungry sound. Tam gives a girlish scream and pulls away from me and we're both laughing as if it's seven years ago and we're that whole bunch of different atoms again.

But then, as I'm laughing, I catch a fleeting glimpse of him looking at me. He is smiling wide, his uniform shirt unbuttoned at the neck, his tie loose. His hand is resting on the table and he's looking straight at me through laughing, appreciative eyes. I know that look and I feel for the jilted girl from the other side of the island. Tam would be easy to misread. When I'm not drunk I might tell him: you come over as straight, Tam. It's an acting job, being who you are. I am good at acting and Tam isn't. He's sending out all the wrong signals.

I'll tell him later. When my lips are working.

We're different people, I slur, every seven years, d'you know that?

He says no and I try to explain, but it's not going very well. Words elude me. When I look up he's very serious.

He says, Else, you're drunk. It's a change of topic from the seven years and he's not pleased I'm drunk.

I can get drunk if I want. You're not the goddam boss, Tam.

Yes, he says, seriously. I *am* the boss. I'm a police officer. You're drunk and you're driving a car. It's all banged up at the back. I am the boss. Where were you going?

I look at him and I think he knows where I was going but I just say nowhere.

I knew when she died you would do something, he says, as if I'm a loose cannon, a crazy person who can't be trusted not to mess everything up unless my mum is there to tick me off. I look up and see the Smirnoff bottle and know that I wouldn't be drinking if she were still alive. The world has been without her for less than twenty-four hours and I'm already drinking and driving and trying to kill people. Being so wrong makes me livid.

I say, So, Tam, you didn't come to see me, you came to *stop* me? I call him a sweary name. What kind of person are you? You don't give a shit about me or my mum.

But Tam's face doesn't even twitch. Don't even try, he says.

Don't even try what, *Tam*?

Don't try to make me feel guilty, Else. You haven't been in touch, you never even wrote to me. You didn't call me and tell me she was dead. What happened to her is the reason I became a policeman so don't even try that crap with me.

But I'm still angry because I'm so wrong and I say things to him that are just crude and mean. A drunken rant and I'm cringing even as I'm shouting. I start crying with shame and frustration because I'm saying things so unkind and nasty. I'm not homophobic. I don't think policemen even do that. I'm just really drunk and my mum's dead and they were so mean to her and Karen had the book all along and it's not fair.

I'm furious and drunk and ashamed and wrong and it's making me cry so much that I'm blind. I can hear Tam breathing gasps. Confusing. By the time the tears clear I can see him doubled over, holding his stomach. I think he's being sick but then I realize that he is laughing, very much, at the things I said about policemen and what he might do with them.

If you saw them! he says, the other policemen! You couldn't, even for a dare!

My mood swings as wildly as a change in wind direction over the open sea. I hope that coffee is for me.

My eyes are trying to kill me. They're stabbing my brain. I wake up in bed this time, in the morning. I've got all my clothes on. I have to keep my eyes shut as I sit up. I get hold of the bedstead to steady myself and tiptoe carefully towards the bathroom. My mouth floods with seawater and I have to run, even with my assassin eyes.

The smell of coffee lingers in the hallway. I'm worried that I've broken something in my olfactory system with all that vodka, unaccustomed as I am, until I get into the kitchen and find Tam making more coffee.

I feel awful.

Good heavens, says Tam, there's a surprise.

It's a nice thing to say, the way he says it. Kind. I slither into a seat and shade my eyes.

He's making scrambled eggs. I won't be able to eat but I'm too comforted by his presence to interrupt him.

You can't drive today, Else, he says. You've still got high alcohol content in your blood and your car lights are all smashed.

I don't answer. I sit with my hand over my eyes and listen to him putting toast on the grill, scraping the eggs in the pan and I think, if this was the fifties we could have been happy in a sexless marriage of convenience, Tam and I.

Who were you going to see last night, Else?

The memory evokes a misery so powerful it almost trumps my hangover. I tell him: I want to kill Karen Little.

He's stopped cooking and is looking at me. I can't look back. Karen?

He puts two plates of scrambled egg down on the table. And takes the toast from the grill and drops a slice on top of each of the yellow mountains.

I pull my plate over to me.

Karen gave me the book back.

Tam is very still. Which book?

The Lichtenstein. She gave it to me at the library yesterday.

She said it was the last book I ever took out of the library. No one had taken it out since. The note was still in it.

Tam sits down. His hands rest either side of his plate like a concert pianist gathering his thoughts before a recital.

Finally he speaks. I'll kill the bitch myself, he says.

The hospital tells me that nothing can be done about my mum today. They need a pathologist to come over from the mainland and do a post mortem, but the ferries are cancelled because a storm is coming. I can sit at home alone or I can go and confront Karen. Tam says let's go.

I'm in Tam's work car, a big police Range Rover. He isn't working today, he says, so it's no bother to drive me around. He's very angry about the book. He wants to know how she got the book to me. I tell him about the ceremony, in front of everyone, how she turned and HAHAHA'd into my face. He gets so angry he has to stop the car and get out and walk around and smoke a cigarette. I watch him out there, walking in the rising wind, his shoulders slumped, orange sparks from the tip of his cigarette against the backdrop of the grey sea like tiny, hopeless flares.

When he gets back in he takes a hip flask out of the glove box. He has a sip and gives it to me, as if drinking in a car is okay now, because he's so angry. I drink to please him. I feel it slide down into me and pinch the sharp edges off my hangover. It is comforting to have my anger matched. He nods at me to drink more and I do. The alcohol warms me and eases my headache and just everything feels a little easier, suddenly. Being angry feels easy and the future feels unimportant. What matters is stopping Karen.

When he finally speaks Tam's face is quite red. He tells me that we will find Karen and take her somewhere. We will not even ask about the note or the book; that would be a chance for her to talk herself out of trouble. If we asked she'd say she

knew nothing about it. She'd blame someone else. She'd plead
ignorance. We will simply get her alone and then, immediately,
we'll do it: we will stab Karen in the neck. We will get away
with it because we'll be together. We will be one another's alibi.
We'll decide which of us will do the stabbing when we get there.
But I already know.

He drives and he asks me about the book and I tell him it had
never been taken out since I recovered it from the gorse bush
and took it back to school. He remembers how upset I was back
then. He says it was devastating for him, too, because I just left
and I was his only friend. She ruined his life, too, because she
chased me away. I know this is true. Back then Tam became
fixated on me to a degree that wasn't comfortable. It wasn't
always benign. *In vino veritas*: if I hadn't had that drink from
his hip flask I might not suddenly know that I didn't really leave
despite Tam. It was partly because of him. He was too intense
back then. His love was overwhelming, and I never realized that
before.

Tam parks in a quiet back street in the town. He has finished
his cigarettes. He needs more so he goes off to the shops while
I go into the school and look for Karen. He says just pretend
that you left something in there. I watch him walk away from
the car and he is scratching his head and his hand is covering
his handsome face.

Karen Little isn't in today. The librarian's position is part time, the
school secretary explains. Karen only works Monday, Tuesday,
and half day on Wednesday. Then she tries to segue into a rant
about government cuts but she can see I'm not listening. Then
she stops and seems to realize that I've been drinking. She waits
for me to speak, cocking her head like a curious seagull. Then
she guesses: did I leave something yesterday? I'm supposed to
say I did but, at just that moment, I think of my mum laying in

a dark drawer in a mortuary fridge and, to be honest, I just sort of turn and walk away.

Out in the car park Tam is waiting with the engine running. I get in. Karen's not there, I tell him. She's at home. He starts to drive and I realize that he knows where she lives. But he's a cop in a small community. He probably knows where everyone lives. And then I wonder why the engine was running, before he knew she wasn't in.

We drive out of town, onto the flat, wind-blown moor. I steal a glimpse at Tam. He's furious. He's chewing his cheek and for some reason I think of Totty. Not about her dying but what she said about being bitter. Tam looks bitter and I pity him that. I catch a glimpse of myself in the side mirror and I'm frowning and I look bitter. This is not what Totty wanted for me.

I know this road. We're heading for Paki Harris's house and I ask why. Karen lives there now, says Tam. She was his only blood left on the island. Karen was related to Paki Harris. I've always known that. Everyone is related to everyone here except us incomers, but I didn't realize she was so closely related to Paki. Second cousins, Tam tells me somberly, just as we're passing a small farmhouse by the roadside with a "For Sale" outside it. The sign flaps in the wind like a rigid surrender flag.

"For Sale" signs are a sorrow on the island. People are born, live, and die in the same house here. A "For Sale" sign means the house owner had no one to leave it to, or maybe only a mainlander. Mainlanders don't understand the houses here. They sell them for cash or use them as holiday homes for two weeks a year, a long weekend at Easter. You can't do that with these houses. They need fires burning in them all the time to keep the damp out. To keep the rot out. These island houses aren't built for sometimes. They need commitment. Karen Little has taken on the commitment of Paki Harris's house.

It was an accident when my mother killed Paki. She ran him over on the main street on a Sunday afternoon in May, just before I was born. The Fatal Accident inquiry found no fault with her. She didn't try to explain what happened. She just ran him straight over, once, completely. She never mentioned it to me, I heard it from just about everyone else, with various embellishments. But the note, that note in the book, was the first version I ever heard that made sense of it. Paki raped her. She got pregnant with me. She killed him. That's why.

Paki Harris was from here. My mother was not. So the island took his side because loyalty isn't rational and, in the end, loyalty is all there is in a place this small.

In the seven years since I left I have often imagined what it was to be my heavily pregnant mother and see a man who had raped her day after day, standing in church, shopping at the supermarket, strolling on the sea front. I would have driven a car at him. The note, though, the note made me realize how deep the bitterness is here. It had never occurred to me that she had a motive until I saw that note. And afterwards, I realized, if they knew, if they all knew that he had raped her and that's why, could they not have found one shred of compassion for her? They spat at her in the street. She couldn't eat in the café because no one would speak when she was in there. She used the library until they banned her for "bringing food in." She had a packet of crisps in her bag. I'm not leaving, she'd say, because wherever you live, life is a race against bitterness and staying makes me run faster.

I feel so sad remembering it all. I feel like a house without a fire in it. I glance at Tam driving down the small road. He looks as if he's had a good old fire burning for the past seven years in him. His cheeks are pink, his eyes are shining. He's upright, sitting proud of the seat back. He's wired with bitterness and ready. I'm a sloucher.

It seems so odd, us being in a car together, driving. Neither of us could drive back then. Tam takes a minor cut-off road and we follow the line of the hill, out towards the furious sea. At the headland, along the coast, the waves are forty feet high, smashing higher than the bare black cliffs. The sea is trying to claw its way onto the land and failing. Each time it retreats to catch its breath it fails. But it keeps trying.

Suddenly we see Paki Harris's house, a stark silhouette against the coming storm. It's one of those Victorian oddities that seem inevitable because they've been there for a hundred and fifty years. It is big, squat, and solid. The roofline is castellated; the windows are big and plentiful. The wind coming straight off the water is perpetual and incessant on this headland. The house is an act of defiance, an elegant one-fingered salute to the wind and the ocean.

Very much like Paki himself, from what I've heard.

Before I knew he might be my father, before the note, I listened to stories about Paki without prejudice. I knew they hated my mum and loved Paki but I didn't see him as anything to do with me. Paki was a wild boy. Paki had bar fights and rode ponies into the town on the Sabbath. Paki pushed a minister into a bush. Paki burned a barn down. I heard a lot of stories about him. He was ugly but wild, and wild is good here.

As we draw up to the house the big heavy car is buffeted by the wind. Tam finds a wind-shaded spot by the side. He drives straight into it and pulls on the hand break. He wants to talk to me before we go in. He gets the hip flask out again. I don't want anymore but he makes me take it. And he tells me quietly what will happen: he will knock on the front door. I will go around behind the house to see if the back door is open. If it is open, I will come in and find the kitchen, first door on the right. There is a knife block with carving knives on it. Karen will come to the front door and let Tam in. Tam will bring Karen into the kitchen where I am hiding behind the door with my knife. I will go for the neck.

He looks at me for confirmation and I nod. I shouldn't be scared, he tells me. He will be right there. He smiles and makes me drink more. He doesn't drink anymore because he is driving. He's a cop. He can't afford to lose his license.

We get out of opposite doors and I slip around to the back of the house. Suddenly, the wind pushes and shoves and pulls at me and I have to crouch low and run for the steps up to the door. It is open. I'm in. I find myself breathless from the pummeling wind and the short sharp run up the worn stone steps.

In the dark stone hallway the house is silent. I don't think Karen is in. This is an eventuality that didn't occur to either of us, so deep were we into our consensus. I flatten myself against the wall and listen to the creaking windows and the hiss of the wind outside. At the far end of the hall I can see the cold white light from the front door spilling into the hallway.

Three knocks. Bam. Bam. Bam. Tam's shadow is on the carpet. Karen isn't even in.

I draw a deep breath.

A creak above. Not wind. A creak of weight on floor above. Karen is standing up somewhere. She takes a step, I feel her wondering if she did hear someone knocking. Then Tam knocks again. Bam. Bam. Bam. She is sure now and comes out to the upstairs hall. At the top of the stairs she pauses, she must be able to see the door from up there. She gives a little "oh" and hurries down to Tam standing outside. She seems a little annoyed by him as she flings the door open.

Why are you knocking? she asks.

Tam keeps his eyes on the hall and slips in, shutting the door behind him, taking her by the elbow and pulling her into a room.

Thomas? She's calling him his formal name, his grown-up name. Why did you wait out in that wind? Did the lawyer call you? She's jabbering like a housewife talking over a garden fence but Tam's saying nothing back.

Their voices move from the hall to nowhere to suddenly coming from the first door on the right. They are in the kitchen. They have gone through a different door into the kitchen and I am supposed to be in there right now with a knife from the knife block.

For the first time in my life, I have missed my cue.

I throw myself at the door and fall into the room. Look up. There is Tam, standing behind Karen, holding her by the elbow, sort of, pushing her forward, toward me.

There, right in front of me, is a worktop with a large knife block on it. A lot of knives, maybe fifteen knives, all sizes, and the wooden handles are pointing straight towards the front of my hand. I can reach out and be holding one in a second.

Karen's mouth is hanging open. Tam's face is a glowering cloud of bitterness behind her shoulder.

I say, Hello, Karen.

No one knows what to do for a moment. We all stand still.

Hello, Else, says Karen.

If I was at home, in London, and a person I had been at school with seven years ago fell through my kitchen door I might have a lot questions for them. Karen just looks around the floor in front of her and says, Cuppa?

It takes a moment to compute. Cuppa? Cup of tea? Hot cup of tea for you?

Actually, I say, looking at Tam who is getting more and more red in the face, A cuppa would be lovely, Karen, thanks.

Expertly, as if she is used to doing it, Karen twists her elbow to snake it out of Tam's grasp and steps away. She picks the kettle up off the range. She turns to look at both of us, thinking about something or other, and then she says, Well, I might as well make a pot of tea.

No one answers. It's the action of the elbow that makes me realize my gut was right. Tam has held her by that elbow before. And Karen has freed herself from that grip many times. He knew she wasn't in school today. I remember his look at me last night, the laughing-eyed assessment of me as he sat at the table.

She has her back to us as she fills it from the tap. Tam nods me towards the knife block. There it is, his face says, over there.

And my face says, What? What are you saying? Oh! There? The knives! Oh, yes! I forgot about a knife! Okay then! But inside I'm saying something quite different. It's not his fault. It's understandable because I'm in a lot of crap on telly. Tam doesn't know I'm a good actor.

Karen gets some mugs down and a packet of biscuits. She's talking. To me.

Else, she says, I heard that your mum died. And I know that she died before you came to the school yesterday.

We look at each other and I see that she is welling up. I'm so sorry, she says and I wonder if she means about the book. But she doesn't. About the talk, she says. You must have felt that you couldn't cancel. Or you were too shocked, I don't know, but I'm sorry.

And then she puts her hand on my forearm. I can see in her eyes that she is really sorry, for my loss, for my mum, and for the sorrows of all daughters and mothers and I start to cry.

Karen's arms are around me, warm and safe, and I hear her tut into my ear and say Oh no, oh no, oh dear. She whispers to me, I hope you like the book. I'm sobbing too hard to pull away and she adds, Tam remembered you liked it back then.

I don't think Tam can hear her. He thinks we are whispering lady things. We stand in this grief clinch for quite a long time, until the whistle of the kettle calls an end to the round.

She sits me down at the table and I gather myself, wipe my face, and look at Tam. Tam is staring hard at the table, frowning furiously. He has given up making eye contact with me or nodding at knives or anything. He hasn't heard it but he has realized that I'm not going to stab her and never was. He doesn't know what to do now. Karen puts a plate of sugary biscuits in front of me and gives me a cup of tea.

And I've put sugar in that for you. I know you don't take sugar probably, but there's sugar in that because you've probably had a bad shock.

Karen sits down, her knees towards me. She picks up her mug and flicks a finger out at him without looking.

Did he tell you?

I sniff, What?

She smiles, *Us*, she says, a wry curl twitching at the side of her mouth.

I shake my head, baffled.

She glances at him. He is staring hard at her but she says it anyway: *Married*.

I lift my sugary tea, for the shock, and drink it though it is too hot. When I put the mug down again, empty, I tell her that my mum never said anything about that.

She hums. It was a secret. They married on the mainland, didn't they, Tam. Tam? Didn't they? In secret. Tam gives her nothing back and that makes her sort of snicker. Because of their families, you know. Because she had a lot of money and houses coming to her and he had nothing. Her family didn't trust him. But, you know, it didn't work out and no kids so, no harm done. They're getting divorced now. Aren't we Tam? Tam? Tam, are you not going to speak at all?

Tam is so uncomfortable that he cannot speak. He is eating biscuit after biscuit to keep his face busy. He is doing a strange thing with this head, not nodding or shaking it but sort of jerking it sideways in a noncommittal gesture.

Karen frowns at him. She doesn't understand. She gives up trying and turns her attention to me. So, what is going to happen with your mum's funeral?

I tell her: I'm flying her out of there. I'm taking her to London and I'm going to have her cremated there. Karen says, Wouldn't it be easier to have her cremated nearby and then take her to London?

Tam came here to kill you, I say.

Karen says do I want another biscuit?

I actually wonder if I said that out loud because she hasn't reacted at all. But then I look at Tam's face and I know I did say it out loud. Karen lifts the plate and offers me another one, her face a perfect question: biscuit? That's how they do things on the island.

Tam stands up then, knocking his chair over behind him. The sharp clatter on the stone floor ricochets around the kitchen. He turns to the door and walks out, through the hall and out of the front door, slamming it behind him. A skirl of wind curls around our ankles.

Apropos of nothing, Karen says to me, This was Paki Harris's house.

I eat a biscuit and when I've finished I say, I know.

Karen nods. I don't know if you ever discussed him with your mum?

No.

She puts a hand on my hand and cringes, tearful again. Do you know who your father is, Else?

We never discussed my father.

Hm. Karen doesn't know what she can and can't say.

It just falls out of my London mouth: You think Paki raped my mum and that's why she ran him over?

Karen sighs. I don't know, she says, I don't know what happened. Not for me to know. But, Else, I think this house might be yours.

I don't want it.

It's worth a bit of money—

I don't want it.

Karen looks at me and I can see she's glad. She likes the house. She belongs here. These are not sometimes houses.

I was so mean to you when we were young. I'm sorry.

And I say, Oh! Forget it! because I'm flustered.

But she can't. She's been thinking about it, a lot, she says. But she is really sorry. She was jealous, because I was an incomer. It seems so free to me back then, she says, to not be part of all of this—

Aren't you worried, Karen? I blurt, Tam invited me here to stab you in the neck! Doesn't that concern you? You've just let him leave. Where's he going?

She looks fondly towards the front door. Gone to get drunk, I think. It's a rough week. Our divorce is final tomorrow.

And I understand finally. He wanted her killed today so he could inherit this house. And if I committed the murder I couldn't inherit from a woman I killed. It would be his outright.

I think he still has a thing about you.

Really?

Yeah.

I don't think so.

Well, you're wrong.

I look at her and realize that she's nice, Karen. She's not bitter. She is tied to this place and always will be. She accepts what it is to be from here and of here. There's no escape for Karen, not from my rapist father's house or from Tam who wanted to kill her. She accepts where she is and who she is and what had happened. She's like my mum. Karen is winning her race.

Let me drive you back to town, Else, as an apology. And as a thank you, for soldiering on yesterday. She pats my hand. Soldiering on is important.

She goes out to the hallway and pulls on a coat and I see past her to the vicious sea. The wind is screeching a ferocious caw. The waves are streaming over the cliffs. The grass on the headland is flattened and salted and Karen looks back at me. She smiles her soft island smile that could mean anything.

I am getting out of here. I am getting away, and this time I'm taking my mum with me.

The Travelling Companion

Ian Rankin

'MY FRENCH ISN'T very good,' I told him.

'The seller's English. You'll be fine.' Mr. Whitman thrust the postcard towards me again. He had insisted I call him George, but I couldn't do that. He was my employer, sort of. Moreover, if the stories were to be believed, he was a descendant of Walt Whitman, and that mattered to me. I had graduated with First Class Honours from the University of Edinburgh that same summer. My focus had been on Scottish rather than American Literature, but still – Whitman was Whitman. And now my employer (of sorts) was asking me to do him a favour. How could I refuse?

I watched as my fingers plucked the postcard from his grip. It was one of the bookstore's own promotional cards. On one side were drawings of Shakespeare and Rue de la Bûcherie, on the other my handwritten destination.

'A five-minute walk,' Mr Whitman assured me. His accent was an American drawl. He was tall, his silver hair swept back from his forehead, his eyes deep-set, cheekbones prominent. The first time we'd met, he had demanded a cigarette. On hearing that I didn't smoke, he had shaken his head as if in general weariness at my generation. This meeting had taken place outside a nearby cous-cous restaurant, where I had been staring at the menu in the window, wondering if I dared go inside. Money wasn't the main issue. I had been rehearsing my few French phrases and considering the possibility that the staff, seeing me for a lone traveller, might mug me for my pocketful of francs before selling the contents of my heavy rucksack at some street market in the vicinity.

'Passing through?' the stranger next to me had inquired, before demanding that I give him one of my 'smokes'.

A little later, as we shared a table and the menu's cheapest options, he had told me about his bookstore.

'I know it,' I'd stammered. 'It's rightly famous.'

He had offered a tired smile, and, when we'd filled our bellies, had produced an empty thermos flask, into which he poured the left-over food before screwing the lid back on.

'No point wasting it,' he had explained. 'The store doesn't pay, you know, but there's the offer of a bed. A bed's all you get.'

'I was going to look for a hotel.'

'You work the till for a few hours, and mop the floor at closing time. Rest of the day's your own, and we do have some interesting books on the shelves...'

Which is how I came to work at Shakespeare and Company, 37 Rue de la Bûcherie, Paris 5. On the postcard we boasted 'the largest stock of antiquarian English books on the continent', and added Henry Miller's comment that we were 'a wonderland of books'.

It wasn't the original shop, of course – not that we trumpeted the fact. Sylvia Beach's Shakespeare and Company had opened in the year 1919 on Rue Dupuytren, before moving to larger premises on Rue de l'Odéon. This was where Joyce, Pound and Hemingway could be found. Mr Whitman had called his own bookstore Le Mistral, before renaming it in Beach's honour – her own Shakespeare and Co. having closed for good during the German occupation of Paris. The new Shakespeare and Company had been a magnet for Beat writers in the 1950s, and writers (of a sort) still visited. I would lie on my hard narrow bed in a curtained-off alcove and listen as poems were workshopped by ex-pats whose names meant nothing to me. Contemporary writing was not my period, however, so I tried hard not to judge.

'You're from Scotland, right?' Mr Whitman had said to me one day.

'Edinburgh, specifically.'

'Walter Scott and Robbie Burns, eh?'

'And Robert Louis Stevenson.'

'Not forgetting that reprobate Trocchi...' He had chuckled to himself.

'Stevenson is my passion. I'm starting my PhD on him in the autumn.'

'Back into academe so soon?'

'I like it there.'

'I can't imagine why.' And he had fixed me with one of his looks, before opening the till to examine the evening's scant takings. It was August, and still hot outside. The tourists were sitting at café tables, fanning themselves with menus and ordering cold drinks. Only one or two people my own age were browsing the shelves of our airless shop. There was an original copy of *Ulysses* in the window, a siren to draw them inside. But this night it was proving ineffectual.

'Was Paris always your destination?' he asked, sliding the drawer closed again.

'I wanted to travel. Stevenson visited France several times.'

'Is that the subject of your PhD?'

'I'm looking at how his health may have affected his writing.'

'Sounds fascinating. But it's hardly living, is it?' I watched him as he turned away and headed for the stairs. Three more hours and I could lock up before heading for bed and the various biting insects who seemed to feast nightly on my ankles and the backs of my knees.

I had sent postcards – Shakespeare and Company postcards – to friends and family, making sure to add a few centimes to the till in payment. I didn't mention the bites, but did make sure that my ongoing adventure sounded as exotic as possible. I had actually sent a first postcard home soon after disembarking from the overnight bus at London's Victoria Coach Station. Another had been purchased and sent from the ferry terminal in Dover. I knew my parents would prefer written communication to an expensive phone call. My father was a Church of Scotland minister, my mother an invaluable member of our local community. I was a rarity of sorts in having stayed at home during the four years of my undergraduate degree. My parents had offered financial assistance towards rent, but my arguments about wasted money had swayed them. Besides, my childhood bedroom suited me, and my mother was the finest cook in the city.

Before leaving, however, I had promised to phone Charlotte every two days, just so she would know I was safe. There was a public phonebox just along the Seine from the store, with a view towards Notre Dame which made up for its general lack of hygiene. With the receiver wrapped in a clean paper serviette from a café, I would spend a few francs telling Charlotte of any new experiences, in between listening to her tell me that she loved me and missed me and couldn't wait until I found a place of my own in time for the start of term back in Edinburgh.

'Absolutely,' I would agree, my mouth suddenly dry.

'Oh, Ronnie,' she would sigh, and I would swallow back the inclination to correct her, since my preference (as she well knew) was for Ronald rather than Ronnie.

My name is Ronald Hastie. I was born in 1960, making me twenty-two. Twenty-two and three months as I stood on the banks of the Seine, surrounded by heat and traffic fumes and a sense that there was another world being kept hidden from me. A series of worlds, actually, only one of them represented by Charlotte and her cropped red hair and freckled complexion. Cous-cous and a famous bookshop and morning espressos (consumed standing at the bar – the cheapest option) – these were all wonders to me that summer. And, yes, the original plan had been to drift much further south, but plans could change, as could people.

'The seller's English,' my employer said, waking me from my reverie. 'You'll be fine, trust me. A five-minute walk...'

His name was Benjamin Turk and he lived in a sprawling apartment at the top of five winding flights of stairs. When he opened his door to me, I stood there breathless, staring past him at a long hallway filled with groaning bookshelves. I felt light-headed, and it seemed in that moment that the shelves were endless, stretching to infinity. Turk slid an arm around my shoulders and guided me into the gloom.

'Whitman sent you but he didn't mention the climb. That's the reason he wouldn't drag his own sorry rump over here, you know.' Laughter boomed from his chest. He was stocky and bald and probably in his fifties or early sixties, with dark bushy eyebrows above eyes filled with sly humour. His voluminous white shirt and crimson waistcoat could have come from a different century, as could their owner. I'd read enough Dickens to see that Mr Turk would have slotted right into one of those comedic episodes from *Copperfield* or *Pickwick*.

'A drink's what's needed,' he went on, steering me down the hall. Varnished parquet floor stretched its length, and it ended eventually at a wall furnished with a large mirror, in which I glimpsed my sweating face. Doorways to left and right, both open, showing a tidy kitchen and a cluttered living-room. We entered this last and Turk positioned me before an armchair, thumping it so hard dust rose into the air.

'Sit!' he commanded, before pouring red wine from a glass decanter. I noticed for the first time that he had a discernible limp.

'I don't really...' I began to apologise.

'Nonsense, lad! This is Paris – you do realise that? Get it down you or I'll have you deported for crimes against the state!'

He had poured himself a glass not quite as generous as mine, and raised his hand in a toast before filling his mouth.

I realised I really was thirsty, so took a sip. The stuff was nectar, unlike the cheap, weak compromises of Edinburgh lunches and dinners. Cherries and blackcurrants replaced the bitter memories, and Turk could tell I was in love. He beamed at me, nodding slowly.

'Delicious,' I said.

'Did you ever doubt it?' And he toasted me again with his glass before settling on the chaise longue opposite. 'Do I detect a Scottish accent?'

'Edinburgh.'

'That most Presbyterian of cities, explaining your aversion to pleasure.'

'I'm not averse to pleasure.' As soon as the words were out, I regretted them, hoping they wouldn't be misinterpreted. To cover my embarrassment, I took more sips of wine, causing Turk to spring to his feet in order to refill my glass.

'Mr Whitman says you're one of his oldest customers,' I stammered.

'We've known one another more years than I care to remember.'

'So you've lived in Paris a long time?'

He smiled, this time a little wistfully. 'How about you?' he asked.

'This is my first visit. I'm taking a break from university.'

'Yes, George said as much – too short a break, he seems to think. Your hero Stevenson didn't let college hold him back, did he?' He saw my surprise. 'George again,' he explained.

'Stevenson completed his studies.'

'And passed the law exam,' Turk said airily. 'But his family expected him to stick to that path, or one very like it, but the bold Louis had other ideas.' My host was swirling the wine in his glass. I found the motion hypnotic, and sensed I was not yet fully recovered from the climb. The room was stuffy, too, with the smell of leatherbound books, old curtains and faded rugs.

'You should take your jacket off,' Turk said. 'Who the hell wears a black velvet jacket in Paris in the heat of summer?'

'It's not velvet,' I mumbled, shrugging my arms out of the sleeves.

'But the nearest you could find?' Turk smiled to himself and I could tell that he knew – knew that Stevenson's nickname at university had been 'Velvet Jacket'.

I lay the jacket across my knees and cleared my throat. 'Mr Whitman says you have some books to sell.'

'A few boxes – mostly bought from George himself. He says you've memorised the stock so will know if they're worth taking or not.'

'He's exaggerating.'

'I think so, too. I know only too well how many books are in that shop of his.'

'You're a collector.' I was looking around the room. Every inch of wall-space was filled with shelving, and those shelves groaned. The books all seemed very old – few had dust jackets. It was impossible to make out any of the titles, but they seemed to be in several languages. 'Are you a professor? A writer?'

'I've been many things.' He paused, watching me above the rim of his glass. 'I'm guessing you'd like to be both some day.'

'I've never thought about writing. I mean to say, I would hope to finish my thesis and try to get it published.'

'A thesis about Stevenson and his ailments?'

'And how they made him the writer he was. He was trying out an experimental drug called ergotine when he got the idea for *Jekyll and Hyde*. It gave him hallucinations. And the Edinburgh he grew up in was all science and rationalism and men who *did* things, while he felt sickly, his only real strength his imagination...' I broke off, fearing I was beginning to lecture my host.

'Interesting,' Turk said, drawing the word out. He rose to fill my glass again, emptying the decanter. My mouth felt furred and sweat was trickling down my forehead. I took out a handkerchief and began to mop at my face. 'He had a nursemaid, didn't he?' Turk asked as he poured. 'She told him ghost stories. Must have frightened the life out of him.'

'He called her "Cummy" – her real name was Alison Cunningham. She told him about the wardrobe in his room.'

'The one made by William Brodie?'

And Turk nodded to himself again, because he knew this story too. Brodie, a respectable man by day but a criminal by night, the Deacon of Wrights who led a gang, breaking into houses, thieving and terrorising, until caught, tried and hanged on a gibbet he had previously crafted by his own hand. The lazy theory was that Stevenson had plundered this story wholesale for *Jekyll and Hyde*, but it comprised only one part of the overall puzzle.

'Maybe we should look at these books,' I said, hoping I wasn't slurring my words.

'Of course.' Turk rose slowly to his feet, and came over to help me up. I followed him into the kitchen. There was a narrow stairway I hadn't noticed and we climbed into the eaves of the building. It was hotter, gloomier and stuffier up here. Two people, no matter how emaciated, could not have passed one another in the corridor. Several doors led off. One seemed to be a bathroom. I guessed there had to be a bedroom, but the room Turk led me into was the study. Three boxes sat on an antique desk. Piles of books lined the walls, threatening to topple as our weight shifted the bare floorboards beneath. I draped my jacket over the room's only chair.

'Shall I leave you to it, then?' Turk inquired.

I looked in vain for a window to open. The sweat was stinging my eyes now and my handkerchief was drenched. Outside, bells were chiming. The scratching noises could have been pigeons on the roof-tiles immediately overhead or rats somewhere below the floor. My lips felt as if they had been glued together. More dust flew into my face as I peeled open the flaps of the first box.

'You don't look well, my boy.' Turk's words seemed to come from far off. Were we still in the attic, or had we somehow moved to that infinite entrance-hall with its books and mirror? I had a sudden vision: a cold drink, something non-alcoholic, in a tall glass filled with ice. I craved it without being able to say the words out loud. There was a book in my hand, but it seemed to weigh far more than its size would suggest, and the title on its spine seemed to be a jumble of letters or hieroglyphs of some kind.

'My boy?'

And then a darkening tunnel.

'Wait, let me...'

And then sleep.

I awoke laid out on a bed. My shirt had been unbuttoned and Benjamin Turk was dabbing at my chest with a damp towel. I sat bolt upright, a hangover pulsing behind my eyes.

It was quite obviously *his* bedroom. My jacket had been placed on a hook on the back of the door, but below it I could see a long red satin bath-robe. There was also a wardrobe whose doors wouldn't quite shut and a bedside table bearing a basin half-filled with water. When I angled my feet off the bed on to the floor, I made contact with several hardcover books lying there.

'Careful you don't faint again,' Turk cautioned as I started to rebutton my shirt.

'I just need some air,' I muttered.

'Of course. Can I help you negotiate the stairs?'

'I'll be fine.'

'I'm relieved to hear it – I had the devil's own job bringing you this far...'

I wasn't sure what he meant until I grabbed my jacket and pulled open the door. We were just inside the front door of the apartment. I must have missed the bedroom on arrival. I stared at Turk, who shrugged.

'It wasn't easy – those steps from the attic are treacherous.' He was holding something out for me to take. I unfolded the piece of paper. 'A list of the books,' he explained, 'so that your employer can be kept in blissful ignorance – if that's what you would like.'

'Thank you,' I said, pocketing the note. He had unlocked the door. The stairwell was a few degrees cooler, but I could still feel sweat clinging to my hair.

'Safe descent,' Benjamin Turk said, giving a little wave of one hand before disappearing behind the closing door. Holding on to the banister, I made my way slowly to the street, pausing outside and filling my lungs with air. A young woman on the pavement opposite seemed to be watching me. She wore a full-length floral-print dress, almost identical to one Charlotte owned. I did a double-take and my jacket slid to the ground. By the time I'd picked it up, she had gone. I began walking back to the shop, aware that my headache was going nowhere. Passing a bar, I headed in and ordered a Perrier with plenty of ice and lemon. Having finished it in two long draughts, I ordered another. I doubted the place would sell painkillers, but then remembered the old saying about the hair of the dog. Kill or cure, I thought to myself, adding a glass of red wine to my order.

And it worked – I could feel the pain easing after just one small measure. It was thin, vinegary stuff, too, the very antithesis of the contents of Turk's decanter, but I felt better for it, and ordered one final glass. While sipping this, I removed the list of books from my pocket and went through it. A solid line had been drawn across the sheet two-thirds of the way down. Underneath was a message from Turk:

> *Not for sale, but possibly of interest:*
> *The Travelling Companion*

I blinked a few times and furrowed my brow. I knew that title, but couldn't immediately place it. The books listed above it could probably find buyers. Historical non-fiction and philosophy titles mostly, with Balzac, Zola and Mann thrown in. Turk omitted to say whether they were first editions, or what condition they were in, and I had only the most fleeting memory of opening the first box. I felt I had let Mr Whitman down somehow – not that he need ever know, unless Turk decided to tell him. But that didn't stop me feeling bad. Preoccupied, I was halfway to the doorway before the barman reminded me I hadn't yet paid. I mumbled an apology and rooted in my pockets for change. Curiously, there seemed a couple of hundred-franc notes there that I thought I'd spent earlier in the week. There would be cous-cous again that evening, rather than a tin of cheap tuna from the supermarket. Heartened, I added a small tip to the bill.

An Australian backpacker called Mike was minding the store on my return. He told me, to my relief, that Mr Whitman would be gone the rest of the day. I resented Mike his broad-shouldered height, perfect teeth and mahogany tan. His hair was blond and curly and he had already made his mark on a couple of female students who liked to hang about the place, reading but never buying. When he ended his shift and I took over, I found that there was a letter for me next to the till. Typical of him not to have mentioned it. It was from my father and I opened it as respectfully as possible. Two small sheets of thin blue airmail. He had news of my mother, my aunt and uncle, my clever cousins – clever in that they both had good jobs in the City of London – and the neighbours on our street. His tone was clipped and precise, much like his sermons, not a word wasted. My mother had added a couple of lines towards the foot of the last page, but seemed to feel that nothing really need be added to my father's update. The return address had been added to the back of the envelope, lest it be lost in transit somehow. As I reread it, I caught a glimpse of someone on the pavement outside, someone wearing the same floral dress as before. I sauntered to the open doorway and looked up and down the street, but she had done her vanishing act again – if it had been her in the first place. What I did see, however, was Australian Mike, stepping briskly in the direction of Notre Dame with an arm draped across the shoulders of a couple of giggling students.

*

Two hours before closing, Mike and his entourage were back.
He had promised the girls a lesson in retail, and informed me
with a wink and a salute that I was 'relieved of all duties'. That
was fine by me. I slipped into my black almost-velvet jacket
and headed out for a late dinner. The staff in the cous-cous
restaurant knew me by now, and there were smiles and bows as
I was escorted to one of the quieter tables. I had lifted a book
from the shelves at Shakespeare and Company – an American
paperback of Conrad's *Heart of Darkness*. There was too much
food and I half-wished I had thought to pack an empty flask.
Instead of which, I refilled my bowl for a third time. The house
wine was thinner than anything I had yet tasted, but I nodded
my appreciation of it when invited to do so by my waiter. And at
meal's end, this same waiter, who had told me a couple of visits
back to call him Harry, signalled that he would meet me at the
restaurant's kitchen door in five minutes. Having paid the bill,
my curiosity piqued, I wound my way down the alley behind
the restaurant and its neighbours. The bins were overflowing
and there was a strong smell of urine. I skidded once or twice,
not daring to look down at whatever was beneath my feet.
Eventually I reached Harry. He stood at the open door of the
kitchen while vocal mayhem ensued within, accompanied by
the clanging of cooking-pots. He was holding a thin cigarette,
which he proceeded to light, sucking deeply on it before offering
it to me.

'Dope?' I said.

'Very good.'

After four years of an arts degree at the University of
Edinburgh, I was no stranger to drugs. I had been to several
parties where a room – usually an underlit bedroom – had been
set aside for use by drug-takers. I'd even watched as joints were
rolled, enjoying the ritual while refusing to partake.

'I'm not sure,' I told Harry, whose real name was more
like Ahmed. 'It's been a strange enough day already.' When he

persisted, however, I lifted the cigarette from him and took a couple of puffs without inhaling. This wasn't good enough for Harry, who used further gestures to instruct me until he was happy that I had sucked the smoke deep into my lungs. Another waiter joined us and it was soon his turn. Then Harry. Then me again. I had expected to feel queasy, but that didn't happen. My cares seemed to melt away, or at least take on a manageable perspective. Once we had finished the joint, Harry produced a small cellophane wrap, inside which was a lump of something brown. He wanted two hundred francs for it, but I shrugged to signal that I didn't have that kind of money about my person. So then he shoved the tiny parcel into my jacket pocket and patted it, gesturing to indicate that I could pay him later.

We then fell silent as two new arrivals entered the alley. They either hadn't noticed that they had an audience, or else they simply weren't bothered. The woman squatted in front of the man and unzipped his trousers. I had seen more than a few prostitutes on my nighttime walks through the city – some of whom had tried tempting me – and here was another, hard at work while the woozy client tipped a bottle of vodka to his mouth.

And suddenly I knew.

The Travelling Companion...

I lifted a hand to my forehead with the shock of it, while my companions took a step back towards their kitchen, perhaps fearing I was about to be sick.

'No,' I whispered to myself. 'That can't be right.' Harry was looking at me, and I returned his stare. 'It doesn't exist,' I told him. 'It doesn't exist.'

Having said which, I weaved my way back towards the mouth of the alley, almost stumbling into the woman and her client. He swore at me, and I swore back, almost pausing to take a swing at him. It wasn't the alcohol or the dope making my head reel as I sought the relative calm of the darkened Shakespeare and Company.

It was Benjamin Turk's message to me...

*

I was unlocking the doors next morning when Mr Whitman called down to tell me I had a phone call.

'And by the way, how did you get on with Ben Turk?'

'I have a note of the books he wants to sell,' I replied, not meeting his eyes.

'He's an interesting character. Anyway, go talk to your woman friend...'

It was Charlotte. She had found work at a theatre box office and was using their phone.

'I need to pass the time somehow. It's so *boring* here without you.'

I was leaning down to rub at the fresh insect-bites above my ankles. The list from Turk was folded up in the back pocket of my trousers. I knew I had to tear a strip from it before showing it to my employer.

'Are you there?' Charlotte was asking into the silence.

'I'm here.'

'Is everything okay? You sound...'

'I'm fine. A glass of wine too many last night.'

I heard her laugh. 'Paris is leading you astray.'

'Maybe just a little.'

'Well, that can be a good thing.' She paused. 'You remember our little chat, the night before you left?'

'Yes.'

'I meant it, you know. I'm ready to take things a bit further. *More* than ready.'

She meant sex. Until now, we had kissed, and gone from fumbling above clothes to rummaging beneath them, but nothing more.

'It's what you want, too, isn't it?' she asked.

'Doesn't everyone?' I was able to answer, my cheeks colouring.

'So when you come back... we'll do something about it, yes?'

'If you're sure. I mean, I don't want to push you into anything.'

More laughter. 'I seem to be the one doing the pushing. I'm thinking of you right now, you know. Thinking of *us* lying together, joined together – tell me you don't think about that, too.'

'I have to go, Charlotte. There are customers...' I looked around the empty upstairs room.

'Soon, Ronnie, soon. Just remember.'

'I will. I'll call you tonight.'

I put the phone down and stared at it, then took the note from my pocket and tore across it. Downstairs, my employer was manning the till.

'You look like hell, by the way,' he said as I handed him the list. 'Did Ben ply you with booze?'

'Do you know much about him?'

'He comes from money. Pitched up here for want of anywhere better – not unlike my good self. Drinks fine wines, buys books he wants to own but not necessarily read.' He was scanning the list. 'He'd probably give these to us for free, you know. I think he just needs space for more of the same.' He paused, fixing me with a look. 'What did *you* think of him?'

'Pleasant enough. Maybe a bit eccentric...' I suppressed a shiver as I remembered waking on Turk's bed, shirt open, and him dabbing at my chest. 'Is he...' I tried to think how to phrase the question. 'A ladies' man?'

Mr Whitman hooted. 'Listen to you,' he said. 'Remind me – which century is this?' After his laughter had subsided, he fixed his eyes on mine again. 'Ladies, gents, fish and fowl and the beasts of field and wood,' he said. 'Now off you go and find yourself some breakfast. I'll manage these heaving crowds somehow.' He waved his arm in the direction of the deserted shop.

It was warm outside, and noisy with tourists and traffic. I slung my jacket over my shoulder as I walked to my usual café, only four shop-fronts away. Benjamin Turk was seated at an outdoor table, finishing a *café au lait* and reading *Le Monde*. A silver-topped walking-stick rested against the rim of the table. He gestured for me to join him, so I dragged out the spare metal chair and sat down, slipping my jacket over the back of my chair.

'It was the local prostitutes who called Stevenson "Velvet Jacket", you know,' Turk said.

The liveried waiter stood ready. I ordered a coffee of my own.

'And an orange juice,' Turk added.

The waiter gave a little bow and headed back inside. Turk folded the newspaper and laid it next to his cup.

'I was coming to check on you,' he said. 'But the lure of caffeine was too strong.'

'I'm fine,' I assured him.

'And you've looked at the list, I presume?'

I took the scrap of paper from my pocket and placed it between us. He gave an indulgent smile.

'It's a book Stevenson wrote,' I said. 'Never quite completed. His publisher liked it well enough but considered the contents too sordid.'

'It concerned a prostitute,' Turk agreed.

'Set in Italy, I think.'

'Some of it.' Turk's eyes were gleaming.

'Fanny made Stevenson put it on the fire,' I said quietly.

'Ah, the formidable Fanny Osbourne. He met her in France, you know. He was visiting Grez. I suppose he became infatuated.' He paused, playing with his cup, moving it in circles around its saucer. 'It wasn't the only book of his she persuaded him to sacrifice...'

'*Jekyll and Hyde*,' I said, as my own coffee arrived, and with it the glass of juice. 'The first draft, written in three days.'

'Yes.'

'Though some commentators say three days is impossible.'

'Despite the author's Presbyterian work ethic. But then he was taking drugs, wasn't he?'

'Ergotine, and possibly cocaine.'

'Quite the cocktail for a writer whose imagination was already inflamed. You know why he consigned it to the flames?'

'Fanny persuaded him. She thought it would ruin his reputation.'

'Because it was too raw, too shocking.' He watched me as I finished the orange juice in two long gulps, watched as I poured hot milk into the viscous black coffee.

'Nobody really knows, though,' I eventually said. 'Because only Stevenson and Fanny saw that first version. Same goes for *The Travelling Companion*.'

'Not quite.'

'Yes, his publisher read that,' I corrected myself.

'Not quite,' Turk repeated, almost in a whisper.

'You're not seriously telling me you have that manuscript?'

'Do you really think any author could burn the only copy of a work they considered worthwhile?'

'Didn't Fanny see it burn in the grate?'

'She saw *something* burn. She saw paper. I'm guessing there would have been plenty of paper in the vicinity.'

Lifting the coffee towards my mouth, I realised my hand was shaking. He waited until I'd taken a first sip.

'I have *both* manuscripts,' he then announced, causing me to splutter. I rubbed the back of my hand across my lips.

'I'm not sure I believe you,' I eventually said.

'Why not?'

'Because they'd be worth a small fortune. Besides, the world would know. It's been almost a century – impossible to have kept them a secret.'

'Nothing is impossible.'

'Then you'll show me them?'

'It can be arranged. But tell me – what would it mean for your doctoral thesis?'

I thought for a moment. 'They'd probably move me from student to full professor.' I laughed at the absurdity of it. Yet I almost believed... almost.

'My understanding,' Turk went on airily, 'is that he entrusted both to his good friend Henley. They found their way into my family because my grandfather bought many of Henley's possessions on his death – they were friends of a sort. There are notations in what seems to be Henley's handwriting. They add... well, you'd need to read them to find out.'

That smile again. I wanted to grab him and shake him.

'I'm not very good at keeping secrets,' I told him.

'Maybe it's time for the truth to be told,' he retorted. 'Wouldn't you say you're as good a vessel as any?' He had taken some coins from his pocket and was counting them on to the table-top as payment for the drinks. 'I should imagine most Stevenson scholars would be on their knees right now, begging to be shown even a few pages.' He paused, reaching into his jacket. 'Pages like these.'

He held them out towards me. Half a dozen sheets.

'Copies rather than the originals, you understand.'

Handwritten on unlined paper.

'The openings to both books,' Turk was saying as my head swam and my eyes strained to retain their focus. 'You'll notice something from the off...'

'Edinburgh,' I mouthed, near-silently.

'The setting for both,' he agreed. 'Well, there *are* some French scenes in *The Travelling Companion*, but our harlot heroine hails from your own fair city, Ronald. And since Jekyll is reputed to be a conflation between Deacon Brodie and the Scottish physician John Hunter, I suppose Edinburgh makes sense – too much sense for Fanny to bear, as it transpired.'

I glanced up at him, seeking his meaning.

'There's too much of Stevenson himself in both works,' he obliged, rising to his feet.

'You could be the victim of a hoax,' I blurted out. 'I mean to say, forgeries maybe.' I held the pages up in front of me, my heart racing.

'Handwriting analysis comes later on in the story,' Turk said, adjusting the cuffs of his pale linen jacket and seeming to sniff the mid-morning air. 'I expect you'll be paying me a visit later – if only to collect those boxes of books.'

'This is insane,' I managed to say, holding the pages by both trembling hands.

'Nevertheless, you'll want to read them. I'm out most of the day, but should be home later this evening.'

He turned and walked away, leaning lightly on his walking-stick. I watched him. He seemed to belong to a different age or culture. It was something about his gait as well as his clothes. I could imagine him with a top hat propped on his head, horse-drawn carriages passing him as he tip-tapped his way down the boulevard. The waiter said '*merci*' as he scooped up the coins and cleared the table, but I was in no rush to leave. I read and reread the excerpts. They revealed little by way of plot, but it was true that Edinburgh was the setting for both, Stevenson's descriptions of his 'precipitous city' as trenchant as ever. It was a place he seemed to have loved and hated in equal measure. I recalled something I'd read about his student years – how he spent his time yoyoing between the strict rationalism of the family home in Heriot Row and the drunken stews of the chaotic Old Town – moving, in other words, between the worlds of Henry Jekyll and Edward Hyde.

When the waiter cleared his throat, alerting me to the fact my premium table was needed by a wealthy American couple, I rolled the sheets of paper into a tube and carried them back to the shop. My employer had ceded his place behind the till to a new arrival, an English woman called Tessa with long brown hair, round glasses, and a prominent nose.

'I'll be upstairs if you need me,' I told her. The curtain had been drawn closed across my alcove. Pulling it back revealed Mike and one of his female friends, both naked from the waist up and sharing slugs from a cheap bottle of wine. The young woman apologised in French-accented English and slipped a t-shirt over her head.

'Ronnie doesn't mind a bit of tit,' Mike told her with a grin. She punched his arm and snatched the bottle from him, offering it to me. I settled on the corner of the bed and took a mouthful.

'What's that you've got?' Mike asked.

'Nothing important,' I lied, stuffing the sheets of paper into my jacket pocket. There was something else in there, and I fished it out. It was the lump of dope.

'That what I think it is?' Mike said, his grin widening. 'Well, now we've got us a proper party!' He leapt up, returning a minute or two later with everything he needed. Cross-legged, he began to assemble the joint. 'You're a dark horse, mate,' he told me. 'Never would have thought you indulged.'

'Then you don't know me very well.' His friend had moved closer, her leg touching mine. I could make out the soft down on her face. When she passed me the lit joint, it was as intimate as any kiss.

'It's not the best I've had,' Mike said, when his turn came. 'But it'll do, *n'est-ce pas, chérie?*'

'It'll do,' his friend echoed.

It was not ergotine, nor yet cocaine, but I found my imagination heightened. I was with Stevenson and his student allies, touring the taverns of Edinburgh, rubbing shoulders with slatterns and sophisticates. I was adrift in France, and sailing to Samoa, and roughing it in Silverado, having survived yet another near-fatal illness. I was weak in body but strong in spirit, and a woman loved me. I was writing *Jekyll and Hyde* as an exorcism of sorts, my demons vanquished, allowing me the less dangerous pleasures of *Kidnapped* less than a year later. External as well as internal adventures were my mainstay – I had to keep moving, ever further from the Edinburgh of my birth and formation. I had to remake myself, renew myself, heal myself, even as mortality drew close. I had to survive.

'What's that?' Mike asked. He was slumped on the bed with his head against the wall.

'I didn't say anything.'

'Something about survival.'

'No.'

He turned to his friend. She had moved next to him so that only her bare unwashed feet now rested near me. 'You heard him,' he nudged her.

'Survival,' she echoed.

'What it's all about,' Mike agreed, nodding slowly, before pulling himself together, the better to roll another joint.

Though I was stoned, I agreed to take over from Tessa while she headed out for food. Mike and Maryse – she had eventually told me her name – decided to go with her. They had the decency to ask if I wanted anything, but I shook my head. I gulped some water from the tap and took up position. A few customers came and went. One or two regulars got comfortable with books they would never buy. Later, a writing group would hold its weekly meeting upstairs. And there she was again. Not just a glimpse this time, but a solidity in the open doorway, in the same floral dress. A willowy figure topped with long blonde hair. Her eyes were on mine, but when I signalled for her to approach, she shook her head, so I walked towards her.

'I've seen you before,' I said.

'You're Ronald,' she stated.

'How do you know my name?'

'Ben told me.'

'You know Benjamin Turk?'

She nodded slowly. 'You mustn't trust him. He likes playing games with people.'

'I've only met him twice.'

'Yet he's already got beneath your skin – don't try to deny it.'

'Who *are* you?'

'I'm Alice.'

'How do you know Mr Turk?'

'Services rendered.'

'I'm not sure I follow.'

'I run errands for him sometimes. I copied those pages he gave you.'

'You know about those?'

'You've already read them, I suppose?'

'Of course.'

'And you need to read more, meaning you'll visit him again?'

'I think so.'

She had lifted her hand and was running the tips of her fingers down my cheek, as if human contact was something new and strange. I leaned back a little, but she took a step forward and pressed her lips against mine, kissing me, her eyes squeezed shut. When she opened them again, I sensed a vast lake of sadness behind them. Tears were forming as she turned and fled down the street. I stood like a statue, shocked to my very core, wondering if I should go after her, but one of the loiterers had decided to break the habit of a lifetime and pay for the book in his hands, so I shrugged off the incident and headed back to the till, not in the least surprised to find that the book being purchased was the copy of *Heart of Darkness* I'd taken with me to the cous-cous restaurant...

It was almost eleven by the time I found myself standing outside Benjamin Turk's building. I stared up towards the top floor. A few lights were burning, but I couldn't be sure which rooms were his. I pushed open the heavy door and began to climb the stairs. I could smell the aftermath of various dinners, and hear conversations – mostly, I guessed, from TV sets. There was a dog behind one door, scratching and complaining softly. Having reached the top floor, and while pausing to catch my breath, I saw a note pinned to Turk's door.

Still out. Come in.

I tried the door. It was unlocked. The overhead light was on in the hallway, but as with most Parisian lighting it seemed woefully underpowered. I called out but received no reply. There was something lying on the floor a few yards into the apartment – further sheets of manuscript, again photocopied. I lifted them and carried them into the living-room, where I settled on the same chair as before. A fresh decanter of wine had been laid out, alongside two crystal glasses.

'In for a centime,' I muttered to myself, pouring some. Then, having rolled up my shirt-sleeves, I began to read.

The two extracts did not follow on from their predecessors. They were from deeper into both books. I soon saw why Turk had chosen them, however – both recounted very similar incidents, vicious attacks on women whose bodies were for sale. In *The Travelling Companion*, it was the courtesan of the title who was brutalised by an unnamed stranger while passing down one of the steep inclines off Edinburgh's High Street. In the version of *Jekyll and Hyde*, the victim's attacker was Edward Hyde. But Hyde's name had replaced another, scored through in ink until it was all but obliterated. Pencilled marginalia, however, indicated that the name Stevenson had originally chosen for his monster was Edwin Hythe. Indeed, the margins of this particular page were filled with notes and comments in various hands – Stevenson's, I felt sure, but maybe also his friend Henley's – and Fanny's, too? Was it she who had written in blunt capital letters 'NOT HYTHE!'?

I poured myself some more wine and began deciphering the scribbles, scrawls and amendments. I was still hard at work when I heard the door at the end of the hallway open and close, footsteps drawing close. Then Benjamin Turk was standing there in the doorway, coat draped over both shoulders. He was dressed to the nines, and had obviously enjoyed his evening, his face filled with colour, eyes almost fiery.

'Ah, my dear young friend,' he said, shrugging off the coat and resting his walking-stick against a pile of books.

'I hope you don't mind,' I replied, indicating the decanter.

He landed heavily in the chair opposite, his girth straining the buttons on his shirt. 'Do you still imagine you're in the presence of a cruel hoax?' he asked, exhaling noisily.

'Not so much, perhaps.'

This caused him to smile, albeit tiredly.

'Do we know who wrote the notes in the margins?'

'The usual suspects.' He rose long enough to pour some wine. 'Edwin Hythe,' he drawled.

'Yes.'

'You won't know who he is?' Settling himself, he studied me over the rim of his glass.

'He's Hyde.'

But Turk shook his head slowly. 'He was a friend of Stevenson's, one of the students he drank with back in the day.'

'That was his real name? And Stevenson was going to use it in the book?' I sounded sceptical because I was.

'I know.' Turk took a sip, savouring the wine. 'Hythe had re-entered Stevenson's life, visiting him in Bournemouth not long before work started on the story you're holding. The two had fallen out at some point and not spoken for several years. There are a couple of portraits of Hythe – I've seen them but don't have copies to hand. I do have this though...' He reached into his jacket and drew out a sheet of printed paper. I took it from him, unfolding it carefully. It was the front page of a newspaper of the time, the *Edinburgh Evening Courant*, from a February edition of 1870. The main story recounted the tale of a 'young woman known to the city's night-dwellers' who had been found 'most grievously slaughtered' in an alley off Cowgate.

'Like Stevenson,' Turk was saying, 'Edwin Hythe was a member of the university's Speculative Society – though whatever speculation they did was accompanied by copious amounts of drink. And don't forget – this was at a time when Edinburgh was noted for scientific and medical experiments, meaning the students had access to pharmaceuticals of all kinds, most of them untested, a few probably lethal. Hythe had a larger appetite than most – for drink, and narcotics, and lively behaviour. He was arrested several times, and charged once for "lewd and libidinous acts".'

'Why are you telling me this?'

'You *know* why.'

'Hyde was Hythe? And the newspaper...?'

'I think you know that, too.'

'Hythe killed her, is that what you're saying? And Stevenson knew?'

'Our dear Louis was probably *there*, Ronald, the guilt gnawing at him until he deals with it by writing *The Travelling Companion*. That particular book gets spiked, but word of it reaches Hythe and he hot-foots it down to Bournemouth to make sure his old pal isn't going to crack. Maybe he leans on him, but my hunch is he finds it a lot easier to enlist Fanny instead. She thinks she's succeeded when Louis shows her the burning pages. He then rewrites the story, shifting location from Edinburgh to London and changing Hythe to Hyde...'

'Was he a doctor?'

'I'm sorry?'

I met Turk's look. 'Was Edwin Hythe a doctor?'

I watched him shake his head. I had emptied my glass and refilled it without thinking. 'How do you know all this?'

'It's a tale passed down through my family.'

'Why, though?'

'As a warning maybe.'

'You're a Hythe,' I stated, maintaining eye contact.

He eventually let out a snort of laughter. 'I sincerely hope not.' And he raised his own glass in a toast.

'Can I see the whole story?'

'Which one?'

'Both.'

'In good time.'

'Why not now?'

'Because I'm not sure you're ready.'

'I don't understand.'

But he just shook his head.

'It's like water torture,' I ploughed on. 'One page, two pages, three...'

'When I said that you weren't ready, I meant me – *I'm* not ready to let go, not just yet.'

'And after all these generations, why me?'

He offered a tired shrug. 'I'm the last of my line. Maybe that's reason enough. How about you?'

'Me?'

'Brothers...? Sisters...?'

'An only child.'

'We have that in common, too, then.' He yawned and stretched. 'Forgive me, I think I need some sleep.'

'I could stay here and read.'

He shook his head again. 'Perhaps tomorrow.' He rose to his feet and gestured for me to do the same. As he accompanied me down the hall, helping me into my jacket, I felt the negative mirror image of his fatigue. I was crackling with energy, a need to be in movement, a need for activity and exertion.

'I saw your friend,' I told him. 'She was passing the shop.'

'Oh?'

'Alice, with the blonde hair.'

'Alice,' he echoed.

'I just thought I'd say.'

'Thank you.' He pulled open the door and I skipped out, almost dancing down the stone stairs. She was waiting, of course – at the same spot across the street, wearing her floral dress and looking cold. I slipped off my jacket and placed it around her, then led her by the hand.

'Where are we going?' she asked.

'The river. I feel like walking.'

There were no tourist boats at this hour, just a few silent lovers and noisy drunks.

'Do you live with him?' I asked her.

'No.'

'So where do you live?'

'Not far.'

'Can we go there?'

'No.' She sounded almost aghast at the idea.

'My room back at the shop then,' I offered.

'Why would I go anywhere with you?'

'Because you kissed me.'

'I shouldn't have done that.'

'I'm glad you did though.' I came to a halt, facing her. 'I'd like it to happen again.'

She took a few moments to make her mind up, then stroked my face again, this time with both hands, as though checking that I really was flesh and blood. I leaned in and our lips met, mouths opening. But partway through, she started to laugh, easing away from me. I tried for a disappointed look, and she had the good grace to look slightly ashamed.

'I'm sorry,' she said. 'It's just...'

'What?'

'Nothing.' She shook her head, but then perked up and grabbed my hand, leading me along the riverfront towards the nearest brightly lit bridge. 'We can cross to the other side.'

'Why would we do that?'

'It's quieter there. Do you have any dope?'

'Just this.' I showed her the remains of the cannabis. 'I don't have any cigarettes or papers though.'

'That doesn't matter.' She peeled away the cellophane and nibbled at a corner. 'You can just eat it. It's almost nice.'

'Almost?' I smiled and bit into the gritty cube. 'Will it have the same effect?'

'We'll know the answer soon enough. Did Harry sell you this?'

'You know him?'

'If you've not paid, offer him half of whatever he asks.'

'What if he doesn't like that?'

She looked me up and down. 'You're bigger than him.'

'He has friends though.'

'So pull a knife.' She mimed the action of drawing a blade from its sheath and lunging with it. 'Straight into his gut and his friends will run for the hills.' She saw the look on my face and burst out laughing, hiding her mouth behind the palm of her hand. I grabbed both her arms and pulled her towards me, waiting until she was ready for our next kiss.

'Keep your eyes open this time,' I said in a whisper. 'I want to see whatever's in them...'

*

For the next week, whenever I walked out of Shakespeare and Company, she was waiting. In deference to the dress she always wore, I'd stopped changing my own clothes, even though Mike had complained, wrinkling his nose as he made a show of sniffing my shoulder.

'Mate, when was the last time you saw the inside of a shower?'

But Alice didn't seem to mind. We would buy a plastic bottle of the cheapest wine and head for the river or the Louvre or the Arc de Triomphe, laughing at the tourists as they posed for their little photos. On one occasion, we indulged in a five-litre cubitainer of red, sharing it with the tramps who congregated near one of the bridges, until a fight broke out and the arrival of the *gendarmes* sent us scurrying. I had stopped shaving, and Alice would run her hands down my cheeks and across my chin, calling me her 'bit of rough'. There was a folded letter in my pocket from my father. I hadn't opened it, and hadn't troubled to call Charlotte. Theirs was another world entirely. I could feel myself changing, growing. When Harry grabbed me one night outside the restaurant to remind me of the money I owed, I laid him out with a single punch, after which I had to keep my distance from the restaurant. Not that this mattered – Alice never ate a thing, and that seemed to suit both of us. With money from the bookshop till, I bought us a few grams of cocaine from an African dealer, which killed any appetite remaining. And when Mike nagged me for missing a shift which he had been obliged to cover, I gave as good as I got, until he backed away, hands held in front of him, fear in his eyes at my clenched fists and gritted teeth.

Oh, yes, I was changing.

I'd been back to Benjamin Turk's apartment, but its door remained locked and unanswered. Alice had advised a shoulder-charge, which had left me with nothing other than a large bruise and a slight deflation of ego.

'I could scale the front wall, window to window,' I'd muttered over more pavement wine, receiving an indulgent smile and a hug.

'He's often gone for a few days,' she'd sympathised. 'He'll be back soon enough.'

And then she'd kissed me.

There hadn't been any sex as yet, which suited both of us. We were happy to wait for the right moment, the most intense moment. Hugs and kisses, the holding of hands, fingers stroking an arm, cheek or the nape of the neck. She seemed to have no other friends, or none she wouldn't give up in order to spend time with me, and I felt the same. I wasn't about to share what we had with Mike or anyone else. Every moment I could, I spent with her.

Until the day I walked downstairs into the shop groggy with sleep and saw Charlotte standing there. She carried a rucksack and a wide-brimmed straw hat and looked hot from walking. Her smile was hesitant.

'Hello, you,' she said. 'We were getting worried.'

'Oh?'

'I phone but you're never here. And your mum and dad...' She broke off. 'Well, do I get a hug?'

I stepped forward and took her by the shoulders, my lips brushing against her damp red hair.

'Bloody hell, Ronnie, look at the state of you. When did you last eat?'

'I'm fine.'

'You're really not. Your friend Mike...'

'Mike?'

'He answered the phone yesterday.'

'And told you to come running? Probably just wanted to size you up as another notch on his bed-post.'

'He was right though; you look ill. Have you seen a doctor?'

'I don't need a doctor. What I need is for everyone to stop bothering me.'

She was silent for a moment, glaring at me. Then she turned

her eyes away. 'A lovely warm welcome for your girlfriend,' she muttered, pretending to study one of the shelves.

I ran a hand through my matted hair. 'Look, I had a bit to drink last night. And the shock of seeing you here...' I broke off. I'd been about to say that I was sorry, but part of me resisted. 'What time is it?'

'Nearly one.'

'I'll buy you something at the café.' I opened the till and lifted out a few notes.

'Is that allowed?' Charlotte asked as I stuffed the money into my pocket.

'I'll put it back later,' I lied.

When we stepped outside there was – for once – no sign of Alice, but Maryse was setting out boxes of cheap paperbacks on the pavement.

'Tell Mike I'll be having a word with him later,' I said, my face set like stone. Then I led Charlotte a few metres along the road, entering the café and taking up position by the counter. Charlotte slid the rucksack from her shoulders.

'Thinking of staying?' I inquired.

'I wasn't about to do Paris and back in a day. Since when did you smoke?'

I looked down at the cigarette I was rolling.

'Not sure,' I admitted. Which was the truth – I had no memory of buying either the pouch of Drum tobacco or the packet of tissue-thin papers. All I knew was that Alice obviously didn't mind. The look on Charlotte's face was properly small-minded and Presbyterian. I could imagine her sitting primly in my parents' drawing-room, holding cup and saucer and allowing herself 'one small slice of cake'. Home baking? Naturally. The conversation stilted and bourgeois and safe. Everything so fucking *safe*.

'What are you thinking?' she asked as I lit the slender cigarette.

'I'm thinking you shouldn't have come.'

Was she really becoming tearful, or merely putting on a show in the hope of sympathy? My espresso had arrived, along with her Perrier. The barman waved a bottle of red in my direction but I shook my head and he seemed to understand.

Pas devant les enfants...

'I wanted to see you,' Charlotte persisted. 'This is Paris, after all. Everyone says it's a romantic city and I've been missing you, Ronnie. I thought maybe this would be the place for us to...'

'What?'

She lowered her eyes and her voice. 'Don't make me say it.'

'Fuck our brains out?'

Her eyes and mouth widened. She glanced at the barman.

'He doesn't have any English,' I reassured her, knowing François would actually have understood every word. He was polishing glasses at the far end of the bar. All of a sudden I craved something alcoholic, so ordered a *pression*. When it arrived, I demolished it in two gulps, and nodded for a refill while Charlotte stared at me.

'You need help,' she eventually said. 'Something's happened to you.'

'Well, you're right about that at least – yes, something's happened to me. For the first time in my life, and I'm all the better for it.'

'You're not though. Look in the mirror.'

As it happened, there was a long narrow mirror running the length of the bar, below the row of optics and shelves of drinks. I hunched down so I could make eye contact with myself and couldn't help grinning.

'Who's that handsome devil?' I chuckled.

'Ronnie...'

'My name's Ronald!' I roared. François clucked and gestured for me to keep it down. I waved a hand in what could have passed for either apology or dismissal of his complaint.

Charlotte's hand was shaking as she lifted her glass of water. I realised that's what she was: carbonated water, while my life had become so much headier and filled with sensation.

'Will you help me find a hotel?' she was asking without making eye contact.

'Of course,' I said quietly.

'I'll change my flight to tomorrow, if I can. I was going to stay a few days, but...'

'They'll be missing you at your work.'

'Oh, I quit the job. My thinking was to do some travelling with you.' Finally she fixed her eyes on mine. 'But that was when you were you.'

'Who am I now?'

'I've really no idea.'

'Well, I'm sorry you had to come all this way to find out.' I placed a fifty-franc note on the counter and made to lift Charlotte's rucksack from the floor.

'No,' she snapped, hoisting it on to her shoulders. 'I can manage perfectly well.'

As we exited the café, I caught sight of a dress I recognised. Just the hem of it as its owner dodged around the corner of a building. We headed in the opposite direction, into the narrow maze of streets behind the bookshop. I looked behind me, but Alice didn't seem to be following. There were plenty of small hotels here, most of them doing good business at the height of the summer. It was twenty minutes before we found one with a vacancy. The owner led Charlotte upstairs to inspect the room while I said I'd wait in the street. I was rolling a fresh cigarette when I heard a scooter come to a stop behind me. I was half-turning in its direction when the passenger launched himself from behind the driver and hit me with what looked like a broken chair-leg. It connected with one of my temples and sent me to my knees. A hand was rummaging in my pockets. It pulled out the notes from the till and rubbed them in my face. Then another smack on the side of the head and Harry climbed back aboard, the driver revving the small engine hard as they fled the scene. Pedestrians had stopped to gawp, but only for a moment. There were no offers of help as I scrabbled to pick up my pouch of tobacco. I got to my feet and felt the world spin. I knew I was grinning, but had no idea why. I lit my cigarette and leaned against the wall, head tilted so I could look at the bluest sky imaginable.

Charlotte came out on to the pavement minus her rucksack, which meant the room had been declared acceptable. When she saw me she let out a screech, covering her mouth with her hand. That was when I noticed the blood dripping down from the cut on my temple. It was staining my already disreputable shirt and trousers, and adding crimson spots to the street beneath.

'What happened?' Charlotte asked.

I took out my handkerchief and pressed it to the cut, feeling it sting for the first time.

'Somebody hit me.' I was still grinning. 'Don't worry, I'll get him back.'

'We need the police.'

'What for?'

'You know who did this?'

'I didn't pay him for the drugs.'

Her eyes hardened. 'Say that again.' And when I didn't, she just nodded slowly, as if a small lump of dope explained everything. She clasped me by one wrist. 'Come upstairs. We need to wash that clean.'

I resisted long enough to finish the cigarette, then allowed myself to be led up a dark twisting stairwell to her room. It was tiny and stifling, the window open and shutters closed in a vain attempt to keep out the afternoon heat. Charlotte's rucksack lay on the bed. She moved it and made me sit down, there being no chair. Then she knelt in front of me, examining the damage.

'It's deep,' she said. There was a thin towel on the end of the bed and she took it with her when she left the room. I could hear water running in the sink of the communal bathroom along the hall. Then she was back, dabbing and wiping.

'Any nausea?' she asked.

'No more than usual.'

She smiled as if I'd made a joke. 'You're being very brave,' she cooed.

'I'm tougher than you think.'

'I'm sure you are.' She made another trip to the bathroom to rinse the towel. This time she wiped it slowly across all of my face, studying my features as she worked. 'You're filthy, Ronald. Really you need a bath.'

'Will you scrub my back?'

'I might.' Her eyes were locked on mine. I leaned forwards and kissed her on the mouth.

'You're bristly,' she said afterwards. 'But I sort of like it.'

So I kissed her again. Then we were standing, arms wrapped around one another. My hands felt beneath her sweat-dampened blouse, running down her spine. Our mouths opened as our tongues got to work, and she gave a small moan. Her fingers brushed the front of my trousers, then started to work at the zip. My eyes were still open but hers were closed, as she concentrated hard on fulfilling the whole purpose of the trip. So greedy and so intent on her own selfish self. I put my hand on hers, squeezing. She opened her eyes.

'I'm going to take that bath,' I said.

'Good idea,' she replied, sounding only half-convinced. 'There's only the one towel though, and it's already wet.'

'I'll be fine.' I gave a smile and a wink and managed to escape the airless room. The bath was old and stained but hot water gushed from its tap. I locked the door before stripping. There were bruises on my body I was at a loss to explain. Piled on the floor, my clothes looked like rags. I sank into the water and slid beneath its surface. I had been soaking only a couple of minutes when Charlotte tried the door.

'I won't be long,' I called out.

'I thought you wanted someone to scrub your back.'

'Another time.'

I could sense her lingering. But she moved away eventually, her bedroom door closing. I was debating my next move. Get dressed and slink away? Would that make me a coward? No, I would talk to her face-to-face and explain everything. I would tell her about Benjamin Turk and Alice and my newly blossoming life. We would part as friends, and I would then pay a visit to Harry and Mike, where both men would learn what happened to people who crossed me.

'Yes,' I said to the bathroom walls, nodding slowly to myself.

And then I closed my eyes and slid below the waterline again.

The water had turned tepid by the time I climbed out. I used the towel as best I could, and slid back into my clinging clothes. Blood still trickled from the cut, so I held the towel as a compress as I unlocked the door and padded down the hall. The door to Charlotte's room stood gaping. Charlotte herself lay on the bed, half-undressed and with a scarf knotted tightly around her neck, digging into the flesh. Her eyes and tongue bulged, her face almost purple. I knew she was dead, and knew, too, the identity of the culprit. She had unpacked one dress from her rucksack, the one almost identical to Alice's. Pushing open the shutters, I looked down on to the courtyard and saw a familiar flash of colour. Alice was heading for the street.

I studied Charlotte a final time, knowing there was nothing to be done, then ran to the stairs, barging past the hotelier, who was on the way up. I crossed the courtyard, scanning the pavement to left and right. Making a decision, I started running again. I didn't know Alice's address or even her surname. Would she head for the Seine and the derelicts we had shared our wine with? Or to the bookshop, where she could wait for me on my infested alcove bed? Bars and cafés and the usual landmarks... We had criss-crossed the city, making it our own.

But there was only one destination I could think of – Turk's apartment.

She wasn't outside, nor was she seated on the stairs. I climbed to the top floor and tried the door – locked, as before. But this time when I hit it with my fist, there were sounds from inside. Benjamin Turk opened the door and studied me from head to foot.

'It looks to me as though you're finally ready,' he said with a thin smile, ushering me in.

'Have you seen Alice?' I demanded.

'Forget about her,' he said, his back to me as he hobbled

towards the living-room. 'I've laid everything out for you.'
He was pointing towards the desk. Various documents lay
there. 'Took me some time and effort, but you'll only begin to
comprehend when you examine them.'

'What are they?'

'The story of Edwin Hythe. Sit down. Read. I'll fetch you a
drink.'

'I don't want a drink.' But I realised that I did – I wanted the
darkest wine in the largest glass imaginable. Turk seemed to
understand this, and returned with a glass filled almost to the
brim. I gulped it down, exhaling only afterwards.

'Does the wound hurt?' he was asking.

I dabbed at my head. 'No,' I said.

'Then you should read.' He pulled over a chair so he could sit
next to me, and while I focused on the various sheets of paper
he explained the significance.

'Stevenson and Hythe were close friends as students,
belonging to the same clubs and drinking in the same low dives
late into the night. Then the murder of a prostitute is recorded
in the newspaper and there's a parting. Hythe disappears from
Stevenson's life. The murderer is never apprehended. When
Stevenson writes a novel about just such a woman, his wife
persuades him it is not going to be good for his reputation. But
Hythe, too, hears about it, and makes his way to Bournemouth.
He comes from money so he stays at the best hotel in town, a
hotel that keeps impeccable records.' He tapped the photocopied
sheet showing Hythe's signature in the guest book, along with
the duration of his stay. 'It's fairly obvious that Hythe was the
killer and that Stevenson was either a witness or else was privy
to his friend's confession. The golden young man Stevenson had
known in Edinburgh was by now a dissolute figure, in trouble
with creditors, disowned by his family, earning a living of sorts
from any number of illegal activities.' He tapped a series of court
reports and newspaper stories. 'Pimping, trafficking, receiving
stolen goods... And with a temper on him. One arrest talks
of the superhuman rage of the man after too much drink had

been taken.' Turk paused. 'And when Hythe left Bournemouth, Stevenson sat down and wrote *Jekyll and Hyde* in three days. Not the version we know, but one set in Edinburgh, where Hythe aka Hyde attacks and kills a harlot rather than trampling a child. Again, he was dissuaded from publishing it. Fanny knew what it would mean – people in Edinburgh would talk. They would remember the killing of the prostitute. They would know the name Hythe and point the finger from him to his close friend Robert Louis Stevenson. That couldn't happen – it would mean prison or even worse. The book had to be destroyed, the story reworked, and Hythe's name changed to Hyde.'

'All right,' I said quietly. Tears were falling from my eyes on to the desk. I was seeing Charlotte, in that horrific pose on her bed, her life snuffed out. I was about to say as much, but Turk was opening a drawer and pulling out more sheets. They comprised a family tree, along with some drawings – portraits of the same man, showing him in his late teens and then in raddled middle age. He looked so familiar to me...

'Edwin Hythe,' Turk was explaining. 'The first time I saw you, I was struck by the resemblance. This was some time back, through the window of the shop. I asked George about you and decided it was no mere coincidence. Which is why I asked him to send you on that particular errand.'

'I don't understand.'

'It's on your mother's side,' he said, running a finger back up the family tree from my name. 'You are descended from Edwin Hythe. His blood in your blood, and with it, unfortunately, his curse.'

'His what?' I was rubbing at my eyes, trying to blink them into some kind of focus.

'Your devil has been long caged, Ronald. He has come out *roaring*!'

There was a mad gleam in his eye as he spoke. I leapt to my feet. 'You're crazy,' I told him. '*You're* the devil here! You and your damned Alice!'

'There is no Alice.'

'She knows you – she runs errands...'

But he was shaking his head. 'There's only you, Ronald. You and the demon that's been sleeping deep inside you, waiting for the right catalyst. Paris is that catalyst.'

'Where are the manuscripts?' I demanded, looking about me. 'The two unpublished novels?'

He gave a shrug. 'You've seen all there is. Nothing more than fragments.'

'You're lying!'

'Believe what you will.'

'Alice is *real*!'

He was chuckling as he shook his head again. His silver-topped walking-stick glinted at me from its resting-place by the desk. I grabbed it and raised it over my head. Rather than shrink from me in fear, his smile seemed to widen. I bared my teeth and struck him across the side of the head. He staggered but stayed on his feet, so I hit him again. He wheeled away from me into the long hallway. I stayed a few footsteps behind him as I continued to rain down blows upon his head and back until he fell, just inside the front door. He was still conscious, but his breathing was ragged, blood bubbling from his mouth. A few more blows and he lay still. I hauled him by his feet away from the door so I could open it and make my escape.

Outside, I could hear sirens. Police cars, probably, heading for a hotel not too far away, where passers-by would be able to describe the bloodied figure running from the scene. Alice was standing on the opposite pavement, her eyes full of understanding. We shared a smile before I looked to left and right. There was plenty of traffic, but I started to cross towards her, knowing it would stop for me. When I looked again, however, she had vanished. Pedestrians and drivers were beginning to stare. I noted the fresh spattering of bright red blood on my shirt, so began to rip at it, throwing it from me until I stood half-naked in the middle of the road, the sirens drawing closer. I stretched out both arms, angled my head to the heavens above, and roared.

Seven Years

Peter Robinson

IT IS ONE of the greatest pleasures of my retirement to set out early on a fine morning for some ancient town or city renowned for the quantity and quality of its second-hand bookshops.

Much of my enjoyment, I will admit, lies in the anticipation of what I might discover on the overflowing shelves of cramped anterooms and attics. I take my time getting to my destination, enjoying the countryside as I drive along. I also combine my book-buying expeditions with a visit to a nearby cathedral, country churchyard, or place of historic interest, and I round off my excursion with a late lunch at a local inn, where I thumb through my day's purchases and enjoy a pint or two of ale with my meal.

Though my tastes are catholic, there are certain subjects I seek out in particular: poetry, literary criticism, and biography being prime among them. I have always been of a literary bent, and in my working life I was an academic, a Professor of Classics at Cambridge, no less. I was good enough at my job, with well-respected translations of Catullus and Ovid to my name, as well as a brief introduction to Latin verse which I am pleased to say has been adopted as a first-year university recommended text. These days, however, I prefer to spend less time poring over dead languages than I do enjoying the writers of my native tongue. Having aspired to poetry once in the long ago days of my youth, I especially enjoy reading verse and accounts of the lives of the great poets.

Naturally, with second-hand books one has to keep an eye out for damage of a physical nature and for other people's scribblings. Underlining of text I detest, especially when it is done in ink, but though I also disdain marginalia in general, there have been occasions when I have chosen a specific copy of a book simply because of the interesting observations of a previous reader. One can feel an astonishing degree of kinship with such anonymous scribblers, whether one agrees or disagrees with them.

One fine English autumn morning, I had been wandering the streets of Beverley, a town hitherto unknown to me, on the eastern fringes of my allotted region. I had been delighted with the magnificent Gothic minster, golden in the late morning sunlight, and it was time to seek for books. I have learned over time that one will usually find the most interesting bookshops in rambling Dickensian structures hidden away in the mazes of narrow crooked alleys behind market squares and main shopping streets, so that was where I headed first.

After a delightful hour or two of exploration, I found myself carrying my weighty book bag into a pub, whose chalked blackboard promised first class food and well-kept cask ales. I bought a pint of Timothy Taylor Golden Best and ordered a plate of gammon, chips and peas and settled contentedly at a wobbly corner table in the small lounge. Rays of sunlight filtered through the windows and caught the motes of dust in their stately dance, the way that the film projectors once did with cigarette smoke in the cinema, and I was thankful that the pub was almost empty and the landlord had foregone the cacophonous allure of slot machines and piped music. As I sipped my ale and savored its bitter taste, I felt that all was well with the world, and I reached for my bag of books.

Imagine my surprise, then, when I found that the selection

of Robert Browning's poetry I had been so thrilled to find had been defaced on the flyleaf. I am usually careful enough to flip through a book before I buy it, but in this instance the pages had stuck together and that prevented me from noticing the inscription on my cursory examination in the shop. As far as I had been able to tell, the book was in mint condition; there were no signs of wear, no price-clipping or creases on the spine, and certainly no tell-tale coffee rings on the cover. In fact, it looked as if it had never been read.

Curious, I sipped some more ale and held open the flyleaf so that I might read the offending scribble:

"Miss Scott,
You know you want to read Browning's poetry. 'My Last Duchess' and 'Porphyria's Lover' in particular. 'The Ring and the Book,' too, perhaps, though that one is rather long and much abbreviated here. No poet quite captures adultery, betrayal, madness and the act of murder the way Browning does. Try this:

'… I found
A thing to do, and all her hair
In one long yellow string I wound
Three times her little throat around,
And strangled her. No pain felt she;
I am quite sure she felt no pain.'
('Porphyria's Lover')

Then she is *his* forever. Don't you just *love* that? Doesn't it sound like fun? I know that I would enjoy it. And don't forget our little bargain. The time is fast approaching!
Happy Reading, Miss Scott!
Barnes"

This highly unusual inscription sent a chill through me, despite the warmth of the day. I felt as if someone had just walked over my grave, as my mother used to say. When the serving girl brought my food and knelt to push a wad of folded beer mat under the table leg to correct the wobble, I pushed the book aside and tucked in, having hardly realized in the morning's excitement just how hungry I was.

But as I ate, I couldn't help but mull over what I had just read.

I realize that at this point you may well be wondering whether I am overreacting to what is, after all, merely a damaged second-hand book. After all, I could always return it to the shop for a refund, or perhaps attempt to slice out the ravaged page with a razor blade at home. I hadn't read Browning in a long time and was looking forward to reacquainting myself with his work, but I certainly didn't think I could enjoy reading this particular copy. It had been defiled. There was something about the tone of the inscription that disturbed me deeply. What sort of person, I wondered, would write something like that in a gift? In a volume of poetry? There seemed a definite aura of taunting cruelty about the words, a certain delight in causing another unease and discomfort. If "Miss Scott" had seen this, no wonder she had dispatched the book to a second-hand shop immediately.

"Porphyria's Lover" had always disturbed me. I remember the frisson of forbidden delights I experienced when I first came across it in the sixth form. Could one really say this sort of thing in poetry? In that same burnished, heightened language of Shakespeare, Shelley and Keats? My pleasure was akin to the thrill of discovering Lord Rochester's sexually explicit verse a few years later, in my student days.

There is something about the matter-of-fact nature of Browning's use of language in "Porphyria's Lover," the contrast between its serene tone and the violent deed itself, the sensuality of the hair and "her little throat." One can easily imagine the murderer sitting there, content with his handiwork, his arm around the beautiful, unfaithful lover he has just strangled, smiling, happy, convinced that he now has possession of her forever.

Perhaps the whole thing was intended as a sick joke, I told myself, but I couldn't stop wondering who these people were, and why this Barnes fellow had written those words. Whatever had Miss Scott done to him to bring about such a deliberate desire to cause her discomfort? And how long ago had this occurred? The book could have been sitting on the shelf for years, as many volumes of poetry often do in second-hand bookshops. In the meantime, what had become of Miss Scott and Barnes? Was there a murder to be investigated?

And who had sold the book to the dealer? Miss Scott, herself? Had she even seen the inscription? It was possible that she hadn't if the pages had been stuck in the same way they were when I flipped through the book. In which case, what had happened next? Had Barnes followed through with his veiled threat? What exactly was "the time fast approaching" for? What was their "bargain?" Was this inscription a sort of warning, or the first salvo in a campaign of terror, something to frighten her, the sort of thing one hears young people do to one another on the Internet these days? And if she had not seen it, had not got the warning, what had become of her?

One of my first thoughts, deduced mostly from the formal address and writer's use of his surname, was that it had been a teacher-pupil relationship, and that the boy was trying to get revenge for the misery he felt his English teacher had inflicted upon him. Perhaps she had forced *The Mayor of Casterbridge* or *Jude the Obscure* on him at too early an age? But what schoolboy buys his teacher a volume of poetry? An apple is one thing, but a book quite another. Was the relationship something more? One of those teacher-pupil affairs one reads about with alarming frequency these days? Had Miss Scott sexually abused Barnes?

Or was Barnes a university student? I remembered my own teaching days, not so far behind me, and I quickly realized that most of those who had passed through my doors had been more than capable of pulling such a prank, if prank it was, though I had never come across a university student who had referred to his professor as "Miss." Was I seriously misjudging the whole business, reading more into it than there was?

I thought I possibly was, so I sipped some more ale, put the book aside and delved deeper into the contents of the rest of the bag. Soon I was on my second pint of Timothy Taylor and enjoying Victoria Glendenning's introduction to her inscription-free biography of Anthony Trollope, the mysterious Barnes and Miss Scott, if not quite forgotten, then at least relegated to a dim antechamber at the back of my mind.

I awoke the following morning from a troubled sleep, the Browning still weighing heavy on my mind. Though I could remember only scraps, I suspected the dreams that had woken me so often during the night were connected with the book's mysterious inscription.

As the days went by, Miss Scott and Barnes crept their way back to the forefront of my thoughts. I found myself, in idle moments, attempting to construct mental pictures of what they looked and sounded like. Miss Scott I saw not as a Miss Jean Brodie type, but more as a Hitchcock blonde with her hair piled high. Tippi Hedren in *The Birds* or Kim Novak in *Vertigo*, without the Hollywood glamour. In my imagination, Miss Scott has the deportment of someone who attended a Swiss finishing school and spent many hours walking the corridors with a volume of Proust balanced on her head. Her voice is low, a husky contralto, and her accent educated, with the broad Yorkshire vowels well hidden behind hours of enunciation lessons. She is private, secretive, even, with a rare but heart-melting smile, and her pale, flawless skin blushes often. Her eyes are dark blue and hard to read. She gains easy control of the classes she teaches, but she does so through the calm strength of her personality and through her elegance and poise, rather than by means of authority and status. It is not that the students are afraid of her; they just don't want to upset or disappoint her. She favors cream tailored jacket and skirt outfits over blue silk blouses, and all her skirts end modestly below her knees, offering just a tantalizing glimpse of her shapely legs.

As for Barnes, he doesn't come through quite so clearly. There's a mischievous look about him, as if he has just got away with something, a naughty boy constantly on the verge of a smirk. His hair is dark, parted on the left, though one restless comma is always slipping over his right eye. He wears a nondescript school uniform, navy blazer, grey trousers, striped tie, black shoes, nicely shined. He's not outwardly scruffy, but he is a boy, after all, perhaps seventeen or eighteen, a sixth former, at any rate, and his pockets are full of a jumble of bits of string, rubber bands, a penknife, loose coins, maybe even a French letter or two, just in case, chewing gum, a packet of cough drops, a crumpled handkerchief and a couple of Bic ballpoints. He keeps a small writing pad in his inside pocket to jot down passing thoughts, mostly unpleasant ones, like the inscription on the book.

That was what I came up with when I let my early-morning imagination run away with me. I wondered whether I would ever get to find out how close my pictures were to the truth because, by then, whether I knew it fully or not, I was determined to find out who Barnes and Miss Scott were and what their relationship was.

In order to begin, I had to return to the bookshop and see if I could find out anything from its owner. Perhaps he would know who they were. What I would do with the information if I got it, I had no idea, but I couldn't simply leave things as they were. I had to know more. It was as if I had been given a teaser, a trailer, the opening chapter of an author's next book tacked on after the end of the one I had just read, and I had to see the film, had to read the next book.

As I drove back to Beverley several days later, I tried to work out what I would say to the shop owner. I could hardly show him the inscription; he would probably think I was insane. Of course, I realized it was more than likely that he would have no idea at all who had sold the book to him. I should imagine people who work in second-hand bookshops get quite a lot of customers dropping in with boxes or shopping bags full of old books. But there was a slim chance, and I didn't want to ruin it from the outset by giving the impression that I was some sort of madman or stalker. No, I had to be careful.

The best approach, I thought, would be to say that I had found something in the book that I wanted to return to its owner. The problem with that was that it gave rise to a lot more difficult questions. What had I found? If it was of value, then why hadn't the owner already returned to ask about it? If it was a letter or some such thing, wouldn't it have the owner's address on it? I could work out answers to most of these questions, but a great deal depended on how long the book had been on the shelf.

Obviously, whatever had been mislaid couldn't be time sensitive and could have been lost elsewhere. By now it might well have been written off as gone forever. But it should be something that the owner would welcome back again, even if she had been able to live without it for some time. To my mind that left only one thing: money.

Perhaps Miss Scott had used a ten pound note as a bookmark and had forgotten about it? That sounded unlikely to me, but I supposed it could have happened. Would the shop owner be suspicious? How many people would drive all the way back to return a ten pound note? Leaving aside the matter of honesty, it would cost me more than that in petrol to return it. But the bookseller needn't know how far I had come. I decided, in the end, that it had to be money. But twenty pounds would make my story more believable than ten. Though unusual, it could be convincing. I had done a similar thing once, myself, slipping a five pound note, a repaid loan, between the pages of a university library book I was carrying at the time. Later, I had returned the book before remembering to remove the note. I was fortunate in having an understanding librarian on that occasion, so I got my money back.

When I had parked my car, I headed first for W.H. Smith's, on the High Street. There I bought the smallest package of envelopes I could find and, back in my car, slipped a twenty pound note into one of them and wrote "window cleaner" on the front, hoping that would convince the bookseller. I know that twenty pounds seems a lot for a window cleaner, but window cleaners are about the only people one pays in cash these days. Perhaps Miss Scott lives in a house with a lot of windows? Putting my concerns aside, I sealed the flap, let it dry, then gently tore it open, as I imagined anyone would do in the real situation of finding such an envelope in a second-hand book.

I had great trouble finding the bookshop again in the labyrinthine alleys, and by mistake first entered the wrong one, the place where I had bought the Trollope biography. I soon realized my error when I saw the man behind the messy front desk, but couldn't stop myself glancing through the new arrivals. After a moment's hesitation, I also couldn't stop myself buying Florence Hardy's life of her husband, Thomas Hardy, which all the experts say he wrote himself. I had a list of books I was "looking for," though not in the sense of actively pursuing them through online sellers or eBay and so on, and this *Life* was on it. Another one I could cross off.

Feeling that much better and strangely more confident after my purchase, I entered into the labyrinth again. It had started to rain rather heavily by then. Just as I was about to give up and return when the weather improved, I found the shop. No wonder it had been hard to locate again. Its facade was narrow and humdrum, its green paint flaking and faded. No hand-painted sign hung over the door; the grimy windows were small, more like those of a terrace house than a shop. When I stood outside, I saw three or four books on display, but there was nothing interesting about them—one had something to do with steam trains, another with numismatics and a third was a coffee-table book on Holy Island. The name over the window was hardly legible, but with a bit of effort, I worked out that it said "Gorman's Antiquarian Bookshop," which was a bit of a cheek, I thought, eyeing the box of tatty paperbacks on a trestle by the door at fifty pence each. Peter Cheyney, Sax Rohmer, Hammond Innes, Erle Stanley Gardner, and "Sapper" do not an antiquarian bookshop make.

Inside, this particular establishment consisted of a warren of small anterooms, connected by narrow passages and short staircases of dry creaking wood, each room stacked from floor to ceiling with books, either upright on shelves or in piles that rivalled the Leaning Tower of Pisa. The uneven floors seemed to meet the walls at odd angles, and I remembered that my footsteps had sounded loud on the uncarpeted floorboards of warped, worn and knotted wood. It was a miracle the whole place didn't just fall down. The smell was not unpleasant, an old bookshop smell of dust and paper, mostly, with an undercurrent of old pipe tobacco and rich leather, like a fine Cabernet, and just a hint of mildew. Gorman kept his stock in decent condition, but with all the will in the world, you can't avoid the rising damp and occasional leaks in an old building like this one. The foistiness was not at all unpleasant, at least not to a habitué like me; it merely adds to the ambience.

I had considered showing Gorman the book I had bought and decided against it. Instead, I had noted down the particulars, including the ISBN number and condition. As he read the sheet of paper I handed him, Gorman scratched his head. A few flakes of dandruff drifted like snow on to the shoulders of his grey pullover. His hair was thin, and what there was of it was uncombed and long unwashed. He clearly hadn't shaved for several days, either.

"Browning?" he said finally, handing back the sheet and pushing his old National Health glasses up on his nose. "Not much call for Browning these days. His literary stock's gone right down, you might say." His chuckle sounded like an automatic coffee maker in its death throes. "Now, your Metaphysicals and your Romantics, that's a different story. Donne, Marvel, Keats and Shelley, they all sell like the proverbial hotcakes. Even old Willie Wordsworth and his daffodils. And your Victorian novelists—Dickens, George Eliot, Hardy, Mrs. Gaskell, and don't forget your Brontë sisters—I can't keep 'em on the shelves. Not that anyone who buys them actually reads them, you understand. I put it down to telly, myself. BBC drama." He shook his head as if pronouncing a verdict on BBC drama. "But your Victorian poets? You can't give 'em away. I don't know why. I quite enjoy a bit of Tennyson myself every now and then. 'Onward, onward, rode the six hundred' and all that. Stirring stuff. Can't say I care much for Browning, though. Bit of a pervert, wasn't he? All that rot about murder and adultery. Take 'My Last Duchess.' Didn't the duke in that one have his wife done away with just because she looked at other blokes?"

"'I gave commands; / Then all smiles stopped together.'" I quoted.

"Yes... er... well, quite. Like I said, not much call for that sort of thing."

"Yes, but would you have any idea from *whom* you bought this particular volume?" I tapped the sheet of paper in my hand.

"Whom?"

"That's right."

He scratched his head again. "Well, I don't rightly know. I mean, I get a lot of people coming in here."

We both cast a glance around the shop when he said that, and when I turned back to him, he continued, "On a good day, like. There's good days and there's bad days."

There had been no-one else in the place the last time I had been there, either, but I saw little point in mentioning that to him. "So there's no possible way you can tell me who sold you this book?"

"I didn't say that, did I? Keep perfectly good records, I do. There's no taxman can fault me on that. You're not—"

"No," I said firmly. "I am not a tax auditor. As a matter of fact, I'm a retired Professor of Classics. Cambridge."

He didn't seem quite as impressed as most people do when I mention the hallowed name of the university. "Professor, eh?" he said. "That explains it, then."

"Explains what?"

He pointed to the sheet of paper. "Browning. I'll bet he knew his classics, didn't he? All those artists and Renaissance stuff. Plenty of fellow perverts back then."

"These records you keep," I said. "Would it be at all possible for you to consult them and try to find out for me who brought this book in?"

"I suppose I could," he said without moving. "But I don't ask customers for their names and addresses. No one likes that. Smacks too much of the police state, being asked for your name and address and telephone number. I mean, you wouldn't like it if I asked you for your personal details when you came in here to buy or sell a book, would you? I think a person should be allowed to buy and sell things in perfect anonymity. That's one of the freedoms our fathers fought for. Within reason, of course. I mean, when it comes to guns or explosives or drugs, that's a different matter. Need a redchester for that sort of thing."

Redchester? I realized he probably meant "register." My heart sank. "Are you telling me," I said slowly, "that you can't do as I ask? I thought you said you could help."

"Up to a point. That's what I meant. Up to a point. I was just explaining that I can't you give you a name and address. Or telephone number. Not that I would if I could. I mean, you say you're not a tax investigator, that you're some sort of professor, but you could be a policeman, for all I know."

"Do I look like a policeman?"

To my dismay, he took my question seriously and studied me from head to foot.

"Well, no," he said. "If you ask me, you rather resemble George Smiley. You know, from the John le Carré books. Not the Alec Guinness version, you understand, or Gary Oldman, but George Smiley as you might imagine he'd look if you didn't see him as Alec Guinness or Gary Oldman, if you follow my drift."

I thought the only thing I had in common with Smiley was that I sometimes appear invisible. People tend not to notice me, or if they do, they mark me down immediately as uninteresting and harmless, then pass me by without a second glance. When some people walk into a room, everyone turns to look at them; when others walk in, no-one bats an eyelid. That's me.

"I suppose you could be a spy," Gorman added. "Like Smiley was."

"Oh, for crying out loud, man," I said. "What would a spy be doing asking for the identity of someone who bought a second-hand book from you?"

"I could think of any number of reasons." He paused. "Why do you want to know?"

Here it was at last, the question I had prepared for but still dreaded. I told him about finding the envelope of money in the book. To my surprise, he took my explanation at face value.

"Well, I must say, sir, that's very honest of you," he said. "Very honest, indeed. And honesty's a quality I appreciate. There's not many as, coming across a twenty pound note, like, wouldn't simply put it in their pocket and spend it down the pub. But you want to return it to its rightful owner."

"Yes," I said, with a sigh. "Indeed I do."

"Commendable. Highly commendable."

"Can you help me?"

"I'm afraid not," Gorman said. "At least, not as much as you'd like me to."

"How, then?"

"I have a list of books bought and sold."

"And what will that tell me?"

He put his finger to his nose. "We'll have to see, won't we?"

And his chair legs scraped against the floorboards as he moved to stand up.

It seemed to take an eternity, but Gorman disappeared into a backroom and reappeared carrying the sort of large hardbound ledger one might expect to encounter in a Dickens novel. He set it down on the counter before him.

Smiling to reveal stained and crooked teeth, he tapped the tome. "If it's to be found, it will be found in here," he said gnomically and started turning the pages, stopping occasionally to mutter to himself, moving back and forth through the ledger, running his index finger down a page, then pausing and turning back to the beginning to inspect some sort of list of contents. I didn't know what system he used to organize his sales and purchases ledger, but it seemed to take him a long time to emit that little "Ah-ha" of success which indicated to me that he had found what he—and I—was looking for.

"What is it?" I asked, leaning forward, finding it impossible to rein in my enthusiasm. "Have you found it?"

He looked up at me. "Now hold your horses a moment," he said. "I think I have. Yes. Like I said right from the start, you're lucky it's Browning. We don't get many of his books in, so this must be the one." He consulted the list with his index finger again, muttering all the while. "Yes," he said, looking up at me. "That's the one. Well, that *is* a surprise."

"What is?"

"The date. That batch only came in a month ago, and there was me thinking Browning had been on the shelf for years." He made that strange dying coffee machine sound again, which I placed halfway between a chuckle and sniffle. Perhaps one should call it "snuckling" or "chiffling?" "Poor old Browning. Left on the shelf. Get it?"

"A month isn't very long. Do you remember who brought it in?"

"Can't say as I do. I told you not to get your hopes up."

"What *do* you remember, then?"

He snuckled again. "You might well end up spending that twenty quid in the pub tonight, after all," he said. "All I can tell you is that your Browning came in on the 28th of September, along with seven other books. Eight in all."

A month was certainly not long. "Do you remember anything at all about the person who sold them to you?" I asked.

"Afraid not. I've got a terrible memory for faces. Besides," he went on, "have you considered that whoever brought the books in to sell might not have been the original owner? Second-hand books go through a lot of hands sometimes. Might be third hand, or fourth hand."

I *had* thought of that and countered it with my own observations and theory. I had examined the book closely and saw no signs of other price markings other than the original Waterstones sticker. Usually a second-hand book dealer will pencil a price on the flyleaf, and pencil marks always leave some traces. But there was nothing. And judging by the book's condition, I had concluded that it hadn't been read, and that it was more than likely Miss Scott had not seen the inscription, as the pages had been somehow stuck together. Gorman had obviously missed it, too. His penciled price appeared on the page *after* the flyleaf.

The only stumbling block to my theory was that Miss Scott must have either been given the book by hand or received it through the post. In either case, the odds were that she knew who had given it to her. Perhaps, if she saw by the postmark that it was from Barnes, she had dropped it straight into the box of items to be taken and sold, wanting nothing to do with him. It was a theory. "Do you have any other useful information?" I asked.

"Depends what you think is useful. The price I paid, which I am not willing to divulge to you, no matter who you might be. And the titles of the accompanying volumes in the batch."

I brightened a little at that. "Accompanying volumes?"

"Yes. Like I said, it came in a box with seven other titles."

"Would you tell me what they are? These titles."

Gorman chewed his lower lip. "I don't see why not," he said finally. "After all, you are a customer. There might be something you're interested in. You might actually buy one or two of them."

I took his hint. "Naturally," I said. "Goes without saying."

He nodded, satisfied, then started to reel off a list of titles, Penguin, Virago or Oxford World's Classics, for the most part, which I jotted down in my notebook. As he said, there was nothing remarkable about any of them—Jane Austen, Emily Brontë, Elizabeth Jane Howard, Elizabeth Taylor, a selection of Rilke's poetry, a biography of Mary Shelley—but I was already thinking that if the books were still in the shop, then one of them might reveal a bit more information about the seller. A slip of paper with an address, used as a bookmark, for example. Wishful thinking, I know, but one can always hope.

"Might I have a look around your shop for them?" I asked.

"Be my guest," said Gorman. "But just so you're not wasting your time, I'll tell you now that *Wuthering Heights* and *Pride and Prejudice* have already been sold. I told you I couldn't keep Victorian fiction on the shelves. And before you get all pedantic with me, yes I know Jane Austen wasn't a Victorian, strictly speaking." I crossed the two novels off my list, which left me five more to find, then I headed into the maze of interconnected rooms along the corridor and got to work.

Though I am used to not being noticed, it did occur to me that a man of my age and appearance, especially in the old mac I was wearing against the chilly rain, might be regarded as somewhat suspicious if seen hanging around a public—which is to say private—school, even a minor one like the Linford School. I determined, therefore, to make my entrance speedy and decisive by driving straight up to the front door and getting out of the car with a confidence and determination that announced I was here for a reasonable and legitimate purpose, and there was no need to call the police.

I had struck it lucky in Gorman's shop on the fourth book, the biography of Mary Shelley. There was no name and address, but there was, on the title page, a stamp bearing the name of the school and its address, a small village just over the Humber Bridge, on the flatlands of northern Lincolnshire. I had been right, I thought, in assuming Miss Scott to be a teacher, and the Linford School was no doubt where she taught. Along with the

Mary Shelley biography, I also bought both Elizabeth Taylor's *In a Summer Season* and Elizabeth Jane Howard's *Falling*—all at what I thought to be a fairly exorbitant price, I must say— just to make Gorman happy, and set off.

The school building, Linford Hall, was Elizabethan or Jacobean in origin, in the "prodigy house" style, a redbrick mansion with a busy roofline, mullioned windows and extensive grounds. Rather than benefitting from the landscaping genius of an Inigo Jones, these grounds had been given over to playing fields and running tracks, deserted on the day of my visit. If Linford Hall didn't quite match the palatial grandeur of Longleat or Temple Newsham, it was still impressive enough to the unsuspecting visitor.

The solid oak door stood atop a flight of stone stairs under an arched brick porch. I hadn't seen anyone about as I drove up the gravel drive, and there was a distinct hush about the place. The staff car park to the right of the main building was almost full, however, so I assumed that classes must be in progress. That was all right with me. I was willing to wait. I carried the Shelley biography, which at the right moment I would say had fallen accidentally into my hands, and as I was passing... I was hoping that one of the teachers would be willing and able to tell me to whom the book had belonged so that I could return it. If necessary, I would bring up the name of Miss Scott somehow. I planned to begin by asking for general information about the school and its teachers.

Once inside the cavernous reception hall, I noticed the odd pair or group of girls moving quietly about the place, carrying books. Footsteps and voices echoed in the grand space. The ceiling was ornate, decorated with Renaissance-style angels radiating outwards from a glittering chandelier, and the wainscoted walls were dotted with large portraits of old families, and perhaps even past headmasters.

"Can I help you, sir?"

I must have looked lost, though I was more struck by wonder at the grandeur of the school, because a young woman had approached me. Her tone was helpful and friendly, rather than accusatory. My harmless appearance was working in my favor. "I wonder if I might have a word with your headmaster?" I said.

She smiled. "I'm afraid *Miss* Morwyn is busy at the moment. We've had a bit of a flu epidemic here, and several of the regular teachers are off sick. I'm sure Ms. Langham, her deputy, will be able to help you out. What is it you're inquiring about?"

"Nothing specific," I said. "I'm just looking for some information and background."

"Very well. If you'll just wait here a moment."

And she clip-clopped off down the broad passage lined with administrative offices. In moments she was back to tell me that Ms. Langham would see me now, though she could spare only fifteen minutes as she had a class to teach at eleven o'clock. I said that would be fine and followed the young woman down the corridor. After a brief knock, she ushered me into a nondescript office, furnished with the usual practicalities of teaching, which these days, of course, included a computer as well as the requisite filing cabinets and bookcases. The room was tidy enough, and it looked out on the playing fields at the back of the school.

Ms. Langham stood up to greet me. She was about my height, which isn't very tall, and slim, with auburn hair loosely tied at the back of her neck, where it fanned out over her shoulders. Her oval face was lightly freckled and her eyes a watchful and intelligent pale blue. A touch of lipstick would have done wonders for her rather thin lips. Her clothes were as conservative as one would expect in such a place as Linford— not tweedy, but a dark skirt over a high-necked blouse. I would have guessed her age to be mid-forties, at the most. She was no conventional beauty, but I have to confess that I found her immediately attractive. She smiled, sat down again and bade me sit opposite her. "Well, Mr....?"

"Aitcheson," I told her. "Donald Aitcheson."

"Well, Mr. Aitcheson, what can we do for you today?"

She sounded more like the girl behind the counter at Starbucks than a teacher. I felt like asking for a double espresso and a blueberry muffin, but instead I said, "I was wondering if you might be able to tell me a little about the school, its history, reputation, staff, standards, courses of study and so on."

"Of course." She paused. "This is quite unusual, however. We don't generally have people calling at the school for a chat about our standards and reputation. But seeing as you're here... Do you mind my asking why you wish to know?"

"I'm looking for a suitable institution to send my son, and I was wondering if Linford might fit the bill."

She stared at me, looking puzzled, for a moment before answering. "Well, Mr. Aitcheson," she said finally, "much as I hate to disappoint you, I'm afraid Linford definitely won't fit the bill. Not in the least."

"Why not?"

She tilted her head and narrowed her eyes. "I would have thought you might have done at least the modicum of research before you came all the way out here, I must say. We're easily Googled."

"I don't understand."

"Linford Hall is a *girls'* boarding school, Mr. Aitcheson. We don't have any boys here."

Then who the hell is Barnes? I almost said out loud. My mind was already spinning in search of alternative explanations. Perhaps we were in a D.H. Lawrence scenario. Barnes as Mellors, the gamekeeper, or something like that. It was a possibility. Surely they must have a few men about the place, if only on a daily basis, to help with the heavy lifting and so forth. Not to mention maintaining the extensive grounds. But would a "Mellors" character be likely to know about Browning and send a teacher a book with the inscription that so intrigued me? I doubted it. I tried not to let my disappointment show.

"Naturally, we employ several men in various capacities," Ms. Langham went on, as if reading my thoughts, "but we most definitely do *not* accept male pupils."

"I see," I said. "Of course not. My mistake."

She smiled, but it wasn't in her eyes. "So sorry to disappoint. Now, if—"

"I can't imagine why my friend never mentioned this," I said, rallying.

"Friend?"

"The friend who told me about this place. I must have got it mixed up with somewhere else." I smiled.

"You have no daughters, then, I assume?"

"None." I didn't have any sons, either, but I wasn't going to tell Ms. Langham that.

"Then I'm afraid I can't help you."

"I also have a book I'd like to return to you, a biography of Mary Shelley, with your school stamp. As I happened to passing this way, I just thought I'd drop in and… well…"

Ms. Langham continued to stare suspiciously at me. I much preferred not being noticed.

I took a deep breath. "She mentioned a Miss Scott, my friend did. When she asked me to return the misplaced library book. Apparently it belonged to a Miss Scott."

Ms. Langham frowned. "Miss Scott?"

"Yes. I think Scott was the name."

"I'm afraid Miss Scott is no longer with us," she said through tightening lips. "Look, what's your game? What's this all about? Why are you really here? Are you a reporter? Is that it? A private detective? One of the parents? We've dealt with the problem."

"Ms. Langham! I don't see why you should leap to such conclusions merely because I asked about Miss Scott. Why assume I'm a reporter? Did she leave under a cloud or something? Was there a scandal?"

"All I can tell you is that Miss Scott is no longer employed at this establishment. And now, if you'll—"

"Where is she?"

"I really have no idea, and even if I did I wouldn't tell you. Now I think it's time you left before I call the police. As you can imagine, we have to take special care to keep an eye open for any suspicious looking males hanging around the premises."

At that, I jumped out of my chair and held out my hand, palm towards her. "There's no need for that. I was just... I mean, I was simply..." I put my hand to my forehead and groaned. "Would you at least tell me *when* she left?"

Her hand hovered over the telephone. "I don't see as it's any of your business, but she left our employ shortly after the beginning of term. Late September. About a month ago. Caused us more than a little trouble finding a replacement at such short notice, if truth be told."

"Was it a sudden departure?"

She touched the handset and lifted it slightly from its rest. "Mr. Aitcheson, you really must leave now."

"All right," I said, sitting down again and opening my briefcase. "All right. Please don't do anything rash. I'm not a reporter or a detective. Just give me one minute, and I'll show you why I'm here, if you're interested. One minute. Please."

I could see her thinking it over. Finally, her curiosity got the better of her. She let the phone drop back in its cradle. "Very well," she said, in the stern tone of a deputy headmistress. "Please illuminate me."

I decided on the spur of the moment to leave Mary Shelley out of it and put my cards on the table. I showed her the edition of Browning with the inscription. She read it, turned a little pale, I thought, then handed the book back to me and said. "There's a decent pub in the village. The George and Dragon. Meet me there at half past twelve." Then she walked over and opened the door. "Now I really must go."

"What did you say your occupation was, Mr. Aitcheson?" Ms. Langham asked as she sat opposite me in the George and Dragon, a rambling old country pub with a whitewashed facade, window boxes full of geraniums and a well-appointed dining room, with white tablecloths and solid, comfortable chairs.

"I didn't," I answered her, "but I'm retired."

"From what?"

"I was Professor of Classics. At Cambridge."

She nodded as if I had answered a question correctly. "Indeed you were."

"You've decided to trust me? You believe I'm not a reporter or a private eye?"

Ms. Langham nodded and smiled. "After class, I Googled you. Quite an impressive career."

"Oh, I wouldn't say that."

"No need for false modesty, Professor Aitcheson. Catullus and Ovid, no less. Two of my favorites. I checked the school library, and we have your translations on our shelves. One of them even has a small author's photograph on the back, which matches your photo on Wikipedia. And you in person, of course, though perhaps it was taken a few years ago?"

"Ah, the computer age," I said. "Yes, it was a few years ago, alas, and I had far more hair and a few less pounds then."

She laughed. "Look, if we're going to talk about this business, we might as well be on a first name basis. I already know your name is Donald. I'm Alice."

"Pleased to meet you, Alice. So there is something to talk about, then?"

Alice frowned. "I'm not sure yet, but I think there might be." She tapped the book I had put on the table between us. "This is quite extraordinary," she said, picking it up and rereading the inscription. "And another book in the same lot led you here?"

"Yes. A biography of Mary Shelley. With the Linford School stamp. I didn't want to mention it at first because... you know..."

"You thought it might get this Miss Scott into trouble?"

"Possibly."

"Very gentlemanly of you to lie to me about it, then. Though as we don't know exactly *who* sold it to the second-hand bookshop, we shouldn't be too fast to point the finger of blame. Perhaps someone stole it from her?"

At this point, a young waitress, barely out her teens, came to take our orders. When I suggested we share a bottle of Chablis, Ms. Langham looked at me apologetically and said, "If I had an alcoholic drink at lunchtime, my pupils would surely smell it on my breath, and my life wouldn't be worth living." She glanced at the waitress and said, "Isn't that right, Andrea?"

The waitress blushed and nodded. "Yes, ma'am."

"I'll have a diet tonic water, please."

I ordered a pint of bitter. "Ex pupil?" I asked, when Andrea had gone.

Ms. Langham nodded. "Not one of our greatest successes, but I'm a firm believer in letting people find their own niche in life. Andrea wants to be an actress, so this is just a temporary stopgap for her. At least she hopes so. I must say, she made a passable Duchess of Malfi in the school production last year."

"I never imagined *The Duchess of Malfi* as the sort of play one performs in a girls' boarding school. Or any school for that matter. A bit too bloodthirsty, surely?"

Ms. Langham smiled. "Times have changed."

"So it would seem. I'm beginning to wonder exactly what sort of school Linford Hal is. *The Duchess of Malfi*? Translations of Catullus and Ovid in the library? 'Porphyria's Lover?'"

She laughed. "You can't blame us for that last one. Besides, we like to think of ourselves as progressive. Though we don't have Ovid's erotic poems, you understand. Just the *Metamorphoses*."

"Even so. I translated both volumes."

"I know."

Our drinks arrived and we gave our food orders to Andrea. I sipped my beer and watched Alice Langham as she read the inscription again. "This is what brought you here?" she asked. "Truly?"

"Yes. I'm curious. Well, probably a bit more than that. You said yourself that you find it extraordinary. There's something distinctly chilling about it, don't you find? The tone of the inscription. The reference to enjoying poems about murder and so on. The 'bargain' and the reference to time approaching.

It could be a taunt, or even a thinly veiled threat, something intended to frighten her."

Alice Langham closed the book and slid it back over the white cloth. "Yes, I agree," she said, giving a little shudder. "It's really quite nasty. That's why it interests me, too."

"Did you know Miss Scott?"

"Oh, yes. I knew Marguerite Scott. Not well, but I knew her."

"And was she the kind to run off with school property?"

"Not as far as I know. I'm sure the book was her own. She simply stamped it as an identifying mark." Alice shrugged. "Even if it did belong to the school library, we'd hardly be bothered enough to hunt her down, or it."

"And the Browning?"

"A gift, it seems."

"Do you know anyone called Barnes?"

She shook her head. "No. That's the puzzling thing. It doesn't ring any bells at all. I mean, it's not an uncommon name. I've racked my brains since we first talked. I'm certain we have had pupils called Barnes in the past, but we don't have any at the moment. Of course, it needn't be anyone connected with the school, though I will admit it sounds rather that way. Do you think Miss Scott is in danger? That reference to the time being near?"

I nodded. "It's possible. The book was sold to Gorman only a month ago, around the time you told me Miss Scott left Linford School, though there's no telling how long she'd had it on her shelves before then, I suppose."

"But the danger could still be imminent, couldn't it, if she sold the Browning as soon as she received it?"

I nodded. "Something may have already happened to her. That's one of the things I want to find out. Where she is. Whether this Barnes fellow has done her any harm. You wouldn't tell me where Miss Scott lives before. Will you tell me now?"

She gave me an address in a village a few miles from Beverley. "Is she still there?" I asked.

"I assume so. Though she wouldn't need to inform the school

of a change of address." She paused. "I remember seeing the place once. We were on our way to Beverley for a talk. Official teachers' professional development day. For some reason, I was giving her a lift, and we passed this… mansion. She said I might not believe it, but it was where she lived. It was quite impressive. As I remember, it's a rather palatial manor house in a desirable location. Her husband used to be something high up in finance. Born into money, too. Very well off, apparently. Anyway, it doesn't sound like the kind of place one gives up so easily."

"I suppose not. Nor does it sound as if the person who lives in such a place needs to cart a box of old books to sell in Beverley. What happened to this husband?"

"He died. Drowned, I believe. A swimming accident. I'm afraid I don't know all the details. She never said any more than that and, well, it wasn't something one pried into, disturbing old feelings and all, probing old wounds."

"Drowning, you say? An accident?"

"That's what she said."

"Hmm. How long ago did it happen?"

"I'm not sure. Seven or eight years, or thereabouts. Before she came to Linford Hall, at any rate."

"Did Miss Scott come from around here?"

"As far as I know, they'd always lived in the same house she's in now, at least since they were married. I don't know where Miss Scott lived before then. I think she taught in Hull for a while before she came here, though."

"I assume she didn't need to work."

"I suppose not. But one thing I will say about Marguerite is that she's an excellent teacher. She loved her job. She wasn't the type to hang about the house all day and… well, do whatever people do when they hang around the house all day."

"I read quite a bit, watch old films, do a little gardening, go for—"

Alice laughed. "I don't mean you. You're retired, and even though you're entitled to be as lazy as you want, I'm sure you use your time most productively. Marguerite was a hard

worker. I think she needed her job. Maybe not for the money,
but because it meant something to her."

"Yet the school let her go. She never remarried?"

"Not that I know of. And I think I would have known. After
all, she was with us for four years. A wedding would have been
hard to overlook."

"And the story behind her abrupt departure from Linford?"

"Aha," said Alice. Thereby hangs a tale. And she put her
finger to her lips as Andrea delivered their meals.

I have to confess that I had been expecting some titillating
story of lesbianism in a girls' boarding school, or perhaps a
confirmation of my *Lady Chatterley's Lover* theory, a sexual
liaison between posh Miss Scott and the school groundskeeper
or gardener. After all, what else could a teacher do that was
terrible enough to lose him or her the job? It turned out that
Linford School was a law unto itself in that respect.

Crushes happened often enough, Alice told me, and in most
cases they could nipped in the bud before they progressed
to a serious level. Students had even had crushes on her, she
admitted. Sexual assault, unwanted fondling and the like were
much rarer, though a games mistress had been fired three years
ago for squeezing a student's breast.

"Did a troublesome student have a crush on Marguerite
Scott?" I asked.

Alice shook her head. "No. Nothing like that. Unless it was
an extremely well-kept secret."

"Which you think is unlikely?"

"Yes. I'm sorry. It would be difficult to keep that sort of
secret around Linford."

It turned out that Marguerite Scott's sins had been of a
very different order: persistent absenteeism and a fondness for
the bottle being the chief among them, which perhaps helped
explain Alice Langham's reluctance to sample a glass of Chablis
at lunchtime. The principal was a strict teetotaler, she told me,

which hadn't helped. Finally, Miss Scott had taken one day off too many and was discovered to be drunk in class after an extended lunch with an old friend. Had she played truant that time, rather than return to school in her inebriated state, her punishment might have been less severe. But not only had she returned to Linford Hall late that afternoon, she had driven her car there and parked it sloppily, scuffing the side of the biology teacher's Toyota as she did so. The students in the one class she attempted to teach that afternoon complained that she was repeating herself, giggling and bumping into her desk, and that her writing on the blackboard was an illegible scrawl. One of them said that when she stood up to leave, Miss Scott pushed her back into her chair roughly.

There was no breathalyzer except the principal herself, who deemed Marguerite Scott unfit to carry out her responsibilities, and as this wasn't her first warning, she was to leave immediately. According to Alice, nobody seemed to have bothered to ask Miss Scott why she had acted in such a manner calculated to result in her dismissal, and it remained a mystery to this day.

"How long had she been behaving that way: drinking, absenteeism?"

"Only since after we got back from the summer holidays. Previous terms she'd been perfectly well behaved, if a little aloof and cool in her manner."

"Not warm and fuzzy, then?"

"Not in the least."

"What happened next?"

"Nothing. That was it. She left without a fuss. In fact, I happened to be quite near Gwyneth's office at the time—that's our principal, Gwyneth Morwyn—and you wouldn't believe the language that came out of Marguerite Scott's mouth. Well, perhaps *you* would, having been at Cambridge and all, but it was quite shocking to me at the time, and I'm no prude. So whether she had any chance at all of keeping her job when she went in for her little chat with Gwyneth, she certainly had ruined any possibility of forgiveness when she emerged."

"And none of you kept in touch with her?"

"No. She wasn't... I mean, she didn't really mix with the rest of the teaching staff. She was polite enough, but like I said, she always remained rather aloof. She made no effort to fit in. She never talked to us about her life, never shared experiences, asked advice or anything."

"The other teachers disliked her?"

"I wouldn't say disliked. Not actively, at any rate. But she certainly wasn't *well* liked. She had no close friends at Linford. There was no strong connection, no sense of her belonging to the community. That time she pointed out her house, it was about all she said during the entire journey."

"And the drinking?"

"Fairly recent, too. Definitely after we returned from the summer holidays. I mean, she wouldn't have lasted as long as she did—which is about four years—if she'd been at the bottle the whole time. You can't hide a thing like that in a closed community like a girls' boarding school. It's hard to keep secrets. I'm not saying she might not have been a secret drinker, at home, though I doubt even that."

"She had other secrets?"

"Well, we all have secrets, Mr. Aitcheson."

"Donald, please."

"Donald, then. Perhaps she did, but they remain secrets. And I'm not only talking about shameful secrets and the like. She didn't even participate in the normal day to day conversations in the staff room. Whether one fancies a particular actor, or actress, what kind of books, films, and music one likes, what one thinks of Brexit or the latest terrorist incident. Marguerite never joined in any of those sorts of discussions, let alone complained about her life, or a love affair, or anything. We didn't even know if she had love affairs. She was a dark horse."

"And her behavior turned self-destructive only in the last few weeks of her tenure, as far as you know?"

"Yes. The drinking, being even more anti-social, taking days off whenever she felt like it and not even bothering to report in sick. Of course, we didn't know at the time, but it was probably because of hangovers." She shook her head slowly.

"What?"

"Sometimes I just think we could have been a bit more... proactive. Because of her attitude, nobody really demonstrated any concern for her, asked her if there was anything wrong, if we could help with her problems in any way." She bit her bottom lip. "Sometimes I feel a bit guilty."

I swirled my beer in the glass and drank some. "And as far as you know," I said, "you're absolutely sure there's nobody involved in this whole business called Barnes?"

"Nobody."

"What was her husband's name?

"George or Gary. Something like that. With a 'G' anyway."

"And her married name, or maiden name, wasn't Barnes?"

"No. According to the school records, her married name was Scott, and her maiden name was Fairbanks. She was always called *Miss* Scott here as a courtesy. No matter what their marital status, no teacher at Linford School is referred to as 'Mrs.'"

"But 'Ms.' is OK?"

She smiled. "It wasn't always."

I rubbed my chin, decided I needed a shave. "So Miss Scott remains a puzzle wrapped inside an enigma, then."

"I'm afraid so. What next?"

"I suppose I shall have to pay her a visit," I said, "assuming she did, as you suggested, keep on the house. I want to make sure she hasn't come to any harm. It sounds as if she was worried about something, perhaps even frightened. The sudden drinking and all. It could have been caused by anxiety, stress or fear. And I don't think she actually *read* the inscription in the Browning, though I'm convinced it was meant for her. There must have been other communications from this Barnes. Ones that did get through to her."

Alice Langham looked at her watch. "Heavens, I really must get back to school or I'll be sharing the same fate as Miss Scott, drink or no drink."

I stood up, shook her hand and thanked her for her time and help.

"Will you... I mean, will you let me know if you find anything out?" she asked me before she left, a slight blush on her cheeks. She wrote something on a beer mat and passed it to me. "Perhaps it would be better if you phoned me at home rather than at the school. I'm in most evenings."

"And if Mr. Langham answers?"

"There is no Mr. Langham. Not for some years."

I didn't enquire any further, partly because I didn't want to know what fate had befallen Mr. Langham. I had long thought my battered old heart damaged beyond repair, but I must confess that the offending organ gave an unexpected flutter when Alice Langham lowered her eyes and handed me the beer mat. While I would never have dared to admit it, hardly even to myself, the prospect of talking to, and even perhaps seeing, the charming Ms. Langham again was not without its appeal. "I most certainly will," I said. "As soon as I find anything out."

As I drove back over the Humber Bridge, I glanced east towards where the estuary widened. Far below me, the Humber pilot's boat guided a large cargo ship out to the North Sea. Once back on the Yorkshire side, I found a garage, filled up with petrol and asked directions to the address Alice Langham had given me.

I thought of Alice as I drove along the country lanes. It was a long time, more years than I cared to remember, since a woman, any woman, had had that sort of effect on me. I can't describe it easily in words, but meeting her, talking with her, had been so natural that I felt as if I had been doing it all my life. Or that I wanted to do it all my life. I told myself there's no fool like an old fool, remembered the days of depression and endless poetic outpourings after Charlotte had abandoned me for an engineering student all those years ago. Remembered how I had finally made the effort, pulled myself together and devoted myself to an academic career, subjugated my feelings and desires to the demands of dead languages and dead poets. Despite the connection I had felt with Alice, I knew I couldn't progress any further. Doing so would involve a move on my part so heavily laden with the risk of rejection that I knew I could never make it.

It was a beautiful, clear day in late October, and the landscape was so flat that I could see for miles around me. I saw what I thought to be Marguerite Scott's house long before I reached it, some distance down the road, standing very much alone in its several acres of grounds. When I got closer, I saw that the grounds were walled, and beyond the wall stood an area of woodland through which a drive wound its way to the front of the house. The house wasn't as large as it had been in my imagination, but it was certainly a substantial dwelling. Victorian, I guessed, with a certain Gothic touch in turrets, gargoyles and gables. It certainly didn't seem as if the place had ever been a farm; more likely it had once belonged to a member of the local gentry, and the family no doubt had to sell it after the war, when it became almost impossible for the old families to cling on to their estates without turning them into zoos or fairgrounds and opening them to the public. Though this place was grand enough, it wasn't quite in that league. Nevertheless, it made me wonder again why somebody who lived in such a mansion would need, or want, to sell books to a second-hand bookshop.

I pulled up outside the front door and rang the bell. After I had been standing there a few moments enjoying the birdsong and the gentle breeze soughing through the leaves, the door opened and a woman I took to be Miss Scott stood before me. She didn't match the version of my imagination in any way, save that her hair was blonde. It wasn't piled up like a Hitchcock ice queen's, however, but expensively layered. She was a slighter figure than I had imagined, too, wearing designer jeans, dangling earrings and black polo neck jumper. She was definitely attractive, but her face had a sort of pinched look about it.

Or perhaps she was simply looking guarded because a stranger stood at her door. Suspicion loomed in her light brown eyes.

"Miss Scott?" I ventured. "Miss Marguerite Scott?"

"Who's asking?"

"My name is Donald Aitcheson. You don't know me, of course, but I assure you that I come only out of friendship and concern." I was so glad to find her alive and well that I was quite forgetting how my arrival might have made her nervous or frightened. I wasn't sure how to put her at her ease.

She frowned. "You what?"

"Perhaps if you'd let me come in I could explain."

At that, she closed the door even more, as if to make a shield between us. "I think I'd rather you explained yourself first," she said. "A woman can't be too careful these days. You might look harmless enough, but…"

Her voice wasn't low and husky, but somewhat nasal, and the Yorkshire vowels were definitely present. I gave her my best smile. "I can assure you, I am exactly as harmless as I look."

"That remains to be seen. What do you want with me? Miss Scott is my school name. If you're selling something I—"

"I'm not a salesman," I said, reaching into my briefcase for the Browning, which I realized would probably be my passport into the house. I could tell that she recognized the book as soon as she saw the cover, but her expression gave no indication that she knew of the sinister and threatening inscription. She looked puzzled rather than apprehensive. I opened it to the flyleaf and held it up for her to see. She frowned as she read the words, put her hand to her mouth.

"Oh, my God," she said. "I never saw that. I…"

"But it was yours?"

"Yes. It was sent to me. Where did you get it? What are you doing here?"

I looked pleadingly at her. "I'll explain everything. May I?"

She stood aside. "Of course. I'm sorry. Please come in, Mr.…?"

"Aitcheson," I reminded her, following her through a

cavernous hall into a cozy and comfortable sitting-room, decorated in light pastels, with a large, empty fireplace on the far wall, in front of which lay a sheepskin rug.

"Please sit down," she said. "How did you find me?"

I sank into a deep armchair. "The school. Linford Hall. There was a book with the name stamped on it in the box you sold to Gorman, a biography of Mary Shelley, along with the Browning, of course, which I bought, also without seeing the inscription."

"Gorman?"

"Yes, the second-hand book dealer."

She looked completely blank, then recognition seemed to dawn. "A second-hand book dealer, you say? Well, well, the little devil."

"I don't understand."

"I distinctly told Martha, the woman who comes in once a week to clean for me, to drop the box off at the Oxfam shop in town. She must have decided she could make a few extra pounds by selling the lot to this Gorman."

"I see. Well, it couldn't have been much. I wouldn't be too hard on her."

"Oh, I have no intention of being hard on her. Good cleaning ladies are hard to find these days. I'll let it go by. And you? Are you the bookseller's assistant or something? Are you here to tell me there was a valuable first edition among my books?"

I laughed. "I'm afraid not. No, I was just intrigued by the inscription. Curiosity got the better of me. I wanted to know who you were, make sure you're all right, find out who Barnes is and what it all means. You must admit, the inscription is rather disturbing."

"It's the first time I've set eyes on it."

"The pages were stuck together," I said. "I missed it, myself, or I probably wouldn't have bought the book. But surely now that you have seen it, it means something to you? Barnes, for example?"

"Have you told anyone else about this?"

Caution impelled me to say no, just in case the thought of my spreading her business about scared her off and caused her to clam up. "They'd probably think I was crazy," I said.

"You say they gave you my address at the school?"

"Yes."

"They shouldn't have done that," she said, and stared at me for a while, as if she couldn't believe it. "There must be some rules about passing on personal information. Ethics or whatever. Did they tell you all about me as well?"

"No," I lied. "Why should they? What is there to tell?"

"I still don't understand why you should be interested in all this. It's nothing but a silly joke."

"Is it? I suppose I've got too much time on my hands, now I'm retired. I was worried about you. And I like puzzles. Are you sure everything's all right, Miss Scott? If I received something like this, I would be more than a little annoyed, if not downright nervous or angry. Why assume that you will like to read about murder? What is it nearly time for?"

"Lots of people are fans of murder mysteries."

"But Browning's poems are a little more disturbing than a murder mystery. And I don't think whoever wrote this—Barnes, I suppose—meant to refer to your taste in fiction. He quotes from 'Porphyria's Lover,' for example, a very creepy soliloquy written from the murderer's point of view."

"Are you trying to tell me you think I'm in some sort of danger, Mr. Aitcheson, that someone is fantasizing about murdering me?"

"I don't mean to scare you unduly, but I do think it's a distinct possibility that whoever wrote this is unbalanced, yes. Have you had any more communications from this Barnes person?"

"This is absurd. I mean it's very sweet of you to be concerned, but really…"

"Tell me about Barnes."

"It's just someone I knew a long time ago."

"The book is quite new, and it was only sold to Gorman a month ago. How did you come to get hold of it?"

"Are you grilling me, Mr. Aitcheson?"

I took a deep breath. "Perhaps I am letting my curiosity get ahead of me. But you have to admit the whole thing is very peculiar. The tone of the inscription piqued my curiosity. Was this Barnes a friend of yours?"

"An old lover, actually," said Miss Scott. She seemed to be more relaxed now, and she leaned back in her armchair and crossed her legs, a slightly mischievous smile playing on her lips and yes, I couldn't have sworn to it, but I thought she was starting to enjoy herself.

"Ah... I... er... I see. Then why... I mean, it's rather an odd thing for an old lover to write, isn't it, and to quote Browning like that?"

She smiled. "What can I say? He's an odd person."

"Does it have anything to do with your husband's death?"

"My husband's death? Who told you about that? What do you know about that?"

"The secretary at Linford School might have mentioned you were a widow," I lied. "He drowned, didn't he? Your husband."

"You know a lot. That was a long time ago."

"And how long ago was Barnes?"

"That's an impertinent question, Mr. Aitcheson. I must say, you're being very perverse about this matter, not to mention persistent. I told you, it's nothing. And even if it were, it would be none of your business."

"Are you sure you're not in any danger, Miss Scott, that you haven't been threatened in any way? Perhaps I can help you?"

"Of course not. And I don't need your help. I told you, it's just a silly joke, that's all. It came through the post about a month ago. I have no idea who sent it. I didn't even see the bloody inscription, and I can't stand Browning. I vaguely remember a few of his poems from university, but that's all. Nor do I read detective novels. I dumped it in the box and asked Martha to take it to the Oxfam shop. Somehow it ended up in the hands of your Mr. Gorman. End of story."

"But you do know someone called Barnes, don't you? You

indicated that it was someone you knew a long time ago. Someone a bit odd. Why has he reappeared in your life now? Was he something to do with your husband's death?"

Miss Scott contemplated me for a moment in some confusion, then she seemed to come to some sort of a decision. She relaxed even more, and her tone softened. "I can see you're not going to give up easily," she said. "Would you like some tea? Or something stronger? Then maybe I'll tell you all about it."

"Tea will be fine," I said.

"Excuse me for a moment, then," she said, and disappeared into the kitchen. I could hear the heavy ticking of the clock on the mantelpiece as I glanced around at the paintings on the walls. I must say I am not a great fan of modern art. I prefer a painting to look like something I can at least recognize. I don't expect my art to be a photographic representation of the world—impressions are all right with me, Monet, Cezanne and the like, even Van Gogh—but these swirls and blobs and lines of color just seemed ugly and pointless. They were no doubt originals, and perhaps even worth a small fortune, but they did nothing for me except perhaps make me feel slightly uncomfortable and dizzy. I kept thinking I could see the walls moving out of the corner of my eye.

Miss Scott returned with the tea, and I realized as she poured that now I had found her I wasn't sure what it was that I really wanted to know. She was right in that I seemed to have a bee in my bonnet about the inscription, even now that I had met her and I knew that she was unharmed. Maybe I had been making a mountain out of a molehill all along? I was beginning to feel rather silly about the whole business.

"I realize it's probably nothing to do with me," I said, after a sip of strong sweet tea, "and I'm sorry for barging in on you like this. But as I said, I've always been interested in puzzles, in solving them, I mean, and for some reason this one just grasped my interest."

"Barnes was a fairly despicable character," she said. "I suppose you were right to some extent to be worried about me. Thank you for that. But I don't think he's a danger to me anymore."

"How did you know him? I know you said he was a…"

"A lover, yes. For a short while."

I sipped more tea. "How long ago?"

"I suppose we met about six or seven months before my husband's death."

I almost choked on my tea. "You're telling me you were having an affair with this Barnes while you were still married?"

She smiled. "One is usually married if one has an affair, Mr. Aitcheson."

"And since?"

"Affairs?"

"Barnes."

She shook her head. "No, we parted company shortly after my husband's death. His usefulness was over, and we seemed to do nothing but argue. I suppose you could say Barnes was my bad boy, and bad boys have their uses, but they don't usually last very long."

"Did you see Barnes again?"

"Not until recently. He came back into my life about six weeks ago. I realize I had told him, seven years before, that I knew he would, but it was still a shock I wasn't quite prepared for."

"What did he want?"

"His share, of course."

I drained my tea cup and put the saucer down on the tray. "His share?"

"Yes. Of the loot. My husband's fortune. I didn't begrudge him it, of course, he'd certainly earned it, but that doesn't mean I was willing to give him it. Not after so long. And he's been quite beastly towards me. I mean, you saw that inscription, and it bothered even you, a stranger."

"But you didn't see it."

"No. But I'm not saying I haven't heard from him. That he hasn't threatened me. That he wasn't blackmailing me."

"What about the names? Miss Scott and Barnes. Isn't that rather an odd form of address?"

"He always called me Miss Scott. I was a school teacher. It was his idea of a joke. He was mocking me. And Barnes happened to be his first name, by the way. Barnes Corrigan."

"And the Browning?"

"Well, Browning *did* write about murder a fair bit, didn't he? Though I never read the book and have only vague memories from university. I suppose Barnes thought it was fitting to remind me of what..."

I was beginning to feel way out of my depth. I must have looked it, too, for Miss Scott leaned forward, patted my hand and said, "Poor Mr. Aitcheson."

"Please explain," I said. My tongue felt thick and furry in my mouth.

"I was going to say that he must have sent the book to remind me of what we'd done together," Miss Scott went on. "Not literally, you understand. Nobody strangled anyone with their own hair, if I remember my 'Porphyria' correctly. But you get the idea. I owed him, and he was reminding me of it. We'd made a bargain, and the time was close for payback. Pity I never saw the bloody inscription."

"What had you done together? You owed him? Payback? For what? Why?"

"Barnes helped me murder my husband. Well, not with the actual murder, I don't think he had the guts for that, so I did it myself, but with the cover up afterwards."

"Why are you telling—"

"Shh. You wanted to hear the story. My husband didn't drown, Mr. Aitcheson. He was already dead. That was Barnes. Well, Barnes didn't really drown, either, but he faked the drowning, and as far as everyone was concerned, he was my husband, and he went for his swim every morning, regular as clockwork. One morning he simply didn't come back. The currents were strong, the sea unpredictable. I was in a small cafe in the village at the time. The perfect alibi. You see, Barnes resembled George to a certain extent, and we were in Cornwall, among strangers, a long way from home, in a rented cottage rather remote from the nearest village. Nobody knew George there, and Barnes made sure he never got especially close to any of the locals. We were very anti-social. We might have gone abroad, but I'm sure they would have asked more questions over there. It was relatively easy in Cornwall. A pile of clothes on the beach. My real husband's, by the way, in case they tested for DNA, which they didn't. Body washed out to sea. Barnes swam to a cave, actually, and made his escape in a small boat he'd previously moored there in a cave for that very purpose."

By this point I was having serious difficulty speaking. Not only that, but my head was throbbing, I felt sick and dizzy and my knees were trembling. I was also starting to have trouble breathing. It was getting difficult to cling on to what little consciousness I had left.

"It won't be long now," Miss Scott said. "This benzodiazepine is fairly quick acting. Then I'll figure out what to do with you."

I could only gape, my mouth wide open.

"It worked a treat," she said. "The only problem is that if you don't want to create a stir and have too many questions asked, then you have to wait seven years before the legal declaration of death. Before you can inherit and cash in the insurance policy. If I'd made too much of a fuss too soon, they might have thought I had done it for the money. Which I had, of course."

"But why?" I gasped. "You were rich already."

"My *husband* was rich, Mr. Aitcheson. That's a different thing. George was a workaholic, and luckily the object of his addiction was making money. Unfortunately for me, though, he liked to hang on to it. He was tight as a... well, you can fill in the blank yourself. I had to negotiate for every bloody penny I got. That's why I had to keep on working. Lucky for me I liked my job. After... when it was over down in Cornwall... all I had to do was keep my cool, and I could do that. All in all, it was rather a lot of money, and well worth waiting for. I didn't mind teaching for seven more years when I knew what was coming to me after that. I was only twenty-six at the time, which means I'm only thirty-three now. Plenty of time ahead of me for fun. And as I had a job and a steady income, it would have looked bad if I'd gone for the money sooner. It wasn't as if I *needed* it. But Barnes and I never got along well after... well, after the deed. Guilt, perhaps. Thieves falling out. The need for secrecy. Whatever the reasons, we agreed to go our separate ways. I told him to come back for his share in seven years, but little did he realize that I had no intention of giving him anything. Anyway, when the seven years were almost up, just before the start of term, he began hounding me for his share. I'd heard from him occasionally over the years. A cryptic postcard here, a hang-up phone call there. I imagine that book was one of his many salvos to keep me on edge. I thank you for bringing it to my intention. Not that it matters any more. I was a little shaken by his other messages and threats of exposure, however. I suppose I acted erratically under the pressure. Drank too much and so on. Naturally, they noticed at school and gave me the sack. But it didn't matter, did it? I had a fortune to inherit." She leaned towards me, resembling nothing more than a pale blob through a fisheye lens. "How are you feeling, Mr. Aitcheson?"

And that was the point at which I wasn't feeling anything anymore. It was as if someone suddenly turned off a switch in my brain.

When I regained consciousness it took me a while to get oriented and work out where I was, where I'd been, and why, but it all came back eventually, bit by bit. I was in a cellar, I realized first of all, lying on the hard concrete floor trussed up like a turkey ready for the oven. And I was here because Miss Scott had drugged my tea. She had done that because I was asking too many questions about a disturbing inscription in the flyleaf of a book, and she was afraid that if she let me go I would press the matter to a point where it would cause serious problems for her. Perhaps I would talk to the police, for example, or the people at Linford School. In other words, she needed to get me out of the picture, remove me from the scene, probably by murder, as it appeared she had done that before, though I was still vague about the details.

I tried to move, but I was well and truly tied up. Various bones and muscles ached as well as my head, and I realized that she had probably dragged rather than carried me down the wooden cellar steps. I was definitely too old for this sort of thing; whether I had ever been young enough was a moot point, but I was certainly too old now. I tried to move again and stiffened with pain. I thought my left ankle might be broken.

I also realized that I was in a house surrounded by woods and a high wall, miles from the nearest village, and I couldn't expect any help to come my way. That was one of my most depressing thoughts as I heard Miss Scott moving about upstairs, no doubt preparing whatever it was she needed to bring about my demise. A bath full of acid, perhaps? Or a wood-chopping machine in the garden? I could try telling her I would let the matter drop, that I didn't really find the Browning quotes and the tone of the inscription frightening or interesting, but I doubted that she would believe me. It was too late for that now. I only had my profession to blame for my ultra-sensitivity to the use of language. Most people would probably have shrugged it off as a bit of a laugh and let it go by.

I thought of Alice Langham and my vain hopes that we would somehow become friends, perhaps even more. I had led a lonely existence for some years, and it now looked very much as if I was going to die a lonely death, too. I had lied to Miss Scott about nobody else knowing what I was up to. Alice knew where I was going, and she thought the inscription as disturbing as I did, so perhaps when she didn't hear from me in a few days, she would call the police. Even if they came here, it would no doubt be too late by then. I hoped she didn't decide to come here by herself. I couldn't bear the thought of her getting killed, too, just because of my stupid curiosity. Not that I would be around to feel sad or guilty.

Perhaps, if I got the chance, I could let Miss Scott know that I wasn't the only one interested in her. In which case she would probably kill me quickly, withdraw all her money from the bank and take the next flight to some tax-free island paradise with no extradition treaty, if such a place existed. Otherwise, she could probably just lie her way out of it all. After all, she had succeeded in murder before.

Whichever way I looked at things, there didn't seem much hope for me.

Then I heard the doorbell ring upstairs.

All I could hear was a distant rumble of voices. I couldn't distinguish a word that was being said, nor who was saying it. Footsteps passed overhead and disappeared into one of the rooms above me. I could still hear the voices, but less distinctly now. I assumed that Miss Scott was one of them, and I had a terrible feeling that Barnes was the other. She must have phoned him while I was out cold and asked him to come and help her get rid of me. I knew they had an unusual relationship from what she had told me before I passed out, but I also got the impression that despite Barnes's taunts and threats, she could manipulate him. And even if it cost her a fraction of her fortune, getting me properly disposed of was probably worth it.

Don't let me give you the impression that these thoughts passing through my foggy brain left me feeling calm and un-ruffled. They didn't. I was terrified, and I never stopped struggling against my bonds, only succeeding in drawing them tight-er around my wrists and ankles. Just in case the visitor *wasn't* Barnes, I even tried to yell out, but nothing got through the gag stuffed in my mouth and held there with my own tie. I tried banging my feet against the floor, but it made no noise and only hurt my damaged ankle. I could find no other way to attract attention, so in the end I simply lay there limp and defeated. There was nothing to do but await my inevitable fate.

*

After a while, things went quiet and I couldn't really tell whether the visitor had left. I was drifting in and out of consciousness. Then I heard another noise from upstairs. This time it sounded like a table or a lamp being knocked over. There was a rumbling sound, then the noise of glass or pottery breaking, someone jumping up and down on the floor above. Then I thought I heard a scream. Were Barnes and Miss Scott fighting?

Whatever was happening, it seemed to go on for a long time, then there was silence again. I heard footsteps above me, almost certainly just one pair, and I couldn't tell whether it was Miss Scott or Barnes who had survived the fight. I wasn't even sure which of them I *hoped* had won. I didn't think it mattered. Either or both would probably want to kill me.

The footsteps receded—upstairs, I thought—and then everything went silent again. Was nobody coming for me? Was I just going to be abandoned to die here of starvation? Left to rot? What if he'd killed her and was just going to leave? Would her weekly cleaning lady find me before I expired? I had no idea.

More footsteps, back on the main floor again. I tried to shout again, but I don't think I produced much noise. All I knew was that I would rather Barnes or Miss Scott kill me here and now than starve to death.

Then the cellar door opened and someone turned on the light.

My breath caught in my throat as I turned slowly and painfully to get a view of who was coming down the stairs. Whether it was Miss Scott or Barnes, I knew I was doomed either way.

But it wasn't either of them; it was Alice Langham stumbling down towards me, holding on to the railing to stop herself from falling. Her blouse and jacket were torn, her hair disheveled, and there was blood smeared on her face and all down her front. Her tights were ripped, too, and she had scratches, cuts and blood on her legs. One shoe was missing.

When she reached the ground, Alice staggered towards me. I couldn't read the expression on her face because of all the blood and her wide eyes, but for one terrifying moment I thought I had misjudged everything, everyone, and had the irrational idea that Alice was party to whatever evil had been going on here.

But she fell to her knees beside me and started fumbling with the ropes at my ankles and wrists. I noticed that some of her fingernails were bloody and torn and realized how hard and painful it must be for her to unfasten the tight ropes. But she managed it. Then she removed my tie from my mouth and pulled out the wadded rag Miss Scott had used as a gag.

When Alice had finally finished and I could sit up and rub the circulation back into my hands, I reached up and touched her cheek and she fell forward into my arms. We stayed like that for some time, a tender tableau, Alice sobbing gently against my chest as I stroked the back of her head and muttered reassuring nonsense in her ear. I don't know which one of us moved first, but it was Alice who said, "We should get out of here. I don't know how long she'll be out. And who knows whether Barnes will turn up?"

"What did you do?" I asked.

"I hit her with the poker."

I was still dizzy, and it took me a little time to regain my sense of balance, but we hobbled and limped our way back upstairs and found Miss Scott still unconscious beside the fireplace in the sitting room, blood matting the side of her head. I found a slow, steady pulse, so she was still alive, but I guessed she would be out for a long time. The place was a wreck, furniture knocked over, the teapot broken in the hearth, a canteen of cutlery scattered about the place, some of the knives red with blood, stained on the carpet and sheepskin rug, a few paintings hanging loose at strange angles on the wall.

"It must have been a hell of a fight," I said to Alice.

She just nodded and winced as she did so.

Then I picked up the telephone to call the police and an ambulance.

We waited outside for the police, sitting on the top step. It was a mild evening, the sky a burnt orange streaked with long grey wisps of cloud. The rain had stopped and the drying brown and lemon leaves rustled in the breeze. I was grateful to be out in the fresh air again. We both sat silently and breathed in deep for a while. I held Alice's hand, which was shaking as much as mine. Then I asked her why she had come to Miss Scott's house and what had happened upstairs.

"I asked to see you," she said. "I'd noticed your car when I arrived. The same one I saw parked outside school earlier today. She tried to tell me you weren't here, that she had two cars. We talked, argued. Then she admitted you'd been here but said you'd started feeling ill and had to lie down."

"That bit's partly true," I said, remembering the sweet strong tea, no doubt masking the taste of whatever drugs she had added. Benzodiazepine, she had said.

"I was more than suspicious by then, so told her I wanted to go up and see you. She asked me if I fancied a drink first. I said no. Things were pretty tense between us, but I didn't expect what happened next. I stood up and said I wanted to go upstairs and see if you were all right now. She came at me with the poker. Luckily I managed to dodge the blow and it smashed a lamp or a vase or something. We struggled, she dropped the poker. I used my knee on her. I don't really remember what happened after that except I've never been in such a fight before. It seemed to go on forever." She shook her head. "I think I got to the point where I didn't care how much I hurt her as long as she stopped trying to hurt me."

"It was a fight for your life," I said, squeezing her hand. She winced at the pain. "Sorry. She'd have killed you, too."

"How could she hope to get away with two murders just like that?"

"She'd gotten away with murder before. She was desperate. Her plan was unravelling. But what made you come here? We thought Miss Scott was Barnes's victim, didn't we?"

"First off, it was just a feeling. You know, like you hear about in those American cop shows. Something stinks, or feels 'hinky.' Is that the right word? Something felt not quite right, anyway, and I was getting more anxious. It was gnawing away at me all the time I was trying to concentrate on teaching my class. I couldn't stop thinking about you and Barnes and Marguerite Scott. After class, I got back on my computer and looked up everything I could find about her husband's disappearance. There wasn't very much, and most of what was there was there because he was a fairly important player in the financial field. Sort of famous. He has his own Wikipedia page, at any rate. He was forty-five at the time of his death, probably about twenty years older than his wife."

I was in my early fifties, having retired early. "Forty-five's not old," I said.

"As that's *my* age, I would have to agree with you. But I said 'older,' not old. Anyway, one thing that leaped out at me was the date of his disappearance. September 28, 2010. That was seven years from the time Marguerite Scott came back from lunch drunk and got her marching orders. I can't prove it, but I'm sure she'd been out with Barnes. Anyway, I knew already that her husband's body had never been found, that he was supposed to have drowned, and I also knew that it takes seven years before an official declaration of death can be issued in absentia. That made me think. The inscription, Marguerite Scott's erratic behavior around that date, her cold and distant manner. I was starting to think by then that I must have misread the whole business, got it backwards, and that Barnes wasn't about to harm Miss Scott but was somehow her accomplice, and perhaps the point of the inscription was to remind her that she really did like killing, or really had killed, not that he was going to kill her. That was when I decided to follow you out here."

"And I'm glad you did," I said.

"I know it wasn't very logical thinking. I mean, the police can't have suspected anything back in 2010, or they would gave questioned her more thoroughly. Besides, she was in a cafe with lots of other people when her husband drowned. Lots of people saw her. She had the ideal alibi."

"Only it wasn't her husband who drowned," I said. "It was Barnes. And he didn't die."

Alice needed a few stitches here and there and some tape around her ribs, while I had my ankle set, which meant I had to walk with a stick for a while. Fortunately for me, Marguerite Scott had dragged me down the cellar steps head first rather than feet, so except for a few bruises around my lower back, I was otherwise in fairly decent shape for a man my age, the doctor said.

A few days after our ordeal, the forensic team dug up two bodies on Marguerite Scott's property. One belonged to her husband, George Scott, who, as I had explained to Alice and the police already, had never made it to Cornwall for the holiday on which he supposedly drowned. The other body, far fresher, was Barnes Corrigan, who had been dead only since the end of September, not so long after he had sent the Browning to Marguerite Scott. Both had their throats cut.

Marguerite Scott was still in hospital under observation. Fortunately, her skull hadn't been fractured, but she was suffering from serious concussion, and she had a hell of a headache. As yet, she hadn't told the police anything, but it was just a matter of time. Besides, the superintendent told us that they already had plenty of evidence to convict her even if she didn't confess.

As regards cause of death, we were informed a little later that the search team had found enough benzodiazepines in Miss Scott's house to knock out a small army. The superintendent also remarked that, given the amount of blood in the soil around the makeshift graves, she must have dumped the bodies in before cutting their throats, so as not to leave traces of blood in the house. As both George and Barnes had not been dead, but merely unconscious, when they were killed, their hearts had still been working to pump blood from the throat wounds. There were no traces of benzodiazepines in what was left of George's body after seven years, but the pathologist had hopes of finding traces still in Barnes's system. Not that it mattered; we could all imagine how she killed her victims. First she incapacitated them with drugs, then she dumped them in a shallow grave and slit their throats before burying them. Nice woman.

And now I knew why Miss Scott had been worried enough about the inscription I had showed her to risk killing me, too. If the wrong people had found out about it, Barnes Corrigan and his whereabouts would have become an issue. Surely someone somewhere would have missed him. Miss Scott had clearly surmised that I wasn't going to stop asking questions about the inscription, and she was right to believe that. I knew when I first saw the words that there was a warped and vindictive intelligence behind them, though I will admit I had no idea that I would experience such an abrupt reversal and discover that the most warped and vindictive intelligence in the whole affair lay elsewhere, in the form of Miss Scott herself. My initial analysis had been terribly flawed, seeing the whole thing as a teacher-student relationship and Barnes as the psychopathic intelligence behind it all. But that wasn't the case at all.

I would like nothing more than to finish by saying that Alice Langham and I were married in such and such a church on such a such a date, but we weren't. Alice had no desire to marry again, and I had no objection to our living together, so I sold my little pile of stones up in Ripon and moved into her bijou Lincolnshire cottage. Alice still teaches at Linford School, where she is something of a celebrity, and I still enjoy the occasional day out browsing the second-hand bookshops, only now I examine what I buy far more closely. Sometimes, in these chilly winter evenings, we sit before the crackling fire and, at Alice's request, I read to her my translations of Ovid. The erotic poems, of course.

Reconciliation Day

Christopher Fowler

FROM THE JOURNAL OF JONATHAN HARKER,
JULY 2ND, 1893

*E*ACH DAY *I expect the count to return. My work cannot be completed if he does not appear. But each day the door remains bolted, and I must return to my work again. I fear now that it will never be complete.*

How well I remember the day I arrived. Never had I felt such a dread ache of melancholy as I experienced upon entering this terrible, desolate place.

The castle is less a schloss than a fortress, and dominates the mountain skyline. It is very old, thirteenth century by my reckoning, and a veritable masterpiece of unadorned ugliness. Little has been added across the years to make the interior more bearable for human habitation.

There is now glass in many of the windows and mouldering tapestries adorn the walls, but at night the noise of their flapping reveals the castle's inadequate protection from the elements. The ramparts and walkways appear unchanged from the time of their construction. I wondered if hot oil was once poured from them onto the heads of disgruntled villagers who came to complain about their murderous taxes.

There is one entrance only, and this at the top of a steep flight of steps, faced with a pair of enormous studded doors. Water is drawn up from a central well in the courtyard by a complicated wooden contraption. Gargoyles sprout like toadstools in every exposed corner. The battlements turn back the snow-laden gales that forever sweep the Carpathian mountains, creating a chill oasis within, so that one may cross the bailey without being blasted into the sky.

But it is the character of the count himself that provides the castle with its most singular feature, a pervading sense of loss and loneliness that would penetrate the bravest heart and break it if admitted. The wind moans like a dying child, and even the weak sunlight that passes into the great hall is drained of life and hope by the stained glass through which it is filtered.

I was advised not to become too well-acquainted with my client. Those in London who have dealings with him remark that he is 'too European' for English tastes. They appreciate the nobility of his lineage, his superior manners and cultivation, but they cannot understand his motives, and I fear his lack of sociability will stand him in poor stead in London, where men prefer to discuss fluctuations of stock and the nature of horses above their own feelings. For his part, the count certainly does not encourage social intercourse. He has not even shaken my hand, and on the few occasions that we have eaten together he has left me alone at the table before ten minutes have passed. I have not seen him consume a morsel of food. It is as if he cannot bear the presence of a stranger such as myself.

I have been here for a month now. My host departed in the middle of June, complaining that the summer air was 'too thin and bright' for him. He has promised to return by the first week in September, when he will release me from my task, and I am to return home to Mina before the mountain paths become impassable for the winter.

This would be an unbearable place to spend even one night were it not for the library. The castle is either cold or hot; most of it is bitter even at noon, but the library has the grandest fireplace I have ever seen. True, it is smaller than the one in *the great hall, were hams were smoked and cauldrons of soup were boiled in happier times, and which now stands as cold and lifeless as a tomb, but it carries the crest of Vlad Drakul at its mantel, and the fire is kept stoked so high by day that it never entirely dies through the night. It is here that I feel safest.*

The count explained that the library had once been cared for by its own custodian and that he had died at a greatly advanced age, and then only through an unfortunate accident. He had fallen into a fast-running river and drowned.

The heat from the fireplace is bad for the books and would dry out their pages if continued through the years, but as I labour in this chamber six days out of every seven, it has proven necessary to provide a habitable temperature for me. The servant brings my meals to the great hall at seven, twelve and eight, thus I am able to keep civilised hours.

Although I came here to arrange the count's estate at the behest of my employer Peter Hawkins, it is the library that has provided me with the greatest challenge of my life, and I often work late into the night, there being little else to do inside the castle, and certainly no-one to do it with.

I travelled here with only two books in my possession; the leather-bound Bible I keep on my bedside table, and the Baedeker provided for my journey by Mina, so for me the library is an enchanted place. Never before, I'll wager, has such a collection of English, Latin and European volumes been assembled beyond London. Indeed, not even that great city can boast such esoteric tastes as those displayed by the count and his forefathers, for here are books that exist in but a single copy, histories of forgotten battles, biographies of disgraced warriors, scandalous romances of distant civilisations, accounts of deeds too shameful to be recorded elsewhere, books of magic, books of mystery, books that detail the events of impossible pasts and possible futures.

Oh, this is no ordinary library.

In truth, I must confess I am surprised that he has allowed

*me such free access to a collection that I feel provides a very
private insight into the life and tastes of its owner. Tall iron
ladders, their base rungs connected to a central rail, shift along
the book-clad walls. Certain shelves nearest the great vaulted
ceiling have brass bars locked over them to keep their contents
away from prying eyes, but the count has provided me with
keys to them all. When I asked him if, for the sake of privacy, he
would care to sort the books before I cast my gaze upon them
(after all, he is a member of the Basarabian aristocracy, and who
knows what family secrets hide there) he demurred, insisting
that I should have full run of the place.*

*He is at times a charming man, but strange and distant in
his thoughts, and altogether too much of an Easterner for me
to ever fully gain his confidence, for I act as the representative
of an Empire far too domesticated for his tastes and, I suspect,
too diminished in his mind. Yes, diminished, for there is little
doubt that he regards the British intellect as soft and satiated,
even though there is much in it that he admires. He comes from
a long line of bloodletting lords who ruled with the sword-
blade and despised any show of compassion, dismissing it as
weakness. He is proud of his heritage and discourses upon it
freely. He has not learned to be humble, even though contrition
is the only civilised response to the sins of the past.*

*I think perhaps he regards this vast library, with its
impossible mythologies and gruesome histories, as part of the
bloody legacy he will have to put behind him when he moves
to our country. He is, after all, the last of his line. I suspect he
is allowing me to catalogue these books with a view to placing
the contents up for auction. The problem, though, is that it is
almost impossible for me to judge the value of such volumes.
Regardless of what is contained within, the bindings themselves
are frequently studded with semi-precious stones, bound in
gold-leaf and green leather, and in one case what appears to be
human skin. There is no precedent to them and therefore there
can be no accurate evaluation.*

How then am I to proceed?

*

A Wizzair flight from London to Romania is deceptively cheap until you realize you can't take any carry-on luggage bigger than a toiletry bag. Once I arrived I found there were compensations; a top-notch three-course meal with wine in Cluj-Napoca set me back around fifteen dollars. Hell, my morning soy-decaf-latte and Danish habit in Manhattan was almost costing me that.

I knew the country wasn't getting many tourist visits at this time of the year because everyone else in the arrivals hall was standing on the Nationals side of the passport line. They were coming home after working in England. I'd come here because of Bram Stoker, or to be more precise, because of *Dracula*.

There are people who'll tell you I'm one of the two greatest experts on that novel in the world. I prefer to think of it as a field of one. Mikaela Klove is the other and she's an antiquarian. Does that make her an expert? She's certainly grown richer on her reputation than I have, but then, it's not a big field.

Dracula's popularity is second only to that of Sherlock Holmes's adventures, but this wasn't always the case. Stoker died broke. He'd written the book in competition with a swindler called Richard Marsh, who guaranteed that he could outsell Stoker and did so that same year with a novel called *The Beetle*. Marsh annually hammered out at least three books published through sixteen different houses, and was hugely popular. *The Beetle* was his best work, but even in this Marsh couldn't resist subterfuge; his vampiric insect is actually an old man in a woman's body who can turn into a giant beetle that alters everyone it comes into contact with, smashing up the social order. Everyone in the tale shapeshifts in some way. *Dracula* was less tricksy, kind of lurid and pulpy, epistolary and fragmentary in form, and published to decidedly mixed reviews. It just couldn't compete.

The pages of the original Stoker manuscript were heavily amended by hand and signed by the author. At that point the novel was titled *The Undead*, and had several marked differences from the published version. In Stoker's manuscript, after Harker and Morris kill Dracula, the count's castle is destroyed in a kind of volcanic eruption. That's not so far-fetched; Transylvania is an earthquake region, although Stoker never went there and only saw Castle Bran, the model for the count's home, in a photograph.

The manuscript had a further significant addition, a chapter concerning Jonathan Harker's work in the castle's library, which we never encounter in the printed edition. But something odd happened—the 529-page manuscript, the only copy, vanished for nearly a century. It reappeared as if from nowhere in 1980 and was auctioned at Christie's in New York, but failed to reach its reserve price and was withdrawn. Nobody knows what happened to it after that. The story of the world's rare objects is a history of secrecy and deception.

However, there was another artifact as rare, if more apocryphal, and two people knew of its whereabouts: an old guy who ran a bookstore in Sighisoara, and Mikaela Klove, who was Lithuanian, and currently halfway through a two-year residence in Transylvania, hence my trip there.

I wouldn't call Mikaela an enemy. I guess we're friendly rivals. But she's attractive and married to a Princeton professor and she's rich enough to be able to take time off from her lecture circuit in order to work on a study of Transylvanian culture, while I'm single and close to broke and can only get a week's break before having to return to my menial day-job in New York. I'm hungrier, and I'm craftier.

You've probably already decided who the villain is in this story. The penniless chancer loses out next to the beautiful high-minded cultural expert. But you know what? Bram Stoker wasn't so high-minded. He was a pulp hack who ended up a pauper, accidentally leaving a hundred thousand critical essays by academics like Mikaela in his wake.

I picked up a hire car at Cluj-Napoca airport and headed off toward Sighisoara, to meet with the guy who had promised to show me how I could find this mythical artefact. In return

I was bringing him a gift for his collection, a very rare edition of Kafka's *The Castle*. It turned out that mine was a forgery, but a very good one. By the time his waning euphoria restored his critical abilities, I'd be on my way. Of course Mikaela knew where the item was as well, but I didn't want to alert her to my interest in it. I was going to casually drop it into the conversation and see her reaction. I figured she might be able to guide me through any access restrictions.

Transylvania is in central Romania, and is bordered by spear-like mountain ranges. The car I hired was a piece of junk called a Dacia Logan, and took hills like an old man with bad lungs climbing a staircase.

I passed through villages that hadn't changed in a thousand years, accessed through avenues of trees in the tops of which sat bushes of leeching mistletoe like cranes' nests. It's tempting to use the vampiric analogy here; it looked like everyone was getting something from someone else. Tucked away from the beauty spots were the smoke-belching factories owned by rich corporations getting a great deal on slave labor, a few of them from my own homeland.

As the Dacia struggled on I was overtaken by guys in black felt hats driving teams of carthorses, hauling logs. It looked as if the whole country ran on burning wood. The other thing I remember most about that journey was the graveyards. Every town had one built right beside its houses, as if to remind folk that they would always be surrounded by the dead.

FROM THE JOURNAL OF JONATHAN HARKER,
JULY 15TH, 1893

Regarding the library: I have devised a system that allows me to create a table of approximate values, and for now that must suffice.

First I examine the binding of the book, noting the use of valuable ornamentation and pigments. Then I make note of the author and the subject,gauging their popularity and historical stature;how many copies have been printed (if indicated)and where; how many editions; the age of the work, its scarcity and length; and finally content,whether scandalous and likely to cause offence,whether of general interest, usefulness and the like. To this end I find myself making odd decisions,putting a history of Romanian road-mapping before The Life and Times of Vlad the Terrible because the former may be of more utility in charting this neglected territory. Thus the banal triumphs over the lurid, the ordinary over the outrageous,the obvious over the obscure. A fanciful mind might imagine that I was somehow robbing the library of its power by reclassifying these tomes in such a prosaic manner, that by quantifying them I am reducing the spell they cast. Fancies grow within these great walls. The castle is conducive to them.

Finally I've started upon the high barred shelves, and what I find there surprises, delights and occasionally revolts me. Little histories, human fables set in centuries gone by or years yet to come, that reveal how little our basest nature changes with the passing decades. These books interest me the most.

I had not intended to begin reading any of the volumes, you understand, for the simple reason that it would slow my rate of progress to a crawl, and there are still so many shelves to document. Many books require handling with the utmost care, for their condition is so delicate that their gossamer pages crumble in the heat of a hand. However, I now permit myself to read in the evenings, in order that I might put from my mind the worsening weather, my poor pining Mina and the thought that I could become a prisoner here.

The light in the library is good, there being a proliferation of candles lit for me, and the great brocaded armchair I had brought down from the bedroom is pulled as close to the fire as I dare, deep and comfortable. I am left a nightly brandy, set down before me in a crystal bowl. Outside I hear the wind loping around the battlements like a wounded wolf, and in the distant hills I hear some of those very creatures lifting their *heads to the sky. The fire shifts, popping and crackling in the grate. The room is bathed in low red light. I open the book I have chosen for the night and begin to read.*

Sighisoara looked shut. Its main attraction was a complete medieval village with covered wooden walkways. Around that was a town with one hipster coffee bar called the Arts Café, lots of bookshops (no English language volumes here), a couple of Russian Orthodox churches, some post-war Communist buildings finished in cheap crumbling concrete and some stunning *fin de siècle* neo-baroque houses painted in odd colors; rust red, custard yellow, lime green. I was told that during high season there were street bars and music festivals and tourists, but not in February, with wet sleet riving across the empty streets. There are a handful of shops selling tourist crap, the weirdest item being the pleading chicken, a china figurine of a bird with its wings pressed together in prayer, begging for its life. Eastern European humor; go figure.

I met up with my bookstore contact, handed the Kafka to him, watched his fingers fluttering through the pages with excitement, received an envelope in return and beat it.

As I headed into the black hills below the Carpathian Mountains the weather changed and visibility dropped. The sleet turned to great powdery flakes of snow the size of paper scraps, and soon began to settle. I spent the next six hours stuck behind filth-encrusted trucks lumbering along single-lane highways, barely getting out of third gear while the locals overtook at hair-raising speeds.

Tired of staring at tarmac and truck wheels, I pulled into a café and ate goulash and pork ribs, sluiced down with Ciuc beer. A wrinkled *babushka* who I swear looked like a crazy old gypsy woman from a Frankenstein movie came over to the table and tried to press a foot-high icon on me. The portrait of the crucified Christ had been badly printed onto plastic and glued to a piece of plywood, and wouldn't have fooled anyone from a distance of half a mile. When I explained that I didn't want to buy it, she swore at me for a couple of minutes before wandering off to sit on the other side of the café, where she ordered a pizza the size of a drain cover and sat glowering at me as she folded pieces into her mouth.

Cursed by an old gypsy woman, I thought with amusement. *All I need now is to be chased by wolves.*

I fell asleep in the Dacia. My phone awoke me nearly an hour later.

"Carter, are you here? It's Mikaela."

"I'm on my way," I said, sitting up and rubbing my eyes. The car park was a white rectangle fenced in by tall black firs. "Are we going to meet up tonight?"

"Sure, but you know I don't have the information you want."

Oh, yeah, I was going to mention that. I may have shared a little too much information with Mikaela in a drunken late-night phone call. I couldn't remember exactly what I'd told her, so I had to be careful.

"I have some leads of my own." I tried to sound as if it was no big deal. I wasn't about to explain what was in the envelope in my glove box.

"You know what you're seeking doesn't exist," she said. "The American copyright loophole was closed and the playscript in the British Library was never—"

"Don't lecture me, Mikaela. I have a pretty good idea where everything is."

"But you don't know where the edition is or if it even exists, do you?" She let the question hang in the air, probing for an answer.

"You know who I thought would be great in a new Dracula role?" I said, quickly changing the subject, "Benedict Cumberbatch. He looks like Henry Irving, don't you think?" It seemed likely that the great Shakespearian actor had been the original inspiration for Stoker's vampire, and Cumberbatch was virtually his reincarnation.

"I can see the resemblance," said Mikaela. "Whereabouts are you?"

"I'm about seventy kilometers southeast of Bran. I think. It's kind of hard to tell. There are no signs and there's a lot of snow coming down."

"It's worse up in the mountains. Call me when you get near the castle. It'll be shut by the time you get here but we can have dinner."

I agreed and hung up, reset my GPS and swung back onto the road, followed by a pack of howling feral dogs.

FROM THE JOURNAL OF JONATHAN HARKER,
AUGUST 30TH, 1893

I have the feeling that I am not alone.

I know there are servants, four I think; a raw-looking woman who cooks and cleans, her silent husband the groom, an addle-pated under-servant born without wits who is only fit for washing and sweeping (he might be the son of the cook; there is a resemblance) and an unsmiling German butler whom I take to be the count's manservant.

But there is someone else here. I sense his presence late at night, when the fire has banked down to an amber glow and the library is at its gloomiest. I can feel him standing silently beyond the windows (an impossibility since they overlook a sheer drop of several hundred feet). When I turn to catch a glimpse of this imagined figure it is gone. Last night the feeling came again. I had just finished cataloguing the top shelves of the library's west wall and was setting the iron ladders back in their place when I became aware of someone staring at my back. A sensation of panic seized me as the hairs stood on my neck, prickling as though charged with electricity, but I forced myself to continue with my task, finally turning in the natural course of my duty and raising my gaze to where I felt this mysterious stranger to be standing.

Of course there was nothing corporeal to see—yet this time the feeling persisted. I made my way across the great room, passing the glowing red escarpment of the fire, until I reached the bank of mullioned windows set in the room's north side. Through the rain that was ticking against the glass I looked out on the most forsaken landscape imaginable, black pines and black rock. I could still feel him somewhere outside the windows, yet how was this possible? I am a man who prides himself on his sensitivity, and fancied that this baleful presence belonged to none other than my host. The count was not due to return for a while yet, having extended his trip to conclude certain pressing business affairs.

This presents me with a new problem, for I am told that winter settles suddenly in the mountains, and is slow to release the province from its numbing grip. Once the blizzards begin the roads will become inundated, making it impossible for me to leave the castle until the end of next spring, a full seven months away. Despite the count's relayed requests that I should write home providing departure dates, I wonder if they will materialise. If not, I would truly be a prisoner here.

With that thought weighing heavily on my mind I returned to my armchair beside the fire, fought down the urge to panic, opened a book and once more began to read.

I must have dozed, for I can only think that what I saw next was a hallucination resulting from a poorly digested piece of mutton. The count was standing in the corner of the library, still dressed in his heavy-weather oilskin. He appeared agitated and ill-at-ease, as if conducting an argument with himself on some point. At length he reached a decision and approached me, gliding across the room like a tall-ship in still seas. Flowing behind him was a rippling wave of fur, as hundreds of rats poured over the chairs and tables in a fanned brown shadow. The rodents watched me with eyes like ebony beads. They cascaded over the count's shoes and formed a great circle around my chair, as if awaiting a signal. But the signal did not come, so they fell upon one another, the strongest tearing into the soft fat bellies of the weakest, and the library carpet turned scarlet as the chamber filled with screams.

I awoke to find my shirt as wet as if it had been dropped into a lake. The book I had been reading lay on the floor at my feet, its spine split. My collar was open, and the silver crucifix I always wear at my neck was hanging on the arm of the chair, its clasp broken beyond repair. I resolved to eat earlier from that night on.

I couldn't have made the journey to the castle more atmospheric if I'd been travelling by stage-coach. Driving through the Carpathian Mountains in a snowstorm was a cool if exhausting experience. With the black firs rising all around me, I passed through endless tiny villages, usually trapped behind black-hatted woodcutters on carthorses.

The arrival at the castle itself was kind of a let-down, as the area proved more suburban than anything in the surrounding region of Brasov. At my first sight of the building I was like, *Is that it?* It was certainly a lot smaller than I'd imagined, and those photographs showing its pointed circular turrets against a background of steep cliffs must have been taken from a very narrow perspective, because it was surrounded by ugly modern houses and what appeared to be a funfair with a boating lake.

Yet when I drew closer I began to appreciate its melancholy grandeur. It was stark and unadorned and imperious.

Mikaela was staying in a three star lodge called the Hotel Extravagance, so I checked in there too. It had a yellow plastic fascia and a life-sized model of a fat chef in an apron holding up a pig's head. We're academics, not movie stars; this was the kind of place we usually got to stay in. The receptionist was a smiling, pretty girl of about twenty who cheerfully admitted that she had been on duty for twenty-four hours. It was the standard length of a shift in these parts, she said. It made me hate kvetchy Manhattan restaurant staff even more.

"You do know it doesn't exist, right?" said Mikaela, smiling with secret knowledge. She raised a glass of *palină* to me. Between us stood a terrifying steeple of pink sausages and pork parts, surrounded by hard-to-identify vegetables in gravy. The *palină* was a local fruit brandy invented in the Middle Ages, and tasted like it, but the local red wine proved sensational.

"Everyone said the manuscript was lost," I reminded her.

"But the missing parts aren't in the official version, which is why it never reached its reserve at the Christie's auction. It just wasn't that collectable, Carter. Stoker was never a great writer, you know that. His prose is purple and really not very interesting."

"I get that." I stabbed another sausage onto my plate. "Everybody said the same thing about the Pre-Raphaelites but look how their stock jumped. And *Dracula* will become more valued in time. You know what makes the difference? Movies. There have been nearly three hundred films made from that one book so far, almost as many as from all of Sherlock Holmes."

"But you have to face the fact that it just doesn't have the same cachet."

"All it will take is one more hit movie. How many rich, dumb collectors now think that Disney's live-action *Alice in Wonderland* characters are from the book? They're not interested in the Tenniel art but they'll pay insane amounts for studio memorabilia."

I needed to play down my own obsession. The last thing I wanted was Mikaela figuring out what I was up to. I'd read the contents of the bookseller's envelope and as I suspected, it wasn't enough to get me there without help. I'd need Mikaela but she had to make the offer unwittingly.

"It was the wrong time for the sale of the annotated manuscript," she said, spearing asparagus. "That's why it was withdrawn. You're right; its value is higher now."

"I still believe the blue edition is out there somewhere. If it's anywhere, it has to be here. I'd just like to see it once."

The blue edition—okay, what happened was this. In May

1897 Constable published the first edition bound in yellow cloth. It wasn't a success. However, an export edition was discussed. It was also to be in English but printed differently, with more widely spaced paragraphs and a blue cloth cover. Stoker approved this second limited run even though the advance was almost nothing, sent off a copy of his manuscript and waited for the paperwork to arrive.

It never came.

The theory is that the company in charge of printing it for the European market, Karnstein-Saxon, had questions about the manuscript Stoker sent them because it was different from the one they'd read in the yellow edition. It was longer—a liability for the export version—and had a different ending. There's a sole piece of correspondence from Stoker, photocopied once but now lost, admitting that he had mistakenly sent them the earlier version complete with the chapter in the library and the immolation at the end. He told them they could edit it for length if they wanted. It was obvious he just wanted the money.

But I was sure they ran off at least one copy without any cuts.

Why did I know this? Because of a little number stuck at the bottom of a page. A copy of the book was placed in a sale catalogue printed in 1905 in Brasov, Transylvania, that totaled 556 pages, not 529 pages. The book was described as having eight woodcuts (which wouldn't fully account for the higher page tally), and a blue cover. It was bought by the priest of a town called Viscria. On the receipt for the copy he had written his reason for the purchase; to form the center of a display showing how Transylvania's fame had reached the world outside. The priest hadn't died until 1979—just before the "official" manuscript failed to meet its reserve. So why would the town have gotten rid of their copy? Did they even know it was different? They'd have hung onto it, hoping it would rise in value. That's what I was counting on.

No other copy of the so-called blue edition had ever surfaced, and the early manuscript was lost. To me, that made it virtually priceless. I've always been an obsessive completist—I can't

collect something without making sure I've got it all, and this
was my Holy Grail. And I guess it was why I'd ended up alone.
No woman was prepared to come second in my life.

"What do you know about a town called Viscria?" I asked
Mikaela as casually as I could.

FROM THE JOURNAL OF JONATHAN HARKER,
SEPTEMBER 22ND, 1893

*The weather has begun to worsen, and there is still no sign of
the count. As the days grow shorter a forlorn darkness descends
upon the castle. The skies are troubled, the clouds heavier now,
ebbing to the west with their bellies full of rain. The library
occupies my waking hours. It is like an origami model of
Chinese paper, ever unfolding into new configurations. Just
when I think I have its measure, new delights and degradations
present themselves. Yesterday I started on a further set of shelves
housing nautical chart-books and maps, and while reaching
across the ladder to pull one stubborn tome free, I triggered the
opening of a mahogany flap built in the rear of the shelf that
folded down to reveal a further hundred volumes!*

*I cleared a space and set these books in stacks according to
their coordinated bindings, and only once they all stood free of
their secret home did I start to examine them.*

*I find that delicacy escapes me at this point; they were lexicons
of erotica, frankly and indecently illustrated, outlining practices
above, below and altogether beyond the boundaries of human
nature, described in such an overt and lascivious manner that
I was forced to return them to their hiding place before the
servant brought me my nightly brandy, for no gentleman would
wish such volumes to fall into the hands of servants.*

*After he had left the room I took time to examine the single
edition I had left out. It was much like the others, designed
more to arouse the senses than to provide practical advice
concerning the physical side of matrimonial duty. The room*

grew hot about me as I turned the pages, and I was forced to move back from the fireplace. The drawings were shameless, representing actions one would scarcely countenance in the darkest woods, here presented in brightest light. More shocking still was the discovery that the book was English, produced in London, presumably for foreign purchasers.

While I was examining this in detail I began to sense the presence once more, and this time I became aware of a scent, a sweet perfume akin to Atar of Roses, a scented water my own dear Mina would often dab at her swan-pale neck. The perfume, filled as it was with memories of home, quite overpowered me and I grew faint, for I fancied I saw a lady—no, a woman— standing on the staircase nearest the windows.

She was tall and handsome rather than beautiful, with a knowing look, her auburn hair swept down across a dress of sheer green gossamer, with emerald jewels at her throat, and nothing at all on her feet. She stood with her left side turned to me, so that I could not help but notice the exaggerated posture of her bosom. It was as though she intended to incite my admiration. The effect was indecent, but nothing to the effect produced when she turned to face me directly, for the front panel of her dress was cut away below her waist to reveal—well, her entire personal female anatomy, the triangle of blackness shocking against her white stomach. Stupefied by such brazenness, wondering if she was perhaps ill, I found myself unable to move as she approached.

Upon reaching my chair she slid the outstretched fingers of her right hand inside my shirt, shearing off several of the buttons with her sharp nails. I was acutely aware that the naked part of her was very close to me. Then, reaching inside the high waistband of my trousers, she grasped at the very root of my reluctantly extended manhood and brought it forward, bursting through the garment's fly buttons as if they afforded no protection. When I saw that she intended to lower her lips to this heated core of my being, every fibre of my body strained to resist her brazen advances.

Here, though, my mind clouds with indistinct but disagreeable impressions. A distant cry of anger is heard, the woman retreats in fear and fury, and I awake, ashamed to discover my desire discharged and my clothing in considerable disarray, the victim of some delirious carphology.

We didn't get drunk. Mikaela's too much of a lady and after a few shots of *palină* I figured I wouldn't be much of a gentleman. So the next morning we breakfasted early and went to Castle Bran. Around its base were dozens of wooden huts selling all kinds of cool trash; Dracula fridge magnets, keyrings, woolen hats, fur waistcoats, a snow-globe containing a castle that swirled with bats when you shook it, T-shirts printed with Christopher Lee's face, the whole schmear. Mamas in shell-suits were waddling around the stands buying vampire teddy bears while feral dogs cruised around the takeout stands, hoping to catch pieces of sausage falling from buns. But I figured hey, all this stuff didn't matter. Shouldn't castles always have peasant huts around their foundations?

Mikaela gave me a little historical background. In 1920 Bran became a royal residence and the favorite home of Queen Marie. The castle was inherited by her daughter, who ran a hospital there in World War II. It was seized by the Communists, who expelled the royal family in 1948. Cut to 2005, when the Romanian government passed a special law allowing restitution claims on properties illegally expropriated. A year later the castle was given to Dominic von Habsburg, the son and heir of Princess Ileana. In 2007, the retrocession of the castle was declared illegal because it supposedly broke the Romanian law on property and succession.

This argument between royals and the government went back and forth. In 2009, the castle administration was transferred again to Archduke Dominic and his sisters. The Habsburgs opened it to the public as a private museum to help safeguard the economic base in the region. Now it was up for private sale, so who knew if it would be safeguarded or closed down for good? It seemed like everything else around here—undervalued and underappreciated. Every town, gallery, beach and beauty spot in France and Italy has been seen to death by cruise-ship tourists. There was no international tourism here, although I'd been told that a few visitors arrived in summer. All of which made me think that the blue edition was gathering dust in a closet somewhere in Viscria. But to get there I had to humor Mikaela, partly because she spoke the language, mostly because she was a familiar face in the area. So we went around Bran and I tried to concentrate while she told me scandalous and entirely unsubstantiated stories about the castle's long-lost library.

The interior of Bran was lacking in grandeur, and none of the mismatched fixtures were original. The bookshelves were all empty. The walls had been painted white, which destroyed the atmosphere—still, it wasn't a film set, just the inspiration for a novel. Re-reading the book on my journey I still found the prose flat and earnest, but the sense of dread accumulating in the tale excited me (HG Wells is the same, not stylistically distinguished but *Kipps* and *The War of the Worlds* always get to me). There were some details I'd forgotten—Jonathan Harker realizes the castle has no staff when he spies Dracula making the beds! The blue edition was supposed to be different in that respect too. Stoker cut the staff for the yellow edition. There was also supposed to be some erotic content the English publisher wouldn't have touched; Stoker had apparently gotten himself a little over-excited and European.

In the courtyard, the castle was criss-crossed with narrow open-sided corridors, winding staircases, spires, turrets and a deep well that conjured up memories of old Hammer films. There were hardly any other visitors.

I was just thinking about how to raise the subject of the book when Mikaela said, "I can take you to Viscria if you want."

FROM THE JOURNAL OF JONATHAN HARKER,
OCTOBER 7TH, 1893

*The snow has started falling. During these increasingly frequent
squalls, all sights and sounds are obscured by a deadening white
veil that seals us in the sky. From my bedroom window I can
see that the road to the castle is already becoming obscured. If
the count does not return soon, I really do not see how I shall
be able to leave. I suppose I could demand that a carriage be
fetched from the nearest village, but I fear that such an action
would offend my host, who must surely reappear any day now.
I am worried about my beloved Mina. I have not heard from
her inside a month, and yet if I am truthful there is a part of
me that is glad to be imprisoned here within the castle, for the
library continues to reveal paths I feel no decent God-fearing
Englishman has ever explored.*

*I do not mean to sound so mysterious, but truly something
strange weighs upon my mind. It is this; by day I follow the
same routine, logging the books and entering them into the
great ledgers my host provided for the purpose, but each night,
after I have supped and read my customary pages beside the
fire, I allow myself to fall into a light sleep and then—*

*—then my freedom begins as I dream or awaken to such
unholy horrors and delights that I can barely bring myself to
describe them.*

*Some nights bring swarms of bats, musty-smelling airborne
rodents with leathery wings, needle teeth and blind eyes.
Sometimes the ancestors of Vlad Drakul appear at the windows
in bloody tableaux, frozen in the act of hacking off the heads
of their enemies. Men appear skewered on tempered spikes,
thrusting themselves deeper onto the razor-sharp poles in the
throes of obscene pleasure. Even the count himself pays his
respects, his bony alabaster features peering at me through the
wintry mist as if trying to bridge the chasm between our two
civilisations. And sometimes the women come.*

Ah, the women.

These females are unlike any we have in England. They do not accompany themselves on the pianoforte, they do not sew demurely by the fire. Their prowess is focussed in an entirely different area. They kneel and disrobe each other before me, and caress themselves, and turn their rumps toward me in expectation. I would like to tell you that I resist, that I think of my fiancée waiting patiently at home, and recite psalms from my Bible to strengthen my will, but I do not, and so I am damned by the actions I take to slake my decadent desires.

Who are these people who come to me in nightly fever-dreams? Do I conjure them or do they draw something from me? It is as if the count knows my innermost thoughts and caters for them accordingly. Yet I know for a fact that he has not returned to the castle, for when I look from the window I see that there are no cart-tracks on the road outside. The snow remains entirely unbroken.

Yesterday I tried the main door and found it locked. Yet there are times when I do not wish to leave this terrible place, for to do so would mean forsaking the library. Presumably it is to be packed and shipped to London, and this gives me hope, that I might travel with the volumes and protect them from division. For the strength of a library exists in the sum of its books. Only by studying it as a whole—indeed, only by reading every single edition contained within—can one hope to divine the true nature of its owner.

"Is this it?"

I tried to see through the windshield but one wiper had stopped working. It was snowing lightly as we passed another walled village that had barely been altered in a millennium. Only a couple of cars parked by a church set us in the present. Everything else looked like a medieval woodcut.

"It's at the end of this road," said Mikaela. "Everyone makes the same mistake with Viscria. The original walled village died and the descendants moved further back to the last town we passed. I thought I'd get to know them. They're helpful when you run out of gas, kind even, but in the year I've been here I haven't gotten to know a single one well. There's too much history. It's hard to comprehend what these people have been through."

"You're going to tell me they hang garlic and crucifixes out at night," I joked, then wished I hadn't, as we passed a seven foot painted Jesus in a field.

"No, the locals aren't vampires," said Mikaela with a straight face, "but they believe in Vlad Drakul. The guy cast a long shadow. That's why you still find paintings in bars and cafés that show him gorily impaling victims. It's his memory they honor, not Bram Stoker's. The book is just a useful means to an end, a way to hook tourists into coming here. It's a pity the area's solely associated with the vampire trade. There's a lot more to discover in places like Sibiu."

I'd heard about Transylvania's capital. It boasted a magnificently rococo French-style square as grand as anything you'd find in Paris or Lyon, but typically the locals didn't feel the need to brag about it, and visitors rarely got that far.

"So what happened to the library at Castle Bran?" I asked.

"What happened to anything here under the Communists?" Mikaela said with a shrug. "It disappeared along with everything and everyone else that genocidal maniac Ceaușescu came into contact with. The one thing he couldn't take from these people was their belief system."

I was thinking of the one thing I could take from them.

We passed a peculiar arrangement of low wooden benches rooted in a circle about thirty yards across, around what looked like a blackened tree with upright branches. The green paint on the benches looked new. "I thought you said that the village was dead."

"It is, but the villagers still gather here several times a year. Old customs never die."

The dirty chalk-white walls of the old village appeared

around the next corner, leaning back from the road and tapering to red clay rooftops. We parked in a sloping field full of turkeys and made our way to the entrance.

An ancient woman with a face like a dried apple greeted us at the gate and took two RON from each of us by way of an entrance fee. On the inside, there were derelict houses beneath the thick circular wall, homes which once afforded the protection of the chapel.

"That's a lard tower," said Mikaela, pointing to one of the many turrets in the wall. "The villagers wrote their house numbers on their lard skins and kept careful accounts. They still live a communal life. And they love their books. The collection is in the Reconciliation Tower, such as it is."

We climbed the dusty plank staircase to the top of the chapel's central tower, past looms and farm instruments. In a single bookcase at the end of the top floor I glimpsed a number of leather-bound volumes. "Reconciliation Tower?"

"Reconciliation Day is when the residents present their annual statement of accounts, costs of births, funerals, crops and so on. It has to be signed by every elder, and there are severe penalties for disrespect and disobedience."

"You mean that's what the burned tree was back there? The elders sit in a circle on their benches and watch while debtors are chained up and set on fire?"

"You've been reading too much Stoker," Mikaela laughed.

I went to the book-cupboard and opened the glass case.

"I don't think you should do that," she said. "I'm just having a little look is all," I told her.

The volumes inside were old but of no interest. Most concerned crop planting and animal husbandry. All were printed in Romanian.

Mikaela seemed to make up her mind about something. "Look out of the window," she said. "See what the babushka is doing."

Old Apple-Face had retired to the outside wall and was sitting on a kitchen chair in the lightly falling snow, wearing just a thin shawl around her shoulders, doing nothing and apparently feeling no cold.

"Okay, come with me." We crossed the tower floor to a rough wooden chest of drawers. "They keep the more valuable items in here," said Mikaela. I studied the chest. It was fastened shut with a fat rusty lock.

"Is there any way we can get inside?" "What? No." Mikaela shook his head. "Absolutely not. I once asked if I could open it and they told me it was not for outsiders."

Mikaela had always been timid and culturally over-respectful. I'd told her she needed to look at the bigger picture and think about how the world might share in the value of these finds.

"You want to get lost for a few minutes?" I asked her.

"No, you can't just break in, Carter. It's a federal offence to remove anything from a state building. You'll go home tomorrow and I still have to live here."

"Go downstairs. I'm not going to steal anything, I swear, I'm just going to take a look, okay? I won't touch a thing."

As soon as she had gone, I dug out my Swiss Army knife and worked on the lock. It slid open with embarrassing ease.

FROM THE JOURNAL OF JONATHAN HARKER,
NOVEMBER 15TH, 1893

Somewhere between dreams and wakefulness, I now know there is another state. A limbo-life more imagined than real. A land of phantoms and sensations. It is a place I visit each night after darkness falls. Sometimes it is sensuous, sometimes painful, sometimes exhilarating, sometimes foul and depraved beyond redemption. It extends only to the borders of the library, and its inhabitants, mostly in states of disrobed arousal, are obscenely perfumed. These creatures insult, entice, distract, disgrace, shame and seduce me, clutching at my clothes until I am drawn among them, enthralled by their touch, degraded by my own eagerness to participate in their rituals.

I think I am ill.

By day, my high stone world is silent and rational. The road to the castle is now quite impassable. It would take a team of mountaineers to scale the sharp gradient of the rock face beneath us. The count has failed to return, and of his impending plans there is no word. The servants will not be drawn on the subject. My task in the library is nearly over. The books—all save one final shelf—have been annotated and explored.

I begin to understand the strangely parasitical nature of my host. His thirst for knowledge and his choice of literature betray his true desires. There are volumes in many languages here, but of the ones I can read, first editions of Nodier's Infernalia, d'Argen's Lettres Juives and Viatte's Sources Occultes du Romantisme are the most familiar. One element unites the works—they are all the product of noble decadence, inward-looking, inbred and unhealthy.

Of course I knew the folk-tales about the count's ancestry. They are bound within the history of his family. How could one travel through this country and not hear them? In their native language they appear less fanciful, but here in the castle confabulations take on substantiality. I have read how the count's forebears slaughtered the offspring of their enemies and drank their blood for strength—who has not read these histories? Why, tales of Eastern barbarism have reached the heart of London society, although they are only spoken of after the ladies have left.

But I had not considered the more lurid legends; how the royal descendants lived on beyond death, how they needed no earthly sustenance, how their senses were so finely attuned that they could divine bad fortune in advance. I had not considered the consequence of such fables; that, should their veracity be proven, they might in the count's case suggest an inherited illness of the kind suffered by royal albinos, a dropsical disease of the blood that keeps him from the light, an anaemia that blanches his eyes and dries his veins, and causes meat to stick in his throat, and drives him from the noisy heat of humanity to the dark sanctum of the sick-chamber.

But if it is merely a medical condition, why am I beset with bestial fantasies? What power could the count possess to hold me in his thrall? I find it harder each day to recall his appearance, for the forbidden revelations of the night have all but overpowered my sense of reality. His essence is here in the library, imbued within each page of his collection. Perhaps I am not ill, but mad. I fear my senses have awoken too sharply, and my rational mind is reeling with their weight.

I have lost much of my girth in the last six weeks. I have always been thin, but the gaunt image that glares back at me in the glass must surely belong to a sick and aged relation. I have no strength by day. I live only for the nights. Beneath the welcoming winter moon my flesh fills, my spirit becomes engorged with an unwholesome strength and I am sound once more.

I really must try to get away from here.

I set the lock on one side.

Inside the drawers were a number of gaudy icons, all fake, priests' robes embroidered with red silk, brocaded white christening dresses, hand-stitched blankets and at the bottom, a few books. I removed the stack, checking out of the window.

Mikaela was stumping about in the courtyard, trying not to look suspicious.

The blue cover jumped out. It was entirely blank, with one gold word embossed on the spine. *Dracula*.

I had to take a moment. After all this time, thinking that maybe it didn't exist—

The book had never been opened—you can always tell a virgin copy by the way the pages seem reluctant to leave one another, the tiny ticking sound the spine makes as it's stretched for the first time, the reluctance of the covers to move further apart. It was unsullied, probably the first and last one, the only one.

Stupidly, I'd forgotten to bring my cotton gloves. I didn't want to release sweat-marks onto the pages, but I had to open it and check. The book's crimson edges had dried so that their coloring had turned powdery and dusted off on my fingertips, but its snow-white interior had no discoloration and the smell of the print was still strong.

The publication date matched. The ending was brief but new to my eyes, describing the utter destruction of the castle. It seemed desultory and flatly written, as if it had been tacked on because the author had no other way of ending the story. I could see why he had subsequently removed it. Turning to the early section, easily the best part of the book in my opinion, I searched to see if there were any other additions. Somehow I already knew what I was going to find. The chapter about Harker and the library was there, intact. I wanted to sit down and read it right then but had to content myself with riffling through the pages, just to prove that I was not hallucinating.

Without wasting another second, I removed the copy I'd had made from my rucksack and put it in the original's place. The only thing I'd failed to realize was that the real edition had painted edges. I felt sure no-one here would know or care, but I wondered if it had been printed that way, or if the priest had marked it himself. Whatever—back home the literary world would sit up and take notice when they saw what I had. My name would live on, forever linked to Stoker's *Dracula*.

Replacing the lock and closing it, I made my way back downstairs—but Mikaela had disappeared and my car had gone.

The babushka was still on her chair, basking in the lightly falling snow as if it was a summer's day. As my fingers were crimson with dye I made sure they were tucked away in my pockets.

"Have you seen my friend?" I asked, but she had no English and would only gesture in the direction of the turkey field.

Mikaela was a heavy smoker. Figuring that she had gone off to find cigarettes I made my way over to where we had parked, the precious cargo in my backpack weighing me down.

The count has finally returned, paradoxically bringing fresh spirits into the castle.

For the life of me I cannot see how he arrived here, as one section of the pathway has fallen away into the valley. Last night he came down to dinner, and was in most excellent health. His melancholy mood had lifted and he was eager to converse. He seemed physically taller, his posture more erect, his colour higher. His travels had taken him on many adventures, so he informed me as he poured himself a goblet of heavy claret, but now he was properly restored to his ancestral home and would be in attendance for the conclusion of my work.

I had not told him I was almost done, although I supposed he might have intuited as much from a visit to the library. He asked that we might finish the work together, before the next sunrise. I was very tired—indeed, at the end of the meal I required a helping hand to lift me from my chair—but agreed to his demand, knowing that there were but a handful of books left for me to classify.

Soon we were seated in the great library, warming ourselves before the crackling fire with bowls of brandy. It was when I studied the count's travelling clothes that I realised the truth. His boots and oil-cloth cape lay across the back of a chair where he has supposedly deposited them after his return. But the boots were new, the soles polished and unworn. I intuited that the count had not been away, and that he had passed his time in the castle here with me.

I had not imagined what I had seen and done. We sat across from each other in the two great armchairs, cradling our

brandies, and I nervously pondered my next move, for it was
clear to me that the count could sense my unease.
   This, I felt sure, was to be our most fateful encounter.

I waited for what felt like an age but Mikaela didn't return.
I started to get cold. The turkeys were now eyeing me with
suspicion. It was beginning to snow more heavily. I set down
the backpack and looked at the low hills surrounding us. At
first I couldn't make sense of what I saw. I thought maybe the
turkeys had escaped to the nearest ridge and were now lining
up to peer down at me.

Then I realized that I was looking at a line of black felt hats.

The hats rose to reveal a row of men, walking steadily
toward me. It looked like a village deputation, the precursor to
a lynching. They were talking quietly with one another. Each
one carried a small leather-bound book.

As they reached me, I was encouraged to walk with them
to the circular benches, which they filled to an exact number,
leaving me without a seat. The men were so timelessly dressed
that they could have existed in any era. They didn't seem to
notice me.

The little books were collected and handed to the group's
oldest man. As the owner of the most luxuriant mustache and
beard I guessed he was the village elder. He began to read
aloud, slowly and very boringly, from the gathered accounts. I
wasn't their prisoner but I didn't think they'd take kindly to me
leaving, especially as I had no car, so I hung around at the edge
of the circle.

I only realized that my backpack was missing when I saw
it being handed in to the elder, who dug around inside it and
extracted every item one by one, laying each on the ground with
exaggerated care, until he came to the blue edition.

Somebody lit the tree behind me.

FROM THE JOURNAL OF JONATHAN HARKER,
DECEMBER 18TH, 1893 (CONTINUED)

'I could not approach you, Jonathan,' the count explained, divining my thoughts as precisely as an entymologist skewers a moth. 'You were simply too English, too Christian, too filled with pious attitudes. The reek of your pride was quite overpowering. I saw the prayer-book by your bed, the crucifix around your neck, the dowdy virgin in your locket. I knew it would be simpler to sacrifice you upon the completion of your task.' His red eyes watched mine intently. 'To suck your blood and throw your carcass to the wolves.' I stared back, not daring to flinch.

'But,' he continued with a heartfelt sigh, 'I did so need a scholar to tend my library. In London I will easily find loyal emissaries to manage my affairs, but the library needs a keeper. To be the custodian of such a rare repository of ideas requires intellect and tact. I decided instead to let you discover me, and in doing so, discover your true self. This is the purpose of the library.'

He raised a long arm, passing it over the shelves, then turned his palms to me. They were entirely covered in tiny scars.

'The library made you understand. You see, the edges of the books are marked with my blood. They just need warm hands to bring them back to life.'

I looked down at my stained and fragrant fingers, noticing for the first time how their skin had withered.

'The books are dangerous to the Christian soul, malignant in their printed ideas. Now you have read my various histories, shared my experiences, and know I am Corruption. Perhaps now you see, also, that we are not so far apart. There is but one barrier left to fall between us.'

He had risen from his chair without my noticing, and had circled behind me. His icy fingers came to rest on my neck one by one, like a spider's legs. He loosened the stiff white collar of my shirt. I heard a collar stud rattle onto the floor beside my chair.

'After tonight you will no longer need to use my library for the fulfilment of your fantasies,' he said, his steel-cold mouth descending to my throat, 'for your fantasies are to be made flesh, just as the nights will replace your days.'

I felt the first hot stab of pain as his teeth met beneath my skin. Through a haze I saw the count wipe purple lips with the back of his bony hand.

'I give you life, little Englishman,' he said, descending again. 'You will make a very loyal custodian.'

I looked from one face to the next as the villagers discussed my case. It didn't take very long for them to reach a decision. Each one in turn held out an upright fist, as if he was carrying an invisible pole.

"You can keep the book," I said, knowing that there was no point in speaking English to them but needing to say something. "If I could just read it, then I'll be on my way." I figured I could at least photograph the pages.

Two of the men walked behind me and lifted the burning tree, gripping it by the stem. When I turned to see what they were doing, I realized that it wasn't a real tree at all but some kind of engraved wooden sculpture. They discarded the upper part, scattering embers. The remaining piece, an elaborately carved hexagonal pole, was left sticking up from the ground. I was prepared to admire its workmanship until I saw that it was a sharpened stake.

Another of the men (little more than a boy, slender-necked and the only one without facial hair) walked over and kicked me onto my back with shocking ease. I landed hard on the grass, which was blackened not by fire but blood.

The men hoisted me up by my hands and feet, held me high and without any ceremony let me fall onto the stake. Crying out in unison, they stepped on my shoulders and pelvis, stamping down with as much force as they could muster.

I guess I must have screamed. I remember lifting my head and seeing this rough wood column pinning me to the earth, the bright red tip protruding from stomach, splinters sticking in my flesh like needles. In my terror I felt nothing more than a weird sensation of invasion.

The whole thing was like one of the paintings I had seen in Castle Bran; the ritual gathering of villagers, the impaling stake, the black mountains behind. All that was missing was the count himself. Past and present collapsed together. I squirmed as they fitted the top of the burning tree-sculpture back onto its base, leaving me like a pinned moth.

I was still writhing in the mud clutching my stomach when Mikaela reappeared. She studied me pityingly for a minute, then pulled me upright and slapped my rucksack against my chest. "Get in the car," she said. "You're going home. And change your jeans first. The guy who rented this out to you will get into trouble if you leave mud everywhere." I looked down at my stomach and found no broken skin, not so much as a torn stitch on my sweater. I was unharmed. We were entirely alone. The strange tree in the circle of benches was intact. There were no footprints anywhere.

My head felt like it was breaking in half. I had to make Mikaela pull over so I could throw up on the road. In my bag was the blue edition with the white edges, the one I'd brought out with me. I looked at my hands. My fingertips were still bright scarlet, and nothing would clean off the stain.

"You really are a piece of work, Carter," she said, lighting a fresh cigarette as she drove. "You come from a country that has never been sucked dry by a parasitic invader. You were raised to think you could have anything you wanted. Well, now you've been denied something, and I hope the experience stays with you."

"You knew the book would do that?" I asked, still pressing my stomach. It had seemed so real.

"Of course. I've read the full version. You wouldn't have

known not to touch it until after you had read it. The priest was smart."

"I don't understand."

"No, Carter, and you'll never be able to," said Mikaela, tapping her ash. "That's going to be your penance."

What hurt most was the realization that I could have sat down with the book and read it without touching its blood-red edges. If I had just been content to do that, I might have finally understood Stoker's true intentions for his gothic romance.

We hardly spoke again until we reached Bran, where Mikaela had left her car. Our parting was cool. She clearly didn't expect to see me again.

I thought about what Mikaela said on the way home, but I still didn't know what she meant. Reading the original version was the one thing I would never be able to do. The story would never be fully revealed to me. After having to live with the novel's impact for over a century the Transylvanians had claimed that right for themselves. To remind me of this failure day and night I only had to look at my hands, which still bore traces of my ordeal.

I went back to New York, and it took another month before I realized that Mikaela had reconciled me to a simple truth; that the story of your life is always incomplete until it's over, and you must accept it as that.

It would be more poetically apt if I could tell you I carried my *Dracula* editions up to the roof of my apartment building in Queens and out into the sunlight, where I watched them burst into flames.

Actually I sold them to an old friend at the Mysterious Bookshop on Warren Street. I made a packet of them. The count isn't coming back. Unlike Jonathan Harker, I'm free of him at last.

Hoodoo Harry

Joe R. Lansdale

T HE SUN WAS falling behind the trees as we came over the
hill in Leonard's pickup, pulling a boat trailer loaded down
with our small boat. We had been fishing and had caught a
few. Our usual method was we terrorized the poor fish and
threw them back at the end of the day, which for the fish, if you
considered the alternative, wasn't so bad.

On this day however we caught about a half dozen good-
sized perch and a couple of bass, and we thought we'd clean
them and dip them in a thick batter and fry them in a deep
Dutch oven full of popping grease.

I've cut back on my fried foods for years now, but once in a
while a bit of fried fish or fried chicken sets me right for quite
a few months and I thought this would be one of those times.
But our intended fish fry was cut short before the fish so much
as got cleaned for frying.

As we came over the hill, the trees crowding in on us from
both sides, we saw there was a blue bus coming down the
road, straddling the middle line. Leonard made with an evasive
maneuver, but by this point the trees on the right side were
gone, and there was a shallow creek visible, one that fed into
the private lake where we had been fishing. There was no other
place to go.

The bus seemed to come for us as we veered, and I saw right before impact that there was a black kid at the wheel, his eyes wild, working the steering wheel with everything he had, but it wasn't enough. He was out of control. The bus hit us with a loud smack and I remember suddenly feeling the odd sensation of the tires leaving the ground and the truck turning over in mid-air. I heard the trailer snap loose and saw the boat sailing along in front of us, and then it was out of sight and we were in the creek, the roof of the truck on the bottom of the creek bed, water coming in through the damaged windows.

I heard a slow groaning of metal and realized the bus was on top of the truck and the roof of the truck was slowly crunching down into the river bed and the floor of the truck was coming down to meet us. Another few seconds and me and Leonard would be pressed like sandwich meat.

I tried to get out of my seat belt, but nothing doing. I might as well have been fastened to that seat with duct tape. I held my breath as the water rushed in through the shattered windows, but the belt still wouldn't come loose. A little, cardboard, pine-tree-shaped air freshener floated in front of my face, a shadowed shape against the dying sunlight leaking in at the edges of the side truck windows. A moment later the belt struggle was too much and I passed out, feeling as if I were drowning. Last thing I remember before going out was Leonard had hold of my arm—

That was it.

When I came to, I was lying on the ground on my side by the edge of the creek. I was dizzy and felt like I'd been swallowed by a snake and shit down a hole. My throat was raw, and I knew I had most likely puked a batch of creek water.

I turned my head and could see the bus, which I realized now was a bookmobile. ROLLING LITERATURE was painted in large white letters on the side. It was sitting with its tires on top of Leonard's truck, the windshield blown out. I could still hear the groaning sound as the weight of it slowly squashed the truck and shoved it deeper into the creek bed. Leonard was holding an open pocket knife in his hand, the one he had used to cut my belt loose. He looked exhausted.

"Good thing you come around," Leonard said. "Mouth to mouth wasn't going to happen, pal. Come to that, I was going to be walking home alone."

"The kid?"

Leonard shook his head. "What's left of him oozed out through the bus's windshield. Glass worked on him like a cheese grater."

"Shit," I said, sitting up.

"I was you, wouldn't go look. You don't need that in your head. Bet he ain't more than twelve years old."

Books were floating out of the shattered windows of the bookmobile and were pushed along gradually by the current like dead fish. The water was either red with sunlight or with blood. Night settled in and the red in the creek turned black as ink and the bus looked like a small island out there in the shallow water.

2

Few days later, Leonard and I attended the funeral of the dead kid. We were fine after the accident, but a little stiff, and Leonard had a bit of a hitch in his git-along. That leg had been giving him trouble for years.

The funeral was attended by a half a dozen people we didn't know. The kid was named James Clifton. He didn't have any real family and had been brought up, or more accurately jerked up, in a variety of foster homes. He lived in a small community called Nesbit. Nesbit was named after the black man who founded the place back in the early nineteen hundreds. At one time Nesbit had been home to over a thousand black people, surviving after the Civil War in their own communities, selling pulp wood to the white folks out and beyond.

Over time the bulk of the community faded, mostly due to an attack on it in the late eighteen-hundreds by ex-Civil War vets and those that wished they had been Confederates. The mob decided to kill everyone in the place over the death of a little white girl. She had been savaged and cut up in a manner that didn't designate any known tool or weapon, but it was immediately assumed that "a nigger done it."

After the raid, only a couple hundred residents survived, and most of them hid out in the nearby deep woods and bottom lands for months. When they returned, the community was a shadow of its former self, with all the houses burned down, the businesses destroyed. Over time it built back up to some degree, but it was never the same. A thousand people may not sound like a lot to begin with, but in those days, it had been a sizable population for an independent black community. After the massacre, its independence was over. The surviving residents went to work for white folks. These days people still lived there, but they didn't even have internet access. A cell phone, forget it. Nesbit was like the ash from a once bright fire.

As a side note, it was later determined the little girl had been savaged by a pack of wild dogs. No apology was made. And in fact there was a sign placed outside of the community on a giant sycamore that said: DEAD NIGGERS ARE GOOD NIGGERS, AND IF THIS SIGN COMES DOWN, THERE WILL BE MORE.

Rumor was it didn't come down until nineteen twenty-five when it became so weathered it could no longer be read. When it was removed no one was killed, but within weeks a new sign with the same words on it went up. In 1965, it was finally removed and never replaced.

Nesbit was now only a post office and a general store, not too unlike the one of old that had been set afire. There were a few other little businesses along the street, a garage and tire shop, a small sawmill and lumber yard, a thrift store.

Our buddy, LaBorde Chief of Police, Marvin Hanson, had filled us in on most of this, and had ended it with, "Thing is, except for the county, maybe a Texas Ranger that wants to bother, there's no law in Nesbit, not even a constable. Well, no official law. Gardner Moost at the general store pretty much takes care of what can legally be done, and some that isn't legal. His wife runs the post office, which means she mostly sits there and reads books. As for Gardner, no one bothers him much if no one gets killed around the place."

"But the kid got killed," I said.

"Not in Nesbit. And not in LaBorde. Sheriff's office will poke around a bit, might find something, but they don't have a good record for that part of the county. There's people in that office that are descendents of the Confederates who burned the place down, killed all those people. Some of them are still fighting the Civil War, least in their minds."

"What about the bookmobile" Leonard asked.

"Eighties bus. Small school bus refurbished to be a bookmobile. It made the route of a number of black communities for years, then disappeared fifteen years ago."

"Wait a minute?" Leonard said. "Jump back on that disappeared part."

"That's the curious part. There was a black lady named Harriet Hoodalay who drove it. Everyone called her Harry. One day she and the bookmobile disappeared. I don't remember all the details, but I remember the story. Anyway, her disappearing like that, like a haint, she came to be called Hoodoo Harry. Nobody calls her anything now. Subject doesn't come up anymore. Pretty much forgotten. And until you guys got run over by the bookmobile, it was forgotten as well."

"That damn sure does fall into the range of peculiar," Leonard said.

"Where's the bookmobile now?" I said.

"Police Department impound. Accident may not have happened in our jurisdiction, but we're the ones that have the storage. We're also the ones that are going to give it a once over and give the info to the county. Odd thing about the bookmobile is except for the window blown out, tires flattened, a few bangs and scrapes, it's in great condition, like it was the day it disappeared."

"What about my truck, the boat?" Leonard said. "Y'all took them in, too."

"Hope you got insurance," Marvin said. "You can collect what's left of them at the junkyard."

Leonard sighed.

"Question is," I said, "how did that kid get the bus? I mean, hell, he couldn't drive. He was all over the place."

"He drove well enough to take it from where it's been all these years, just not well enough to keep it in his lane," Marvin said. "You boys are lucky you're alive."

"Yeah," I said, "but poor James wasn't that lucky."

"Since it was us he run over," Leonard said, "can we can take a peek at that bus?"

"Not legally," Hanson said.

"How about illegally, but we don't call it illegal?" Leonard said.

Hanson pondered on that. After what seemed long enough for all life on Earth to die off, he said, "Tell you what, if you'll wear gloves and footies, and don't touch anything—and I'm especially talking to you, Hap—we might can do that. Come to the impound around midnight."

"I don't touch things," I said.

Leonard and Marvin stared at me.

"Sometimes," I said.

3

Before it was time to go over to the impound, we did a bit of research, taking advantage of other friendships at the cop shop, the local newspaper, and the paper over in Camp Rapture. In some cases they gave us connections to people who had a bit of information they didn't have. What we got when we put it all together still wasn't much.

We discovered that James had been born in Nesbit. His father ran off when he was born, and his mother died of heart disease. Then his grandparents took him in, but when he was ten the grandfather died, and just six months before he ran over Leonard's truck with the blue bus and got himself killed, James's grandmother died. Since then, he'd been couch surfing with his relatives and friends of his relatives. Child Protective Services had missed a beat. No one knew where he'd been staying the last week. He had been out of sight and out of mind, and was now resting in a pauper's grave in Nesbit cemetery. But before he was sent there, his body was examined and it was discovered he had been tortured with burns and cuts and pokes from sharp instruments. He was also malnourished.

Online we read some old newspaper accounts about the disappearance of the bookmobile. It originated out of LaBorde, but its driver, the aforementioned Hoodoo Harry, kept it where she lived. One morning folks woke up to find she was gone, and so was the bookmobile. And no one knew where either one of them were. Or at least no one admitted it. She was supposed to go off on a vacation to visit her sister that day, catch a bus, but if she left she must have left in the bookmobile, as her car remained at home. She never arrived at her sister's.

I went over to Leonard's apartment around ten p.m. and we had a cup of coffee to stretch our night out more comfortably, and then about ten minutes before midnight, we drove from Leonard's apartment to the city compound, which was more or less just down the street. When we got there, Hanson's car was parked in its place, and out back was the compound fence and there was light poking out of the windows of a large garage tucked at the back of the property. The lot within the fence was filled with cars and trucks and even a couple of boats on blocks.

I pulled out my cell and gave Hanson a call. A few minutes later he came out of the garage and took his time strolling toward the fence.

"It's okay," Leonard called out to Hanson. "Take your

time. We're going to set up camp in a bit anyway. We brought supplies."

As Hanson arrived at the gate in the fence, he said, "You're lucky I'm letting you do this. I'm putting my ass on the line."

"Bullshit," Leonard said. "You're the police chief."

"But I'm not Police God."

"In our book you are," I said, "and oh so precious."

Hanson let us in without whacking either of us on the head with a rubber hose, and we all walked over to the garage. Inside it was so brightly lit you could almost see germs crawling on the floor. A man and a woman in evidence protection gear were wandering about.

There was a motorcycle and a few cars inside, but at the back of the place was the bookmobile, mine and Leonard's Moby Dick. The window had been replaced and the side door was open, and water still leaking out of it. There was a small smear of oil visible to the side of it where it had run out of the bottom of the bus. They had either repaired or replaced the tires to make it easier to maneuver and examine.

A short man, who might have been thirty or fifty, wearing a protective gown, gloves and footies, was standing near the bookmobile. He had a gray face shaped like the blade of a well-used axe, and his build like a stack of mud. The mud flowed when he moved, but he moved very little, just enough to reveal his natural shimmy as we introduced ourselves without shaking hands.

When we told him our names, he said, "Stump. Get suited out."

In a back room full of fresh and folded evidence suits, we dressed along with Hanson.

"Stump isn't much for lengthy conversation, is he?" I asked.

"No," Hanson said. "Bricks in his presence have died of boredom."

"Aren't bricks already dead?" Leonard asked.

"I was reaching," Hanson said.

"You got any news on the kid, or the bookmobile's sudden appearance?" I asked.

"Nope," Hanson said. "You know more than I know."

He said that because while we dressed we informed him the bits and pieces we had discovered, not revealing that in some cases they were people in his department speaking out of school.

When we were dressed we went back to the bookmobile.

Stump was standing pretty much where we had left him. I think he had moved a few inches to the right. Maybe he had peed in the old spot.

"What can you tell us?" Hanson said.

"I can tell you don't screw up my evidence, which is the whole damn bus. They got to do this, Captain?"

"No," Hanson said, "but believe it or not, they have solved a few things in their time. They don't have as much to do as we do, and they are dogged."

"Yeah, well, I guess that's some kind of reason," Stump said.

We went up the metal steps of the bookmobile and eased our way inside. I stood by the steering wheel and looked back through the bus. Though water still leaked from the bottom of the bus, the inside had been dried out after evidence was collected. There were lights strung in there. The books were all gone, and the shelves had warped a bit. In the back there was a curved metal hull that had been put in, perhaps to house a larger fuel tank. A small door was off to the right of where I was looking. The toilet.

It was so clean, I said, "Looks like you've already collected evidence."

Stump, who was behind us, standing on the top step into the bookmobile, said, "I have. But I don't want you adding any evidence that isn't evidence. Get me?"

"Yep," Leonard said. "We got you."

"That hull at the back," Leonard said, touching on what I had noticed first off, "what's it for?"

"Usually they put that kind of thing in to have a large gas tank, all the traveling they do out in the country. That was probably put in the minute it became a bookmobile."

"I've never heard of that," Hanson said.

"You an expert on bookmobiles?" Stump said.

"Point taken," Hanson said.

"Actually, I only seen a few buses and such with that," Stump said. "Sometimes it isn't a gas tank, but a crapper tank. That way the toilet doesn't need to be emptied out as often. Toilet works, by the way. Everything worked on this thing before it went off the road and took a swim. It has a bit of an oil leak that could be due to the wreck, but I don't think so. From looking it over I think that's been an ongoing problem, but other than the window and the original tires gone flat, it's in remarkably good shape."

I walked toward the back, looking left and right as I went.

"You two ace detectives find anything, please let me know," Stump said. "I wouldn't want to not learn a thing or two from the experts."

"You don't know our lives," Leonard said. "We could actually be smart."

Stump made a grunting sound. "I got a pretty good idea about your lives, and I'm thinking it isn't pretty."

"So you been over every inch?" I said.

"I might have missed a centimeter under the shitter, but yeah," Stump said. "You see, it's my job."

I ran my gloved hand over the top of the backend section, the place where the tank would be contained. "What if it isn't a tank in here?"

"What else would it be?" Stump said.

"Always ask questions," I said, "that is the path to wisdom."

"Fucking Confucius?" Stump said

"Hap Collins," I said.

"Look, I was about to take the bolts out of that thing. I was even going to lift off the top and look inside. Thought that up all by myself before you got here."

"Now," Leonard said, "don't start selling yourself for more than you are."

Stump grunted again and left the bookmobile.

"He seems to like you guys," Hanson said.

A moment later, the man and the woman we had seen wandering the garage entered with battery powered tools, pushed past us, went to the back, removed the bolts, and lifted the top off the covering. They carried it away with them without even looking inside. Curiosity would not kill those cool cats.

When they left the bus with the metal top, Stump reappeared and waddled down the aisle toward the now open container. He had a flashlight in his hand. He turned it on and looked inside, turned his head from left to right, said, "Huh."

We went over and looked. Stacked from left to right, six in a row, were oil-covered, time-withered little bodies, and one larger one.

"How about that?" Stump said.

"We told you that you ought to look," Leonard said.

"And I told you I was about to," Stump said.

"You say that now," Leonard said.

"I hate both you bastards," Stump said.

"You now belong to a sizable club," Hanson said.

4

You can bet that threw a wrench into things. Where before there was the problem of the long missing bookmobile and its return due to a twelve-year-old boy driving it for reasons unknown, not to mention his death by accident, now we had six oil-covered bodies to identify, tucked up in the back of the bookmobile.

Who put those bodies there? Where had the bookmobile been for all those years, and why did it look brand new? And while we're making a list, where was Hoodoo Harry? Was hers the larger oil-soaked body?

Well, I'd like to tell you it all came together, mysteries solved, but it didn't. In fact, a few weeks passed by. They examined the corpses and sent off DNA samples from the bodies, five off which turned out to be kids, but that was all they knew. No DNA matches. The sixth one was a female adult, but if it was Hoodoo Harry, no one had yet tracked down a relative to make the determination. But the search was in progress.

Complication on complication multiplied by more complications.

Me and Leonard felt pretty smart for a few weeks about the bookmobile container, but truth was, we weren't expecting bodies at all. And further truth was, Stump and his forensic crew were minutes from discovering what was there. So had we not shown up, they'd have found the bodies anyway.

As the weeks went by, I began to feel agitated, and had trouble sleeping at night. One night, lying in bed with Brett, I was tossing and turning, and she flipped on the night stand light, rolled over and lifted herself on one elbow and looked at me.

"What the hell, Hap? You been acting like a jumping bean for a week. Moan and groan all night."

"I moan and groan?" I said, sitting up in bed, looking at the beautiful Brett, her flame-red hair tied back in a pony tail.

"Yep."

"I'm bothering you?"

"Only when I'm trying to sleep. Or lie still. And you go to the toilet all night. What's up with that?"

"Poo-poo."

"Six, seven times a night?"

"Well, I go in there and read."

"Why can't you sleep?"

"I don't know."

"It's the kid, isn't it?"

"Guess it is. Think about him a lot. I close my eyes, I see his eyes, looking out of the windshield of that bookmobile."

Brett fluffed her pillow and folded it against the headboard and put her back against it.

"You been looking into it?" she asked.

"No. Hanson said it was his case to investigate."

"That's never stopped you and Leonard before."

"It hasn't, but, I guess we didn't know where to go with this."

Brett pursed her lips, said, "You know what? Just look up the old route of the bookmobile, and follow it."

"Marvin's done that."

"But he isn't you, Hap."

"No. He isn't. He's smarter and a good investigator."

"Yeah, well, you do have that going against you. But is he more dogged than you and Leonard?"

"Hanson used the same word. But I think he's the one that's dogged."

"More dogged than you and your bro?"

"I'm not sure how you measure things on a dogged scale. I'm not sure I know what a dogged scale is. I'm not sure there is one."

"I'll tell you right now, you are more dogged. You and Leonard need to get back on the trail and figure things out so I can get a good night's sleep. And here's another idea. How about you look up Cason Statler's friend, the one who runs the newspaper morgue in Camp Rapture. Have him check into things for you. He can find more in a day than the law can find in a month. That guy, isn't his name Mars, something like that?"

"Mercury."

"He has the mind for looking into conspiracies, or whatever is going on here. No one knows odd information and can evaluate it better than that guy. Or so you've told me. Get him to do some kind of... I don't know, chart about the route of the bookmobile, then look into missing persons in that area, on the route. Might be something in that."

"You're smart," I said.

"I know that," she said.

"Since you're awake, want to fool around?"

"No. And if you ever expect to again, you better quit tossing, moaning and groaning and talking to yourself."

"I talk to myself, too?"

"Yep."

Brett turned out the light. "Now, close your little Hap eyes and shut your little Hap mouth, and go the fuck to sleep."

5

Cason Staler is a Pulitzer Prize winning writer that works at the Camp Rapture newspaper. We've known him for awhile. Handsome and quirky, quick of wit, he can also hold his own in a fist fight. He's a guy with a bunch of odd friends. Including us. He's a big dog over at the paper. His friend, Mercury, works downstairs in the news morgue, sometimes known as the first level of Hell. Mercury is a kind of a genius. Cason told him about us, explained our problem, and left us to it.

Down there they have all the back issues of the paper, as well as all manner of stuff, stacked up this way and that. You have to wind your way through it all to find Mercury. Down there he was king. Of course, he was the only one that worked down there, so the job position was easily filled.

Mercury was blond and pale, but looked strong. His job was to put all the old newspapers on the computer, then send the originals off to somewhere where they were collected by someone for some reason unknown. In his spare time, Mercury conducted investigations of his own. Some of them were nutty. Crop circles. Flying saucers. The Kennedy assassination, involving everyone but Bigfoot, though in time he might work him in as well. But he was smart and helpful, if you could point his nose in the right direction. He loved a good mystery, and he had a way of calculating odd situations into a recognizable patterns.

After we wound our way through the stacks and came up on Mercury, he said, "Welcome to the center of the earth."

The overhead light was thin back there, but there was a bright lamp on his desk, and there was another on a table that was pushed up against it. Both lamps had metal shades over the bulbs, but those had been tilted so as to let more of the light leak out.

On the table were books, assorted newspapers, clippings, an old microfilm machine, and on a chair was a small TV and an old fashioned VCR. The VCR cord was fastened to the back of the TV and plugged into a plastic power strip on the floor. The wire from his computer was plugged to the bar as well.

"How are you men?" he said.

"We're fine," Leonard said. "Cason says you can help us."

"That depends. He told me what you're looking for, and I've pulled out a few things, got some stuff on the computer I can show you."

Mercury inched over to it, seated himself in front of it, touched a button. The computer lit up like a Christmas display. "There's not a lot here, but what's here is of interest. Here is the path of the bookmobile."

We took a gander at the place he was pointing, a map with a moving arrow.

"You can see that it covered quite a bit of ground, but most if it, the places where Harriet stopped, were right near Nesbit. Made a few stops in areas where there were neighborhoods, if you can call a half-dozen houses neighborhoods. Folks wanted books, they either had to be in town at the post office at the right time, or they had to be at one of these stop areas. Six altogether. Last two stops were well out in the country. Wasn't like it was a money-making business, driving the bookmobile. Harry came once a week, three times a month, then there was a week off. When she wasn't making this run through Nesbit and the surrounding area, she was on other routes. She drove four days a week, three weeks a month."

Mercury showed us a few more routes around LaBorde, a spot or two out in the country that were destinations.

"Those are routes on days when she worked outside of the Nesbit area. Way I'd think about it is Harry was from Nesbit, so that would be the hub of everything for her. Also, there have been missing persons cases around Nesbit in the last few years, couple of kids, and Harriet Hoodalay."

"Quite a coincidence," Leonard said.

Mercury considered for a moment.

"Place small as Nesbit, you want to connect anyone to the missing kids, you could make the case for everyone there, the community being so small, being so few people. And the missing kids came from the area. Also possible none of what happened in and around Nesbit is related, but that's where you can make the case that there might be too much coincidence. The law of averages come into play. Someone in, or around Nesbit, is most likely responsible for the kids, but are they responsible for Harriet and the bookmobile? Still likely."

"Harry and the bookmobile could have come up missing on one of the other routes," I said.

"Merely saying the most likely scenario is it happened near her home, near Nesbit, and probably someone who knew her, and the two missing kids are related to it all, because that's who a bookmobile is specifically designed for. Anyone can check out a book, but it's bored kids, kids that don't have library access, that they are trying to appeal to. Thing is, now even poor kids have computers and the internet, and with all the lights and bells and whistles, books get lost to a time when we had more patience and less to distract us."

"We found more than two kids in the bookmobile," Leonard said.

"Can't help you there, but if you nose around a bit, you might find more missing than have been reported. I'm going to strongly guess they are all from the same area, and what you're dealing with is a child predator, someone who likes to stick close to the place he knows. Way it usually works in these cases.

And one reason you may not know about the other kids, is they may not have been reported. Neglect is just the thing that puts them in a bad spot, causes them to fall between the cracks. Not the only thing, but a major factor."

"Think it could have been Harry?" Leonard asked.

"Could be, but then we got to ask, where has she been all this time? After she disappeared there were no more child abduction cases reported, so that leans toward her possibly being responsible, but she doesn't fit the profile, and nothing was known about the bookmobile until it nearly ran you over. The kid inside, that leans toward him being a victim as well, or a potential victim. An escapee. But I go back to what I said before. Just because we have a report of two children doesn't mean that's all there is. You found six bodies, and one not a child, that could be folks who haven't been reported, and the adult could just be Harry."

Mercury paused, tapped the keys. A new image came up. It was of a middle-aged black woman.

"Harriet Hoodalay," he said. "What I found from looking through older microfilm. You know about her supposedly taking a bus trip to see her sister, I assume. Her not arriving?"

"Do you know who first reported her missing?"

"Gardner Moost."

"General store guy?" Leonard said.

"Correct," Mercury said. "Said he got that information from her husband, Tom Hoodalay. Tom didn't report her missing when her vacation ended and she didn't come back. Gardner asked why she hadn't come home and Tom told Moost he figured Harriet had run off from him."

"What's Harriet's sister say?"

"She never arrived, but she did buy a bus ticket. No one was doing a head count when it came time to get on the bus, and the bus line closed down its hub here years ago. Whoever worked there back then has scattered to the wind."

"Maybe Harriet found out something about her husband," I said. "Like how Tom was using her connection to children to do something he wasn't supposed to. She decided to get away from him, go see her sister. He was afraid she'd spill the beans to the law, so he killed her."

"Possible, but unknown," Mercury said. "But Nesbit, that's where you begin."

6

We drove over to Nesbit in my car.

It was a nice drive and a nice day. Not too warm for the time of year. We cruised along the highway for several miles, and into an area where the trees grew thick and the houses were far apart.

Nesbit was off the highway, down a roughly paved road. As we came into the community we saw the post office on one side, general store on the other. Tire and mechanic shop, and so on, were all nearby. We were through the place before we knew it, and I had to turn around and drive us back. First place we stopped was the general store.

It was like stepping back in time. The place was chock-full of cool items, things that I forgot existed, like mule plowing equipment. Not a lot of it, but even some was surprising. There were long shelves of canned goods, prepared by locals, sold on consignment, and there were the sort of things you expected. High shelves with bolts of cloth. Tools. There was a series of bins in the middle of the store, stuffed with fresh vegetables, and according to a sign, locally raised.

There was a counter with a lot of old candies and soft drinks I had forgotten about. There was a break in the piles of goods on that counter, and there was an old fashioned cash register with a black man behind it, sitting on a stool. He was a big fellow, and though he was sitting, I could tell he would tower over both me and Leonard. He had shoulders as wide as a bank vault. He had a red tone to his skin, what in the old days they used to refer to as a red bone Negro, when they were being polite. He had reddish freckles scattered on his cheeks. His hands, which were clutched around a hunting magazine, were about the size of catcher's mitts. He looked to be in his sixties, had a fringe of white hair around his head, just over his ears and nowhere else.

At the counter we greeted him. He put down his magazine and eyed us carefully.

"I help you fellas?" he said.

"Maybe," I said. "We work for a private detective agency out of LaBorde. We're trying to find out about James Clifton. I'm Hap Collins, and this is my associate, Leonard Pine."

"Gardner Moost," he said. "Yeah. Sad story. But what can be done for him now?"

"What we're trying to figure out," Leonard said, "is how he came by a bookmobile that had been missing for years, and what was he doing driving it?"

"Don't know what I can tell you. Poor boy was hard luck. Lost most of his family. Good kid, though. Had him a little part time job at the tire shop. You know, picking up things a couple hours after school. Old tires, this and that. He was sleeping at different homes. He slept in the back here a few times. I was thinking of letting him stay full time. Maybe give him a little work on the weekends. Tire shop didn't use him all week. As for the rest, I don't know. I don't think I saw him around the week he ended up gone. I doubt he was going to school. Was supposed to be, but I'd see him walking down the road, not really seeming to be going anywhere. An hour later, you'd see him walk back. I guess I saw him last on a Monday. Then the rest of the week he wasn't about. Didn't think much of it. Reason I know he was missing is because he finished up at the tire shop, he'd come over, buy him a pop and a candy bar. Every day. Next thing I know he's dead, and I hear he was in that old bookmobile. Beyond that, I don't know a thing about him or the missing bookmobile."

"Did you know Harriet Hoodalay?" I said.

That gave Moost pause.

"Yes. I did know Harry. Lovely woman."

"Do you know her husband?" I said. I knew he did, from what Mercury had told us, but I wanted to see where he'd go with it.

He nodded. "Yeah."

"We ask," said Leonard, "because Harriet used to drive the bookmobile, then she disappeared. Supposed to be going up North to see her sister but never made it."

"I never believed that story," Moost said.

"Oh," I said, "and why is that?"

"I think she might have meant to see her sister, but I don't think the bus took a wrong turn at Amarillo and let her out in a pasture, or some such. I think her husband killed her. Tom's a mean sonofabitch. Me and him don't get along. He shops somewhere other than here. I banned him from the store when Harry came up missing those years back."

"You say he's mean," Leonard said. "But how mean?"

"He beat on her from time to time."

"So you and her were close?" I said.

"Look, if you two are going to be snooping about, might as well tell you. Me and Harry, we had a thing. Went on for awhile. She told me Tom was brutal. I saw the bruises. She was going to take a bus and see her sister, all right, but the plan was me and her would get together later. She'd get a divorce and we'd marry. But she didn't get a divorce, and she didn't come back. At first, at least a little, I thought she had changed her mind, didn't want what I thought she wanted. But deep down, always figured her husband did her in. Told the cops that, some sheriff's deputy, but they didn't find anything to prove it. They dropped it. I told Tom last time he was in here, years ago, not to come back, just because I didn't like him. Later, I married. Still married. Happily. But me and Harry, we had our moment."

"Slightly off the subject," I said, "but the bookmobile. Did she like that work? Every have any problems?"

"She mentioned a bit of this and that. Kids stealing a book, acting up. But nothing special. She did seem tense days before she was supposed to catch that bus."

"Tense?" Leonard said.

"Maybe her husband was worrying her. He didn't know she wasn't coming back, but I think right before she left, she might have told him. Couldn't hold it in. Figure they got in a fight, he killed her, and she's buried somewhere out in the woods behind their house."

I didn't say we thought she might have ended up in a compartment in the bookmobile.

"Anything special you remember about the bookmobile from that time?" Leonard said.

"That's been awhile."

"Anything?" Leonard said.

"Just that Turner, over there at the tire and mechanic shop, was going to fix the bookmobile up. Needed new tires, some general maintenance. Always leaked oil. No matter what they did to it, it leaked oil."

"So her route was closed out for her vacation?" I said.

"They had another driver, and I think Harry was supposed to drive the bookmobile over to him, but then the bookmobile disappeared, and that was it. People out of LaBorde who had been paying for it decided they weren't going to try and replace it, so that was all she wrote.

"Who was this new driver?" Leonard asked.

"Will Turner, works over at the tire shop."

7

Will Turner was a skinny man that I judged to be in his early forties, dark of skin, almost as dark as Leonard. He had a pleasant face and skinned knuckles, probably from dealing with tools and tires day in and day out, though it was hard for me to imagine a lot of business in Nesbit.

"Yeah," Will Turner said. "I took the job, but then the bookmobile got stolen, and that was the end of it. So I just work here for Donnie James. I been working here since I was a kid, started just like James did, doing odd jobs."

"What kind of kid was James?" I asked.

"Quiet. Never said much, so you never knew much about him. Did his work, couple hours a day. Except for that, he was kind of wandering about, sleeping and eating where he could. I don't really know much about him."

We were standing inside the doorway of the tire and mechanic shop. It was one of those doors that was wide and made of the same aluminum as the building. End of the day you pulled it closed and padlocked it. It was a small building, and it was stuffed with tires, and there was an upper deck supported by a series of two by eights, and one in particular looked as if it was about to retire from the job. It looked as if insects had been at it. There was a long aluminum building out back of the garage. We could see it through the open back section of the shop. Having the doors open on both ends was a good choice, because a nice breeze was blowing.

"That post there," I said, "it looks as if it's about to give up the ghost."

Will looked toward it. "Yep. I have to go up there and get a tire, mostly for older foreign cars, I'm always a little nervous. Take it slow and easy. Been on Donnie for a year to get it fixed. He can be cheap."

"If you don't mind me asking," I said, "you get a lot of business here in Nesbit?"

Will laughed. "Nope. Still, we got a reputation, and folks bring their cars in from miles around. We mostly make money on mechanic work, but we sell a few tires too. But a lot of business? No."

"Moost was telling us you been working here a long time," Leonard said.

"I have. That's a fact."

"Let me ask you something about Harriet Hoodalay and the bookmobile. She was supposed to pass that job to you, right?"

"That's right. I was only a kid then, twenty-three, working part time here, and I needed extra money. Driving the bookmobile wasn't much, but hey, it was something to add to the pot."

"Did Harriet drop the bookmobile off with you?" I said.

"Was supposed to, that night. She didn't show, though. Thought she might have got tied up with something and I'd find out about it the next day. Figured she could have left it for me here at the garage. We discussed that as an option and I was figuring maybe she got confused on what we had finally decided. Next day I found out she and the bookmobile had gone missing. And I was out some easy money."

"Did you know Harriet well?" Leonard said.

"Not really. Nice lady, far as I could tell. Saw her around. Knew she drove the bookmobile. She brought it here to be worked on time or two. We talked a little. You know, small talk. Nothing special. I think she liked the job, liked kids. Never had any of her own."

"Okay," I said, "we'd like to talk to your boss, Mr. James."

Will looked at his watch. "Back about two. On lunch break. Takes longer breaks these days."

"What's the building out back?"

"Oh, boss has a tractor, some equipment for this and that. He goes around and does farm work from time to time. Breaking up gardens, sometimes large fields. Side work."

"Where would Donnie be having lunch? Home?"

"Naw. He's not married and he's a terrible cook. He can't put a peanut butter and jelly sandwich together without it tasting like tar paper. There's a little place down the road. Ethel's. Not much to it, open for lunch and dinner. Used to be open for breakfast, but stopped doing that last year. Alright food. Ethel and her husband Bernard run it."

"Thanks, Will," I said, and me and Leonard went out.

8

Ethel's was indeed small. A little, yellow frame house. What would have normally been the living room had been turned into a dining area. A few tables and chairs were scattered about. A counter had been put in, as well as an opening into the kitchen; a cut out in the wall where the food could be passed to the waitress, who I assumed was Ethel. She was petite, had a look on her face of perpetual worry, as if she feared forgetting a French fry order. Through the gap in the wall we could see a big black man, possibly Bernard, standing in front of an old fashioned grill, flipping burgers. He looked big enough to turn over the grill.

Waitress said, "Pick a seat."

That was easy, the place was packed, except for one small table in the corner, and we took that. The table wobbled when I put my hands on it.

"Shall we eat?" Leonard said.

"Yep. Let's hope the food is better than the furniture."

"It's packed here," he said. "That's a good sign."

"Choices are limited."

I looked around trying to spot someone I thought might be Donnie. That was easy. A man with Tire and Mechanic Shop written across the back of a khaki work shirt was moving toward the cash register, his ticket in hand.

I got up, went over, said, "Are you Donnie James?"

He nodded.

I gave him the synopsis version of what me and Leonard were doing convinced him to sit down with us, but not before I agreed to pay his check.

"I got to get back to work, fellas," he said. "Make this quick. I don't think I know a thing that could help. Thanks for lunch, by the way. I hope you find out who did what to those children. Saw in the paper about all those kids, and the woman in the bookmobile. Terrible. Coated in oil. Why would anyone do that?"

"Preserve the bodies a little," I said. "I think whoever did it liked looking at them. Oil probably killed some of the stink."

"I guess so," Donnie said.

"How well did you know Harriet?" Leonard asked.

"Not too well. Except for driving the bookmobile, Tom kept her on a pretty tight leash. I was you, he's the one I'd talk to. I figure he's got her in a fifty gallon drum under his front porch. Tom's a jerk. Always thought men were trying to take Harry from him. One time, right here, they got into it at supper time over something. He called her a bitch. She got up and went outside and stood by their pickup until he paid up and went out. I was sitting over there by the window. I saw him grab her arm and push her into the truck. He's a bully, even at his age, retired and always on his front porch or he's out back in the yard lifting weights. Old as he is, I seen him get into it at the post office with a young man over something. I don't know what. I'm sure it was Tom started things. But he whipped that young man like he was a heavy bag. Hit him at will, and finally dropped him. Gardner Moost stood up to him, though, about how he treated Harry. I mean, hell, everyone here knows everyone else's business. Gardner's owner of the General store."

"We've met," Leonard said.

"Then you've seen Gardner. Tom's afraid of him, and with good reason. When he was younger, Gardner cleaned out a few bars down Houston way, or so I've heard. But Tom is no slouch either. Got a bum knee, but I think Gardner could take him. Someone like you two, he'd run you together so hard he'd make one of you."

"We talked to Moost," Leonard said. "He told us about Tom, how he banned him. Another thing. James Clifton. What kind of kid was he?"

"Didn't say much. Did some little clean up jobs for me. Knew he had it rough, so I was trying to help him out. That's about all I got. Who works for who, here? You the boss, white man?"

"I want to be, but he won't let me," I said.

"And he won't let me," Leonard said. "Brett Sawyer is our boss."

"Who's he?"

"She," I said.

"Ah," he said. "Well, good luck finding out what happened to Harry. She was good people. Like me, she cared about children. That's why I fixed that bookmobile on my own time, even donated tires. It was mostly children got something out of that bookmobile. Me, I was never much of a reader. Always figured by not being I missed out on things. Might be doing something other than a tire shop if I'd gotten a real education. Then again, folks need tires and they need cars fixed."

"No disagreement there," Leonard said.

"I got to go. Good luck."

Donnie got up and went out.

Leonard said, "Tom Hoodalay seems to get a lot of bad marks."

"Maybe we ought to check Tom's report card personally," I said.

"Not until I get a burger. I'm so hungry I could eat the ass out of a menstruating mule."

9

The burgers were good. Much better than I assumed the ass of a menstruating mule would be. We ate, and found out from Ethel, who was indeed the waitress, where Tom Hoodalay lived.

It was a small house not far off the road near the center of Nesbit. It was a down a narrow, cracked, concrete drive, and at the end of the drive was a small, dilapidated house with an old brown pickup in the yard.

Weeds grew waist high on both sides of the house, out to the edge of the drive, and the drive seemed to be fighting a losing battle against the weeds growing up between the cracks in the concrete. Another few months, you could film a Tarzan movie out there. There was a small overhang porch, and there was a long wooden bench on the porch, and on the bench sat a man I took for Tom Hoodalay. He was crouched there like a frog on steroids.

We parked in the drive next to the pickup, got out and walked up to the steps. There were chunks of concrete breaking off in the drive next to the step. Leonard put his foot on a chunk and wobbled it with his boot.

"Who the hell are you?" the man said.

Up close I could tell he was in his sixties, but it was a powerful sixties. He had a head like a soccer ball. It was shaved and smooth as an oiled doorknob and glistened in the sunlight. He had a lot of white teeth and his eyes were both red where they should be white. His pupils, swimming in the middle of all that redness, were chocolate colored. He had very little neck and was almost as wide as Gardner Moost. I thought the two of them went at it, it might be a close fight. Nesbit seemed to have a lot of large people.

"We're Avon," Leonard said.

"The hell you are," the man said.

"Naw, just messing with you," Leonard said. "You Tom Hoodalay?"

"What if I am?"

"Might be a prize involved," Leonard said.

This had already gone south. Leonard obviously didn't like the guy on sight. I wasn't fond of him either, and all he had said so far was "Who the hell are you?"

"We work for a private detective agency out of LaBorde," I said. "We are looking into the death of a child, James Clifton."

"That worthless little nigger? Shit, he better off dead."

"Why would that be?" Leonard said.

"Ain't got nobody, ain't got no future," Tom Hoodalay said.

"He wrecked a bookmobile that had been missing for fifteen years, one your former wife used to drive," I said.

"Heard about that," he said.

"Any idea where the bookmobile was all these years?" I asked.

"How the fuck would I know? I been asked that already. Years ago."

"Your wife used to drive it," I said. "I thought you might have some clue."

"I ain't got nothing to do with where she went, or where that damn bookmobile went. I ain't got no concern about neither."

"You're saying the kid was better off dead, huh?" Leonard said.

"What I said, ain't it?"

"Cause you wouldn't want James to end up... Like you?"

"What the fuck you talking about, nigger?"

With that, Tom Hoodalay stood up. He was even bigger than I thought.

"Way we got it figured," Leonard said, "is you used to slap your wife around, because you could. What happened Tommy? Wife catch you with your dick up a kid's ass?"

Tom actually yelled. More of a bellow really. He turned, and slammed his fist down on the long bench. It shattered, some of the fragments hitting me in the chest.

"Damn," I said.

"You showed that bench," Leonard said.

My man Leonard is never one to use common sense in an excitable moment. He's more akin to the guy that throws gasoline on a fire, then goes to get more.

Tom Hoodalay was coming off the porch. He limped a little, an old injury was my guess. He brought a leg of the bench with him, and he was swinging it about, and he wasn't all the way down the steps yet.

Leonard picked up the chunk of concrete under his foot, cocked it back, said, "Bet you flinch," and threw it.

The sunlight caught the white concrete and made it shine,

and then it hit Hoodalay right between the eyes. He staggered, came tripping along and collapsed to his knees. David had just knocked the shit out of Goliath.

Hoodalay loosened his grip on the bench leg. Leonard sprang forward, grabbed the leg, said, "Give me that."

And then Leonard swung the leg, caught Tom Hoodalay right upside the head, causing him to go face down into the driveway.

"There's your prize," Leonard said.

"So much for asking questions," I said.

Leonard tossed the bench leg away and looked down at Tom's unconscious body. "He wasn't gonna tell us anything anyway."

"You hit him pretty hard," I said. "Maybe too hard."

"I just stunned the hippopotamus," Leonard said. "Wakes up, he'll wish he hadn't torn up a perfectly good bench."

"Or got hit between the eyes with a piece of concrete and then battered with a board."

"That too," Leonard said.

10

As I was driving us away, Leonard said, "I don't like that bastard, but I don't think he killed the kids. Call it instinct, and also the fact that though he's big, he gets around like a pig on stilts. Maybe he killed his wife, but a guy like him strangles his wife, then tells the cops it was self-defense. She came at him with a paring knife, or some such. I don't think he's smart enough to plan what to do with the body, and certainly not smart enough to stay quiet about it all these years. He's the kind of dumb ass brags about a thing like that."

"Maybe," I said.

I drove us around a bit, nothing really in mind. We tossed out an idea or two, but we arrived at nothing. Anybody we had spoken to could have done it, and none of them could have done it.

I finally convinced Leonard to let me drive back to Tom's place, just to make sure he wasn't collecting vultures.

"He might shoot at us this time," Leonard said.

I drove back there anyway, and as we came up the drive, I could see that he was no longer lying where we left him. Fragments of the bench had been gathered up and stacked by the porch steps.

"All right," I said. "He lives."

We backed out, and I drove us back to LaBorde. There wasn't anything else left for us to do. I dropped Leonard off at his place, and then I called Brett. She was at the office, finishing up some paperwork on a divorce case she had been working. I hated that kind of stuff, but frankly it was the sort of business they kept us in biscuits.

When I arrived at our office and parked in the lot, the bicycle shop lady downstairs was wearing her shorts, as usual. I noticed, as usual, because I'm biologically driven to do so, then I went upstairs and saw the only woman that really matters to me in that kind of way.

Brett said, "So, find out anything?"

"Found out we don't know anything."

Brett was sitting behind the desk with her hair pulled back into a ponytail. She was working on some papers with a pen. She was dressed in jeans and an oversized tee-shirt, had on slip-on, white, tennis shoes.

"I got a little bit of paperwork left, then we can get something to eat. Nothing fancy, obviously. I want to stay sloppy."

"LaBorde doesn't have much that's fancy," I said.

"True," she said, and got busy on her paperwork.

I picked up the newspaper on the edge of the desk, started reading. The bookmobile and the murder of James Clifton weren't even on the second page. Third page, at the bottom. The article was thin. James had been driving, he ran off the road, hit a truck (occupants unnamed, but unhurt), and there was an investigation into his death and into the mystery of where the bookmobile had been all these years. Some bodies had been found.

By the time I had finished reading the rest of the paper, which didn't take long, Brett was up and we were out. We traveled in my car. After dinner, I would drop her back at the office to pick up hers.

We went to a small joint that served Ecuadorian food. It was off Universal Street, and it was good. After I dropped Brett back at her car, we met up at the house. It seemed a little empty when we first came in. My daughter Chance had been living with us, along with a rescue mutt we named Buffy. Actually, Leonard had rescued her, but I had ended up with the dog. Now Buffy was with Chance. Until last year, I didn't know I had a daughter. I missed her. I missed Buffy.

We watched a couple TV shows, then we went to bed. I fell asleep quickly. I didn't sleep long. When I awoke it was still solid dark. I had dreamed I was reaching for a butterfly that kept flittering out of the way. I had an uncomfortable feeling that butterfly was representative of me having knowledge I didn't understand. A common problem. Then again, I might have merely been dreaming about butterflies. Thing was, now, I was wide awake.

To keep from tossing and turning, I slipped out of bed, went downstairs and made an early breakfast. After I finished my oatmeal, I sat and sipped coffee, glancing out the kitchen window at the darkness. I tried to collect my thoughts, tried to catch my butterfly. I thought about all of the people we had talked to, thought back on that poor kid's face as the bookmobile barreled down on us. I thought back to finding those oily bodies in the container in the bookmobile. And then I thought, wait a minute.

I called Leonard on my cell. He was none too happy to hear from me.

"It's dark outside," he said.

"All the better for clandestine activity," I said. "Get dressed. I'm coming to pick you up."

"You don't dare come this way for an hour," he said. "I'm going to eat and shower, but right before that, me, and the extra-nice Officer Carroll, are going to play rodeo."

Officer Carroll, as we both called him, was Leonard's new love interest. Nice guy and a nice cop, one of Marvin's people.

"Don't get any rope burns," I said. "But an hour is too late. It still needs to be dark when we get where we're going."

"Twenty minutes, then," Leonard said.

"Bring protection."

"We use protection."

"No. Bring it, and I don't mean the kind you're talking about. You show up with a Trojan and I'll beat you to death."

"I use one of those big garbage bags, you know, something that'll hold the meat."

"Yeah, right."

I had another cup of coffee, took a quick shower, wrote Brett a note, dressed and drove over to Leonard's apartment. Officer Carroll was coming out as I arrived. He's constructed like a large artillery shell.

"I hope you boys aren't going to get in trouble," he said.

"Us? Heaven forbid."

"Don't tell me anything. I know it's best I don't know."

After I got Leonard hustling along, a granola bar in one fist, a cup of coffee in the other, I told him what had come to me, and then I drove us back to Nesbit.

11

It was still dark, and in East Texas, wandering about near people's homes and places of business during the night is the sort of thing that could get you shot. Growing up I had been able to walk to people's houses if the need came about and ask to borrow their phone, or some such, without expecting to be shot into Swiss cheese by some fearful and angry home owner. The days of close neighbors had almost passed, and in its place was a cloud of anger and suspicion and a lot of hardware of the killing kind.

Still, we parked to the side of the General store and chanced it, walked between the store and the tire shop, wandered out to the big building at the back of Donnie James' place. There was a night light in front and back of the building, and we stood out like bugs in a porch light. I took out my handy little lock pick kit, and easily defeated the padlock. Once we pulled the door aside, there was yet another door, and its locks were a little more difficult.

"Hold it," Leonard said. "Alarm system."

Leonard had discovered a little black panel on the inside of the second door fastened to the wall. He took out his pocket knife and popped the cover, used the blade to cut a wire.

"Might as well have been on the honor system," he said.

We got that door slid aside as well, then closed it behind us. I took out my penlight and flashed it around. There was a big tractor in the center of the building, some farm equipment attachments, and not much else.

We walked around for awhile, but no clues jumped at us.

"Okay," Leonard said. "What are we looking for?"

"I don't know exactly, but I have a strong feeling it's here."

Leonard pulled out his own penlight, and we split up and went around the building looking for whatever might look like a clue.

Reason we were there was I had thought about Donnie James. He had mentioned the boy's and the woman's body in the bookmobile, but then reading the paper, where he said he got his news, I realized that the bodies in the bookmobile had not been mentioned. Marvin had most likely not revealed those things on purpose, to have one up on the killer, so how had Donnie James known about it?

It was possible someone leaked the information, but if they

had, I doubted it went all the way to Nesbit and to the owner of a tire shop. Again, possible, but not likely. Marvin ran a tight ship.

We met up by the tractor, turned off our penlights and stood there a moment.

"Nothing," Leonard said.

"Same."

After a brief moment, Leonard turned back on his penlight, said, "Place looks bigger on the outside."

"Yeah."

"Because it is," he said.

I turned on my light again, flashed it around. On the right there were windows in the wall, and on the left there were not. That could have merely been a builder's choice, but something didn't seem right.

I started over to that wall, and Leonard went along with me. When we got there he tapped on it with his fist.

"Okay," he said. "Pretty sure it's hollow."

"No doors. No windows, but a hollow wall means another room."

"Uh-huh. And this aluminum looks fresh, like it's been added lately. Maybe after the kid stole the bus and ran off with it."

That got me excited.

We walked along the length of the wall, and near the front of the building I thought it looked a little odd. I pressed against it. The wall moved a little. There was a separate piece of aluminum that had been used to fill out the wall; it looked all of one piece if you weren't paying attention. I worked with it some more and it slid aside on rollers. It left a gap big enough to walk through, but there was a chain and lock through it and the main wall. We could have slipped under the chain, but I decided to make it easier.

I took out my lock-pick kit and snapped the padlock open. Once that was done, we were able to push it wider. We slipped in behind it.

Using my penlight, I found a switch and flipped it. Lights

came on along the stretch of hidden chamber. It was a full twelve feet wide, and maybe forty feet long. On the concrete floor was a dark oil stain, and at the far end of the room was a metal chair bolted to the floor. There were leather straps on the arm rest and at the base of the chair. There was a freezer behind the chair, and off to the side a metal box with air holes in it.

It was pretty obvious then. Recently the wall had been put up to hide what had formerly been in the open. Unlikely anyone was ever let in, but after James escaped, paranoia set in, and the wall was built to hide where the bookmobile had been parked, where the kidnapped boys were kept, and obviously tortured. I felt sick to my stomach.

Leonard walked over to the freezer and looked inside.

"Empty," he said. That caused me to let out a sigh of relief.

I went over to the box and lifted the lid. It too was empty. At least there weren't any others.

The bookmobile had been setting here for years, part of Donnie's murderous ritual, that and the oiled bodies that he had eventually put in the tank in the bookmobile, along with Harriet Hoodalay.

"Fits," Leonard said. "Donnie has a bad thing for boys, somehow Harry must have delivered the bookmobile here one night, night she was supposed to drop it off at Will's place, got her wires crossed about where, and in the process of leaving it at the tire shop she must have seen something that got her killed. Donnie hid her body and the bookmobile in here. Must have dug up those early bodies, oiled them all down and put them in the bookmobile with Harry's corpse."

"Sounds right," I said.

"Kept the bookmobile running and in good shape, checked on the bodies from time to time, see how they were marinating."

"Jesus," I said. I could visualize Donnie sitting in the bookmobile, starting it up, listening to the motor hum, feeling the thrill of being in control of the machine that brought children to it; that struck me as something the sick bastard might enjoy thinking about.

Leonard was still piecing it out. "He grabbed James, had him here awhile, but somehow James got loose while they were out, opened the door, stole the bookmobile and got away. Or tried to. Goddam. Donnie is one sick fuck."

"Not sick, just different," a voice said.

We turned, and there was Donnie standing near the open section of the wall. He had slipped in quietly. He was holding a flat, black automatic.

"I thought I was pretty clever," he said, "way I built this room after the kid escaped. Lucked out he killed himself. If only you two had been killed, that would have ended my problems."

"You almost had me convinced it was Tom," I said.

"What was it, the newspaper?"

"Yep," I said.

"I thought about it later, hoped you wouldn't think about it too hard. You know, I don't mean to do the things I do, but I can't help myself."

"Yeah you can," Leonard said. "You don't want to."

"You could be right," Donnie said.

"There's another alarm, ain't there?" Leonard said.

"Yeah. You killed the obvious one, but there's another. You tamper with one, it sets off the spare. Goes off at the house. Somehow, I figured it was you two. That newspaper slip I made."

Will glided in through the gap in the wall and came up behind Donnie. For a brief moment I thought we had lucked out, but he walked up and stood by his partner.

"Took you long enough," Donnie said to him.

"Came fast as I could," he said.

And then I got the rest of it. Will had worked for Donnie for years, been groomed, and then he became part of the operation. Donnie had created Will in his image. It was the two of them doing the torturing, the killing. I was waiting for the inevitable.

That's when a gun went off. I expected I had been shot, but that's not what happened. I watched as Donnie sagged, slightly. There was another shot, and he went down on one knee and dropped his gun. Blood seeped out of his right shoulder and out of his right leg, splashed onto the floor, looked orange in the harsh light.

Will had darted out of the gap at the sound of the first shot.

I turned. Leonard was holding a little revolver in his hand, an old-fashioned snub nose twenty-two. I looked back at Donnie. He was trying to pick up his gun.

"Nope, nope, nope," Leonard said, "or the next one gives you a hole in the head. Did you see that, Hap? I didn't miss either shot. Course I was aiming for his head with the first one."

I had forgotten I told Leonard to bring protection, and hadn't noticed the gun tucked beneath his shirt. I was glad, that for once, he had listened to me.

"Go get Will," Leonard said. "I got this one."

I raced past Donnie, kicking his gun to the side as I went, then I darted out the gap in the wall, through the front door and into the crisp night air. I could see Will running toward the tire shop. He was almost there. I jogged after him.

When I got to the shop, Will had already opened the door and slipped inside. I eased into the dark building and fetched up behind some tires on racks. There was a shot and a chunk of rubber flew out of one of the tires and hit me in the face, hard. That shot had missed me by inches.

I kept moving behind the rows of tires. The son-of-a-bitch had run in here to get a gun, and I had followed him inside, the way he had wanted. I was a duck in a shooting gallery.

There were three more pops, but all they did was ruin a couple more tires. At least he was a bad shot. I bent down behind the tires and tried to peek between a gap in them. It took a moment for my eyes to adjust, and I could make out his shape on the landing above, framed by the moonlight slipping past a little window up there. He was squatting, the gun pointing in my general direction, waiting for me to stick my head out.

I pushed a tire loose from the top rack. It bounced when it hit the floor, and when it did Will popped off a nervous shot. I was already moving, back along the row of tires, and then under the landing above. I rushed my way along until I was pretty near under him. I glanced at the sagging timber that helped hold the top floor up. I charged it, hit it with my shoulder, heard it crack; the board, not my shoulder, though I was certainly feeling pain. I hit it again, and I could feel it move this time, and then a third time and it came down in an explosion of lumber, tires, dust and unidentified crap. I tried to get out from under it, but I was too slow. I don't know anyone could have been fast enough.

Junk was lying on me. It was heavy. I was trapped. Looking out from under the debris, I saw Will rise up from the floor uninjured. I had only succeeded in making him fall, and pinning myself under the wreckage. He looked about, spotted what he could see of me under the junk, and lifted his gun. There was a shot, and Will did a bit of sideways dance, then toppled to the floor.

I heard Leonard say, "Got 'em Boscoe," and then I passed out for awhile.

12

Leonard dragged me outside and propped my back against the tire shop. That's where I was when he slapped me awake.

"Damn, quit that," I said.

"How do you feel?" he said.

"Like a bunch of lumber fell on me and then my brother started slapping my face."

"I enjoyed that a little," Leonard said.

"Did you kill Will?"

"Boy did I."

"Donnie?"

"Yeah. I went ahead and shot him too. He kind of died in a gunfight, but I was the only one shooting. Wasn't like I could tie him up. I knew you needed help. I could hear the gunshots."

"Jesus, Leonard."

"Wasn't like he needed a room with a bunk for the rest of his life, sitting in some cell breathing stale air and making turds.

He needed a bullet. You dumb ass, you should have took his gun with you."

"I didn't want to kill anyone."

"That's all right," Leonard said. "I did it for the both of us. I'm going to go back down there and fire off his gun a few times to make sure it looked like he put up a fight."

"That's cold," Leonard. "He was unarmed when you killed him."

"Yeah. He was."

13

A crowd of people showed up, due to all the shooting. A light was shone in my face.

Before their arrival, Leonard had fired off Donnie's gun so he could claim there was a shootout and that he had prevailed. The noise, along with all the other racket we had made, stirred the locals. By the time they arrived, Leonard was leaning against the wall next to me, his gun lying on the ground six feet away. Donnie's gun was back in the formerly secret room, probably firmly placed in his hand by Leonard.

The county was called out. We ended up in the back of a deputy sheriff's car, watching the car hood shimmer in the red-and-blue from the light bar. In time they brought us in for questioning and locked us up in county for a few days. Leonard at least had a conceal carry license, so illegally carrying a firearm wasn't added to the list.

Brett came to visit. They let her give us food she brought from outside. I don't think they're supposed to do that, but once the county realized what Donnie and Will had been doing, they treated us well. They had discovered photographs of the kids that dated all the way back to the first murder, and the photos had been ugly. The poor kids' dead and rotting bodies had been stacked in seats in the bookmobile and a timer on a camera had snapped away with Will and Donnie posing beside their wrecked remains like hunting trophies, which, in a way, I guess they were. There were all manner of things found on internet files. There were torture devices in Donnie's house. It was a pretty slam-door case. I don't know if they believed Leonard's story about the shoot-out. But if they didn't, no one said a word. There was also the fact that Donnie and Will had kept records of who the boys and how long they had kept them, as well as all they had done to them. Their records solved all the murders. The victims, with the exception of Harriet, (a relative's DNA proved it was her) were unwanted kids, lost and forgotten, tossed out like used condoms.

I guess Tom Hoodalay still remains an asshole, and Nesbit needs a new owner for the tire and mechanic shop, not to mention some renovation.

We were back home pretty quick, though there was a bit of talk about us getting into trouble for breaking and entering, maybe a fine, a little jail time. That idea got shuffled and forgotten, thank goodness. No one really wanted to punish us for what happened to those two, not even for the lesser charges.

I brooded for a few days over Leonard shooting Donnie in cold blood, stayed home and didn't go visit with him, didn't even take his calls. Then Brett said, "Get over it. Leonard saved your life. And it isn't the first time."

"I know," I said, "but I got to get right in the head. Killing doesn't bother him. Me, I feel different."

"You've killed, Hap, and if you had to, you'd do it again. Quit feeling sorry for yourself. I'm glad Leonard made sure you came home. Stop being a jackass."

She was right. I called Leonard later that day. He answered, said, "You been pouting, haven't you?"

"I have."

"Yeah, well, I knew you'd get over it."

"When it involves you, I always do."

"Yep."

"One question," I said. "After all that, after all the things we've done, the deaths, how do you sleep?"

"Deeply."

"I don't."

"I know."

"But, thanks, Leonard."

"You're welcome. Still sore from all that crap falling on you?"

"A little. Nothing serious. Thanks for pulling that off of me too."

"Welcome again. But you owe me. We working out today?"

"I need another day to feel bad about who I am."

"How about you take this day to know that there won't be anymore kids abused and murdered by those two, and you don't have a hole in your head and about six feet of dirt over you? Want to do that?"

"That's exactly what I'll do," I said.

"Alright, then. And Hap?"

"Yeah."

"Go fuck yourself. Talk tomorrow."

"Goodnight," I said.